THE HARLEQUIN CREW SERIES

THE HARLEQUIN CREW SERIES

CAROLINE PECKHAM
&
SUSANNE VALENTI

This book is dedicated to all the cops in Sunset Cove who turn a blind eye to the violent, theatrical crimes that happen all across town.

Did they show up when fucking Shawn blasted off several heads at the Rosewood Estate and hung them on the balcony? Doubtful.

Did they blink an eye when Greg reported that his moustache had been ripped off and fed to a man-eating starfish?

Not even an eyelash twitched.

Did they call in backup when several huge explosions ripped through a cliffside and brought an entire building down on the heads of half the youth in town?

Not even pushover Jerry who said he'd be available if there were any disturbances in the night.

Thanks SCPD! You allow the gangs in the Cove to run riot, set off grenades, chop off heads and feed people to sharks without even a hint of an investigation! Are you corrupt? Of course. But do you beat yourselves up about that at night? Nah, those distant explosion rumbles help rock you to sleep, don't they? Keep up the good work!

CHAPTER ONE

I wished my pain had given way to numbness, but it hadn't. It split me open like a butcher's knife beneath my ribs, carving out the last shreds of my heart.

I stared at the open water as rain dripped over me, my gaze fixed on the shore of Sunset Cove. This was an agony equal to death, because it came served with a hopelessness that made my life seem so fucking pointless.

What was back there for me on that shore anymore? There was nothing left of me and my boys, nothing left of my family.

Rogue was gone, her job well and truly done as she left us in tatters in her wake. And I didn't know how to feel about her anymore because on the one hand, I knew I deserved this, and on the other, the thought of her returning to the arms of that monster made me want to tear the world apart to get her back. But she wasn't mine to reclaim, she'd made that more than clear when she'd driven her point home like an arrow shot straight into my chest.

"Fox?" JJ rasped, but I didn't respond, just standing there staring and staring into the abyss. Because that was what Sunset Cove was now. Empty. Hollow. An echoing chamber where so much goddamn love and joy had once lived only to be scraped out and left bare.

Maverick's men had started work on returning the boats to the Isle, lining them up before us on the jetty. They stared between us occasionally, but none spoke a word about the fact that Maverick was right here among his mortal enemies and was making no move against us. He was still sitting on the jetty, his head in his hands, his aura so dark I could feel it crashing over me like a shadow across the sun, demanding I give him my attention.

But I wasn't his brother anymore. He didn't want anything from me and what I wanted from him had long since ceased to be possible. So we all just remained there in silence as the storm beat against us and picked up in ferocity.

Mutt sat beside Maverick, staring at the horizon and releasing the occasional whine of yearning which pierced right through me.

JJ's phone had died so there was no chance of getting a call from my father to inform us of whether or not he'd caught up to Rogue. And I wasn't sure I wanted to know if he had anyway. What difference did it make? She wanted Shawn Mackenzie. I could drag her to Harlequin House, cuff and chain her there, but for what? She'd never love me. Never had and never would. And it was so much worse than that because now I knew the depths to which she hated me.

I knew she'd been angry before, but this…this was a venomous kind of abhorrence that wanted to exterminate me like vermin. And it had. Because this man wasn't the one who loved Rogue Easton to the ends of the earth. This man was the one who'd been ruined by her.

"We should go inside, the storm's picking up," JJ said in a rough, broken tone.

I ignored him, but my mind refocused for a moment and my gaze settled on a speedboat as one of Maverick's men pulled it up beside the jetty and jumped off it, moving to tie it up. I started walking at a fierce pace as I made a snap decision, approaching the man and snatching the keys from his hand before jumping down into the boat.

"Hey!" he barked, then looked to Maverick. "Orders, boss?" His hand was on his gun but he didn't draw it, waiting for Maverick to give him the go ahead, but my brother just remained deadly silent.

Before I started the engine, I found my head turning, looking back at JJ with an ache of longing.

"Are you coming?" I gritted out, my heart starting to thrash. I hated him. I did. But if he stayed here, that was it. It was the end of us, and after everything I just wasn't ready to let go of the last fragments of my family.

JJ stepped toward me with desperation in his eyes, then his gaze fell to Maverick who was still locked in some trance, his face buried in his hands. "I…think we should stay here."

"There's no 'we' in that scenario. If you stay, that's it, Johnny James. You're out of the Crew." It was harsh. A punishment I hadn't even meant to deliver, but there it was, rolling off my tongue all the same, coated in his betrayal.

JJ's eyebrows arched and even I was surprised at those awful words which would be impossible to take back the moment his choice was made. But I was forcing him to do it, because it was me or Maverick now. So he'd choose and that would be that.

"Fox, wait," JJ pleaded, the emotion in his eyes pulling on some deep rooted cord in my chest. "We should stay together, we-"

"There is no we," I snarled again. "It's me and you, or you and him. So which is it?"

Maverick had shown his true colours again and again, and tonight he'd gone too far. He'd forced me to watch as he fucked the girl I loved. He'd known he was destroying me, he'd *wanted* to.

JJ took another step toward me and a little flame of hope filled me, because I knew this shit was bad. And I didn't know how I'd ever forgive him for lying to me, for laying a claim on Rogue all this time, but now she'd broken all of us, maybe I could find a way to do it. Maybe if he just came home-

"I'm staying," he said, his voice tight and if I'd thought I'd been shattered enough tonight, a few more pieces of my heart manage to chip off and die all the same.

I nodded stiffly as I accepted his rejection of me, casting aside all we were and all we ever had been with those two cutting words. I turned to face the horizon to hide the pain in my expression over that decision.

I've lost everything.

"Fox, listen to me," JJ growled, his tone full of dominance that made my alpha male instincts prickle and my spine straighten. I turned my head back, glowering at him as I waited for him to speak, though I didn't know why I was wasting more of my time. He'd made his choice and it wasn't me. "If you leave, Rogue wins. She gets what she wants. She'll have us broken forever. But if we stay and fight for what's left of us, maybe-"

"There is nothing left of us," I talked over him, but he barrelled on, raising his voice.

"I know I shouldn't have lied to you and I'm sorry for that, but you never had a right to tell me I couldn't love her. You never had the right to demand anything of me when it came to her. It wasn't Harlequin business. I'm not your subordinate when it comes to our family. And just because you think you loved her harder and fiercer than the rest of us did all these years, that doesn't make it true."

I chewed the inside of my cheek as I stared at him, his words seeping through my skin and settling within me. I nodded slowly, seeing that he was probably right, but it did fuck all to change things now.

"The problem is, JJ, you bottled all of that up inside because apparently you're so afraid of me that you'd rather lie to my face and fuck Rogue behind my back than have it out with me before you broke my goddamn heart," I said bitterly.

"You really think you would have listened?" he barked, his eyes flaring. "If I'd been upfront from the start, you would have kicked me out of the Crew a long time ago."

"You never gave me the chance to try," I spat and Mutt's ears twitched before he barked at us, apparently not liking the confrontation. Maverick still just sat there like a statue, acting as if he couldn't even hear what we were saying as he stayed captured in his own pain over the girl we'd all lost for the second time.

"No, Fox," JJ snapped. "I didn't. Because we lost Rogue for ten years and you never realised that I was in love with her. That I *am* in love with her and was just as broken as you over losing her. I spent those ten years hunting for her as ferociously as you did and you never saw it."

"You never told me!" I bellowed, my hands beginning to shake.

"I shouldn't have had to!" he roared back. "And if I had, do you really think anything would have been different? You would have forced me out of our family, you would have forced me to let you have her."

Silence settled between us once more and the rain washed over me harder, chilling me to the centre of my being. Mutt continued to bark, the sound twisting away into the wind.

"Well I guess we'll never know now, will we?" I started the engine and JJ didn't even try to stop me as I turned my back on him and drove out across the choppy water.

I glanced back, finding him kneeling down beside Maverick with worry lining his expression and I ground my jaw before forcing my gaze back to the ocean.

He'd made his choice. He'd made plenty of fucking choices when it came to her apparently. And I must have just been the fool too fucking blinded by my love for all of them to see it.

My heart beat rampantly and emotion burned the back of my throat as I pressed the throttle and left the last piece of my family behind, knowing that from this moment onward I was going to be alone. And nothing would ever change that.

When I made it to shore, I found Harlequin House swarming with my dad's men and as I tied off the boat, my Great Uncle Nigel came running toward me down the beach.

"Fox!" Nigel gasped, his eyes wild with fear, and dread knotted my gut at his expression.

"What?" I demanded, quickening my stride towards him.

"It's your dad," he said. "He's been shot. That bitch of yours shot him."

"What?" I repeated, lower, harsher, unable to draw in a single ounce of air as my mind worked around those words.

"Rogue fucking Easton shot him, I saw it myself – though I didn't manage to end her for it like I wanted to," he growled passionately. "He's in a bad way. He's at the general hospital in the upper quarter but…you need to get there. I don't think he's gonna make it."

Those final words threaded through my mind and opened a gaping chasm of fear in my chest. I darted past him, running for the house, the garage, my truck.

Panic clutched onto every piece of me as I drove out of Harlequin House and through the gates where a bunch of my men stared at me with worry in their eyes.

I drove so fast, the world was a blur and my mind worked up into a frantic, desperate panic that was just a jumble of incoherent thoughts.

Rogue shot my dad??

She wouldn't. How could she?

By the time I made it to the hospital, anxiety was a living creature beneath my ribs thrashing and screaming and clawing at my insides. I parked up haphazardly on the curb out front, throwing the door open and flat out running inside. I hated my dad, but fuck I loved him too. And I didn't want him to die. I couldn't picture a world without Luther Harlequin in it. He may have made mistakes, but he'd been trying to work on them, we'd made progress lately. We'd laughed together, he'd been working to make things right. But I'd told him they never would be, I'd told him I hated him.

Please, please don't let him die thinking I hated him.

A receptionist directed me upstairs and after jamming my thumb on the elevator button ten times, I abandoned it and took the stairs, moving so fast, I couldn't catch my breath. But I didn't give a fuck. I didn't wanna breathe again until I saw that he was okay. I had to know he hadn't died here alone in this goddamn place with too white walls surrounded by strangers.

I made it to the operating theatre and tried to march straight through the double doors that led to the operating rooms.

"Sir!" a nurse dove out from behind her desk, grabbing my arm. "You can't go that way."

"My dad's down there," I barked, yanking my arm free of her grip and knocking her aside.

"Sir!" she cried again as I shoved through the doors, breaking into a sprint again as I ran down the hall, glancing through the windows in the doors surrounding me.

"Dad!" I called, knowing he couldn't answer but I was just so fucking desperate to find him.

"Sir, you must return to the waiting room!" the nurse shouted from behind me then started calling for security.

I made it to a room at the end of the corridor and my body seemed to freeze as I gazed through the window in the door, seeing my dad laid out on a table with a tube in his mouth, his face horribly pale, his eyes shut as several doctors worked to operate on his chest. There was blood and gauze and masked up surgeons, but I couldn't focus on anything except the stillness of his face.

"No, no, no," I croaked, reaching for the door, but suddenly strong arms caught hold of me, yanking me backwards and I didn't have the strength to even try and fight them off.

"Don't die," I begged of my dad. "Please don't fucking die."

I was half dragged back to a waiting room where I sank into a chair and someone planted a cup of water in my hand.

I just sat there, falling into shock and slipping into what felt like an alternate reality where all my nightmares were coming true at once. And the worst part of it all was the empty chairs around me. No JJ, no Chase, no Maverick, no Rogue. I couldn't remember a time before they'd been there at my side. They'd had my back through thick and thin, through shit like this when I needed them most. And I knew with complete certainty, that I wasn't strong enough to survive losing my dad alone.

Dead Man's Isle

MAVERICK

CHAPTER TWO

"You have to get up," JJ's voice found me in the dark and his hand pressed to my shoulder, cutting through some of the cloying fog of rage and hurt clinging to my chest.

I lifted my head, not feeling any of the chill of the rain as it washed over us, and I found Johnny James kneeling in front of me with droplets running down his face as he stared at me intently. His eyes were full of his destruction, and I was sure my own was mirrored back to him.

I shoved to my feet and JJ got up too, moving after me like a magnet.

Mutt stared up at us both with a whine in his throat and wet fur plastered to his body. I had to pity the thing for being left here on rejects island, there was no joy here for him.

"Well it was fun while it lasted, right?" I said dryly, finally cutting off the piece of me who cared about this. Fuck her. She wanted me broken? Well she'd arrived far too fucking late to the party to make a damn bit of difference anyway. She'd coiled herself into the shell of my body, trying to claw at something which still thrived, but I'd been emptied out a long time ago, and there'd been nothing left there to harm.

"Don't do that," JJ hissed and I shrugged like I didn't know what he meant, turning my back on him and heading toward the hotel. I was fine. Just fucking fine.

Every step I took felt heavier than the last. I could feel the distance dividing me and Rogue now and it was a far vaster plane than it had ever been before.

I was just her foolish little tool in all of this, her puppet on a string. The one thing I'd tried so hard not to become under Luther's rule, yet I'd allowed her to do it to me, actually deluding myself into thinking she could really love me as this fucked up, broken man. Well more fool me.

Hadn't Luther tried to warn me of that? Hadn't he said that this was what women like her did to men like us? Chewed us up, spat us out and left us even more damaged on the other side of their destruction than we had been when they'd arrived. Men like us weren't supposed to have love like the kind I'd tried to believe I owned with her. We were damaged, dangerous brutes and the good in this world was never meant to be ours.

"What are we gonna do?" JJ asked, picking up Mutt and hugging him to his chest, trying to shield him from the pressing rain. The little dog shivered in his arms, leaning to the side so he could keep his gaze locked on the stormy sea where the girl he pined for had disappeared.

"Dunno what you're gonna do, brother, but I'm thinking I might play Russian roulette with the gun fully loaded." I shrugged lightly as I considered it and JJ quickened his stride, planting himself in front of me with fear in his eyes, making Mutt growl as he was crushed between us.

"What?" he gasped, his eyes ablaze with worry like he actually gave a fuck.

"Just kidding, Johnny James. You always take things so seriously," I said, but my tone was dead and flat. I wanted to play this all off like I didn't give a fuck, but Rogue had well and truly ripped my black, decayed heart out of my chest. Maybe she'd wear it on her necklace alongside my key.

"We need to make a plan," JJ said firmly, clearly needing the order of his Crew to deal with this stress, but he was cut loose now. A man adrift. Just like me.

"There ain't no plan to make. She's gone. She fucked us. Accept it." I shouldered past him and Mutt yapped angrily like he was siding with JJ.

"I don't mean about Rogue," he said, his tone full of pain as he spoke her name. "I mean about Chase."

At that name, I found my feet stalling and my heart thumping unevenly in my chest. Yeah, alright, I had thought about him once or twice since I'd found out Fox had banished him again. I'd decided in my head that he'd found his place in life on a cattle ranch, milking the cows by hand and learning how to ride a horse. He'd figured out how to toss a lasso and started wearing a cowboy hat everywhere he went, tipping it low to hide the scars of his past beneath the brim. Seemed unlikely, but it sure helped keep him outa my thoughts.

"What about him?" I muttered, turning my head halfway back towards JJ as the rain slid down my cheeks like tears which I would never shed.

"We have to find him. We have to mend what Rogue broke."

"Don't go fooling yourself into thinking this was all Rogue's doing, idiot," I hissed. "We were wrecked the first time she left, and this will be the last time I'm destroyed by her or any of you assholes."

"I'm sorry," JJ croaked. "Sorry I wasn't there for you in prison, sorry I couldn't be. Sorry for playing my part in steering our fate here. But you gotta own what you did too. It's the only way we're gonna fix this, Maverick."

"JJ," I sighed, shaking my head at him. Poor, fucking foolish Johnny James. He was so goddamn hopeful, that was his problem. Always had been. Whenever a storm had blown into Sunset Cove, he'd see the opportunity in it, he'd talk about the high waves we'd get to surf after it hit and how we could all watch the lightning from Sinners' Playground when it arrived, or he'd be all excited about what treasures might wash up on the beach once it was gone. That was the way his mind worked. He found the cracks of light when the rest of us couldn't see anything but black. I'd loved him for that once. But this time, there was no light to find, and it was time he faced the truth of the dark.

"You need to let it go. It's done. Go back to shore, find something to live for. 'Cause there ain't nothin' here for you."

I kept walking, but JJ caught me again, grabbing my arm and wheeling me around with surprising strength. I guessed all that dancing made him into a foxtrotting powerhouse.

I squared up to him as a snarl built on my lips, but he didn't back down, he just glared at me through the sheet of rain with a fierceness in his eyes that rivalled the storm around us.

"You've given up on everything, on all of us, and I'm sick of it, Rick," he snapped. "Don't you get it yet? We need each other. We're brothers. Are you really happy to leave Chase out on his own somewhere, just like Rogue was left all those years ago? He has nothing, and no one, he's suffering from all that fucking Shawn put him through, and how long do you think it'll be before he starts drinking himself into an early grave?"

"Why are you so convinced that I give a fuck?" I asked coolly and JJ shifted closer, his hand sliding up to my shoulder where he squeezed hard. I felt it then, it was impossible to ignore, the thrumming of an age old bond between us that echoed of the childhood we'd spent together, of endless days in each other's company, of promises made and kept. There was a time when we would have done anything for one another. A better fucking time. A time that demanded respect and implored me to make good on it now.

I sighed as Mutt started growling at me again, his little brown eyes begging me to listen to the motherfucker holding him. I wasn't exactly looking for life coaching from a tiny dog though, even if he did seem to have his shit together better than I did.

"We're not those kids anymore," I gritted out in one last bid to try and dissuade him from convincing me on this.

"Well maybe I want to be them again because I'm tired of being these men, and I'm tired of the world hating us," JJ said, his jaw ticking. "Or maybe I want to be the men they always promised they'd be. But I can't do that without you, without Chase…Fox. Rogue's gone." His voice cracked. "And if we all fall apart, I'll never forgive myself for letting her in, for letting her break us."

"Fox is out of the equation," I hissed, latching onto the one part of his words I could wield to my favour in this argument, and my heart thumped awkwardly in my chest over my adopted brother, but I refused to acknowledge it.

"But Chase isn't," JJ growled. Not a question, a fact, a fucking proclamation. Because he could see in my eyes that I was being worn down to agreeing to this. Maybe I was a damn idiot to be tempted in by the last scraps of a future I could see shining in his gaze, a future I'd discarded years ago. But Rogue had already proven I was a fool, so maybe I'd embrace my foolishness in a last-ditch attempt to claim something good in this world. Fuck knew that if I didn't, I had nothing else left.

I nodded once as I gave in and JJ wrapped his arm around me, crushing me in his hold as Mutt growled then savaged my goddamn nipple for being stuck between us.

"Argh, you little beast." I tugged away from JJ's embrace and shoved him in the shoulder to push him back and Mutt looked up at me innocently. "We find Chase. We can start tomorrow," I muttered. "But that doesn't mean I want to be Team Besties again, asshole."

"What does it mean then, Rick?" JJ asked, arching a brow at me as he tried to summon something playful into his expression, but it was coated with darkness, his pain as clear as my own.

I shrugged and turned away. JJ followed like a sheep after his shepherd and we walked inside, my men eyeing us curiously but not daring to ask any questions. I trudged upstairs, trailing mud through the halls as JJ kept close and I worked as hard as I could not to fall to pieces over the girl who'd mauled my heart like a ravenous wolf tonight.

I pulled off my clothes as we stepped into my bedroom and tugged on some dry sweatpants before tossing a pair to JJ. He put Mutt down and the small dog ran to sit by the balcony doors, staring out at the storm and the sea, like he was hoping to see a glimmer of his rainbow haired girl returning. Part of me wanted to join him there, but it would be akin to staring down the barrel of a smoking gun. Rogue was the bullet I'd never seen coming, driving deep into my flesh and leaving me bleeding out behind her. *I hope it tasted sweet when you pulled that trigger, beautiful. I hope you got what you came for.*

The darkness in my mind deepened until I felt the creeping of fingers sliding up my spine and a heavy breath in my ear that belonged to Krasinski. I doubled over the bed, my hands fisting in the sheets as I squeezed my eyes shut and tried not to drown, but it was already too late, my lungs were labouring and I was falling, falling, falling-

"Did you miss me, pretty boy? I missed you," Krasinski panted, his hands sliding around my waistband as I pressed my palms to the wall. If I fought, he'd beat me. And it was always so much worse after that. He'd beat me down and then his body would linger on mine longer, his hands would roam

and try to coax my own cock into stirring for him, though it never did. This way was the simplest, the quickest.

I remained silent, lips sealed as I fixed my mind on Rogue. My sweet sinner girl from the Cove. Her laughter rippled through my mind like the calm waters of the ocean and my heart slowed as I left my body behind and disappeared into a vast and perfect sea with her.

Krasinski's shadow swallowed me up, but I was gone, far away where he couldn't reach me.

"Maverick," JJ called from somewhere near but too distant for me to find.

I tried to cling to Rogue again, to wield the memories which always saved me from my monster. But I was losing my grip on them, finding them tainted and discoloured. Instead, I saw that video playing in front of my eyes again and heard her words directed at me.

You became my weapon, Rick.

I was just a tool. Just a machine turned against the others and she'd played me beautifully. I'd tortured Fox for her and it didn't matter that I'd enjoyed it too, because now it left a sour taste in my mouth which I couldn't shift.

Panic was twisting my chest up like a corkscrew and when someone's hand landed on my back, I lost it, snapping like a half severed rope. I wheeled towards my attacker, seeing nothing but Krasinski's face as I threw my weight against him, taking him to the floor with a bellow of anger. I started punching, fighting, the thought of being pinned down again unbearable. I had to win. I had to kill him before he could defile me. Before his shadow consumed me and never let go.

He fought back, trying to push me off, but I pressed my weight down and found his throat, my hands binding around it and locking into place. I crushed his windpipe as adrenaline poured through my body and the demons in my mind urged me to end this.

Show him who the biggest man in the room is.

Make him pay.

Deliver him to the Devil firsthand.

Mutt's teeth drove into my arm and I blinked, my head twisting towards the dog as he barked furiously at me. My gaze shifted to JJ beneath me before he took advantage of my distraction and broke the choke hold I had on him, coughing and spluttering. I shoved off of him, scrambling back to the bed and half falling against it as I swiped a hand down my face.

"I didn't mean…" I trailed off, the darkness still circling like a vulture within me, waiting for another piece of me to die so it could come and feast on it.

JJ pushed himself upright and I expected him to attack me, but for some unknown reason he didn't. He looked at me like he understood, or at least like he wanted to and I couldn't turn away from him, clinging onto his presence in this room and finding that it anchored me here. Away from Krasinski, away from the dark.

"Sometimes it seems so real," I said in a low voice and JJ nodded, his fingers trailing over the reddened marks on his neck as his eyebrows tugged together.

Mutt came and sat in my lap, licking my bare chest and drawing my attention to the little animal. He whined gently, nuzzling my hand as if trying to steal some affection from it, and I petted him, the motion somehow grounding me even more.

"Rogue told me that you…that sometimes you zone out like that," he said and a flash of Rogue beneath me surged through my head, her lips pressing to mine, her fingers brushing over my skin and her eyes full of a need to heal me. It had all been an act. All just a way to rip me apart further. She was the cuckoo in my nest and I'd been blind to her, feeding her all of my darkest secrets and handing her the means to destroy me.

"If you don't like it, you can leave," I growled, hardening my tone again as I felt heat crawling up my neck at what I'd let him see in me.

"Well I'm usually the one doing the choking and getting paid good money for it too, but I think I'd let you dom me for the right price," he said and a surprised grin pulled at my lips.

He always had known how to break the tension in the shittiest of situations. He cracked a small smile back at me for half a second before both of us descended into a pressing, brooding, insufferable silence over Rogue.

We sat there for so long, the quiet started to fester and all I could feel in this room was pain. JJ's heartbroken expression was somehow worse than feeling it myself. We were in pieces, scattered to the wind like debris in a bomb blast.

JJ tapped his foot against mine to get my attention again and I looked at him with a heavy lump in my throat.

"She really fucked us, didn't she?" he breathed and I nodded, my chest torn to ribbons again as I pictured her malicious expression in that video message. Hatred, that was the long and short of it. A sickening, guttural hatred for each and every one of us. We'd left her high and dry, so she'd offered us the same courtesy in repayment. There were no winners in this game, just five losers all cut adrift from the past we used to call home, left floating in a sea of pain so far from land that we couldn't even see it beyond the horizon anymore.

"We deserve it, don't we?" JJ whispered darkly and I frowned at him.

I would have wished this on him a thousand times over alongside Foxy boy before today. But now that the sword had actually swung and gutted us all, I couldn't find it in me to enjoy their fall from grace. This made me feel somehow even more empty than I had before.

"Yeah," I grunted, the claws of her revenge still so damn sharp within me, but I embraced them, knowing it was what I'd been owed for never finding her, never protecting her when she needed me most all those years ago. "But all men fall, brother. And if I had to pick a hand to fall by, then it would always be hers."

Rejects Park

ROGUE

CHAPTER THREE

The room I was in was cold and dim, the single bulb doing little to banish the shadows which coated the walls and clung to the corners of the cold space. Shawn had kissed me on the cheek and told me to 'hold tight for a bit.' Whatever the fuck that meant. Then he'd left me down here, walking out the door half hanging off its hinges before a bolt slid into place on the other door which stood at the top of the stairs.

I was in the basement. Alone in a room with a single chair and a hook hanging from the ceiling above. That was it. This was where he'd been keeping Chase for all that time. I recognised it from Chase's description alone. And the dark stains on the stone floor marked the time he'd spent here, his blood decorating the space and his pain clinging to the walls.

I didn't mind that though. There was a peace in knowing I was in a place that he'd occupied for so long. The cold which wrapped itself around my body was the same cold that had kept him company while he'd been trapped down here. Me tasting even this small amount of his suffering was right. I deserved it. I had been the reason for him ever ending up here after all.

I traced my fingers along the rough stone and tried not to think of my boys. Tried not to wonder if they'd bought my lies. Tried not to hope they had just as powerfully as I was hoping they hadn't.

It hadn't been much of a plan. Just one dumb girl's desperate hope to reset the pieces on the board and let the game have a chance at a different outcome.

I'd been the trump card playing against them for too long. But now it was time for me to become the ace they'd been keeping back to play in reserve. I didn't know if it would work. Didn't know if any of it stood any real chance of playing out the way I was praying it would. But there was still a chance.

A chance that without me clouding their vision, my boys might find a way to reconnect with one another again.

A chance that Shawn might be blinded by his idea of victory enough to buy my lies.

A chance - albeit a slim one - that Shawn might even keep to his word and end this war in return for me giving myself up to him.

And a chance that I might just be able to pull off what I was planning and end it all for good.

I didn't know if it would really change much of that, but I did know that this way there was a slim ray of hope. Even if I had to be the sacrifice that made it possible.

I'd been down here for hours. So long I wondered if he'd forgotten me. If the world might have forgotten me. And I wondered what would happen if it did. Would I just fade away? Become nothing more than a ghost which used to haunt these streets who no one could recall anymore.

There had only ever been four people who had truly known I existed anyway, so maybe that would be true. It certainly would be once they were gone too. The Harlequin boys and me, a legend forgotten by everyone aside from the five of us who had lived it.

I moved towards the door to the room, my damp clothes making me shiver as the evidence of the storm refused to leave me in the cold and unforgiving room. Shawn hadn't locked it when he'd left. And I hadn't opened it until now because I didn't have anywhere to go. I wasn't a prisoner here. I'd made this choice. So I wasn't even sure why he'd bothered to lock me up at all.

Though I guessed he wasn't stupid enough to trust me, even if his ego was bigger than the house we were currently in.

The door juddered across the concrete outside it as I pushed it wide and I looked between the stairs which led back up to the main house where a locked door stood to keep me down here and the open door across the small hall from mine beyond the rocking chair that sat there.

Chase had told me that that was where poor old Miss Mabel had been living ever since that motherfucker Kaiser had come back here to steal his inheritance by faking her death.

Tears pricked the back of my eyes as I thought of her, cold and alone down here for the final years of her life. She hadn't deserved that. She'd been good. Probably the only truly good person I'd known in my entire miserable existence. She'd been worth more than being stuck down here in the dark without company or entertainment for the last years she'd been gifted on this cruel planet.

I crossed the little space at the foot of the stairs and pushed open the door to the rooms she'd been trapped in before her death, the scent of lilacs clinging to the air as I entered and driving me back into memories I had of much happier times.

"Come on, tell me. I'm old and I need something to make my tired heart flutter," Miss Mabel whispered conspiratorially as I sat on her porch swing with her, drinking the lemonade she'd made through a paper straw.

She wore a big blue sun hat which shaded her entire little body and her bare feet rested on the coffee table in front of us as she used her toes to rock the swing seat back and forth gently.

"None of them," I protested, my cheeks heating with a blush as I tried not to look at my boys where they were all working together to mow the lawn and pick up the cuttings. They'd rib me for ducking out on the hard work later, but they were also happy for Miss Mabel to have someone to talk to so they wouldn't call me out on it now.

"Oh come on, a bunch of strapping young lads like them? You must get all of a flap around at least one of them. They've all got the big eyes for you, young lady," she teased and I died a little inside.

"They're like my brothers," I protested, glancing over at Rick just as he pulled his shirt off. His body had been changing recently, his shoulders getting broader and the muscles of his arms becoming more defined. Not that I'd been

paying attention to anything like that.

I cut my gaze away from him and found JJ and Fox wrestling shirtless in a pile of freshly cut grass while arguing over something to do with the mower and my blush deepened. Chase was up a tree collecting apples above them and he'd paused to sit and eat one, looking like a savage as he ripped a huge bite out of the fruit, something about that action making my stomach clench.

"Maybe it's not about just one of them then?" Miss Mabel pushed. "Could be you've got the flutters for them all?"

I groaned, burying my face in my hands while my weak protests spilled out around my fingers and she laughed at me.

"Enjoy it while you're young, child. Before you know it, you'll be an old woman like me and you can trust me when I say, the things you look back on and regret are always the things you didn't do. Not the ones you did. So be wild, be free, live fast and love hard. Or at least have another glass of lemonade while you decide which one of them you'll be kissing first."

A smile touched my lips at the memory as I stepped further into the rooms where she'd been held before her death.

They were a lot nicer than the empty chamber I'd been left in. There was wooden furniture, a rug, a small bathroom set off to one end and even a television to the side of the space. The blankets were piled on the bed which looked soft and cosy and there was a little kitchenette built into the far wall.

I moved over to the closet and opened it, the scent of lilacs increasing as I ran my fingers over the row of skirts and dresses which hung there, waiting for her to return to them as if she could be back at any moment.

A tear tracked down my cheek as I shut the closet again and I headed over to the kitchenette. There was food in the cupboards and a coffee machine on the side and my hands automatically got to work making a cup as I tried to think about what I was going to do next.

I'd been ready for Shawn to be all over me. I'd thought he'd want me close, be looking to punish me or put me back in line or whatever the fuck he'd been going on about. But I hadn't expected this. Was he up to something else? Why had I just been forgotten down here?

I finished making my coffee and moved back towards the bed, sinking down on it as my mind reeled with ideas for how I was going to proceed from here while I kept fighting off the urge to fall apart over running out on my boys.

But as my ass hit something hard in the bed, a startled cry came from within the blankets and I screamed in alarm as someone moved beneath me.

The coffee went flying and I fell on my ass next to the bed, snatching a heavy book from a low table by the door and scrambling to back up as an honest to shit ghost emerged from within the sheets.

"Who's there?!" Miss Mabel yelled, brandishing a fist as her other hand scrambled for the lamp beside her bed.

The light clicked on and my eyes widened to saucers as I stared up at her in shock, the book I'd grabbed to use as a weapon tumbling from my hand onto the rug beside me.

"You're dead," I gasped, pointing a shaking finger at her.

"Not yet I'm not," she huffed, squinting at me before lowering her own fist. "Is that my little Rogue?" she asked more softly, reaching out a hand and I somehow managed to push myself upright to approach her again.

"I saw your head on a spike outside the house," I breathed, my gaze roaming all over her as I drank in this new reality. A reality where one of the worst truths I'd known wasn't even true at all. "How?"

"Well it clearly wasn't *my* head, though I dare say I must look a state if you thought a rotting head had a look of me about it. What are you doing loitering there anyway? Get on over here girl and let me look at ya."

Miss Mabel beckoned me closer and I rushed forward, climbing onto the bed and holding her in my arms as the tears I'd been so far from shedding started falling free and fast down my cheeks.

She hushed me softly, stroking my hair and holding me tight like I'd always imagined my mother might have if she'd wanted me. But that was yet another thing I'd never known in this brutal, fucked up life I'd led.

"Tell me about it," Miss Mabel urged as I let myself fall apart in her arms, relief filling me over finding her here. Alive. My long lost friend. "Come on now, it can't be all that bad."

CHAPTER FOUR

I woke with the taste of regret on my tongue alongside the tang of too much tequila. Rolling over on the bed, I found Maverick sprawled out beside me, his face drawn in a frown as he slept.

Mutt was by the window again, his ears pricking up with every sound, his eyes falling closed for a split second moments before they flickered open once more. The poor dog was damned to pine for a woman who would never return for him. And I knew the fucking feeling.

I'd drunk with Maverick long into the night, draining his tequila and talking about anything but Rogue, unable to bear her name anytime it crossed one of our lips. I couldn't even say for sure what we'd spoken about, only that it had felt like being with my old friend again, the one I knew and loved when I was a kid. But waking up beside him was sobering because it came with the weight of this new, unbearable life that had seen Rogue return to it only to leave us once more. My heart had combusted, no trace of it left except a gaping wound that throbbed with the loss of her.

I pushed out of bed, walking into the adjoining bathroom as my stomach churned and I was pretty sure the alcohol wasn't to blame.

Johnny James, you were the easiest. I thought you'd be the best place to start as fucking comes so naturally to you these days, but I was surprised to find out you're just the same pathetic, lovesick boy you were for me when we were kids.

I retched over the toilet, though nothing came up, no food there to eject itself. I was empty through and fucking through, and part of me wished I could cough up the chunks remaining of my heart and flush them away so it wouldn't hurt anymore.

Pathetic.

Lovesick

Boy.

I was all of those things, just a stupid, stupid kid who'd fallen for her all over again. Hook, line, and goddamn sinker.

I rinsed my mouth out with mouthwash and drank what felt like a gallon of water from the tap. Then I forced myself to look at my reflection in the mirror as I braced my hands on the sink and my shoulders tensed.

My eyes were ringed with darkness and I could practically see the shattered remnants of my former self in my pupils. Rogue had done a real number on me, shattered me from the inside out. And I should have hated her for it, should have wanted her to feel this torturous pain in payment for how she made me feel now, but I didn't. I just fucking missed her. Sure, I was angry at her, fucking raging, but every time my eyes closed for even a second, I felt her soft hands on me, heard her laughter, pictured her beneath me with a tumble of rainbow hair around her and light dancing in her eyes. Was it all fake? Or had she felt some of it? Had I meant anything to her at all in this quest for vengeance, or had it really all been an act?

Then I thought of fucking Shawn, of her returning to his arms, his bed, and I cringed, my whole body rejecting the image and making bile rise in my throat again.

How could you do this, pretty girl? How could you want him? He's a monster straight from hell.

Maverick shoved into the room, grunting at me in vague acknowledgement before whipping his tattooed cock out and taking a piss without a flicker of a care in his eyes over me being there. I was used to that in my line of work, the strippers often walking around naked at the club, and as me and Maverick had shared Rogue several times, there was hardly any point for modesty between us now. He tugged up his boxers when he was done, elbowing me away from the sink as he washed his hands before gargling enough mouth wash to drown a rat. When he was done, he strode straight past me to the walk-in shower, dropping his boxers and kicking them away.

"We'll head to the mainland as soon as we're ready to leave," he said gruffly and relief ran through my chest. He was keeping his word. We were going to find Chase. And I wouldn't rest until I caught up to him, then the three of us would find a way to rebuild something. In time, maybe Fox would talk to me. Maybe we could resolve things…

I was still so angry at him for taking Chase out of town without telling me, but after everything that had happened since, knowing he'd watched me and Maverick fuck Rogue, knowing the pain he must have been in over that…I just couldn't find it in me to hate him. I always forgave my brothers too easily, because I knew how much we needed each other even when they couldn't see it too. And I guessed the time for me hating Maverick had passed as well.

When he stepped out of the shower, I tossed him a towel and he rubbed it over his damp hair, his inked body tight with tension as I walked past him into the shower, dropping my sweatpants and just letting the heated water rinse away some of the discomfort in my body.

But the longer I stood there in the flow, the more thoughts invaded my head of her.

She was wrapped around me, whispering in my ear, my wild, untamed girl who I'd lost and somehow found. And for a moment there, I'd been convinced she'd loved me. But I'd just been an animal receiving affection from its hunter. She'd played me, lured me into her trap and I'd fallen so damn hard into it because the possibility of her loving me back was too tempting to resist. She'd offered me the one thing I'd desired my whole life. Her. Every, beautiful, broken piece of her.

Fucking idiot. You stupid, fucking prick.

I didn't even realise I was slamming my fist against the wall until Maverick's arms surrounded me, dragging me out of the shower and turning me to look at him. His hand locked over my jaw, his grip as firm as iron as he forced me to look at him. My fingers remained curled up in bruised fists, my right hand worse than the left, my middle knuckle split open and bleeding. I knew if I'd kept going I would have broken something for sure, but I didn't care, I just didn't fucking care.

"Find something good to ground you, JJ," Maverick commanded. "That's what you're best at. So fucking find whatever it is you need to stay here."

"What did *you* find?" I asked through my teeth, realising I was shaking, my shoulders practically vibrating as the rage in me spilled into my flesh.

"What?" he growled.

"Last night, you found something to ground you. What was it?" I demanded, wondering if whatever he had latched onto could offer me the same comfort.

"Nothin'," he muttered.

"Rick," I hissed, trying to pull away, but his hand remained locked on my jaw.

"You, you asshole," he snapped, his temple pulsing and the shaking in me started to cease as I stared at his furious expression. Something shifted in his eyes for a moment, letting me see beneath the untouchable man he presented to the world. And instead I saw the boy I knew, the one whose soul was latched to mine and anchored me here to this room. This island. This life.

A long breath left me and Maverick released me as the anxiety attack eased off and he roughly handed me a towel.

"Don't fucking look at me like that," Rick muttered then turned and left me there.

Then don't look back at me like you're my best friend again, asshole.

I dried off then wrapped the towel around my waist and followed him back to his room, clinging to the single purpose left to us. *Stay together, find Chase.* If we did that, things would be okay. Somehow, they'd be okay.

Maverick gave me some clothes and disappeared off to speak with his men. By the time I was dressed in the white t-shirt and black sweatpants, the rain had eased off and the sun was peering through the clouds. Mutt still hadn't moved from his position by the window and I walked over to him, crouching down to rub his head. He released a distressed noise and my heart squeezed at his expression.

"She's not coming back, buddy," I said quietly, those words as crushingly heavy as a tank on my chest.

Mutt continued to stare at the ocean and I hated that I couldn't explain this to him. That he was gonna keep waiting and waiting on her to come home. And she never would.

I love you, Johnny James. I love you so much it terrifies me. It makes my skin burn and my heart race. But it makes my gut knot and my palms clammy too because loving you means risking my heart on you all over again. But this time I know it's not the same. This time I'm all in, which means that if you throw me away again there won't be anything left of me to keep on going.

Liar.

Fucking. Liar.

I ground my jaw, hating her for that lie most of all. Because all I'd ever wanted was her love, and my greatest fear was not being good enough for it. But now I didn't know what to think. She hadn't even been the girl I'd fallen for years ago, it had all been a cruel act. *So why had it felt so fucking real?*

I scratched Mutt's ears, trying to soothe the little dog, but he just continued to whine and growl, his eyes set on the horizon.

A sharp whistle caught my ear and I turned, finding Maverick there, jerking his head at me in a command to leave.

I scooped Mutt into my arms, following him out the door. We walked in silence downstairs, passing his men who shifted guns in their hands and eyed me curiously. But none made any move against me and I guessed Maverick must have told them not to. I wondered if he'd offered them any explanation or if he'd simply barked the order and let their minds churn over what that meant. Either way, they were clearly going to follow his command, their fear and respect for him so potent you could taste it on the air whenever he passed them by. I wondered if he even realised how like Luther he'd become in that regard, though in fairness, Rick's aura was probably even darker than the leader of the Harlequins' these days.

We headed out into the compound where a black SUV was waiting for us. Maverick climbed in the driver's side and I got in the other with Mutt on my lap as he drove us onto a boat waiting there on the dock.

I took my phone from my pocket, turning it on for the first time after charging it last night and found a bunch of messages waiting for me from the Crew.

"Fuck," I gasped, my grip tightening on my phone as my heart lurched in shock.

"What?" Maverick demanded, looking over at me as I scrolled through the messages.

"Luther was shot last night. By Rogue."

A burning kind of silence followed my words and I frantically read through more of the messages, my heart thumping unevenly.

"It's bad, Rick." I looked over at him as worry pooled in me over Fox.

Maverick said nothing, though his knuckles were turning white as he gripped the steering wheel and the blood had drained from his face.

We stayed in the car as the boat sailed out across the water and I brought up the number to Fox's backup phone seeing as Maverick had taken his main one, pressing call and hoping he had it on him. There may have been a lot of shit between us right now, but that didn't change the fact that he needed me. He was alone while his father was in hospital and those messages were old, what if Luther hadn't made it? What if Fox had had to go through all of this by himself? I couldn't bear it.

"Answer, brother," I hissed under my breath as the call rang out and I hit dial again.

Maverick remained silent the entire boat journey and I called Fox at least fifty times before he finally answered.

"What, JJ?" he demanded, though his voice sounded weak, exhausted.

"I just heard about Luther," I said, terror knotting up my chest. "Is he alright?"

"He's alive. For now," he said, his voice thick.

"Where are you?"

"The hospital," he murmured.

"I'm coming there now," I said firmly.

He sighed and I expected him to fight, refuse me, start giving me orders. But he didn't. He just hung up.

"Get to the hospital," I begged of Maverick as we docked on the mainland and he put the car into drive before bombing it off the boat, not hesitating for a second to do as I asked.

Maverick kept up his silence and I stole glances at his expression as his jaw ticked. Mutt whimpered and I swear the little creature could sense the shift in our mood, like he knew what had happened.

"Are you alright?" I asked in a low voice.

"Of course I'm alright," he said aggressively. "Why wouldn't I be?"

"Luther-"

"Fuck Luther," he spat. "I'm only hurrying there because if he's teetering on the edge of death, I want to be present to see him go outa this world."

I didn't know what to say to that, so I turned my attention to the window and scraped a hand through my hair. "Rogue shot him. Rogue did this," I rasped and I felt Maverick's whole body tensing, though he still maintained his silence on the subject.

He drove so fast, we made it to the upper quarter in record time and as we pulled up in the hospital parking lot, my anxiety spiked.

I stepped out of the car and strode to the door with Mutt clutched against my body. Maverick walked half a step behind me, putting on a baseball cap and pulling it low as if it would do much to hide his identity.

"You can't bring a dog in here!" a receptionist cried as I walked straight up to her.

"Where's Luther Harlequin?" I barked and she shrank back from my tone, the name Harlequin enough to make the strongest of backbones bend.

"Level three, room twelve," she stammered, pointing towards the elevator and I rushed into it with Maverick in tow.

Upstairs, we ran along a corridor full of private rooms and I followed the numbers until I reached Luther's, rapping my knuckles on the door.

It yanked open a beat later and I came eye to eye with an exhausted looking Fox, still wearing the same clothes from yesterday. He didn't even look angry anymore, he looked empty. Like some vital piece of him had been taken and he couldn't function properly without it.

I moved forward, wrapping my arms around him and he just stood there in my hold until I let him go.

"It's alright, we're here," I swore.

"We?" he whispered in a deadly voice.

I glanced over my shoulder as I released him, finding Maverick was lingering a little further down the corridor. I beckoned him closer and he stepped up beside me, peering into the room and trying to get a look past Fox.

Fox backed up, his stance protective as he stood in front of Luther's prone form on the bed. He had a tube down his throat and his inked chest was heavily bandaged. The beeping of a heart monitor and the rasping suction of a ventilator told me all I needed to know. This was bad. Seriously fucking bad.

"You here to gloat?" Fox shot at Maverick.

I stole a glance at Rick, but he didn't have any of the bravado he usually had about him. His arms hung at his sides, his brow fixed in a frown and his eyes pinned on the man who had raised him.

"Is he gonna die?" Maverick spoke at last and he sounded so young and boyish in that moment that Fox seemed to drop his defences a little too.

"I don't know," Fox admitted, his eyes full of fear as he followed Maverick's gaze to Luther.

Mutt struggled in my arms so hard that I had to let him down and he rushed past Fox, leaping up onto the bed and nuzzling Luther's hand as if looking for a stroke. When he didn't get one, he whimpered, curling up beside him and resting his chin on his arm, staring at his face as if waiting for Luther to wake up.

My throat thickened at seeing Luther like that. He'd been a constant in my life, and maybe I'd hated him sometimes, but not always. He was like family. The only semblance of a father figure I'd ever really known. And seeing him laid out at death's door hurt more than I'd expected.

Maverick shifted closer to the bed and Fox's posture straightened.

"I'm not gonna kill a man who's unconscious, Foxy," Maverick said darkly, his eyes moving to Luther again. "You need to get better so I can kill you properly, don't you old man?" He nudged Luther's arm, getting no response and Maverick's brow lowered further.

As Fox accepted that Maverick wasn't gonna try and rip out Luther's breathing tube or something crazy, he sank down into the chair beside the bed and stared at his father with worry in his eyes.

"She did this," Fox said in a broken tone. "Rogue pulled the trigger on him."

"She hated him," Maverick said, though he sounded angry not pleased. His love for Luther was clear to me right then, it filled this room, tangling with the love of his brother. But it was all so goddamn broken now, I didn't know if it could ever be healed. I guessed I knew now that you could love someone while hating them to your core.

"How long until he wakes up?" Maverick asked.

"I don't know," Fox said, the weight of the world seeming to rest on him.

"We have to go. So call JJ when he does. Or if he doesn't. Either way just let me know," Maverick commanded of his brother and Fox raised his eyes to him in surprise, hatred still simmering between them.

"Why? So you can turn up to ruin the funeral if he doesn't make it?" Fox sneered.

"Just do as you're told, asshole," Maverick snarled.

"Don't fight," I begged, rubbing my temple where a headache was starting to brew and for once they listened to me. "Fox..." I took a step towards him. "I know you don't owe me anything, but I need you to tell me something."

Fox's dark green gaze shifted onto me, full of so much pain it made me bleed inside. "What?" he murmured.

"Where'd you leave Chase?" I asked, desperate for the answer and Fox's gaze slid over my expression before he looked back at his father.

"The Lazy Shore Motel," he said simply, hopelessness clouding around him. It was like he didn't care anymore, like he'd discarded his Harlequin crown in the mud and was just a man now. A broken, lonely man.

"Thank you," I sighed, backing up to the door and Maverick came with me. "Come on, Mutt."

The dog didn't move and when I stepped forward to get him, he growled, snapping his teeth at me in a clear refusal.

"He can stay if he wants," Fox said flatly.

"He's probably hungry," I muttered and Fox nodded, his gaze not wavering from his father again.

We stepped out of the room and the door swung closed, seeming to form a solid, unbreachable wall between us once more. My fingers lingered on the door handle then I turned and walked away with Maverick, my pulse thrashing beneath my flesh as I left one shattered brother behind to go in search of another.

Maverick didn't speak about Luther again, and I sensed pushing him to talk about it wasn't gonna get me anywhere. So we just returned to his car and headed onto the road, this task providing us a purpose I was sure we both needed.

I prayed we got lucky today and found Chase soon. After all, how hard could it be to track down a guy with one eye who was covered in scars and had a limp?

It turned out, it was seriously fucking hard to find a guy with one eye who was covered in scars and had a limp.

"Dammit, you must know something," I snapped, slamming my hand down on the motel owner's desk. She was chewing gum and filing her nails, apparently used to scary assholes threatening her because all she did was roll her eyes at me.

"I told you. He only stayed one night. Do you want me to lie to you, pretty boy?" she tossed at me, her eyes sliding to Maverick who stood silently beside me with his arms folded. "I don't lie to gangbangers with muscles bigger than my head. Kinda keeps me alive 'round here."

I sighed heavily, my head falling forward as I rested my hands on the desk. "I should chop you up and feed you to my starfish," I muttered.

"Go right ahead," she said, snatching a magazine from her desk and leaning back in her seat as she flipped it open. "It'll make my day more interesting."

"Gimme the key to the room he stayed in," I growled, holding my hand out to the girl. She plucked it off a hook behind her and handed it straight over, her eyes immediately going back to the article she was reading. A tank of a rockstar stared at me from the cover of it, his leather jacket hanging off his bare shoulders, holding his balls and squeezing while he stuck out his tongue and a girl poured rum directly onto it. Cannon Keller. The guy's band was actually half fucking decent, but I swear I always expected his next headline to be news of his death after he leapt off a bridge into some shallow water or some other equally dangerous shit he enjoyed.

"Have a good day now," she said in a falsely polite way as she noticed where my attention had fallen. "Or are you planning on taking my magazine to give you some ideas for roleplaying as Keller with your boyfriend?"

"Hey-" I started but Maverick took hold of my arm and tugged me out the door while I continued to glare over my shoulder at the infuriating woman. When we were outside, I pulled my arm out of his grip and stalked up to the room where Chase had stayed, walking inside as I unlocked it.

The space was small with floral sheets on the double bed and faded wallpaper on the walls. It smelled of countless cigarettes and had stains on the ceiling which proved how many people had smoked in here over the years. Had Chase smoked in here too? Had he started drinking again? Had he sat on that bed, thinking no one in the world wanted him and believing no one ever would again as he drowned himself in nicotine and alcohol?

Maverick lingered by the door as I strode to the nightstand, checking the drawer then shoving the mattress up and knocking the bedding flying.

"What are you doing?" Maverick asked.

"Maybe he left something. A clue to where he's gone." I searched more frantically, tearing the place apart as I hunted for some lasting sign of him. Something that marked the next step on his trail. Where would he go? What would he do? How much cash had he had on him? Could he live from motel room to motel room for a while or was he gonna need to pull a job?

Yeah, that's what he'd do. He'd boost a car. It was what he was best at. Then he'd sell it on for more cash and keep doing it until he could afford somewhere to live. He was born in the gutter and he knew how to take advantage of the rats.

"This isn't some Dan Brown novel, asshole," Maverick said. "There ain't gonna be clues hidden behind secret hatches and mystical fucking symbols pointing us to our next destination. Chase left. He ain't here. And he ain't coming back. He hasn't laid out breadcrumbs for anyone because he doesn't think anyone's coming."

His words cut my chest to ribbons and I picked up the lamp in anger, hurling it across the room with a bellow that tore at my lungs.

"If *she* hadn't come back then this wouldn't have happened," I forced the bitter words out through the lump in my throat. "He knew she'd ruin us, he *knew*, and he tried to warn me, but I didn't listen. Now look what's happened to him."

It was obvious Maverick didn't wanna talk about Rogue. Neither of us did. But it was clear it was all either of us were thinking about too.

His heavy footfalls moved across the carpet and he laid a hand on my shoulder. My brother. My friend. He was the one good thing that had come out of this, and I was too much of a pussy to tell him I didn't hate him anymore. Not since I'd found out what had happened to him in prison. How could I? He must have had so many demons living in him, he rivalled hell itself.

"We'll find him," he said, his voice just a low rumble.

"And then what?" I hissed.

"You and him can start over. You could leave the Cove-"

I whirled on him, my brows pulling tight together. "What about you?"

His eyes clouded with shadows and the muscles in his throat worked. "I've got a new purpose, Johnny James. Shawn Mackenzie's death is mine. I'll make dirty work of it. And I'll make him pay for every scar on Chase's body, and for stealing our fucking girl from us, don't you worry about that."

"I thought you didn't give a shit about us?" I scoffed lightly.

"I don't," he grunted. "I'm just sayin'. You can leave town knowing it'll be done."

I shook my head at him. "You really think I'm just gonna leave town? You don't think I might wanna be there when Shawn's blood is spilled, when his screams puncture the air?" I took a step towards him, bloodlust lacing my tongue and darkness churning in my chest like a forbidding sea. "I may have sold countless pieces of myself to the people of Sunset Cove, Rick, but I never sold my loyalty to my family, or my vow to do anything and everything to protect them. Shawn is *our* enemy, the biggest threat we've ever faced. And we'll face him together whether you like it or not. Because that man tainted Rogue, he tortured Chase, and now he's moved into the heart of our town and is infecting it like a disease. So I'll be there when he dies, and I'll fight for what's left of us afterwards because I know what most people's lives look like on the inside. I'm the product that's paid for to fill that void in them, but it never lasts. Because they don't have what we once had. What we can still have."

"What's that?" he asked, his eyes glued on mine, seeming to search for the piece of his soul within them that I still owned.

"A place in this godforsaken world, Rick. It's never been about the Cove. It's always been about us. We're each other's home. And that's why it hurts so goddamn bad being apart. That's why you've never shot a bullet straight at any of us, and why we never shot back. And I know it's never gonna be the same again. I know we'll never have Rogue and maybe you and Fox will never be able to love each other again either, but there's something still here worth holding onto and you already know what losing it feels like, so do you really wanna go through that again?"

Maverick's adam's apple bobbed and he finally cast his gaze away from me, a line of tension forming on his brow.

"I don't see the point of it without her," he said darkly and my chest crushed in a vice.

"The point is, it's better to be a shell with nothing inside, than one that's been crushed to pieces and lost to the sea." I walked past him out the door and he followed a beat later.

I left the key in the door and we got into Maverick's vehicle, heading onto the highway with the plan to ask about Chase at every motel we came across.

Though the sun was shining, beating down on the hood of the car, my world felt like it was stuck in an eternal night. And I realised that was because Rogue had felt like the sun to me, her warmth giving me life unlike anything else I'd ever had. But now she was gone, and it turned out her warmth had been a lie. So I was left frozen to the bone and missing the heat of a girl I'd never really had.

Rejects Park

ROGUE

CHAPTER FIVE

By the time me and Miss Mabel had caught ourselves up on the last ten years - and most importantly the last few months since I'd returned to the Cove and the place I'd once called home - it was midday. We'd eaten a meal together, though my appetite was definitely not what it normally was, and I'd just choked down a few bites of toast before giving up on the food altogether.

We didn't exactly have much of a plan, but I understood a little more about the way this place operated now.

Shawn was living in the house here and he allowed a few of his closest men to stay inside too. But for the most part he had them camping out in the grounds or coming and going when they needed to sleep. It seemed odd to me that he would rather risk them moving back and forth outside this stronghold than just allow them inside the building. There were plenty of rooms here for at least twenty of them to stay full time but for some reason he was keeping them out.

Aside from that, Mabel didn't know a whole lot. She was given food and was even allowed up into the house on occasion when Shawn wanted an audience for his boasting, but nothing he'd told her had seemed useful to me in any way. Mostly he just liked to blow smoke up his own ass and talk about the way the world was all coming together for him, and Miss Mabel admitted she'd turned her hearing aid off more than once while he droned on.

A heavy knock sounded on the door at the top of the stairs and I flinched, glancing at Miss Mabel as she reached out to take my hand and gave my fingers a reassuring squeeze.

"You've got this, sweet girl," she whispered and I nodded, not entirely sure if that was true or not but needing to believe it was.

I pushed to my feet, smoothing down the long, floral dress Miss Mabel had leant me. I was taller than her but the material was baggy and all in all I was swamped within it. But the clothes I'd worn here last night were wet and filthy so if Shawn had a problem with this then he was going to have to find his own solution to it.

The heavy knock came at the door again and I pushed myself to my feet, not wanting Shawn to come down here while Miss Mabel was with me. I knew he hadn't hurt her yet, but I wasn't going to trust him with anything, let alone the life of someone I cared about.

I moved out of Miss Mabel's rooms and hurried up the cold stairs on bare feet, swallowing a thick lump in my throat before calling out to let him know I was here.

"The point of knocking is to get someone to open the door, but it's locked on your side, not mine. So why don't you just open it?" I asked.

There was a pause and then the sound of a bolt sliding open rattled through the metal door before the thing was pulled wide.

I raised my chin, ready for a showdown with the Devil before falling still as I found myself looking at Shawn's man instead of him. In fact, I knew this guy. Travis hadn't changed a whole lot since I'd last seen him up close like this, though the tattoo sleeve on his right arm had been finished off and my gaze trailed over the ink that lined his muscular bicep. His dark skin gleamed with droplets of moisture which also clung to his black hair, little drips sliding down the short dreadlocks and splashing my bare feet as he took me in.

He towered over me and he definitely had that whole intimidating gangster vibe going for him, the aura of 'I'll kill you if you blink at me wrong' hanging heavily on his shoulders. But I didn't think he was here to kill me despite the baseball bat which currently rested against his shoulder, held loosely in his grasp.

"I assumed you were Shawn," I said in explanation for my snark. "Where is he?"

Travis raised a brow at my tone but didn't seem offended by my lack of terror.

"He sent me to come get you," he explained, his gaze moving past me and giving me a little more time to inspect him. His white tank was damp too, clinging to his abs which I could sort of see through it and I glanced towards the window, wondering if it was still raining out. But no, the sun was shining again. So why was he all wet? "Does the old lady need any more food or is she good?"

"Miss Mabel?" I asked, surprised at the softness of his tone which suggested he gave a shit about her. "Yeah she said she's gonna make herself some lunch now. Why do you care?"

"Well if I didn't then I doubt anyone around here would remember to make sure she'd got food down there."

I looked up at this scary dude with the gang tats and 'I could kill you with my pinky finger' glower and cocked my head to one side as I reassessed him. If he was the one looking after Miss Mabel then he couldn't be all bad. Then again, Shawn had never wanted his men to spend much time around me, so it wasn't like I'd ever had the opportunity to figure that out for myself before now. But that one time we'd shared a beer I remembered him making me smile and when Shawn had been threatening him for spending time with me, he hadn't even looked at me like he blamed me for it the way most men like him would.

"That's...thank you. For looking after her," I said, unsure of myself now that I knew that about him.

"It's the right thing," Travis replied without inflection before reaching out to tug the door closed behind me and bolt it again. He glanced down the hallway for a moment before leaning in closer to me and speaking in my ear. "You should never have come here."

I turned to look at him in surprise but he'd already drawn back, turning away from me and striding further into the house. I glanced about for a moment then hurried to follow him, wanting to ask why he'd said that but not having the chance as more Dead Dogs appeared, heavily armed and giving me the kinds of appraising looks which made me glad to be wearing a granny dress.

We moved right through the enormous house until Travis pushed open the door to the large sunroom where Shawn was reclining in an armchair by the window while wearing a navy smoking jacket over his bare chest and puffing on a cigar.

He looked up from his cell phone as we entered the room, his eyebrow arching as he took me in.

"Well don't you look like a sack of shit?" he said, his gaze moving all over me. "I'm just sitting here wondering how my cock ever got hard enough to find its way inside you, sweet cheeks. If you came back here thinking to seduce me, you're failing miserably."

"I happen to think my dress looks fucking amazing," I replied, my tongue running away from me before I could help myself. I'd been out of his company for too long and I'd forgotten how easily his temper could be triggered.

"Is that so?" Shawn asked, his blue eyes flashing with anger. "Well, it's a good thing I got someone here who can fix you up for me - Mimi, get your ass over here, poppet!"

I startled as a shadow rose from a position in the corner of the room and my eyes widened in surprise as I found Mia hurrying towards Shawn, her black bob perfectly styled and a fitted black dress plastered to her body which seemed more appropriate for a night out than hanging out in here. We'd assumed the other head up on those spikes had been hers, but I guessed we'd gotten that wrong too and she'd been here the whole time. Though it looked like Shawn had taken a whole lot more interest in her than he had in Miss Mabel.

"Yes, Shawn?" she asked, her voice barely more than a whisper and none of that bitchy fire I'd hated so much in her present anymore. But this was worse. She wasn't some annoying skank now - she was just this vacant looking thing. Her eyes were red rimmed and puffy like she'd been crying but her cheeks were currently dry and there was something about her that just made me feel sorry for her. He'd killed her mom and stepdad, so the cause of her grief was pretty obvious, and my gut churned as I realised he'd kept her here like a little broken toy ever since he'd murdered them. I might not have liked the girl, but she didn't deserve that.

"Be a good girl and go get my sugarpie something hot to wear. My eyes are offended by the state of her right now." Shawn shuddered in an exaggerated way and I scowled at him in reply.

Mia nodded, moving towards me and taking my wrist as she led me back to the door. Shawn picked up his phone dismissively and I gave in to this bullshit as I let Mia tug me from the room. Travis followed us as we walked away through the house and she led me upstairs, but when we made it to her room, he just waited outside.

Mia released me and hurried to her closet, the sound of clothes being rummaged through reaching me as I looked around at the huge space. It was decorated garishly, the walls violent pink with zebra print accents over her bed and on a feature wall, making me wrinkle my nose in distaste. This house was beautiful and old, steeped in history which ached to be honoured and highlighted, not hidden behind this modern brightly coloured bullshit.

"Mia, what's going on here?" I asked her. I moved across the room to the closet just as she appeared with a couple of dresses in her arms. "I thought you were dead. Then again, I thought Miss Mabel was dead too, so-"

"Pick one, hurry up," she said, her gaze shooting to the door nervously.

"Mia," I growled, trying to force her to look at me but she just shoved the dresses into my arms and hurried over to a rack of shoes, grabbing some and bringing them over for me too. "Tell me what you're doing here. Didn't Shawn kill your family? Why are you still alive? Fuck that, why are you still *here?*"

Mia blanched at my words, looking towards the door again before hurrying right up to me.

"It'll all be fine so long as you're good," she whispered. "Just behave. Be a good girl. He likes that. And when he's happy he's so generous… Just don't make him angry, okay?"

I nodded along because Mia looked likely to freak out if I didn't agree and she almost smiled before hurrying out of the door again and leaving me to get changed.

Her style really wasn't my style and I had curves where she was all tall and willowy, but I pulled on a white shirt dress with a chunky belt and paired it with some high heeled black pumps which were thankfully my size.

When I made it back into the corridor, Mia was gone but Travis was still waiting, the baseball bat hanging loosely from his fingertips and his hair no longer dripping.

"Why were you all wet when you came to get me?" I asked him as I moved to walk at his side and we headed back downstairs.

"Boss decided he wanted you thirty seconds after I got my ass in the shower. He felt that using a towel would slow me down," he replied with a shrug and I frowned.

"And why didn't you just tell him to get fucked?"

Travis snorted a laugh. "Because if I'm gonna die, I'd rather it was over something a little more important than my use of a fucking towel."

I had to admit he had a point there so I just nodded, my attention fixing on the room at the end of the hall where Shawn was waiting for me.

Shawn looked up as I entered, exhaling a low whistle as he looked me over and tossed his phone aside.

"Well look at you," he said. "Don't she clean up nice, Trav? Now I remember why I enjoyed fucking you so damn often, sugarpie. You look like a girl who just loves dick, doesn't she Trav?"

"I dunno, boss," Travis said, moving to the far side of the room and keeping his gaze away from me. "I ain't looking at your girl."

Shawn boomed a laugh, slapping his thigh like that was just so fucking hilarious to him before shoving to his feet and falling silent so suddenly that Mia shrieked from her corner before clasping her hands over her mouth. Shawn ignored her entirely though, his attention fully fixed on me.

"But you're not my girl, are you sugarpie?" he asked, tilting his head to one side and prowling towards me like a big cat closing in on a baby deer. "My girl wouldn't fuck a dirty Harlequin. Would she?"

I said nothing, my gut prickling as the mood he was in settled over me and I felt the danger in the air. This was the Shawn I hated. The vindictive, cruel version of him who somehow managed to make me feel so impossibly small. My walls were up and I was primed for the blow I knew was coming but I doubted it would make it sting any less. He just had a way of worming beneath my skin and making the cruelty of his words stick there no matter how much I wanted to deny them. And over the years, I'd come to the conclusion that that was because no matter how much I wanted to deny the things he said about me, he always managed to taint them with enough truth that it was impossible to fully refute them.

"Come on, sugarpie, don't be shy. You spread those bronze thighs of yours and took them good, didn't ya? Did they pass you about like a sex doll? Did you fuck Daddy H before letting his boy plough you next?"

"What if I did?" I asked, keeping my chin raised as I refused to back down this time, refused to let him break me the way he'd always liked to try to.

Shawn smiled widely, moving right into my personal space and filling my air with his presence. It was a cold, malicious thing which made my lungs constrict as I breathed it in, but I kept my gaze defiant and my face impassive as I worked to ignore the cloying feeling of his aura soaking over mine.

"Well, if all you're good for these days is serving gang cock, then I have more than a few men who would gladly take you up on that offer. I could set you up with a nice room and help you out by tying your ankles to the corners of the bed for you so that when you get tired you won't have to try and hold your legs open anymore. I could hand you out as a prize for good behaviour to my men whenever they please me - or just let them take turns with you as often as they like, seeing as that's what you're best at these days."

"You said you wanted me back," I said in a firm voice, refusing to give his threats any of my attention. "You said you'd end the war if I returned to you. So here I am."

"Mmmhmm," he agreed, reaching out to pluck a strand of my pink and purple hair into his grip and inspecting it in the light. "Out of interest, sugarpie, why the fuck have you done this to your hair? I feel like it's gonna be mighty distracting when I'm peering down at you on your knees for me and I have to look at all this vibrant nonsense."

"Says the man in the bright blue smoking jacket," I hissed. "Stop changing the subject. I came back because you said you'd finish the war with the Harlequins if I did. So are you a man of your word or am I leaving again?"

"Oh you think you'll just leave, do ya?" he asked, releasing my hair and moving away from me to the French doors at the far side of the room. "Because I don't think you want freedom any more than my sweet little Mimi wants it."

Shawn tossed the doors wide, letting a summer breeze slip in through them and the sound of birdsong filtered in too. He stepped aside, gesturing for me to walk on out but I held my ground. I hadn't done what I'd come here for yet. And I didn't believe for one second that I was really free to leave anyway.

"You said Mia was free to go?" I asked, glancing across the room to the clam vag, who I was actually feeling kinda sorry for as she tried to fade into the background.

"Of course," Shawn said loudly. "I'm not a monster. Am I Mimi?"

"No," she breathed though the terror in her gaze called her a liar.

He beckoned her closer and she quickly got up, scurrying to his side and staring at him with wide eyes like he was the only thing in this room that mattered.

"If you wish to leave, Mimi, you are more than welcome to go. I'll miss you dearly and I'll be most disappointed. But I promise no harm will befall you if you choose to move on with your life. So go. Unless there's something else you would rather do?"

Mia hesitated, glancing between me, Shawn and the open door. She looked like a deer caught in headlights, unable to move from the spot even though death was approaching on swift and certain wings.

"Just go," I encouraged her and she flinched like I'd struck her.

"What...would make you happiest?" she asked Shawn in a small voice and my frown deepened as I wondered what the fuck he'd been doing to her to make her behave like this. The girl I'd known when she'd been seeing Maverick was catty and full of herself, unafraid and unapologetic. This creature before me was nothing but a broken shadow of that girl now.

"Well, I'm not entirely certain," Shawn said thoughtfully. "I'm just so het up over my little sugarpie coming back here with her hair all fucked up that I can't settle myself. So any suggestions you might have on how to satisfy this pent up energy in me would be most welcome, Mimi."

Mia looked towards the door again, her hands fisting and releasing a few times before she suddenly dropped to her knees in front of him and started tugging his belt undone. My lips popped open in surprise as I watched her fingers slipping on his belt as she scrambled to undo it quickly and Shawn grinned broadly, his eyes never leaving me while he just let her do it.

"Well shit, I guess she learned her party trick from you, hey sweet cheeks?" Shawn called to me as he didn't even look down at her while she tugged his cock out and dropped her mouth over it. "Though I will admit that you'll be a hard act to follow in this department – I've never known a girl who can suck cock as good as you, sugarpie."

I glanced at the open door again, wondering what the fuck I'd been thinking by coming back here. But then it all just hit me at once. My boys. Me. All the ways I'd fucked them over intentionally and unintentionally…the reason I'd decided to walk into this monster's house and the fact that I hadn't achieved a single thing with my return yet.

"I thought you killed Mia and Miss Mabel," I hissed, looking down at the girl who was sucking his cock before meeting his cold gaze again. "There were four heads up on that balcony, so who-"

"Well four heads look better than two all lined up, don't they?" Shawn said, rolling his eyes at me like that was obvious. "And a couple of Kaiser's men didn't wanna jump onto my ship like the rest, so I added them to the line-up. Besides, there was little more than a scrap of hair left after I blew sweet Jasmine's head off, so I needed a few skulls with a little more meat to them. I'm still lamenting the fact that the stench got so bad I had to take them down."

Mia whimpered at the casual mention of her dead mother but as Shawn cleared his throat she started moving again, bobbing her head as she sucked him off while my gut twisted uncomfortably.

"Luther is in the hospital," Shawn said casually, practically ignoring the way Mia was sucking on his dick. "Rumour around town is that you went and shot him."

I sucked in a sharp breath. "That's bullshit and you know it. You were the one who put a bullet in him," I growled.

"Yeah, I know it," Shawn said with a grin. "I know you fired a little warning shot to try and get him to leave and I followed up with one intended to be a whole lot more lethal. But the funny thing is - his men seem to have focused on the fact that you were pointing a gun at him at the time and put two and two together to get ten. And would ya look at that - you're now the HC enemy number one. They want your head, sugarpie, and I don't think there's much they wouldn't do to get it at this point."

I tried not to panic at those words, at the fear they sent racing through me. Did they all think that I'd done that? Did Fox? I'd wanted my boys to believe my lies because I'd needed to be certain they wouldn't try to chase me here, but believing I was a manipulative bitch who'd been out for revenge and them thinking I'd actually tried to murder the king of The Harlequin Crew were two very different things. Shit. Shit, shit, *shit*.

"Don't look so freaked out about it, Rogue," Shawn cooed. "You don't have to worry while you're here with me. Unless you were starting to consider walking out that door?"

I shook my head, glancing to the table where there was some food laid out as I tried to focus my thoughts. I was going to lose my mind over Luther Harlequin being close to death and his whole crew blaming me for it later. Right now I needed to keep my composure and focus on what mattered which was facing off against the man in front of me.

"What does Luther being in hospital have to do with anything?" I asked, my gaze dropping to Mia as Shawn fisted her hair roughly and started forcing her to take his cock deeper. She began making some gagging noises as she gripped his thighs like she might fall down if she didn't steady herself, but he ignored her.

"Well I can't very well end the war while the kingpin is out of action, can I?" Shawn asked, looking at me like I was an idiot while I tried to ignore the girl choking on his dick. "I have to wait for him to die and the new king to ascend so that I can deal with him directly. Or I guess Luther might recover and I can deal with him after all. Either way, seems like my hands are tied until that situation resolves itself."

I gritted my teeth angrily at his bullshit and Shawn sighed irritably, shoving Mia off of him and pushing his still hard dick back into his pants before buckling his belt again.

She fell onto her ass and gaped up at him with fearful eyes and my whole body tensed as I felt his anger permeating the room like rainfall on an expanse of dried out soil.

"Go find another cock to practice on," he snapped at her. "You suck dick like you're trying to husk an ear of corn. If you're no good for that then you're gonna have to think long and hard about what you *are* good for because this is supremely disappointing. I mean, what good is a whore who can't even make a guy come?"

I frowned at Mia as she stammered apologies and scrambled back to her feet, looking fucking terrified.

"It's alright, poppet," Shawn said to her, moving forward and cupping her cheek in his hand. "But maybe you should go take some time to think about what this makes you, yeah? Because a slut who can't fuck for shit might just be better off not existing at all, don't ya think?"

Mia nodded profusely then turned and ran from the room with a sob breaking past her lips and I had to force myself to remain still and just let her go. She was better off away from Shawn anyway so taking his attention off of her was probably the best help I could offer.

I caught Travis's eyes as he watched her go and he cleared his throat, looking more than a little uncomfortable, though he made no move to intervene in any way. I guessed he really was just a good little lap dog after all, though I wasn't sure what else I'd been expecting. This was how gangs like The Dead Dogs worked. There was a king and everyone else just fell in beneath him in whatever position they managed to claim for themselves. So unless Travis wanted to make a play for the position of top dog, he wasn't gonna go against the man who owned him.

"So what now?" I asked, remaining where I was and trying to assess Shawn's mood. He was grinning, looking so fucking pleased with himself that it made me uncomfortable and I could tell he had all kinds of cruel plans in mind for me.

"Now we eat, sugarpie," he said, moving to the table and pulling out a chair for me. "I want to hear all about the time you spent sleeping with my enemies."

I wet my lips and moved to join him, sinking into the chair he held out and stiffening as he leaned down to speak into my ear, his fingers running down my bare arms so that I was fully encompassed in his shadow and reminded of just how much bigger than me he was.

"And if I don't like the sound of the answers you give me, then maybe we'll have to rethink the pleasantries I'm offering you and start considering burning those ugly as fuck tattoos off of the backs of your thighs," he breathed, his lips brushing against my ear and making me shudder.

I swallowed the lump that had lodged in my throat and looked up at him from the corner of my eyes.

"I don't know what you want me to say," I murmured, placing my hands either side of the plate he'd laid out for me and sliding them forward slowly as I hunted for a knife or even a fork to use against him. That was my best bet here, to strike hard and fast at the first opportunity I could get. A fork could be lethal if wielded right and I had nothing left to lose anymore. "The Harlequins treat their business the way you do. They didn't talk about it around me. They didn't want me to know any of the details of their organisation."

"Mmm. That may be so. But I'm sure you have at least a few juicy bits of information for me. After all, I'm a curious man and I do love to learn about my enemies as intimately as I can. Isn't that right, Travis?" He looked up at the man as he approached us and I met Travis's gaze too, wondering what he was thinking beneath the careful mask he kept his features arranged into.

"Yes, boss," Travis agreed as he dropped down into the chair opposite me and laid his bat on the chair beside his. "Just like when you cut that asshole open last week to get to know him as intimately as you could."

Shawn barked a laugh, straightening suddenly before dropping into the chair at the head of the table between me and Travis. "That I did. Would you like to hear the story of how I came to need to know that fella as intimately as I did, sugarpie?"

My fingers finally connected with the knife that had been laid out for me and I picked it up with my heart sinking as I looked at the flimsy, disposable piece of plastic.

"Oh I see you've found your special bought cutlery," Shawn said, smirking widely as I lifted the knife up to get a look at it. "Premium cheap as fuck disposable - you can't even cut a fucker's eye out with that thing. Believe me - I tried. Not on your Chase of course - I made sure to use a good sharp one for that because I tell you now, that fucker you're holding in your delicate little hand wouldn't have gotten that job done. It's as blunt as shit and breaks under pressure. Just in case you got any crazy ideas into your pretty little head about murdering me over my meal."

"Heaven forbid," I muttered, trying to ignore the way my chest tightened at his words. He'd seen through me. Of course he'd seen through me. I'd offered myself up with no resistance after refusing point blank to come back to him time and again. But that didn't mean I was going to give up. I'd just have to get more creative than stabbing him with my dinner knife.

"Alright then, where were we?" Shawn asked, spearing his meal with his own metal fork and grinning at me as he began cutting it with a particularly sharp looking knife too. My gaze fell on the bracelets he wore as they slid down his wrist while he carved into his food with his knife and my gut tightened as I recognised them. They belonged to Chase and he'd worn them since we were kids. I gritted my teeth, silently vowing to remove them from his body once I killed this motherfucker.

I focused on the new scar he had marking his cheek thanks to me and managed to regain some of my composure as I smiled back at him.

"I think you wanted to tell me about the man you carved up," I supplied.

"Oh yes," he agreed. "Well settle in, sugarpie, because this is one helluva story and you're gonna wanna hold onto your hat."

CHAPTER SIX

"*Can we keep it?*" *Maverick asked, bouncing around Dad, his feet kicking up sand and making the seagull squawk angrily. "I'm gonna call it Gullbert."*

"No, it's a wild animal," Dad said, holding the bird still while I sat beside him in my swim shorts, holding out his pen knife. The bird had a plastic beer ring around its neck and me and Maverick had been trying to catch it for the past hour to get it off. Dad had shown up ten minutes ago, laughing at our attempts before heading up the beach to buy some churros and offering one to the creature. The bird had gone right up to him and snatched the churro from his hand before Dad took hold of it.

"You do it, kid," Dad said, nodding to me encouragement and my eyebrows raised as I shifted a little closer with the knife.

"I don't wanna hurt it," I muttered.

"You won't. You got this, Fox." Dad gave me a firm look and I took a breath, sliding the knife carefully between its feathers and the plastic.

"How comes he gets to do it?" Maverick dropped down onto the sand beside me with a frown.

"Because you can't both do it," Dad said. "And Fox already has the

knife. You can free the next animal you find wrapped in trash."

"I'm gonna free a hammerhead shark," Maverick said with a grin.

I cut through the plastic and Dad looked to Rick. "Why don't you pull it off?"

Maverick nodded eagerly, reaching out before pulling the plastic away from the gull's neck and we shared a triumphant look.

"Rick's right. I wanna keep it. But we're not calling it Gullbert," I said and he elbowed me in the ribs.

"You can't keep it," Dad insisted, but I was too busy diving on Rick and getting payback for that elbow.

He growled as we rolled and thrashed, punching and kicking each other.

"Gullbert's a stupid name!" I snapped.

"You're a stupid name," Maverick snapped back, his fist driving into my ribs.

"You're scaring it," Dad hissed and we both looked over at him, sand falling from my hair as I pressed Maverick down beneath me. The gull was wriggling in his grip, looking at us with panic in its eyes. "You two are like the sun and the moon, when you work together there's harmony, but if you go against one another it's total chaos."

I huffed, making a lock of hair over my eyes flutter upwards and Maverick's head dropped back onto the sand in defeat.

"Come here and sit quietly or I'll let it go somewhere where there aren't two kids scaring the shit outa it," Dad said sternly and we shuffled our way back over to him, bowing our heads.

"Look what your hands can do when they work together," he said, his tone softening as he stroked his fingers over the bird's feathers. "Some people would have seen a doomed bird when they looked at this gull, but you both saw one that needed saving and acted to help it. That's rare, boys. And I'm proud of you for it." Dad smiled at us and warmth filled my chest. "You're both gonna rule this town one day and I know you'll do good so long as you work together."

"Dad," I groaned and he smirked while Maverick mimed throwing up.

"Right, let's free this little guy, yeah?" Dad suggested and we nodded eagerly, watching as he let go of the bird's wings and I was surprised when it *didn't immediately fly off.*

"What's it doing?" I whispered.

"Gullbert's decided to be our pet," Maverick said under his breath.

"He feels safe with us," Dad said then nudged the bird and it regarded him for a moment before flexing its wings and flying away with a squawk, the wind lifting it away from us towards the bright blue sky.

My eyes were closed but my mind was wide awake, burning with a thousand memories and even more regrets. My fingers were locked around Dad's as I sat beside his hospital bed, the steady rhythm of his heartbeat through the monitor the only thing keeping me sane.

I was a terrible king. The kind who'd become his job. I'd been so intent on keeping everything running the way I wanted it run, of ensuring my family were kept safe, that I hadn't once stopped to ask if that was what they wanted. I'd been chasing an imaginary point in time where we'd all be okay again, but it had just been an illusion on the horizon, cast there by foolish beliefs. The regrets stretched back a lifetime, but dwelling on them did nothing because I couldn't change the point in time I was currently idling at. It felt like a crossroads, one route leading me further down this destructive path. And the other...

I rubbed my temples. The other was an equally dark road, but perhaps the one I deserved after everything.

Dad's fingers flexed around mine and my eyes shot open, a wave of hope crashing against my chest.

He cleared his throat, the noise fast turning into a groan and my hand tightened on his.

"Dad?" I rasped. "I'm here. You're okay."

His eyes cracked open, revealing the deep shade of green that mirrored my own. "Hey, kid."

Fuck, I never thought I'd be glad to hear him calling me that.

Mutt yapped, jumping up from beside him and started licking his face, making Dad laugh his deep laugh which sent an ache through my chest. I reared forward, wrapping my arms around him as Mutt wedged himself between us and Dad pulled me close as I breathed in his familiar scent of coffee and earth, his stubble scraping against mine.

The next hour was a blur of nurses and doctors checking on him while I sat and stared at the man I'd been so afraid to lose. I held Mutt on my lap after he kept nipping the hands of anyone who tried to get close to Dad and figured the little beast was going to get his ass kicked out of here if he didn't behave. One of the nurses had already tried to tell me that we couldn't have a dog in here, but one thinly veiled death threat had made her back down sharpish and I was willing to bet she'd warned the other hospital staff not to say anything further on the subject. He bit my fingers more than once, but I didn't give a shit, holding tightly onto him while he growled and grumbled at the sea of staff helping Dad. When they finally left us alone again, Dad had eaten some food and a little colour had returned to his cheeks.

He was propped upright in the bed, looking moody from all the fuss that he'd been drowned in. Luther Harlequin was a prideful man, especially when it came to women. And there hadn't been a single man among the people helping him. But considering his condition he couldn't exactly refuse their help – though he'd made a vague attempt at trying to convince the doctor to sign him off and let me take care of him at home. He was literally half stitched together right now and had zero chance of that happening, but that was Luther.

"Do you remember what happened?" I asked as he scraped the last bite of his pudding out of the pot with his spoon, about to devour it when he saw Mutt staring at the morsel. I'd had one of the Harlequins bring Mutt's dog chow here, but he was still a beggar when it came to people food.

"Here you go, boy." Dad offered it to him and I opened my mouth to protest that he needed the energy more than the dog who'd been eating chicken treats all morning, but Mutt savaged my hand and dove straight from my lap onto the bed to claim his prize.

I rolled my eyes as Dad spoon fed the damn dog and Mutt wagged his tail happily before curling up beside him and laying his head on Dad's arm.

"Good boy." Dad stroked his head and I swear Mutt smiled.

"He's not a good boy," I muttered, sucking the bite mark on my thumb which was now bleeding. "He's the Devil in a tiny fluffy package. If he was a full sized dog, he'd have a death count higher than me by now."

Dad chuckled, scruffing Mutt's fur like he was proud of him over that.

Great, now I was jealous of a dog.

The door banged open and I was on my feet in a heartbeat, yanking the pistol from the pack of my pants and aiming it at the goon who stomped into the room not seeming to care one bit that I had a gun ready to blast his brains out.

"Who the hell are you?" I demanded as he ignored me, looking around as if checking the corners to make sure no one else was here and as I took a step closer to him, the door pushed open again and the click of high heels sounded before Carmen Ortega strode into the room looking like she thought she owned the fucking place.

"Calm down, Pepito, I hardly think Mr Harlequin would have concocted a plan this elaborate just to set up an assassination on me," she said, her Mexican accent touching the words and giving them a little more bite as she set her eyes on my dad who looked paler than he had before she'd shown up. She was dressed in a figure hugging blue dress which looked like it cost more than my car and her dark hair fell in loosely bouncing coils around her stunningly beautiful face.

"What are you doing here, Carmen?" Dad asked, grasping the edge of his bed covers in his tattooed fist before releasing them again like he wasn't sure if he should try to hide the bandages plastered to his chest from the gunshot wound. He despised showing any kind of weakness, especially to people he saw as rivals, and extra especially to rivals who were women, so I was willing to bet he was pissed as all hell now.

"I just came to check that you were still kicking," she said with a shrug, drawing closer to the foot of his bed and cocking her head to one side. "You work for us after all. It's in our interest to make certain you are still capable of performing to the standard we require."

"There's nothing wrong with my performance," Dad growled, scraping a hand over the unshaven scruff on his jaw self-consciously.

"Did you wanna sit?" I asked her, lowering my gun and indicating the only chair in the room for her to take.

"That won't be necessary," she replied, her gaze moving to me and skimming over me in a way that made me feel utterly exposed, like she could see all of my strengths and weaknesses laid out right there before her and had already figured out what way she would exploit them if she needed to.

The huge fucker with curly black hair who I had to assume was her bodyguard quickly dropped to his hands and knees at the side of the bed as if he'd been commanded to, and Carmen proceeded to sit on his back as if it were a fucking bench. What the fuck?

Dad shot me a look which told me to hold my tongue on that strange fucking display and Carmen reached out to take his hand, squeezing his fingers for a moment as she leaned closer to speak with him.

"You had me worried for a moment when I heard the news," she purred and Luther swallowed thickly as he frowned at that statement.

"You were worried about me?" he asked, clearing his throat and shooting me a death glare like I'd done something wrong. Fuck knew what though.

"Of course," she replied, giving him a private smile which I almost wanted to look away from as I felt like I was intruding on something, but as she leaned closer and my dad shifted in the bed, I couldn't help but keep watching. "If you died, this place would be so very fucking boring after all."

"Nice to know you give a shit," Dad said gruffly and she laughed, leaning back and taking her hand from his.

"Do I?" she asked curiously and Luther frowned.

"So you…just came to see if I was okay?" he asked, seeming perplexed by that and Carmen laughed again, tossing her brunette hair and shaking her head like he was the funniest thing she'd seen in a long time - which was damn weird because it didn't seem to me like he'd said anything remotely funny.

"No, chico tonto," she replied, that softness entirely gone from her gaze as she looked down at him in his hospital bed with a predator's gaze. "I am not the type of woman to come visiting sick old men on their death beds. I came to make sure you are still capable of handling the next shipment destined for your shores. Because if you aren't, there is another player on the board who is very keen to take your place."

"You just called me a silly boy and an old man in the same breath," Luther ground out and her smile widened as she baited him.

I cleared my throat, trying to remind him to watch his temper with her and his jaw ticked as he worked to heed my warning and hold his tongue.

"So I did," she mused. "But you didn't answer me."

"Yeah, I can handle the shipment," he ground out.

"Perfecto." She clapped her hands together and stood in a fluid motion. "Then you must hurry to get back to your full strength and on your feet again. I need to know you're as powerful as always so that I can make use of you the way I want to."

"You want to make use of me?" Luther asked his voice taking on a deeper tone.

"Always, Mr Harlequin," she said, her gaze roaming over him. "Our business relationship requires you to have plenty of stamina after all. Fox." She nodded to me and turned for the door, leaving Pepito to shove himself to his feet and hurry after her like some weird, whipped little bitch while she ignored him entirely.

"Bye, Carmen," I called after her, instantly feeling like an idiot and wishing I hadn't said it while Dad remained silent in the bed.

Mutt didn't seem to have any kind of opinion on her which was a fucking first for that judgemental little asshole and he was content to just continue licking the old pudding pot from his position on the bed while the door swung closed behind her.

"She's…a lot," I muttered, relaxing back into my chair while Luther grumbled something about devil women showing up unannounced while a man was trying to get some damn rest. He hadn't seemed so full of things to say about her while she was here though.

I sighed, pushing my hand into my blonde hair which must have looked like a bird's nest from how much I'd been clawing my fingers through it. I didn't want to have this next conversation, but I needed to. And I might as well get it over with.

"Do you remember what happened?" I asked and Dad frowned, slowly nodding.

"Shawn shot me," he growled.

"And Rogue," I said, her name holding so much weight I could barely push it off of my tongue.

He shook his head. "No, she didn't."

My thoughts jarred. "She...didn't?" I croaked, trying to wrap my head around that. I'd sat here for days blaming her for placing my father in this hospital bed alongside that motherfucker Shawn, but she hadn't done this?

"But some of the Harlequins saw, they said-"

"I ain't blind, kid. I know who shot me, I was the one being shot," he said and I stared at him, my tired brain taking an age to process that news.

"What happened?" I asked in desperation. I'd heard the story from my dad's men, but he'd been there front and centre, maybe he knew more.

His forehead pinched and he dropped his gaze to Mutt as he rubbed his thumb over his head in slow circles, sending him to sleep. "I caught up with her in my truck, but I lost control of the vehicle and veered off the road. The next thing I knew, I was waking up, seeing her there walking away from me. Maybe she figured I was dead, I dunno."

My chest tightened like it was in a vice.

"I managed to get out, to go after her," he continued. "But by the time I caught up we were close to Shawn's gates. I shouted out for her to stop before she made it to them, I figured I could bring her back even if I had to do it at gun point. But then she aimed her own gun at me and said something about her being a curse as she begged me to let her go. That was when Shawn showed up outa those gates."

Dread slid down my spine like icy water as I drank in every detail of this story.

"Rogue spoke to him, but I didn't catch what they said. I tried to make Shawn step away from her, but I wasn't exactly holding many cards at that point, kid." He gave me a look that swore he really had tried to stop her and I nodded, my teeth clenching tightly together. "Rogue fired a warning shot to make me leave, but I always was a stubborn motherfucker. That was when Shawn shot me and it was lights out for me from there. Did you...get her back?"

I shook my head, unable to look at him again in that moment, feeling myself unravelling all over again. She'd tried to make him leave? What did that even mean? Even after she'd abandoned me, I was still left with these fucking mind games and questions I had no answer to. "She's gone. She's with him still."

"I'm sorry, Fox," he said in a low voice. "Really, I am."

I nodded vaguely.

"I thought she was better than that, she fooled us all," he said, a bite of anger to his tone, and I knew what that meant. She was officially on his kill list. An enemy to The Harlequin Crew as assuredly as fucking Shawn was. But despite everything, I still couldn't bear the idea of her being killed, shot down in some gang war. It would be akin to ripping my heart from my chest and putting it in a meat grinder.

"She's not to be killed, Luther," I growled in the most commanding voice I had. "No matter what she's done to me, no matter her betrayal. I will not see her die."

He took in my expression like he pitied me. "If she's working against us, against you, then you know I'll step in."

"Well it ain't your call, it's mine," I said darkly and silence settled between us for a minute. I wasn't sure if he was agreeing, but I'd make sure of it when he was back on his feet.

"What's the situation anyway? Are we at war with The Dead Dogs?" he asked.

"Not exactly. They've gone quiet and there's been cops out on the streets since your shooting," I said and he nodded.

"Is Maverick okay?" Luther asked, glancing at the door like he hoped his other son would walk through it.

"Yeah. He came to see you," I revealed and his eyes widened, full of hope.

"He did?" he asked, his love for his traitor son blazing in his eyes.

I nodded stiffly. "Him and JJ," I muttered.

"What's going on, kid?" he asked and I took a breath, ready to say what needed to be said. To start heading down the path that I knew I had to take.

"I'm done, Dad," I said heavily. "All I ever cared about was my boys and Rogue, and the Crew gave me a way to protect what was left of my family all these years. But I fucked up because I got so lost in protecting them that I started ruling their lives, acting like you did with me and Maverick."

"Fox-" he started, but I cut over him as I continued.

"I get why you did it," I said earnestly. "I do. It's why I did it too. But love's not a good enough reason to trap the people you care about because you think it'll keep them close. You sent Rogue away and initiated us into the Crew to make sure me and Rick didn't leave. And I guess it worked for a while, but in the end it broke us."

"Look, kid, I have my regrets, I do, but you've gotta understand-"

"I do understand," I said seriously. "That's what I'm telling you. But the problem was, you never asked what we wanted, you locked us in a jar and prayed in time we'd stop looking for a way out. And now I've gone and done the same thing to my family, and I've lost everyone I've ever loved."

"I know I messed up," Luther tried.

"I know you did too. And I think after this, I can forgive you for it. But I don't forgive myself for doing it to them because I should have known better." Emotion burned a hole in my heart and Mutt whined like he could feel the pain in my words.

"I'm sorry I set a terrible fucking example," he said, reaching for my hand and I let him take it, his fingers tight around mine. "I don't want this for you. There's something about bleeding out on the back seats of a car that puts shit in perspective. Anytime I regained consciousness, all I could think about was you and Rick and how I'd never have you under one roof again, smiling and laughing like we used to when you were kids. I thought I was gonna die alone with both of you hating me and hating each other too, and maybe that's still my fate, but it ain't gonna be yours, Fox. You love those boys and yeah, maybe you've lost the girl, but the rest of them…it can be fixed. You just need to find a way to make them happy again."

"It's fucked, Dad," I said, shaking my head. "They're never gonna want me around again. And it's not like they're all innocent in this."

"Well, the first question is, can you forgive them? And do they still deserve the happiness you once wanted for them?" Dad asked and I took a long time to think on that.

Rogue was gone, and her admission about destroying us all was clear enough. I'd seen JJ and Maverick break as clear as day, and I'd broken Chase first hand.

"I think so…I'm just so fucking angry." I swallowed the sharp lump in my throat and Dad nodded like he understood.

"You can be angry and still want someone to be happy. That's what love is, kid."

I nodded, hanging my head.

"You gotta forget about holding onto them because the tighter you squeeze now, the further they'll run," Dad pressed.

"They're never gonna want me around again." I looked up at him, finding him looking back with an expression that told me exactly what he was about to say, and it scared the hell out of me.

"I'm afraid that ain't the point, kid. I think I've finally figured that out too."

"I have to let them go," I exhaled, the idea of that tearing my heart in two.

"If you get lucky, they'll come back, Fox," he said, but fate had never been that kind to me. It was already too fucked. I knew I had to try and fix what I'd broken, give my boys each other, make sure Chase was found, and ensure they found a home between the three of them. But that didn't mean I'd get them back too.

I rose from my seat and Mutt jumped up, looking up at me with a bark that seemed to say he was onboard with my decision.

"I'm out of the Harlequins," I said decisively and Dad's lips parted on a speech I didn't wanna hear. "It's done. I'll stick around to help kill Shawn, but when he's dead, I'm gonna leave the Cove."

"Wait, son-" he started frantically, but I was already walking out the door with Mutt running at my heels.

It was over. All of it. And like a farmer scorching the land to ensure more things could grow in future, I needed to light the match and watch it burn.

I headed out of the hospital, climbing into my truck and letting Mutt dive in after me. I frowned at the little dog then started up the engine and drove out of the parking lot onto the streets of the upper quarter. The sun was blazing, glinting off the glitzy glass buildings and making the world sparkle like this whole part of town was made of diamonds.

I turned down the roads until I made it to a stone building with the words Sunset Cove Animal Shelter curving above the doorway. The sound of barking dogs carried from inside and I looked to Mutt, suddenly seeing Chase staring back at me as he whined.

"Don't look at me like that," I muttered. "Rogue's gone. There's no one left to look after you."

He barked sharply at me and I cursed, turning to look out the window as I killed the engine. "What am I supposed to do, huh? You hate me, why would you wanna stay? Luther's not gonna be fit to take care of an animal for a long time and he doesn't have time for a pet anyway. He'll be running the Crew. It's too dangerous."

Mutt yipped and I looked back at him, an ache in my chest at letting him go. But this was the point, wasn't it? Letting them all go to find a better life. I was the problem. The one suffocating everyone, and Mutt was just gonna be another casualty if he stayed.

"Some little old grandma will adopt you and give you steak for breakfast," I tried. "You'll get to live in some luxury seaside villa or fancy ass apartment around here."

Mutt bared his teeth at me like that idea was shit. But I couldn't give him what he really wanted.

"She's not coming back," I said, those words tearing into my own chest. "She's gone. She left you behind." I wasn't sure if I was even talking to the dog anymore or myself, all I knew was that I lost it in that second, throwing my fist into the dashboard. Over and over until my knuckles split.

I popped the glove compartment open, hunting for cigarettes and finding a pack there that must have belonged to Chase once. I grabbed it, my fingers catching on a letter that fell out onto the floor. Chase's letter. For Rogue.

I stared at it for several heartbeats before jamming a cigarette into the corner of my lips and dropping the window as I lit it up. Then I snatched the letter from the footwell and held the lighter underneath it. These words weren't for me. And Rogue didn't need them now anyway. She'd fucked him over just like she had the rest of us. And whatever pain was contained within this letter did no one any good anymore.

I hesitated too long, the flame dancing beneath the envelope like it was hungry to do my bidding. I cursed before shoving the letter back into the glove compartment and scoring a palm down my face and tossing the lighter away.

That's not my decision to make.

I had to stop controlling the world around me. I had to let other people make their own choices. And this letter was intended for Rogue, so maybe one day I'd find a way to deliver it to her like Chase had wanted.

Mutt watched me as I dragged down a lungful of smoke and let it pour from my lips in a slow stream.

"What?" I demanded of him and I swear the dog rolled his eyes at me. "You'd have a good life if you went in there." I pointed at the shelter with my smoke. "A better one than I can give you."

He yawned provocatively then turned his face away from me.

"What's that supposed to mean?" I grumbled.

He gave me the side eye and I sighed.

"If I keep you I'm an asshole, if I give you up I'm an asshole. I can't fucking win." I shoved the door open and whistled at him to follow. He reluctantly jumped out and, as insane as my next idea was, maybe I didn't give a fuck. I scooped Mutt up, earning myself a bite to the thumb before carrying him to the porch of the shelter and placing him down.

"Now listen," I said around my cigarette as he sat in my shadow, glaring up at me. "You want a better life, you sit here and stay like a good boy. You wanna run off and live the street life again? Go right ahead. And if you want to stay with me – which let's be honest, I think you'd rather eat a turd on the street – then I'll be waiting in my truck. It's up to you."

"Um, sir?" a woman's voice made my head snap up and I found her standing in the doorway to the shelter. "Would you like me to take him for you?"

"Don't touch him. He's making this decision for himself," I said firmly and her eyes darted left and right like she was looking for the crazy police to come collect me. "Don't you touch him," I warned again as I backed off and Mutt glared after me.

I got back in my truck, reaching across and shoving the passenger door open for him if he wanted to come. I finished my cigarette as I waited for him to move, the two of us in a stare-off as the girl behind him hovered like an awkward butterfly.

"You staying there then?" I called to him. "Is that your decision?"

Mutt turned around, promptly taking a piss on the door of the shelter and making the woman dive out of the firing line before he trotted down onto the sidewalk and strutted off along it with his ass shaking at me. He had as much attitude as Rogue did. Had. *Fuck.*

Street dog it is then.

I reached across the seats, pulling the passenger door shut with a snap that echoed through my soul. Why was letting him go so hard?

I put the truck in drive, forcing myself to let him leave but then I frowned as I spotted him turning back with something in his mouth.

"What the fuck…" I murmured as he took his sweet time trotting back towards me before stepping into the road and sitting in front of my truck.

I pushed the door open, exiting and rounding the vehicle to see what he had. I dropped into a crouch, holding out my hand for it and he dropped whatever it was on my palm. I grimaced as I found a dried out, decaying frog and Mutt barked like he was laughing at me before running off.

"Ergh. You little bastard." I tossed the gross thing away and turned around, finding him looking out at me from the driver's seat of my truck with his paws up on the wheel. He continued barking, clearly amused by that stunt and I moved to wipe my hand off on some grass as I muttered angrily at him under my breath.

"You're staying then, are you?" I demanded, half aware I was still being watched by the woman in the doorway of the shelter who must have been pretty concerned for my mental wellbeing right about now.

Mutt hopped aside as I got in the truck then dove back onto my lap and stuck his head out the window, shutting his eyes as he sniffed the breeze.

"Looks like I'm stuck with you then, huh?" I murmured, unable to help a smile as I scratched his ears and he pretended not to notice the fuss I was giving him. My smile died just as fast as I accelerated in the direction of the lower quarter and all my thoughts turned to the girl who'd left us. The girl my heart would eternally pine for now she was gone again. The girl who'd wrecked me worse than a ship dashed to pieces on sharp rocks. And I'd lay broken in her waters until the end of time.

I took the long route home, driving aimlessly down lanes and streets, memories of a life long lost echoing around me on all of them. I saw the past like it was somehow closer today and I yearned for it in a way I hadn't for a long time. I'd give anything to go back to the days before our precious world was obliterated. To hide there in the haven of my youth and relive it over and over, never to age a single year. But I guessed that was a pointless hope that belonged in Neverland. I'd been trying to hold onto them all so hard, keep what few fragments remained of that time clenched in my fist. But maybe fate had been telling me all along that I had to let go.

As I turned a corner, I realised I was driving up the graffiti covered street that led to Rejects Park and my gaze snagged on the park owner Joe McCreevy. He was standing outside the park with a table set up before him and clothes laid out all over it. Clothes I would have recognised in any world, in any lifetime. Rosie was there with Jake, the bitch holding a bright pink tank top up to her tits and asking for her friend's opinion as he toyed with a bag of jellybeans in his hand.

"Rogue's," the word gritted out between my teeth and I swung the wheel hard, mounting the curb across the street from them as I saw nothing but a red storm clouding my vision.

Mutt barked out the window at Joe like he was pissed at that asshole too and the guy looked over at us in confusion. But worse than Joe trying to make a quick buck off of clothes that weren't his to sell was the fact Carter Jenson was there, thumbing through the selection of her underwear in a wooden box.

I shoved the door open and Mutt jumped out as I stalked after him, crossing the road without even looking and a wailing horn said I'd walked into oncoming traffic. Mutt was already across the road, diving on Carter and savaging his ankle, but as he tried to shake the dog off, he still didn't seem to realise the danger lurking behind him.

The blood drained from Joe's face and he slicked a hand over his oily black hair. "Now listen a second, M-Mr Harlequin, she didn't pay her rent and that makes whatever's in that trailer mine. Besides, she's Shawn Mackenzie's girl now, ain't she? So she's gone against ya and-"

I grabbed hold of the table and flipped it up with a snarl, sending clothes flying everywhere and Carter screamed like a girl as he tried to run. I caught him by the back of the shirt, wheeling him around as my eyes fell on the Green Power Ranger panties in his grip.

No. Oh Fucking hell no.

I knew Rogue had betrayed me. I knew she was gone to the arms of a man I despised, a man who'd shot my father, who'd killed good people. But something about seeing her clothes laid out for vultures like Carter to claim still didn't sit right with me. This stuff, these clothes. They were hers. Not his.

My fist connected with Carter's jaw, knocking him clean onto his back with a hard thump as he hit the sidewalk. He tried to throw Rogue's GPRPs away, but they were tangled on his fingers so I stamped my boot on his wrist, making him squeal like a pig before I reached down and snatched them from his hand.

A scream behind me made my head snap around and I found Mutt biting Rosie's legs and clawing at her sneakers. *Good boy.*

"It's rabid!" she wailed and Jake stared around at the mayhem, casually pushing a jellybean between his lips instead of helping her. "Jake, kill it! Kill it!" She kicked at Mutt who leapt aside and I left Carter on the ground, new prey locked in my sights as she almost caught the dog in the face.

Rage burned through my veins like acid and my fists curled with the urge to punch this bitch and silence her shrieking voice. But as tempting as that was, punching a defenceless woman in the face seemed a bit overkill – even if the woman in question grated my nerves to shreds on a semi-regular basis.

I grabbed the crop top from her hand and pointed in her face. "You ever try to kick my dog again or ask your jellybean eating fuckwit of a friend to kill him, I'll put you in the ground Rosie Morgan," I hissed and she fell silent, her lower lip wobbling as tears spilled from her eyes. "Do you fucking understand me?"

"Y-yes," she stammered and I glanced over her shoulder, noticing Mutt taking a shit on the sidewalk right behind her.

"Then apologise to him. On your knees. Right now." I took hold of her shoulders, spinning her around at high speed and making her shriek in alarm.

Jake continued to munch his way through his jellybeans as he watched with wide eyes, apparently in no way inclined to step in and help Rosie and as he hadn't been interested in Rogue's belongings, I left him be.

Mutt stopped shitting and moved to sit looking up at us and I shoved Rosie down to the ground, her right knee sinking fully into the dog shit and making her release a wild sob.

"Say it," I snarled, my fingers twitching for a gun as I fell into the darkest river of violence inside me. This was a kindness. She had no fucking idea how close I was to fetching my pistol from the truck and blowing her brains out along with anyone else who'd touched Rogue's clothes. I was having a goddamn shitstorm of a day and I needed an outlet which brought me some kind of relief.

"S-sorry," Rosie choked out.

"Louder!" I barked, realising we were gathering a sizeable crowd now from the trailer park and some of the girls from JJ's club were there among them.

"I'M SORRY!" Rosie cried, falling apart into hysterics as Mutt gazed blandly at her. I swear that dog was as psychotic as I was.

Sniggers sounded from the crowd but one sharp look from me shut them up. I sought out Joe, finding him gathering up the clothes he'd been selling, placing them into a couple of plastic bags.

"Here, take 'em," he said, offering them to me as his hands trembled.

I ran my tongue across my teeth, taking them from him and adding the panties in my hand to the bag.

"Her trailer is now property of the Harlequins," I gritted out, uncertain why I was doing this, just sure I couldn't let any other asshole claim ownership of it. "If anyone touches it or any item in it, I'll be taking it up with you, Joe," I warned and he nodded, wiping sweat from his brow.

"S-sure thing," he forced out.

I turned my back on him, feeling eyes on me from every direction. I slapped Jake's jellybeans out of his hand and sent the multicoloured candies flying everywhere before I crossed the road and whistled for Mutt to follow.

I placed Rogue's stuff in the back of the truck, got in the cab and accelerated in the direction of home.

A cold sort of numbness took hold of me by the time I arrived back at Harlequin House and I sat in the truck for way too long after I'd switched the engine off, staring at nothing, feeling nothing.

I could sense the emptiness of the house above me and realised this place had never been home to me. Home was my friends. Home was JJ making margaritas and dancing around the kitchen like he was mid-show, home was Chase working out on the patio to rock music and lifting weights as he worked to beat his PB. But nothing was home more than the past. A place where I still had my brother, a place where Rogue was whole, a place where she loved me, even if it wasn't the type of love I'd always wished for from her. Maybe it was more than I'd ever deserved.

Rejects Park

ROGUE

CHAPTER SEVEN

I jolted awake to the feeling of a hand locking around my throat and a scream tried to rip its way from my lungs before the fingers tightened and cut the sound off at its roots.

"There it is," Shawn purred, his blue eyes lighting excitedly as he loomed over me, his weight dropping on top of me as he sat on my chest, ignoring the way I was thrashing against him.

I tried to jerk back into my pillows and when that made no difference, I swung my fists into his sides and tried clawing at his hands to wrench him off of me.

"Shh," Shawn hushed, ignoring every attempt I made to free myself of him. "You want me to let go then you gotta stop fighting, sugarpie. Accept it. Give me full control over your fate and maybe I'll let you breathe again."

My heart thrashed like a bird trapped in a too small cage and my lungs burned with an impossible fire as the need for oxygen overwhelmed me. I was back at his mercy just like the first time he'd done this. When he'd meant to kill me and only some strange twist of fate had kept me alive against his will.

Inside my head I was screaming. But as my panicked gaze locked on the heat in his eyes and I felt the excitement thrumming through him, I knew he wasn't going to stop unless I did as he wanted.

A shudder ran down my spine and my muscles locked up tight as I forced myself to release him. I closed my eyes and thought of my boys, somehow finding the strength to let my arms fall to the bed either side of me.

"Eyes on me, sugarpie," Shawn growled, his grip not loosening in the slightest.

I didn't want to look at him. I didn't want him to be the last thing I saw if this wasn't just some game. But I knew I had no choice if I wanted any chance of winning against him, so I forced my eyes to flutter open and watched a cruel smile spread across his face.

"Good girl," he growled, holding on tight for another long second before releasing me and sitting back.

I sucked in a huge breath, instantly starting to cough as he let his weight rest on my chest, making it harder for me to get all the air I needed into my lungs.

"Maybe there's hope for you after all," Shawn purred, shifting back a little more as he looked down at me.

I'd slept in a silky black teddy that Mia had given me and Shawn's gaze dropped to my tits as they threatened to spill out of it, his hands roaming down to grope them roughly through the fabric before he tugged it hard enough to force them free. Disgust twisted my gut and made bile rise in my throat.

"Doesn't it feel better to be good?" he asked me in a low tone, his eyes on my tits though he made no further attempt to touch my bare flesh. "Maybe your little brush with death there has you in the mood to make me even happier..."

A sneer pulled at my lips and before I could stop myself, I spat at him, a wad of saliva hitting him in the face and sliding down his cheek.

Shawn stared down at me in surprise for a moment then broke into a peal of wild laughter as he reached up to wipe the spit from his cheek.

I recoiled as he reached for me, wiping the saliva down the centre of my tits before gripping the left one hard and digging his fingers into my skin until a whimper of pain built in my throat. But I refused to let it pass my lips, glaring up at him and waiting for him to do his worst. I couldn't overpower him like this. I couldn't do a damn thing, but if he wanted to get off on the power he held over me, then I wasn't going to be giving him ammo in the form of my fear. He wasn't going to get that from me. Not ever again.

"I can't wait to douse that fire in your eyes, sugarpie," he hissed, leaning close and speaking right into my ear so that the tobacco and musk scent of his skin overwhelmed me and tried to launch me right back into my past.

I fought off the memories though, refusing to let him force me back into the skin of the girl I'd been for him then. Because I'd tasted a life so much sweeter since he'd left me for dead in that ditch. A life I thought had been stolen from me for good. And even if I'd set a match to that existence in payment for their protection from this beast, I still had that taste lingering on my tongue and it was a heated, passionate kind of obsession which a man like Shawn Mackenzie could never understand or compare to.

Shawn shoved himself away from me, pushing himself to stand beside the small bed he'd brought down into the cellar for me to sleep on. Miss Mabel had wanted me to join her in her rooms, but I'd refused, knowing this motherfucker would come for me and not wanting her close when he did. Besides, I was in the company of Chase's agony in this basement and I was at home with it embracing my own suffering.

"Get up, sweet cheeks, and get dressed. You look like a cheap hooker laying there with your tits out like that. You've got three minutes to make yourself presentable and you won't like what happens if you keep me waitin'."

He turned and strode out of the room, leaving me to push myself upright as I watched him walk away.

I swallowed thickly, feeling the tenderness of my throat against the motion and knowing I was going to have bruises to rival the ones he'd given me before by the morning. I ran my fingers over the skin he'd ravaged, curling my hand against a tremble in my fingers and pushing back the violation I felt over what he'd done.

There was a three legged stool by the door and a dress lay over it alongside a pair of white sneakers. I stepped out of the silk teddy and pulled the red dress on, finding it tight fitting but stretchy so I could move in it okay, even if it was a size too small - no doubt because it belonged to Mia. I hadn't been offered any underwear so I had to go without and I couldn't help but feel a little more vulnerable without it, though I knew it made no real difference.

Mind games. Twisted fucking mind games. I knew them well and I had to fight off the urge to play into them, reminding myself over and over again that I wasn't that girl anymore. I wasn't his plaything. I wasn't his anything. Aside from his death.

I made it to the top of the stairs and Shawn was there waiting for me, leaning against the wall with his foot kicked back against it and whistling like he didn't have a care in the goddamn world.

"Let's go," he said, offering me his arm like a proper gent and I reluctantly took it while sweeping my gaze over him and trying to figure out if he had a weapon concealed anywhere on him which I might have been able to get my hands on. He was wearing a white t-shirt and a pair of pale blue jeans, the fabric of his shirt hanging low enough to conceal his waistband so that it was hard to tell if he was armed or not.

"Where are we going?" I asked as he tugged me along the corridor which led through the main part of the house.

"Out. I figured you and me could take a turn about my new empire, sweet cheeks, take in the local sights, that kind of thing."

"I thought you were going to end the war with the Harlequins? How is this your empire if you're leaving town?" I asked.

"Ending the war doesn't have to equal me vacating the premises," Shawn said with a shrug. "But don't you worry your pretty little head about politics, sugarpie. There are so many other things that could be filling it after all."

I frowned at him as he smiled serenely, no sign at all of his inner psychopath on show, just the charming asshole I'd fallen for way back when I was so alone that he seemed like the best option I'd had in a long damn time.

I tried not to think too much about the place I'd been in when I'd met him, the way I'd been so fucking lonely and hopeless that his attention had actually felt like taking a breath of fresh air after years spent beneath ground.

I'd been at some house party in a not so shitty part of town and to this day I still couldn't remember how I'd ended up there. I'd probably been invited by some asshole who wanted to get into my panties, but all I really remembered from that night was how fucking low I'd been feeling. How fucking pointless everything had seemed.

At some point I'd headed up to the roof on my own, swigging on a bottle of rum and looking out at the darkening sky while I just tried to feel...anything.

I'd stepped up onto the edge and looked down at the drop below, wondering if it would kill me if I fell. Wondering if I'd even feel that.

"Well?" a man's voice spoke behind me and I startled a little at the realisation that I wasn't alone.

"Well what?" I asked, looking back over my shoulder at him and arching a brow as I took in his muscular build, heavily tattooed skin and the dark look in his eyes which said he knew the taste of pain intimately, and he enjoyed dishing it out too.

I knew who he was. I'd been in town long enough to figure out that The Dead Dogs were the biggest players around here and Shawn Mackenzie was a man who liked the limelight. He drew attention to himself at all times and I could admit I'd looked before. But this was the first time I'd noticed him looking back.

"Don't keep a man in suspense, sugarpie. Jump or don't. I'm waiting to hear how prettily you'll scream on the way down." He gave me a smirk which said he really would enjoy the show if I decided on jumping.

"Maybe you could give a girl a push?" I asked. "Seems like I'm having trouble pulling the trigger on my own."

"And why is that?" Shawn asked, toking on his cigarette so that the cherry glowed in his blue eyes and made him look even more like the demon he was.

"Because I find I don't care about dying any more than I care about living. So it seems kinda pointless to me," I replied in a flat tone, swigging from my rum again and feeling it burn all the way down.

Shawn stepped closer, flicking his cigarette aside and tilting his head as he regarded me with a keener interest than he had before.

"Well look at you," he murmured. "You really are the most beautifully kind of broken, aren't you?"

I shrugged. There was truth in that statement though it still didn't mean anything to me. Nothing had meant anything to me in a really, really long time.

He stopped before me, still watching me with that predatory look in his eyes while I stared impassively back. His hand locked around my throat and he shoved me backwards, making my heart lurch as I was held out over the edge of the rooftop, my back to the drop below.

I grabbed his wrist on instinct as my heart kept thumping at a rampant pace, my body wanting me to fight to live even if I found it hard to care about it myself.

Shawn held me there, a smile pulling up the corners of his mouth as he watched me.

"So what would I have to do to earn that scream from your pretty lips?" he asked in low drawl which had my skin prickling. This man was dangerous. I should have been trying to get as far from him as possible. But maybe that was exactly what I needed - a little bit of fear in my life. Because I sure as fuck had trouble feeling any other kind of emotion.

"If I knew then maybe I'd have jumped already," I breathed, watching the way his eyes lit at the idea of him just letting go. And maybe that would be for the best. Because at least then it would be over. I wouldn't be wasting my life waiting for something which I knew I'd never find. I wouldn't be left hanging in this place between emotions where I found it hard to care about anything at all. I'd just be done.

Shawn broke a laugh and yanked me upright, shifting his grip on me to the back of my neck.

"I think I wanna play with you, sugarpie. Tell me your name so I know what to groan when I'm coming inside you in five minutes," Shawn said roughly, every word a threat I knew I should have been running from. But I was so sick of fucking running.

"Rogue," I said, wondering if he might just be the key to making me feel something again. Or at least if he might be the key to me waking the fuck up.

"Well, Rogue, how about you and me do somethin' interesting?" he purred, his thumb dragging over my bottom lip hard enough to smudge my lipstick and as he tugged me closer so that he could take a kiss from me, I let him. Because I knew he was a bad decision, but making it felt like the only thing left to me aside from jumping from that damn roof and seeing if it even hurt when I hit the ground.

Shawn led me through the front door and I glanced around at his men who stood watch by it, but none of them said a word as we passed.

He walked me straight to an unassuming looking black Ford with tinted windows and opened the driver's door before shoving me in.

I scrambled across the seats as he followed me, falling into the passenger seat as he closed the door and started the engine.

"Did I ever tell you about the time I spent with your boy Chase down in that basement, sweet cheeks?" Shawn asked casually as we started driving, and I cast him a wary look as we drove out of the gates and away from Rosewood Manor without a single member of his gang in tow.

"No," I replied, looking away from him to inspect the car around me in search of anything I might be able to use as a weapon.

"It was quite beautiful really," Shawn said thoughtfully, his eyes on the road. "Me and him found this sense of nirvana between us which really touched my soul. There's beauty in that kind of bond you know - between a killer and the man at his mercy. And you know what the strangest thing of all was?"

"No," I muttered again, wishing I didn't have to listen to this while trying not to show how much it was getting to me.

"Your boy *wanted* me to do all those terrible things to him. It's true. He is one fucked up little hellion, that's for sure. So full of rage and self hatred, guilt and this wonderful kind of acceptance. He knew what he was worth, you see. He knew a death by my hand would be more than he deserved." Shawn smiled like he was reliving some happy memory and my gut churned.

I bit my tongue against the bile rising in my throat at his words because I knew at least in part that was the truth. Chase had always thought so little of himself thanks to the upbringing his piece of shit father had offered him. He'd always been trying to prove himself worthy while endlessly convinced that he never would be. There had been a time when I'd tried to do all I could to show him how much value he held, but he'd never truly accepted that. And after seeing the way he'd looked on the beach when Fox had been going to shoot him, I knew he still felt those same doubts, harboured that same belief that he was worthless, no matter how much anyone else tried to convince him of the opposite.

I dropped my hand into the pocket of the door beside me as subtly as I could, and a little thrill of adrenaline surged through my veins as my fingers grazed against something cold and metallic inside it.

"It made it all kinds of interesting to torture him - which is why he ended up staying alive I suppose. I went soft over him. I enjoyed doling out the punishment he ached for so much that I let it go on longer than I should have. Though I suppose you'd know all about that, wouldn't you sugarpie?"

"All about what?" I asked as I hooked the metal item into my hand, my heart dropping a little as I realised it was only a pen, but it was still sharp and hard. I could make it work.

"About me helping you to accept the truth of yourself. The same way you always loved to spread your legs for me like a good little whore no matter how many times I scolded you for how willingly you begged for cock. It's because deep down inside you know that you're a dirty, ruined thing, don't you? And you know that me fucking you like the whore you are just helps you to accept that about yourself. You know it's what you deserve. Just like Chase knew that he deserved it when I cut his eye from his pathetic, self-loathing face because he knows how utterly worthless he-"

A furious snarl escaped me and I lunged at him with the pen in my hand and the desire for his death consuming every piece of me.

I'd been aiming for his neck, but the tip of the metal slammed into the meat of his shoulder as he tried to lurch away from me.

The car swerved violently and I was knocked into the steering wheel, but I didn't give a fuck. There was only one thing left for me to do with this son of a bitch and I'd given up everything I'd ever dreamed of for a chance to achieve it. I wasn't going to back down now. I wasn't going to fail at this after all the pain I'd caused to achieve it.

I ripped the pen free and started stabbing him wildly, my strikes driving into his right arm repeatedly as he fought to ward me off before I managed to slam it into his cheek too.

Shawn roared in pain and jerked the steering wheel so hard that I was thrown back and half fell into the footwell. I scrambled back onto my seat and dove at him once more but a second later, a huge crash sounded as the car slammed into a wall and I screamed as I was hurled through the car, colliding with the passenger door as glass shattered around me and my head impacted with something hard enough to knock me out.

I wasn't sure if I lingered in the dark for minutes or seconds, but a fist wrapping itself in my hair and hauling me from the wreckage woke me up sharply.

"I tried playing nice, sugarpie," Shawn snarled at me as he dragged me out of the car and across the asphalt. I had to fight to scramble along at his feet while the agony in my skull almost blinded me. "But I'm okay with playing rough too."

The hard road gave way to wooden boards and I was tossed against a metal gate that clanged loudly as I hit it and fell to my ass before it.

I blinked up at the dark sky above as I rolled onto my back, taking note of the agony in my body and trying to figure out if I'd broken anything. There were cuts and scrapes along my left arm and a burning pain radiated from somewhere close to my hairline by my temple.

Shawn stood over me with blood staining his right arm and the wound on his face bleeding steadily as he lifted a set of bolt cutters and used them to cut through the chain securing the gates before us.

I blinked at my surroundings as the taste of salt on the air and the crash of waves called to me, and I realised where we were. Sinners' Playground. One of the few places where me and my boys had ever felt truly safe and secure together as one. Where no one could find us and intrude on our love and the days were filled with the endless sunshine of my past.

Shawn dropped the bolt cutters as he shoved the gates open and he picked up a can of gasoline before grabbing a fistful of my hair and dragging me through them.

Blinding pain scored through my skull and I belatedly felt the wetness trickling out of my hair from my temple as I scrambled along at his mercy, his boots stomping along the old boardwalk I'd once loved so much.

It felt like every step he took on this space tainted it, leaving the mark of his dirty soul upon it and stealing the innocence of the love I'd found here piece by piece.

He dragged me through the amusement arcade that filled the central part of the pier and we emerged on the other side of it where the motionless rides waited for us and the sea was visible beyond the abandoned Ferris wheel.

Shawn released me with a shove that sent me thumping down onto my ass as he stood in front of the carousel where JJ had found me hiding not so long ago and made me feel like I might just have somewhere to belong again after all this time.

The memory of his arms around me, his flesh against mine and his sweet words in my ear made a shiver run down my spine as I tried to cling onto that feeling and use it to strengthen me for what was going to come next.

"While young Chase and I were enjoying the perks of each other's company, he would on occasion mutter some pain induced nonsense which held very little value to me aside from to prove how truly fucked up he was inside," Shawn mused. "He would murmur things to dear Fox Harlequin and his buddy Johnny James and even that traitor Maverick on occasion. Just silly things about how sorry he was and how he wished he could go back in time to how it used to be. How it used to be with *you* in particular. And on more than one occasion he mentioned the strangest name - Sinners' Playground. And I have to admit that got me all kinds of curious," Shawn said, his lips tilting up in a savage grin as he watched me cower at his feet.

"Looks like you found it then," I muttered as I scoured my brain, trying to figure out if there was anything here that I might be able to use against him, any way that I might finish what I'd started despite this turn in my luck.

"Mmhmm," he agreed, gazing around with a decidedly unimpressed look on his face. "Turns out this old shit pit is something of a let down on closer inspection. In fact, the whole thing seems primed for demolition if you were to ask me."

My pulse leapt with fear at that casual statement and I had to fight to keep the emotion off of my face as I stared up at him.

Shawn watched me like he was drinking in my pain and devouring it entirely before he ever so slowly unscrewed the cap on the gas can.

"It's been quite some time since you came back to me, sugarpie," he said casually as he tipped the can up and began walking while he poured the pungent, flammable liquid over the dry boards and headed towards the teacups ride with it. "And the Harlequins certainly know where you are."

"So what?" I asked, pushing myself to my feet while trying to ignore the dizziness in my skull as I did so.

"I'm just wonderin' how long you expected them to take?" he went on as he splashed the ride with gasoline then continued walking, drenching the boards and heading towards the fortune teller machine where I could see one final card waiting inside it to be drawn.

"Who?" I asked, playing dumb but he just offered me a wolf's smile in return.

"Did you think it was different with them?" he asked, moving behind me and splashing more gasoline as he went. "Did they whisper sweet promises in your ears as they fucked you raw? Did they tell you they loved you while you took their cocks like a good, useful little whore?"

I swallowed thickly as I tried to block out his words, pushing away the memories of me and my boys and the things we'd been doing since I returned to this place as I tried to focus on him instead and figure out what the hell I was going to do here.

"Pretty words are so easy, aren't they?" Shawn murmured, tossing the gas can aside as he finished pouring it and completed the circle surrounding us, leaving one small patch of boardwalk clear to our left with a view of the sea beyond it. "They're candy laced with poison, so easy to feed to hungry mouths."

"You should know," I said. "You spout poison as easily as you breathe."

Shawn chuckled as he moved to stand at my back, his fingers teasing into my hair as he tugged it over my shoulder and away from my ear. My skin prickled at the contact - not in any good way but the way it would if I found myself lost in the wilderness and realised there was a mountain lion at my back.

"Did they tell you that you were their one and only?" he asked in a low voice, his mouth brushing my ear as he leaned over me and his arms moved to circle my body, something hidden in each hand as he held them before me. "How did it feel to hear such sweet lies before they passed you along to the next throbbing dick in line?"

"It isn't like that," I hissed.

"No?" Shawn asked, feigning surprise at my words. "So you didn't fuck any of them then? You didn't do what you do best and spread those pretty thighs so that they could gain all the access they might have wanted to that wet, wet, pussy of yours?"

I swallowed the words that rose in my throat, knowing he was baiting me and fighting against the urge to rise to it.

"You are a damn good lay, sugarpie, no one is denying that. You found your calling in fucking, you really did. But deep down, I think you and I both know that that's all you're really good for, isn't it?" Shawn pressed, his breath sickly hot against my neck as he moved even closer to me so that I could feel his hard cock driving against my ass.

"It's not," I breathed, unable to help myself as I bit back at him.

"Are you sure?" he asked, his words slipping beneath my skin and wrapping around my shattered heart despite every effort I made to keep them out. "So where are they then? Why haven't they come for you if you mean so much to them?"

"I don't need rescuing," I said with as much grit as I could muster. "I told them not to follow me."

"Oh. So I suppose love would stop them from coming for you then? They love you so damn much that they just can't bear to go against your wishes, no matter what you might be getting up to with me. Do you think I'm a fool, sugarpie? You think I can't see you wishing for my death every time you turn those big blues my way? You think I wasn't expecting you to try and kill me like you did tonight?"

"You tried to kill me once - seems like I'm within my rights to want you dead in return."

Shawn laughed, nuzzling my hair and making me recoil, but as I was trapped in the cage of his arms I only ended up pressing my back to his chest more firmly, making the swell of his cock against my ass more apparent.

"So they agreed to let you come after me, did they? The sacrificial lamb sent to try and kill the big old bad guy? How many times did they say you should let me come inside you in the pursuit of my downfall then?"

"They didn't tell me to come back to you," I snapped. "They didn't want that. You saw the way the Harlequins were trying to stop me at the gates to the manor. You know-"

"Then that only brings us back to my first question, sugarpie. Why haven't they come for you?"

Shawn's words hung in the air around me and I was forced to face them as the sound of the sea crashing against the shore below us filled the silence and left my heart aching.

"Did they tell you they loved you?" he murmured, his hands dropping to mine as he pressed the things he was holding into my grasp. "Did those words taste so sweet to your poor, empty soul?"

I swallowed thickly, blinking against the tears that were trying to spring to life in my eyes as I fought against what he was saying, but he wouldn't stop and no matter how hard I tried, I couldn't block him out.

"What good are those professions of love to you now, sugarpie? Do they keep you safe from monsters like me? Do they still warm your soul when you know how empty they must have been?"

"They weren't-"

"Shhh." Shawn pressed a kiss to my cheek in a gesture that almost seemed like it was supposed to be comforting, but as he moved his mouth back to my ear, I knew it was just a cushion for the blow of his next words. "You're a dirty, broken thing with nice tits and the kind of ass men would fight to ram their cock into, sweet cheeks. You got a mouth just made for suckin' cock, and a pussy that's always wet and willing. Men will say a whole lot of things to fuck a girl like you - a beautiful, broken doll hunting for something to fill her up and make her whole again. But no matter how good your cunt might have felt wrapped tight around their cocks, they haven't so much as sent me a threatening letter on your behalf since you came to me. I haven't heard a word. Not a fucking peep. And I think you know why that is, don't you?"

I shook my head, biting my tongue as I fought to keep the venom of his words out of my ears.

"I told them I'd chosen you," I said. "I made them believe it."

"Oh is that how love works then?" he taunted with a soft laugh. "Undying declarations so easily forgotten in the face of some pretty lies? How fickle that love must have been...or how false."

"You don't know what you're talking about," I hissed, trying to ignore the way my pulse was pounding in my ears and the way my chest felt altogether too tight at his words.

"Don't I? Because it wasn't so long ago that I was whispering sugar-coated words into your ears and making good use of this tight body of yours."

"Don't try to pretend there was even a hint of love between us," I said waspishly, knowing the truth of that clearly enough. Neither one of us had ever come close to wanting that or making those kinds of professions. There had never been any kind of soft emotion between me and him.

"Oh no, sugarpie, I'm not going to pretend that I loved you. Truth be told, the only person I think I've ever truly loved is myself. My brother came close, but I would have always chosen myself over him and I certainly never would have tried to claim love for a woman. Not even my own momma – you know for yourself how judgemental that bitch can be, though of course a boy needs his momma all the same. But don't you see? That's what makes me so good at what I do and what I see in others. I don't get caught up with *feelings* so I can identify people easily because I am not clouded by my own cares or desires when I look upon them. That's how I know what you are. And it's why you'll always end up right back here with me in the end. Because despite all of your silly dreams of the woman you might wish to be, you know that there is only one who you ever *will* be, and I won't lie to you about seeing her in your eyes."

"I'm more than that girl you think you know so well," I insisted but my voice was weak and full of every doubt I'd ever had about myself as he broke through the walls I'd been working so hard to construct around my heart.

"No, sugarpie, you're not," Shawn said, his mouth grazing my ear again. "Which is why they ain't here. It's why they forgot you so damn easily. Because hot, eager pussy is still just pussy at the end of the day. And there isn't a pussy on this planet worth a man dying over. Certainly not yours. They haven't come for you because they know what you are as well as I do. They believed your lies because they weren't lies at all. They didn't need convincing that you were nothing more than a wandering cunt because they already knew that. Just like they all know you'll be back serving my cock just as soon as you remember your place in this game. The only thing holding you back is yourself." Shawn pushed the items fully into my hands before dropping his fingers to my waist and pulling my ass back against his hard on again.

I didn't need to look down at the single match and matchbook he'd given me to know what they were and despite how small and insignificant those items were, they felt like they weighed more than I could bear to hold.

"Let it go, sugarpie," Shawn commanded in a low, rough voice which somehow crept into my deepest fears about myself and curled all around them. "You're the girl who no one wanted - do you remember telling me that?"

I nodded mutely, wondering why I'd ever let myself admit things like that to him, but he'd always been like this, able to crawl beneath my skin and peel my insecurities out from under it.

"They believed the worst of you so easily, didn't they? And why is that, do you suppose?" Shawn's hands slid onto my wrists and my body trembled at his touch, the familiar cloying sense of hopelessness pushing in on me as I remembered what it had been like to be his girl. To have no vision of anything better out there because I knew there was nothing better first-hand. To be the girl he kept telling me I was and knowing that at least in part he was right about her. About me.

Unwillingly, I thought of my boys. Of the things Johnny James had said to me to make my heart race or the way Rick had kissed me like his soul would set on fire if he didn't, of the way Chase had hated me so hard it tore us in two, and the way Fox had wanted to burn the world down for me a thousand times. Those things I'd felt with them were real. They had to be real. But then why were Shawn's words spreading within my veins, making me doubt every moment I'd stolen with them? Making me wonder if he had a point.

If they knew me the way I wanted to believe they knew me then why would they so easily believe that video I'd made? I'd hit them all with it as hard as I'd known how to and I hated myself for it, but I'd been trying to keep them safe. Trying to keep them away from Shawn and his sadistic games while giving myself a chance to play against him and win.

But I wasn't winning, was I? I was here in the cage of Shawn's arms, standing in one of the few places on this earth where I'd ever truly felt happy and he was guiding my hand to strike a match against it.

"Let the past burn, sugarpie," he breathed in my ear. "Let it all burn up so that you can rise from the ashes of your past as the creature you were always born to be. Stop running from what you know you are."

My heart was beating so fast that I was having trouble catching my breath and my eyes burned with tears I didn't want to let fall as the weight of every dark thought I'd ever had about myself came crashing down on me at once until I was drowning in all that self-loathing and doubt and the undeniable knowledge that I was just the girl who was so easy to throw away.

And that was all I ever would be now.

Shawn's strong hand gripped mine and he forced me to strike the match, though I didn't have the strength in my limbs to fight him anymore anyway.

"Come on then, Rogue," he growled, using my name for once and making my limbs lock up with fear as I looked at the lit match in my hand and scented the gasoline on the air surrounding us. "Are you gonna jump, or do you need a push?"

My gaze flicked up from the match to the pier surrounding us and the echoes of all the memories I'd had in this place which hung so close, I could almost step right back into them. I looked up at the Ferris wheel where I'd spent so many nights watching the sun set with one or all of my boys, the gilded waves calling out my name and making me feel at peace. This place was a part of my soul. And no matter what I was or what my boys truly felt or thought about that, nothing could steal those memories from me.

I tried to raise my hand to blow the match out, but Shawn jerked it away, flicking the match from my fingertips with a snarl of, "Push it is then."

A whoosh of flames engulfed us just as thunder crashed overhead and I cried out in agony as the pier I'd loved so much went up in a blaze of flames.

Shawn laughed loudly as we were surrounded by fire, the heat of it licking at my skin and making me recoil into him despite me knowing that he was far more dangerous than any spark.

"Nice work, sugarpie!" Shawn cawed, his hand smacking my ass so hard I knew he'd left a print before he caught me by the wrist and dragged me towards the gap he'd left in the flames beside the railings on our left.

My heart was shredding into a thousand pieces as my numb feet stumbled over the boardwalk which had held so much of my heart, and pain ripped through my core as a strangled cry of grief and loss escaped me.

Shawn only laughed louder at my pain and the next thing I knew, he was shoving me so hard that I fell from the side of the burning pier with a scream tearing from my throat.

I hit the water hard and shot below it as my scream turned into a stream of bubbles and I sank lower and lower into the dark.

I made no effort to swim for the surface, curling into a ball instead and willing the tide to take me, to wash me away to some faraway shore where none of this had ever happened and I could pretend to be someone new. Someone better. Someone who fucking mattered.

But of course my fate wasn't as kind as that and as Shawn's rough hand closed around my arm and started dragging me towards the surface, everything suddenly became so clear to me.

I'd been a fucking fool to think that I could go to him and end this war by cutting the head from the monster himself. I'd been an idiot to run from the only men I'd ever loved in hopes of saving them from this tyrant. Because he was never going to stop, and I was never going to win. And I was struck with the very real fear that sooner or later he really would break me and there would be nothing left inside me apart from the girl he claimed I was.

Broken. Ruined. Unwanted. Dirty. *His.*

CHAPTER EIGHT

Maverick was sleeping beside me in the truck with his baseball cap pulled down over his eyes as I queued up to the drive-thru. We hadn't eaten since breakfast and as it was after two am now, my stomach was growling for something substantial. The asshole in front of me in his swanky black Cadillac Escalade was taking his sweet time ordering and I was getting seriously impatient.

I opened my window, honking my horn. "Move it!"

"Perfect, now you're upsetting the hicks," a low male voice drawled from inside the car, carrying from the open windows of the vehicle, though I couldn't see the person speaking through the blacked out rear windshield.

"We'll get four burgers – one veggie -, three chocolate milkshakes and a vanilla one for my brother who's afraid of staining his Prada shirt." A tattooed arm hung out the front window, their deep voice making recognition prickle at my senses, and I suddenly realised who was in that car.

"Don't forget the fries!" a girl cried from somewhere inside the vehicle.

"And four portions of fries for the wife," the tattooed guy added and I opened my door, stepping out and leaving the truck idling as I walked up beside them and leaned my forearms on the open back window, peering inside.

A fist swung at me so fast, I almost didn't move in time to avoid it, but I did, barking a laugh at Saint Memphis as he glowered out at me.

"Just thought I'd say hi, assholes. I'm Fox Harlequin's…" The word 'second' died on my lips and I regretted this instantly as I met Saint's cool gaze.

"I hear you are an ex-Harlequin these days, Johnny James," he stated like those words weren't devastating.

Tatum reached around from the front seat, swatting his arm. Of course he knew that. This guy made it his business to know everything.

"Be nice," Tatum warned.

"The word nice isn't in my vocabulary, siren. Just like the word 'drive-thru' isn't in my vocabulary. The least I expect from an establishment I am purchasing food from is proper spelling."

"I think they spell it like that so the signs are cheaper for the company to buy," the tattooed guy called from the front.

"I am quite aware of the reasoning, you hillbilly, that doesn't make it any more acceptable. If one cannot spend money on good grammar then they shouldn't have money at all," Saint said sharply and I snorted a laugh, earning me another cutting look from him.

"Have you heard anything from Rogue?" Tatum asked, her brow pinching with concern that told me Saint Memphis knew all about that fucking fiasco too. Though I guessed as the entire Harlequin Crew were out for her blood it wasn't exactly a secret that she'd betrayed us and run back to The Dead Dogs.

"No," I replied coldly, my mood plummeting at the mention of her name.

"Do you have something else to say then?" Saint asked irritably.

"Maybe move along, yeah? You're holding up the line." I patted the roof of the expensive car, nodding to the others and walking back to the truck before climbing in.

Maverick was awake, his gun in his grip and his eyes clouded with demons.

"You alright, man?" I asked and he nodded stiffly.

"You know those people?" he asked.

"We've run a few jobs for them," I said with a nod, the word 'we' leaving a bitter taste in my mouth.

We ordered our food and soon collected it from the serving window, and I ate my burger with one hand while driving us through the upper quarter in the direction of the cliff roads that led down to Harlequin territory.

We'd searched day and night for Chase in every place we could think of and had finally come up with the idea to head back and search the outer edges of Sunset Cove in case Chase had decided to stick around town. He had a vendetta against Shawn after all, so maybe he'd be gunning for his death like the rest of us were. It was worth a shot anyway.

The bright lights of the upper quarter were soon left behind as I took the dark roads along the cliffs and the feeling of arriving home sent a rush of warmth through my chest. But it was quickly followed by a chill as I remembered there was no real home here for me anymore. Harlequin House was out of bounds. Fox wouldn't want anything to do with me, Rogue had betrayed us, Chase was gone. And it made me want to hold onto Maverick as tight as I could for fear that I'd lose him too.

It was strange how quickly we'd fallen into our old ways, how comfortable I was around him, and I realised how fiercely I'd missed him too. He'd always been a part of me, just like they all had. And I'd be damned if I'd let anyone take him from me again.

I glanced over at Maverick, finding his food untouched in his lap, his baseball cap now twisted backwards onto his head as he stared out at the dark sky, rivalling it with the darkness in his own eyes. I didn't need to ask what he was thinking about. That ache was as familiar to me as breathing by now. It was what we were constantly not talking about. The rainbow haired elephant in the room.

The way his fingers gripped the revolver in his hand made me sure he was thinking about firing it, but I didn't know who the target was in his mind. Shawn? Rogue? Himself?

As broken as I felt over Rogue, I was clinging to the barest hope that I could keep the last fragments of our family together. But maybe I was just a dead man holding onto a dream of life. Maybe this hunt for Chase and these days we were spending sleeping in motel rooms and service stations was just something to keep my spirit alive. Because I was sure if I paused to think too long, I'd give in to the desperate grief inside me and find it impossible to keep moving.

I reached out, pressing a hand to Maverick's shoulder, knowing he needed me even if he wouldn't say it. But all that did was remind me that Chase was out there on his own without anyone to tell him shit would get better. He was alone, abandoned. And fuck I hated Fox for that. I hated him so much it burned. And I missed him so bad it made me hurt. And then it all boiled down to her again. Rogue. The name carved into every ruined piece of my heart. Sometimes I wanted to cut it clean from my chest just so I didn't have to feel any of it anymore. Because all the while it still beat, it ached for something it was never gonna get.

"Get your hand off me, JJ," Maverick growled. "I'm not a child needing a fucking comfort blanket."

"No, but you're my brother and I love you," I said in a low voice and I felt his eyes on me at those words, boring into my skull. I didn't care. What difference did it make if he knew that? That I loved him as deeply now as I had when we were kids. "We're family," I gritted out and he shoved my hand off of him.

"I ain't got no family. Never did, Johnny James," he said.

I tutted, shaking my head at him. "You're as stubborn as her." Fuck, I shouldn't have brought her up. The second I did, the temperature seemed to plummet and the energy shifted between us.

"Is that why you won't leave my side, hounding after me like a stray dog looking for scraps just like you always did with her?" he said bitterly and anger daggered through me.

I pulled over at the edge of the cliff, tugging up the parking brake so hard that the wheels skidded and kicked out dust behind the car before I shoved the door open.

"Fuck you," I hissed. "You want me to go? Fine. I'm done trying with you." I stepped out of the truck, tossing the keys into his lap and starting to walk down the track.

"Don't be a bitch about it," he called after me, but I ignored him, my fists clenching and my teeth grinding. Half of me wanted to hurl myself off the cliff to my left, and the other half wanted me to keep walking until my feet bled. I was exhausted and had felt drawn as tightly as a wire these past few days, and now the pressure had become too much and I'd snapped.

"JJ!" Rick roared as I kept going, leaving the glow of the headlights behind as I rounded a corner and started climbing a steep hill.

The pounding of heavy footfalls sounded behind me, but I didn't turn back until Maverick fisted the back of my shirt and dragged me to a halt.

"Fuck off, Rick," I snarled, tugging out of his grip and continuing up the hill.

He fell into step with me, his arm rubbing mine. "Don't leave," he muttered, so low I barely caught it and there was so much pain in those two words I nearly gave in to them.

"I'm done playing this bullshit game with you. You wanna pretend you despise me? Despise Chase? Then go back to Dead Man's Isle and sit in your villain's hideout alone. I've reached my tolerance for lies," I said icily, thinking of Rogue and I swear my heart broke all over again.

Maverick gripped my arm so tight I was sure he was gonna leave bruises as he forced me to face him and a flash of lightning cut through the dark sky, lighting his features. The air was pregnant with a storm, the hairs rising on my arms as static crackled against my skin. For a moment there was a scent of smoke on the air and I wondered if hell was going to open up at our feet and swallow down our sinning souls.

"Fine," he hissed. "I don't want you to leave. But you will. When we find Chase and the dust settles between you and Fox, you'll go back to Harlequin House. Where I can't follow. Where I don't want to follow. Because deep down you know this is temporary. But in the end, you're Fox's boy and I ain't."

"Rick..." I started, but a glow caught my eye in my periphery and I turned, frowning as I jogged up the last few feet to crest the hill, my breath becoming trapped in my lungs never to be let out again.

A fire blazed out in the water beyond Sunset Beach, Sinners' Playground consumed in a glow as deep and red as the Devil himself. Maverick took to my side, a horrified curse leaving his lips and panic spilled through my flesh as I watched our beloved sanctuary burn.

No!

I turned, running back towards the truck with Maverick hot on my heels. We leapt into it and I grabbed the keys from the seat, starting it up and accelerating down the road as fast as I could. I didn't know what I was planning, only that I had to get there. Had to try and stop the blaze. I couldn't lose that piece of our past. I couldn't watch it turn to ash and crumble into the ocean, washed away and lost forever.

"No, no, no," I bit out, tearing down the roads into the lower quarter as my pulse ricocheted inside my skull.

I grabbed my phone from the dash, bringing up Fox's number and hitting call as my throat constricted. It rang out twice before he answered on the third attempt.

"What?" he demanded and I was so surprised that he'd actually answered that it took me a moment to reply.

"Sinners' Playground is burning," I gasped and silence stretched out on the line. "Fox!"

"I'm coming," he bit out then cut the call.

I accelerated down The Mile, speeding alongside the boardwalk as the raging inferno out in the water seemed to billow up into the sky itself.

The sound of a fire truck blared nearby and as I pulled up by the beach and the two of us jumped out, it arrived. I ran down onto the sand, the heat of the fire licking my skin and seeming to find its way right beneath it too.

My hands trembled as I stared uselessly on at the blaze as the firefighters tried to tackle it from the end of the pier. Maverick's hand landed on my back and I glanced at him, finding his face pale, the fire reflecting in his dark eyes.

"Let it go, J," he murmured and I shook my head in despair, because I knew he meant more than that. That this was the end of it all. The final knife buried in the belly of our childhood. There was nothing left of the past, all that remained was a broken future where the five of us would never come together again.

Fox appeared running down the beach in sweatpants and sneakers with Mutt on his heels, slowing as he approached us, his face full of horror as he stared up at the monstrous flames consuming our favourite place on earth.

He stumbled past us, his fair hair glinting with the reflection of the fire as he kept walking towards it like he was going to burn with it. Then he sank down to sit and watch our world end and I moved after him, dropping down at his side, knowing this might be the last moment we shared together. He said nothing, gazing on at the devastation and a beat later Maverick sat on my other side.

The wood cracked suddenly and the firefighters shouted out at us to move, but none of us did as a strut gave out in the shallows and part of the arcade came tumbling down into the water. A loud hiss sounded as some of the flames went under and smoke plumed higher into the sky, the wind carrying it in the opposite direction to us.

"It's over," I muttered, knowing it deep in my soul. All of it was gone. Finished. And nothing would grow from these ashes. There was no phoenix to be reborn, no hope to be renewed.

"Yeah," Fox agreed darkly, his gaze not moving from the fire.

I glint of white caught my gaze among the ash cascading through the sky and I followed it with my eyes as a charred fortune card came tumbling down to land right at my feet. I hooked it out of the sand, the corners singed and the writing on it smeared in black, but as I dragged my thumb across it to wipe it away, the words became clear.

Losing sight of the stars is the only way to know their worth.

"This is the exact opposite of how I wanted things to end up," I said quietly, regret gnawing at my gut as the heavens opened up and rain started to pour down on us. But it wouldn't be enough to save our precious amusement park which was already crumbling before our eyes.

"Happily ever afters are for fairy tales," Maverick growled. "This is how a real story ends."

CHAPTER NINE

I'd been numb for the drive back to Rosewood Manor, my soaking wet clothes clinging to my flesh and making me shiver despite the fact that I could hardly even feel the cold. The cut to my temple burned from the salt water but it had thankfully stopped bleeding now, just leaving me with a raw and painful wound in my hairline which would no doubt look even worse tomorrow when the bruising blossomed all around it.

Sinners' Playground was gone. Just like everything else good in my life was gone. And yet again, I'd been the thing that caused its destruction. This was exactly why my boys were better off away from me. Because I was so broken that everything I touched broke too.

The rain crashed in on me through the window that had shattered when I'd forced Shawn to crash earlier but I didn't make any attempt to move away from it, letting it chill me to the bone and paint my cheeks in more water to try and wash away my tears.

We drove through the gates at Rosewood Manor and Shawn parked up right in front of the house as rain from the storm thundered down on the car.

He'd been singing to himself the whole way back here, pleased with the havoc he'd wreaked on me tonight and no doubt satisfied with the way I was curling in on myself and lost in the silent darkness of my own thoughts.

A couple of his men stood watch by the door, but none of them made any comment on the state of the car with its cracked windscreen and broken window. They didn't even mention the fact that Shawn had a bleeding wound on his cheek from the pen I'd stabbed him with. They just nodded respectfully, a touch of fear to their postures as we passed by and Shawn cried out loudly, "Honey! I'm home!"

I wasn't sure who he was aiming that greeting at because no one replied. All I really wanted was to return to the basement where Miss Mabel was waiting and try to steal some comfort from her arms even though I knew I didn't deserve it. But instead of leading me back to the basement, Shawn caught my arm and pulled me up the stairs then along the landing at the top of them.

"That's my room," Shawn said casually, pointing at the door ahead of us at the end of the corridor before turning me sharply and opening the one to the left of it. "So I'll be close by at all times, don't you worry about that."

I said nothing, knowing that would get to him far more than any pointless words I threw at him. He wanted a rise from me. Wanted to know he was getting beneath my skin. My silence was better than any insult I could hurl his way.

"And this is where you'll be sleeping - nice and close for when you wanna call out in the night for me to come ride you like the good little whore I know you're just aching to be for me again." Shawn slapped my ass hard enough to hurt, the wet material of my dress making the noise even louder, then he flicked the lights on. He'd been doing that a lot, striking my right ass cheek in the same spot over and over so that a bruise was flourishing and each crack of his palm against my flesh hurt a little more than the last.

The room was thankfully untouched by Kaiser and his gross sense of interior design, and I found myself looking at a simple guest suite with full length windows which led out to the iron balcony beyond. It had old wooden furniture, a double bed and floral wallpaper lining the walls.

"I know it's hard for you to adjust back into your place at my side, sugarpie," Shawn murmured, his hands moving to my shoulders as he began to massage them for me, but it was anything other than relaxing. His touch on my skin made bile rise in my throat and a shudder of disgust race down my spine. "You'll feel better as time goes on. Once you get back to yourself again."

I stayed silent, my gaze roaming over the room as I tried to hunt out a weapon of any kind, something I could use against him as I fought my hardest to keep hold of the girl I knew I was instead of letting the one he wanted me to be slip back under my skin. But after what he'd made me be a part of tonight, I was finding it harder than ever to cling onto that girl.

"Come on, give the bed a try and see what you think of it." Shawn shoved me forward and I stumbled a little as I was forced towards it.

My head was ringing with the words he'd spoken to me at Sinners' Playground and all the worst things I ever felt about myself kept pouring in on me so fast and deep that it was all I could do to keep my head above the ocean of them, to try and maintain a hold on the girl I knew I wanted to be while the weight of the one he saw in me tried to drag me down.

I hardly even noticed he'd shoved me onto all fours on the bed until I felt his hand dragging the wet skirt of my dress up and a shiver of pure horror raced through me.

I tried to scramble away, a noise of protest escaping me as he caught my ankle and hauled me back.

"Just wondering if you're back to yourself yet, sugarpie," Shawn cooed, the back of his hand colliding with the side of my face as I tried to scramble away again in a casual blow that knocked me onto my side. "You always did manage to get so wet for me when that dead look surfaced in your eyes like it has now."

He laughed as he yanked me back towards him again, ignoring me as I managed to kick him and thrusting his hand up my skirt roughly.

His fingers scraped across my bare pussy and a note of panic escaped me as for a moment I thought he was going to force himself on me after all, the savage look in his ice cold eyes bleeding terror through my heart.

The door banged open behind us and I choked out a relieved sob as Shawn pulled his hand away from me as fast as it had landed against my flesh, whirling to glare at the interruption to his sick games.

"Sorry, boss," Travis muttered, keeping his eyes downcast as I looked around to find out who I had to thank for that interruption. "But there's been a report of someone trying to break in down by the gates."

Shawn sucked his teeth in frustration then pushed himself off of me, casting a look at me as I managed to roll onto my back and scramble up the bed away from him with my thighs tightly locked together, shoving my dress back down.

"For someone all covered in water, your pussy is as dry as the Sahara, sugarpie," he said cruelly, his eyes lighting with the challenge I presented him and looking in no way put off by the fact that I clearly wasn't turned on by him. "So I guess we've still got a lot more work to do to get you back to yourself." He tapped his fingers against a box I hadn't noticed which sat on the nightstand and my eyes widened as I spotted the brunette hair dye.

Shawn turned and strode from the room without another word to me, barking an order at Travis to remain there to keep an eye on me and I managed to breathe again the moment he was gone.

Travis didn't immediately close the door between us, his gaze pinning me in it as his brow pinched a little. Was I completely insane to wonder if he'd just saved my ass on purpose?

"Is it the Harlequins?" I asked, hating myself for the desperate tone of hope that coloured my words at that question. I'd made my choice in coming here, but in that moment I couldn't help but hope for a knight or two in shining armour – or dressed in brutal lines of ink - to come rescue me.

"No," he replied, his voice low and rough and sending a crack of pain resounding right through my broken heart.

I'd known it wasn't them before I'd even asked. Shawn had at least been telling the truth about that - they hadn't come for me. Hadn't made any attempt to contact me. And maybe now they really would forget me too.

I guessed I deserved that even though the pain of it cut me so deeply that I wasn't entirely sure how I was still breathing.

"Then who-" I began, but Travis cut me off.

"One of The Dead Dogs got shot in the face," he said. "Or so I heard. Looks like there's no trace of who did it though."

I frowned at that, my gaze catching on his grey shirt and the red speckles colouring the collar of it. He stiffened as he noticed where my attention had fallen then stepped back, a warning in his eyes which told me not to question him.

"Get some rest. I'll knock if I hear him heading back this way."

The door closed between us before I could reply, and I was left alone in the room with a box of hair dye designed to stamp out the lingering remains of the girl I wished I could be and more than a few unanswered questions about the man who stood guarding my door.

My mind turned to my boys and I wondered what they must be thinking of me right now. How much they hated me. And how little it was worth if I couldn't even kill the motherfucker who had come here to hurt them.

I pushed myself off the bed and looked around the small room. There was a little bathroom to one side of it and a closet sat open with a small selection of clothes inside.

My gut twisted as I slowly reached out and took the box of brunette hair dye from the nightstand before walking towards the bathroom on shaky legs.

I placed the box down on the edge of the sink and stripped out of my saturated dress before looking at myself in the mirror. My gaze slowly dragged over my body, taking in the feminine curves and peaks of my nipples, the seductive lines of dark ink on my tanned skin and the tilt of my full lips.

If only I'd been born a boy. Things would have been so much simpler then. Me and the Harlequins would have loved each other so much more easily. Axel never would have desired me. He wouldn't have tried to rape me, so none of the shit that had caused me to leave town ever would have happened. My boys wouldn't have fought over me either. They never would have desired me in that way, so our love could have remained untainted by lust.

I ran my fingers across myself slowly, reliving the touches of their skin against mine and the way my body ignited for each of them at the faintest caress. The love I felt for them was so consuming that it had tried to devour them too. This body of mine had created a divide I would have given anything to destroy. It had put me in Shawn's firing line too. Because he was right. I was good for one thing. One single thing about me had caused almost every problem I'd ever faced. The fact that I'd been born with a pussy that men wanted to take ownership of had been the reason for so much destruction in my life.

But now my boys had had a taste of me or had realised that wanting a taste had been a fatal move and either way they weren't here. They hadn't come. I'd destroyed all hope of that just like I destroyed everything else in my path.

But that only made my mission here more vital. Because if I caused destruction everywhere I went then that meant I could cause fucking Shawn's destruction too. Even if that meant I had to be his whore again.

I sneered at the sight of my naked body in the mirror, hating the girl who stared back at me. But she could be good for this one thing.

So with one last, lingering look at the rainbow colours of my wet hair, I said goodbye to the girl I'd been fighting so hard to become and embraced the one I was. Because this whore was going to be charging a whole lot for her services from now on. And the only client I was taking on would be buying my soul at the cost of his life.

I grabbed the box of hair dye and tore it open. It was time to let go of the girl who had died the night I was run out of Sunset Cove all those years ago. And the bitch who was born in her place was ready to rise from the ashes of her corpse.

CHAPTER TEN

Turned out hitch-hiking was all but impossible when you looked like a zombie pirate who'd hobbled inland for its next meal. No one wanted to let a big, muscular, one-eyed, scarred up, gang tatted guy into their vehicle, and I couldn't really blame them. I looked like a serial killer about to go on his first spree. And I had the dark soul to match.

I was getting far too used to the stares, but it was the fear in people's eyes that was the real kicker. It was like I had an invisible shield around me, repelling people for ten feet in every direction. But despite the twist in my chest that had caused at first, I realised it suited me alright, considering the only people I gave a fuck about liking me were long gone, firmly in my past now. But it did make moving around a helluva lot more difficult than I'd been prepared for. Especially when the voices in my head grew so loud it was nearly impossible to block them out. Without them here to chase away the nightmares, they were always present. My father, Shawn, myself. There were a thousand cutting words on a loop in my head, accompanied by the memories of fists pounding my body, blades slitting open my skin. It was all becoming a violent blur already until I didn't know where my childhood horrors ended and Shawn's torture began.

I'd spent my last dollar paying a cab driver to get me to Sterling this morning and now the night was already drawing in and it looked like I'd be sleeping on the streets if I couldn't get hold of some cash. I hated when the sun set. I hated the way it felt like fingers sliding around my throat, holding me hostage until dawn. At least I could function in the daytime. But at night, I was fighting a losing battle with the demons in my head. So I needed to get hold of some cash so I at least wouldn't end up curled up in a doorway tonight. I needed a room, no matter how small or shitty it was. Just somewhere I could put the lights on.

Robbing people wasn't out of the question, but I was so fucking recognisable now, I'd likely be rounded up by the cops in no time if anyone gave them my description.

I focused my attention on a couple of teen boys as they flashed some cash to their friends a few yards away. I was sitting on a bench in a park under a tree, my hood firmly up and even though I looked shady as shit, I wouldn't be seen here easily in the shadows. And there was no law against sitting on a park bench with your hood up.

Where the fuck did they get cash like that?

Thieves, most likely. And maybe this was my answer. A thief wouldn't go crying to the cops about his stolen cash. But there were eight of them and though I could have taken it at gunpoint, it didn't quite sit right with me. Besides, some teenage boys liked to play hero – I'd know, having been one of them at that age. Especially with the girls hanging around them. The boys were already playing up, acting like the big tough men they wished they were. *Trust me, kids, they won't want you then either.*

Ah shit, I was becoming a bitter old man already. My destiny was looking a lot like my father's right about now. But fuck if I'd grow old and get stuck in a chair with nothing but cheap alcohol for company. I'd put a bullet in my skull before that happened. In the meantime, I was doing my best to fix the dodgy leg that would secure my fate as a grouchy old chair-ridden man by doing the exercises the doctor had recommended daily, plus adding in a gruelling calisthenics workout at the ass crack of dawn every day too. The movements were slow, requiring balance and strength built around my body weight only. I missed the gym, but this was something. And as I couldn't even go for a run, it would have to do. I swear I'd seen a little improvement in my leg already, but it always seemed to seize up in the evening again. I didn't take my painkillers though; they made my head fuzzy, and when it got fuzzy all I saw was her.

I felt her everywhere, always. But at least when my mind was sharp, I could keep her out enough not to break down over her. Leaving her behind felt like I'd taken a gunshot directly to my heart, and the wound was oozing, pulsing blood, forever ripped open. But letting her go was the right choice. Letting them all go was the right choice.

I just hoped Fox had listened to me and would find a way to keep Rogue and JJ close when he found out about them. Because he would. It was fucking inevitable.

"You racing tonight, bro?" asked one of the guys among the group.

"Yeah, I'm gonna smash Big Benny," his friend answered, swaggering around between his friends.

The one with the cash waved it at him. "I'm betting on you, asshole, you'd better win this time."

"I'm the best driver in Sterling," the guy said cockily and my brows arched as they started chatting about the street race he was taking part in tonight.

No, buddy, I'm *the best driver in Sterling. And the entire west coast for that matter.*

They kept talking about it and I kept listening until I took note of the time and location then grabbed my bag off the bench and made my way towards the gate that led onto the street.

It was getting dark and an air of danger hung around the place as I walked deeper into Dead Dog territory.

"I'm gonna crawl into those cracks I see in you and you'll never get me out."

Shawn's voice echoed around my head and I had to stop walking for a second as I felt him everywhere. He'd been right about that. He was in me now and I'd never get him out. The harder I fought, the worse the panic got. But I had to keep it together. I was so close to achieving what I'd come here for.

I drew in a low breath and filled my head up to the brim with Rogue. It was the only thing that ever helped and as I remembered her laugh and the light that glittered in her eyes like sun on the waves, it became easier to breathe.

I started walking again, my muscles tight and my scars seeming to burn. This was Shawn Mackenzie's old hunting grounds, which was the precise reason I was here and I wasn't worried about his goons recognising me. He was way down in the south and I was just a long forgotten torture victim he wouldn't have bothered to have his men lookout for. I was a ghost blown in from Sunset Cove and if I played my cards right, I'd be heading back there soon to haunt fucking Shawn's ass and put it in the ground too.

But first I needed cash. And it looked like I finally had a way to get it.

I pulled up behind a bunch of douchebags in their douchebag cars which were souped up with flashy shit, riding so low to the ground that they were one speed bump away from taking the exhaust pipes off. I'd picked out an old, beat up silver Jaguar which looked like a piece of crap but had an engine that could give me the boost I needed to leave these assholes in my dust. It kinda reminded me of myself, all beat up with one purpose left to it.

The teenagers turned to look at the new arrival, wrinkling their noses at my car and hollering laughs. One kid strutted up to my window, his pants riding low over his ass. *Fuck me, did I look that douchey at his age?*

He knocked his knuckles on my window, leaning down as I dropped it, a smirk on his lips like he was about to cut me down to size. But I pushed my hood back, letting him see my face, the eyepatch, the few scars cut into my forearms where my sleeves were rolled back. Was it a serial killer move? Yeah. But if I couldn't play the scary asshole card then what did I even have anymore?

He legit nearly tripped over his own feet as he backed up into a bunch of girls behind him and they all turned to stare at me. One girl bit her lip, apparently the ringleader of their group, her denim jacket hanging open and revealing nothing but a lacy bra beneath it. "Holy shit, who invited the hot pirate?"

"I'm racing," I told the guy, ignoring the girl as she slid her jacket off and gave me a show of her half naked body. She had to have a death wish.

Her friends apparently decided to fall in line and pretend I was hot too as they batted their lashes and started coming up with dark backstories for me. I started to grow uncomfortable from the attention I was receiving and my muscles bunched as I shifted my attention back onto the boy.

"You need to buy in, bro," the guy said, twisting the cap on his head so it sat backwards. "Fifty bucks."

Shit.

"Take it out of my winnings," I said with a shrug.

"No can do, Captain," he said, his eyes sliding over my eyepatch.

"Oooh, I like that name," the queen bee said beside him. "Let him race, Alex." She prodded him. "Don't be boring."

"I can't, Melissa. Rules are rules," he said, slinging an arm over her shoulder.

She scowled, shoving him off. "Fine. I guess you can suck on someone else's tits tonight. Maybe your mom's." She tossed her hair, turning her back on him and he gawped at her.

I inclined my head, raising an eyebrow at him as he huffed.

"Fine," he snarled, ushering me forward to join the starting line.

I smirked, hitting the button to close my window and laughter rang out as I rolled my car up beside some asshole-mobile. I pulled my hood up again, retreating into the shadows of it as people angled their phones at the racers.

Melissa appeared with a flag made from a pair of red panties, standing in front of us and waving it above her head.

I readied my foot on the gas, my jaw clenched with determination as I waited for the race to begin. There was a decent sized crowd either side of the street, made up mostly of teens and a few local gangsters who'd come to watch the show.

I tightened my grip on the wheel as someone blew a whistle and the girl waved the pantie flag before lowering it dramatically and I slammed my foot to the gas, speeding past her towards the sharp turn at the end of the road.

Everyone else was so concerned about scratching their cars, that all I had to do was swerve towards them to get ahead. And in a few seconds, I was out in front, speeding around the corner with a whoop leaving my lungs as I remembered how much I fucking loved driving. I gave her all the gas she needed to tear up the road and put a decent lead between me and the assholes on my tail, following the blue markers which had been drawn on carboard and hung up at every turn.

My heart thundered in my chest and I felt more alive than I had in so fucking long. I could almost hear Rogue's laughter dancing around me from when we used to do this as kids. I'd take Fox's truck up to race the rich kids in the upper quarter with all five of us piled in the front and we'd thrash every one of them and take the winnings home to buy as much takeaway food as we could stomach.

The faster I drove now, the closer I felt to them. I could hear their cheers, their cries urging me on and a grin split across my face as I bombed it down another narrow street, the headlights behind me fading away. I was a king in the driver's seat. I'd gotten my boys away from countless jobs, lost the cops in the backstreets of Sunset Cove countless times.

The engine roared and the scent of gasoline and fucking freedom filled my senses as I took corner after corner at high speed. I had no fear driving this fast. There was nothing but pure adrenaline coursing through my veins and reminding me I wasn't fucking dead yet.

The finish line came into view and I sailed almost leisurely up to it, rolling over the line and dropping my window as I held out my hand for the winnings.

Alex dropped a wad of cash into my palm with a huff as the crowd whooped and clapped. I offered him a two fingered salute then forged my way through the crowd and turned down a street in the direction of any motel that would take me in tonight.

My leg was aching, but the fire in my blood was worth it. It gave me the energy I needed to get on and do what I'd come here to do. Because I'd gotten a list of local Mrs Mackenzies online and I was going to start visiting them tomorrow. Then the right one would be coming all the way back to Sunset Cove with me.

Rejects Park

ROGUE

CHAPTER ELEVEN

My bedroom door crashed open and I stifled the panicked cry that rose in my throat as I scrambled upright, brunette hair falling all around my shoulders as Shawn ripped the bed covers off of me.

"Get up and take your clothes off. I wanna know you ain't armed, sugarpie," he snapped, his eyes blazing with an excitement that made my heart race.

Travis stood in the door behind him, his short dreadlocks pushed out of his face and his brow pinching slightly as I scrambled off the bed and put it between me and Shawn as I tried to get my bearings.

I'd spent most of last night searching this place from top to bottom for something I could use as a weapon, but all I'd come up with was the somewhat weak idea of tearing my bedsheet to create a strip of fabric that I could use as a garrotte. But as Shawn had arrived here with backup, I couldn't believe I'd be granted the time it would take to strangle him even if I did somehow manage to hook the torn sheet around his neck.

"Now," Shawn barked and I raised my chin as I pushed the straps of the silk nightdress I'd been given to sleep in off of my shoulders and let the fabric slide from my body.

Travis pushed his tongue into his cheek, looking like he was holding back on saying something as he turned to lean against the doorframe and looked away from my nudity. I wasn't sure what to make of him. On the one hand, he didn't seem to be much of a fan of Shawn's methods, but on the other, he clearly wasn't planning on going against him in any way either. Unless my suspicions over the man who had been shot the other night were correct. But why would he have killed some random gangbanger to help save me from Shawn's temper if he had no intention of taking on the man himself?

Perhaps I should have been considering trying to make an ally out of him. But what was I gonna do? Try to convince him to kill Shawn? Then what? It wasn't like I could offer him any kind of immunity or money or anything at all of value. Hell, I was safer here than I would be away from this psychopath anyway now that I was sitting pretty at the top of The Harlequin Crew's hit list.

Shawn stalked towards me, reaching out to fist his hand in my hair and yanking my head back as he let his gaze travel down my exposed body.

"Looks like you're starting to get the right idea, sweet cheeks," he murmured, leaning in and inhaling the scent of my hair while my skin crawled at the contact. "I always did have a thing for brunettes."

I held my tongue, knowing I wasn't able to say anything he would like and feeling too vulnerable in this position to want to test him.

"Are you starting to feel more like yourself again now?" he asked, his free hand skimming down my side as bile rose in my throat at his touch.

"Yes," I said in a low tone, because I *was* feeling more like myself. At least the version of myself that Shawn had known. More like the jaded, fucked up thing I'd been for the last ten years. And that was a good thing because it meant I didn't have to feel all of the hurt and heartbreak of the girl who loved the Harlequin boys. I could just focus on my desire to end the bastard in front of me instead.

"Enough like yourself for me to take you for a ride?" he taunted, his blue eyes sparking at the undisguised disgust that swept across my features.

"You have me at your mercy, Shawn. That doesn't mean I'm suddenly going to start wanting to fuck you again," I growled, holding firm on my feelings over that. If he wanted my body he would have to take it by force and though I feared he might do just that, I still held hope that he enjoyed the game of trying to break me too much to give in to the desire to do that.

He cocked his head as he regarded me, giving me a clearer view of the stab wound I'd given him when I drove that pen into his cheek and his grip on me tightened as he realised where my attention had fallen.

"You're treading a fine line with me, sugarpie," he warned. "Don't think I'm above pinning you beneath me and taking whatever the fuck I want from your flesh."

"I know you're not above anything, Shawn," I drawled. "But I also know that raping girls isn't your style - you're too full of yourself for that."

"You're right," he agreed with a cruel smile before shoving his hand between my thighs and pushing his fingers inside me.

I cried out despite having promised myself I wouldn't, my nails biting into the flesh of his arm as I tried to fight him off, but he yanked his hand back again just as fast, tugging on my hair to pull me off of him.

"Gotta check you haven't stashed any pens or other sharp objects anywhere, sugarpie. But if you like that then you can suck my dick for me when I'm done checking you over."

"I haven't got any-"

Shawn twisted me around and shoved me face first onto the bed, keeping his hand fisted in my hair as he crushed my face to the mattress and I tried to fight my way upright again.

He shoved his fingers into my ass so suddenly that I screamed again, burning pain forcing tears to prick my eyes as I tried to kick and fight my way upright, but he thankfully withdrew his hand and released his hold on me a moment later.

I rolled over and scrambled away from him with my chest heaving and wild, fearful eyes fixed on his face as he grinned at me.

"You fancy taking my cock like a good girl now then, sugarpie?" he asked casually as he straightened his blue shirt sleeves over his tattooed forearms.

"Fuck you," I spat and he laughed.

"All in good time. You know I'll have you begging before long." Shawn turned and strode towards the door where Travis still stood, though it looked like his second in command was having trouble keeping his cool as his muscular body bunched with tension and his jaw was locked so tight he seemed in danger of cracking a tooth.

"Eyes on my girl, Trav," Shawn commanded and Travis only hesitated a beat before turning his dark gaze on me where I still knelt on the bed, cradling a pillow over my naked body like it might somehow help me. "I want you watching her while she makes herself pretty for me. If she manages to stash a weapon somewhere then I'll be taking your head in payment for it. Bring her down to the car in five minutes and don't keep me waiting."

"Yes, boss," Travis agreed in a low tone and Shawn tossed me a taunting grin before turning and striding away down the corridor while singing Teenage Dirtbag by Wheatus like a fucking psycho as he went.

Travis and I just looked at each other while his singing faded away into the distance then the big man released a sigh.

"Why the fuck would you walk back into his hands?" he growled at me, anger flaring in his gaze as he stalked into the room and snatched a dress I hadn't noticed from the chair close to the door.

I recoiled a little as he closed in on me, his big frame intimidating especially while I was feeling so violated, but all he did was hold out the white material for me to take.

"I came back because he needs to die," I muttered, snatching the dress while keeping the pillow pressed to my chest. "And I figured I'm no good for anything else, so maybe I could at least do that one good thing."

I wasn't sure what I expected Travis to say to that, but it wasn't like I hadn't made it clear that I wanted Shawn dead when I'd tried to murder him with a pen, so I wasn't exactly afraid of him telling tales on me.

"Well next time, buttercup, maybe try a little harder, yeah?" he cocked his head at me and I blinked in surprise. Was he...encouraging me to kill the leader of his gang? What the fuck was that about?

"If you want him dead then why don't you just do it?" I suggested, giving the gun jammed into his waistband a pointed look.

"My agenda isn't your business," he said with a shrug. "But I won't get in the way of yours if you don't get in the way of mine."

I regarded him for a long moment, but I had no real reason to doubt him. Of course, I had no reason to trust him either, but he hadn't done a thing to hurt me and I knew that he was the one looking after Miss Mabel so I nodded.

Seeing as Shawn had given him strict instructions not to take his eyes off of me, I gritted my teeth and dropped the pillow, before quickly tugging the white dress over my head. To Travis's credit, his gaze didn't slip from my face even with my tits right in front of him and I silently thanked him for not being a total sleaze.

The dress was low cut but pretty long and the white fabric clung to my figure before dropping all the way to my toes. Once again, I wasn't given any underwear but as I was pretty sure I was still being dressed in Mia's clothes, I wasn't going to complain about that.

Travis pointed out a pair of sandals by the door and I moved over to slip them on before falling into step with him as we left the room and headed out to meet Shawn and find out what he had in store for me today.

The sun was shining as we exited the huge house and Travis led the way to a big black SUV which was parked up and waiting for us at the foot of the long porch.

He pulled the back door open and I moved to climb into the car before pausing as I spotted Mia sitting on Shawn's lap inside.

"Come on, sugarpie, we don't have all day," Shawn drawled, beckoning me to get inside and I bit my tongue as I climbed in too.

Travis shut the door behind me then headed around to get in the driver's seat while another one of Shawn's men sat shotgun beside him. I couldn't help but notice that all the men in the car were pretty heavily armed, but despite the questions sitting on the tip of my tongue, I didn't ask where we were going. This was just another game and it didn't matter to me anyway - I only needed to focus on getting hold of a weapon.

"Did I ever tell you about the time me and my brother Nolan went fishing up in Catfall Springs, Trav?" Shawn called and my gaze flicked to his number two just in time for me to see his jaw tighten the tiniest amount. I was willing to bet he didn't much like being called *Trav*.

"No, boss," he replied, no hint of irritation in his tone.

"Oh, that was a blinder of a time. We met this family who owned a big old farm up there and invited ourselves into their home. They had this pretty little thing of a daughter, not far past twenty one who had these big come fuck me eyes. I can tell you, I was balls deep in her not long after we'd all finished up our dessert and I tell ya now, that girl was a screamer in the sack."

"Nice," the dude sitting beside Travis chuckled, licking his thick lips as he looked over his shoulder at me before his gaze trailed to Mia. The lust in his eyes darkened as he looked to her and I found myself glancing over too, seeing Shawn's hands between her thighs and her skirt hiked up high enough that I was pretty certain Thick Lips could see what she'd eaten for breakfast.

"It was," Shawn agreed, a sigh escaping him. "Of course, Nolan may have overstepped the boundaries of their hospitality when he gutted her parents in their beds, but he always was a wild one."

My gut twisted and I tore my eyes away again, supremely glad that Luther Harlequin had put an end to the life of that sick fuck. Who knew what him and Shawn might have gotten up to together if he was still around, getting off on butchering people for fun? Not that Shawn was much better on his own, but at least I only had one of them to watch out for.

I looked out of my window, noticing familiar streets pass us by before they gave way to some of the long roads which led out of town towards the south. The trees hung thick around the edges of the streets but the brightness spilling through them spoke of the heat of the sun which awaited me outside this air-conditioned box.

"Anyway, the funny thing was, that girl came with us when we left. She came with us and kept riding my dick like a cowboy on a bull every chance she got. Can you imagine that? The brother of the man who had killed her family. There was something special about that, when she begged me for more and looked at me like I was her entire world. Of course she was a little cracked in the head after seeing what her parents looked like inside out, but there was something raw and beautiful about the connection me and her had. Kinda like you and me, hey poppet?" Shawn patted Mia's thigh and she nodded.

"Yes," she breathed and I couldn't help but look at her again as her bottom lip quivered and he gave her a little shove forward so that she was gripping the back of Travis's seat.

"You hear that, sugarpie?" Shawn asked, looking to me as he took a condom from his pocket and turned it over between his fingers. "My little Mimi feels it. That pull to the dark. Just like you always did."

I looked at Mia, her gaze meeting mine as tears swam in her eyes for a moment and something in me stirred with an anger so deep it was a wonder I didn't just lunge at Shawn then and there and try to strangle the fucking life out of him.

"Let her go, Shawn. She's fucking terrified," I hissed and Shawn laughed.

"Oh is that right? Are you terrified, Mimi? Do you wanna go? Or was there something else you were hoping to ask me for?" Shawn asked her, his blue eyes on me as he grinned wickedly.

I looked at Mia again and her eyes watered more for a moment before she blinked the tears away.

"I want your cock, Shawn," she breathed, her gaze going flat and dead and making the anger in me rise even further.

"Shawn," I growled, moving towards him, but he just laughed, shoving my shoulder hard enough to knock me back into my seat.

"Pete, be a lamb and point a gun at my girl there, would you? I'm getting the feeling her jealousy might cause her to do something foolish in a moment," Shawn said and Thick Lips quickly pulled a glock from his belt and aimed it at my face.

"Jealousy?" I scoffed, but my gaze was on Mia again as Shawn gave her another shove to get her where he wanted her and the emptiness in her eyes made my chest tighten.

Pete the fat lipped dragon kept his gun aimed at me and my heart began to pound as I looked around for an ally which I knew wasn't here. My gaze briefly met Travis's in the rear view mirror but despite the tension around his dark eyes, I could tell he wasn't going to do anything about what was happening any more than I could with a gun pointing at my face.

"What was it I wanted you to call me again, poppet?" Shawn asked Mia as he unzipped his fly and rolled the condom over his hard dick, his taunting gaze on me the whole time.

"Daddy Kaiser," she whispered and my stomach turned as his grin grew darker.

"Oh yeah, that was it." Shawn tugged her down onto his lap, keeping her facing away from him and she gasped as he drove his cock into her. "Let's hear it then."

"Fuck me, Daddy Kaiser," she gasped, gripping the back of Pete's chair to stop herself from falling as he barked a laugh and gripped her ass to get her positioned where he wanted her.

The car bounced a little as he fucked her, his brutish grunts mixing with her gasps and murmurs of 'more, Daddy Kaiser' while he fucking laughed every time she said it.

"What's it feel like to fuck the man who blew your momma's head clean off?" Shawn growled and a tear slipped down Mia's cheek as she gripped the back of Pete's seat and said nothing, but that single tear was enough to break something in me.

Pete's jaw was slack and he was practically drooling as he stared at his boss fucking a girl right there in the back seat of the car and his grip on the gun had visibly loosened.

My fingers twitched and adrenaline spiked in my limbs, but as a whimper slipped from Mia's mouth, I lost all sense of self preservation and just fucking went for it.

I surged forward, slamming my fist down on Pete's hard cock with one hand and ripping the gun from his grip with the other.

A shot went off as his finger latched around the trigger and I screamed as the rear window shattered, but I lurched back with my prize in hand and aimed it at fucking Shawn's fucking face as I leaned back against my door.

Travis slammed on the brakes, but I was ready for it, bracing myself with my foot on the back of his seat and baring my teeth at Shawn as he fell still with his cock still buried inside the crying girl on his lap.

"Let her out," I snarled, my finger itching on the trigger, but I didn't dare pull it while Mia was blocking my view of the man I needed dead.

Nobody dared move, but Pete groaned as he cupped his balls and I could feel Travis's gaze boring a hole in the side of my head as he started shifting a hand towards the gun he had at his hip.

"Don't fucking move," I barked, keeping my gaze firmly on Shawn. "And let her *out.*"

Travis froze and Shawn whistled long and low as he wrapped a hand around Mia's throat, tugging her closer to him to use as a human shield.

"You really give a damn about this girl, sugarpie?" he asked me, tilting his head a little, though not enough to give me a clear shot and despite how fucking tempting it was to pull the trigger and hope for the best, I wasn't going to risk her life after all she'd been through at the hands of this monster.

"Let her out, Shawn, or so help me I'll shoot."

"You heard her, poppet," Shawn said, his voice dropping to a low and dangerous thing. "Fuck all the way off." He opened the door and Mia practically fell out onto the road, leaving him there with his condom wrapped cock out and still rock solid in his lap.

"Mia?" I called out and she stared at me with her lips parted, not seeming to have a fucking clue what to do now. "Get your ass to Afterlife and ask for Di or Lyla. Tell them I said to look after you, okay? They'll give you somewhere to go."

She didn't reply but she nodded slowly and that was about the best I could hope for.

"Close the door, Shawn," I commanded. "And put your fucking dick away," I barked. "And start driving again," I added to Travis who glanced at Shawn for confirmation before pulling away again as Shawn nodded to him.

I spared a single glance out the shattered rear window, watching as Mia shrank away into the distance as I bought her a little time to get the fuck away from what was going to happen next.

"So what now, sugarpie?" Shawn purred as he zipped his fly up and tossed the condom into the footwell. "You gonna just shoot me in cold blood?"

I raised my chin and aimed the gun right at his smug fucking face, a dark and hungry smile filling my lips as I drank in this moment at long fucking last.

I didn't bother to reply to his taunting or acknowledge the look on his face which said he didn't think I'd really do it. Because he might have wanted to believe that I was his broken creature, all fucked up and bound to him in all the ways he wanted, but he was dead fucking wrong about that. I may have been broken, but I didn't belong to him. Four boys had taken ownership of my soul long before I'd ever laid eyes on this piece of shit and there had never been any question of anyone owning it other than them.

I pulled the trigger with my heart soaring and a rush of relief flooding through me at this finally being the end. Even if it meant Travis or Pete would kill me for it, or if I ran and the Harlequins got me for what they thought I'd done to Luther - I didn't care. Because this motherfucker would be dead and gone and he wouldn't be able to hurt my boys ever again.

Except that wasn't what happened. His brains didn't splatter all over the car, the smug smile wasn't obliterated and the raging beast inside me wasn't rewarded with the taste of his death on the air.

The gun clicked loudly but the bullet didn't fire and I had all of half a second for my eyes to widen in horror before Shawn slammed into me, cracking my head against the window behind me and ripping the weapon from my hand with a howl of laughter.

"Ho-ly mother of a goose! I was almost a goner right then and there, did you see that, Pete?" he cried, thumping back down into his seat and emptying the cartridge into his hand. "Your piece of shit, dirty as fuck gun just went and misfired and saved my damn life!"

"Oh shit, boss," Pete gasped, his eyes wide as he looked at Shawn and I just stared at him with the most crippling sense of failure crushing my heart to dust in my chest as my one fucking shot at destroying this monster disappeared like sand running through my fingers, impossible to catch again. "You're one lucky son of a bitch!"

"That I am, Pete," Shawn cooed, flicking the faulty bullet onto the floor before reloading the gun. "That I fucking am."

I flinched as he fired three times in quick succession and Pete's blood splattered my white dress as Travis jerked on the wheel in surprise, making the car veer over the road and bump up onto the verge for a moment before he righted it. There was a wild psychotic amusement in Shawn's eyes as he did it like he was pleased that an opportunity to kill had presented itself and all I could do was gape at him as he smiled widely.

"Hurry the fuck up, Trav, we're gonna be late at this rate," Shawn snapped at him as he quickly straightened the wheel, muttering a curse beneath his breath as Pete's body slumped in his seat and blood stained the upholstery.

"Oh, sugarpie," Shawn breathed, leaning in close to me and trailing the heated barrel of the gun down the side of my face. "You are gonna regret being such a bad girl."

"The only thing I regret is the fact that your head is still attached to your shoulders," I hissed venomously and he smiled wider at me like he loved the challenge I presented him with.

The car pulled up outside a huge white building in the middle of goddamn nowhere and Shawn promptly got out, taking hold of my hand and dragging me after him.

"Grab the box from the trunk, Trav, yeah?" he said as Travis got out too and I tried to catch his eye as he moved to do what Shawn had told him.

Travis didn't appear to be bothered about the blood splattering his right side, so I had to assume he hadn't been a fan of Pete - which hopefully meant he still had the potential to be a friend of mine. But so far, he was giving me no solid signs to say he was.

Shawn strode up to the gate which blocked off the entrance to the white house before us and I craned my neck to look up at the beautiful building. It was one of those old plantation houses with tall pillars and long balconies and it just fucking oozed money.

Before we could make another move, four men strode out of the house and walked down the long drive towards us, their scowls deep and bodies loaded up with enough fire power to blast us clean out of existence.

"Please kindly tell Miss Ortega that Shawn Mackenzie has a gift for her," Shawn called loudly, his words discussed in Spanish by the men who continued to glower at us before one of them strode away towards the house again.

Travis came to stand on my other side while Shawn kept a tight hold of my wrist.

I cast a curious glance at the box Travis now held in his arms, the heavy wooden thing almost looking like a pirate's chest.

Before I could consider asking what was in it, one of the men who stood glaring at us received a call on his phone and he wordlessly listened to whoever was on the other end of the line before hanging up and walking towards us.

"Miss Ortega will speak with you," he said, his Mexican accent curling around the words as he swung the gate open and indicated for the three of us to head inside.

Shawn dragged me along, but it was unnecessary. I wasn't dumb enough to try and run off while a member of the Castillo Cartel was waiting for me. Besides, I was almost certain my last run in with the drop dead gorgeous cartel front woman had ended up with her liking me. So how bad could this really be?

The men flanked us as we headed up to the house, three more of them appearing as we reached the front door where they frisked us and removed Shawn and Travis's weapons from them before letting us inside.

We crossed an open entrance hall with a sweeping staircase dominating the centre of it, our footsteps loud against the white tiled floor. I looked around curiously at the minimalistic decoration in the house, my gaze roaming over the artwork which hung from the walls, each piece decadent and dripping sex. There was something empowering about each of the women in the paintings, their positions dominant and the men at their sides worshipping them.

The man leading our group opened a door which led out to the back of the property and we strode along a wooden balcony towards the far end where a large seating area was nestled behind bamboo privacy screens.

Carmen sat in a white armchair, her dark hair perfectly styled and navy designer dress clinging to her curves. She was drinking from a martini glass with golden liquid filling it and a strawberry perched on its edge, and I noticed her manicured nails, painted red and sharpened to points.

Her attention was fixed on the laptop she had perched on a little white table beside her and she didn't bother to look our way as we approached.

Fuck I'd forgotten how big of a girl crush I had on this woman. I swear every man here was equally panting over her and shitting their pants at the thought of pissing her off. She just screamed power and sex appeal and yeah, okay, I might have been pissing my pants a little too because she was seriously fucking scary.

"What makes the man who lost thousands of dollars worth of our merchandise think it is a good idea to stroll into my house looking like a freshly primped peacock with a smile like that on your face?" she asked slowly, her accent wrapping around the words as she lifted her eyes to drag an unimpressed look over Shawn as he raised his chin.

"I've been working on something to make up for my, err...mistakes," Shawn replied and I could feel how pissed off he was for having to admit that he was anything other than perfect. "And I think you'll like what it is I found."

Carmen clucked her tongue, her gaze shifting away from him dismissively before sliding onto me. She arched one perfectly manicured eyebrow at me as her gaze slid over my hair and, took in the speckles of blood on my dress then trailed down to the place where Shawn was still gripping my wrist.

"I don't tolerate men who abuse women in my home," she said, her attention turning back to Shawn and a flicker of fire in her eyes that was seriously fucking intimidating. "It is a weak man who resorts to a show of physical strength to try and overpower a member of the dominant sex. And weakness in all forms disgusts me."

"My sugarpie here ain't no innocent lady, and I can promise you I haven't abused my physicality with her. Have I?" he shot at me and I shrugged.

"Sure, you're the perfect gent," I drawled sarcastically and Shawn barked a laugh, squeezing my arm tightly in warning before releasing me and stepping forward to take the attention from me and place it back on himself.

The men who had all fanned out to surround us stiffened as he drew a little closer to Carmen, but he fell still short of getting close enough to touch her.

"Believe me, darlin', you won't care for this girl's safety all that much when I show you what I brought you." Shawn pointed to the box Travis still held in his arms and Carmen turned her attention his way while taking a sip of her cocktail.

She wrinkled her nose for a second then her eyes snapped to the men behind us. "Pepito," she beckoned a huge, muscular man with curly black hair forward and he scurried over like he was the size of an ant.

"Yes, señora?" he asked, bowing low to her like she was a freaking queen.

"This cocktail tastes like it has been concocted by a monkey. Are you a monkey, Pepito?" she snarled harshly.

"Yes, señora. I am a loathsome, dirty little monke-"

She cut him off by throwing the cocktail in his face and the liquid dripped down onto his shirt. He let out a noise that was almost sexual and shivered like he was mid fucking orgasm. *What the actual fuck? I think I just fell in love with her even harder.*

"Go and think on your failings, Pepito," she commanded, directing him away with a swipe of her hand and he grabbed the glass from her before hightailing it off of the balcony with his chin tucked to his chest. She rested back in her seat, not seeming to give one shit about making a scene.

There were plenty of other chairs surrounding her, but as she hadn't offered us one, we all stayed on our feet.

"So… the box?" Shawn reminded her.

"Oh yes, I wondered why you were just standing there holding that like a lost delivery boy," she drawled, her gaze sliding over Travis in what I could have sworn was an appreciative way as she took in his dark skin and muscular body, but her interest zeroed in on the box he held so quickly that I might have imagined it. "Oh and Mr Mackenzie?" she clipped.

"Yeah?" he answered.

"Call me *darling* again and I shall have your balls fed to the dogs, do you understand me?"

"Yes, ma'am," he said tightly and I seriously enjoyed the whipped bitch look on his face.

Carmen sighed like we were testing her patience then flicked her blood red nails at the coffee table which sat between the rest of the chairs. "Well don't go keeping all of us in suspense," she said and Shawn snapped his fingers at Travis to get him to place the box down. "But, Mr Mackenzie, I hope you know what you're doing. Because if you don't have something extremely impressive hidden in that box, I can assure you that you won't be leaving here in one piece. You'll be finding out first hand why they call me la viuda negra."

"The black widow?" I asked, perking up at the name and she flashed me a smile which seemed even more dangerous than her scowl.

"Yes, rainbow child, many men are afraid of falling prey to me," she agreed, her nickname for me making it clear she knew who I was despite the freshly dyed brown hair.

Shawn cleared his throat, clearly not liking the attention I was getting even though he was the one who had brought me here and Carmen let him reclaim her interest as he moved to open the box for her to see inside.

The way he was standing meant that my view of its contents were blocked, but as Carmen fell unnaturally still, a prickle of fear raced down my spine.

"Where did you find this?" she hissed, barking something in Spanish which had the men surrounding her scurrying away while two of them moved to stand behind Shawn and level guns at his head.

"Easy now," Shawn said, raising his hands in innocence. "This here had nothing to do with me. I was locked up in the state penitentiary when these items went missing which you can certify easily enough."

"So explain yourself quickly, Mr Mackenzie, or I'll rid myself of you and figure out the rest of the details for myself." Carmen took a big ass handgun from the side of her chair and pointed it right at his head.

My heart leapt with the dizzying idea that she might solve my fucking Shawn problem for me right here and now, but as he opened his poisonous mouth, all thoughts of that fled me and nothing but pure terror ran through my veins.

"I found The Harlequin Crew's little stash," Shawn said excitedly, his mouth pulling into a wicked grin as his gaze shifted from Carmen to bore right into me. "Turns out, years ago they were naughty, naughty kids. They had all kinds of nefarious items locked up in an old crypt at Rosewood Manor, but as soon as I realised what this was, I figured out what it meant - because the cartel have been hunting for the people who sunk this yacht and killed the people onboard it for a long damn time, haven't you?"

Carmen's ice cold gaze hardened and a flash of something dark and terrifying sped through her eyes a moment before she locked it away.

"What do you want in return for this information?" she demanded, her gaze never leaving the box of stolen items which incriminated me and my boys in the murder of ten of the cartel's most influential players.

My heart was thrashing in my chest, the need to run, to warn them, to do something to save them from the wrath of these people consuming me as utter panic broke through my body. I'd once planned on releasing this secret myself, but now that I was looking it dead in the eye, I knew I never would have gone through with it. If I'd gotten hold of all those keys, the only thing I would have done with the contents of that crypt would have been to destroy every single item hidden within it. But now it was too late for that. Too late to hide our involvement in whatever had happened that night. And too late to hope that the truth might earn us any kind of leeway with the monstrous people who ran this organisation.

"I want your backing against the Harlequins," Shawn replied smugly.

"I want you to help me end this war by making sure there isn't a single one of them left to fight in it. I want their turf and the money you were paying them to help you move your product into our beautiful country. And if I'm being totally honest, I wouldn't mind a shiny new boat too."

Carmen's upper lip curled back and she pushed to her feet in a fluid move that I would have struggled to replicate in heels that damn high. She slammed the box shut and strode towards Shawn, tipping her chin up to glare at him as she pressed the barrel of her gun to his chest.

"I don't like people who think they're funny, Mr Mackenzie," she growled. "And I don't like men who try to push their luck with me. The Castillo Cartel have you marked because you fucked up. You lost our product and cost us money. So no, I won't be giving you a fucking boat. And I won't be helping you to win your petty turf war either. But if this information proves to be true then you can be certain that The Harlequin Crew will meet a swift and bloody end by our hands. No one crosses us and gets away with it. So all this information does is buy you back your life. For now. And seeing as The Harlequin Crew are likely to be out of commission soon enough, we may be in touch about the distribution of our product in due course. In the meantime, I suggest you fuck off before I change my mind about being so generous and take you to my playroom for some one on one time with my butcher's block."

Shawn swallowed thickly before tipping an imaginary hat to her and swiftly turning away. He caught my arm as he went, dragging me along a few steps while Travis held back, his gaze on Carmen like he was expecting her to strike while our backs were turned. Though fuck knew what he thought he'd be able to do about it if she did.

"Wait," I gasped, tripping over my feet as Shawn hauled me along. I wasn't even sure what I was going to say, but I couldn't just leave. I had to try something. She had to know that my boys hadn't been responsible for killing the people onboard that boat all those years ago. It had just been a stupid fucking coincidence.

"Come on, sugarpie, we don't wanna outstay our welcome," Shawn growled, moving faster as he continued to pull me after him.

"Hold on," Carmen barked and Shawn fell still like a whipped little bitch, but I was too concerned about my boys to take any joy in seeing him brought to heel again. "I want a word with the girl."

Shawn's fingers flexed around my arm and he narrowed his eyes on me suspiciously before replying to her. "Of course." He tugged me closer and leaned in to speak in my ear before letting me go though. "Remember, sugarpie, I could tell her here and now that you were involved in that theft too. Seems to me like you'd end up deader than dead if she knew that. And let's not forget - I promised you I'd end the war if you came back to me. No one ever said I couldn't do that by winning it."

I jerked my arm out of his grip and scowled at him as I felt my hatred for him rise to impossibly higher levels and I strode back towards Carmen as quickly as I could.

She snapped her fingers at the two men who had remained in the room with us and one of them grabbed the box of evidence against me and my boys before the two of them ushered Shawn and Travis towards the door.

Travis looked back at us as he was encouraged further down the veranda and the intensity of his gaze on Carmen made my skin prickle before he tore his attention away and walked off.

"Speak," Carmen instructed, her lips pursed like she was half tempted to kill everyone in this room and be done with the bother of us.

I glanced back at Shawn, wondering if he really would sell me out and risk losing his favourite plaything before realising I didn't even give a fuck if he did. Because not speaking up was far worse than what might happen to me for admitting the truth. So if these were the last words that might ever pass my lips then so be it. Because I would speak them out of love and in the sincerest hope that they might just be enough to save the boys who had been my entire world for as long as I could remember.

"Those men were already dead when we found that boat," I breathed, making sure to pitch my voice low so it wouldn't carry beyond me and the ice cold cartel enforcer before me. "I swear it. We didn't do anything to them. We had no idea it was your boat, we were just dumb kids who set a fire by accident and-"

"You set the fire?" she asked sharply, though she kept her words for me alone too.

"We didn't mean to. We'd just realised whose boat we were on and in the panic-"

"Enough," she snapped, taking a step closer to me and gripping my chin between the points of her red taloned fingernails. "I see you, rainbow child, hiding beneath the hurt and shame of what you've survived. I see you. And I don't think it's time for your flame to gutter out."

My eyes widened at her words, some tangible, fractured piece of my soul shivering at the brutal honesty of them as she seemed to scrape aside all of the bullshit in me and peer right into the fucking truth of me instead.

"Hold on to that fire in your heart," she hissed. "And use it to burn everyone who tries to put it out." Her gaze snapped to Shawn who was looking fairly close to pissing himself as he watched us from the far end of the balcony and for a moment I felt like she really had seen every truth of me. Like she knew exactly who I was and why I was here and was standing front and centre like the world's most badass cheerleader waiting for me to finish what I'd come for.

"How did you-" I began but she cut me off.

"We learn to recognise our own, don't we? The forgotten, broken girls. But we are so much more than that. Embrace it. Own it. Become who you were born to be. Life is too short to spend it accepting your place in the gutter when there are stars just waiting for you to rise up and claim them. And I swear, when you ascend, there will be no man on this earth powerful enough to pull you from the throne you build for yourself."

My lips parted at the power of her words and somehow it felt like they reached right into the darkest, loneliest places inside me and strengthened them with bars of pure iron. Carmen jerked her chin towards Shawn and Travis who still waited for me then turned and strode away, heading into the house through another door without a backwards glance.

I followed her instructions and moved to re-join Shawn, but her words stayed lodged inside me and I knew that she was right. I'd spent too fucking long hurting and aching and wishing my life could be different. So I was going to stop moping and start working on becoming the woman I knew I could be. And the first thing I had to do to achieve that was kill fucking Shawn. So I planned on doing that ASAP.

Dead Man's Isle

MAVERICK

CHAPTER TWELVE

G ravel seemed to roll inside my throat as I toked on a cigarette on the balcony of my bedroom, watching the sea. The morning air was filled with the promise of a burningly hot day and I half wished the sun would blaze so hot today it melted the flesh from my bones and turned the rest of me to dust.

There was no wind. No air to breathe. Or maybe that was just the way every day felt without her. Like my lungs knew there was nothing worth pumping for anymore.

I toyed with the idea of playing Russian roulette with my life, but one glance back towards the bedroom made my eyes fall on JJ in my bed, sleeping with anxiety written into his features.

Apparently I was making a habit out of that. Sleeping in a bed with a guy who'd been absent from my life for ten years. Even when we'd checked into motels outside of Sunset Cove, we'd gotten one bed. Like that was perfectly normal. The two of us craving the company of the other, like if it went missing we'd die.

I took another long toke on my cigarette then flicked it away from me in a cascade of sparks as it tumbled through the air and hit the patio far below. The smoke spilled from my lips as a grimace pulled at my face. Nicotine wasn't giving me what I needed. My addiction didn't lie with a pack of Marlboros. It was out there, across that sea, up in a manor I couldn't gain access to. And right about now, it was probably laying in a bed with Shawn Mackenzie, letting his cock fill her up and please her in some way I'd never been capable of.

A shudder crawled up my spine and made my lips peel back. I'd kill that man. I'd kill him for twisting my Rogue into a vengeful, bitter creature, and I'd paint his blood across the walls of my kingdom to show her who the bigger monster in this town was. If she thought he could take over the Cove, she was delusional. I may have despised every Harlequin in this town, but I'd stand with them against our common enemy and let every one of The Damned Men lay their life down for the cause. I'd cut out the heart of his empire and squeeze it bloody in my fist.

"Morning." JJ's voice snapped me out of my dark reverie as he joined me, resting his elbows on the balcony and pushing his floppy black hair out of his eyes. His shoulder rubbed mine as he mimicked my stance and some ancient part of me purred like a lion whose brother had returned to his side.

I grunted in some semblance of a greeting as he stared out at the husk of Sinners' Playground on the shore. The end of the pier had survived, the Ferris wheel still standing tall, but the rest was lost to the fire and the sea. Even from here, I could see the blackened boards and smoke licked metal of the old fairground stands. It was tainted, all but ruined. Just like us.

"I had a dream," JJ murmured.

"Yeah?" I muttered.

He'd been doing this lately, most mornings telling me about his dreams and for some reason I listened. For some reason I liked to listen. Maybe because I was damn curious about what it was like not to have dreams riddled with darkness, with fingers tearing into my flesh and hot breaths huffed against my ear. Even now, JJ's dreams held light in them that mine never could. So I lived a little vicariously through him as I imagined a night without terror awaiting me behind closed eyes. Sleeping with Rogue, I'd found the most peace I'd ever known in sleep. But I'd never dreamed something sweet.

"We were out in the water surfing," he said and he didn't have to say he meant the five of us, because JJ's dreams always meant the five of us. "There was a shark circling us and everyone was freaking out. Then you dove in and punched it in the head." He breathed a laugh and I cracked something of a grin.

"Did I kill it?" I asked.

"No, it ate you," he chuckled.

"Not a very realistic dream then," I pointed out and his smile grew.

"You know, you may hate Luther, but you sure as shit inherited his arrogance."

At Luther's name, my mood took a darker turn. I'd asked Fox in clipped words whether he was alive or dead before he'd left the beach the other night, and I'd found myself disgustingly relieved over him living. I tried to tell myself that was because I still wanted to kill him myself, but my lies were getting thinner these days. I was finding I was unable to convince myself of much because it took too much goddamn energy. And I'd been hunting for Chase like a man possessed. I knew what that really meant. I knew my traitor self was taking over and I wasn't sure who I was even pretending for anymore. JJ knew. And JJ was all I had. So why even fucking lie?

That hadn't been the only thing Fox had told me either, he'd said Rogue hadn't been the one to fire the bullet that had landed Luther in surgery. Hadn't been the reason he could have ended up as worm food. In fact, she'd fired a fucking warning shot before Shawn had been the one to lay him out half dead. And I found myself quietly relieved I didn't have to hate her to my core for almost ending the man who'd raised me. Because his life belonged to me, of course. Though why she'd tried to spare him, I guess I'd never fucking know.

"I was thinking we could head to the woods out that way today." I pointed over at the mainland where my territory lay. "If he's keeping out of the Harlequins' way, he might have risked staying on my turf."

JJ nodded, his eyes still fixed on Sinners' Playground. "Rick, do you… think she's okay?"

A shard of glass seemed to lodge in my throat at those words and I clenched my jaw.

"What's it matter?" I shot back. But it mattered. I knew it fucking mattered. It mattered so much it made me want to rip the sky down so I might read her fate among the fabric of the universe. I had to know. It fucking killed me thinking of her in Shawn's arms, even if that was where she wanted to be.

He wasn't capable of loving her. He was vicious, heartless. And I may have been a lot of those things too, but I would have loved Rogue Easton until the world ended.

"You know it does," JJ hissed. "I can't stand it. Thinking of her. With *him*." Acid coated his words and I nodded, tasting it on my tongue too.

"She's not okay," I said honestly, my skin turning icily cold despite the sun on my flesh. "She hasn't been okay since we were kids. And all of this shit is our fault, maybe it's hers in ways too, I don't fucking know. All I know for sure is, this is what real life looks like. Gritty and flawed and so fucking painful it makes you want to slit your own throat just so you don't have to keep living it anymore."

"So why are you still standing here?" JJ demanded, clearly not agreeing with my pretty grim outlook on life.

I shrugged and he turned toward me, shoving my arm.

"Not good enough," he growled, standing upright and I noticed how much of a man he was these days. I used to look down on him when we were kids, his height not keeping up with ours, but that had changed. He'd bulked up too, but that wasn't what made him a man. It was the look in his eyes. A rawness there that spoke of all he'd experienced since we were just boys playing on Sunset Beach. Johnny James had tasted the bitter side of fate as well as I had, maybe in different ways, but he knew what it was like to crawl through the dirt looking for something worth living for in the muck. And I reckoned he'd found it in Rogue like I had, so I supposed that meant we were back in the dirt again, but at least he was with me this time.

I stood upright too, my jaw working as he waited for me to give him a proper answer.

"Purpose, Johnny James," I said firmly. "I've got a list of things I need to check off before I check out."

He shook his head at me then frowned as his phone started ringing back in my room.

I followed him inside as he hurried to grab it and he hit speaker as he picked up.

"Hello?" JJ asked and I noticed the caller ID was unknown.

"Hey J," Chase's voice sounded down the line and what was left of my heart thumped harder.

I took a step closer as JJ's face split into the first real smile I'd seen on him since Rogue had left.

"Oh thank fuck," JJ sighed in relief, carving his fingers through his hair. "Where are you brother? Are you alright?"

"Yeah, you know…surviving. I've got a gift for you," Chase said and I frowned.

"We'll come pick you up," JJ said quickly. "Look man, shit's happened. We need to talk."

"We can talk when you get here," Chase said. "I'll text you the address."

He hung up and a heavy breath fell from my lungs. JJ looked up at me, a fucking rainbow seeming to break through the clouds in his eyes then he lunged forward and snared me in a hug. I resisted it for all of two seconds then crushed him in my arms as I let myself just feel the relief of finding Chase. Fuck it, why fight it anymore? This was what we'd hoped for for so long and just like that, we had him.

I didn't know how long I was gonna stick around on this earth, but I couldn't deny the bond I had to JJ anymore. It felt so fucking good to have one of my brothers back. And maybe I was about to get a second.

"Come on," I muttered, letting him go and JJ all but bounced across the room to get dressed.

I smiled at his back, but flattened it by the time he turned around again as I grabbed some of my own clothes and pulled them on.

Maybe today wasn't going to be another shit show after all.

I made JJ ride on the back of my motorcycle in the bitch seat instead of taking the truck so we could get to Chase faster. He soon got comfy with his arms wrapped around me and his thighs gripping mine though, so I had to think the guy was enjoying it more than he let on.

Chase had given us a location beyond the upper quarter where there was a stretch of wetland beyond the fancy ass beach houses.

I drove so fast, the world was a blur and adrenaline bloomed in my veins like tinder catching light.

We were soon sailing through the wetland on a winding road, driving deeper and deeper into the deserted land. I knew for a fact that Luther Harlequin had hidden bodies out here because I'd been there when he'd done it, showing me the best spots to hide them in the deep pools where the heat and moisture would help them rot away quickly while hiding them from discovery.

The chirrup of birds and ribbet of frogs called around us as I spotted a beat up silver Jaguar pulled up at the side of the road.

I slowed my bike, pulling up behind it and killing the engine as JJ jumped off and tossed his helmet onto the bike handle. I got off too, removing my helmet and taking a gun from the hidden box beneath the saddle just in case this was a trap. But as the driver's door opened and Chase stepped out, I lowered it, staring at him from his dark curls to the eyepatch he wore.

JJ rushed at him like a dog who'd been separated from his owner for a year, wrapping his arms around him and nearly knocking Chase on his ass as he stumbled on his bad leg.

I stood there, frozen as they laughed and clung to each other, feeling like an awkward turd left to bake here in the sun.

When JJ finally released him, I found my feet moving forward with intent and I yanked Chase into my arms before I could take a second to consider it.

He stiffened in surprise like he thought I was about to drive a knife between his shoulder blades then his arms wrapped around me and he hugged me back. My neck burned and I didn't look at fucking JJ who was definitely smirking at me. I just crushed my brother in my arms and said nothing.

"It's good to see you too, Rick," Chase said and I released him, shrugging like I didn't care. Which was kind of pointless now, but my pride wouldn't let me admit I'd been fucking worried about him since Fox had kicked him out of town.

"Rick's learning to be a teddy bear again, aren't you Rick?" JJ elbowed me and I rolled my eyes.

"It's cute that you think I wouldn't empty my gun into you, J," I taunted.

"I bet you would." JJ winked at me and I snorted a laugh, shoving his arm.

Chase looked between us, a grin playing around his mouth. "So what's the news? How's Rogue?"

The mood took an instant turn and I swear a cloud drifted over the sun at that very moment, blotting out all the light that had just been shining in the world.

"Ace..." JJ started, a frown creasing his brow. "Rogue, she...she betrayed us. All of us. This whole thing, this whole time- he started getting worked up into an emotional state so I stepped in for him.

"She's Shawn's girl. Always was."

"What?" Chase scoffed, half laughing as he looked between us for the joke.

I tugged the phone from JJ's pocket, bringing up the video she'd left us and holding it out for him, hating to have to pop his little Rogue bubble, but it had to be done. "She left and went back to him. This is her confession. She fucked with us for revenge."

Chase took the phone, watching the video and I tried to block out the sound of Rogue saying those sharp words all over again. They drove a knife into my heart repeatedly until it was weeping blood and I missed her almost as much as I despised her for what she'd done.

Chase's face paled as he watched then he slowly handed the phone back to JJ, seeming to take a moment to process what he'd just watched.

"So she's with Shawn?" he rasped in fear and I nodded. "Hang on, are you actually telling me you watched this video then let her go to that psychotic motherfucker?" There was an edge to his tone like a rage was building in him, and I hoped he wasn't about to have a meltdown. Even I could admit the guy deserved a break after all the shit he'd faced, so I didn't take any pleasure in ruining his day.

"It wasn't a choice, Ace," JJ said, clawing at his hair. "She fucking left and then we found this. She wants to be with him. They're together."

Chase gaped at us for several long seconds, then words exploded from him in a roar. "Are you fucking idiots?!" he bellowed.

"No?" JJ said like he wasn't sure.

Chase grabbed JJ's shirt in his fists, yanking him nose to nose with him. "She lied to you, you moron."

"I – what?" JJ stammered in confusion.

Poor fucking fool. I'd expected a breakdown, but it looked like he was going with denial instead.

"Get your hands off of him." I pushed Chase back, but he came at me next, locking a hand around my throat.

"Maverick, are you really telling me you swallowed that horseshit?" he snapped.

"You're being naïve!" I barked, shoving his hand off of me. "Of course she fucking lied. Why would she want anything to do with us after what we did to her? This makes perfect sense, you're just trying to deny it to yourself."

Chase released a manic sort of laugh that was all psycho. "Oh my god, this is our problem, isn't it?" he said in realisation. "All of us think we're so fucking worthless that we'd rather swallow a lie that proves that than acknowledge that maybe Rogue fucking Easton actually still loves us."

"What?" JJ balked in confusion as Chase turned his manic gaze on him.

"Don't you get it, J?" Chase barked, taking hold of his shoulders. "She lied to fucking save you. To save all of you."

"She wouldn't-" I started, but Chase cut over me.

"She would," he growled furiously. "She told me herself one night in my room. She said she was considering going to Shawn to end the war. To protect us. She swore she wouldn't go through with it and made me swear I would stay too. So if I lied, then you'd better believe she did too."

A weight of lead seemed to drop in my gut as I stared at him, refusing to accept those words. Because if they were true, if there was even an ounce of truth to them, it meant Rogue had walked into the lion's den alone and was no doubt being shredded by the beast's claws right at this fucking second.

"No," I gritted out.

"Yes," Chase tossed back, his features twisting in fear. "What the fuck have you done?"

JJ backed up into the road, crouching down and clawing his hands into his hair.

My hands shook and I turned, making a sudden decision as I made a beeline for my bike.

"*Wait*." Chase caught up to me, taking hold of my arm and I glanced back at him, hesitating as I took in the scar peeking beneath the eyepatch over his right eye. He'd been butchered at the hands of Shawn and now my girl could be facing the same fate. And it was all my fucking fault.

"Take a breath," he commanded, gripping my face in his hands.

"I have to get her out," I said, panic shredding everything inside my chest.

"We will. But not by marching up to his door with nothing but a gun in your hand," he growled and I managed to see sense enough to know I'd only end up dead in that scenario and then I'd be no use to her.

"JJ, get up." Chase commanded and JJ scraped himself off the road, looking to us in dismay, like he needed to fix this, but he didn't know how.

"Luckily for you assholes, I've got a plan," Chase went on. "I was gonna lure Shawn to me with her, but I say we use her for a trade instead."

"Who are you talking about?" I demanded as Chase walked to the trunk of his car, popping it open and revealing an unconscious middle aged, redhaired woman in there with her wrists and ankles bound. "Say hello to Shawn Mackenzie's mother."

"Holy shit," JJ gasped as he stepped between us, gazing down at our answer to getting Rogue back. My mind was spinning, a haze of utter rage clouding all my thoughts as I tried to process what Rogue had done. What I'd been stupid enough to let her do.

"Are you sure we're not making a mistake?" JJ aired his fears. "Do you really think she was lying?"

"I know she was," Chase said firmly and I cussed her out under my breath. Fuck that beautiful bitch. I'd teach her a lesson she'd never forget when she was back in my arms. She wanted to save me? Well I was long beyond saving, my soul already bid for and won by the Devil himself. So when I tore her back from the arms of Shawn Mackenzie, I'd be sure to show her the depths I could stoop to in her name. I'd show her the tarnished creature she'd given her life for alongside the Harlequins and demand she acknowledge the worth she held. Because it was far more valuable than any coveted treasure that existed. And if she really thought she could place a price on her head to save us all, then I was going to spend each breath left to me on this green earth making her count every priceless fragment of her being.

And when I was done, I'd claim her as mine. My perfectly broken girl. And I'd whisper the truth to her, confessing that she was theirs too. Because I knew in my bones that she was never meant to belong to one entity. Not me, not the sea, nor the sky. But she was ours. That, she wouldn't fucking deny.

"We need to contact Shawn," Chase said, slamming the trunk shut and looking to us. There was a strength about him now that seemed to have grown from the darkness Shawn had dragged him into. Like every word he spoke was weighted with his survival of all that pain and suffering. Like he'd seen the inner rings of hell and walked back from them with his demons bowing at his feet. And there was power in that. A power that his father had lacked, a power that he had lacked too all these years. Chase had seen the worst life had to offer and had conquered all fear because of it. And I had to fucking respect him for it.

"I know a guy who'll be able to get in touch with him. He doesn't live too far from here," JJ said.

"Well let's fucking move. I want Rogue back by sundown with her ass reddened by my handprint," I gritted out.

"We don't know what she's been through," JJ hissed. "We're not going to punish her for this."

"Speak for yourself," I said with a shrug. "I'll spank her if I feel she deserves it."

"What if Shawn's…" JJ trailed off and Chase took in a shuddering breath like he was back in Shawn's clutches for a second.

"If he's touched her, raped her, or harmed her in any way, I'll cut his cock off and feed it to him," I said darkly, meaning every word of that. Mostly, I was planning on not thinking about the worst-case scenarios right now. I just needed to act. Needed to burn off the energy raging in my muscles. It was the sweet need of bloodlust coursing through me that wanted the most attention. Shawn's blood would be spilled today if I got my way. I just had to be patient.

"Come on, let's go," Chase urged and JJ got into the car with him.

I tossed the spare helmet into the back of his car then pulled mine on and swung my leg over my bike.

Chase turned his car around and I accelerated after him down the winding roads, leading the way back towards the shore and speeding past the huge beach houses there. They eventually turned into a place with towering gates in front of it, beyond which was a huge white house that looked like a church. Rich assholes really gave no fucking shits.

JJ got out of the car, pressing the buzzer at the gate and waiting for a reply.

"Hello?" a girl answered.

"Tatum, it's JJ. Sorry to drop in on you like this, but I wondered if Saint's around? We need help with getting hold of someone."

"I'm busy," a sharp voice sounded in the background.

"It's important," JJ said urgently. "It could be life or death for Rogue."

"Come in," Tatum said instantly and the gates started parting for us.

I followed them inside and Chase and I parked up before I took off my helmet and followed them to the huge wooden door, wrinkling my nose at the monstrous place. I'd have robbed this kind of house blind when I was a kid if I could've gotten away with it.

The door opened and a blonde girl appeared in a pink bikini with a dark figure standing in the shadows behind her like a supervillain – especially as he seemed to be holding a black cat and stroking its head.

The girl led us inside and the guy stepped into the light, revealing a handsome face and built shoulders that filled out a crisp white shirt.

We followed Tatum through the intensely clean house to a lounge with white couches and a TV the size of a car on the wall.

"So what's going on?" Tatum asked anxiously as she dropped onto the couch, gesturing for us to sit opposite her on another four-seater.

I glanced back at the man following us as we sat down and his lips twitched irritably as his gaze hooked on our shoes sinking into the thick rug. He took up a position standing behind us and I felt his eyes burning holes in the back of my head like lasers. This guy was fucking intense.

JJ filled Tatum in on what was happening and her eyes widened in horror as she sat forward, worry crossing her features.

"So we need to contact Shawn," Chase clarified. "JJ thought you might be able to help?"

"Saint?" Tatum asked hopefully, looking at the guy behind us.

"Able, yes. Willing? Hmm…" he muttered. "What am I to gain from it?"

"Rogue's in trouble," Tatum growled and Saint sighed.

"Yes, indeed. She is. A trouble she decided upon getting into. So are sure you want to make decisions for the girl? She wouldn't have made the choice she did without her reasons," he said tightly. Rain started splattering against the window as a storm picked up outside and I cursed this tempestuous weather that was plaguing the town.

"She thinks she's saving us," I bit out. "But if you're not gonna help, then you're wasting our time."

I got to my feet, a growl in my throat as I formed my own plan. Head to the manor, shoot as many Dead Dogs as I could until I got to Rogue. Simple.

Saint stepped smoothly into my way and the cat jumped out of his arms, coiling itself around my legs. "Are you a buffoon, Maverick Stone?"

"A what?" I snapped.

"A buffoon. A ridiculous but amusing person," he deadpanned.

"Are you mocking me, asshole?" I growled.

"I asked a simple question," Saint said, examining his nails. "If you don't have an answer, then perhaps I have misjudged you. You are not a buffoon, you are an ignoramus."

I brought my fist up with a snarl on my lips, about to knock this posh motherfucker on his ass when JJ caught my arm.

"Stop," he hissed, stepping toward Saint. "Can you help us or not?"

"As I said, I am able to," Saint said.

"And will you?" Chase snapped.

Saint wet his lips, seeming to enjoy holding all the power in the room for a moment before he inclined his head. "I suppose so. You can leave, I need silence to do my work. I'll call you when I have the information you require."

"We can't leave," Chase muttered. "We aren't welcome with the Harlequins anymore and Shawn has taken control of the town with The Dead Dogs."

Saint sighed like those words made him weary.

"Then stay," Tatum urged. "We're actually heading out of town for the weekend, but Saint can get you the information you need and I'll give you a key. No one would think to look for you here."

"Are you sure?" JJ asked. "Because that would actually be pretty fucking perfect."

"Of course."

Saint pinched the bridge of his nose and muttered something about needing strength to deal with the halfwits in his home.

I scowled at him and Tatum rolled her eyes, urging him to go do his work somewhere quiet if he needed silence.

He exited the room and the cat padded after him, its tail flicking left and right sharply like it was as irritated as Saint.

My fist was still clenched and frustration boiled inside me as we turned to look at Tatum and she gave us an innocent bat of her lashes over her neurotic boyfriend. "Coffee?"

CHAPTER THIRTEEN

I poured some premium treats into the bowl under Mutt's nose and he took one sniff then turned his head away from them like they were rancid. He trotted off through the kitchen to sit by my dad's feet at the breakfast bar and Luther promptly handed him some bacon from his plate. Mutt wolfed it down, yipping appraisingly and I scowled. I swear that dog was holding a grudge against me. If he wasn't pissing on the new toys I'd bought him, he was chewing up my favourite shoes or leaving strategically placed turds outside my bedroom door. And if I so much as rose my voice a single notch, my dad chewed me out for it like I was the one with the problem while the dog gave me this smug little look which seemed perfectly designed to goad me.

Worse than Mutt's moody attitude with me was the fact that Maverick had thought it was a great idea to send me the recording of him and JJ fucking Rogue last night. I'd clicked play only to instantly regret it and nearly smashed my phone with how hard I'd thrown it across the room. I may have slept on my rage, but it had done very little to shift my anger.

Fucking asshole.

I grabbed my plate of eggs and toast, sitting down at the breakfast bar beside dad and stuffing a large mouthful between my lips in annoyance.

"You okay, kid?" Dad asked and I shrugged.

I was never okay anymore. Rogue had obliterated my heart and the pieces left behind had been taken by my boys when they'd left too. Now my chest was just an empty building with nothing but pain as a resident.

I'd stopped running, stopped eating right, stopped giving a general fuck about any of it. Who was it for now? Me? So what if I was healthy? I didn't have anyone to protect anymore.

"Do you wanna talk about it?" Dad asked.

"Talk about what? There's nothing to say," I said dismissively, my eyes on my food. Despite having cooked it well, it tasted of nothing in my mouth. With her gone, the world was tasteless again. No light, no colour, no flavour.

"I know you must be hurting over Rogue," he said gently. "And JJ... what exactly happened with him?"

I stiffened, shaking my head as I thought of the moment I'd found him with his cock deep inside Rogue. "It doesn't matter."

"It does," he pushed. "You might feel better if you talk about it, kid."

"Feel better?" I scoffed bitterly. "There's no 'better' now."

"You and your friends were always so dramatic. I'm sure you can work it out with your boys. With Maverick," he said hopefully and I growled under my breath, thumping my fist down on the surface.

"When are you going to accept that me and him are never going to be brothers again?" I demanded, glaring him in the eye and a frown pulled his dark blonde brows together.

"You will," he bit back and I just huffed out a breath, tired of having this same old argument.

"Then you'll both rule the Harlequins together and-"

"I'm not a Harlequin anymore," I told him for the fiftieth time since I'd brought him home from hospital. He was doing much better now, but he was still on a lot of painkillers as his body healed from the surgery and he definitely wasn't up for running the Crew fully yet. That didn't stop him attempting it though, acting like he was invincible and trying to prove that not even a bullet could put the great Luther Harlequin out of action.

I saw his pain through the act, the winces he tried to hide, the way he slept longer and took naps in the afternoon – though whenever I caught him resting he jumped to alert and pretended it hadn't happened. It was ridiculous, like he couldn't even allow his own son to see him weakened after a damn gunshot and major surgery. But I knew what that was like. Being a leader came with so much responsibility that it was difficult to let go of it, even when necessary.

I just wished Dad would find something that meant more to him than his gang, something outside of me or Maverick too. He needed a life of his own, something that was his and no one else's, but I couldn't exactly give any decent advice on that when I had fuck all to show for trying to claim something like that for myself and failing. I may have had it once, but I'd fucked it up supremely now.

"Sure you are, you're just taking a break," he said dismissively and I shoved out of my seat, sick of his same old shit.

"I hope I'm not breaking up this little breakfast party," a sultry woman's voice sounded behind me and I whipped around, grabbing my pistol from my hip and aiming it at her head in less than a heartbeat.

Luther had his gun raised too and Mutt's hackles were up as we all stared at the intruder. Carmen Ortega. A lieutenant of the Castillo Cartel who ruled over this territory. She wore a fitted red dress, her feet bare and a pair of high heels in her grip. She slowly slipped them back on, smirking at us.

"You really ought to get better security, Luther," she said, her Mexican accent thick. "I have the men who were guarding your back door tied up in a boat out on your little private beach." She smoothed a hand through her long dark hair, approaching us on her killer heels. "I come unarmed." She raised her hands and did a slow twirl for us though knowing how deadly this woman was, I wouldn't have been surprised if she was concealing blades everywhere beneath that dress and possibly in her hair too.

I glanced at my dad who nodded to me, lowering his gun and pawing at his bed hair as he tried to flatten it, though why he gave a fuck what it looked like I had no idea.

"This is not appreciated, Carmen," he growled.

"No?" she said in mock surprise. "I've done you a favour, Luther. I've highlighted the weak spots in your security. And I've shown up here to warn you over a threat that could see you destroyed by midday. But if that's not of interest to you, I'll just head on my way." She turned to leave as my stomach knotted.

"What threat?" Dad demanded, pushing to his feet so that he towered over her and Carmen took her sweet time turning back, examining a photo on the wall of me and my father at a wedding.

"There's an old saying in my family," she said casually, the power she exuded somehow rivalling the power my father held. I could feel the tension in the air like it was thicker than the oxygen we were all breathing in. "No se puede hacer buen vino con mala fruta," she said in a lyrical tone. "You can't make good wine out of bad fruit."

"Uhuh, and you're telling me this why exactly?" Dad pushed and she finally turned to look at us again, raising her chin as her dark eyes roamed from my father to me.

"Your family produces good fruit, Luther," she said. "You're useful to me. And you may have your flaws, as all men do, but you are not entirely detestable to me."

"Cut to the chase of this love song, yeah?" Dad growled and her lips twisted up at one corner.

"Shawn Mackenzie is planning to take over Sunset Cove today. He will shortly be on his way here with enough men to dismember you and your son within moments of their arrival. To add to this, he brought me evidence that your son and his friends were involved in the attack which took place on La Princesa," she added. "And as such, I'm afraid I had to put a price on your heads too – though my men have not yet been told why they are hunting for you."

"What?" I gasped, realising what this meant, that fucking Shawn had gotten into the crypt and found the evidence that linked us back to that fucking yacht. "I need to explain-" I began but she cut me off.

"There is no time for that right now," she said, her eyes flicking from me to my dad as she strode right up to him, not seeming the least bit intimidated by the way his powerful body dwarfed hers as she tilted her head back to look up at him. "I am giving you this one chance to escape. You cannot win the fight, so I have organised for you both to be smuggled out of town to safety."

"What?" I gritted out, panic lacing my tone. Was she serious? How many goddamn men was Shawn sending? And why was she warning us about the cartel coming for us when she was openly admitting that she was also the one who had set them after us?

"Why would you do this for us?" Dad demanded in clear distrust of her.

She shrugged. "Shawn is bad fruta. He leaves a bitter taste in my mouth."

"That doesn't explain why you're helping us," Luther growled.

"Or why you haven't killed us if you really believe we had something to do with the deaths of the men on La Princesa," I added fiercely, but Carmen started shaking her head.

"I told you, you don't have time to waste asking foolish questions now. But if you wish to live another day, then you can take the offer I have on the table. Or not. It's really up to you." She said like she really didn't care either way but then why the fuck was she even here? And why was her gaze lingering on Luther like he was a whole lot more interesting to her than she was admitting?

"I'm not running like some frightened dog," I ground out and Mutt yapped in agreement of those words.

"Then stay here and get gutted, chico tonto," she said with a light shrug like she gave no shits either way. But clearly she did or she wouldn't have been here offering us a bone.

She casually checked the slim silver watch on her wrist and clucked her tongue. "You're almost out of time. While Shawn's cutting your nose from your face, be good boys and keep your tongues from telling tales on me today, hm?" She turned and headed out of the room in the direction of the back door.

"Wait!" Luther barked, moving to chase after her and cursing as he jolted his injuries. "Fuck that devil woman," he cursed, grasping his side and bracing himself against the wall.

"I think that devil woman's trying to help us," I muttered anxiously.

"Then go catch her. We can't take the risk of staying here. Carmen wouldn't have come here if she wasn't serious about saving our asses. I'll pack a bag," Luther growled decisively and I nodded, jogging after Carmen and finding her walking down onto the beach.

Black clouds were thickening overhead and the first drops of rain peppered my cheeks as I hurried after her. A boat was docked at our jetty for her manned by the large guy Pepito, but I caught her before she made it to him, twisting her back to face me.

"Remove your hand from me, Fox Harlequin," she commanded and I did so. Despite her being notably smaller than me, she still somehow seemed as big as a goddess standing there with the wind tussling her long hair and a demon peering out of her big, dark eyes.

"Where do we go?" I demanded.

"Oh good, all of that testosterone hasn't made you entirely dense," she said cuttingly. "My cousin will wait for you with a boat at the Sailor's Eye Lighthouse for the next thirty minutes. I suggest you go on foot because the roads are being watched. If you can make it there in time, he'll get you away from Sunset Cove. You will need his help to cross the water because there will be many men out on the sea to ensure you don't escape."

"How do you know all of this?" I asked in dismay.

She tutted, shaking her head at me. "Chico tonto," she muttered then walked away, boarding her boat and Pepito lifted the two Harlequins who'd been guarding the back of the house out of the boat, tossing them onto the jetty bound and gagged. *Jesus.*

Carmen disappeared into the cabin as it tore out across the water and the reality of our situation struck me like a heart attack.

Fuck.

I ran back to the house as thunder boomed in the heavens and I cursed this wild weather we were having lately. One second the sun was shining, and the next the clouds were rolling in and unleashing hell on our town.

I made it inside, finding Luther with a couple of bags at his feet. "Here, get Mutt in there." He held out a backpack for him and I stooped down to put the dog in it, then Dad threw a blanket at me full force.

"Not without his snuggle," he said in horror. "And he needs Mr Squeakeasy. Where the fuck is it?" He rifled through the mountains of dog toys which I'd bought Mutt and had been rejected. Hard.

"Who the hell is Mr Squeakeasy?" I demanded. We needed to go. There was no time for finding some random dog toy. "Just grab one of those." I picked up a banana toy from the pile and Mutt snapped at my hand as I tried to put it in the bag with him.

"Ah, here it is!" Dad exclaimed, pulling the thing out of one of my sneakers by the door which had been half chewed to shit. He squeaked the toy that looked like a broccoli with a smiley face on it, stroking Mutt's head and putting it in the bag and Mutt licked Dad's hand like he was thanking him.

I scowled at the dog for his continued rejection of me, though I knew this was the least of my worries right now. I zipped up the backpack, leaving a hole big enough for him to stick his nose through before placing it on my back. Dad put on his own backpack, grunting as the movement made his wounds ache and I slung the final bag over my shoulder.

"I've directed our men to lock the house once we're out of here then they'll make their own way out of town. They'll wait for me to call them once the dust has settled and we've figured out a game plan. We'll come back to fight another day, kid," Dad said and though I despised having to leave the house behind, it was just bricks and mortar. The heart of it was long gone now that my family had left, and so long as Dad and Mutt were with me, there was no one else left in this town who mattered to me.

We headed down to the beach and I led the way as we waded out into the shallows, making it off of our property around a craggy rock wall, then moving to the fence that lined the perimeter up on dry land. Dad took out some bolt cutters, quickly clipping a hole in the wire and ushering me through before following.

I kept a gun in my grip the whole time, my ears pricking at any sound of men's voices in the distance. Shots were fired somewhere in the town and my pulse thundered in my ears as we started jogging down side streets and alleys, sticking to the less trodden paths of Sunset Cove. I'd grown up on these streets, and my dad had too. We'd know our way around it blind, so we at least had that advantage over Shawn today.

When the lighthouse came into view, we were in luck, this side of town only dotted with a few people, most of them hurrying to shelter from the rain and paying us little attention. As we made it to the beach, we broke into a run and scaled the black rocks surrounding the lighthouse. A fishing boat was docked beyond them, bobbing in the choppy waves of the water as the rain started to pick up in intensity.

A huge guy stood on the deck with bronzed skin and intense, murderous eyes that flashed onto us in an instant. There was a girl beside him wearing a rainbow mermaid bikini, pink fishnet stockings and big biker boots, her black hair whipping around her in the wind. She had a fluffy blue lead in her hand which led to the meanest asshole of a dog I'd ever seen, its collar blue to match the lead with metal spikes sticking out of it. The animal was grey, covered in scars and looked like a cross between a pitbull and a grizzly bear.

"Ahoy there!" the girl cried, waving like we couldn't see them even though she stood out like a unicorn in a field of miniature ponies. The man jerked his head to beckon us down to them and we scrambled across the rocks to get to the water.

"Raise the gang plank, drop the sails!" the girl cried orders to seemingly no one as the huge guy took to the helm and steered the boat a little closer to us with a rev of the engine.

"Are you Carmen's man?" Dad called to him and the man grunted vaguely in affirmation.

"This is Mateo," the girl introduced him as we clambered aboard the boat. "And I'm Brooklyn with a B."

"What else would you spell it with?" I asked in confusion.

"A silent H, obviously." She snorted like I was an idiot and her massive dog growled at me so deeply it seemed to rumble right from its belly. "This is Brutus. You can pet him if you want. He doesn't bite."

"He does," Mateo warned, his voice laced with a Mexican accent like his cousin's. "He has eaten many men and will eat many more." He turned his back on us as he steered the boat out onto the waves and Brooklyn laughed wildly like Mateo had made a joke. I hoped he had. But the look in the dog's eyes said it was no joke.

"Carmen says you're her cousin. Are you part of the cartel?" Dad called to Mateo over the roar of the storm.

Mateo glanced at him and I swear I could see countless deaths reflecting back at me. I knew souls like my own, the kind dipped in blood and dark deeds. He looked like he'd faced the seven deadly sins hand to hand and emerged victorious, and that kind of power commanded respect.

"No, I am not part of the cartel," he growled, some ominous undertone to his voice almost suggesting he despised their organisation. But if he was related to Carmen, I didn't imagine that was very likely.

Brooklyn moved to his side and he locked a possessive arm around her, dropping his mouth to her ear. "It's very wet up here, mi sol."

"Very wet," she agreed, biting her lip as she gazed up at him and he slid his fingers around her throat, holding her gently but the power he emanated made her shiver like she couldn't get enough of his touch.

"Take our guests below deck," he ordered and she nodded, batting her lashes several times before he released her and she hurried toward us looking flustered.

"Come on, you can hide down here. There's a little hidey hole. Don't worry, there's no squirrels in here to peep on you." Brooklyn beckoned us after her into a small cabin, picking up a fishing net and throwing it over my dad. "There. No one will see you now, Mr Man. They'll just think we caught a big fat, tattooed fish." She laughed manically and Dad pulled the net off of him, sharing a confused glance with me as Brooklyn started dancing. She let go of the leash tethered to her dog and I stiffened as the beast took a step towards us, baring rows of sharp teeth.

"And she danced in a meadow and she danced in a tree, and she danced like a widow in a nice cup of tea," Brooklyn sang and I started to think we'd made a mistake taking Carmen's help. Who the hell was this lunatic? "Come on, you know the song! Join in!" she cried.

"We really don't," Dad said, moving to sit down as the boat ride grew choppier. I took my pack from my shoulders, leaning against the wall with it in my arms instead and keeping my gun in my grip, feeling safer on my feet while that dog kept looking at us like we were its next meal.

"Holy nipples, batman." Brooklyn stopped dancing abruptly, pointing at the pack in my arms. "Your bag's alive! It's wriggling."

"It's just my dog," I muttered, clutching the bag tighter. I didn't wanna let Mutt out around that other hellhound. He might eat him.

"Awwww. Can I see?" she asked, rushing over in a blur and taking hold of one of the straps. "Animals love me. I woke up with a ferret called Angus in my sleeping bag once. That was back when I used to sleep on the streets. Well I mean…he looked like a ferret. I suppose he could have been a really long rat. Who'd called a rat Angus though, amIright?"

"Err," I struggled with how to respond to that.

"Lemme see the secret puppy." She took hold of the zipper and I let her open it enough for Mutt's head to pop out.

"He might bite," I warned, but Mutt – traitor that he was – immediately started licking her hand like he was the friendliest dog in the world.

"What's his name?" she asked, then squealed before I could answer. "No wait! Let me guess. Voldemort?"

"No," I balked.

"Right, right, he's more of a Gryffindor kinda dude. Gotcha." She winked. "I'm a Slytherin. Mateo's a total Hufflepuff but don't tell him that – he thinks he's a Ravenclaw. As if." She snorted. "Niall's a Slytherin too, obvi."

"Who?" I asked in confusion, my head rattling with the speed this girl talked. She whipped out her phone from god knew where seeing as she was hardly wearing any clothes and waved a photo at me on the screen. The man in the photo was stacked, with blonde hair and colourful tattoos coating his body alongside enough scars to let me know he'd come damn close to death more than a few times in his life. He was also butt ass naked apart from a pink tutu that did nothing to cover his giant, hard, pierced cock.

"Jesus," I cursed, shoving the phone away from my face.

"Miss you, Hellfire." She kissed the screen – right on his dick. "This pic was his idea. So I'd remember him always." She sighed wistfully then proceeded to start dancing again. Which was fine by me as that seemed to keep her distracted from showing me anymore naked pictures of dudes and she sang a song under her breath about Brutus chewing off Harry Potter's legs.

The boat suddenly crested a wave, slamming down hard and my heart lurched into my throat as Mateo whooped up on the deck.

"Sounds fun up there," Brooklyn said with a wild glint in her eyes. "Brutus, sit." She commanded and the dog ignored her. "Good boy." She petted his head then kissed him all over his face as he growled a deadly growl. "Look after our special guests, kay?"

She ran out the door back up to the deck and my throat thickened as Brutus advanced on us.

"What the fuck was Carmen thinking sending us here?" Dad hissed, wincing as the violent boat journey jostled him about and made his injuries flare.

"Where are they even taking us?"

"Maybe they'll drop us off beyond the upper quarter," Dad said hopefully, reaching into his bag and taking out a handful of dog treats. "Here now, good boy." He tossed them to Brutus and they sprinkled over his face, not distracting him one bit. This beast looked like it wanted blood for dinner. Our blood.

"If we make it that far," I gritted out, holding onto a rope hanging from the low roof above me to keep my balance. "If we don't capsize in this storm and drown, I'm pretty sure we'll be ripped to pieces by this dog."

"Land whore!" Brooklyn cried from up top.

"It's land ho," Mateo corrected her.

"Right, I knew the land was a slut, I just couldn't remember which type," she said with a giggle.

"What?" I asked in confusion. "We can't have gotten beyond the Cove that fast."

Brutus turned and bounded upstairs onto the deck and I helped Dad to his feet as he fought a wince, his jaw flexing as I guided him along. The rain sheeted down on us as we made it up top and my gaze fell on the half sunk wreckage of The Mariner.

Realisation struck me like a slap to the face and I shook my head in horror.

"You idiots, you've taken us to an enemy stronghold," I barked. Dead Man's fucking Isle? What the hell were they thinking? "Take us up the coast," I said in a fierce order.

"That would be best," Dad agreed, though he didn't seem as unsettled by our location as I was.

"No," Mateo said, his brow lowering to shadow his intense eyes and my instincts prickled for a weapon to defend myself against the fight I saw brewing in him. Though something told me this man preferred to kill with his bare hands and maybe his teeth too. Between the merciless darkness in his eyes to the muscles which clad his body like armour, he looked like a warrior dressed in sin.

"Yup. No can do, Mr Man," Brooklyn agreed, not seeming affected by the rain drenching every inch of her as she casually eye-fucked her boyfriend.

Mateo dropped an arm around her shoulders as he stared coolly at us, his gaze warning of our deaths which he looked more than willing to try and hand out.

"We cannot take you any further than this. The cartel has boats in the water all around of Sunset Cove," he said in his deep, lilting tone. "It's here or nowhere. And if you would like to keep my knife out of your throat, I strongly suggest you never talk to mi sol like that again."

"Then it's nowhere, because you've as good as bought our deaths," I snarled, but Luther gripped my arm, turning me to look at him as he frowned.

"Maverick will take us in," he said, looking like he actually believed that shit pouring from his lips.

"Fuck Maverick," I snapped. "I'd rather take my chances with the sharks."

"But sharks are snappy and like to eat people feet," Brooklyn gasped in horror.

"Especially feet that have been cut from the legs of disrespectful hijo de putas," Mateo added, giving me a forbidding look. But I had dealt with assholes like him before and I had absolutely zero hesitation about going up against him. In fact, I'd relish the fucking fight.

"Son, this ain't up for discussion. Let's move," Dad ordered, directing me off the boat by dragging me away from the guy who was squaring up to me.

Mateo dropped the anchor as the boat rocked and swayed violently beneath us, looking out at the lurching waves with a frown. "We'll have to wait with them, chica loca. Until the storm settles."

"Okay, Mateo." She leaned up, sinking her tongue between his lips as he lifted her into his arms and shoved her against the side of the boat. They started grinding on each other like we weren't there and they were about to start fucking right here on the deck.

I gave in to the inevitable and climbed off the boat into the shallow water, the cold wrapping around me as I helped Dad down and we walked along the rocky shore. I spotted a bunch of Dead Dogs out patrolling the perimeter of the complex and tugged Dad into the relative shelter of The Mariner's husk with my pulse skipping.

"We'd better call Maverick before we try and march in there," I muttered angrily.

I was not on board with this plan, but we were stuck between a rock and a hard place now, so I needed to get on with it. We could stay here until the storm died down then take another boat, head out to sea and circle around to the mainland further down the coast. I'd have to stomach Maverick for a few hours and try not think too much about the last time I'd been here on this island with him. I could already see it too clearly though. Him buried in my girl, sharing her with JJ. And then everything after that before I lost her for good.

I forced back the painful memories as Brooklyn and Mateo appeared with Brutus, stepping under the old wooden hull with us to keep dry.

Dad took out his phone, dialling Maverick's number, but there was no answer no matter how many times he tried.

"Great," I said through my teeth.

"It's okay, Mr Man Junior," Brooklyn said earnestly as Mateo pulled her under his arm to keep her warm. "I can put on a show for you and the hours will fly by. Whiz, whiz, whiz, one after the other."

"We're fine without a show," Dad tried.

"You will watch the show until it's over," Mateo growled, a deadly promise in his eyes as he touched the gun at his hip. Brooklyn pulled away from him, starting up some exotic dance and Mateo watched her like she was the most alluring creature to ever live.

I rubbed my eyes, hugging Mutt's bag tighter to my chest as I watched this craziness play out and prayed for the storm to end soon.

"This is a dance rendition of Lord of the Rings," Brooklyn announced, waving her arms in the air. "There once was a small, hairy footed hobbling called Frondor who had a magical wand and went to school with a beardy man called Dumbledolf…"

CHAPTER FOURTEEN

Shawn was in full on cocky showboating mode, and I was just gritting my teeth against the fear that he had every right to be feeling that way.

We drove through Sunset Cove while rain hammered down on the car, Shawn and some unknown goon in the front while Travis kept me company in the back.

My wrists and ankles had been secured with thick zip ties before we headed out and Travis had been given clear instructions to watch me like a hawk while Shawn played his winning hand in this war.

My gut churned with fear for my boys and my mind raced with ideas for how I might be able to stop this, to do something that might help them or give them a chance to escape. But Shawn had clearly figured out that I would try something, hence my new restraints and bodyguard.

Gunfire erupted ahead of us and Shawn whooped wildly as he dropped his window and leaned out, aiming a rifle into the rain as we sped towards Harlequin House.

"Hold onto your hats, boys!" he cried, revving the engine and aiming it straight for the gates.

A scream tore from my throat and I recoiled into my seat a moment before we collided with them, the sound of screeching metal and breaking glass meeting with the force of the impact rocking through the car.

Travis grabbed me as I was thrown forward, his strong arms banding around me as he tugged me down and shielded my head from the broken glass that came crashing through the car as well as any bullets that might have been aimed our way.

But before I could work myself up into too much of a panic over my boys being out there in a gun fight, Shawn's cries had hope slipping through my veins.

"Well shit, it looks like the rats already ran from the ship," he cursed, though the glee in his voice was unmistakeable as he threw his car door open and got out into the rain.

Travis released me, not saying a word about the fact that he'd just protected me like that as he turned his attention towards the quiet house too.

More Dead Dogs piled from the vehicles that had come here with us and I was forced to watch with my heart in my mouth as Shawn led a small army right up to the front door before smashing it open.

The Dead Dogs all rushed inside and their triumphant cries were soon followed by the sounds of things breaking before most of the noise was stolen from me by the continued roar of the storm hammering down on the roof of the car.

I was trembling from head to toe, hoping against all the odds that Shawn had been right and the Harlequins truly weren't here, while terrified that it might just be some ruse and that they'd leap out at any moment and bullets would start firing yet again.

"Your boy and his dad got out over an hour ago," Travis said in a low voice and my gaze sped from the house to his face as hope and confusion washed through me.

"What do you mean? How can you know that?" I demanded, lurching towards him like I planned on shaking the answers from his mouth, though my seatbelt just tightened and held me back.

"Trust me, rainbow child," he said with a knowing smirk before looking back out into the storm again.

"Wait. Why did you just call me-"

"The Harlequins have fled like the cowards they are!" Shawn cried from the front door as he strode back out into the rain, his rifle slung over one shoulder and his bright blue shirt plastered to his broad frame. "So you can come on in now, sugarpie."

Travis got out and circled the car to open my door for me next. I couldn't exactly walk with the zip ties securing my ankles, so he just looped one strong arm beneath my legs and the other behind my back before heaving me against his chest and walking to meet Shawn.

We followed the leader of The Dead Dogs into the house I'd grown so familiar with, and I had to fight a wince at the sight of the gang members crawling all over it, pawing at things and destroying shit. One guy was pissing on the couch while another was ripping open cupboard doors and tossing the contents everywhere.

Shawn directed Travis to sit me down on the kitchen island and I fought to keep my expression blank as my psychotic ex-boyfriend closed in on me with a wide smile on his face.

"Just think, sugarpie, you could fuck me right here in the heart of the Harlequin's kingdom as a part of my coronation. Or would you rather wait until I get done spilling the blood of all of your past conquests before we consummate our union?"

"I'd sooner cut my own heart out," I hissed, my fingers flexing against the restraint of the zip tie surrounding my wrists as I subtly tried to shift to my left. There was one mistake that Shawn had made in bringing me here after all - I knew where all the weapons were hidden inside this house. And I fully intended to get my hands on one of them and end his miserable fucking life.

Shawn grinned like my rejection amused him then reached out to the knife block and grabbed a sharp little fucker of a blade from it before cutting through the ties restraining me and letting them fall to the kitchen floor.

I tried to lunge at him but he instantly pressed the knife to my throat, grinning as he leaned in to speak in my ear.

"Every time you try to kill me, I take note of it, sugarpie," he breathed. "And for each and every attempt, I intend to make your sweet Harlequins suffer all the more at my hands. When I catch those cowardly assholes, I'm gonna string them up and skin them slowly, making sure you get a front row seat to the show. Because one way or another I'm gonna be breaking you in again, sweet cheeks. The only question left is about the methods I'll have to resort to to get the job done."

My defiant gaze locked with his icy blue eyes and he smiled widely before pulling back. But I was so far past the point of self-preservation that I only needed those few inches of safety from the knife in his hand before I lunged to my side and snatched another blade from the block.

Shawn cursed as I swung it at him, his forearm colliding with mine as he managed to deflect the blow and his own knife swiped across the shoulder of my other arm before I could do anything to avoid it.

I cursed at the pain which blossomed through my skin as blood spilled down my arm, but I ignored it in favour of swinging my knife at him again. Some asshole caught my wrist before I could sink my knife into Shawn's black heart and the next thing I knew, I was flat on my back on the kitchen island with Shawn's hand locked around my throat as he reared over me while his man ripped the knife from my hand and defeat crashed through me again.

"Fuck, I wanna break your pretty little neck sometimes, you know that?" Shawn demanded, his grip tightening as my fingers latched around his wrist and I fought against his hold on me. "If I wasn't looking forward to breaking you so damn much then I'd do it."

I couldn't reply with his grip cutting off my airway, but I glared at him with enough venom to let him see how fucking much I hated him. My fingers continued to bite into the flesh of his wrist and as the leather bracelets he wore there tangled in my grip, I found a sliver of comfort, like Chase was here lending me his strength for a single moment.

Shawn took another second to enjoy the feeling of me being pinned beneath him before rearing back suddenly. My fingers were still tangled in Chase's bracelets though, so as he ripped his hand away, they came free and I was left with them in my grasp.

"Get her out of my fucking sight," Shawn barked. "Or I may just end up cutting her open to see how prettily she bleeds."

Strong arms heaved me off the kitchen island and I was relieved to find Travis there as he tugged me away from Shawn and started leading me through the house. He didn't say anything as he seemingly picked a door at random before leading me through it and drawing me down into the garage.

I slipped Chase's bracelets onto my own wrist as I stumbled down after him, feeling the smallest sense of victory at claiming them back even if I'd failed once again to do anything to really harm fucking Shawn.

The lights came on as we descended the stairs and my racing heart settled a little as we stole a bit of peace down away from the rest of The Dead Dogs and their destruction upstairs.

Travis released me and I wrapped my arms around myself as I stood beside Fox's truck, a chill finding me as I stood there in the short black dress Shawn had given me to wear. The material was damp from the rain and a shiver passed through me as I hugged my chest and berated myself for failing once again.

Blood continued to trickle down my arm from the cut to my shoulder and I gritted my teeth against the pain of it.

I didn't pay Travis much attention as he moved around the garage, opening Fox's truck and rummaging around inside, sliding his hands beneath the seats and checking the glove box before stepping back and pointing me towards it.

"You won't find any weapons in there, but it might be a bit warmer than standing around on the concrete floor," he suggested, his voice low and gaze full of secrets which I could tell he wouldn't be sharing with me.

I climbed into the truck but hesitated short of closing the door between us, looking up at him as he pushed his short dreadlocks away from his face.

"Why do you keep being less than an asshole to me?" I asked him and he snorted softly as he wrapped his hand around the top of the truck door and peered in at me.

"Things aren't always as they seem," he replied with a shrug before swinging the door closed between us and leaving me confused inside the truck.

But as I shifted against the seats, a familiar scent wrapped itself around me and I closed my eyes, breathing it in and feeling the ache in my chest over the man it belonged to. Where was Fox now? How had he known to run? Was he even safe out there? Because there were far worse people than Shawn Mackenzie hunting him now and if he'd fallen into the hands of the cartel...

I scrunched my eyes up and forced myself to reject that idea as forcefully as I could manage. I couldn't waste energy on worrying about things that may or may not have happened. All I could focus on was what was right here in front of me.

I opened my eyes again and my gaze caught on the glove box which Travis had left hanging open after his search of the truck, a white envelope sitting inside it with my name scrawled across the front of it.

I sucked in a breath as I recognised Chase's handwriting and reached out to pull it into my grasp. My fingers trembled a little as I broke the seal and pulled the letter free, but as I read the words inside it, my heart began to pound with a whole new kind of ache and longing because I was so broken over these boys. And every word in that letter only made me break a little more over the knowledge that I'd ruined any chance there might have been of having them in my life again.

Little one,

I never thought I'd survive saying goodbye to you once, so now I have to do it twice, I hope the words in this letter are enough to do our end justice.

The first thing I have to say is what I should have said to you a thousand times. What I should have replied to you with down in the Dollhouse when I feared we wouldn't have another day in the sun together.

I love you. But not in the way you deserve to be loved. My love is and always has been selfish, destructive and all consuming. I have drowned in the vastness of it and have been twisted into a demon because of it. So there's something I really need you to do for me. When you read this, when you want to hate Fox for what he did, please find a way to forgive him. Everything Fox does is to protect his family. To protect you. Even when he has to protect us from each other. The truth is, I can't give you what you need, but Fox can. JJ too. Maybe even Maverick. And I know you'll find a way to make it work together somehow.

So don't come looking for me, little one. And don't waste tears on me either. I spent day after day in the dark with nothing but pain and cold and fucking Shawn for company, and I bartered with every divine force in the universe to give me one more moment with you and my boys before I died. But I got far more than that Rogue. I got weeks and weeks surrounded by all of you.

I had you in my arms again, I got to look into the eyes that have possessed me since before I can remember, and I got to remember what it was like to love you before I tried to hate you.

I have stitched every moment of that time together into my soul because I always knew it was going to be limited, little one. And that's okay. Because even though I'm alone now, I will forever be full. Full of you and them and every piece of light you gave me when I was suffocating in the dark.

So I'm going to put my regrets to bed, because what's done is done and I'm tired of suffering over the past. When I think of you, I will always think of the good. And the only thing I ask of you, is that you try to do the same when you think of me.

I know I'll never stop loving you, but I promise to love you peacefully now, the way I should have loved you all along.

This is my last apology, Rogue.
I hope it's enough to heal the wounds I made in you.

Ace

I bit my lip as I crumpled the letting in my hand, pressing it to my heart and trying to fight the tears that burned in the backs of my eyes at the beauty of the confession I'd just read. My Ace, my poor, broken saviour had told me that he loved me and the most heart breaking thing about that was that it was too late. For him, for me, for us. And the only thing I could really offer him in return for that love was the death of the man who had tried to ruin him. But I was starting to doubt I'd ever be able to complete that task.

CHAPTER FIFTEEN

I swaggered into Fox Harlequin's bedroom, sucking the inside of my cheek as I took in his king of the world space and threw myself down on his bed with a sigh. My temper was high thanks to my sugarpie, but this win over my enemies certainly helped sate the animal in me. I quietly preferred that Fox and his daddy had hightailed it outa here. It made the thrill of the chase even more appetising. No satisfying battle was ever won easy. I'd be sure to make a meal of this game, catch my prey one by one and make them wriggle and squeal before I cut off their heads.

My victory was gonna be even sweeter when I found those diamonds Kaiser had been hunting. I was having wet dreams about them daily and though his diary hadn't led me to them yet, I had a sixth sense about these kinda things, and I was sure they were destined for me.

"What do you keep in your drawers, I wonder?" I tugged open the drawer in Fox's nightstand, finding a knife and a book called Dark Fae with some hot purple haired chick on the cover of it. "The fuck is this?" I flicked it open to a random page, but before I could explore any further, my phone started ringing and I lifted my hips to tug it from my ass pocket, finding an unknown caller ID staring back at me.

"Well I wonder if my day's about to get a little more interesting…" I answered it, holding it to my ear as I leaned back against Fox's pillows. "And who might I be speaking to?"

"Your death," a deep voice growled down the line and my lips tipped into a smirk as I recognised Maverick Harlequin.

"And which one o' my deaths might that be, boy? The Grim Reaper sent a whole army after me. Can't say any of them have caused me much trouble yet."

"Picture this, Shawn," he went on and the satisfied undertone to his voice intrigued me. "I'm looking down into the trunk of a car where a little woman lays bound and gagged. She's pretty for her age, all that red hair looking so damn good messed up like that."

I stilled as a thought crossed my mind that sent a furious earthquake ripping down my spine.

I remained silent, letting this piece of shit play his cards to be absolutely sure of what I suspected he was telling me.

"Hey, Mrs Mackenzie," Maverick said and tension knotted every muscle in my body. "Ever sucked a ten inch cock before?"

A growl tore from my throat. "Now I know you ain't talking about my momma, boy, 'cause if you were, then you'd be as good as signing your own death warrant this very moment."

"I signed that a long time ago, motherfucker. Oh hey, I guess I'll be a real motherfucker too soon if you don't do exactly as I say."

"You lay a hand on her and I'll fucking-" I started but he cut me off.

"You'll fucking what? Cut out my friend's eye? Keep my girl captive? Nah, I think you're done doing bad shit actually Shawn. Now we're gonna play my game because I'm tired of playing yours, so if you want your sweet little momma back before I decide to see how quickly my cock gives her Stockholm syndrome, you're gonna pack up my little unicorn nice and gently in lots and lots of bubble wrap, then drive her out to trade her to me."

My jaw ticked as I worked over every solution to this in my mind, bloodlust coiling through my body like a viper and demanding I let it strike. And oh honey, I would. I'd strike and strike and strike until there was nothing left of Maverick Harlequin but blood and bone.

"Where are you?" I hissed.

"I'll text you the address. Come alone. If you try to pull anything, I swear to god I'll plant six bullets in Mommy's skull before you can say boo," he warned.

We'll see about that.

"You're gonna regret this, boy," I warned.

"I doubt that," he said then hung up on me.

I clenched the phone so hard in my fist it almost cracked, then a bellow exploded from my throat that made the walls shake. Two of my men came running into the room, looking fearful for my life, but I shoved to my feet and stormed past them, marching downstairs as rage bit into my veins.

I made it to the garage door, throwing it open and jogging down to where Travis was guarding Rogue. She was in Fox's truck and her eyes widened as I approached her, the bitch lunging to lock the doors before I could get her out.

"Oh you think that'll stop me, sweet cheeks?" I said, grabbing the gun from Travis's hip and whacking the butt of it against the window hard enough to shatter it.

Rogue gasped, trying to get out the door on the opposite side of the truck but I tossed the gun back at Trav and caught hold of her ankle, wrenching her towards me and dragging her through the broken window.

"Let go!" she screamed as I threw her to the ground, but I wouldn't be doing that, no siree.

I dropped over her, pinning her wrists to the concrete by kneeling on them either side of her.

I pinched her nose and covered her mouth with my hand in the same movement, baring my teeth at her as I glared into the fearful eyes of the whore who seemed to hypnotise every powerful man in this town with her pussy. She thrashed and bucked, trying to fight me off but she wasn't strong enough.

Fuck, I wanted to kill her. I wanted to steal away the precious thing Maverick longed for, that they all fucking longed for. I'd break all the Harlequin boys forever with this one act and I'd enjoy every second of watching the light go out in her eyes.

But then I thought of my poor momma held hostage by that son of a bitch and my muscles got twitchy, telling me to let go.

I felt Travis shifting behind me and wondered if he was moving closer to enjoy the show. I wanted to put one on, I really did, but instead, as she started to lose the fight in her limbs, I released her, shoving to my feet with a snarl.

She gulped down air, half rolling over as her shoulders shook and I had to look away from her to hunt out something to distract me from the blissful idea of ending her fucking existence.

My gaze hooked on a piece of paper that was lying on the driver's seat of the truck and I grabbed it with a sneer on my lips. I read through the letter from my little pretty eyed torture victim, and I had to admit it cheered me up somewhat.

I strode in front of Rogue, crouching down by her head and dangling the letter in front of her eyes, her brows pulling together at the sight of my newly claimed treasure while she remained kneeling at my feet where she belonged, her hair all fucked up and her eyes full of fire as she continued to gasp down breaths.

"Oh my goodness, he's more pathetic than I thought. That boy showed gumption in my basement, but this?" My upper lip curled. "I have to say it's lost me some respect for him, sugarpie. Men really will say anything for premium pussy." I tsked then jerked my head at Travis. "Fetch me a comforter and some duct tape, Trav."

"Yes, boss," he said, taking his sweet time heading out the door.

"Don't come looking for me, little one. And don't waste tears on me either," I read out Chase's words and Rogue glared at me. "Holy moly, that boy is playing one helluva manipulation game, sweet cheeks. Did you really buy this?"

"Shut up," she bit out.

I went on. "The truth is, I can't give you what you need, but Fox can. JJ too. Maybe even Maverick. And I know you'll find a way to make it work together somehow." I roared a laugh. "You see that right there? He's giving you the green light to fuck his friends. You think that's the words of a man who *loves* you?" I scoffed. "They're all in on it, sugarpie. If you went back to them, they'd be double-dicking you by sundown."

"Get fucked Shawn," she snarled, pushing herself to her feet and I followed, cocking my head to one side as I regarded her.

"Oh darlin', it's pathetic seeing you swallow this horseshit. I know the minds of men. Take it from a man who speaks nothin' but the truth." I placed a hand over my heart, giving her an earnest look. "Men don't love women, they fuck them and spin lies into the most beautiful webs they can weave to keep fucking them. And you know whose fault that is?" I stalked toward her, gripping her chin and making her look at me as poison poured from her eyes. "Yours. Women's. You enable men by swallowing their lies. Because you so desperately wanna believe the words comin' outa their mouths." I ran my thumb over her lower lip. "It's nature, darlin'. A woman's purpose in life is to breed, so you all come up with pretty stories in your heads to make yourselves feel better about the fact that all men care about is using your body to get a quick high. Our value to you is far higher than yours is to us. It's just the way it is. But there ain't no shame in it. In fact, once you accept your place in the world and realise I'm the best thing you're ever gonna get, you'll find peace sugarpie." I pushed my fingers into her hair, liking the deep chestnut colour far better than all that garish colour.

Her eyes swirled as she tried to fight against my words, but I could see them sinking in and I enjoyed every second of it. I was stamping myself there again, writing myself into every crevice of her mind, and no matter how this day went down, I knew she'd be left aching for me when it was done. Because I was becoming the centre of her world again, slowly, bit by bit. And it was so fucking beautiful to watch her fall in line.

She lunged for the letter suddenly, but I was faster, holding it above her head as a smirk twisted my lips.

"Don't be a dumbass," I taunted her, shaking my head. "It's nothing but words on a page, sweet cheeks."

"Yeah?" she snarled, and her knee suddenly drove up between my thighs, crushing my balls and making me cry out and drop the letter. "Well that's nothing but a knee to the balls."

I shoved her to the ground, clutching my manhood as I cursed through my teeth. She grabbed the letter just as Travis appeared with the comforter and the duct tape I'd asked for.

"Get that letter off of her," I commanded him and he dropped the shit he was holding, striding toward us as I groaned through the pain still radiating through my balls. Man, this fucking day was taking a turn. I needed a win. And fast.

Rogue turned her big eyes on Travis, but he was a good boy and wrestled the letter from her hand before keeping a tight hold of her arm. I straightened, prowling toward her with intent and ripping her out of Travis's grip. I forced her to lay down on the comforter and started rolling her up like a burrito as she shrieked and thrashed. I whistled at Travis to help me and we soon had her wrapped up good and tight, the duct tape keeping her trapped inside it with just her head poking out the top. I laughed as I took Chase's letter from Travis, making sure she was watching as I shoved it into my mouth and started eating it.

"You fucking prick!" she screamed.

"Tastes like a desperate man with a sad, sad soul," I mused, chomping through every bit of it and swallowing it down.

My phone buzzed and I moved to sit on top of Rogue, finding she made a rather comfy seating area as I read the text from Maverick.

Unknown:

Meet at Lucia Beach in thirty minutes. We'll take the north road in, you take the south.

And for every minute you're late, your momma will take another inch of my cock.

I spat a snarl, my mind settling on a plan of how this little exchange was gonna go today.

Because Lucia beach may have been just a small strip of sand with only a couple of dirt roads that led in and out of there, but it was about to become the site of a bloodbath.

"Round up the men, Trav," I commanded. "We're going hunting."

CHAPTER SIXTEEN

"**D**id you really have to keep threatening to rape his mother?" JJ asked Maverick as he passed JJ his phone back to him, his own one out of battery.

I was driving us towards Lucia Beach in my stolen Jaguar, anticipation splintering through my veins.

"Yes, Johnny James," Maverick said from the back seat. "I did."

"That's dark, man." JJ shook his head as he loaded the pistol in his grip.

"What's darker is the fact that I'd actually do it if it'd get Rogue away from fucking Shawn," Maverick said smoothly.

"*Rick*," JJ snapped and I snorted.

"He's joking," I said. "Aren't you?"

"Nothing funny about rape, Chase," Maverick said seriously and JJ shot him a frown.

"Ahhhhhhhhh!" a wild scream came from the trunk.

"Mrs Mackenzie's awake," Maverick pointed out.

"No shit," I deadpanned and he smirked at me in the rear view mirror. His eyes were full of a psychotic need for death as we closed in on the location where Shawn would be meeting us with Rogue, but I didn't know if he'd get the chance to fulfil it. I damn well hoped so.

My pulse was erratic, my grip on the steering wheel tightening as I drove us off the main streets and started taking the winding backroads towards Lucia Beach as the rain pummelled the windshield.

"Are we sure the only guy in this car with no depth perception should be driving us right now?" Maverick mused like a cocky asshole.

"I'd still drive better than the two of you combined even if I had both eyes torn clean from my face," I shot back.

"Just keep telling yourself that, bud." JJ patted me on the shoulder and my skin ached for more contact as he drew his hand away. Fuck, I'd been alone too damn long. It was pathetic.

"Let me out! Please!" Shawn's mom wailed.

"If you don't shut up, Sandra, we're gonna carve you up and feed you to the nearest animal we find," I called and she fell dead quiet.

"Bullshit, I'm not giving her to some random racoon. We'll bring her home to Sparkle," JJ said. "I'm not training up a man-eating starfish for nothing."

"Jesus, you've still got that thing?" I asked.

"That *thing* is called Sparkle and he's a part of the family. He's basically your older brother, Ace."

"Older brother?" I balked. "How'd you figure that?"

"Starfishes live up to thirty five years and he's at least twenty eight," JJ said with a shrug.

"How the hell can you tell how old a starfish is?" I demanded, happy to indulge in this ridiculous conversation to keep my mind off the fact that we were about to see Rogue again. Because shit, I was not even remotely ready for that.

"God, Ace, you can see it in his eyes," JJ said like I was the irrational one here.

"They don't have fucking eyes," I said, turning so I could see him properly, my blind side keeping him from view.

"Uh, yes they do," he said with a tut.

"They've got more eyes than you do, Chase," Maverick chipped in with a bark of wicked laughter, kicking the back of my seat.

"Asshole," I ground out, but I didn't really give a shit. In fact, I was quietly enjoying every damn second of their company. It was keeping all the shadows at bay which was what I desperately needed right now because I was about to see the man who'd tortured his way beneath my flesh again and I wasn't sure I'd be able to face it without my brothers here. *I just wish Fox was here too.*

"Just so everyone's clear, if I get a chance to kill Shawn today, I'm taking it," I said in a low voice and the mood immediately shifted in the car.

"Agreed," Maverick growled and JJ nodded.

"But our priority is Rogue," JJ added.

"Obviously," Maverick muttered.

I turned onto the dirt road that led to the beach and silence pooled between us as the tension rose in the car. My breaths became shallow as I pinned my thoughts on Rogue. I was so fucking angry she'd gone to Shawn, but I knew why she'd done it too. We didn't deserve that girl's sacrifice though, she deserved to be placed on an altar where we could worship her day after day. Instead, she'd been suffering at the hands of fucking Shawn and I was terrified of what state we were about to find her in.

"If he's hurt her-" JJ started but I cut over him.

"He has," I said gruffly. "That's what he does." Bitterness coated my tongue and I heard Maverick priming his revolver, an animal growl leaving him.

"I'll never fucking forgive myself for this," JJ said under his breath and I frowned. Yeah he'd been a fucking idiot, they all had. But I couldn't blame him for swallowing Rogue's lies. That girl knew how to act, and it wasn't like any of them had had much reason to contradict what she'd told them after how shitty we'd treated her in the past. But I'd seen the worry in her eyes when she'd confided in me about considering going to Shawn, how much she really cared about us.

She was loyal to us just like she had been when we were kids. And I'd show her that loyalty in kind by being there for her today because fuck if we had some making up to do over all of this. After that, I didn't know what the world held for me. So long as she had JJ and Maverick, I'd find a way to be content enough to leave again. I couldn't stay in the Cove after all, but I also hated the idea of leaving when our family was in such a mess. JJ had confided in me about what had happened with him and Fox, and I was so fucking pissed at Fox for breaking his promise to me to keep our family together. Though I guessed I wasn't surprised. This was exactly how I'd expected things to end up, but it didn't make it right. I just hated the idea that Fox was on his own now and we were all so fractured in ways I didn't even know how to heal.

Just focus on Rogue. Bring her home first then fix the rest later.

We passed through tall sand dunes and I pulled over before the track got too sandy to traverse, taking a gun from the glove compartment and keeping it tight in my grip as we all got out of the car.

The rain was still pouring and the choppy waves of the sea churned beneath the black clouds above. The rain soaked me through in an instant, but I barely felt it as we moved to the trunk together to get Sandra.

Maverick popped it open and she screamed like a banshee as he hauled her into his arms and tossed her over his shoulder, her ankles and wrists still bound.

I shoved the trunk closed and we walked together down to the beach, our weapons in hand and my senses prickling with the need for violence. I just had to see her, be sure the fire in her eyes still burned. Because if it didn't, I'd break more deeply than Shawn had ever broken me.

Please be okay, little one. You're so fucking strong. I know you can survive him.

I marched down the beach beside JJ with Maverick leading the way and as we made it past a large dune to our left, I spotted Fox's red truck out on the beach with Shawn leaning against the hood, his shotgun propped on his left shoulder. Beside him was a guy with short dreadlocks and dark skin, holding an umbrella above Shawn's head while the rain beat down on him.

"We told you to come alone!" JJ barked.

"Well now that's hardly fair. I am still a man down on you three after all," Shawn said with a shrug and I clenched my teeth.

"Where's Rogue?" Maverick boomed and Shawn smirked, making my hackles raise as I was immediately cast back into that basement with him marring my flesh.

Whenever you shut your eyes, I'll be there until I'm all you can see.

The memory of his voice sent a tremor through my chest but I kept walking, trying to force myself not to limp a single step and show weakness in front of him.

"Well hey, pretty eyes," he purred. "Long time no *see*." He roared a laugh at his own joke and I glowered, my finger getting really fucking twitchy on the trigger of my gun. "That's no way to greet an old friend, is it? I thought you were long gone. What brings you back to town? Surely not little old me?" Shawn asked as we stopped ten feet away from him.

"I'm here for Rogue," I spat and he smirked, the look on his face making my head ring with dark memories.

"Is that you, bubba bear?" Sandra wailed from where she still hung over Maverick's shoulder, unable to see around his ass and I wrinkled my nose.

"It's me, Momma," Shawn replied, his tone softening to something almost tender. It didn't sound right on him at all. And it made me want to slit her throat just to take away something precious to him like he had to all of us. "Don't you worry about those there men, Momma, you'll be back with your bubba shortly."

"Where's. Rogue?" Maverick ground out again.

"Right where you wanted her to be, Maverick," Shawn strode around the truck and his man followed him with the umbrella, covering his back as my finger slid onto the trigger of my gun.

Shawn handed his shotgun to his man then pulled a huge rolled up comforter out of the truck bed and tucked it under one arm. My lips parted as I spotted Rogue's head sticking out of it, her hair dyed dark, sticking to her cheeks from the rain.

"Rogue!" JJ stepped forward but I caught his arm and dragged him back, my jaw flexing. My heart was hammering and Shawn's torture was echoing through my skin, making me ache for vengeance.

"She's all wrapped up safe and sound, just like you asked," Shawn said. "I'll sure miss seeing her bouncy ass every morning, but ain't no son worth his salt if he don't protect his momma, boys. You remember that."

Shawn launched Rogue toward us through the air and I cursed as she screamed, slamming onto the sand and skidding along in it so she landed half way between us and our enemies.

Shawn grabbed his shotgun back from his man, quickly aiming it at us. "Now hand over my momma. Slowly like. No false moves or my finger might get jumpy on this here trigger."

Maverick walked forward to stand beside Rogue, laying Sandra on the ground beside her.

I gazed at Rogue as she craned her neck to try and look up at Maverick, jerking against the duct tape holding her in that thing. The fury in her eyes made me burn. I wanted to go to her, to pull her into my arms and never fucking let go ever again. But I remained there, rooted to the spot with my hand clenching the gun so tight, it was a miracle it hadn't gone off. I'd never felt so thirsty for someone's death as I did for Shawn Mackenzie's. And I didn't just want him to die, I wanted him to suffer. To bleed until he couldn't bleed anymore.

Shawn jerked his chin at his man. "Go get her, Travis."

Travis walked forward as Maverick ripped open the tape holding the comforter around Rogue with his bare hands. He had to roll it out to get her free and she cursed as she scrambled out of the folds.

Maverick didn't let her get up, instead grabbing hold of her and flipping her over his shoulder, locking his arm over her legs like a fucking caveman claiming his mate.

I was surprised when she didn't fight it, curling around him and clinging to his back as he backed up toward us and Travis helped Sandra to her feet.

"Now a trade's a trade o' course, but if my sugarpie comes crawling back to my bed of her own fruition again, then that's her choice, boys, understand?" Shawn said with a taunting smirk.

"She'll never return to you," I spat and his eyes snapped onto me.

"You sure about that, pretty eyes?" Shawn smiled widely, all confidence.

JJ's arm rubbed mine as he kept close and it was his presence alone that stopped me from falling into the darkest place inside me where nothing but the devil before me lived.

"Your death's coming for you, Shawn," JJ called as Maverick made it back to us.

Shawn laughed loudly as Travis opened the door to Fox's truck for him and he slipped inside.

We turned, moving swiftly back to the car and Rogue looked up at me and JJ where she hung over Maverick's shoulder. Her eyes brimmed with tears and she immediately looked away again, making my heart tug so violently I swear it was going to tear free of my chest.

We made it back to the car and Maverick climbed into the back, pulling Rogue into his lap as JJ and I hurried into the front.

I started up the engine, wanting to get her the fuck away from Shawn as fast as possible.

"I'm so sorry," she croaked and I hated how broken she sounded.

I turned the car around, driving it back up the dirt road, the wipers swinging back and forth as the rain somehow worsened.

JJ turned, placing his hand on her knee as she curled up in Maverick's lap and he stroked her back as she clung onto him.

The car suddenly bumped over something and I cried out as the tyres deflated at once, sending us spinning off the road towards a high dune at the side of it.

"Fuck!" I shouted, slamming on the brakes as we skidded and bumped over the sand before coming to a halt.

Half a second of silence passed before gunfire tore it apart and I grabbed hold of JJ beside me, flinging my door open and dragging him out onto the ground to take cover. Maverick had done the same with Rogue, the two of them huddling against the side of the vehicle as it was shot to shit and I lifted my gun as glass shattered over us and fired again and again through the broken windows.

Adrenaline bled through my body as Maverick and JJ returned fire too and the noise reverberated through my skull.

"We have to run for it," I said over the cacophony.

"Take Rogue." Maverick shoved her into my arms. "You're a shit shot anyway."

"Fuck you," I growled.

"I'm not leaving any of you," Rogue snapped. "Give me a weapon. I'll kill that motherfucker."

"The weapon bag is in the back," JJ said as he fired another few rounds.

Maverick yanked the door open again, pulling the bag out and tossing it down as JJ and I covered his ass. Rogue caught hold of it, taking out a flashbang and I grabbed another one, and her eyes lit up with that glorious fucking inferno I'd prayed still lived in her. She nodded to me as we jumped up, throwing the two flashbangs in opposing directions towards where the gunfire was coming from up in the dunes.

Two bangs rang out followed by cries of confusion and fright and the gunfire died in an instant.

We turned and ran as Maverick shouldered the bag and the four of us scaled the dune behind us fast, leaping over the top of it and tearing along the animal tracks winding through the long grass and growing among the sand. Shouts and gunshots started up again at our back, but we'd gotten a head start. We could make it.

My bad leg ached, but I didn't let the pain stop me as I pushed through it. Despite that, I couldn't quite keep up with the others and I clenched my jaw as I fired over my shoulder at anyone who dared try to take pot shots at my family.

The rain made the sand clumpy and thick at my feet, my shoes sinking in and making it even harder to run across it. Rogue was ahead of me with JJ's hand locked around hers and Maverick leading the way forward, but the gap was growing between us and I was only going to slow them down if they noticed I was lagging.

Fuck it.

I turned back as we crested a dune, dropping onto my stomach and lining up the pursing men in my sights.

I picked the first one off with a clean headshot that made him crash to the ground and the second tripped over his friend's body. I finished him with two more bullets, slipping ammo from my pocket and reloading swiftly as I aimed at the next asshole to crest the dune.

"Ace!" Rogue screamed suddenly as she realised I wasn't behind her.

"Keep going!" I bellowed without turning back. "I'll catch up."

I saw a shadow whirling through the sky in my periphery and my gaze locked onto the grenade as it sailed in the direction of Rogue and my brothers.

I twisted around, shoving myself upright, finding JJ and Maverick fighting a battle of their own ahead of us as they took cover behind a bank and tried to hold off whoever was firing from the other side of it. The grenade seemed to fall in slow motion towards the girl running towards me with a flare of desperation in her eyes.

I ran to meet her, the two of us colliding as I knocked her sideways over a steep bank and we tumbled away from the explosion as it ripped through the dune with a tremendous boom.

We kept rolling over and over, hitting the base of the high dune we'd fallen from and the breath was driven from my lungs as she landed on top of me.

"You okay, little one?" I asked, cupping her cheek as she lifted her head, the rain still hammering down on us.

"Define okay." She shoved herself upright, pulling me with her and gunfire tore the sand apart just beyond us.

I fired back as four men poured over the hill, racing toward us and I took out two of them, leaving Travis and a bearded guy remaining.

Rogue dragged me around the side of the next dune and I forced myself to run as hard as I could as I followed her, the two of us taking a winding path through the dunes as gunshots echoed out from every direction.

Our fingers remained interlocked as we ran on and I hoped JJ and Maverick were okay, but all we could do was run for our lives as the men behind us shouted out at us to stop. I wouldn't let them get hold of Rogue again. I'd fucking die first.

We ran on for what seemed like an age and my shin burned where the break had been in it, this amount of strain almost too much for it.

I gritted my teeth through the pain, focusing on the girl I had to protect at all costs as I fired another shot over my shoulder to keep our enemies at bay.

We rounded a sharp bend in the narrow track, finding ourselves in a dead end surrounded by high walls of sand.

"Shit," Rogue gasped, turning back but footfalls were already pounding this way. We were out of time.

I grabbed hold of her, lifting her up and trying to shove her up the bank to my left. "Go. Get out of here," I growled.

She wriggled in my arms, trying to shake me off. "I'm not leaving you."

"I left you," I reminded her. "I'm owed this one." I shoved her harder, but she kicked me in the chest and I stumbled backwards as she skidded back down to the ground in front of me.

A huge, bearded asshole appeared and I raised my gun, firing without a single thought as I pushed Rogue behind me. The guy winced as my gun rang empty and horror washed into my chest. *No.*

"You can kill me, just let her go," I tried and the guy laughed coldly.

"It doesn't look like you have any bargaining chips left," he said with a sneer.

Rogue tried to pull me aside as he aimed at my head and I feared my death more than I ever had, because it would equal my girl being recaptured by her villain.

A bang rang right through the centre of me and for a second, I was so fucking sure I was dead, but then I felt the heated splatter of blood against my face and the bearded asshole slumped to the ground with a bullet hole carved into his temple. Travis appeared beyond him, confusing the complete fuck outa me.

"Stay back," I commanded.

"It's okay," Rogue said, stepping around me, her fingers tight on my arm.

"You need to run," Travis said in a low tone. "Head as far south as you can then circle back to the road." He pointed, stepping aside to let us pass.

"What the fuck?" I muttered, my pulse thrashing in my ears as Rogue gripped my fingers and tugged me past him.

"Thank you," she whispered to him and he nodded before we ran on, following the directions he'd given us.

I slipped my phone out of my pocket, finding a message from JJ saying they were alright and that they were taking shelter in some trees further south. They'd have to lie low for a while, and there was really only one place we could head now, so I hoped they'd get there soon. I shot him a reply to say we were okay too and that we'd meet them there, then tucked my phone away.

"You've really got a way with savage men, little one," I murmured as we ran together, our hands still clamped in each other's.

"What?" she asked, shooting me a frown.

"That guy back there, you made a friend of him?"

She shook her head. "He's got his own agenda, fuck knows what it is though. I just hope it ends with Shawn's blood on his hands – assuming I don't get his blood first."

"Or me," I agreed and we shared a dark look as we raced further south and left the sounds of shouting men behind.

The lack of gunshots helped my heart rate settle, because so long as they weren't firing that meant they didn't have any targets. I just had to hope Maverick and JJ stayed off their radar and got to safety soon.

We eventually reached the road and crossed into the trees on the other side of it, following it along as far as we could before we came to somewhere even close to urban. There were few large houses dotted around and an old Ford sat outside one, looking ripe for the picking.

It didn't take me long to jack it and we were soon driving along in the direction of Tatum's house, the wipers racing back and forth across the windscreen to try and clear the rain while Rogue used my phone to call JJ.

"Are you okay?" she asked breathlessly as he answered in a low whisper over speakerphone.

"Yeah, we're good, pretty girl. They've blocked the road this way though so we're gonna have to take the long way round. Are you sure you're not being followed?"

I threw a cautious look in the rear view mirror but we hadn't seen any sign of anyone for miles.

"We're good," Rogue promised.

"Then we'll see you soon." JJ hung up and I released a relieved breath, the tension falling from my shoulders.

We ditched the car half a mile from Tatum's house and ran down their private beach in the rain the rest of the way just to be sure we wouldn't be spotted.

I kept my hand locked tightly around Rogue's as we hurried up to the side gates of Tatum's house, tapping in the code she'd given us to gain access. My heart was pounding and I knew the adrenaline wasn't entirely to do with the gunfight we'd just been a part of. The feel of Rogue's hand in mine was making my pulse thrash to a furious, almost violent tune. I didn't look at her as I towed her up to the side door, taking out the key to unlock it and guiding her inside.

The second she pushed the door closed and the noise it made echoed around the vast, empty house, I swear the tension between us spiked.

I couldn't help but stare at her for a stolen moment, drinking in the sight of her shivering and soaked through, her brunette hair clinging to her cheeks and raindrops caressing her full lips. The short black dress she wore was tight on her, pushing her tits up so that I couldn't help but notice the swell of them, but my gaze instantly returned to her ocean eyes and the depths of a storm even more turbulent than the one battering the windows which raged inside them.

I ran my thumb over the back of her hand, the silken feel of her skin like a drug calling me in. But I forced myself to release her and back up, adjusting the eyepatch covering the ugly side of my face.

"Did he hurt you?" I gritted out, forcing myself to look at her and face whatever horrors might lay in her eyes. Shawn had left his mark on us both, and though I was painfully glad to see she didn't bear any scars to indicate weeks of torture on her flesh, I knew there were far worse things he could have done than use weapons on her body. She did have a few injuries, a healing wound in her hairline which left yellow and blue bruising covering her temple as well as a cut on her shoulder which was bleeding, red droplets mixing with the rain as it ran down her arm. My gaze caught on the marks surrounding her throat, the clear bands put there by tightly clasped fingers which reminded me so clearly of the injuries she'd had when she'd first come back here.

How had I looked at those wounds on her flesh then and seen a threat? How hadn't I realised in that instant that she hadn't come back to hurt us but that she was there, begging for help and the love of the only family she'd ever known despite how much we'd hurt her before she left us? Shame mixed with a potent kind of fury within me as my muscles bunched and my hatred for fucking Shawn impossibly grew deeper, the need in me for his bloody end all consuming as I took in not only the wounds on her, but the darkness in her gaze which he'd put there while he held her.

"He's Shawn Mackenzie," she said icily. "Hurt is what he does. But he didn't fuck me if that's what you're asking."

I nodded stiffly, rage prickling along my limbs as the need to murder that motherfucker burned through my body. I'd been afraid to ask her that question, knowing it was already going to be near impossible for me to mend the wounds he'd given her but relieved that at least she hadn't had to endure that from him. It was something. Not much, but enough to give me hope that we could fix the rest of it.

The cut on her arm was bleeding quite badly and sand and dirt from our escape was probably trapped within it now too. I frowned, capturing her hand again and guiding her through the cavernous house to the kitchen which was fitted with every modern appliance known to man.

I caught hold of Rogue's waist, lifting her and gently planting her down by the sink before grabbing a cloth and dousing it in some premium vodka I found in the fridge.

"Here," I murmured, reaching out and pressing it to the wound, making her suck in a sharp breath between her teeth.

The quiet between us was eating me alive and I wished JJ was here because I knew he'd know what to do, what to say, how to be there for her. I was the last person who could soothe the pain I saw in her eyes because it was housed in me too, and I'd failed miserably at healing from Shawn's torture, so how could I do anything to help her?

She was almost the same height as me sitting up there and I felt her eyes scouring my face, making the blood rise to my cheeks as I tried to turn my head so she couldn't glimpse the gross scar peeking out from beneath my eyepatch.

"Don't you dare look away from me, Chase Cohen," she growled, catching hold of my chin and forcing my head around so my gaze slammed into hers.

I free-fell into the endless blue pool of her eyes and my heart thumped out a desperate beat, begging me to pull her closer, to act on every urge I'd ever had towards this girl. It was all mounting up like water against a dam and I felt weaker than I ever had in my life against those desires. I'd never thought I'd see her again. I never thought I'd be this close, be able to taste every sweet, broken thing about her in the air between us. But she wasn't mine and never would be.

I placed the cloth down, my fingers scoring a line up to her throat, brushing over the bruises there as hate for Shawn spilled so deeply into my skin I was sure I'd never be rid of it.

"I'm sorry for my part in this," I sighed and a shiver gripped her body as I traced my fingers down her arm, goosebumps rising wherever my skin touched.

"It's not your fault," she whispered.

"It is in ways, little one. But I will atone for it." My fingers paused on the leather bracelets on her wrist and my eyebrows arched.

"Here," she said, pulling them from her wrist and sliding them onto mine and I felt instantly comforted by being reunited with this old piece of me. It was like regaining a fraction of my family, each one representing the four of them. They were supposed to bind your soulmate to you, and though the guy I'd got them from had probably just been full of shit I'd still bought into their apparent meaning.

"This one represents you," I told Rogue as she plucked at the leather band around my wrist which was braided in an intricate pattern with a line of silver running through it. It was the prettiest one, so obviously it belonged to her.

"What about this one?" she asked, pulling at another one which was a thick band with random lines etched all along it. "It's complete chaos so it's Maverick."

"And this?" she asked, tugging at the next one which was a complex design of interwoven bands with knots tying the different sections together.

"JJ," I said. "Because he's the peacekeeper, these knots are like the way he holds us together." I glanced up at Rogue, feeling a bit self-conscious about the stupid way I'd decided these bands represented each of my friends, but she just smiled, her eyes lighting up as she nodded.

"Oh yeah!" she agreed and I grinned as her finger slid onto the last one for Fox. It was a simple band, but thick and sturdy with coils of black string glued tightly around it at various points.

"Fox is the order to Maverick's chaos," I murmured and Rogue hooked her finger through them all, drawing them together, the slightest touch of her skin against mine starting a fire in my chest.

"What about you?" She pouted.

"Well I'm wearing them," I laughed.

"You need one for you," she huffed then Maverick appeared, kicking sand over her legs and bouncing a volleyball off of my head.

"You playing, or what? Those upper quarter kids think they can take us on, so we need to whoop their asses and send them back to their fancy beaches where they belong." He pointed at the group of teenagers who'd blown in from the upper quarter, clearly trying to show off by coming down to this dodgy end of town. And fuck if I was gonna let them think they had anything on us.

"Thank you…" I offered her a sad sort of smile, thinking of the past and what we'd all once been. "The others will probably be here soon," I said, trying to swallow back the lump rising in my throat. "JJ will be here," I confirmed and she frowned, glancing away from me and I could see her shattering, see the mark Shawn had left on her as clearly as I could see it in myself.

"Rogue," I rasped, wishing I could be what she needed right now, but there was too much lacking in me. She needed JJ, Maverick, hell even Fox would know how to deal with this better than I could.

"I just wanna feel you," she said, her voice cracking and it didn't matter if I felt broken inside, I had to give her what I could.

My forehead fell to hers and I gripped the sides of her thighs, my fingers locking tight as I dragged her closer and she wrapped her legs around me, the two of us suddenly locked in a tight embrace. I buried my face in her neck and her hands dragged down my back, her heartbeats drumming powerfully between us as I practically scooped her off the surface, holding her as tight as I could. Our wet clothes clung to each other like they were in on the embrace too and somehow just that simple contact between us seemed to chase out the chill the storm had left in my bones.

"I'm here," I told her, knowing how desperately I had ached for one of my family when I'd been locked away in Shawn's basement. She needed to be surrounded by someone who loved her and I could offer her that if nothing else, even if I could never love her the way she needed to be loved.

"I read your letter," she said breathlessly and my stomach knotted.

Oh fuck, she knows everything.

"I wasn't supposed to come back," I said against her neck and she tilted her head as my mouth brushed her skin. Just that smallest of tastes lit a fire on my tongue and my hands balled as I fought the urge to take more. I wasn't this girl's knight in shining armour, I wasn't even the dragon who hoarded her in his tower, I was the beast who would have cast her out of it to survive on her own in the wilderness, and I would never stop hating myself for that.

"But you did," she said, her nails tearing into my shoulder blades and a hungry, unfulfilled need for her rang demandingly through my body like a gong. But I wouldn't answer it, because this girl was not and never had been mine.

"*Rogue*," I warned, my cock growing hard in my pants and giving myself away to her.

I lifted my head, about to let go when she slid her fingers into my hair, fisting them tightly and her lips brushed mine for half a heartbeat. Every touch from her was like purest energy dripping into my blood. I was almost shivering with the need for more of it, my skin too used to the bite of steel and leather and fists. It was begging for her feather soft lips and the silken caress of her hands, but I couldn't take more of it, it wasn't mine to have, and yet I couldn't pull away.

"I'm tired of the lies and the bullshit," she exhaled. "So don't lie a damn fucking word to me anymore, Ace. You said you loved me in that letter so is that true? Or is it another lie put there to drive me insane?" Her eyes glimmered and my throat thickened at the desperation in her gaze, the fear.

"It's true," I said firmly, exposing myself to her because what did it really matter anymore? "But I don't want anything in return for that love, little one. It's an admission I owed you and myself, and I didn't wanna leave town with it never having been said. But I don't expect anything for it. You're JJ's, I know that-"

"I'm not JJ's," she cut in, her nails biting into my scalp as she still clung to my hair. "I can't belong to one of you without belonging to all of you, that's how it is. It's how it always was with us and maybe it doesn't make sense now we're grown up, but it doesn't change the fact that it's true."

"I'm not one of *us* anymore," I said, pushing a lock of dark hair behind her ear, both missing the vibrant rainbow colours and relishing this small taste of the girl from my past.

"If you're not a part of us then there is no us, Chase Cohen," she growled.

"I betrayed you," I said, trying to pull away but she wouldn't let go.

"And I forgave you. And since then, you've shown who you really are. The survivor, the one who'd bleed for me and his boys and offer his life to a monster to protect us." She caught hold of my eyepatch, trying to tug it from my face and I jerked my head back, catching her wrist to stop her as my muscles tensed.

"Don't," I snarled, her sweet words wasted on me as I retreated into the shame I felt over the scars laying beneath that eyepatch, the repulsive opaque, unseeing eye.

"I want to see," she demanded, some dark, powerful goddess seeming to blaze within her eyes, capturing my entire attention. "I want to see every scar, every mark, because it's beautiful to me. It's your strength written into your skin."

My throat bobbed and for once I couldn't avoid the truth in her eyes, couldn't stand in denial of the worth I could see she held for me. Rogue. The girl I'd wanted my whole life, the girl who'd driven me to the edge of insanity and back again. The one who lived in every dream and nightmare I'd ever had. She was the possessor of my soul. But the strength she saw in me was a farce, because beneath it all was Shawn picking me apart, my father towering above the small boy who still cowered inside my chest. And now that weakness could be seen on the outside too, bared for the whole world to see.

"It's Shawn written into my skin," I said. "He's here, always. And I could bear that burden before, but now I see him in you too." I brushed my fingers over the arch of her eyes, my fingertips brushing the edges of her bruises and hating the echo of his cruelty I saw staring back at me. "And it makes me want to commit a murder so brutal, it would rival the sins of Lucifer himself."

"We can destroy him together," she breathed and those words filled me up with a light I'd been missing for so long. I could feel us bound by them and I nodded, a promise twisting between us to kill that motherfucker in the most gruesome way we could think up. And damn the fucking consequences, because I had a feeling the only way I could free Rogue from his snare was with his end.

"Once we have him, I'll do anything you want. I'll cut off pieces of him until he's screaming, I'll gut him slowly, I'll rip his wicked tongue from his mouth and burn it to ash for you." My voice was rough with grit and her eyes lit up with excitement at my words, an excitement I felt deep down to my bones too.

"Yes," she practically moaned and the sound made me so hard, a growl left me in response.

My thoughts scattered and I tracked my fingers up her outer thigh, pushing the saturated material of her dress higher, every wall crashing down between us and leaving us bare. I couldn't stop staring at that blazing hope in her eyes, the possibility of Shawn's death lighting us both up from the inside out.

"I want him torn to bits, I want nothing left of him," she panted and I nodded eagerly, the image giving me renewed fucking life just like she was.

"There's no length I wouldn't go to, little one. I'll be his worst nightmare brought to life, and you'll be the queen who rules me," I growled and another breathy moan left her, her thighs tightening around my hips, her heels pressing to the backs of my thighs and drawing me flush against her.

There was nothing but honesty and maddening tension between us that was building into a force of nature. She was making me feel as though I looked like I always had, and I wanted so fucking much to be that man before her that I tried to believe it too.

I scored my thumb across her lower lip as a noise of desire left me.

"Take it off," she begged, biting her lip as her gaze hooked on my eyepatch.

My heart jackhammered as I obeyed her, clenching my jaw and pulling the eyepatch from my face before tossing it onto the surface beside her.

"When we kill him, you can't wear it," she said huskily, gazing at the butchered side of my face while my pulse pounded loudly in my ears and I fought the urge to cover up again. "I want him to see the powerful creature he couldn't break."

She smiled at me and I lost my fucking mind at the strength that look gave me. All reasonable thought left my head as I lunged forward and crushed my lips to hers, wanting to taste that smile and brand it to my memory forever. Her tongue met mine and thunder boomed beyond the house, sending the walls shuddering and my heart skipping. Our kiss healed something deeply broken in me over her and I dragged her tighter against me, her mouth chasing mine until we were two entities becoming one. I could feel her heart beating as if it lived within my own chest, I could sense the time lost between us becoming nothing, insignificant as it bowed to this single moment of perfection we shared. It was earth-shattering and like a tonic to my fucking soul, and something told me if I could only keep this girl, there was no damage in me that couldn't mend.

Rogue half ripped my shirt off of me and I let it fall to floor as she broke our kiss, her lips parted and glistening as her eyes lowered to take in the marks left there by our enemy. It made no fucking sense to me why she didn't recoil from my scars, but as she leaned forward and pressed her mouth to an old cigarette burn at the hollow of my throat then moved to a crescent shaped mark on my right pec put there by a blade, I tried to find new meaning in them. Because every one her mouth touched seemed to brand it with this new, sweet memory, overwriting the sting of the old one.

I drew in a rampant breath, aching with how hard I was as Rogue took her time running her mouth all over my chest.

When I was at breaking point, I gripped her hair and tugged her head back, making her look up at me.

"Did Shawn make you wear this dress, little one?" I asked, a murderous edge to my tone as I took in the tight black material which didn't look anything like her own style.

She nodded, her pupils dilating and I grabbed a sharp knife from the kitchen block, finding the thing had a metal handle with the words *my siren, my light, my life* engraved into it. But I had far better things to focus on than those words.

"C'mere," I said, wrapping my arms around her and she held onto me as I lifted her, carrying her to the large white couch in the lounge. I lay her down, watching as she bit her lip, her eyes following every movement I made and making adrenaline rush through me.

I knelt between her thighs, taking hold of the hem of the dress and shearing through it with the knife right up the centre, needing to strip her of anything else left there by Shawn. She gasped as it fell open in the middle, staring up at me as she panted. Her body was still covered by the pieces and I hesitated a moment, wondering if I should have done that, if she really wanted this.

"We don't have to," I back-peddled, thinking of the hell she must have been through with that asshole and not wanting to cross a line. My insecurities started rising again too and I turned, looking for a blanket to offer her when she took hold of my waistband to get my attention again and I stared down at her, transfixed as she drew the material of the dress apart, baring herself to me in a move so fucking sexy it made me curse.

She shrugged out of it, her body bare beneath it and my gaze roamed from her perfectly round breasts to her pussy as she spread her thighs for me.

"Rogue," I managed to say around the lump in my throat. I was a teenager again in that second, awkward and lost and pining for a girl I'd thought I'd never have. But now she was offering herself to me and I wasn't anything like the man I'd hoped I'd be if this day ever came.

"Show me what you'd do to him," she asked, taking my wrist and guiding the knife in my hand to her throat. "Show me where you'd make him bleed first."

I positioned my knee between her thighs, lowering over her and grazing the knife down to her collarbone, giving into that desperate need in her eyes. It was a lust for blood, revenge for the monsters he'd made of us. And I needed it too.

Rogue inhaled sharply, though she knew I wouldn't cut her, I would never draw blood on this girl's flesh. I circled the blade around her left breast and she moaned, biting down on her lower lip as the tension between us grew palpable, rivalling the energy in the storm beyond these walls.

I ran the blade down the centre of her body, skimming her navel and watching the way goosebumps travelled across her skin and her nipples peaked at the contact with the cold blade.

"I'd slice him open just like this," I murmured, moving the blade slowly as I watched her shiver beneath me. "Let him scream as his flesh peeled apart and relish the hot spill of his blood on my hands."

"Yes," she moaned, her voice rough and filled with a heady kind of desire as sex and bloodlust collided within her and I couldn't tear my eyes away from the perfection of her laying beneath me, bared and willing, her eyes filled with desire as I ran the knife over her skin.

"The second I thought his agony was waning, I'd start again, punching holes in him and listening to each and every scream that escaped him, adding them up until they equalled the ones he's torn from my lips and yours," I said, pressing the tip of the blade to her side lightly, moving it up her body as I repeated the move again and again, her heavy breaths and the shivers dancing across her letting me know how much she wanted that too.

"Then when he was in so much pain it coloured the world black, I'd slit his throat." I grazed the knife along the curve of her throat, her eyes misted with lust and making the tip of my cock twitch and throb. "And he'd die choking on his own blood, his voice forever fucking silenced." My gaze hooked on the way her sun kissed skin reflected in the silver blade and my breaths came unevenly.

"Fuck him," she croaked and I looked up, finding a tear tracking down her cheek.

The sight of it punched a hole right through my chest and I leaned in, kissing it away and cupping her face as she gazed at me through a haze of unshed tears.

"I'll find you some clothes, we can sit here and watch the storm, little one," I said, my heart full of pain for her. I needed her to be alright again, I'd do anything to make her okay.

"No," she said before I could pull away, her hand sliding around the back of my neck to hold me there. "I want you. I want to drown in you and forget what he did to us. Please Chase. I need you."

I hesitated, frozen by her want for me. But those words were my undoing and I vowed to give her what she needed, to offer her as much pleasure as I could and steal away the pain in her eyes. Even if it only lasted a little while.

I leaned down, sucking her nipple into my mouth with a groan as I fulfilled a fantasy I'd been having over this girl for so long that I couldn't remember a time before it. Every woman I'd been with in her absence had been nothing but a Bandaid I'd used to try and stem that ache in me for her, every time I'd closed my eyes and fantasised about anyone it had always ended up being her. She was it for me, a pure fucking daydream of a need I'd never thought I'd get to claim and my head spun as I tried to come to terms with the fact that this was real. That the heat of her body beneath mine was no fantasy and that she really wanted me just like I wanted her.

I grazed the blade down her side and she urged me on as she moaned my name. Her back arched and goosebumps tumbled across her flesh as I teased her, flicking my tongue back and forth as I pressed my knee harder between her thighs. She started grinding on my jeans, desperate for friction on her clit but I could do better than that for her.

I kissed my way down her stomach then pushed her thighs wider for me, bringing the knife to her inner thigh and circling it there, drawing a whimper from her lips that made my head spin.

I grazed my thumb over her clit and she cursed as I slid my hand lower and my fingers sank into the soaking heat of her pussy. A deep groan left me as I pushed two fingers inside her, curling them and pumping them in and out of her in a slow rhythm as I watched her. This siren set to lure me in and take control of my heart, my flesh, my desires. She was everything, fucking everything and here she was, falling to ruin at my touch and moaning my name as she kept her gaze fixed on my destroyed face like I was as intoxicating to her as she was to me.

"More," she demanded, her hips bucking to try and get what she wanted, and I pulled my fingers free, driving the smooth hilt of the knife into her instead.

She half sat upright as she gasped at the new sensation and I dropped my mouth to her clit, giving her no time to recover as I took a taste of what I'd been aching for for so fucking long. I groaned as her sweetness coated my lips, my cock throbbing with need as I licked and sucked, continuing to tease the knife handle in and out of her.

She gripped my hair, moaning so loud it was all I could hear and I turned into a starved beast at the taste of her, needing more, far fucking more. I dragged the pad of my tongue back and forth over her clit again and again, feeling her building for me as I got closer and closer to bringing her to ruin.

She mounted toward the brink of pleasure and I watched her as her head tipped back, her eyes on me as she pawed at her breasts, about to fall into oblivion, but then she reached for me, an urgency in her gaze that begged for more of me.

"Chase," she panted and I knew what she wanted, what she fucking needed as desperately as I did too.

I tugged the knife free of her pussy and tossed it away as I freed my cock from my pants, shoving the wet material off of me so that there was nothing left dividing us anymore aside from the taste of the unknown and the need in our souls.

I gripped the back of her knee, drawing her leg around my waist as I lined the tip of my cock up with her pussy, our eyes locked and the air seeming so thick I couldn't breathe at all.

I pushed inside her, inch by inch, her pupils dilating as I drove in deeper and deeper, making me lose my goddamn mind at how good she felt.

"Fuck," I gritted out as I filled her completely, thrusting every inch of my cock inside her and one further drive of my hips sent her over the edge. She came, her pussy squeezing my length so hard I swear I was a gonna be a goner far too fucking soon.

She cried out as I started fucking her in slow and firm drives of my hips, the noises leaving her getting me so turned on I almost followed her over the edge as my dick swelled even further. But I was a damn pro when it came to delayed gratification, and I hadn't waited my whole damn life to claim this girl just to blow my load in three seconds. Besides, this was for her more than me. I wanted to banish the ghosts in her eyes and make her feel so good she momentarily forgot about Shawn and all that she'd been through while she was with him.

I braced my hand on the arm rest behind her, fucking her breathless as she wound her legs around me and cried out for more. She felt so good wrapped around me, so hot and tight I teetered on the brink of madness.

A few dark curls fell forward to cover my bad eye and she immediately pushed them back, looking at me like the sight of my scars turned her on even more. It made my heart riot with a furious kind of energy and as hard as it was to just let her look, it was easy to feel better about my eye when I was deep inside her with her pussy pulsing with the aftershocks of coming all over my cock, and to top it all off she was looking at me like *that*.

I could already feel her building again, her body tensing as she clung to me and the intensity between us made my ears fucking ring. I circled my hips, hitting that sweet spot inside her over and over until she was saying my name like it belonged to a god. And fuck if it wasn't the best feeling in the entire goddamn world.

I forgot about Shawn, I forgot about my scars, and I forgot every blackened, tarred thing inside me that was left there by him. I was one with Rogue and there was nothing but light between us as we held onto each other like the ocean would rise and swallow us up if we let go. Every part of me was hers and I'd never felt so whole in all my life.

Her hips rose to meet every drive of mine and when she fell apart again with a sexy as fuck moan, I let myself fall with her, thrusting in deep and coming so hard I swear I half blacked out.

I could feel the heat of my cum spilling from her, making a complete mess of the couch and I growled against her lips, loving how good that felt.

"Mine," I claimed her. Claimed her like I had no right to fucking claim her, but I did anyway because it was all I'd wanted to do since forever and I didn't care what that meant after this.

"Mine," she replied, her fingers tracking up my cheek and I leaned down, kissing her slowly, enjoying the way our tongues worked in perfect harmony with one another.

I could already feel myself getting hard again inside her and I knew nothing would ever sate me of this girl. I smiled against her lips as I slowly pulled out of her, her body going slack beneath me. But I'd promised to help her forget the darkness awaiting her beyond this, so I was going to hold it at bay for as long as possible.

I pulled her to her feet, towing her over to the glass doors where the rain was hammering against it and the wild grey storm surged beyond it. Then I picked her up, wrapping her thighs around me and pressing her against the glass as I sank inside her once more in a slow, teasing move that made her look at me like I held some untold power.

She sighed my name just as thunder crashed once more and I was sure I felt the lightning that followed right down to my soul as I pressed one hand to the glass above her head and claimed her like the sky was about to come tumbling down to crush us into oblivion.

I felt somehow remade by this girl, built up into a leviathan that could take on the world and bring it to its knees just for her. But there was only one man who would face the wrath of this new power in me, and when he died, I'd free Rogue from the shackles he'd put on the inside of her flesh, and maybe then I'd finally make up for some of my deepest regrets.

CHAPTER SEVENTEEN

I lay in the enormous bed which Tatum and her men had clearly gotten made especially for them all to share with Chase's arm wrapped tight around me and my head resting on his chest.

My body hummed with the afterglow of the pleasure he'd delivered to me, but my mind felt like it was full of whispers which I couldn't block out no matter how hard I tried.

That's it, little whore, show him what you're good for.

Shawn's voice wouldn't stop rattling around inside my skull and no matter how many times I tried to remind myself that my boys weren't like that, that they thought more of me than that, I couldn't keep the words out.

I'd been with him too long and as much as I'd tried to steel myself against the poison of his words, it was clear that I hadn't done a good enough job of keeping them out.

Thunder boomed beyond the windows and I glanced over at the clock, seeing it was almost four in the morning and giving up on the idea of sleep as I carefully untangled myself from Chase's arms and climbed out of bed. The lamp was on and Chase's arm was stretched vaguely in its direction as if even in sleep he feared the light might go out. I hated that for him, that Shawn had infected the dark for my sweet Harlequin boy.

My bare feet met with the cool wooden floor and I walked beneath the arching roof of the stunning house feeling like I was a demon creeping through a house of God. I knew the place wasn't really a church but with its vaulting ceilings and stained glass windows, not to mention the damn spire, it was hard to remember that in the dark.

I moved to the balcony doors sweeping aside the long, white curtains so that I could look out into the storm and watch the choppy waves crash against the beach while I worked to clear my mind.

The storm clouds were thick and only the occasional fork of lightning gave any real illumination to the turbulent waves and sheeting rain. I shivered, wondering if Rick and JJ had found somewhere dry to wait out the storm and hoping that they were okay. The last we'd heard from them, they were safe and laying low, not wanting to risk leading any of Shawn's men to us here and I just had to have faith that they were still there, waiting to return to us once it was safe to.

I closed my eyes and tried to concentrate on nothing aside from the sound of the storm raging outside as my bare skin prickled in the cool, air-conditioned room but as soon as I did, I was back in that basement with Miss Mabel. And my guilt over escaping without her was even worse than the whispers of Shawn's poison in my ears.

I snapped my eyes open again, silently vowing to do whatever it took to break Miss Mabel out of that fucking house and blinking back tears at the thought of what Shawn might do to her in the meantime. He hadn't shown any real interest in her while I'd been trapped in that place and he hadn't seemed to notice my connection to her either, so I was just going to have to hope she would remain safe enough while I worked on a plan to get her out. I didn't know what the hell Travis was up to, but I did know that he was making sure Miss Mabel got enough food and supplies down there, so I had to trust that he would continue to do that.

I focused on the puzzle that was Travis as I tiptoed across the huge master bedroom and slipped through the door to the enormous bathroom attached to it. At the far end of the white space, a big claw foot bath stood before a long window which looked down on the beach and I crossed the cold white tiles to it and set the water running right away. I wasn't sure what else I needed to help me get past the clawing feeling of Shawn's hands on my skin, but a hot bath sounded like a damn good start to me.

I perched my ass on the edge of the tub as it began to fill with steaming water, leaving the lights off so that I was left in the near complete darkness of the room. The window was made of red stained glass, the image of a fallen angel dominating it as he knelt on the ground and raised his hands towards the heavens. There was something achingly sad about the image, especially as the rain washed down the other side of it, making it seem like he was crying.

There were only a few theories about Travis which made any real sense to me. He was clearly up to something within Shawn's ranks, and I had to guess that either he was there with a vendetta against the man in charge or... *shit*. He was undercover. I'd been accepting help from a fucking cop.

I groaned as I took that in, adding fancy bath salts and bubblebath to the running water before finding a pot of red petals and scattering them across the top of the water too. Tatum had some fancy shit in this place.

But if Travis was a cop then why hadn't Shawn been arrested yet? He'd been with him for years and I knew for a fact that he'd witnessed Shawn killing more than a few men. He had to have more than enough evidence against him after all this time. So why hadn't he made his move?

I shut off the running water and stepped into it, sighing as I sank down and got myself comfortable in the huge tub, my toes barely reaching the far end of it.

Travis was young. I'd guess maybe a few years younger than me. But he'd been with Shawn since well before I'd come on the scene. I'd have to guess he'd been in The Dead Dogs for at least six years from the things I'd overheard in my time with him which meant he'd probably been around seventeen or so when he'd joined the gang. So how had he managed to go through his cop training and shit and ended up in deep cover like that? I felt like I was missing something, but I just couldn't grasp it. Maybe he wasn't as young as he was making out? But he wasn't exactly a small dude, so I wasn't sure how he would have been able to fake his age by much. I guessed it was possible though, if he was really a few years older than he claimed then he would have had time to do the police academy shit. I still wasn't sure it all added up, but what else could it be? I was going to have to warn the others about him either way. But I couldn't risk any of them trying to kill him when I did - cop or not, I owed him.

I sighed, letting the mystery of Travis go as I lay back in the water and willed it to wash this unclean feeling from my flesh. But it wasn't just about the memory of the way Shawn had manhandled me. It was the cloying sense of suffocation that his words had left inside my skull. He'd told me time and again that I was a good little whore and that was all I was good for.

I didn't want to let his words touch the memory of Chase and I finally claiming one another, but it was so hard to force them from my mind.

Why hadn't they come for me sooner? Had he gotten what he'd wanted from me now? Was that really all I was worth to him, to all of them?

I didn't want to believe it, I wanted to bask in the memory of the love I'd felt for my boys for my entire life and trust in the power of it, but even as I tried to do that, Shawn's voice crawled through my mind and dripped more vile poison into my veins.

They threw you away back then too. Their so called love for you has limits, but yours for them has none. Would they even want you back if they couldn't fuck you as often as they please? What else can you really offer them anyway?

I scrunched my eyes up tight in denial of those words, but I couldn't do anything to hold back the tears that burned their way free and started racing down my cheeks. I was so fucking damaged. And I didn't even know if there was anything I would ever be able to do to fix that now. I didn't have an answer to that question either. What was I to them if I took my body from the equation? They all kept secrets from me, tried to keep me out of things that I had every right to be involved in, told me pretty truths to avoid the ugly ones.

Was I a fool to hope that things might be different now? Was I being totally naive to even want that? And if I was then what choices was I even left with? If I had to face the reality that my appeal to them was limited, that my voice wasn't wanted, that their love came with conditions, what then? Would I accept it? Just be their whore because it gave me a taste of the love I craved so much even if it was a watered-down version? Or would I refuse it and run again? Run away into the arms of nothing and no-one and try to find something else out there despite the fact that I'd never managed to find it before.

The door cracked open behind me and I flinched as I looked over my shoulder, finding Chase standing there silhouetted in the dim light of the room beyond.

"Hey," he murmured, his voice low and rough, a caress to my senses.

My heart jolted in alarm and my throat locked up as I tried to form a proper response to his greeting, but my mind was so scrambled and my doubts so present that I couldn't seem to even make my tongue bend around a simple greeting.

"Can I join you?" he asked, a little of the boy I once knew in his voice, a touch of hesitation, self-awareness, like he was worried I might turn him away.

But I couldn't turn him away no matter how much I might have been breaking in that moment.

"It's dark in here," I whispered, knowing he could never have the lights off since Shawn had locked him up in the pitch black for so long.

"I'd face any demon in the dark for you," he said, his tone low and sending a tremor down my spine, leaving me without words to answer.

He stepped inside, closing the door behind him and blocking out all the light from the room beyond so that we were plunged into complete obsidian. I knew what he was offering by giving me this, braving the dark for me and it made me almost believe my flesh was worth more to him than the pleasure it could give him.

In the few seconds it took my eyes to adjust, I heard him moving closer, his feet padding across the tiles towards me and making my skin prickle with recognition of his body closing in on mine.

I took a deep breath and dunked my head beneath the water, pushing my dark hair back out of my face as I emerged again and hoping it would be enough to hide any evidence of the tears which wouldn't stop running down my cheeks.

Chase came to stand beside the tub, his shadow looming over me as the silence stretched between us and I looked up at the outline of his powerful body, scouring the darkness to try and see his eyes.

My wish was granted as lightning flashed in the raging sky beyond the window and for a few brief seconds, his features were thrown into focus. He'd fallen asleep in bed naked so his entire body was on show for me to see, all of the scars that Shawn had given him alongside the ink he'd chosen to mark his skin with. My gaze fell to a shark tattoo on his left thigh, its mouth open as it swum beneath a turbulent sea, razor sharp teeth looking to eat me up and swallow me whole. Every hard ridge and line of his muscular body was lined in the glow of light and for a moment I was struck by just how beautiful he was, like an impossibly imperfect god sent down from the heavens to bring ruin to us all. Or maybe just to me.

But as the light fell away, I was left with the image of his sea blue eyes, one razor sharp and one clouded with blindness burning into mine, all of my own pain mirrored back to me in them so sharply that I couldn't help the sob that broke free of my chest.

I clapped a hand to my mouth to try and hide it, but Chase was already moving, taking hold of me and moving me so that he could climb into the huge bathtub behind me, his arms holding me tight as he nestled me back against his broad chest.

"I know," he murmured, his lips brushing my ear through strands of wet hair as his strong arms banded around me and I fell apart.

I curled my legs up against my chest as my body gave way to the inevitability of my meltdown and all the worst things I'd endured with Shawn alongside all of the shit I'd survived in the last ten years came crashing down on me. It wasn't the first time I'd lost my shit like this over the years. In fact, it happened more frequently than I would have liked to admit to myself. But it was the first time that I'd had someone here to hold me while I fell apart.

Chase's fingers pushed through my hair, stroking me soothingly over and over again while the strength of his other arm locked tight around me helped me feel like he might just be holding me together. He didn't say anything, just held me while I broke and placed kisses against my temple as I turned into his embrace.

The storm continued to rage beyond the window but as time went on, I somehow found the strength to end the tears streaming from my eyes and the sobs rattling my chest.

When I'd been quiet for several minutes, Chase shifted beneath me, making the hot water slosh around the two of us as he encouraged me to unravel my limbs and sit upright between his legs again with my back still to his chest.

I sank lower in the water as I stretched my legs out, laying my head against his shoulder so the rough stubble of his jaw grazed against my temple as he spoke.

"When that monster had me at his mercy, it was like all the worst things I'd ever felt about myself were somehow painted across every wall, written out in great detail and offered up to him for his amusement to use as tools against me," he murmured, the rumble of his voice passing through his chest and sinking into my body, making me feel calm and safe in his arms. "I fought to keep him out of my head and I never spoke a single word that could ever be used to hurt any of you. But he found the truth of me all the same."

He shifted behind me again, clearly feeling uncomfortable about speaking these words, but somehow, here in the dark with my back to his chest so that we couldn't even look each other in the eye while admitting this damage, it seemed simpler, easier. So I gave him a piece of my truth in reply.

"He always had a way of doing that," I breathed. "Of seeing the things I felt most insecure about and bringing them to the light, of exposing any weakness he could find and making it into a weapon."

Chase growled, this low deep, pain fill sound which made my heart ache as his arms tightened around me and he held me closer.

"I'm so sorry you ended up with him, little one. I'm so fucking sorry that we never found you, that we were too afraid to even try for so fucking long. I told you the apology in my letter would be my last, but it's not. Not even close. I'll never be done apologising to you or repenting for what I did. Because I'm so fucking sorry that I gave up on you, that I tried to hate you so hard and fight against the truth of what I've always known in my heart."

"And what's that?" I asked, not wanting to go over and over the past anymore because it never changed anything. Even if I understood it all so much better now, it didn't undo any of it. But I was done being angry with them for it. All I wanted now was to figure out whether or not there was any chance for us to find our way back to the kind of happiness I dreamed of. Because even a small taste of the sunshine of our youth would be more than I ever could have hoped for a few years ago.

"That I love you, Rogue Easton. I've been so irrevocably and helplessly in love with you for so long that I let it twist me up inside. I let it turn me cruel and jaded and so fucking angry because..."

He let his words fall away but my heart was pounding with the desperate need for him to finish that sentence.

"Because of what?" I asked.

Chase sighed, his fingers flexing a little so that he was caressing my stomach and making my skin hum with that simple pleasure.

"Because I always knew I wasn't good enough for you. And Shawn figured that out too. He saw exactly what I was and what I was worth, and he gave me the punishment I deserved for it."

"Don't ever say that," I hissed, turning in his arms so that I could glare at him, but his grip tightened around my waist to stop me and his jaw pressed firmly against my cheek so that the rough bite of his stubble seared across my flesh again.

"I might hate him for what he did to me, little one," Chase growled. "But I know that a lot of what he saw in me was the truth. I am weak. I am broken. I am useless. I am the reason for so much of the bad you and the others have suffered since you came back into our lives and I might hate all of that about myself, but it doesn't stop it from being the truth."

"No," I disagreed, turning my head so that I could look up at him and force him to admit to the truth in my words. "You might have made some mistakes, you might have even been a total fucking asshole a whole lot of the time and yeah, that stunt you pulled on the ferry made me wanna cut your damn balls off and wear them as earrings." Chase winced at that thought but I ploughed on before he could interrupt me. "But you're not broken, Chase, and you're definitely not useless. Those aren't your words, they're Shawn's and they're your dad's and maybe they've worked their way into your fears and insecurities but they're not true. When we were kids, you and me were the ones who really had nothing. JJ's mom might not have been rich, but she loved him and kept him fed and in clean clothes. Fox and Rick always had so much from Luther that I don't think they'll ever fully understand what it was like for us, but you and me knew what it was to be unwanted, to be hungry, to feel so fucking alone in the world that it hurt. And yet you were still always the first to think of the rest of us before yourself. You always shared your food with me even when your stomach was rumbling so damn loud that even the seagulls took pity on you and didn't come begging for scraps. You risked your dad's rage more than once by doing things to help the rest of us."

"You're making me out to be better than you and the others and that's not true," he grumbled, but I wasn't done.

"Chase, you were the one who stole your mom's car to come get me in the rain even when you knew how much trouble you'd be in for it. You were the one who showed up with bruises and always tried to hide them because you thought they made you look weak, when really all they ever did was prove how strong you were because you still managed to smile through the pain of them-"

"You were the ones who made me smile," he interrupted. "All four of you. You were everything to me."

"You were everything to me too," I breathed and silence fell between us again as we let the weight of all we'd lost press down on us. "It's never going to be like that again, is it?"

Chase sighed but didn't reply because we both knew it wasn't. How could it be? And yet in that moment it was painfully clear that it was the one thing the two of us wished for above all else.

"Tell me what Shawn did to you, little one," he asked after a few minutes and my spine stiffened as I fought the urge to just shut down, block him out, run away. But I was so fucking tired of running and I'd made a promise to myself that I wasn't going to be that girl anymore.

So I set my gaze on the rain dashed window and looked out to the storm beyond it through the coloured glass as I forced myself to admit my weakness out loud in the dark.

"Shawn likes fucking pretty, broken girls," I said slowly. "I didn't realise that when I first met him...or maybe I did. I dunno. I guess back then I didn't really care either way."

"Tell me," Chase urged and I could tell how desperately he wanted to understand this. Understand me. So I forced myself to look at my pain face on and speak it aloud.

"After I left that fucking place where Luther had dumped me, I told you where I ended up."

"Living with some asshole wannabe gangster boyfriend," Chase muttered and I nodded.

"Yeah. Cody. He was the first man who I ever met who really made me understand what it was to be desired for my body above all else. He made it clear what he wanted from me pretty early on, his hands always wandering when he was kissing me, and the nicest things he ever said to me were always geared towards how hot I looked or how much he wanted me. But I guess I just wanted to be wanted after feeling so rejected by all of you and having had months of no one at all even caring if I lived or died. Sex had seemed like such a big deal to me when I was living here, but I think that was because I'd known that once any of us started fucking other people it would change everything."

"The only girl any of us ever wanted was you," Chase said, the truth in his words making me blush like I was that girl again, stealing looks at my boys and fearing the feelings I was developing for them. "It should have been one of us, not some fucking Cody asshole."

"If it had been one of you then it would have meant me choosing and I was never going to do that," I reminded him, but he just shook his head.

"So, what was it like then?"

"Losing my virginity?"

"Yeah."

I thought back on that night, on the rumpled bed sheets and Cody's lust filled breaths in my ear, of the sting of pain I'd felt and the rush of panic as he'd started thrusting his hips between my thighs.

"We were alone in his apartment and we were kissing on his bed," I said slowly. "I was into it enough and it was nice to feel something other than the pain of being alone all the time. He said something about wanting to fuck me so bad and I agreed because I knew I couldn't keep stringing him along. He was older than me - twenty-one and he knew what he wanted, so if I wanted to stay with him then I'd already realised I'd have to give it to him. He got my clothes off of me so fast that I didn't even really have time to freak out over it or anything like that. Then suddenly he was rolling a condom on and grinning down at me where I lay naked beneath him, drinking in the sight of my body while I tried not to squirm and pretty much just stared at his cock, wondering what it was going to feel like. Then I started freaking out about not knowing what I was doing so I just blurted it out and told him I was a virgin."

"What did he say to that?" Chase asked and I could tell from the tension in his posture that he fucking hated hearing this, but he was managing to hold his tongue for the most part.

"He just drove his dick inside me and said 'not anymore'." I cleared my throat while Chase's grip on me tightened almost to the point of pain. "It didn't last all that long anyway, and I realised later on that his dick was pretty small, so I got away with that fairly lightly. But he was so much nicer to me after that. He wanted me around a lot and he let me crash at his place, he gave me shit - mostly food but sometimes he stole jewellery for me. Nothing flashy or whatever but for a while there, I felt kinda important. Until the shine wore off, I guess."

"So you left him in your dust, and then what?" Chase asked and I knew he had to be wondering how this led into what Shawn had done to me, but he had to understand all of it to understand that.

"On to the next guy," I admitted. "And the next. I figured out pretty quick that I could use sex to my advantage, and it wasn't like I didn't enjoy it once I figured it all out a bit more. For a while, I think I was hoping I'd find someone to love me, but I never came close to that and the more I realised that men coveted my body above all else I might have had to offer, the less I thought of myself. I just ended up in this cycle of partying and living from meal to meal, using guys when it suited me and letting them use me right back. It didn't really matter to me. But the longer it went on the emptier I felt inside, and by the time I met Shawn I was so fucking alone that I was just relieved to find someone who actually saw me when he looked at me. Even if all he saw was my damage. Even if that was all he liked about me. He still fucking saw it."

Chase pressed his lips to the side of my head and I could tell he was biting back the words he wanted to speak in favour of hearing me out so I kept going.

"Shawn likes broken things, but what he really wants is to become the centre of their world. I'm sure he only kept me around for so long because he never managed to achieve that with me. He called me out on all the worst things I thought about myself, made me feel like the best thing I could offer up was sex, but I didn't even care. I liked sex. I liked feeling something aside from the emptiness in me. But he wanted more than that, he wanted my devotion, my adoration, I don't even fucking know really. But he didn't like the fact that he couldn't get it and he was determined to take it if he could."

"So he didn't rape you because he wanted you to want it?" Chase asked and I was surprised at how much he seemed to understand that. "He wanted you to beg for it?"

"Yeah," I whispered.

"He wanted that with me too. Whenever he came to torture me, he practically made me want it. He made me remember all the worst things about myself and he got so deep inside my head that sometimes I swear he's still there."

I hated that so fucking much, but I felt it too, I knew what it was like to have him in your damn head. And I had no idea how to get him out again.

"He told me the only thing any of you really wants me for is sex," I admitted in a voice so low I wasn't sure he'd even hear it, but the way his muscles flexed told me he had.

"Fuck that," Chase spat. "You have to know that's not true, little one."

I wanted to lie to take the hurt from his words, but I knew that I couldn't do that anymore. I had to be honest with him, I had to give him the truth and hope that I could find some peace in his response to it.

"I don't know that, Ace," I muttered. "Since I've been back here, I've had to face so much about our past and come to terms with so many things that have changed, but there is one thing between all of us now which wasn't there before. Or at least it wasn't like this. There are so many things that all of you have lied to me about or even just concealed from me and when Shawn kept telling me that that was because the only thing any of you really wanted from me now was my body...it's hard for me to completely deny that."

"So you think I just used you tonight?" he asked, the hurt in his voice making me hurt too and I shook my head hard in refusal of that.

"No," I disagreed. "I've just been wanting to feel loved by all of you again for so long that I'm afraid of believing in it. If I wasn't a girl then none of this would have anything to do with what we all have, but because I am it's impossible for me to disconnect one thing from another. And I don't know how I'm supposed to truly believe you all think I'm worth something more when I have trouble believing that myself."

"Then I'll prove it to you," Chase swore.

"And I'll prove it to you too," I promised, turning my head so that I could look up at him in the darkness.

His brow pinched and his good eye scoured my face, lightning flashing beyond the window again and illuminating the want in both of us to believe in that. I cupped his cheek in my hand, my thumb gently tracing the edge of the scar that cut through his right eye and he sighed, closing his eyes and leaning into my touch.

I tilted my chin up and captured his lips with mine, the kiss we shared so sweet that I felt it in every single inch of my body as his strong arms around me made me feel safe. He kissed me like he was aching for it, like he was trying to breathe me in and hold me inside his chest where I would be protected from the world and all the hurt it tried to throw at us. My heart thundered with the depth of all I felt for him and I let myself get lost in that kiss, wishing I'd taken it from him long before this and silently swearing not to let any more time be stolen from us anymore.

And for a moment we were just a pair of kids again, hanging out in his mom's car while the rain crashed down on the roof and we shared the kiss we should have had then, with our hearts beating hard for one another and the storm locked outside of our perfect moment. His soul reached out to caress mine and I was his, all his and he was mine. Just two kids in a car with nothing to live for aside from the dreams we shared and the love which bound us to one another.

CHAPTER EIGHTEEN

"**A**aaand then there was a big bushy spider monster who was like rah!" Brooklyn cried, spinning around and pretending to be a big spider as she waved her arms at us.

I was dog tired. Scrap that, I was fucking pull-my-eyes-from-my-head-and-stomp-on-them tired. This night had been the longest of my life, hunkered up next to Dad against the cold wind as the storm raged on and he tried to call Maverick time and again.

I'd been two seconds from marching out onto the Isle and risking a bullet from my brother's men in a bid to find him, but then Brooklyn had finally curled up in Mateo's lap and gone to sleep for a while, announcing she'd continue her rendition of what seemed to be a very mashed up version of Lord of the Rings and Harry Potter with occasional scenes from The Fast and the Furious and Fight Club mixed in.

Mateo hadn't slept, instead glaring at us all night while she slept on him like a cat, his arm around her protectively as he made it more than clear that he valued her above all else in this world and he would sacrifice anything and everything to keep her safe. Watching them like that made my chest hurt, the emptiness inside me where Rogue belonged seeming to bleed agony through me until I turned my gaze to the holes in the hull of the shipwreck we were hunkered in and watched the storm instead.

I'd caught about three winks of sleep and now that Brooklyn had woken up again and continued with her show, I was about ten seconds from walking out of here and risking a gunshot over this hell. *I might even just shoot myself and be done with it.*

"Oh noooo, I forgot about the bit with the flying car and Brad Pitt riding on an eagle." Brooklyn stomped her foot with a pout. "No wait, that's not right. Brad Pitt came into it later and punched Voldemort in the face. That's how he lost his nose. Pow, right in the kisser!" She punched the air. "Take that you filthy mudhobbling!"

"This is all wildly inaccurate," Dad muttered to me like I wasn't aware of that, but Brooklyn heard him, whipping around with an accusing stare.

"What did you say?" she asked, her eyes brimming with tears as Brutus started growling at us from beside Mateo.

"It's just you have a few scenes mixed up from various movies," Dad explained and I shot him a glare that said *really? You're questioning the crazy girl with the man-eating dog?*

"You are mistaken," Mateo said in his gravelly voice, flashing us a warning glare which said he would willingly cut our throats over that fact if we objected any further, then nodded to Brooklyn. "Continue, chica loca."

She smiled again and carried on and Dad rubbed his eyes, trying to call Maverick for the millionth time, but there was no answer.

I held on to Mutt, only having let him down for a few minutes during the night to take a piss, but apart from that I wasn't letting him go anywhere near that dog who could eat him in one bite. Because with his attitude problem, Mutt would likely end up taking the beast on and would finally figure out how small he is once he was locked in Brutus's jaws and it was far too late.

"Oh - then that was that opera scene when they're all floating down the river and the woman is singing like ahhhhhhhhhhh!" Brooklyn tried and failed to do opera and my ears rang from the noise.

"You're gonna give us away." Luther got to his feet, about to grab her when Mateo stepped into his way like a warrior ready to die on this hill.

"I dare you to lay a hand on her," Mateo snarled, his hand on the hilt of a hunting knife which was hanging from his belt.

Luther looked inclined to take him up on that offer of a fight, but we didn't need the fucking bloodshed on top of freezing our asses off out here in this storm.

"That's it," I snarled, pushing to my feet. "I'm done." I passed Mutt into Luther's arms, stealing his attention from the psychotic cartel asshole and effectively stopping him from grabbing onto me as I strode outside.

"Fox," Luther hissed. "Get back here."

Nope. I was done. If Maverick's men shot me then so be it.

I raised my hands above my head, my gun stuffed in the back of my waistband as I strode up the beach in the pouring rain and headed towards the compound. I'd washed up half dead here before and survived, so I reckoned my chances of being killed on sight weren't too high. Couldn't rule it out though.

"*Fox*," Luther growled from behind me and I glanced back, finding him following me with anxiety in his eyes, one arm locked around Mutt and the other raised in the air like mine.

"Hey!" one of The Damned Men barked as he spotted us, aiming a gun at my head. "Stay right there!"

I stopped walking, waiting for him to bring a little gang of Damned Men down to the beach and as I glanced back, I saw Mateo and Brooklyn walking towards us with their hands raised. Brooklyn had the biggest smile on her face like this was all some wild adventure and if I'd thought she was semi-insane before, now I was pretty sure she was fully cracked.

"Is Maverick here?" I asked as the men disarmed us.

"What's it to you, Harlequin scum?" asked the guy who seemed to be in charge. He was a big, greasy-looking man with Grim Reaper tattoos covering his neck to represent his gang affiliation and he had a piercing in his eyebrow that looked like a fishhook. All in all, not someone you'd want serving you coffee at the local diner.

"We're here to see him," Luther answered for me.

"Well he ain't here," Fishhook said, sneering at us. "So you can sit pretty until he gets back and decides whether or not to peel your skin from your bones." He shoved me ahead of him to make me move, leaning in close to speak in my ear. "Or maybe I'll get bored and start the peeling process myself. I'd open you up like a banana, Harlequin prince."

"Oooh, I'm hungry. Do you have any bananas?" Brooklyn asked, appearing beside me as she listened in on what the brute was saying.

He glanced her way with a scowl. "I've got one in my pants for you, love."

Mateo collided with him so fast, he seemed to come out of nowhere, smashing his head down on the guy's forehead and making the fishhook cut into his face.

Brutus barked loudly as Brooklyn caught his collar and fought to keep him from the fight, and Mateo swung his fist into Fishhook's face so hard I heard something crack.

"Ah, you motherfucker!" Fishhook roared, raising his gun to shoot, but I rammed my shoulder against his to throw him off balance and the bullet went wide as he dropped his gun.

"Te destripare con ese gancho en tu cara." Mateo looked like he was about to kill the guy, not even flinching as that gun went off and Brooklyn made him look at her, stopping his advance.

Brutus trotted to her side, snarling viciously and looking fucking terrifying as he bared all of his teeth in a clear warning as Fishhook backed away, hunting for his gun which had fallen into the sand by his feet.

"Enough, baby," Brooklyn breathed and Mateo came out of his murderous trance as he looked into her eyes, taking a deep breath and murmuring something in Spanish which had a blush rising in her cheeks.

I hadn't heard him clearly enough to translate it, but the passion of his words made my skin prickle and the way he was looking at her like she was the sole reason for his existence made the ache in me sharpen once more. *Fuck, I miss Rogue.*

"Hey Gregory!" a girl's voice cut through the air. "You fire another fucking bullet and I'll report you to the boss when he's back."

I spotted the red haired girl further up in the beach, wearing all denim with a glare that could have melted glass. "You know his orders when it comes to those men. Them and anyone they're with get dealt with by him and only him." She pointed from me to Luther and I frowned, glancing at Gregory as he dabbed at his bleeding eyebrow with a pout and retrieved his gun from the sand.

Mateo moved to walk beside Brooklyn, a dangerous energy rolling off of him as he hounded her like a dark protector with Brutus stalking along beside her like he felt the exact same way.

"Thank you, Mr Man Junior," Brooklyn whispered to me as Brutus licked her hand. "You saved my Mateo."

"It's Fox," I told her. "And it was just instinct is all."

"Even better," she said excitedly. "I think this means we should all be best friends."

"Sure," I muttered and she let out a small squeal as we were taken inside and up some stairs.

Fishhook guided us to a hotel room on the fourth floor, gesturing with his gun for us to go inside. The double bed was dressed in plain white sheets and there was a dusty scent about the place like it hadn't been used in a long time. The curtains were open, revealing a padlock and chain on the balcony doors.

"Stop it, Mutt," Luther begged and I turned, finding Mutt wriggling wildly in his arms, trying to get free. He bit his hand and Luther dropped him with a curse, the little dog charging through the legs of Fishhook, farting as he went then sprinting off down the corridor out of sight.

"Mutt!" I called anxiously, trying to go after him, but Fishhook was blocking the door, raising his gun as I got closer.

"Well I guess my day just got a little more interesting. Because no one said anything about me not shooting the vermin you brought with you. Looks like I'm going rat hunting."

A snarl tore from my lips as I lunged at him but he slammed the door in my face, locking it tight as he boomed a laugh.

"C'mere little ratty!" he called, his footsteps heading off down the corridor and making my heart jerk furiously in my chest.

"Shit." I punched the door, panic pulling on the strings of my heart at the thought of him hurting my dog.

"It's okay, Wolf," Brooklyn said, laying a hand on my shoulder and I didn't bother to correct her on my name. "He seems like a really fast little dog,

I bet he'll whiz far away from that stinky man."

I rested my forehead to the door, on the brink of breaking, the fear over Mutt, my exhaustion and the complete shit storm that was my life closing in on me on all sides.

"She's right, kid," Dad tried, but I just stayed there with my head against the door as I tried to think of a way to get to him. He felt like my last link to the girl I'd loved so fucking deeply and failing him was one of the final nails in the coffin of all the mistakes I'd made in regards to her.

I didn't know how long I stood there like that, but the longer I did, the more I felt like I'd simply turn to stone and never move again. Everything was so fucked. We'd lost Harlequin House, the Cove, Sinners' Playground, but none of that even compared to the loss of Rogue and my boys. There was a cavernous void in my chest which kept getting bigger and bigger and I was on the verge of being swallowed by it, never to escape.

"Have you still got those cookies, Mateo?" Brooklyn asked.

"Yes, chica loca," he replied. "Here."

Where the hell had he been stashing cookies?

I listened to them eating for a while and my stomach growled demandingly, making me glance around in hopes of getting some sugar. Maybe I could think clearer if I ate something because my head was spinning and I didn't wanna be on the verge of passing out by the time Maverick showed up.

Brutus was on the huge bed, curled up asleep and Brooklyn and Mateo sat on the floor beside the balcony window as Mateo inspected the padlock keeping the doors closed.

Luther leaned against the wall as he ate a cookie and looked completely zoned out. "This isn't so bad," he murmured. "I once hid under a tarp for fourteen hours with the shits."

"Holy tits," Brooklyn gasped. "Can you tell me the story?"

Luther started telling it while I hunted down the cookies, finding the empty packet before spotting two left on the end of the bed, presumably for me. I swiped them up, chewing them down in a few bites while Brooklyn moved to sit cross legged at my dad's feet, giving him her full attention as she listened to his tale.

"-there were enemies hunting me high and low," he said with a smirk, telling the story the way he always had when me and Maverick were kids. Making gang showdowns and shootouts sound like superhero tales and great adventures. I used to think he was the coolest, bravest man in all the world – at least until I figured out that he had really just been a villain in a story without a happy ending. "And I was so badly poisoned, I could hardly see straight. When my men finally showed up to get me, I was half dead, covered in my own shit, but goddamn alive." He barked a laugh and Brooklyn clapped.

"Ah, here we go, chica loca. When the storm dies down, we can leave this way." Mateo took the padlock off the balcony doors, clearly having picked it with what looked like a small, bent nail he must have gotten from somewhere.

"I quite like it here," Brooklyn said brightly.

I blinked as my head became swimmy, rubbing my eyes as the room seemed to pop with colour.

"Oh good boy, you ate your special weshel medicine, didn't you baby?" Brooklyn said as she climbed onto the bed with Brutus, tickling his ears as he growled in his sleep.

"What medicine?" I asked, a laugh building in my throat as a dust mote floated past me, looking like a tiny cartwheeling badger. *Weeeeee, bye tiny badger.*

"It's for his angries," Brooklyn said. "It makes him a happy little chappy all squishy and squeezy. Of course, he's super big, so we have to get him a dose intended for horses, but we know a man who gets us them on the double down low." She stroked his head and he growled deeper in his chest. "When he doesn't take his medicine he can be kinda murder, and though I don't really like taking pills to quiet the voices- on account of me having been locked up in that horrible hospital before and me quite liking what the voices have to say sometimes – Bruty-tooty really can't control the urge to kill without them. So it's best he numbs them up, although he does try not to. But look, he ate the medicine all the way down in his cookies like a good, squishy boy."

"Cookies?" I mumbled, my gaze fixing on the rain washing down on the balcony and the way it seemed to spark with light as every raindrop hit the ground. "Wow…" I moved to the window, pressing my face to the cold glass and I swear the storm was filled with rainbows, hidden between all the darkness. "Do you see them? All the hiding rainbows?"

"What's that, kid?" Dad asked.

"See, there's one!" I pointed, my hand slamming into the glass. It was so cool and nice on my face. I opened my mouth, taking a little taste. Oh my god, it tasted like Coca Cola. I ran the full pad of my tongue up the window, wanting to get all the goodness out of it.

"What's up with, Coyote?" Brooklyn stage whispered somewhere behind me.

I gazed out at the ocean as it swirled and writhed, remembering swimming out there in calmer waters with my friends.

I bet all that water would feel so good racing over my skin.

I pulled my shirt off, kicking off my shoes and socks next then heading outside into the rain, tilting my head back to look at the sky. I felt so wishy and washy and all the happy calm things I hadn't felt since I was a kid. *Look at that raindrop! Weee there it goes, splish-splashing onto the ground taking all my worries with it.*

"Fox, what the hell are you doing?" Dad called as I opened my mouth wide, catching the drops on my tongue as I started spinning. I laughed as the raindrops tickled my skin and my brain did a loop-the-loop in my skull. *Weeeee.*

"Um, sorry to bother you Mr Man Junior, but I think you ate my dog's angry horse medicine." Brooklyn appeared out on the balcony and I caught her hand, making her spin with me.

That sounded like a lot of frightening words, but I didn't feel very worried at all.

"I wanna catch all of them. Help me!" I demanded, unbuckling my pants and trying to catch the rain in them as I tugged out my waistband. *Oh look at dick dancing between my legs, left, right, left, right, ding-dong dangle dance.*

Brooklyn shrugged, raising her hands in the air as she tried to catch them too, but then a strong hand caught hold of me and tugged me inside.

"Daaad," I said through a wide smile, face planting his chest before he righted me, a frown on his face that said he was going to go full father on me.

"You need to throw up," he said anxiously.

I batted him away. "No, I have rainbows to catch," I growled. "You wouldn't take away my rainbows, would you? Not again. You took my brightest rainbow and now she's living in a jar she hates."

Luther frowned and I spun away from him, heading into the bathroom and grabbing a folded white towel there. I looked at myself in the mirror as I wrapped one end around my neck and tied it in place to make a cape. "Not all heroes wear capes, this one wears a towel." I spun back out of the bathroom with a flourish, heading to the balcony.

"What are you doing?" Dad tried to catch my arm as Mateo watched me from the corner of the room with intrigue. I street danced my way past him so he couldn't catch me, pulling off moves Johnny James would have been so fucking jealous of. *You're not the only dancer around here, JJ, look at my foxtrot.*

I trotted through the door with my knees flying high and as I made it outside, I climbed onto the railing to the right of the balcony. *So much wind and air and water.*

"Fox!" Luther bellowed just before I jumped.

Weeeee.

I landed on the next balcony, crashing to my knees and rolling like a rock star at the best concert of his life. Pain blossomed along my legs and back, but it washed away as fast as the rain had come and then I was back on my feet, walking into the room, whipping my cape back with dramatic flair.

"Wait for me!" Brooklyn cried.

"Chica loca, be careful!" Mateo called.

Brooklyn appeared beside me a beat later as I moved to the room door and tried the handle.

Open. *Yes.*

"Where are we going?" Brooklyn whispered keenly.

"Shhhhh." I pressed a hand to the lower half of her face. "We're going to rescue my floof."

"Your little brown and white floof?" she asked against my palm.

"My little brown and white floof," I confirmed, dropping my hand and taking hold of the door handle.

I cracked it open, glancing out into the hallway and finding it empty. I slipped out into it and Brooklyn kept close to me like she knew the drill on how to stay covert on a mission like this. I picked up the pace as we reached the end of the corridor, listening for any sounds of approach.

"Are you good at hide and seek, Brooklyn?" I breathed.

"The best. I can curl up really, really tiny. One time, I took out all the drawers in our freezer at home, hid them in the garden then got in the freezer. I almost died before Mateo found me." She stifled a laugh and I looked down at her with a grin.

Wow, I'd never have found her in the freezer. She'd have died and turned into a big lump of ice. I smothered a laugh.

"Are you good at the seeking part too?"

"The best, best," she said with a firm nod.

"I used to play it with my friends at an old amusement park at night. Last one to be found got to dare all the rest of us to do stupid shit." I chuckled. "I used to be fun, Brooklyn. Can you imagine that?"

She squinted at me, bringing up her finger and thumb to my face in an L shape as if measuring up the straightness of a painting on a wall. "Nope, can't picture it. Your funs must be buried really, really, really, really, really, really-"

"Shh," I hushed her as footsteps sounded and she held her breath as we pressed back against the wall. A tall guy walked past us, his eyes on his phone as he scrolled through TikTok, chuckling under his breath at a cat with sunglasses on its butt. That shit was pretty funny, I almost cracked a laugh and got our brains blown out because of it. *Bad kitty.*

When he disappeared around the next corner, Brooklyn let out a long breath.

"-really, really, *really* deep," she finished what she'd been saying. "But don't worry, Labrador, I'm good at digging people's funs out. You want me to try?"

"I don't think it'll do much good," I sighed. "I'm boring. Like dry oatmeal, no sugar, no honey, no nothing." I led the way down the corridor to the right, heading for the stairwell as I listened for Mutt barking, but I couldn't hear anything and my heart scrunched up in my chest at the fear of why that might have been. But I couldn't dwell on that, I had to keep walking, had to find my floof.

"Boring people don't wear towels as capes," Brooklyn pointed out.

"I don't usually wear towel capes," I admitted. "I wear jeans and shirts and moody expressions and no one likes me."

"I like you, Dingo," Brooklyn said, patting my arm. "You saved my Mateo. Before that I thought you had a bit of a stick up your butt. And maybe you do, but butt sticks aren't permanent, you know? You can pull that right out with a bit of jiggling."

"Thanks." I smiled as we made it to the stairwell, slipping into it and listening for sounds of any men nearby, but all was quiet. The light seemed really bright in here and I squinted against it as colours seem to burst all across the walls.

I walked over to the closest one, trailing my fingers across it as the colours seemed to follow the movement of my hands. It reminded me of Rogue's hair and I pressed my cheek to it, dragging it along the wall as I tried to capture the feel of her again.

"She's gone," I whispered. "She hates me and she's gone." I started walking downstairs and Brooklyn followed closely, watching me as I continued to rub my face along the wall.

"Your floof?" she asked.

"No...not him," I said sadly. "She ditched him too."

"Who's this she? She sounds like a meanie bambini."

"She's not really. I mean, she is now. But that's because of me. Once upon a time, she was a unicorn who came out of the sea and I got to be her friend for a while. We all did. Me and my boys. Then we hurt her and lost her and we looked really hard, but we couldn't find her and when she finally came back, she hated us for failing her. So she ripped our hearts out one by one and ate them raw."

"Wooow," Brooklyn cooed. "She sounds awesome."

"Yeah," I agreed. "Have you ever dived at the cove?"

"No, is there fishes down there? I'd love to see the fishes."

"There's so many fishes, they're silver and gold and green and pink and every colour you can think up."

"Even jallaberry blue?" she whispered.

"I don't know what that is, but yes," I said, turning a corner as we wound downstairs and I kept my face against the wall. "Rogue's like the cove. You'd think you'd seen the most beautiful place on Earth on the surface, the beach, the rocks, the way the light falls so perfectly in that corner of the town when the sun sets. But then you dive under the water, you realise you've never seen real beauty, because it was all hidden away for only lucky people to find."

"And you were one of the lucky ones?" Brooklyn asked.

"Yeah, I was one fucky motherlucker, I mean lucky motherflucker, no, motherfl-" My foot slipped on a step and I started tumbling down the stairs, rolling ass over head, my cape slapping me in the face before I hit the bottom level flat on my back.

"Ow," I groaned and Brooklyn rushed down the steps, leaning over me as her long, dark hair swung forward over her shoulders.

"Are you okay, Jackal?" she asked anxiously, offering me her hand.

I started laughing, the urge rising up and taking over me, becoming uncontrollable as heaves of laughter ripped through my body.

Brooklyn's eyes widened and she glanced left and right in concern before dropping down and sitting on my chest, crushing the laughter right out of my throat.

"You'll give us away, Mr Man Junior," she hissed.

"*Fox,*" I wheezed.

"Where?" She looked around as if a fox might present itself and another laugh tried to tug its way out of my chest, but I couldn't manage it with her making it so hard for me to breathe.

The familiar sound of Mutt's bark carried to my ears and hope rushed through me as I gasped.

Brooklyn jumped up and I sprang up after her, stumbling into the railing at the bottom of the stairs with a clang that reverberated through the space.

"D'ya hear that, Phil?" a voice sounded from beyond the door to our left.

I glanced around for a way out and Brooklyn grabbed me by the back of my jeans, towing me toward a cupboard under the stairs and I went assways into it as she pulled me after her.

The door swung shut behind us just as footsteps pounded into the stairwell and I picked up the nearest item in the dark, my hand closing around a handle which could have belonged to a broom or a mop. Whatever it was, it was going to beat anyone to death who tried to stop me reaching Mutt.

I'm coming, little bro. I'll shove this handle up anyone's ass who tries

236

to get in my way.

"Let's check upstairs," the guy said and a grunt of agreement sounded before the men's footsteps sounded up and away from us.

Brooklyn stepped past me, cracking the door open to check the area was definitely vacant, the light spilling in and showing me I'd claimed a mop as a weapon.

"The ghost is clear," she said, slipping outside with a dustpan and brush in her hands, wielded like blades.

The mention of a ghost made me think of Chase calling Rogue that and I hugged my mop to my chest as I thought of all the shitty things that had gone down between them. Us. I thought of saying goodbye to Chase and a fresh shoot of hatred for myself planted in my gut, growing roots so deep I'd never be able to pull them out.

"My friend lost his eye and I dumped him at a motel," I told Brooklyn in a strained voice, letting her take the lead as we headed to the door that must have led outside.

"Oh no, did he ever find his eye?" she asked.

"No, I mean, it's still in his face he just can't see out of it anymore," I said with a sharp tug in my chest.

"Why did you dump him at a motel? Was there a doctor there to fix his eye?" she asked as we slipped along an alley where white walls led us in the direction of Mutt's distant barking.

"No, there was nothing there for him but loneliness," I said, my throat burning with emotion.

"I hope you gave the motel a bad rating," Brooklyn said, glancing back at me with a frown. "Then picked your friend up and gave him a warm hug."

"I didn't," I admitted. "I'm a horrible person."

She turned around, halting me by placing a hand on my chest. She was a really tiny person so I could have knocked her aside if I wanted to keep going, but the way she was glaring at me made me pause.

"Look, Panda," she huffed, apparently having lost her grasp on my name entirely. "No one likes mopey people, and you're moping more than a Moping Mandy on a Moped. So pull yourself together." She slapped me with the dustpan on every one of those final words and my brain rattled in my skull.

"If you're in love with this one-eyed man, then you have to tell him."

"I'm not in love with-"

"Fine! Keep lying to yourself, but I think if you just apologised to your pirate boyfriend and gave him a couple of decent BJs, he'd forgive you. And if you want a few tips on good blowjobs, I'll go down on Mateo when we get back to our room and show you how to blow his mind, kay?"

"I don't need blowjob pointers."

"That's the spirit." She clapped me on the arm and hurried on.

I raised my mop, taking a determined breath as I jogged after her, ready to save Mutt as we rounded into the pool area.

"Get back here you little rat," Gregory's voice sounded from up ahead.

I bared my teeth in a snarl as I spotted him on the other side of the pool where rain cascaded across the water. He headed through a gate, his gun raised as he chased after my dog and I started running full pelt after him, the rain hiding the sound of my approach.

I leapt the gate like a fucking ninja as I spotted Mutt cornered against two old beer barrels, Gregory's gun raised right at him and with one furious whack of my mop handle, I split his temple open and knocked him to the ground.

"Yes!" Brooklyn whooped as she dove on him, dropping her dustpan and brush and throwing her fists into his face over and over as I leaned down and snatched the gun from his grip, throwing it into the pool.

Mutt yipped in greeting, sprinting over and savaging the man's leg as he tried to push Brooklyn off, clearly dazed from the strike of my mop - though she also seemed weirdly strong for such a small thing.

She grabbed the brush from beside the dustpan and managed to force it into his mouth, her eyes wild with excitement as she shoved her weight down on the handle and began to choke him with it.

"I'm gonna sweep your tonsils right down to your asshole," she growled, a feral look in her eyes that said she was hungering for this kill with the brutal need of a true killer.

"That's enough," I said, calling her off and Brooklyn leapt to her feet, prowling back and forth like a lioness as she wet her lips for the kill. But this asshole had tried to murder my dog, so his death was mine.

He coughed and heaved as he yanked the brush from his mouth and I grabbed him by the throat, dragging him back to the gate and using his head as a battering ram to open it. He kicked and flailed as I hauled him to the pool and thrust his head over the side so it went underwater, moving to straddle him and hold his face beneath the surface.

Brooklyn started dancing around the pool in the rain, waving her arms back and forth like some sort of death dance and Mutt moved to bite the man's fingers as he thrashed.

Adrenaline buzzed inside my blood and light bounced like gumballs before my eyes, wild laughs spilling from my lips as I watched him die, die, die for what he'd done.

He's my dog. Mine. And no one hurts what's mine.

A sick satisfaction filled me as he stopped kicking and I held him under a minute longer to be sure the job was done before I let go. The rain washed down my back, my breaths coming raggedly as I stood up and kicked his huge body into the water.

No one hunts my fucking dog and gets away with it.

A whistle caught my ear and I looked up, finding Dad and Mateo leaning over a balcony several floors up. Brooklyn started waving and as Dad beckoned furiously for us to get back there, I saluted him, joining Brooklyn in her maddening dance for a moment before we ran back to the alley with Mutt chasing us.

We slipped back into the stairwell, sprinting upstairs as we suppressed our laughter and colours burst before my eyes once more. I was high on the kill and I wished my friends were here to celebrate with me. But then I remembered Maverick and JJ touching Rogue, fucking her, making her moan and beg and pant their names and my smile died a thousand bloody deaths.

I'm a bossy, bothersome badger and no one wants me.

We miraculously made it back without being caught, climbing onto our balcony, using a ledge this time that spanned the gap between the two rooms. Then we slipped inside as I held Mutt in my arms and Dad gazed at me in concern before I placed the little dog down on the bed and face planted it a second later beside Brutus.

My limbs were growing heavy and I couldn't find the strength to move.

It was so comfy, like laying in an ocean of candyfloss.

"I'll lock the balcony doors again. They won't know we got out," Mateo said.

"I'm gonna sleep now," I mumbled into the sheets as Brutus started growling. "Please don't eat me."

Brooklyn rubbed my back. "That's it, sleep off the dog medicine, little Koala."

"Is he gonna be okay?" Dad asked anxiously as Mutt licked my ear. *Ahh, stop.*

"Yeah, once the happies wear off, the sleepies come. He'll probably be out for a while," Brooklyn said. "He might pee himself though, so we could take his clothes off and put his dick in a jar. Does anyone have a jar?"

Nooooo. I don't want a dick jar.

I tried to say that, but sleep was stealing me away and the promise of peace within it made me stop fighting. My dreams were immediately vivid and so real, I wanted to stay in them forever. Because I was a kid in Sunset Cove again with my family and I was no longer a boring, grumpy old asshole who no one wanted to be around.

Here, I was free. And I wished I'd never, ever wake up again.

Rejects Park

ROGUE

CHAPTER NINETEEN

By the time the bath got cold around us and we finally had to give up on our little stolen piece of solace, the storm clouds were beginning to let some light through them while they raged. There didn't seem to be any sign of the weather breaking, but the sun was rising over the Cove, and I could officially give up on any attempts at sleep.

I borrowed a long, white robe from Tatum's things and loosely braided my freshly washed hair to keep the dark strands away from my eyes. Every time I looked at the brunette colour of it, I was reminded of Shawn and I hated that, but I wasn't sure if rainbow really fit me anymore either. So for now, I was going to tie it back so that I didn't have to look at it and I'd just worry about it another day.

I paused on my way down the stairs in the huge house, moving to the door of a balcony which looked out towards the road and chewing on my bottom lip as I searched for any sign of JJ or Rick arriving. They'd been stuck out there in that storm all damn night and the fact that they still hadn't appeared yet was making my gut churn with worry for them. Rick's phone was dead and although we could keep in touch with JJ, he was on the last of his battery too so we hadn't been able to call him for a while.

"Breakfast?" Chase asked, making me jump a little as he appeared behind me and I looked over my shoulder at him.

He'd borrowed clothes from the closet upstairs and was wearing a pair of designer jeans with a white polo shirt which not only looked ridiculously expensive, but also made him look stupidly hot. Even if preppy wasn't really his go to look. His freshly washed dark curls fell in a purposefully messy style on top of his head and I smiled a little to see that he'd put that much effort into his appearance. He'd always done his hair and cared about what he wore before Shawn had tortured him, and it was nice to see that little piece of himself reappearing.

Even if he was wearing the damn eye patch again. First chance I got I was decorating that thing – most likely with a picture of a butthole.

"Yes please," I replied to his question, letting my attention travel to his arms where the sleeves of the polo shirt strained around them before snapping my gaze away again.

My libido and my internalised self-doubts were at war with one another this morning and I didn't know whether I wanted to get closer to him or pull away. I might have been able to work through a lot of Shawn's bullshit with Chase last night, but the lingering belief that he'd made valid points about my value to these boys of mine wouldn't be shifted entirely.

Chase nodded, reaching out and brushing his fingers against my arm for the briefest of seconds before pulling back again and continuing down the sweeping staircase. I swallowed a lump in my throat, wanting to call him back as I felt that distance between us growing with every step he took, but I wasn't sure what to say or how to say it.

I love you. I want you. I'm terrified of having you and not being enough for you.

I didn't know why it had been so easy to confess so much to him in the dark of that bathtub last night, but it suddenly felt like I was choking on my own oxygen as I hunted for the right words to say to him now. I could tell he was offering me space after what I'd admitted to him about Shawn, and as much as a part of me ached to tell him that the last thing I wanted was space, another part of me was still just a terrified little girl who had already lost these boys once.

I looked down at the road once more and sucked in a sharp breath as I spotted two dark shadows running along the edge of the wall which approached the house.

They were little more than silhouettes through the pouring rain and dim morning light, but I would have recognised them anywhere.

"Chase!" I called, breaking into a run and hurrying down the stairs. "They're here!"

Chase whipped around from his position by the kitchen door and his eyebrows rose in relief.

"Really?" he asked, moving towards me as I leapt from the bottom of the stairs and ran for the front door.

"Really," I confirmed, reaching the door and disabling the locks on it before throwing it open just as the two drenched and exhausted looking men reached it.

Their eyes widened as they spotted me and a hesitant smile graced my lips a beat before JJ came at me. His body collided with mine so hard that I was knocked from my feet and only managed to remain upright because his arms locked tight around me as I was crushed to his chest.

He was freezing cold and drenched through, the water from his body quickly soaking into the thin gown I wore, but I didn't give a shit about that because the feeling of his arms being locked tight around me was one of the best feelings in all the world.

A breath of laughter escaped me as I inhaled the almond oil scent of his skin and I wound my arms tight around him in response, needing to cling onto him for a moment to believe that this was real.

"Fuck, pretty girl, we've been losing our minds over you," he murmured, his face nuzzling into my hair until I could feel the heat of his breath against my neck and the press of his cold lips brushing my ear.

I wanted to stay there like that, locked up safe in the cage of his arms forever. But as he drew back suddenly and I was forced to look him in the eyes, I could see that this wasn't just some instant fix to all the hurt that hung between us.

I could see the pain I'd placed in him when I'd left that video for them to find, and I could tell that my words had cut him just as deeply as the loss of them had cut me.

"I'm so sorry, J," I whispered, knowing it wasn't close to enough and flinching as he blinked hard and I practically felt him trying to shut me out.

JJ took half a step back, but I caught his arms as he tried to release me, my fingers biting into his cold skin as I held on tight and looked up at him, willing him to see how much I knew I'd screwed up, how much I fucking loved him and how devastatingly sorry I was for that pain I'd caused him.

Rick wasn't saying anything or doing anything, remaining in the doorway like a wraith while the atmosphere in the room seemed to plummet like I'd been dropped into a snowstorm.

"I..." JJ began before shaking his head and glancing over at Chase who was standing awkwardly to the side of us. I swear you could smell the sex in the room from last night and the thin white gown I'd stolen from Tatum wasn't doing a whole hell of a lot to cover up the fact that I was naked beneath it, especially now that it was wet too.

"Did Shawn hurt you?" JJ asked instead of saying whatever else he'd been going to say, his hands lingering on my waist, though I could feel the tension in his posture which implied he half wanted to move away.

I didn't know how to reply to that. On the one hand, I didn't want this fragile state of relief that hung between us to be ruined by the truth, but on the other I was so done with all the lies and half-truths that always hung between me and these men. I knew they deserved the truth of what it had been like for me while stuck with that animal, but all I really wanted right now was a little bit of time to bask in the relief of having them all here, safe.

"I can handle Shawn," I promised him instead of trying to downplay what it had been like to be stuck with that monster for the last few weeks.

"Not good enough," Rick snarled, drawing my attention to him where he still stood by the front door, not so much as an inch further into the huge house than that. He tossed it closed with a bang and I flinched as the dim light from beyond it was stolen from the room.

I'd been a coward up until that point, focusing on Johnny James because I knew his soft heart would be so much more willing to forgive me than Rick's broken one would be. I hated myself for the things I'd said to him in that video and a tremble of fear passed through me as I forced myself to look at him at last, to own what I'd done and to accept whatever consequences there were to that.

The only light on in the room was a single lamp in the far corner of the wide space so I couldn't see his eyes, but I could feel the anger pouring off of him in waves as he glared at me and the guilt and pain I felt over that sliced right into my heart.

"Rick-" I began but he cut me off.

"Give us the full answer. Did that motherfucker lay his hands on you? Did he hit you? Did he touch you?" he demanded and my lips parted on an answer which got stuck in my throat because I was afraid of what he might do when I gave it but I knew I couldn't lie to any of them now.

Maverick clearly wasn't feeling patient though and he strode across the room towards me, knocking Chase aside as he tried to intercept him before throwing his shoulder against Johnny's to make him move too.

I stumbled back a step as JJ released me, but my entire attention was stolen by Maverick as he closed in on me so fast that I could do nothing but raise my chin and hope he saw how fucking sorry I was in my eyes as he looked back at me.

Rick gripped my chin in his tattooed hand, the feeling of his skin against mine igniting the most sinful kind of heat in me as he tilted my head back so that he could inspect my face. I knew it was fucked up after everything I'd been through, but I couldn't help how it made me feel when one of my boys manhandled me like that. When they forced my body to bend to their will and took exactly what they needed from me. And right now, Rick needed answers.

His expression was cold, dead, furious and unforgiving as his eyes roamed over every inch of my face, his free hand pushing into my braided hair and making me whimper as the brunette strands tugged on the wound I had there from the car crash.

A low noise like an animalistic growl escaped him as he inspected the healing cut in my hairline and the yellowing bruises around it before he released his grip on my chin and inspected my neck instead.

He fell terrifyingly still as he drank in the sight of the bruises which marked my throat - by far the most angry looking injury I'd gained from my time in Shawn's company and no doubt they looked even worse after a night where the bruises had time to blossom fully.

A part of me wanted to duck my head in shame over the injuries I'd sustained while failing to kill that asshole. I'd done all that I'd done with that one, clear goal in mind. I'd sacrificed so fucking much for the chance to drive a knife into his black heart and save my boys from the violence he had brought to our paradise town and all I had to show for it were bruises on the inside and out. I'd failed. One fucking job to do to fix so much of the shit that had befallen us and I'd fucked it up. So what did I even have to show for all I'd put them through?

Maverick reached between us and I made no move to stop him as he tugged my gown open to reveal my naked body, his gaze roaming over every inch of flesh in search of fresh wounds. It wasn't sexual. It was just this primal, protective need in him to know that I was alright and for me to submit to what he had to do.

I let him tug the gown all the way off of me, feeling Chase and JJ's eyes on me too as Maverick took hold of my arms, inspecting them in turn, snarling at the cut on my shoulder before grasping my hips and making me face the window on the far side of the room.

I gripped the back of the white couch as I stood there and let him continue his inspection, my nails biting into the soft material as I watched the rain crash against the glass as his fingertips trailed down my spine. A slight sting made me wince as he brushed them against the angry bruise on my ass where Shawn had liked to smack me. He'd done it often enough and hard enough that it had caused that injury and I'd had to fight a whimper of pain every time he repeated it since the bruising had formed.

A length of silence passed between all of us as I just watched the rain pounding the glass and felt their eyes on my flesh. I was sure I had more injuries, healing bruises and scratches, but it was nothing too serious. Nothing compared to what Chase had endured. Though the weight of their stares on my skin had me shivering beneath the rage I felt simmering from them all the same.

Maverick picked up the white gown and held it up for me as he moved to stand so close that I could feel his breath on the back of my neck and I obediently slid my arms back into the material for him.

He stepped closer still so that his body pressed to my spine as he wrapped his arms around my waist before he slowly tied a bow to secure my gown for me.

"Rick," I murmured in a low plea, a shiver chasing down my spine as he finished tying the bow and lingered there for a moment, his lips pressing to my temple as he drew in a deep breath and his hold on me tightened for the briefest of moments.

I closed my eyes, a single tear tracking down my cheek as I felt the weight of the pain I'd caused him and regrets flowed through me in a never ending river. I wanted to take it all back, to return to the night when I'd made the foolish decision to try and take Shawn on myself and stay with them instead. Or better yet, to go back to the night I'd killed Axel and do everything differently so that I could have had all of them this whole time. But that was the foolish dream of a broken girl and there was no easy fix for the things any of us had done.

Rick released me suddenly, turning me around to face him again and taking a measured step back as he glared at me, no sign of any sweetness or love in his dark eyes at all as he folded his ink stained arms over his saturated shirt and raised his chin in accusation.

"Chase said that we were fucking fools for believing the things you said in that video," Maverick growled, his eyes on the bruises that surrounded my neck. "Is that true? Did you lie? I need to hear it from your mouth."

The pain in his voice was barely disguised and agony tore through my heart as I felt the hurt of what I'd done to him. What I'd done to all of them. My gaze skipped from him to JJ and lastly to Chase who at least wasn't looking at me like I was the worst person he'd ever known. And what a fucking role reversal that was for the three of them.

I forced myself to look at Rick again as I gave him my answer, knowing it was a cop out to focus on Chase.

"I lied," I admitted, a sob catching in my throat as tears slipped down my cheeks. "I lied because I couldn't stand being the thing that caused all of you so much pain anymore. I couldn't stand worrying about what Shawn was going to do to all of you and I thought that maybe...just maybe if I could get close enough to him then I could kill him myself and end all of this without any of you having to put yourselves in more danger than you had to."

Maverick's dark eyes lifted to mine but there was nothing inside them but pain and darkness. I'd done that to him. He'd shown me how deep the hurt ran in him, and I'd still run and left him to face it without me. But at the time, I hadn't seen another way. I hadn't wanted to keep getting between him and the men who always should have been his brothers.

"Did you fuck him?" he asked in a low tone which made a shiver track down my body.

"No. I would sooner die than let him touch me like that ever again," I breathed, and I swear I felt the others relax a little at that statement, but Rick didn't relax one bit.

"Did he rape you then?" he demanded instead. "Did he force himself on you, place his hands on your body or take what he wanted against your wishes?"

I opened my lips to deny it but hesitated the briefest of moments as I remembered the way Shawn's hands had groped between my thighs, how his fingers had been forced inside me and how fucking violated I'd felt from his touch. Rick took that beat of hesitation as some kind of confirmation and a roar of fury escaped him as he moved away from me and whirled towards the door, grabbing a chair and hurling it across the room as he went.

"Wait!" I begged, chasing after him and grabbing his arm as the others ran to get between him and the exit as well, knowing we couldn't let him head out there after Shawn now.

"Please Rick, don't walk out on me," I gasped and he turned those pain filled eyes on me again, before gripping my face between his hands and making me look up at him.

"Tell me the worst of it," he begged. "I can't bear the thoughts inside my head. I need the truth. All of it."

"It doesn't matter now," I tried, but none of them were going to let me get away with that.

"It does," Chase said firmly. "You need to get it out. No more fucking secrets."

"No more secrets," I agreed, another tear racing down my cheek as I looked over to my poor, beautiful Ace and what that fucking monster had done to him. I wasn't going to let Shawn win by allowing the time I'd spent with him to come between me and the men in this room. I wasn't going to lie for him either. They wanted the truth? Then I was going to give it to them. Every last piece.

"He was rough with me, pushed me around a little and groped me a bit. He…" I hesitated as the memory of his fingers pushing into my body against my will surfaced in my mind and bile lined my mouth, but I forced myself to tell them all of this. "He shoved his fingers inside me claiming he was checking I wasn't hiding any weapons from him, but he kept his dick away from me and it only lasted a few seconds."

"That doesn't make it any better," Rick snarled savagely and I nodded, fighting back tears at the memory.

"I know," I whispered. "But he didn't go further than that. That's not the way he works - he wanted to get into my head, fuck me up and break me until I was putty in his hands. He wanted me begging him to fuck me because I thought that was all I was good for… And maybe once that shit would have worked on me, but since I came back here, the four of you made me remember the girl I used to want to be. And I found the strength I needed in that knowledge to fight off the poison he tried to spread beneath my skin. I won't ever be the girl he used to know again."

"Pretty girl…" JJ said softly, moving closer to touch my arm, but I wasn't done.

"I won't be that girl," I said firmly. "And I won't be the one you all used to know either. They may be a part of me, but those parts are in my past and it's time I fucking grew up. I know the kind of woman I want to become and that isn't one who lets fear rule over her. So I'm sorry I fucked up again and I'm sorry that I hurt all of you, I really am. But I won't apologise for trying to protect you or for loving you enough to risk my own life for you. Because if it had taken my death to secure your lives then I'd have accepted that, and I need you all to understand me on that fact."

"Yeah?" Maverick asked bitterly, his gaze darkening as he drank in my words and I could already tell he didn't like the taste of them. "And what exactly did you think would become of us if you had died? If the only good thing any of us has ever tried to lay claim to had been ripped out of this world by that piece of shit? What then? You think it all would have been peace and rainbows and some happily ever after that didn't include you? How many times and in how many ways do I have to prove to you that you're all I ever have and all I ever will want? Why is it so hard for you to understand that without you I wouldn't want a fucking thing?"

"That's not true, Rick," I said firmly, holding his eye despite the pain I felt at his accusations. "I was never all you had. You had your boys too. It was never me and you, or me and J, or me and Chase, or even me and Fox. It was all of us."

"Always has been, always will be," JJ muttered like an echo of the words we'd spoken countless times in our past, though I could hear the mocking lilt to his voice.

"Yeah, Johnny James, it has," I snapped. "So we just need to figure out what the fuck that means for all of us now."

We all stared between each other in silence as the rain continued to pound against the enormous glass windows which fronted the house and lightning flashed to illuminate the crests of the waves in the roiling sea beyond them.

Maverick stared at me long and hard, this desperate kind of longing in his gaze which I thought for a hopeless moment might just have been enough for us to find a way past this. But with a harsh shake of his head and a snarl of anger, he turned away from me and stalked towards the glass doors which led out onto the veranda that overlooked the beach.

"I need a fucking drink," he growled, snatching a bottle of expensive looking liquor from a cabinet close to the door before wrenching it wide and stepping back out into the storm.

I made a move to follow him, but Chase caught my arm, shaking his head. "I'll go, little one. I think me and him are long overdue this chat anyway."

I fell still as Chase released me and headed out into the rain after the man he used to call his brother and as the glass door slid closed between us, I hugged my arms around my chest, trying not to feel the hopelessness that was attempting to drown me.

"Rogue," JJ said slowly behind me and I turned tearstained eyes on him as he reached out to brush his fingers down the side of my face. "Just…give us a little time. Yeah?"

My lips parted on a protest to that, but what could I really say? I'd fucked up. I knew it. They had every right to hate me if that was how they felt, and I had no right to expect them not to. So despite how much it hurt me to do it, I nodded my agreement and accepted the ache that tore through me as JJ withdrew his hand and turned away.

He headed up the stairs and soon the sound of a shower reached me as I stayed rooted to the spot, not knowing what I should even do with myself.

After a few more seconds of standing there in the damp gown, I crossed the room to one of the huge couches, grabbed a throw from the back of it and curled up beneath it, with nothing but my own guilt and failure to keep me company.

Dead Man's Isle

MAVERICK

CHAPTER TWENTY

The wind whipped around me as I took a seat on the veranda, the rain pouring down beyond it from the balcony above me and washing onto the beach. I rested my elbows on my knees, clawing my hands into my hair as I grappled with the knowledge that Shawn had not only touched my girl, left marks on her skin and did god knew what fucking else, but she'd fucking chosen to go to him. To hand herself up to him like a virgin sacrifice to King fucking Kong, and now the damage of that was spreading through all of us like a disease.

I didn't know what I wanted more; to fire a bullet into my own head, to get creative with a knife and Shawn's face, to see Rogue kneel for me and beg for forgiveness, or to just drag everyone in that house into the raging ocean and let it drown us all.

But for all the things I wanted to do, I did nothing.

I sat there and I fell into a wasteland of regret and devastation in my mind where all the mistakes of my past lived.

When fingers curled over my shoulder, something snapped in my brain like an elastic band against the inside of my skull and I grabbed the motherfucker, thinking of Krasinski as I reared to my feet and locked a hand around their throat.

Chase lost his balance on his bad leg, stumbling back into a white pillar holding up the balcony as I dropped my hand, my fingers burning with what I'd done.

"Fucking hell, Maverick," he growled under his breath, steadying himself as blood coloured his cheeks.

I hated that. His shame. Maybe I should have revelled in it after everything, but I was running out of excuses to hate these boys and the few I held onto were wearing thin. Chase may have betrayed Rogue, but fuck if he hadn't paid the price for it ten times over.

"You shouldn't sneak up on me," I snarled, ever the asshole. I wasn't going to apologise, because…well, maybe I was just stubbornly holding onto the hate in me. It was all I'd known for a very long time, and letting it go felt like it had all been for nothing. And maybe it fucking had been for all I knew.

"I wasn't sneaking. I said your name three times," he said, taking out a pack of cigarettes and lighting one up.

"Whatever. Here," I said gruffly, gripping his arm and pulling him down to sit on the bench beside me, not looking him in the eye.

I grabbed a cigarette from him, pushing it into the corner of my lips and lighting it as his thigh pressed to mine. The heat of his body was the only warm thing in my entire universe in that moment and I shamelessly leaned more firmly against him, some deep need in me demanding it.

Smoke coiled between us as we sat there watching the storm, the silence stretching, the rain as loud as a jet engine yet not nearly loud enough to fill the void between us.

"Do you wanna talk about it?" he muttered after a while.

"Talk about what?" I grunted dismissively.

"Fine, be a coward," he said on an exhale of smoke.

"Coward?" I spat.

"Did I stutter?" he asked, leaning back in his seat, looking like he had absolutely nothing to lose by goading me. But he sure fucking did; there was one good eye right there on his face for the taking.

"How'd you figure that?" I snarled.

He turned to me and I fought the instinct to look at him for several seconds before caving and letting my eyes drift to his face. His scars. They as good as cut me open and let my guts pool out on the ground.

"What are you so afraid of, Maverick?" he asked, not answering my question. "Is it so bad to admit you're still a human being with emotions?"

"What do you want? You want me to cry on your shoulder and ask for a back rub?" I scoffed.

"I just wanna have a conversation with you that doesn't involve you deflecting every real thing I try to talk about with humour or anger," he said, shrugging as he turned away. "But if you can't do that then…"

I was so sure he was going to leave and so quietly desperate that he wouldn't, that my hand snapped out of its own accord, locking around his arm to keep him there.

He looked at me once more, his eyebrows arching and my gaze travelled from his eyepatch to his good eye which was so familiar to me.

"He hurt her," I gritted out. "And it's her fault for going back to him after she ripped my heart clean from my chest. How the fuck am I supposed to deal with that, Ace? Tell me. Because I don't see a fucking answer to all this."

He swallowed, leaning back against me and it helped calm the furious animal in me.

"Honestly? I don't know," he said, toking on his cigarette again. "But I think it starts with trying to be something again. Somehow. For her."

"I don't know if I can, there's just so much shit in my head," I breathed, my fingers still tight around his arm as anxiety warred in my body.

"Then let it out," he urged.

I glanced away, my free hand balling into a fist. "It's like no matter what paths I take, I keep ending up on the road to hell. Look what's gone down since she's come back here. It shoulda been the best thing that ever happened but it's just a new way to be tormented. The nightmares in my own head were bad enough, but now they're playing out in real time and nothing I do seems to make any difference." I flicked my cigarette away, watching the sparks cascade through the air then the butt sizzle out as it hit the wet sand beyond the veranda. "I'd endure every day in prison again if it meant that girl was never broken, that she grew up happy and knew the taste of love everywhere she went. But instead of that, she's on self-destruct mode and fate seems more than happy to help her in her quest to be ruined. I get that she was trying to save us with what she did, but that's worse, Ace. Because I'd have given my life to stop her ending up in Shawn's hands again, but instead we're here sitting in the wake of her shitty decisions and I feel like I'm fucking bleeding inside."

Chase dropped an arm around my shoulders and I glanced at him in surprise, about to tell him to back off when I saw so much of my own pain mirrored in his gaze that it was a strange kind of comfort to remain there.

"We've all made shitty decisions," he said and I saw the regret in his gaze over that. "But Shawn is the reason for a lot of our suffering." His expression reminded me he knew about what had happened to me in prison, that Shawn had supposedly told him he was responsible for the guards who'd tormented me in there, the ones who'd placed me in the hands of Krasinski. And I'd been holding on to the rejection of that truth because I'd been so blinded by my hate for Luther, that I didn't even realise until Chase brought it up now that I had accepted that fact at last. My adopted father hadn't sent men to break me in prison, fucking Shawn had, and in doing so he'd driven a permanent wedge between me and my family. And I'd played right into his fucking hands.

"If we fall apart, Shawn wins," Chase said icily, dropping his arm from my shoulders as he took out another cigarette, flicking away his butt and lighting up the next. "And all I know is, Rogue's in that house feeling alone and miserable and fucking remorseful, and we've all goddamn been there because of Shawn, so instead of falling apart again like he wants, we need to start building something he can never break again."

"You really think there's anything salvageable here?" I asked, wanting to see it, though fuck if I knew how to even begin to move forward from this. But goddammit, I wanted there to be a way.

I was so tired of walking through this world alone, marching towards some inevitable lonely death that would mean nothing to nobody. My vendetta against the Harlequins had burned to ash before my eyes and I was only holding onto it now to try and give myself purpose, but there was no denying the truth anymore.

I still hated Luther for sending Rogue away when we were kids, but how could I really be angry at my boys anymore for not going after her? We'd been sixteen, and Luther would have been a step ahead of them at every turn.

Of course, Fox was still an asshole in his own right, acting like the king of the world, sending Chase out of town after he'd paid his debt in blood, treating Rogue like a possession he'd been owed his whole life. Nah, fuck Fox. But the rest of them…that was a different story.

"I guess we won't know unless we try," Chase said.

I released a heavy sigh, scoring my hand over my face. "Alright," I gave in to this madness, not having a whole lot of hope for this situation, but fuck it I'd try. I had one last push in me, and I'd give it to this, and if the world fucked us again, then I'd know it was time to take out my revolver for one last game of roulette.

"Come and talk to her," Chase said, rising to his feet and I nodded stiffly, getting up and wondering what the fuck I was even going to say. I couldn't just get over my anger, but I also knew she needed us right now, so I'd have to find a way to work through it.

I followed Chase inside and Rogue looked up from the couch where she was wrapped in a blanket, though I could see her shivering beneath it. She looked so like the young girl I'd known as a child with her hair dark, her face bare of makeup and her eyes wide and full of a thousand oceans.

Chase and I walked towards her and her eyebrows lifted as I caught hold of the thin blanket, tugging it off of her and dropping down beside her. Chase took her other side and I pulled her legs over my lap as she leaned against his shoulder and I draped the blanket back over us. I rubbed her calves as she curled them up against me then took her frozen feet and wrapped my hands around them.

"Are you still angry?" she asked me in a small voice.

"Fuming," I said simply and she nodded as Chase wrapped his arms around her from behind.

"Do you want to talk about it?" she whispered and I watched as Chase brushed his hand down her arm and she shivered, arching into his touch.

"You two had sex," JJ's voice filled the room and the three of us turned to look at him where he was standing in the doorway, his features cast in shadow.

I looked to Rogue with a frown, surprised as her cheeks touched with colour.

"Did you?" I asked in shock, my eyes flashing up to Chase as he adjusted

259

the eyepatch on his face, seeming all too fucking occupied by it.

"Yes," Rogue admitted, looking from me to Johnny James as she assessed our reactions to that.

I observed Chase, seeing the truth written all over his face as he gave up trying to pretend he needed to adjust his damn eyepatch any longer and looked JJ in the eye.

"How the hell did you know that?" I shot at J.

"Sex is what I do, man," JJ said like some mysterious fucking sex witch.

"JJ," Chase started. "I know you and her-"

"There's no me and her, is there pretty girl?" he said, folding his arms and looking like a damn psycho lurking over there in the shadows. He moved forward into the room and Rogue's face twisted in pain over what he'd said.

"Isn't there?" she breathed hopelessly.

"No," he said darkly, moving to the back of the couch and looking down at us, exuding power. "It's just *us*, right? There's no fragments, no jagged edges. There's you, me, Maverick, Chase…and Fox."

"Fuck Fox," I growled, my fingers clenching around Rogue's feet. "We don't need him. The four of us is enough."

JJ dropped his hand to Rogue's hair, gently brushing his fingers over her braid as she stared at me with a taut frown on her brow.

"It's always been all of us," she pushed.

"Not always," I scoffed. "You reap what you sow, and he sowed poorly."

"We all sowed poorly," Chase muttered.

"He's right," JJ agreed. "Fox has made mistakes like the rest of us, why should he be left out in the cold because of it?"

"And it's not like you didn't make him pay already, Rick," Rogue said, an edge to her tone over me getting Foxy boy to watch me and JJ fuck her.

I shrugged, stubborn as a goddamn mule. "Payback's a bitch, and don't you know it, beautiful."

I felt her shrink from my razor sharp words and I knew I wasn't gonna let go of what she'd done anytime soon. But I wasn't done with her. It didn't look like I was done with Chase or JJ either.

"You wanna play happy families? I'm in," I said, holding onto Rogue's feet as she tried to pull them out of my grip. "But I'm signing up for three best friends again, not four."

Rogue managed to wriggle her feet free and she pushed herself forward, climbing into my lap, wrapping her arms around my neck. "I'm sorry, Rick. Those hateful words I said about you were just that. Words. Letters strung cruelly together to forge a weapon powerful enough to pierce your heart. I only knew what it would take because I see who you are right down to the bones of you, and I thought wounding you once was better than the alternative."

Well damn, it was hard to hold onto my anger when she spoke to me like that. But I just about managed it, nodding stiffly and as she leaned forward to kiss me, I offered her my cheek like a prick.

She didn't complain though, her lips pressing to my skin and making my heart gallop like a thoroughbred racehorse. I wrapped my arms around her as she straddled me, holding her tight and inhaling her coconut scent.

"So what's the deal, beautiful? Are you fucking Chase now?" I asked.

"It was a one time thing," Chase offered.

"Yeah right," I growled under my breath. If I was being honest, I didn't really care that he'd had sex with her. The guy needed her as much as we all did, maybe even a little more. And I was quietly glad they'd sorted their shit out at last. "So what are we? Some sort of foursome?" I asked in confusion.

"Let's try being a family," Chase said, hope filling his expression.

"I'd really like that," Rogue sighed, sounding exhausted as she curled into my body, resting her head against my shoulder as she stole the warmth from my flesh and I offered it up to her on a platter.

"Sounds good to me." JJ climbed over the back of the couch, dropping into the space she'd vacated and wrapping the blanket around us all again as he scruffed Chase's hair.

Chase smirked, shoving his arm as they started tussling and I closed my eyes as JJ broke a laugh and the tension in the room lifted, allowing a small pocket of peace to arise.

I knew there were a thousand issues we hadn't dealt with but for now, I just wanted to hold my baby girl tight in my arms and make sure she knew she was safe. And when this storm finally blew out, I hoped some of our issues would be cast away with it.

Rejects Park

ROGUE

CHAPTER TWENTY ONE

"**D**o it!" I shouted, always the voice of encouragement instead of caution.

JJ winced beside me but said nothing as we watched Fox and Rick climbing the frame of the Ferris wheel, racing each other to the top while the old metal groaned and squealed its protests.

"Twenty bucks says one of them falls," Chase said, tossing a handful of popcorn into his mouth before offering the bag to me.

My stomach was growling after Mary Beth made me miss dinner in favour of scrubbing the bathroom floor because fucking Rosie had told tales on me for sneaking out with the boys last night. Stupid bitch was just jealous. No doubt I'd be in even more trouble now that I'd gone out again, but fuck staying in that dumb house with that dumb troll Rosie all night when I could be out watching the sun set with my boys. Mine. Not hers. Never fucking hers.

I took a handful of popcorn, tasting the sweetness of it on my tongue and knowing it only tasted better for the fact that we'd stolen it. JJ had expertly distracted the vendor who was set up on the rich end of the beach by falling over right in front of his stand and screaming loudly about his ankle being broken while Chase and I had dashed in and filled the biggest bag we could *grab with a mix of sweet and salty. Rick and Fox had been keeping watch but we hadn't even needed the backup in the end, and we'd run for it before the guy ever even noticed us. JJ had then made a miraculous recovery and caught up to us here at Sinners' Playground where we were all splitting the spoils of war.*

That said, as JJ took a single piece of popcorn from the fistful I'd just claimed for myself and placed it between his lips, I realised that he, Fox and Rick had barely touched it. Chase gave me a knowing look as he stuffed popcorn between his own lips and I shrugged. It made my heart feel all warm and full inside when the others did things like this, showing they cared without making a fuss. I knew Chase hated it for the fact that it was charity, but he never really blamed the guys for it. The problem wasn't them pitying us. The problem was the reason for us to be pitied. And as there wasn't exactly a cure for our own personal levels of poverty, I was willing to accept a little charity from people who loved me. Hell, I was just glad I had people who loved me.

"You don't even have twenty bucks," JJ protested and we all winced as Rick slipped, his left foot swinging free for a moment before he managed to haul himself back into place.

"I will when one of them falls," Chase pointed out.

"No deal," Johnny replied. "You still owe me ten bucks from the last bet."

"That doesn't count."

"Does too. I told you she was gonna get her tits out and she did."

"Her bathing suit broke, you can't count that," Chase growled and I rolled my eyes as they started up this argument again. It was pretty much all I'd heard about this entire week. We'd been people watching down on Sunset Beach last Sunday and we'd been making dumb bets on the kinds of beach goers they were. JJ had picked some wrinkled, over sun tanned woman for a nude sunbather while Chase had claimed she wasn't. Then by some random twist of fate, the woman's top had come undone and her tits had fallen out of it for the whole world to see. She promptly put them back away again, but they'd been arguing the toss over which one of them had won ever since.

"Jesus, anyone would think neither of you had ever seen a pair of tits before," I muttered. "If I get mine out do I get the ten bucks?"

I laughed at my own joke but the two of them stared at me, their eyes widening and making me blush as I realised what I'd just said.

"I didn't really mean-"

"Yes," Chase cut me off and JJ instantly thumped him in the arm, making him drop the bag of popcorn.

"Hey!" Chase complained, the three of us dropping down to try and salvage the bag as the wind worked to claim it and the seagulls swooped in.

JJ and Chase bashed heads, swearing as they lurched apart again and I snatched the paper bag, grabbing the last handful of popcorn from the bottom of it and shoving it into my mouth.

"Asshole," Chase snarled at me and I laughed as I chewed, fishing in the bottom of the bag and finding one single, golden piece left just as JJ caught the bag and ripped it away from me.

"It's all gone," JJ groaned and I scrambled back, holding up the last piece for them to see.

"Not quite," I taunted, waving it before them and I squealed as they both dove on me, pinning me to the wooden boardwalk as I tried to hold the piece of popcorn away from them.

"Give it here," Chase demanded playfully while JJ started tickling me and making me squeal louder.

"Never," I gasped, pushing the piece of popcorn between my teeth and grinning at them to give them one final look at my prize.

"You wouldn't." JJ gasped and I laughed just as Chase launched himself at me, grabbing my arms and pinning them down either side of my head as I tried to hold him back. He lurched towards me and my eyes widened a moment before I shut my lips over the piece of popcorn to keep it from him. But as he'd been going to snatch the damn thing from my mouth with his freaking teeth, that meant that his mouth hit mine.

It was a single second, a crash of lips and teeth and noses. But that second was enough to make my breath seize up in my lungs and my eyes go as wide as saucers.

He lurched backwards again, breaking the contact as suddenly as it had begun.

"Sorry," he said hurriedly, pressing two fingers to his own lips as I felt mine tingling with the sensation of his mouth against them.

"Did we just..." I trailed off, my gaze darting to J and back to Chase again as he scrambled off of me and started vehemently shaking his head.

"Can one of you fuckers tell him that I won?" Fox yelled and Chase jerked around to look back up to the top of the Ferris wheel where both he and Rick now stood, precariously balancing on the huge frame.

"Errr...it was a draw?" I suggested as JJ offered me his hand to heave me upright.

"Did Ace just try to kiss you?" he hissed, his brow drawn low as he tugged me to my feet.

"No," I gasped at the same moment as Chase did.

Fox and Rick were arguing over the win again and hurling insults down at us for not paying attention while Chase clasped the back of his neck and his cheeks darkened with colour.

JJ frowned between us but the sound of Maverick and Fox whooping excitedly drew my attention back to them just as they launched themselves from the top of the Ferris wheel and off the edge of the pier towards the sea below.

"Holy shit," I said, shoving between Chase and JJ as I raced to the edge of the pier, just managing to see the moment the two of them hit the water and disappeared beneath the surf.

Chase and JJ ran to grasp the railing either side of me as we all leaned out to watch for the others to emerge and the moment they did, a huge smile broke across my face.

Chase started cheering as the boys pumped the air with their fists, laughing at their daring and I grinned so big my cheeks hurt.

A startled cry made me jump as JJ caught hold of Chase's legs and shoved him over the edge so that he fell down into the water with wheeling arms and a cry of fright. I laughed louder at the huge splash which followed and JJ caught my hand in his, spinning me away from the view of the water down below and the sounds of the others starting up a violent splash war so that I was looking at him.

"Did he kiss you, pretty girl?" he asked seriously and I shook my head even though my lips were still tingling.

"He was trying to steal the popcorn. It was an accident," I replied though I couldn't help but squirm under the seriousness of JJ's gaze.

But then his frown turned into a smile and his fingers twisted between mine as he took my hand. "Then I want a kiss too," he said, making my heart pitter patter in my chest as I blinked way too many times at my gorgeous best friend and my unwilling gaze dropped to his mouth.

"What?" I breathed in surprise, but he was already leaning in and I was still staring at his mouth and for some insane reason, I wasn't jerking away or pushing him back or doing any of the things I should have been doing.

JJ's mouth landed against my cheek before I had time to process anything other than panic, his lips hot against my skin and making my stomach flip over in that brief moment of contact before they were gone again.

"There," he announced, his fingers tightening around mine as he drew back, his face a few inches from mine as we stared at each other for several seconds.

"Was it as gross as you expected?" I murmured.

"Worse," he breathed in reply, the corner of his lips twitching into a smile a moment before the two of us fell into laughter.

We looked down at the water where the others had entered into a wrestling match, dunking each other beneath the waves and splashing like crazy while their laughter echoed all around us.

I kicked my shoes off and JJ followed suit, the two of us climbing over the railings while still holding hands, and on the count of three we jumped together, the wind whipping all around us, sun blazing as it sank beneath the horizon and so much happiness in my heart that I knew I'd never need anything else in my life so long as I always had this.

"Is she still out of it?" JJ's voice drew me back from my dreams and I inhaled deeply, the scent of wood and leather wrapping around me as tightly as the strong arms I lay in and Maverick's deep voice rumbled through the chest I was currently using as a pillow, letting me know without a doubt that I was with him.

"She sleeps like the fucking dead. I could always toss her beneath a cold shower if you want her awake though?"

"Don't be an asshole," Chase muttered from somewhere nearby as the scent of cooking food reached me.

"Can't help it," Rick replied with a shrug.

"Food," I murmured, coming around a little more as the smell hit me more firmly.

"Should have known that would wake you," Maverick said with a snort of amusement.

I cracked my eyes open and pushed myself upright, finding mine and Rick's bodies tangled together and our hearts beating in time, even if the darkness in his eyes was still just as deep as it had been last night.

"I texted Tatum to let her know that we were still here," JJ said, drawing my attention to him as he strode into the room with two huge bowls of pasta in his hands and set them down on the coffee table. "She said to make ourselves at home and to borrow whatever clothes and shit we need."

"That's because she's awesome," I announced, pushing myself to my feet and cringing at the feeling of the slightly damp gown against my skin. It was particularly wet around my legs where I'd been crushed against Rick's drenched jeans while we slept.

I really wanted to demolish that food, but I needed clean clothes and to pee, so I scurried up the stairs instead, barking a warning at the others not to eat my food before I got back.

I made use of their fancy bathroom, stole a toothbrush from a pack of new ones I found in the medicine cabinet and rummaged through Tatum's enormous walk-in closet in hunt of something to wear. But as my hands skimmed across fancy dresses and designer jeans, I found myself aching for the comfort of something less pretty. Shawn had enjoyed dressing me up in skin tight cocktail dresses for his own twisted pleasure and right now all I wanted was comfort.

I hunted until I found a bunch of casual clothes, digging out a pair of loose fitting running shorts before stealing an oversized white tank with huge arm holes from one of her guys' things. There was a fancy ass accessories drawer where I managed to find an elastic for my hair too, and I tied my brunette hair into a high ponytail to replace the braid which was coming loose. Lastly, I claimed a pair of thick red and white football socks which probably belonged to another one of her guys and rolled them up to my knees.

As I jogged back out of the closet which was bigger than any bedroom I'd ever owned, I heard the sound of running water and glanced into the bathroom as I reached the open door.

Maverick stood beneath the flow of hot water, steam rising all around him as soap slid down his inked skin and I could only stare at him for several long seconds which made my heart twist up in my chest like it was being forced through a meat grinder.

He turned, seeming to sense my gaze on him and I licked my bottom lip as I fell into the trap of his dark eyes and the pain that waited there. I wanted to go to him, to wrap my arms around him and make it all okay again, but as my eyes fell to his body and his dick which was already at half mast, I hesitated, hearing Shawn's whispered words in my head and second guessing myself.

Rick fisted his cock like it was irritating him then turned his back on me, letting the water race over his dark hair as he tipped his face up to the shower head.

I tried to swallow the thick lump his dismissal left in my throat then turned and slipped away back downstairs towards the food. I'd fucked up. I got it. But it still fucking hurt to feel the brunt of his anger towards me simmering over.

Chase and JJ were sitting on the white couch, eating their own big bowls of pasta and they looked up as they spotted me.

JJ smiled, though it didn't fully reach his eyes and Chase patted the couch between them in invitation.

"Looking good, pretty girl," Johnny said, his eyes slipping over my comfy and seriously understated look and I grinned at him.

"I could do with some new GPRPs but it feels damn nice to be wearing something comfortable at least."

"I swear, if I never have to see the Green Power Ranger ever again, I'll die a happy man," Chase muttered and I gasped in outrage, punching him in the bicep as I dropped down between the two of them.

"Fuck you, Chase Cohen. Don't ever speak ill of the man."

"The man?" he scoffed. "He's the fucking man now, is he?"

"You were at the signing, Chase, so you know he's the fucking man."

I grabbed my bowl of pasta, crossing my legs as I set it in my lap, my knees resting on their thighs and neither of them complaining over the contact. I quickly began eating as much of it as I could as fast as I could manage, sighing in relief as the nagging ache in my stomach was satisfied.

Silence fell among us as we demolished our food, but it was the comfortable kind, the safe kind, that peaceful sort of solitude that you could only really achieve when surrounded by people you loved.

I twisted my fork through the final few mouthfuls of my meal, missing Mutt as I thought about tossing him the scraps. JJ had told me that Fox was looking after him and I was glad of that in a way because at least Fox had him. But I still missed my scrappy little companion so much that my heart wouldn't stop aching for him. I wondered when I'd see him again, but as no one currently had any idea of where Fox or Luther were, all I could really do was hope that they were all still okay and together somewhere safe.

Rick appeared just as I was finishing my meal, snatching his bowl from the table and dropping into an armchair opposite us as he began eating it.

"Thought I'd better hurry before the brat ate mine too," he said, jerking his chin at me in accusation as I scowled at his shorts and backwards baseball cap combo. No shirt. Nada. Just those ink drizzled cut abs and broad chest of his bare and drool worthy working to claim my attention. He was doing it on fucking purpose, I swear.

"I'm not that bad," I protested, but I hadn't quite finished my mouthful of food and a piece of penne dropped from my lips to land slap on the middle of the ice white couch cushion, instantly staining it with red sauce. "Oh shit."

We all looked between each other in alarm before bursting into laughter at the stupidity of the situation. Here we were, a bunch of assholes muddled up in gangs, vendettas and with the fucking cartel hunting us down, and we were worried about staining a couch cushion.

"It's fine, I'll just flip it over," JJ said. "They'll never know."

"Good plan," I agreed, finishing up my food and grabbing empty bowls from the others before heading out to the kitchen with them.

I dumped everything in the dishwasher then hunted in the freezer where I found some fancy salted caramel ice cream hiding in the back and grabbed five spoons from the kitchen drawer before heading back to the front room.

I took my spot back between Chase and JJ on the couch, sitting on the freshly flipped cushion and dumping the spoons down on the coffee table for everyone to grab as I sank my own into the ice cream and moaned around a mouthful of it with my eyes closed.

"You got too many spoons," Rick said, making my eyes snap open as I spotted the final spoon still laying on the table unclaimed and my heart sank like a stone in my chest.

"No," I replied. "That one is for Fox."

No one said anything for a few awkward seconds then JJ sank his spoon into the tub of ice cream which I still held in my hand. "Well, he'd better hurry the fuck up then. Because I'm not saving him any if he's late."

I grinned as Chase dug into the ice cream too, his shoulder knocking mine as he leaned in to claim a spoonful.

"If this is gone before he gets here then that's his own fault," Chase agreed and though Maverick shook his head like we were all delusional, he didn't disagree, just claimed his own spoonful of ice cream the way we always used to and sat back in his chair to enjoy it.

"I found a deck of cards upstairs," Rick said as we continued to demolish the ice cream. "I figured we need to clear the damn air. So high card offers up a truth. Low card takes a shot."

"I'm not really drinking at the moment," Chase said, glancing between the rest of us with a shrug. "So I can't play that game."

I smiled at him, proud of how seriously he'd taken his vow to quit drinking, but Rick sighed dramatically and started shuffling the deck of cards before tossing one face down in front of each of us. "Okay. So as Chase is being a little bitch, low card can take a shot *or* a dare."

"Seems like you'll all just end up shit faced watching me make a damn fool of myself," Chase pointed out, but there was a smile hanging around the corner of his lips which made something inside me settle into place as I just breathed in their company and let myself bathe in the fact that I was back here with them once more. Where I fucking belonged. And I wouldn't be dumb enough to fuck that up again.

Rick and Chase started bickering over how fair that made the game and I leaned back on the couch beside JJ as we took the opportunity to hoard the ice cream while they were distracted.

We watched each other over the tub, our spoons dipping into the slowly melting treat in turn.

"What?" I asked as his honey brown gaze intensified and a softness filled his expression.

"I missed you so fucking much, pretty girl. For a long time, missing you has just been this big part of me so now that you're here again, I find myself unable to look away. Like you might vanish again at any moment."

The unspoken hurt hung between us as we both thought of the way I'd walked out on him to go to Shawn, and I chewed on my bottom lip as I tried to think of a way to express how freaking sorry I was to him.

"I missed you too, Johnny James," I said instead, knowing that right now there was nothing I could do to fix the divide between us other than stay right here with him and prove that I wasn't going to leave again.

JJ blew out a breath and slung an arm around me, dragging me closer before leaning down to eat the ice cream from my spoon instead of his own.

I squealed and fought him, trying to get hold of his spoon while he kept his lips sealed around mine and we wrestled like a pair of dogs fighting over a bone before I managed to steal his spoon and take it hostage in my mouth too.

"Cut it out," Maverick demanded, smacking JJ over the head with a cushion before spanking my unbruised ass cheek hard enough to make me yelp and stealing our ice cream while we were distracted.

Chase laughed as Rick strode away and I scrambled to get out of JJ's hold so that I could hunt down my frozen sugar fix. But Chase caught my ankle as I started kicking and I found myself pinned beneath the two of them as they started tickling me instead.

I spat the spoon from my mouth and screamed as I kicked and thrashed, trying to escape the torture while they worked together against me, and I was only saved by the heavy thud of a bottle being placed on the coffee table as Rick returned.

The guys released me and I scrambled upright, finding myself bookended by them as they shifted closer on either side of me, my knees laying over their thighs as I crossed my legs again.

"How about I just keep hold of you like this?" JJ suggested, dropping a heavy arm around my shoulders. "That way you can't run even when your feet get itchy."

"I don't get itchy feet," I replied.

"You should have been an athlete," Chase objected. "You could have won marathons with all the running you do these days."

I pouted but I couldn't really deny it either. "Well I'm done running now. For better or worse, this place, this town and most of all, the four of you, you're it for me. I'm not going to deny it anymore. I'm home. So you're stuck with me whether you like it or not."

The three of them all looked at me like they wanted that to be true more than anything in all the deep dark world, and yet they also looked at me with mistrust, like they couldn't bring themselves to believe those words either. And that was on me. I was the one who had fucked up. I was the one who had broken their trust with my dumb ass plan that didn't even work.

"We like it," Chase said in a low voice, his hand landing on my thigh and squeezing for a moment before he pulled away again. I smiled up at him, reaching out to take the eyepatch from his face and casually snapping the elastic that secured it in two so that he couldn't put it back on before I tossed it away from me.

"Asshole," Chase muttered, reaching up to twist his fingers into his curls like he planned on tugging them low to conceal his face again, but I batted his hand away and leaned in to kiss the edge of his scar before dropping my mouth to his ear.

"If you cover your face with your hair, Chase Cohen, I'm going to take a pair of clippers to it while you're sleeping." I patted him on the head like he was a good dog and he huffed irritably but the corner of his lips twitched too.

"Well I'm not kissing you," Maverick said as Chase glanced his way, clearly feeling more conscious of his scars with the others than he was with me after all I'd done to prove to him how much I liked seeing them. "But I will make endless pirate jokes if you put the eyepatch back on. We can call it negative reinforcement."

"Great," Chase deadpanned and we all laughed as JJ gave me a little squeeze which I knew was in thanks for bringing a smile back to Chase's lips. But that wasn't just on me. It was us. Always had been.

"Let's see the cards then," Rick said, flipping his over to reveal a ten. JJ got a nine, I got a queen and Chase got a two.

"Of course I got the fucking low card," Chase grumbled, tossing it back towards Rick so that he could return it to the deck.

"Come on then, Ace, let's see you dance like Johnny James," Rick dared, grinning widely in a way that let me know he'd been fully fucking aware of who would get which cards. I bet the asshole had been stacking the deck while pretending to shuffle it, making sure every round fell in his favour too.

"For fuck's sake," Chase grumbled, pushing up out of his chair and calling out to Alexa to put Drop It Like It's Hot by Snoop Dogg and Pharrell Williams on for him. And of course the fancy ass house had a full surround sound system built into the damn walls so we were instantly gifted the song on full blast.

"Come on, dude, don't forget to roll your pelvis," JJ called while Chase cut me a slightly embarrassed look before shrugging and starting up a seriously exaggerated version of JJ's dance moves, complete with crotch grabs and overtly sexual faces that had us all howling and calling Johnny out until he joined in too.

By the time the song ended, I was bouncing up and down in my seat, wanting to get up and dance too and we left the music playing as Rick jerked his chin at me in a command, the sight of his bossy, domineering attitude accompanied by that damn backwards baseball cap making me want to do pretty much anything he told me to.

"We'll be having a truth from you now then, beautiful," he said. "No bullshit. Just something real."

I nodded my head, understanding the rules he'd laid out as I looked between my boys one at a time. "I love you," I said firmly. "All of you. And I really am done with running."

CHAPTER TWENTY TWO

I woke to the sound of running water and the scent of coconut under my nose. It was the first moment of utter peace I'd known in a long time and I held onto it with everything I had, keeping my eyes clamped shut as I drew Rogue back against me, my fingers brushing Maverick's arm where he held her too.

The huge bed we were in was big enough for us to all spread out, but we were folded together as tightly as if we were in a single.

After spending the rest of the day playing that damn game yesterday and me, Rick and Rogue predictably ending up wasted, the four of us had eventually headed up here to watch a movie on the enormous flat screen at the foot of the bed and I guessed we'd all crashed out together. Maverick had been straight up naked at the time after we'd dared him to do a naked opera show in the music room downstairs, and now his bare ass cheeks were peeking at me from the comforter which was pushed half off of him.

A grin pulled at my mouth. It felt like we'd stolen a day from our past, all of us just hanging out and laughing together like we had nothing to do and nowhere to be other than in each other's company. It was bliss. And the only thing that would have made it any better would have been if Fox had been here with us too.

The need for a piss was messing with my tranquillity so I sighed as I gave in to the demands of nature and opened my eyes, letting go of Rogue and slipping out of bed. Chase was missing and as I pushed through into the cavernous en-suite, I found him stepping out of the shower, scrubbing a bath towel through his damp curls. When he saw me, he clamped the towel tight in his fist, holding it against his chest so it hung to cover most of his body.

"You good, man?" I asked, heading to the toilet and taking the leak I was desperate for. I tipped my head back with a breath of relief as I finished and tucked my dick back into my boxers, glancing over at Chase when he didn't answer.

He was standing with his back to me by the long mirrors on the wall, buckling up his jeans and reaching for his shirt, though he was still dripping wet.

My gaze fell to the whip mark scars torn through the inked map of Sunset Cove on his back and my gut tugged with rage at the thought of Shawn doing that to my brother. I glanced up, finding him watching me in the mirror and he hurriedly pulled his eyepatch on, the strings that Rogue had snapped now retied together. Realisation struck me and I frowned as I strode over to him before he could yank the shirt over his head to cover up.

I gripped his shoulder, tugging him forcefully around to face me and ripping the shirt from his fingers.

"Don't," I growled. "You don't need to hide your scars. Rogue loves you as you are. *I* fucking love you as you are."

"JJ…" he sighed, looking away from me but I grabbed hold of his face and made him look me in the eye. "These scars don't just make me ugly, they've changed me. I'm never gonna be the guy I was. And Rogue needs better than what this version of me can give her."

"I think it's time we let Rogue speak for herself on that, don't you?" I pushed.

"Yeah," Rogue's voice reached us as she entered the room wearing a long black t-shirt that didn't belong to any of us. My jaw ground at seeing her in some other man's clothes. It wasn't like she could wear any of our shit considering it was dirty, but still. I was irrationally pissed about it.

"Morning, pretty girl," I purred as she walked over to us, her eyes hooded and her hair fucked up from sleeping in a heap with us. It looked damn good on her.

I caught her hand, drawing her into the arc of my body and she reached out to place her hand on Chase's bare chest.

"I told you," she said firmly, leaning in to place a brief kiss a scar on the side of his neck, making him stiffen at the contact. "I love all of this."

"I don't," he said and a snarl pulled back my lips.

I caught his chin, making him look at me. "You're a fucking warrior, Ace. We'll never be able to repay you for what you did for us, and if you think your scars make you ugly then you ain't seeing them right."

I leaned down, tracing my mouth over the scar Rogue had kissed too and Chase inhaled sharply as both mine and Rogue's fingers moved over the scars on his chest.

"JJ," Chase rasped. "Rogue…"

The door flew open before he could finish that thought and a shadow dominated nearly the whole doorway and for a moment I could have sworn Lord Voldemort had come to avada kedavra our asses.

"What in the ever loving fuck have you been doing to my house?!" Saint boomed.

Before we could answer, a tank seemed to collide with him from behind and a butt ass naked Maverick suddenly appeared as he knocked Saint to the bathroom floor, pinning him down and locking his throat in a choke hold.

"Rick!" Rogue cried. "That's Saint!"

Saint threw an elbow back into Rick's gut just as a tattooed beast of a guy with a topknot dove on Maverick with a roar, sandwiching his naked ass between them. I recognised him as the one of Tatum's boyfriends who'd gotten us to steal a squid statue and I was pretty sure his name was Kyan.

"Get your cock off of my Armani suit," Saint wheezed out from the pressure of both huge guys crushing him. "And get off of me this instant or I will have you both fucking executed."

"What the hell's going on?" Tatum appeared in a fitted pink dress, her eyes widening as Maverick and Kyan rolled off of Saint and started pounding on each other. Saint rose to his feet like the undead, brushing off his knees and

279

I swear his hands were shaking with rage.

"You have desecrated our home," Saint spat, turning around so fast I almost got whiplash, and Rogue hurried over to Tatum as her boyfriend stalked out into the bedroom.

"I'm sorry, we didn't mean to make such a mess of the place. We'll clean up," she said.

"Your standards of cleanliness will never be enough to purge this place," Saint cursed and I followed Rogue as she and Tatum jogged after Saint while Chase dropped down to try and break up the fight going on on the floor.

Saint was kicking doors open, crying out in disgust when he found any sign of us having been in there. I didn't know how the guy could tell where we'd been though, there weren't any obvious signs that I could see, but our dare games had led to a few explorations last night and we might have a spilled a bit of alcohol around the place.

When we made it downstairs and he prowled on, Rogue threw me a look that said oh shit and I threw her a wink back, finding this whole situation kinda fucking funny.

"Oh holy mother of fuck!" Saint lamented as he headed over to the grand piano. "Crumbs on my Bechstein piano. They're between the keys, I'll never get them all out!"

Oh yeah...I forgot we ate that whole pack of cookies in there while Maverick put on his naked concert.

"Is that a bare ass print on the seat?!" Saint screamed "It'll never buff out."

Tatum bit her lip, looking to us. "He'll erm, need some time to process this. He gets a bit of a bug up his butt about cleanliness."

"Sorry, we got carried away," Rogue murmured, her cheeks flushing and I smirked, biting down on a chuckle.

Tatum pulled her into a hug. "It's fine, really. I'm just glad you're okay."

Rogue squeezed her back just as Saint flung the door open again and came striding past us like a hurricane, holding his phone to his ear. "Rebecca, you need to come to The Temple this instant – I don't care if it's your mother's birthday, this is an emergency. You'll need to bring the strongest bleach you have and that custom made collection of vacuum cleaner attachments I bought you. If you do this for me, I will send you and your mother to any destination in the world with a ten thousand dollar spending budget – yes even Britain, Ireland, the whole of Europe if you want. Just be here within fifteen minutes." He hung up, heading into the kitchen where another cry of anguish left him.

"The couch cushion – oh no," he snarled then his footsteps pounded further away. "Argh – one of the silver knives I bought for your birthday is over here and it's sticky! Oh fuck me, they've been smoking on the veranda too! Tatum! Get Debussy back in the car. We'll have to go to the Saint Laurent hotel while the place is redecorated."

"Don't worry, I'll calm him down." Tatum winked, jogging away into the kitchen and I couldn't hold my laughter in any longer as Rogue turned to me with wide eyes.

I caught her arm, tugging her closer as she broke a laugh too, burying her face in my chest to hide the sound. "Maybe he won't notice the ass prints on the window."

"Goddammit! Look at the window, siren – look at the fucking window! That's premium tempered glass," Saint cried and I fell apart, catching Rogue's hand and running for the stairs.

"Come on, we'd better get our shit and make a break for it."

"Just like when we were kids, except instead of leaving firecrackers now we're leaving ass prints and pasta stains," she said with a snort.

"The ass prints he can polish up, but the pasta stains? They're gonna be a bitch to get out," I snorted and Rogue cupped a hand to her mouth as another laugh tumbled from her throat.

We met Kyan walking down the hall with a smirk on his lips and he held out a hand to fist bump me. "Hey, tell your friend to come to Slammers sometime. If he can come that close to beating me with his cock out while half awake, I'd love to see what he can do in the ring."

"Will do," I agreed as he headed downstairs, whistling lightly like he was enjoying the chaos and we stepped back into their bedroom. Maverick was pulling on clothes and Chase was fully dressed, bagging up the small amount of shit we'd brought with us.

"Kyan said we can borrow some of their clothes." Chase pointed to the pile of stuff I guessed he'd left out for us and Rogue grabbed the denim shorts and pink cami among them, whipping off the shirt she was wearing and immediately grabbing all of our attention.

"You'd better stop looking at me like that. I'm pretty sure Saint would murder us one by one if we fucked on his bed," she joked, but none of us laughed, all staring at her so intensely, I was surprised my ears didn't pop from the change of pressure in the air. Her smile fell away and a blush coloured her cheeks.

"Well you're safe from my cock, sweetheart," Maverick said.

"Shut up, Rick," Chase bit at him and Rogue chewed her lower lip.

I wasn't even sure what any of us were with her anymore, but I sure as shit didn't plan on making a move on her anytime soon. She'd gone through hell, and honestly? I felt like the dynamic had shifted with us after what she'd done. I didn't even know how to get my head around it, and though I wanted to let go of all the anger I felt over her breaking my heart, I couldn't simply turn it off.

"Let's just get dressed and get out of here," I urged.

I grabbed some jeans and a blue shirt from the pile, pulling on the designer gear while the others did the same.

When we had all of our shit together, we headed downstairs as a unit, finding Saint in the hallway, stroking his black cat's head and glaring at us as he pointed to the door. "I will bill you for Debussy's therapy session."

Maverick barked a laugh and I snorted, but it didn't look like Saint was joking as the cat turned its face away from us.

"And the ice cream I had imported from Italy for Tatum's birthday," Saint added.

Tatum rolled her eyes at him then waved to us. "We'll see you soon."

"Unlikely," Saint said coolly.

"Thanks for letting us stay here," Rogue said. "Sorry for the um, mess."

Saint's jaw ticked as we headed out the door and before it swung shut behind us, I saw Tatum sinking down to her knees behind him and bowing her head. *O...kay.*

We gathered outside the house and I frowned as I realised we had no plan.

"Well we could try and squeeze onto my motorcycle," Maverick suggested, nodding to it. "But I don't want either of your cocks pressing into my ass, so JJ and Chase will have to straddle each other on the back and Rogue can straddle me."

"Yeah, how about no, dickface?" I said, folding my arms and he flashed me a teasing smile which I couldn't help but return.

Rogue looked up at me and my mouth hooked up at the corner as I realised I didn't give a fuck where we ended up so long as she and my brothers were with me. Nothing was right yet, and I knew there were a few serious conversations we really needed to have, but I felt we were somehow on the right track to something good at last. But then I thought of Fox and missed him so bad it fucking broke me.

A whistle caught my ear and we all turned, finding Kyan watching us from the side of the house. He beckoned us over, dangling a key on his index finger. "I'll give you a boat if you do me a favour."

"What kind of favour?" Maverick asked, a smirk on his lips saying he was up for mischief. For a second he looked just like the boy I'd grown up with, always looking to get into trouble. "You want me to beat your ass again, big man?"

"I think we both know that's not what happened." Kyan grinned and Maverick grinned back. Dudes were bro bonding if ever I saw it.

"Where's this boat then, tats?" Rogue asked. "And what do you want for it?"

"Follow me." He turned and led the way down the side of the house, pushing through a side gate and leading us out onto the private beach. Maverick rolled his bike after us, clearly not planning on leaving it behind.

Kyan pointed to a jetty further along the beach where a speed boat was docked up beside a huge fucking yacht and hope filled me.

"You can borrow Speedy Gonzales." Kyan tossed the keys to Rogue and she caught them out of the air. "*But,* you have to fly this off the back of it when you leave." He moved to a large plastic bag on the ground, picking it up and taking out some folded red fabric. He unfolded it and the thing just seemed to get bigger and bigger until a life-size giant squid kite was revealed with several long tentacles blowing in the wind and flicking Chase in the face.

"What the fuck is that?" I asked in amusement.

Kyan beamed. "What's it look like, brother?"

"A giant fucking squid," I said and he smiled wider, looking like a predator as he showed more teeth.

"What's with you guys and squids?" I asked in confusion.

"Its meaning is important to our family," he answered with a shrug.

"Which is...?" Chase asked.

"How can you not know that?" Rogue asked him. "What are you, like eighty?"

Chase frowned at her before looking to the rest of us for an explanation we didn't offer.

Kyan laughed loudly, winking at Rogue as she grinned back then offered the squid kite to Maverick who gripped it in his fist, looking more than up for complying with this crazy request.

"Enjoy the boat. Bring it back whenever. I'll just go make sure Saint and Tatum are watching so they see the kite go up." Kyan grinned at us then ran off up the beach with a low chuckle.

We headed to the jetty and I helped Maverick get his bike on the boat before capturing Rogue's hand on instinct, pulling her down beside me on a seat at the back. I released it just as quickly, flexing my fingers from the electricity rolling through them, unsure how things were with us now.

Maverick moved to tie the squid kite to the back of the vessel before laying it down on the floor but when he started up the engine, I realised Chase hadn't boarded and spotted him standing beside the boat looking like a lost coconut.

"Ace, what are you doing?" Rogue jumped up, moving to the edge of the boat and holding out her hand for him. "Get in." There was a note of anxiety in her tone that made my heart clench.

"I...can't go back to Sunset Cove."

"First off, yes you can because fuck Fox up the ass with a dead goat," Maverick growled. "And second, Dead Man's Isle ain't Sunset Cove in my eyes, it's my domain. So you get on this fucking boat Chase Cohen and RSVP yes to my invite or I'll drag you back there as my prisoner and put you in my murder freezer. Your choice."

"The murder freezer sucks," Rogue added by way of convincing him.

Chase's jaw flexed and he looked between all of us, his gaze locking firmly on Rogue. "I can stay?"

"You don't need permission," she said. "This is your home. You belong with us and you're never leaving again."

Chase's gaze brightened at that and I smiled as he stepped down into the boat, letting Rogue steady him for a second. He'd overdone it on his bad leg when escaping Shawn's men and I knew it was troubling him this morning, but he'd grin and bear it just like he had with all the wounds his evil old daddy had placed on him when he was a kid.

Rogue tiptoed up to kiss him on the cheek and he slid his hand around the back of her neck, pressing his forehead to hers, the two of them looking so fucking right together I kinda wanted to snap a photo. So I figured fuck it and took one because good moments came far too infrequently for us these days, so why not make the good ones last?

Rogue fell still as she looked down the coast towards Sinners' Playground, the very end of the blackened pier just visible from where we were.

"Last I heard the cops were saying it was arson," Chase muttered, noticing where her attention had fallen.

"It was," she breathed, swallowing thickly. "Shawn dragged me up there and tried to force me to light the match myself. When I wouldn't, he did it for me. I couldn't stop him, but I keep thinking back on it and thinking I should have fought harder to-"

"None of that," I growled powerfully as I stood and tugged her into my arms, hating that she'd had to go through that.

"It was only rotting wood and old memories anyway, beautiful," Maverick added, leaning in to press a kiss to her hair for a moment before pulling away again. "And that fucker can't steal the memories from us no matter what he does."

"I'm so sorry." She dropped her head against my shoulder and Chase rubbed her back.

"None of us blames you for it," Chase growled.

"Nah. We'll just add it to the list of reasons we have to make fucking Shawn's death really hurt," Maverick added in a dark tone and I nodded my agreement, shifting her back to hold her at arm's length and make sure she wasn't still beating herself up over it.

"Just another reason to make him bleed," I reiterated and she nodded firmly, fighting off the tears I could see brimming in her eyes before I sat down again.

"Come on, little one. Why don't you forget about that asshole and launch the squid?" Chase suggested, the corner of his lips quirking in amusement.

I knew what he was doing. Our girl always valued a good game over anything, and putting her in the driving seat of this prank was precisely the distraction she needed to focus her mind on the good things we had going again. And as she smiled at the task he'd set her, my heart lightened, knowing it had worked.

Chase moved to sit beside me and Rogue picked up the kite, a laugh falling from her throat as she held it up and Maverick drove us out over the waves at full speed. A whoop left me as she lifted it above her head, letting go and it shot up toward the sky, the tentacles slapping me and Chase as it whizzed over our heads before climbing ever higher.

"Do you think they can see it?" Rogue called.

"I think the whole of the Cove will see it, pretty girl," I cried over the roar of the wind and the crash of the water as we tore across it.

"What if Shawn sends his men after us?" Chased shouted.

"I'd like to see them try to catch us in this thing," Maverick called, clearly enjoying being in control of such a powerful speedboat as it ripped across the ocean like a bullet.

I caught Rogue as she stumbled forward and our eyes met, full of so many unspoken words that they almost burst free from my tongue. But instead, I guided her down onto the seat beside me and offered her something from our past, trying to bring those days to life again once more.

"Would you rather have the body of a dolphin but the arms, legs and head of a person or have the body of a person but the head of a dolphin, a tail and fins?"

She turned to look at me with amusement glittering in her eyes. "I'd take the body of the dolphin so I could stay living on dry land, otherwise you guys would have to move to the ocean."

She leaned against me and took Chase's hand in hers, shutting her eyes like she was soaking in this moment. I forgot the game as I watched her, enjoying the wild wind and the feel of my family around me as Dead Man's Isle loomed ahead of us. And I basked in the peace that had eluded me for so long, silently swearing that if this lasted, I would never take a single second of it for granted. I'd show up every day for Rogue and be the man I imagined I'd grow into before the world had cursed us. And we'd build something beautiful from the ruins of our past, something unbreakable.

CHAPTER TWENTY THREE

I groaned as I woke, a headache sliding into my skull like a faucet of pain had been turned on and left running.

"Oooh, he's waking up. And he didn't even pee in the dick jar!" Brooklyn's excited voice reached me.

"Please tell me my dick's not in a jar," I said into the mattress.

"Okay, your dick's not in a jar," Brooklyn said loudly, then stage whispered to the others in the room. "Shall I tell him it's in a coffee pot or leave it as a surprise?"

"Nooo," I groaned, raising my head and finding my dad frowning at me from where he was sat with his back to the wall beside the bed.

"You alright, kid?" he asked and I glanced over my shoulder, finding my pants around my ankles, my ass bare and a coffee pot shoved up between my legs which my cock was chilling out in.

"I don't really know how to answer that right now, Dad," I said as I propped myself on my elbows and grabbed the coffee pot on my junk.

"If it makes you feel any better, Mateo put it in the jar, he said you'd prefer him to do it than for me to put my hand on your filthy stranger cock," Brooklyn said.

"Oh yeah, knowing a huge guy had his hands on my dick while I was unconscious makes me feel loads better," I deadpanned.

"Good," Brooklyn said brightly.

"I couldn't convince her against it," Dad muttered, not seeming nearly sorry enough about my predicament. "And I figured it was better than you peeing yourself."

"Well I didn't pee myself, did I?" I grumbled as I double checked that the pot was empty to make sure of that.

"Look away, chica loca," Mateo said from behind me as I tossed the pot aside and took hold of my pants, pulling them back up. I got to my feet, turning around and finding Brutus lying beside Brooklyn and Mateo with Mutt between his paws as he washed his head like he was some kind of dog royalty. The fuck?

"Do you feel better now, Mr Man Junior?" Brooklyn asked, twirling a dark lock of hair around her finger. "You had a really long snooze. At one point we thought you were dead and your dad started crying."

"I did not start crying," Luther hissed.

"He did too, didn't he Mateo?" Brooklyn nudged her huge boyfriend.

"Yes, chica loca."

"He agrees with everything you say," Luther said accusingly.

"No he doesn't, do you Mateo?" Brooklyn asked.

"No, chica loca."

"See," Brooklyn said, folding her arms. "Anyway, after he realised you were still breathing and you didn't die shamefully with your dick in a coffee pot, I continued with my show to cheer him up. And after he blubbered for a bit, it really worked, didn't it Luther?"

"I didn't blubber," he snarled.

"I don't know what else you'd call making a noise like this. My son, my sooooon!" she wailed then grinned widely as my dad glared at her. "Anyway, you're just in time for the end of my show, Pigeon." She clapped her hands and I assumed I was 'Pigeon.'

"Great," I said through my teeth, running a palm over my face as I moved to the window, looking out over the sea. "Did the dead guy get found?"

"Yeah, a couple of assholes came here to check on us, but they're assuming he fell in and drowned," Dad said and I smirked. That was one good thing anyway, that motherfucker deserved nothing less.

Brooklyn had started up her show again, leaping onto the bed and using the TV remote as a wand.

"Ex-smelly-armpits!" she cried like she was casting a spell. "Then he was all like pow – kapow – bam." She started punching the air. "And the Weasel boy went pop!"

The sound of a speedboat caught my ear and my heart raced as I tried to catch sight of it out in the water, but it must have been coming in from the south. Some of Maverick's men gathered at the edge of the beach and the way they were jumping to attention made me hopeful that my brother was the reason for that.

"I think Maverick's finally here," I told Dad and his eyes brightened as he stroked Mutt's head.

"Hopefully he'll charge his damn phone soon then," Luther said, taking out his own phone which he must have somehow kept from The Damned Men when they'd brought us up here. I did not need to know where he'd hidden that shit.

"And then! This woman with crazy hair was all like, "Your sister has to go to the Hunger Games," and Harry Potter was like, "that's not my sister, that's Barty Crouch Junior!"

"Ring him now," I demanded of Dad, unable to bear any more of this show with my head feeling like it was a casualty in a train crash. "Just keep trying until he answers."

He nodded several times, dialling Maverick's number over and over. *Come on, come on.*

"Then Cedric Diggory turned into a vampire and this sexy yet haunting music started playing that was like ba-ba-dum dum dum da da da spider monkey dum dum dum da da-"

"Hello?" Maverick's voice sounded down the line and I was so goddamn relieved that I snatched the phone from my dad and answered for him.

"Maverick, we're being held in one of the hotel rooms on Dead Man's Isle by your men and I swear to fuck if you don't let us out I'm going to climb down from the balcony and go on a murderous rampage across this whole island."

"Ooooh," Brooklyn breathed, pausing in her story. "Can I come?"

"Foxy?" Maverick laughed. "What the fuck are you doing here?"

"I'll explain when you let us out."

"Who's us?"

"Me, Dad and some…friends." Brooklyn and Mateo were a bit odd – mostly Brooklyn – but I'd sort of warmed to them too, though friends might have been a strong word to use.

"Hmmm. Nah I'm good. See ya-"

"Wait, you fucking-"

He hung up and I hit redial, grinding my teeth together as Dad watched me with a frown.

Maverick answered again on the fifth ring as if he wasn't right with his goddamn phone.

"Hello?" he asked like he didn't know who was calling. God he was an asshole.

"Let us out," I growled, trying to keep my tone level.

"And why would I do that?" he mused.

"Look, we just need a boat and we'll go. There's a couple of members of the cartel here who need to get off your island without any trouble."

"I see," Maverick said lightly. "Well I suppose I'll let you out then, brother."

"Good," I exhaled, my shoulders dropping.

"Just as soon as I hear you apologise," he continued.

"Apologise?" I spat. "What for? You're the asshole who-" I glanced at my dad, preferring not to go into the whole being-tied-to-a-chair-and-watching-the-girl-I-love-be-pounded-by-two-of-my-ex-friends situation. "Did you know what."

"Uhuh. Which you deserved for being an entitled prick," he pointed out. "But I never got an apology for you being a massive cunt of a sibling. So…"

"Just do it," Luther hissed at me and Mutt yapped his agreement as he nuzzled Brutus like the dog was his new best friend.

I sighed, running my fingers through my unruly hair. "Fine. I'm sorry."

"For?" Maverick pushed and anger seeped through my chest.

"Being a massive cunt of a sibling." *Fuck my life.*

Brooklyn had stopped performing, instead sitting on Mateo's lap and watching me like I was her new favourite TV show.

Maverick laughed loudly down the line and I blew out a breath of rage as he continued to laugh and laugh.

"You done?" I snapped and he finally reined it in.

"Alright, I'm done. I'll let my men know you can leave and have your cartel buddies escorted off the Isle. Oh, and I don't forgive you by the way." He hung up and I swore furiously, tossing the phone back to my dad.

"I'm not spending more than five minutes with him," I muttered.

"We might have to, kid," Luther said, rising to his feet.

The door unlocked a minute later and a guy with a tattooed face jerked his head at us in an order to come out.

Brooklyn dove forward to hug me and my eyebrows arched in surprise.

"I've had a wonderful time," she said, squeezing me tight and dammit, I couldn't deny I sort of liked the girl. "The best ever! I hope we can do it again sometime. Maybe we can camp somewhere cooler on the next trip. Like in one of those tree tents that dangle from branches! How fun would that be?" She pulled away, running to Mateo and fisting his shirt in her hands. "Can we get one? Can we? Can we?"

"If it'll make you happy, chica loca," he said and I couldn't deny their bond was weirdly cute in a psychotic kind of way.

There was another man waiting beyond the door who beckoned Brooklyn and Mateo to follow him and Brooklyn waved to us as they left with him, Brutus padding after them, his short tail wagging.

A couple of Maverick's men led us in the opposite direction along the corridor and Mutt snapped and growled at them whenever they got too close to him in Luther's arms.

We were escorted up a stairway to a large lounge that had a balcony overlooking the sea. My eyes fell on Maverick man-spreading in an armchair with JJ standing by the window and Chase beside him. I noticed they were all wearing some seriously preppy clothes and had to wonder what the fuck was going on. They looked like they were about to attend some sort of fashion shoot for Entitled Pricks Weekly.

"Ace." I stepped toward him with intention, my heart lurching into my throat in surprise before I stopped myself from going any further.

He's here. They found him.

Fuck, I missed him.

Chase looked over at me with a hopeful smile twitching his lips, but I lost sight of him as Maverick stood up, glaring at me as he approached.

"Look who it isn't," he growled. "It isn't the man who commands any respect from the men in this room, it isn't the man who deserves a shred of welcome in my home and it isn't anyone I give a fuck about. That goes for you too, old man." He gestured to Dad with his chin.

"Don't be unreasonable, Rick," Dad tried in vain as Mutt surveyed the room with a cool attitude.

"Unreasonable?" Maverick laughed. "You haven't seen me unreasonable, Luther." He spread his arms wide. "But I'll sure give you a show if that's what you're here for."

"Rick," JJ tried. "This isn't helping. Look at them, they've clearly been through hell." He walked over to Maverick's side and my throat constricted at how outcasted I felt from them all. But this was how it had to be now. And I was glad they'd found Chase, that he had them in his life. Because I was done playing king of the world and I wasn't gonna control their fates anymore.

"What happened?" JJ asked us and I released a long breath as I started explaining how Carmen had shown up and told us to leave town.

"You having some trouble with fucking Shawn, little Harlequin prince?" Maverick taunted me. "Do you need the help of your big brother to beat down your bully?"

"I don't need anything from you but a boat," I growled. "And I'm not the Harlequin prince anymore. I'm out of the Crew."

"Temporarily," Luther added and I shot him a glare.

"Permanently," I corrected and JJ's eyebrows arched.

"Really Fox?" JJ asked in shock and I nodded, unable to look at him directly too long without remembering seeing him with Rogue in that fortune teller's tent, her body bowing to his as she looked at him like the world began and ended with him.

Chase moved to stand beside them and my fists clenched as I took in the scarred X across his eye.

"Are you alright?" I asked in a low tone, guilt clawing at me over everything that had happened between us. The ruler of the Harlequins was partly responsible for that, the vicious son of a bitch who resided in me whenever I took charge. And I didn't wanna be him anymore.

"Yeah...look, Fox, something's happened," Chase started.

"I don't see why we should tell him," Maverick cut in.

"He deserves to know," JJ hissed, cutting him a sharp look.

"Know what?" I demanded, not liking being kept out of the loop here. I felt like I was standing on the opposite side of a ravine to them and it hurt like a bitch. But they had each other now and things were too fucked between us to change, so I guessed I had to get used to it.

"Rogue didn't betray us," JJ blurted and Maverick rolled his eyes, turning and dropping back into his seat.

I frowned, trying to figure out what the game was here. "Is that meant to be funny?" I spat, stepping forward but Luther's hand locked over my shoulder to stop me advancing.

"Fox...hear them out," he muttered to me and I took a breath to clear the rage in my head as I waited to see where the hell they were going with this.

"She lied," Chase went on. "I saw the video and knew straight away. When I was recovering at Harlequin House, she told me she was thinking about going to Shawn to end the war. I made her promise she wouldn't but...I guess she decided to make the sacrifice for you guys anyway."

I hunted all of their eyes, waiting for them to start laughing their asses off at me as I grew almost as desperate to believe those words as I was to reject them. Because if they were true, she'd handed herself over to fucking Shawn as a prisoner. He could have beat her, tortured her, *raped* her.

"You're lying!" I bellowed, panic slashing through my chest.

"We're not," JJ said, pity twisting his features as he stepped toward me. "But it's alright. We got her back. She's safe. She's here."

"Here?" I rasped, my pulse blaring like a siren in my ears, my hands beginning to shake.

Mutt started wriggling wildly in Luther's arms then sank his little teeth into his hand, forcing him to let go and diving from his arms. He hit the floor and sprinted out of the room with a bark of excitement like he'd understood what JJ had said. And suddenly I was following him, running out the door with a burning ache in me to see the girl I was so painfully in love with it was like an axe to my chest. "Rogue!"

Rejects Park

ROGUE

CHAPTER TWENTY FOUR

I spent way longer than necessary in the huge shower in Rick's suite, letting the hot water scald my skin pink and washing away any and all lingering remnants of the feeling of Shawn's hands on my skin, his words in my ears, the tainted taste of poison which hung in the air all around him.

He'd done a damn good job of trying to fuck me up while I was stuck in his company, but last night, between the arms of three of my boys, I'd found more than one way to chase him out again. And every time those thoughts or feelings he'd tried to force on me tried to creep into my head, I only had to remember what it was like to be held in their arms or the way they'd looked at me or the words they'd spoken to me to know that he'd been wrong about all of those things.

Maybe once upon a time I'd been that girl for Shawn Mackenzie, but with the Harlequin boys, I was always going to be so much more. And there really wasn't another opinion on this sweet Earth that I gave a shit about beyond theirs.

I finally decided that it was time to give up on my mega shower in case I turned so pruny I just slid right down the drain, and shut the water off before stepping out and drying myself on one of the fluffy hotel towels.

The steam had fogged up the mirror so I swiped a hand across it and tilted my head as I took in the brunette colour of my hair for a few moments, noticing the uneven spread of the colour where the cheap dye was already starting to fade and the rainbow beneath was working to peek back through. I'd only even coloured my hair like that in the first place to irritate Fox but now that I was back to my old, dark colour it was funny how much I found I missed my rainbow.

I wasn't sure if that meant I should colour it again or not though. I didn't want to be the girl Shawn had tried to break, but I didn't want to be the one who had shown up here jaded and hateful too. It had been a long summer. So fucking much had changed. So was I the vengeful, rainbow haired girl now or the broken brunette? Maybe I would have been better to just shave it all off and become a bald headed badass. It would certainly make my morning routine a lot simpler.

I glanced around for a set of clippers, but before I could go all Britney Spears on my long locks, a shout from somewhere outside the suite caught my attention.

I scrubbed the towel through my hair to catch any last drips then strode out into Maverick's room, grabbing one of his black tanks from a drawer as I went and making myself a dress out of it as I moved towards the continued shouts.

"Help me!" Rupert bawled and I frowned at the frantic tone to the gangbanger's voice as another one of Maverick's men shouted in reply.

"Ah! He bit me! You catch him, Dave!"

An angry snarl and a furious little bark followed his words accompanied by panicked yells and an all-out girlish scream from one of the men.

I rushed forward as my heart lifted with hope and recognition.

"Mutt?!" I cried, yanking the door open just as Rupert managed to grab my little white and tan buddy and heave him into the air by his scruff. "Hey!" I yelled, rushing out into the corridor. "Get the fuck off of him!"

Mutt snarled ferociously and started pissing with enough force that it splattered the front of Rupert's shirt. He swore loudly, shaking Mutt aggressively and I grabbed a lamp from a side table and took a wild swing at his head.

The lamp smashed against his thick skull and Rupert dropped Mutt who managed to hit the other guy during his fall and promptly sank his teeth into his leg so that he hung suspended from the dude's thigh while he swore to high heaven.

Rupert took a swing at my little buddy, but I shoved him hard and he slipped in the puddle of piss as I knocked him off balance before slamming into the other guy.

Mutt leapt away as they went crashing to the ground and he raced towards me with an excited yip.

I smiled widely, ducking down and opening my arms to him as he leapt at me before catching him and lifting him up to squeeze him tight to my chest.

His doggy tongue started licking me all over my face and I laughed as my heart swelled with love for my little friend and the relief of being reunited with him at last.

"I'm so sorry, boy," I murmured, squeezing him as tears pierced the backs of my eyes.

Rupert and the other asshole were scrambling to their feet and scowling at me, but I gave no fucks about them, so I just turned my back on them and headed straight into Maverick's suite.

I kicked the door shut behind me and continued to murmur apologies to Mutt while he wagged his tail so hard that his whole body wriggled and he continued to lick every piece of my skin that he could find.

"Of course the fucking dog forgives you for abandoning him," Fox's voice cut through my happy reunion with my dog and I froze, feeling his eyes on my back as my heart went to war with my ribs. "The little asshole won't forgive me for yelling at him *one time*, but he's all over you despite being left to fend for his fucking self when you ran off back to your ex."

I turned around slowly, my pulse this frantic, terrified pounding while my stupid muscles bunched and tensed as I fought the desire to just run to him and throw my arms around him, because I could see in his face that he wasn't looking for that. But it was Fox. *My* Fox. And I'd missed him so damn much I could hardly even breathe as I looked at him now.

"Is that really what you think?" I whispered, setting Mutt down as he started snarling at Fox and I whistled to make him back off. He obediently did as instructed and strutted away in the direction of the bed, leaving me and my badger alone to talk.

"Yes. You let him think he had something real in his life. You took him in off of the streets, got him used to regular meals and having a roof over his head, to feeling the intensity of your presence and bathing in the glow of having your attention on him. You made him fall head over heels in fucking love with you and then just like that you dropped him and ran the fuck away." Fox glared at me with such venom that my breath caught.

"Are you still talking about the dog?" I asked, folding my arms across my chest as I drank in the sight of him even if he was clearly furious with me. In all honesty he looked like shit. His dirty blonde hair was all messed up and there was sand sticking to his shorts. His muscular chest was bare, his tanned flesh marked with cuts and bruises and when I forced myself to meet his blazing green eyes, I found them bloodshot and rimmed with dark bags like he'd been out partying all night. Though I could tell that wasn't it. He'd clearly been through hell before somehow washing up on Maverick's island and yet I could tell he wasn't badly injured, so I was able to drink in the relief I felt at seeing him again even if it came with a heavy dose of anger from him too. He looked like he wanted to eat me alive, and I had to admit that this roughed up, savage version of my badger looked good enough for me to want to let him take a bite or two.

"Yes I'm talking about the fucking dog," Fox snapped. "You made him think you loved him, you made him think you'd always be there and then you just fucking left. Again." His voice cracked on the last word and he definitely wasn't talking about the dog, the pain in his eyes making the wounds in my heart splinter and break open.

"Fox," I breathed, stepping forward and reaching for him but he practically flinched, backing up a step which was enough to let me know how welcome my touch would be, so I dropped my hand instead. "Look...I know I fucked up," I started instead, chewing on my bottom lip as I tried to figure out how to even begin with him.

"Well I think at this point we can admit that we both fucked up," he bit out, tipping his chin up so that I was forced to look up at him and take in the difference in our heights. But I was plenty used to big men working to intimidate me and I wasn't going to feel small in front of a boy I'd literally watched tackle puberty from the front lines. His balls might have been big now, but I'd been around when they'd dropped and made his voice go all funny at random intervals for months on end, so he wasn't scaring me.

"Yeah, we can. So where do we go from here?" I asked.

Fox's brows tightened like he hadn't been expecting me to ask him that and I tried not to fidget nervously before him as I waited for his answer.

"I don't know. I want to see Shawn dead but after that...I guess we'll just admit that things between us were never gonna be what I wanted them to be, and I'll get out of your way," he said, defeat and acceptance falling across his features.

"What's that supposed to mean? I'm done running, Fox. So you're going to have to deal with me sticking around. And it's not like I *want* to be away from you, so why are you-"

"Well maybe this isn't about what *you* want," he replied firmly. "Because not everything in this world has to be."

My lips popped open in hurt at that accusation and I found myself falling back into the same old cycle I always seemed to fall into with this infuriating fucking man where he opened his mouth too many fucking times and I ended up wanting to punch him in it.

"How is *everything* about me?" I demanded, anger flooding through me as easily as breathing around him. And I knew why. It was all the unsaid things, the unfulfilled potential and the potent goddamn energy that bounced between us endlessly, aching for us to just give in to it.

"Open your fucking eyes, Rogue. Everything has always been about you. Even when we were kids, me and the others only ever had eyes for you. Yeah we loved each other, but we loved you more. We wanted you more. You were this thing placed up on a pedestal higher than all of us and we were all competing to win you." Fox swiped a hand down his face, cutting his gaze away from me then back again, like looking at me hurt him but not looking hurt even more. I knew the feeling.

"That's bullshit, Fox. That's not how it was. The five of us belonged together. It had nothing to do with me alone. That's why you, Chase and JJ were still together when I came back to town. Why Maverick was so caught up on trying to hate all of you for so fucking long, why my heart never stopped hurting over any of you in all the time that I was gone." Tears pricked the backs of my eyes but I fought them hard, needing to have this out with him and hold myself steady while I did so.

"Yeah? Well, my heart hurt over you," he said firmly. "Just you. You were it for me and I stupidly thought that maybe I could be it for you too. But after watching you with Maverick and JJ, it was made abundantly clear to me that you never gave a single fuck about that, did you? You just stormed right back into my life to tear my fucking heart from my chest before skipping back to fucking Shawn-"

"I went there to try and kill him! I wanted to protect all of you from him and I stupidly thought that taking myself away from you might protect you from each other too. I never wanted it to be just you and me because there was never an us without the others. It's supposed to be all of us, Fox. Can't you just forget about this fake, fantasy version of me which you've created in your head and try to remember the real me? If you did, you'd know that this was always how it was. That I always wanted all of you equally and I-"

"How can you expect me to just accept that? What hot blooded man can stand to watch the woman he loves being with another man? How am I supposed to just come to terms with that like it's normal?"

"It is normal," I hissed. "Normal for the five of us. We were always meant to be together, you know that in your heart. And yeah, now that we're all grown up that's added another dynamic to our group but why should it be any different just because sex ended up in the equation?"

I swallowed thickly, not knowing how we'd even reached this point again, but it was the one that he clearly couldn't get past. Not that I even knew if I was hooking up with any of the others anymore. In fact, I'd been making a point of not thinking about sex up until this moment where I was being forced to confront it again. For now, all I wanted was my friends back. I wanted to feel their love without their lust for at least a little while and remember the way we'd always been with each other. Figure out how to force Shawn's accusations from my mind and just *be*.

Fox fell entirely still as he stared at me and for a moment I had no idea what he was thinking, but when he spoke again it became more than clear that he wasn't able to hear anything beyond the possessive bullshit which raged inside his caveman head.

"Five of us?" he asked in a low voice and I realised what I'd just admitted to because clearly he hadn't known about Chase until now. And I could see how much that dawning realisation was hurting him again and that just cut me open. I hadn't wanted to hurt him any more than he'd already been hurt and no matter how much I'd been aching for this reunion, it wasn't going the way I'd been hoping at all.

"What do you want from me?" I asked in a low voice, so sick of always being the thing that let them down, that caused them pain, that failed them. "You want me to say I'm sorry?"

"No," Fox snarled. "Sorry is bullshit and we both know it. Sorry doesn't undo any of it. Sorry doesn't change it. I don't want empty apologies from you."

"So what do you want?" I demanded of him, losing the fine hold I had on my self restraint and striding towards him, shoving him hard in his stupidly solid chest and failing to make him back up so much as a step.

"I want you to be real with me. No more lies, Rogue. No half truths or attempts to save my feelings or protect your own ass. I want you to be fucking real with me for the first time since you came back here. Lay it all out. You owe me that much," he snarled, dropping his chin so that we were eye to eye and I was left with nothing between us anymore. Not the rage or the heartache or betrayal, not the pain or the accusations or the self loathing. There was only me and him and if he wanted me to be real then he could have every drop of my truth. Then we'd find out if he choked on it or if he had a taste for my brand of poison.

The anger slipped back out of me as I looked at him, my hands still pressed to his chest where I'd shoved him while he kept his arms firmly crossed beneath the point where I was touching him. I could feel his heart pounding through the hard muscle of his pec and I swear my own heart was racing to the same frantic tune.

"Fox, I..." I paused for a moment, caught in the depths of his deep green eyes while he tried to keep his guard up against me. But I could see him. I had always been able to see through all their bullshit, and I knew the truth of them.

He was my boy and he was hurting because of me.

"Don't try to spare my feelings, Rogue," he ground out. "Give me all of it right now or I really will know that you don't give a damn about me."

"That's not true," I breathed. "Fox, you're everything to me. For so many years I was out there just existing, pining for the feeling of your hand in mine, your arms around me, the security I always felt in your presence." My hands fisted against his flesh and I moved closer to him, breathing in his air as my whole body warmed with the nearness of him. "Being without you was like going without the sun - I learned to survive in the dark, learned to find a way through, but I never felt truly warm, never felt awake the way I do when I'm here with you."

"So why have you been fighting against me every step of the way since the moment you returned?" he asked, his arms finally uncrossing as I inched closer, moving my grip to his biceps and pulling us together while I clung on tightly in fear that we would be torn apart again at any moment. My attention fell on the hummingbird tattoo he'd gotten for me on his forearm and a shiver danced along my spine.

"Because I love you," I admitted finally, my gaze flicking up from that tattoo to his eyes again and his pupils dilated at my words. "I've been in love with you for my entire life and after you threw me away, I was terrified of reliving that heartbreak. I was so afraid that you'd just do it again the moment you realised I wasn't the girl you remembered. When your pretty fantasy version of me shattered and you got a good look at the fucked up, broken creature who was left in her wake."

"I don't want some fantasy version of you," Fox growled, his hands catching my waist before tugging me a step closer so that our bodies were only a breath away from being pressed together. "I just want you, baby. I want every dark and depraved piece of your soul alongside the light and the beautiful pieces too. You weren't the only one left adrift in the ocean when you left Sunset Cove. There has been an ache in my heart which never once stopped bleeding in all the time that you were gone. When you came back here, I only had to take one look at you to know that nothing had changed for me in all that time. You're it for me. You always were, like my fucking destiny, written in the sand on Sunset Beach, carved into the struts that hold up Sinners' Playground, tattooed into every inch of my flesh. You were always inevitable to me, which is why it's so impossibly fucking hard to accept that I was never inevitable to you."

He reeled me in a little more, his hands making the material of Maverick's shirt bunch around my thighs as his grip on me tightened. I could almost taste the kiss we were both aching for on my lips, but he had wanted me to be real with him and I wasn't going to back out on that, no matter how much I feared his reaction to my truth.

"I love you, Fox," I repeated and his throat bobbed as he took in those words. "But I love them too."

Silence fell between us like the strike of an axe and my grip on his arms tightened as I felt the tension radiating through him.

"Please, just hear me out," I begged, my fingers digging into his skin as the tightness of his posture only grew and the pain in those green eyes sharpened to points that cut right into my heart. "Think about it, Fox. Think about all the time we spent together growing up. About all the things we did together, the places we went, the laughter we shared, all of it. It was always all of us. I never picked a favourite because you were all my favourite. You have to know that in your heart, you have to feel it too. Surely when you were missing me you were missing Maverick just as much-"

"No," he barked, backing up a step and releasing his hold on me, but I kept my grip on him and followed, refusing to let him run. "I missed the person I thought he was. But I was furious with him too. When he selfishly decided to take off chasing after you, he put your life at risk - that's the kind of love he offers people. The selfish kind where nothing matters at all to him beyond his own desires. He cared more about getting you back for himself than he did about putting you at risk by coming for you-"

"And *you* care more about your stubborn, masochistic urge to claim ownership of me than you do about making me truly happy," I bit back. "About all of us being truly happy again."

"By entering into some kind of fucked up ménage à cocks where I have to watch my girl fucking my best friends whenever the urge strikes them?" he sneered and I flinched at that assessment of the love I felt for them. Like it was dirty, sordid, the exact kind of thing Shawn claimed it would be and what I'd been working so hard to convince myself it wasn't.

I wanted him to see it the way that I did. The way I was almost certain the others did. But I could already tell that this was never going to work for him, that he would never be able to put aside his stubborn sense of male pride for long enough to even consider what me and the others had come to figure out - that this had always been meant to be all of us. That none of us would ever be truly happy unless we were all in this together. And it fucking killed me that he was pulling away from the idea with such vehemence. But at the same time, I wasn't surprised either. Because this was Fox Harlequin I was talking to and he either got what he wanted, or heads rolled to satisfy his fury.

"It's not about the sex," I tried, but he was shaking his head and as he stepped back again, he pushed my hands off of him.

"That's not how it seemed when I was tied up and forced to watch you fucking JJ and Maverick while begging for more with every thrust of their cocks inside you," he spat.

I bit my lip, my anger over that fucking stunt Rick had pulled clouding my thoughts for a moment. I couldn't even think of the right things to say while Shawn's mocking laughter echoed inside my head, and I wanted to scream against the assessment in Fox's gaze which said I was a whore. "Fox please, it wouldn't have to be like that with you and me-"

He barked a cruel laugh and shook his head as he backed up again. "Yeah, just you and me when we're alone and the knowledge that whenever you're not in my direct line of sight one or more of my best friends probably has their dick inside you."

I shook my head, but what else could I even say? I wasn't going to give any of the others up. I couldn't. And if he couldn't accept that then there was nothing I could do about it. I didn't want to force him into something that would make him miserable, but the idea of giving up on him was ripping me apart inside.

Fox blew out a harsh breath and swiped a hand down his face. "Look, I only came here because I needed to know that you were okay. I didn't want to get into all of...well I don't even know what to fucking call it, but whatever your situation is with the others, I hope it makes you happy. All of you. That's all I ever wanted for you anyway, to know that you were happy, so I'm glad you found a way to be that." The honesty in his eyes surprised me, and I hated that I could see him giving up on me. No more possessive demands came from his lips, no more fight. He was letting me go.

I could already feel him shutting me out and the idea of that hurt so much that I was damn tempted to break down and start sobbing. But I couldn't put that heartache on him. If he was certain that he couldn't handle the idea of me and the others then I couldn't try to force him to accept it, even if I didn't know what it was I had with them anymore. I only knew in my heart that nothing was off the cards when it came down to me and the Harlequin boys and I wasn't going to make promises I couldn't keep.

"I just want to see Shawn dead now. I told my dad that after that I'm done with the Harlequins - he can hunt me down and try to kill me for it if he feels he has to, but I'm out. Once Shawn is dead, I'll be gone and the rest of you will be free to live happily ever after without me coming in and fucking it all up for you."

"What?" I gasped, my head reeling with that announcement, but he was already turning and striding towards the door, taking a chunk of my heart with him as he moved to walk out on me.

I chased after him, but I was too slow to catch him before he wrenched it open and there was a cry of surprise as JJ almost fell through the door, only avoiding landing on his ass because Chase caught the back of his shirt. Rick was with them too, the three of them so clearly eavesdropping that for a moment all I could do was stare at their guilty expressions before Fox snarled some angry comment at them and shoved his way between them.

"Fox, wait," JJ called as his old friend stormed away and I ran the last few paces to the door to watch as he just kept going, acting as though he hadn't even heard him.

"Shit," Chase muttered while Maverick sighed.

"That dude seriously needs to get laid," Rick muttered and I smacked his arm irritably.

"Stop being an asshole," I snapped, while my heart twisted with pain and my eyes burned with unshed tears. I needed to do something to fix this, but it seemed like everything I'd said had only made things worse.

"I'd better go after him," JJ said anxiously, making a move to walk away but Rick caught his arm to stop him.

"No. I'll go. I think it's time me and Foxy got a few things out in the open."

My eyebrows arched but Rick just ignored the shock the rest of us were expressing and turned to walk after Fox.

"That's either going to go great or end in one of them dying," Chase muttered. "My bet is on the bloodbath."

"Maybe we should follow them?" I suggested. "We don't have to get involved, but maybe we should be close by just in case it goes to shit?"

"Yeah, that makes sense," JJ agreed and the three of us headed out of the room.

I glanced back at Mutt but he just hopped onto Maverick's bed and rolled over with his legs in the air, clearly deciding he'd rather stay here and snooze than deal with our drama.

Fox had already disappeared up ahead of us and even as we broke into a jog, we didn't catch up to him on the stairwell, though we caught up to Rick as we made it to the ground floor.

As we reached the main foyer of the hotel, a voice called out to me which made me pause and had the others closing in around me.

"Nice to see you again, traitor," Luther's deep voice made the hairs raise along the back of my neck and I froze as I turned to look at him where he sat by the bar drinking from a whiskey glass with the bottle sitting beside it.

Maverick and JJ stepped forward like they were planning on shielding me or something dumb like that, but I just shoved them out of my way and took off toward the scary gang leader who I'd been terrified Shawn had killed.

Luther arched an eyebrow as he spotted me coming, his intimidating gangster vibe cracking as surprise broke over his face at my bold approach, though as I was only wearing Rick's shirt it was pretty obvious I wasn't armed.

I threw my arms around his neck and he grunted in surprise as I squeezed him tight, a laugh of relief escaping me.

"For someone who I used to dream was dead, I sure did freak out when I thought you really might have been," I breathed, releasing him and blushing a little as he looked at me like I was insane.

"Rogue, step away from him," Maverick growled behind me and I turned my head to look back over my shoulder at him.

"It's okay, Rick, I'm a big girl and I was going to have to face the music over this at some point," I replied, looking back to Luther and wondering if I might have been speaking too soon. My gaze fell to Luther's tattooed hands and I couldn't help but wonder how many people he'd killed with them. How much blood he'd spilled. I guessed I had to hope that mine might be more valuable to him while running through my veins.

"You already made sure I was unarmed, what exactly do you think I'm going to do to her in a room full of your men?" Luther asked curiously and Maverick's gaze narrowed.

"You know as well as I do that you're in no need of a weapon to kill someone, old man. And that the fuckers standing around us would be no match for you if you decided that you were feeling murderous." Maverick's hand grasped my shoulder, but I resisted him as he tried to tug me back a step.

"Less of the old," Luther muttered, pushing his fingers into his blonde hair. "I was a kid when I became a father to the two of you and forty is the new thirty."

"Yeah, so what's forty-seven then?" Rick taunted and Luther broke a laugh.

"Still young enough to kick your punk ass if I had to," he retorted.

"We need to go find Fox," JJ urged.

Luther raised his glass of whiskey, using it to point towards the door. "My other son was heading that way when he came storming through here like he had a crab up his ass. By all means, go help him pull it back out again. But I need a word with the wildcat."

Luther gave me a look which made it clear this wasn't optional and I could feel the others bristling behind me as they heard the command in his tone too. Chase's hand brushed against my arm like he was tempted to drag me away but wanted me to make my own choice too.

"It's fine," I said firmly, knowing I had to deal with this. The Harlequins were out for my blood thanks to my part in getting this man shot. I needed him to call the dogs off if I wanted any chance of being able to stay in Sunset Cove and that meant facing the music. I had to place myself in his hands and hope he was feeling merciful. That meant trust which meant no guard dogs

311

surrounding me for this conversation. "You guys should go find Fox. He needs you right now."

Luther arched a brow at that comment but didn't ask me for more details on it, he just waited to see what would happen.

"I'll go after Fox," Maverick answered for all of them. "You two can stay here and keep an eye on my dear old dad." His words were filled with a mocking kind of disdain, but Luther only seemed to hear the paternal reference and his lips hooked into a smug kind of smile.

"It's a private conversation I want," Luther reaffirmed. "But if you two wanna go sit on the other side of the bar and watch us have it for your own peace of minds then I don't give enough of a fuck about that to stop you."

I waited out the tense look the others exchanged while they decided what to do, and with a curse from Rick and some reassurances from Chase and JJ, they finally fell into line.

"We'll be right over there," Chase warned Luther while Maverick leaned down to press a kiss to my hair. I looked up at him as my heart fluttered at the gentle touch, wondering if he might be ready to forgive me for what I'd put him through, but the dark possessiveness in his eyes told me that wasn't the case and he was just affirming his feelings towards me in front of Luther as a warning.

"You lay a single finger on her and you're a fucking dead man," he warned his adopted father, the threat in his gaze proving he meant every word of that vow.

"You have my word, son," Luther replied and Rick scoffed like that meant little more than shit to him before he turned and strode out of the lobby in the direction Fox had taken.

Chase and JJ took a pair of seats by the long window which looked out onto the pool and I hesitantly dropped my ass onto the bar stool beside Luther's.

"Give me a glass for the wildcat then get some music playing loud enough to hide our words before fucking off outa my space," Luther said to the Damned Man playing barman.

He bowed his head to the authority in the rival gang leader's tone, slapped a glass down on the bar for me then strode away.

Luther took his sweet time refilling his own glass before filling mine up for me too and I watched his powerful frame for any sign of him being poised to strike, but aside from the slightly careful lilt to his movements which I guessed had to do with his gunshot wounds, he seemed perfectly at ease. Then again, so did a snake in the grass before it struck so I wasn't going to be letting my guard down too easily.

Bad Man by Easterly started playing loudly through the bar speakers and Luther took a long sip of his drink before setting it down on the bar and fixing his green eyes on me.

"I already heard an explanation of your actions from Johnny James," he began. "So I know the story you're selling them. But I wanna hear it from your mouth before I buy it myself. So tell me, trouble maker, why did you run on over to our enemies and how come you're still alive to tell the tale if you didn't truly turn coats on us?"

I blew out a heavy breath as I tried to think up a simple answer to that question and knocked back the contents of my drink before I gave it. The whiskey burned all the way down and I winced, scrunching my nose up against the strength of it before tapping the rim of glass in a demand for more.

Luther seemed on the verge of being amused as he obliged me and refilled my glass, but I left it waiting for me as I gave him his answer.

"I went back to Shawn because I know how he works. I know what he hungers for and I thought - admittedly foolishly, that I might just be able to play him at his own game and win. He wanted to break me down, put me in my place and try to prove that he could own me, and I thought that maybe I could take advantage of his arrogance and kill him. End this fucking war, take my goddamn shot at him and win."

Luther nodded thoughtfully and I took the opportunity to sink my next whiskey before looking him face on again.

"You shouldn't have gotten mixed up in it when I went to him," I said, hoping he could tell how fucking shitty I felt over what had happened to him because he'd been trying to save me. "I didn't want anyone to get hurt. And I swear I wasn't the one who shot you, I aimed wide - I just wanted you to run."

"Yeah, I know you weren't the one to put a bullet in me, wildcat," Luther agreed. "And let's say I'm inclined to believe the rest of your story. Why then does Shawn Mackenzie still draw breath?"

I sighed in frustration and shrugged. "Because unlike you, apparently I can't kill a man with my bare hands. At least not that one. But I gave it a good shot with a pen which stabbed a hole through his cheek, and I managed to misfire a gun at him. What can I say? That motherfucker is one lucky asshole. Maybe I'll have better luck next time."

"You won't be running off to him again," Luther said firmly. "I can promise you that. My boy has been a fucking mess ever since you walked into that fucker's arms. I won't watch him suffer that again."

"I'm not planning on going back to him," I agreed, though I absolutely was planning on getting Miss Mabel the hell out of his clutches. It probably wasn't the best moment to mention that though.

"Good. I'll call my men off then. Can't have them killing you right when you're starting to get things done." Luther took another sip of his whiskey and I frowned in confusion.

"You're losing me," I admitted.

"With my boys," he said like that should have been obvious. "Look at how much has changed since you started working to reunite them. Rick and Fox are off talking to each other now after years of being at each other's throats. We're here on Dead Man's Isle and I can tell it won't be long before The Harlequins and The Damned Men are united fully. You're doing good, wildcat."

"Errr...thanks?" I shrugged because I wasn't really sure that any of that was down to me trying to fulfil my end of the bargain I'd made with him, but if it was keeping my head off of the chopping block then I wasn't going to complain about it.

"So now I just need you to fix this shit with Fox. I ain't ever seen that boy looking as downhearted as he's been of late and I need him back on point. Stop all of this nonsense talk of him leaving the gang and put a smile on his slapped ass face, would ya?"

"I'm not sure he wants anything to do with me right now," I admitted because what he was suggesting seemed seriously unlikely to work to me. Fox was never going to accept what I had with the rest of my boys and I was at a total loss as to how I was supposed to make him smile again when I was the absolute cause of his distress.

"Nonsense." Luther reached out to ruffle my hair and though it was damn odd it was also kinda...nice? I'd never really had a parental type figure and though I was pretty certain he wouldn't be onboard with me deciding to start calling him daddy, I had to admit I didn't hate it when he showed signs of being proud of me. I probably should have been thinking about getting counselling for that sad little need in me, but for now I was gonna go with smirking like a smug bitch as my hair was scrubbed by my murderous gang leader pseudo-papa and not over think it. "You'll figure it out. I got faith in you, wildcat."

"I'll try," I said with a shrug, feeling Chase and JJ's eyes on us as Luther grinned and I lifted my whiskey glass to my lips again. "So what now? Am I dismissed or are we getting shit faced and dancing on this bar together?"

"Wildcat, if you think you can get me drunk enough to dance on a bar then by all means, give it a try. But when you're passed out on the floor and have to be carried back to your bed blackout drunk, don't come crying to me about your hangover."

"Ohhh, it's like that is it?" I asked, snatching the bottle and filling his glass to the brim for him. "Well bring it on, big man, because I wanna see you shaking your tattooed ass on this bar before lunchtime."

"You're on." Luther tapped his glass to mine and I smirked at him as we held each other's eyes and sank our drinks.

Was I likely to lose this game? Well, considering the fact that he was at least twice the size of me in muscle alone and seemed thoroughly amused by the prospect of me trying to win this, I would have to go with yes. But would I risk puking my guts up and collapsing on this floor for the minuscule chance of seeing him dance on a bar for me? Also yes. So it was game on, baby.

MAVERICK

CHAPTER TWENTY FIVE

I strode after Fox, following him at a distance as he stormed out the front exit and started heading in the direction of the beach.

My men stepped forward to apprehend him and he threw a punch at one of them, knocking him on his ass only to find himself at the end of several gun barrels.

"Let him through," I boomed and The Damned Men looked to me in confusion for a moment before doing as I ordered.

Fox didn't even look back at me, stalking down the path to the gate and I gestured for my men to open it as I continued to hound him. Why I was following him was a mystery to us both, but as he made it onto the beach with tension lining his shoulders, I realised what I was gonna do.

I started running, charging the motherfucker down and football tackling him onto the sand.

"What the-" he started in a snarl then cursed as I threw a punch into his kidney.

He rolled over, bucking me off of him and swinging a fist that smashed into my chest and knocked me backwards.

I dove at him again, cracking my forehead against his as he slammed onto his back beneath my weight.

"What's your problem?!" he shouted, shoving me hard enough to unbalance me on top of him before landing a rib-crunching punch to my side and I toppled onto my back beside him.

He shoved to his feet, sand clinging to him and his eyes full of some raw emotion.

"What do you want?" Fox snapped. "Do you want my flesh? Because here, take it. I don't give a fuck anymore." He opened his arms, offering himself to me and it kinda took the fun out of the fight.

"Oh, chill out, Foxy boy." I pushed myself to my feet, shaking sand out of my hair. "You're the master of your own fate. If you try and control the world long enough, it'll eventually break free and bite you in the ass. This is your comeuppance, and you can't stomach it because no one messes with the great Fox Harlequin's divine plans. Not even the universe."

"You've got the first part right." He shrugged, and I was kind of annoyed at how indifferent he seemed over me pushing his buttons. Like his buttons weren't attached to anything anymore. And goddammit that was no fun. "But the second part's always where you got me wrong. I don't think I'm the great anything. The reason I've done the things I have is because I thought I was protecting the people around me."

"Ha, and look where that got us all," I taunted, looking for the spark of rage in his eyes that I loved igniting in him. But there wasn't a spark, there was just a dark kind of acceptance.

"I know," he said, looking out toward the husk of Sinners' Playground across the water, an ocean of regret in his eyes. "I fucked everything up."

Sad, pathetic little Foxy wasn't nearly as amusing to me as stick-up-his-ass Foxy had been. What was his deal? Where was the possessive caveman who sought to steal my woman? Where was the guy who'd tried to rip the whole Cove apart to find her while I'd stolen her away and made her mine right beneath his nose? Where was my nemesis who I loved playing villain with?

This wouldn't fucking do. I wanted him crying over Rogue being back in our family and him being left on the outside where he deserved to be because he was a cock.

"Yeah, you did," I agreed. "You lost all your boys and Rogue. Now they're mine. And you're not getting them back." *Fight me for them.*

He nodded, his eyes still on Sunset Cove like he could see all his mistakes crawling through the streets and glaring back at him. "I think that's how it should be."

"What?" I blurted, shoving his arm. "You're just giving them up? Letting me fucking win?"

"It's not about winning or losing." He rounded on me and his eyes blazed, but not with the fight I wanted from him. "It's about them being happy. It's about there being a life for them that isn't full of pain and longing and loss."

"So you're giving *her* up?" I asked, my tone lowering as I realised the weight of what he was really saying. He was done. And maybe it was killing him inside, but he'd made the decision anyway because he thought it was the best thing to do. And for a second I remembered the boy I'd grown up with, how he'd always put the rest of us first and I wondered if that was genuinely what he'd been trying to do all these years. Even when it made him into a massive douchebag.

"Yes," he confirmed, not blinking, no hint of a lie in his eyes. "And I don't like you Rick, but she's told me straight she wants all of you around her again and I don't fit into that scenario."

"You could," the words slipped out before I even realised I'd said them. The fuck? No he couldn't.

He frowned, studying my expression and I found myself not taking them back, my teeth locking down on my tongue instead. Was that what I wanted? My brother to be a part of this? Surely fucking not.

"No, Rick," he said slowly. "It's not who I am."

"It used to be," I said, feeling my jester's mask slipping as I stared at my brother's pain and found I wasn't able to mock him for it. It was a damn travesty. "We all shared her once, maybe not in the way it is now that there's sex involved, but it ain't all that different really."

"Yeah, but if she'd chosen one of us back then it would have broken us just the same," he said.

"Don't you get it yet? She was never gonna choose," I hissed. "It was always all of us. And you may be a massive veiny cock wearing a crown, but she still wants you to be part of our family for some reason, so why don't you stop bitching and go make her happy?"

"I'm not like you, Maverick," he snapped. "I'm not made to share. It isn't who I am. I can't play happy families with you all and not want to steal her away. It wouldn't work."

"So you're content to let us all keep her and it doesn't bother you one bit?" I pushed him and his lips twitched at every one of those words, his hands curling into fists.

"I want her happy. I want all of you happy. And whatever shit's between us, I also know what you've been through and can admit you deserve a slice of something good too. So take it. I won't interfere. I won't say a word. I'm not your problem anymore. When Shawn's dead I'll get out of town for good and I'll never darken your door again."

But I quite like the door darkening.

I huffed out a breath, this whole situation boring as fuck.

"You're really out of the Harlequins?" I asked, confused as shit over that.

"Yeah. I took the crown off my veiny cock head," he deadpanned and he caught me off guard, making a laugh burst from my throat.

"I bet Luther's losing his shit over that," I chuckled.

"He's in denial. Just like he's in denial about us," Fox said, breaking some semblance of a smile, though it did nothing to brighten his eyes.

"Well he's always been as tunnel visioned as you are. Once he's got a goal in mind, there ain't no changing his view on it."

"Mm," he sounded his agreement. "So are you gonna fuck off back to your castle now?"

I thought on that for a second then shook my head. "Nah, you can't go wandering across my island alone finding all my secrets."

"Pfft, what secrets?" he scoffed.

"Well they wouldn't be secrets if I told you about them, would they?"

He rolled his eyes, his gaze falling to the Cove again. "Give me a boat Maverick. I'll take Dad and we'll head out to sea, avoid the cartel and circle around to dock somewhere up the coast."

I thought on that, scratching the stubble on my jaw. "Nah, I'm good."

His gaze snapped onto me, fury in those dark green eyes. "What? Why not?"

"I don't have a boat to spare."

"Bullshit," he growled.

"Yeah, it's bullshit," I laughed obnoxiously. "But I still ain't giving you one. Come on, asshole." I turned away from him, beckoning him along after me and I was kinda surprised when he followed.

"Where are we going?"

"Can you ever just not be in control anymore?" I tossed back. "Chill out, go along for the ride, what's the worst that could happen?"

"You'll lead me into that shed and shoot me in the face," he said flatly, pointing to the shed I was guiding him towards.

"Nah, I'm more theatrical than that. When I kill you, it'll be in front of all your loved ones. Bang, bam, bloodbath."

"Still planning on my death then?" he muttered.

"Always, Foxy. Always." I shot him a wink and he frowned.

I led him up to the shed at the crest of the beach and twisted the numbers on the padlock to unlock it, slipping inside and grabbing my surfboard before pointing Fox to another one in there. Since Rogue had bought me the board, I'd picked up the hobby again and I had to say it did me almost as much good as a nice bloody kill for my stress levels.

"There's a decent swell after that storm," I said. "Better make the most of those waves. You in?"

Fox hesitated, seeming confused by my ever changing moods and I was glad I could still keep him on his toes even when he was being an indifferent asshole.

"What are you playing at, Rick?" he asked, seeming defeated and I didn't much like that. I'd spent a long time trying to defeat my brother, but now that it seemed like I'd won, the victory tasted kind of bitter.

"Surf with me," I pushed and his jaw ticked as he considered his answer.

He grabbed a board and I smirked, leading the way down the beach to where the best waves were. I stripped down to my shorts, the two of us heading out into the water and paddling beyond the break without another word passing between us.

As we turned our boards, ready to catch the wave rising behind us, I made a decision to cut through this accepting bullshit Fox was feeding me. Because I wanted him trying to steal my woman away in the night like the possessor of her soul he'd always believed he was. I wanted to dangle her in front of him and awaken that fierce creature in him who would never have given her up for any prize. And if I had to be a prime asshole to do it, then all the better. Because being an asshole was what I did best.

By the time we headed back to the hotel, we were dripping wet and the sun was beating down on our backs as we made it to the front gate. We hadn't really spoken much apart from the odd comment about the surf, so I'd used the time to come up with my wicked plans to get my arch enemy brother back. Which mostly involved baiting him to no end.

After we'd showered and dressed in some dry shorts and shirts, we sought out the others, finding them all gathered in the lounge.

Luther was sat alone on one side of the space, looking like he was dozing in his chair, his head bowed low and his phone loose between his fingers.

Rogue was lying on a couch with her head in Chase's lap and her feet draped over JJ, giggling at something they were saying. They looked over as we entered and Fox split off from me to go and sit near Luther, moving like a soldier on a mission of war. I strode casually over to join the others scooping Rogue up and sitting between JJ and Chase as I placed her down beside me.

"Where've you been?" she murmured, sniffing me like she could smell the soap on my flesh and I caught the scent of whiskey on her in return.

"Me and Foxy boy went for a surf," I said with a shrug and she smiled hopefully, leaning in to whisper to me.

"Did you make up with him? Is he gonna be my badger again?"

"Nope," I said and her smile vanished.

Having her this close was the darkest kind of temptation and my eyes lingered way too long on her mouth, the urge to steal a kiss almost enough to break me. But I didn't, I held firm, my anger with her too sharp to be ignored and I turned away, finding Foxy boy watching us. Well I couldn't kiss her, but I could sure as fuck touch her.

I laid my hand on her knee and heard her breath hitch a little as I dug my fingers in. It felt so fucking good, this contact, but I wasn't fool enough to take it further. Fox watched our interaction with green, green envy in his eyes, though he locked that shit down faster than a seagull's asshole in the face of an approaching storm.

"I should talk to him." Rogue tried to get up, but I pressed my hand down harder, not letting her go.

"Nah, he's good. Aren't you Foxy?" I asked loudly.

He grunted in response and JJ looked at me in my periphery, shifting forward in his seat anxiously like he wanted to go over to Fox and I had to pity the asshole. I swear he was pining for the guy.

"Have you been drinking, beautiful?" I asked curiously and Chase chuckled darkly as she shook her head in false innocence.

"She's shit faced," he supplied. "She started a drinking game with Luther after they kissed and made up."

"Is that so?" I asked, eyeing Luther with interest and noting the fact that he hadn't roused despite us arriving and talking loudly right by him.

"I won." Rogue grinned at me and I was once again damn tempted to kiss those smiling lips, devour that taste of happiness on her mouth and steal it for my own.

I managed not to, satisfying my need for her by tightening my hold on her instead.

"She didn't," JJ said. "Which is a damn shame because I would have loved to see your dad dancing on that bar."

My lips twitched with a smile and I found myself wishing she'd won too.

"He's not my dad," I muttered but I didn't bother making more of a fuss than that.

Luther's phone started ringing and he jerked awake in his seat, looking like he was about to start a fight before he realised what had happened.

I released a dark laugh. "You alright there, old man? Nodded off for a second, did ya?"

"Fuck off. I ain't old. I got no sleep last night," Luther said, shooting me a parental glare.

"Sure, sure. I don't see Foxy curling up in a chair with a blanket though," I teased.

"I don't have a fucking blanket," he said, shoving one of my hoodies off his knees onto the floor like that proved he hadn't been snuggling up with it. He pawed at his hair as he looked at his phone, the thing continuing to ring.

"You gonna answer that?" Fox asked.

"Yeah, yeah just gimme a sec." Luther continued patting his hair down and smoothing the dark blonde beard covering his chin.

I watched the display in confusion, trying to figure out what he was playing at. Was he...preening? I swear to fuck, I had never seen my adopted father give a damn about what he looked like a day in my life. Apart from keeping himself vaguely neat and tidy, he spent all of ten seconds looking in the mirror in the mornings. So what the hell was this?

"Who is it, Luther?" Rogue asked, seeming excited about something as she got to her feet and padded across the room to him.

"Carmen Ortega," he said offhandedly, but my eyes locked with Fox in that second as he thought the same thing. Does Luther Harlequin have a fucking crush on the cartel boss bitch? There was no way. He hated women.

"Oooooh," Rogue cooed and I pushed to my feet, moving closer so that I could watch this video call play out from the front lines.

"Shut up," Luther muttered then hit answer at last and Carmen's stunning face filled the screen.

"If you ever keep me waiting that long again, Luther, I will castrate you," Carmen said icily and Luther's face twisted into a deep frown.

"I was busy, Carmen. I'm not always at your beck and call."

"Busy doing his hair," JJ murmured and I snorted.

Had Luther really developed a crush on the most ruthless woman on the west coast? Jesus fucking Christ. Talk about unobtainable. I wouldn't have been surprised if she ate the heads of the men she fucked like a praying mantis. I supposed that would solve my little Daddy issue though if he could get her into bed, but it wouldn't be as satisfying as killing him myself.

My eyes drifted to him again and I cursed myself out in my head. He was right there. I could have carved him up fifty ways by now, but had I? No, I continued to let him keep breathing. And fuck knew why.

"I'm glad you're all together because it is time for you to repay me for saving your lives. Listen to me closely because I will only say this once," Carmen said sharply, gaining the attention of everyone in the room.

Rogue drifted nearer to peek over Luther's shoulder, raising her fingers in a little wave that Carmen actually fucking returned. What the hell? Was that because of the alcohol swimming in her system or was she actually on friendly terms with that woman?

"The boat that Rogue and her friends sunk all those years ago held a ledger on it full of incriminating information against the Castillo Cartel," she said, her voice dipped in poison. "They don't care about the people who died on its decks, it's the lost ledger they are hunting for. And they fear whoever sank that boat has it."

"We don't have anything. Shawn gave you the only things we took from that boat, I swear," Rogue said as Fox moved to stand beside her so he could be in on the conversation. Their arms brushed and they both jolted a little before Fox pulled away and I could practically see the energy charged in the air between them.

"Si, I am quite aware of that," Carmen said. "It was in a watertight safe, the combination of which was known only by very few people. The cartel have been searching for the site of the wreck for many years, only there were no witnesses to its sinking…until now. I am not fool enough to believe you have exact coordinates, but if you have even a vague location-"

"We don't have coordinates exactly, but we do have a location," Chase piped up and we all looked over at him with a frown.

Chase stood up, turning around and lifting his shirt, pointing to the base of his back where the inked shore of Sunset Cove met with the sea. Within the curling waves which were sliced through with scars was an island shaped like a tiger's head with jagged rocks splitting out of the water around it and one in particular arched up like a jagged claw.

"Isla Tigre," JJ breathed and Chase nodded, dropping his shirt as he turned around again.

"It wasn't far from there, I remember that rock formation was close because JJ said it looked like a whale's cock and Rogue said-"

"That it was more like a beluga dick!" she cried excitedly and Chase chuckled as my lips tipped up in a smirk.

"And I said that's the same thing because a beluga is a whale," JJ said with a grin and I could see this old argument was about to break out again.

"It's an overgrown dolphin," Rogue pushed.

"So you have a location?" Carmen cut in, a note of excitement to her voice though there was no hint of it on her face.

"I guess so," Fox said with a shrug.

"If the cartel get that ledger back, are my family off the hook?" Luther asked and I had the feeling he was including everyone in this room in that word. Family? Fuck off.

Carmen laughed wickedly, shaking her head. "Oh Luther, you silly boy."

Luther's jaw tensed and the back of his neck reddened with anger.

"The cartel will do no such thing," Carmen went on. "But if those who lost that ledger were to find it…well, perhaps the cartel would not be so hungry for blood anymore."

"So if we get it, we can go back to the Cove?" Rogue asked keenly and I saw the bloodlust in her eyes. There was only one reason she wanted to get back there so soon and I knew it was Shawn's death. It made my cock harden at the thought of seeing her standing over his bloody corpse, a knife in hand and a look of wild, unbridled violence in her gaze. Yeah, I might just be forgiving enough to fuck her over his dead body the second he stopped breathing. Maybe a little before.

"If you can retrieve it, I highly doubt the cartel will care much what you do. I might even be able to encourage them to leave town, so that only me and my closest men remain once more and then Shawn will be exposed and who knows what will happen next? That is really up to you, rainbow child."

"Alright, I'll figure this out, then I can round up my men and return the town to its rightful owners," Luther said firmly.

Carmen turned her gaze on Luther again and all the warmth she aimed at Rogue fled from her expression. "Perhaps you'd do better listening to the plans of the only female member of your Crew, Luther. You built your castle on the sand and your empire has fallen to ruin beneath your feet when faced with a single wave of adversity. I suggest you seek better foundations in future."

She hung up and silence fell hard. I could almost hear the metaphorical slap to Luther's face and started laughing at his expense as his fingernails tore into the arm of the chair.

"I really hate that woman," he growled, shoving to his feet.

"Really? I'm kind of in love with her," Rogue sighed. "I bet if someone punched her in the face she'd just stand there smiling and bleeding. She's such a badass."

Luther grumbled something then caught Fox's arm, drawing him toward the door.

"And where the fuck do you think you two are going?" I demanded, rising from my seat.

"To talk business," Luther said. "You're welcome to join too, Rick. In fact, there's something I need to talk to you both about anyway."

"You talk in front of all of us or not at all," I gritted out.

"It sounds sort of boring anyway, so I'm gonna head to the pool," Rogue said, heading for the door, stumbling a little thanks to the drinks she'd consumed.

JJ hopped up too and pulled Chase up after him. "We're coming."

She smiled at them as they followed her out of the room and I went to follow too before Luther stepped into my way.

"Rick, this really is important," he said, his brows drawing together. "After I was shot, I thought on this a lot. And I really think it's time we discussed it."

"I'm not interested," I said with a shrug, skirting around him and striding to the door.

"It's about where you came from," he called after me, making my heart trip over itself and fall down a flight of fifty stairs.

"What d'you say?" I growled, not turning back but my feet had halted.

"Your father wasn't some random crew member, Rick," Luther said in a low voice.

"What are you talking about?" Fox asked in confusion and despite myself, I turned back to look at my adopted father.

Luther moved to sit on the couch, gesturing for us to sit opposite him and both of us resisted. But the weight of the secrets I could feel hanging in the air made me go against my better instincts and move to sit down. Fox sat beside me but we didn't look at each other, we stared straight at Luther and waited for answers.

"Start talking, old man, or I might get bored and blow your brains out." My gut pulled ever so slightly at those words, but I ignored that weird ass reaction and continued to glare at him.

"Shut your mouth," Fox snarled at me.

"Listen kids," Luther started and I pursed my lips at that word. "I ain't been entirely honest with you both. And there's reasons for that…it's complicated. But I've tasted death now and I woke up thinking…fuck, what if I'd died with this secret? What if that had really been it for me? I'd have left way too much unfinished business here in Sunset Cove and I know you two have issues, I'm not blind. I've tried to be optimistic about this situation, but I need you both to understand the implications of this feud between you continuing."

"Stop babbling and get to the point," I insisted.

Luther let out a long breath as he decided how to start explaining whatever was on his mind. "My brother Deke and I fell out too a long time ago. You see, Fox, your mother-"

Fox was on his feet so fast, I swear he'd moved with the speed of the wind.

"I don't wanna hear shit about my mother," he said and I frowned at him. After all these years, Foxy still couldn't bear the thought that his mother had been anything other than a loving, perfect angel in his mind. But angels didn't live in the Cove. This place was full of sinners and their bad deeds were written into the stone. If he thought he'd been born of purity, he was a fucking idiot.

I caught his arm, forcing him to sit back down beside me. "Don't be a little bitch. The time for closing your ears is long gone, brother."

He looked at me and I looked back, my hand still locked around his wrist. I felt the old bond we had flare between us and tried to snuff out the flames that started to rekindle in the pile of blackened ash that remained of it.

His throat worked as he stared at me and slowly, he gave in, turning back to look at Luther as I released his arm.

Luther glanced between us with hope in his gaze and I ran my tongue over my teeth, assuring him with my glare that that interaction had meant nothing.

"Go on then," I pushed him. "Give us the truth."

"Fox, I loved your mother very much," he said in a way that sounded bitter and full of hurt.

"But?" I pushed, guessing there was one helluva but to this story and Fox stiffened in his seat beside me. *Sorry, Foxy boy, you can put lipstick and a nice dress on the truth, but it'll still be as ugly as a hairy ballsack.*

"But when you were very young, Fox, she had an affair," Luther said, the pain of this fact still clear in his deep green eyes. "With my brother, Deke."

"Holy fuck," I breathed, glancing at Fox and I swear I saw his sweet little vision of his momma pop right before his eyes like a balloon. *Ouch.*

"When I found out, I told her to choose between me and you...or him. And she chose us, kid. She did. And I would've forgiven her eventually, I think. But then she went and told Deke she wanted us and that he needed to leave town. I guess he thought he'd try and deal with his problem with violence because when I found her, she was already dead."

My heart rate picked up and I glanced at Fox again, finding his shoulders rising and falling with the furious breaths he was taking in. And shit, I felt sorry for the asshole as another part of his world crumbled and was lost. Dammit, why couldn't I just enjoy his misery anymore? Why did I keep getting these strange pangs whenever he looked like a kicked puppy?

"She loved you, Fox," Luther went on. "Despite what she did, despite how hurt I was, I could never fault her as a mother."

Fox's lips flattened into a hard line and he hung his head, his fingers pushing into his hair as he tried to process this.

"What did you do next?" I asked.

"I shot him," Luther gritted out. "Dead between the eyes. And I didn't feel much of anything about it either. I just needed him to stop existing. It's why I know there's hope for you two, because I know what true hate feels like. And it feels like nothing. Like a cold, empty *nothing*. But you hate each other

329

with passion and fury that speaks of what you really feel for each other. And you may be hurt by what each of you have done, but it's because deep down you love each other."

"Yeah, yeah," I muttered, ignoring the yank in my chest at those words. "So what's your brother being a cunt got to do with where I came from, old man?"

Luther's gaze moved to me as Fox looked up, as curious as I was to know what he was going to say next. "It matters because Deke is your father, Rick."

I stilled, an arctic coldness running deep into my bones as I absorbed those words. Great, now I was getting shit shovelled at me.

"A month or so after Fox's mother died, a woman turned up at my door with a little boy in her arms. She was in a state, I thought maybe she was on drugs at first, the way she was acting like someone might be about to sneak up on her from behind, but once I let her in the house, I realised she was just terrified."

"Of what?" Fox asked, taking over on the questioning as I suddenly couldn't seem to form a sentence, the tables having definitely turned.

"She said someone was hunting her," Luther said darkly. "And that she needed to hide you, Rick. She needed someone to protect you from whoever was after you both."

"Well who the fuck was it?" Fox growled.

"She never said," Luther sighed. "She told me you were Deke's boy, that he'd knocked her up a while back and washed his hands of her the moment she'd told him she was pregnant."

Nice. I'll just add that to the shitty list of traits my father possessed. Fuck.

"So you just took me in?" I blurted, finding my voice again as confusion ripped through me. "Why would you do that?"

"You were just a little boy. And when I looked at you, I knew you were family. I had Fox in my arms and all he wanted to do was get closer to you. It was like he sensed it."

I glanced at Fox who frowned at me and I scored my thumbs over my eyes.

"Trust me, it didn't make any sense for me to take on another kid when I was working around the clock to keep the gang in order and be a decent dad. I was struggling. Fox's mom had done the brunt of the childcare, I was up to my ears in diapers and toys and storybooks. I was attending all kinds of toddler classes to make sure I didn't fuck things up. It was chaos. And yeah, I had the Crew to help out sometimes, and your grandpa was still alive back then to babysit when I needed him to, but it wasn't exactly ideal. And yet…I couldn't turn you away, Rick. It was instinct. I just knew I'd find room somehow, I'd find a way to cope and raise you both together."

"So what happened to my mother?" I asked the most urgent question burning in my mind.

He frowned and I had the awful feeling I knew where this was going. "I never heard a word from her again, but if the terror she'd shown me was real then I'd guess she either ran a long way away or whatever she was running from caught up to her. I tried offering her help but she insisted the only thing she needed was for someone to take you who would never be connected back to her. She wanted you hidden where no one would ever think to look," he said, his brow taut like he didn't want to upset me with those words. But I could stomach them. I'd never expected this to be a good story. There were very few in life that were.

"I never did figure out who was supposedly after you or even who your mother was," Luther said sadly. "But I vowed to protect you from whoever it was with the full weight of the Crew. We were untouchable, and I wanted to raise you both to be able to protect yourselves from any enemy who might seek to harm you. But the strongest protection you've ever had is each other. You look after one another like nothing I've ever seen before. My siblings and I were never close like you two were, it was fucking beautiful," he said, emotion pooling in his gaze and for a moment I missed the constant, solid presence of Fox I'd always had when I was younger. It made me think of what he'd told me before. That Shawn had been the one responsible for everything that had happened to me in prison, and though I'd stubbornly refused to believe those words, looking at Luther now, I knew they were true. Because this man may not have been perfect, and he sure as shit had made countless mistakes in his life, but I could see that he had moved heaven and earth to protect me once upon a time, and it looked like that instinct in him still burned brighter than ever.

"So we're cousins?" Fox rasped and Luther nodded.

"You were always a Harlequin, Rick," Luther said. "Your blood is our blood. And your father was a lot of bad things, but your heart is your mother's. I didn't know her, but she gave you up to save you even though I could tell it broke her heart, and that kind of love and loyalty lives in you more fiercely than you even know."

I rose to my feet, needing to move, to think. My brain was overloaded and I was finding it hard to process all of this, wondering if it really changed anything at all or if it changed absolutely fuck all. I moved to the window, the sound of Rogue's laughter carrying up from the pool helping to calm the rampant pulsing of my heart.

Then I set my gaze on Sunset Cove, the land which I'd been born and raised on. Where I'd met Rogue, JJ, Chase. Where we'd had countless adventures and woven our fates into the fabric of the sand. And for the first time in a very, very long time, I wanted to go home.

CHAPTER TWENTY SIX

"Well now, bubba bear, I'm just so dang proud of you," my momma gushed as she set to work cooking my dinner while I sat at the kitchen island. "My baby Shawn, the lord of this here manor. I knew you'd make somethin' of yourself one day, it just makes my heart fill with sunshine and rainbows to see it, it truly does."

I beamed with pride as momma walked over to make a fuss of me, pushing my hair back from my face and placing a soft kiss on my cheek. "Look at my strapping boy, how comes you're still unmarried? You must have women trying to break down your door daily here to put a ring on your finger."

"There ain't no woman who matches up to you, that's why Momma," I said and she grinned, patting my shoulder. Sandra Mackenzie was the epitome of a good woman. She knew her place in this world and she fulfilled it with everything she was, putting hot meals on the table three times a day, making sure my clothes were waiting out for me in the morning, keeping the house spotless and all with a smile on her face. In fact, I shoulda thought to bring her here sooner. She'd even gone and miraculously forgotten about the ordeal it took to get her here, apparently having no recollection of the three assholes who had kidnapped her and making no acknowledgement of any kind of nefarious activities which I may or may not have been involved with. It was a damn blessing for all concerned, though I noticed she flinched at loud noises and seemed a little uneasy from time to time. No doubt she'd get past that soon enough.

"Well I can't deny that," Momma said, striding back to the stove to cook up what was smelling like one mighty fine stew. "Girls these days got too many ideas in their heads. They're either spreading their legs for every man who glances their way in the name of their so-called liberation, or dressin' in suits and tryna compete with men in the workplace. It's ludicrous, bubba. Whatever happened to that nice girlfriend of yours, Rogue? You don't bring her round my house no more."

"We're having a few…difficulties. But she'll come home soon, Momma."

"Well that's good. You make sure you sort it out with her, she was a real sweetheart. And when she comes to her senses, she'd better give you all the love you need, then maybe you'll make a grandmomma outa me, huh?"

"Sure thing, Momma," I said then continued reading through Kaiser's diary which I had laid out in front of me. The asshole sure did prattle on a lot, but at the very least most pages seemed to rule out a location or two for my diamonds, so it was worth the time investment. I was in need of a win after losing Rogue, and my mood was constantly sour. I could play this to my advantage though. Let the little bitch off her leash for a while and let her gain some confidence back. It would make it all the sweeter when I crushed it right out of her again. And this time, I'd be taking the most ruthless path I knew. Because I'd decided on killing me some Harlequins soon and I planned on taking down the big, bad Fox first and foremost. I wasn't sure how I'd do it yet, only that when I did, I'd make quite the spectacle of it. Rogue was gonna see her Fox skinned alive and made into a fur hat just for me. And I might just bake his innards in a pie too and feed it to a couple of hungry dogs.

You think you've won, sugarpie? *Oh baby, you just bought yourself hell on earth. If you thought I was cruel before, prepare to see how black my heart truly is.*

As I turned another page and listened to my momma humming contentedly while she cooked for me, my gaze snagged on some words that made my mind spin.

The direct heir is my main issue now. Mabel is getting old and she won't say anything about the diamonds, though I'm sure she knows where they are. That wouldn't matter much if I was certain that my claim on her fortune was ironclad, but recently I found out something that could put my entire inheritance in jeopardy.

Before my Aunt Rhonda disappeared, long before I tracked her down and made sure she would no longer be a problem for me, she had a secret. The kind of secret that could blow my entire plans asunder if anyone were to discover it.

Years ago, she had an heir of her own, a baby born without a soul knowing of its existence which subsequently disappeared as quickly as it had appeared. I only found out about it at all thanks to a chance discovery of some old hospital records detailing the birth and try as I might, I cannot figure out where the child ended up. I will continue my hunt for this missing heir, but in the meantime, I'll guard the secret of their existence closely and just hope that no one ever discovers what I have. Mabel can never find out she has a grandchild. So if I can't discover and dispose of the brat soon, I may have to consider other options for safeguarding my claim to the diamonds.

Kaiser moved on to writing about the various places he checked out after that, but I didn't keep reading, curiosity curling through my brain. A secret little Rosewood baby? Then where was it now?

I got to my feet, heading from the room, stalking to the basement and unlocking the door. I jogged down the steps into Miss Mabel's rooms and found her knitting in a rocking chair.

"Good evening, Miss Mabel," I purred and she scowled at me, pausing her knitting.

"What do you want, Shawn?" she demanded. Despite how frail she looked, there sure was fire in the old gal's belly.

I slowly prowled toward her, cocking my head to one side. "Just to have a friendly little chat about your family. I recently happened across a rather interesting detail in your nephew's diary."

"What kind of detail?" she asked, her eyes narrowing.

"A snot-nosed baby of a detail." I smirked, watching her expression closely and confusion twisted her wrinkly old face. She remained quiet so I strode right up to her, casting her in my giant shadow and leaning down to smile widely at her. "Now correct me if I'm wrong, Miss Mabel, but if your daughter had a baby right before she disappeared, then that baby would be all grown up now. A man, some might call him. Or a woman if it was a girl. And that would make them around hmm, twenty-six years old I'd guess. The question is, did they come a-visiting before Kaiser locked you up in this here house? And did you entrust that child with a secret or two that you didn't want your nephew finding out?"

Mabel stared at me in shock, shaking her head and seeming to struggle for words. "My Rhonda didn't have a child."

"Now, now, don't go acting dumb." I reached down, locking my hand around her throat, squeezing gently in a little warning. Nothing too rough. I wasn't a monster or nothin' when it came to old people.

"I'm not acting, you blaggard," she snarled and my eyebrows arched. "There was no child. Rhonda didn't have any children before she – she-" Her voice cracked.

"Went missing like a fart in the wind?" I finished for her with a mock look of sympathy.

"How dare you?" she croaked.

"Oh I do dare, Miss Mabel. Now lemme see if you're lying…" I pulled a flick knife from my pocket, replacing my hold on her throat by holding the blade there instead. "It don't please me to watch an old woman bleed out at my feet, but I assure you I am up to the task if you are. Now answer me again, did you or did you not know about your daughter's baby?"

"I didn't!" she cried, her eyes flaring with defiance but there was some fear there too.

I pulled the knife away, scratching at the stubble on my jaw. "Hm."

"But Lord have mercy, if there is a child out there who holds Rosewood blood in their veins, the child of my beloved Rhonda, then that means…"

"They're the only surviving heir to those diamonds," I finished for her, tapping the blade against my lips.

"Yes," she said breathlessly, hope seeming to climb into her eyes, though I had no idea why. The old gal was stuck down here for the foreseeable future, and once I had my diamonds I'd hardly be keeping her around like a weird old budgie I had to feed twice a day. Not that I took on that personal duty myself, but still. I wasn't a man of charity.

"And lemme guess," I said thoughtfully. "The baby's the only one you'll tell the location of the diamonds too."

"Of course," she rasped. "I'd die before I see them in your hands or anyone else unworthy."

"Uhuh." I nodded, fully aware of that.

The old bird had nearly died the first time I'd tried to force the location out of her by holding a plastic bag over her head. I'd learned quick enough that she really would die with that knowledge in her head no matter what I did to her. But now it looked like another solution was presenting itself to me. It couldn't be that hard to find out where Rhonda's baby ended up, the cops or child services or the like would have some record of it. And lucky for me, I had corrupt friends in high places. So it looked like I was on the trail of a diamond heir.

CHAPTER TWENTY SEVEN

The night was dark and the water calm after yet another day of blazing sunshine in Sunset Cove. I was wearing a black sweatshirt and sweatpants combo over my bikini, and I slipped my feet into a pair of black trainers as I prepared to head out with my boys.

Chase and JJ were sitting out on the balcony in Maverick's room, their gaze on the distant lights of the Cove while they spoke in low voices which carried in to me on the warm breeze.

Maverick was off somewhere giving his men instructions on what he wanted them to do while we were gone, and I hadn't seen Fox since the day we'd arrived back here and he'd basically told me he wanted nothing more to do with me.

That hurt. But I got it. And if he was sure he didn't want anything to do with me now then I was going to have to try and respect that. But it didn't stop me aching for him all the same.

I blew out a breath and Mutt perked up from his position in the middle of the bed, cocking his head at me in question.

"Men," I muttered to him and I swear he rolled his eyes sympathetically before flopping onto his side and raising a leg in hopes of a belly rub. I caved and moved closer to tickle him, grinning as his tongue hung out the side of his mouth and he closed his eyes in pleasure.

"It's not that simple," Chase muttered, his voice drifting in on the breeze and catching my attention. "That asshole has a way of getting into your fucking head and laying eggs there. It's hard to explain. But we just need to make sure she stays the fuck away from him from now on."

"That much is obvious at least," JJ agreed and my chest tightened at the concern in his voice. "I feel like such a fucking idiot for not realising what she was up to sooner, but the things she said in that video..."

Guilt burned a path beneath my skin and I drew back from Mutt, slipping out to the balcony doors and hesitating as I reached them. The night was dark and full of stars which glimmered overhead, but there was no sign of the moon as I swept my gaze over the blackness of the sky.

Chase and JJ sat side by side on the rattan couch with their backs to me as they looked out over the water, the only light on the balcony cast by the orange glow of Chase's cigarette where it hung from his fingertips as he let his arm dangle down beside the couch.

"Hey," I said softly, drawing their attention to me and making them both look around.

"Is it time to go?" JJ asked, making a move to get up but I shook my head and stepped out to join them instead, leaving Mutt to enjoy the warmth of the bed inside.

"I haven't heard anything yet," I confirmed. "I just wanted to come see you guys. If that's okay?"

"When have you ever needed to ask, pretty girl?" JJ replied, patting the spot between the two of them in invitation and I stepped out into the cooler air to join them.

I walked up to the back of the couch and climbed over, dropping down between them and smiling at them as they both looked at me, but I could feel the hurt in the air tonight, the pain from me and Chase surviving Shawn, the pain of the words I'd cut JJ with when I'd run from him. It was all fucked. And yet it wasn't at the same time, because here we sat, together, owning our love for each other even if it was more than a little bruised right now.

"You all ready to go?" Chase asked me, changing the subject smoothly as he lifted his cigarette to his lips and took a drag from it.

"Yeah," I agreed, reaching out to steal the smoke and filling my lungs with nicotine as I let my eyes fall closed and just enjoyed the feeling of their arms pressing up against me, the sound of the waves lapping the shore and the taste of freedom in the air.

I exhaled and turned to JJ, offering up the smoke as I looked at him and he tipped his chin in agreement as I lifted it to his lips. I looked into his eyes as he took a drag, my fingers lingering against his mouth, his stubble grazing my palm and the fire between us flaring bright before dimming again as he drew back and exhaled the smoke for the wind to catch.

"I didn't mean it," I breathed, passing the cigarette back to Chase who ashed it in a glass tray beside him before placing a hand on my thigh, giving me a gentle squeeze of encouragement.

"I know," JJ replied but the look in his eyes said he didn't know that at all and it fucking killed me to know I'd done that to him, used his insecurities against him and left him to bleed over them.

"No, Johnny James, you don't. Being with you wasn't a part of some fucked up game. It was like tasting salt water on my tongue again after spending years stuck on land. It was simple and beautiful and ours. I didn't have any agenda. In fact, the only promise I made myself at all when I came back to this place was that I wouldn't let a single one of you get under my skin again. That I'd make you all pay for the past and hurt like you'd hurt me. But I get it now. I still hate it, but I get it. And now the only thing I want out of being back here is the thing I lost when I left. You. All of you."

"Rogue," JJ rasped, his hand coming up to touch my face, his fingers drifting down the side of my jaw as he studied me.

Chase sighed, giving me a little nudge like he was growing impatient and I glanced around at him in question. He arched an eyebrow at me, letting me know he thought I was a fucking idiot and I frowned at him in reply before looking back to JJ.

"I don't have a whole lot to offer," I said slowly, reaching down and taking JJ's hand before lifting it to rest over my heart which was thrashing like a bird in a cage, desperate to get out and meet with his. I couldn't let him believe those vile things I'd said. I wouldn't. "But this is the truth. You make my heart race and my fingers tremble. You make me smile when I thought I never could again. You make my pulse race and my words come out all jumbled and I might have called you a lovesick boy, but I have always just been a lovesick girl when it comes to you."

The hardness of JJ's expression softened at my words, his fingers flexing over my chest where he was still touching me, still feeling that thundering beat.

"Do you remember when you thought Chase kissed me when we were fifteen?" I asked.

"When he tried to take a piece of popcorn from your mouth with his and 'accidentally' planted his lips on yours?" JJ deadpanned, shooting a look over my shoulder at Chase who snorted a laugh.

"Well the competition for her attention was pretty fierce," he replied shamelessly. "I had to steal it somehow."

"You meant to do that?" I asked, whipping my head around to look at him as he just smirked.

"It wasn't exactly premeditated, but I can't say I regretted it. I still count that as my first kiss."

"You can't count a stolen kiss as your first," JJ said, shaking his head and drawing my attention back to him.

"You told me you had to kiss me too," I said, getting back to the point I'd been trying to make.

"You kissed her after you pushed me off the fucking pier?" Chase asked in outrage and I slapped his chest to shut him up.

"Let me finish, asshole," I shot at him and he raised his hands in innocence, looking back out over the water before dropping his hand to my thigh again, his fingers making the material of my sweatpants shift and bunch against my skin.

"I wanted to give you a real kiss so fucking bad that day," JJ said as my gaze met his again. "I was such a dumb kid. I'd been aching for you for so fucking long and there you were, looking at me and waiting for a kiss and I just...choked."

"I wanted you to kiss me then, Johnny James," I said, remembering the way my heart had raced and my palms had grown slick, the way I'd looked at his mouth and felt an ache in me for something that I'd been denying and fearing ever since I'd discovered it. "I wanted you to kiss me so much that I felt like I might burst if you didn't. So if you were just a lovesick boy then it wasn't a bad thing because I was so lovesick for you that it hurt sometimes. I was so lovesick for you that in ten long years I never got over you at all. And from the very first moment that I saw you again, I wanted you all over again. Because no matter how many women came after me, you were mine first. All mine. And when I gave you my body it wasn't some fucking game or trick or even just an empty act of lust. It was you and me, J. Please tell me that still means something to you too."

His brow furrowed like he still had trouble believing that and my heart twisted at the thought of it.

"I didn't mean it, JJ," I said, my gaze holding his and the way he looked at me made all the pain inside me ache more sharply because I could see it in him too and I knew I'd been the one to put it there. "I only wanted to keep you safe. From Shawn, from the pain you were causing each other, and most of all from me too. I didn't want you to lose all the good things you had for yourself over me."

JJ stared at me as he drank in my words, his hand pressed to my chest while my heart continued to beat out a tune entirely for him.

"Well then you're a damn idiot, pretty girl," he said fiercely, some anger colouring his words as his gaze intensified and the golden tones in his eyes flare with the power of his words. "Because the only thing I've ever been terrified of in my whole life was losing you. And I can't do it again. I won't. Maybe I would have been willing to sacrifice everything else I had to keep you, but this right here is so much better because if I can have you and my brothers can have you too then I think there really might be a future for us where we could truly be happy again. And I just want to see you smile the way you used to."

When his hand curled into a fist and he pulled me towards him by the fabric of my sweatshirt, I went more than willingly.

His lips crashed against mine and a moan rode up in my throat, this painful, bitter relief that he still wanted me like this, that he still needed me too. Our mouths moved together, almost hesitantly at first, tasting, feeling, exploring the reality of our love for one another before the thin hold we had on our restraint snapped and he was pushing me back, rearing over me and kissing me harder.

I melted for him, relief and gratitude and so many nights of pining for him when I was on my own out there in the world all tumbling together until I felt like I wouldn't be able to breathe unless I had him. JJ groaned into our kiss, his lips parting and tongue caressing mine in a slow and decadent way that had my damn knees trembling as he showed me just how much he wanted me with nothing but his mouth.

I used to lay alone in whatever bed I could call my own and think of my boys, of the way their kisses would have felt against my lips or how their bodies would have felt destroying mine.

But no fantasy I'd ever had could ever come close to the reality. And as JJ stole my breath away with a kiss so fucking full of love and emotion, I swear I broke all over again. But this time my pieces weren't sharp and brittle shards meant to cut and hurt, they were all soft edges and liquid silk, looking to mould back together more seamlessly than they ever had before.

That kiss was a promise between us. An end and a beginning too. We were done being the kids who had been too afraid to love like this. And we were done being the jaded, hurting adults those kids had grown into without each other. This here was where we belonged and there wasn't going to be anymore hiding from it or hurting from it or fucking fearing it.

He lit me up and made me burn and I was walking willingly into those flames and begging them to consume me.

When he pulled back, leaving me panting and needy beneath him, my flesh aching for more of his touch, I could see the love in his eyes. And as he placed his hand over Chase's which still gripped my thigh, I knew what he was saying too. He was all in if I was. If *we* were.

I turned my head, my chest still heaving from that kiss as my gaze roamed over Chase's expression in the dark and I found no anger there, no hurt or sense of betrayal, only a want and need of his own and the reflection of all my own scars in the pain that lived inside him.

"We're late," Chase grunted, wetting his lips and drawing my gaze to his mouth as the hunger in me for these boys grew out of control. I wanted to draw him closer, draw both of them closer and show them how much I needed them.

But even as the thought of that occurred to me and my panties began to grow damp with arousal, the sound of Shawn's voice rang through my ears. The accusations he'd thrown at me and the marks he'd left inside my head.

I pulled back the tiniest amount but they saw it, the two of them stiffening either side me as if I'd screamed instead of flinched and JJ leaned back, blowing out a breath and nodding like he agreed though I hadn't said a damn word.

"Come on," he offered, holding a hand out to me as he stood and not even bothering to try and hide the way his dick was tenting his sweatpants like a fucking leviathan looking to feast on virgin souls.

"Sorry," I muttered, letting him pull me up and Chase stood too.

"None of that," Chase growled, catching my chin in his calloused hand and making me look up into his mismatched eyes. I knew that he was blind in the right one now, but something about the way the pale orb seemed to look right inside of me made me feel like it could see my soul even if it couldn't see my face. "If you can look at my damage without flinching then you can face what that asshole did to you too. Don't let him make you feel like that, little one. Not ever."

"Okay," I breathed, wishing it was that easy and he sighed because he knew just as well as I did that it wasn't.

"We got you, pretty girl," JJ added, tugging me into a walk as he kept hold of my hand and Chase threw his arm around my shoulders too.

"I got you, too," I replied and Chase smiled, placing a kiss on the side of my head as we made our way inside.

I squinted in the light of the bedroom after the dark of the night, but after a bit of aggressive blinking and letting the boys steer me along, my eyes adjusted again.

I whistled for Mutt and he leapt from the bed, scampering after us as we made it to the door and headed down to meet Rick and Fox at the boat.

The sounds of their voices reached us before we spotted them.

"That's because you've forgotten how to catch a wave in the years you've spent running around trying to be king of the Cove," Rick mocked and Fox snorted derisively.

"Says the guy who wiped out when the swell got too big. Face it, asshole, all that time in prison made you rusty," Fox replied, the teasing lilt to his tone making my heart lift and hope swell within me. Were they…getting along?

"Yeah, as rusty as the spoon I'm gonna use to carve your liver from your chest," Rick said and Fox laughed loudly.

"My liver isn't in my fucking chest, idiot."

"No. But I'm gonna go in that way just to make it hurt more," Maverick tossed back his own amusement clear and bringing a grin to my lips.

"Anyone else excited for the five of us to be heading out on an adventure together again at last?" JJ asked loudly as we made it to them, breaking up their ridiculous discussion and making them turn to look at us.

"You make us sound like Enid Blyton characters," Chase muttered.

"Err, yeah I think that's accurate - we're totally the hotter, more badass version of the Famous Five," JJ said shrugging. "We've even got our own tiny Timmy the dog."

Mutt yipped like he agreed with that and started chasing his tail excitedly, his little claws tapping against the jetty as he ran.

"Who does that make me then?" Fox asked, his gaze skimming over the three of us and seeming to settle on the points of contact where Chase's arm still draped around my shoulders and JJ still held my hand. He didn't say anything about it though, just kept that shuttered gaze of his and focused his attention on JJ's face.

"Julian," Rick answered for him. "The pompous prick who thinks he's in charge all the time and has a great big stick up his ass. You're such a Julian."

"Well Rogue is obviously Anne - pretty girl with all the best ideas who the guys clearly all have a thing for," Chase interrupted as Fox scowled at that assessment.

"I'm like eighty percent sure that they were all siblings, dude," JJ said and I snorted a laugh.

When we'd been about eight or nine, we'd gotten our hands on a box set of the old English TV series based on the Famous Five books and had watched them back to back in JJ's house while his mom banged a line of clients upstairs. We'd cranked the volume up but had been yelled at for putting the clients off their game with the sound of children laughing. After that, JJ had gone to the local library and gotten a bunch of the books to read and had made us go on random 'adventures' with him after getting kinda obsessed.

"Well I'm Dick, obviously," Maverick said. "Partly because he was the one who always got into trouble and partly because of my massive cock making that name so fucking appropriate for me."

I really laughed then and even Fox twitched a smile.

"And Johnny James is George because he's still trying to convince everyone he's a boy," Rick added and I groaned, remembering the way he'd ribbed JJ over that when we were kids, taunting him about it and always telling him should get his dick out to prove he was a boy if he didn't like the rumours. The only rumours were from Rick's asshole mouth, but it had been enough to cause the two of them to end up in a brawl on the beach one night and Maverick had lost a tooth.

"I will quite happily convince you of my manhood if you want me to, Rick," JJ said suggestively and Maverick rolled his eyes.

"Nah, you're good. I got the message when I watched our girl choke on your dick multiple times."

The lightness of the conversation fell away as Fox tensed up and everyone glanced at him warily. The uncomfortable silence was only tainted by Rick snickering like the asshole he was, and I narrowed my eyes on him with promised violence.

"Well who the hell am I then if you guys claimed all the main characters already?" Chase asked, taking his arm from my shoulders and folding his arms across his chest as he attempted to break the tension.

"Easy," Fox replied and I swear I could hear a little of my light-hearted best friend in his tone as he grinned again. "You're Aunt Fanny."

We all laughed again as Chase cursed him out and Fox led the way onto the large speedboat we were clearly going to be using in our search for the cartel's ledger.

Chase and JJ followed him onto the boat and the three of them kept chatting amongst one another as they got ready to leave, but I caught Rick's arm before he could follow them onboard.

He turned to look down at me and I punched him solidly in the bicep, making my knuckles flare with pain from how goddamn hard his muscles were beneath my strike.

"I'm still pissed at you over that sex tape stunt," I growled at him.

Maverick caught my wrist and tugged me closer, making my chest bump against his as I craned my neck back to maintain eye contact with him as he scowled down at me.

"Yeah? Well I'm still pissed at you for running out on me. So I guess we're even on that front," he replied in a dark tone designed to send a shiver down my spine.

"That's between you and me," I said firmly. "So you can stop being an asshole to Fox."

Maverick tipped his head to one side, his dark eyes seeming to drink in all the light surrounding us until I felt like I was adrift in a pitch black sea. "What are you going to do about it, beautiful?"

"Well I can start with punching you in the dick the next time I hear you baiting him over that fucking tape."

"Maybe you should be asking Foxy why he kept the copy of it if he really hates it so much," he shot back.

"Why would he have a copy? You live streamed it."

"Yeah. And I recorded it as well. I told you I was going to, and I was right about that idea too - it is seriously fucking hot. You have no idea how many times I've jacked off while watching it." I knew that he was baiting me, but I couldn't help the blush that rose to my cheeks all the same because I knew him and I knew when he was lying to get a rise out of someone and the heat in his gaze told me clear as day that that was no lie.

"You sent that to Fox?" I hissed in alarm, glancing around at the boat where the others were doing a good job of pretending they hadn't noticed us lingering on the jetty.

"Sure did. And if he really hated it as much as he claims to, he'll have deleted it. Ten bucks says he hasn't though." Rick raised his brows at me and my blush deepened.

"I mean it, Maverick," I hissed, falling back on my original point and sticking to it, because I seriously wasn't in the headspace to start discussing the idea of him pleasuring himself while watching a video of me, him and JJ fucking, let alone wondering if Fox really had been watching it again too. "Fox is one of us. I don't want him to be hurt any more than he already has been by us."

"Us? What exactly is us right now, beautiful?" he asked, ignoring the bulk of what I'd said as he leaned in closer and made it hard for me to breathe without the taste of him coating my tongue.

I only had one answer for him that made sense to me and as I breathed life into the word, I swear I felt a pulse of pure energy passing between us. "Everything."

Rick remained silent for long enough that I began to fidget, but as his large hands closed around my waist and he dropped his mouth to my ear, I fell utterly still again.

"Then it sounds to me like you and I have unfinished business to attend to soon, baby girl. But you'd better be sure you mean that statement, because when this anger between us reaches its limit, you're going to really meet the monster in me, and it will be far too late for you to turn your back on me then."

The deep timbre of his voice sent a shiver of desire coursing through me so potently that as he pulled his hands away from my body, a moan of protest escaped my lips, making an explosion light his dark eyes.

"Come on, *friend*, it's time to go." Rick flicked me in the chest, his expert aim striking against my rock hard nipple and making a needy whimper escape my lips before I could lock it away inside my throat.

He smirked knowingly then turned away and jumped onto the boat with the others, leaving me to follow on slightly weak knees with Mutt diving aboard beside me.

The boat was bobbing heavily in the water from Rick's landing and I stumbled as I climbed in, almost falling before Fox caught me and heaved me upright again.

"Thanks," I said, glancing up at him as he gave me a nod then released his hold on me, leaving my skin tingling from his touch.

The mood quietened between all of us. Maverick started up the boat and I dropped down onto a seat beside Fox as we pulled away from the jetty and headed out to sea.

The boys all had weapons with them and Fox silently handed me a pistol as the speedboat hit the open water and we picked up the pace, racing towards the spot where La Princesa had been burning before we abandoned it.

Memories of that night surfaced in me as we shot across the water and

I gripped the pistol tight in my fist. Carmen may have promised to have the cartel looking the other way for us tonight, but I wasn't ever going to let my guard down when it came to them. Besides, Shawn was still hunting us and there was always a chance we could run across him. We needed to keep our guard up until this was handled and even then, I wasn't going to sleep easy until fucking Shawn was resting in an early grave.

A shudder ran down my spine as I thought about him and the things I knew he'd do to my boys if he got his hands on any one of them again and I lifted my chin, trying to fight off the fear of that reality. I fixed my gaze on the darkness of the sea ahead and the glimmering lights of Sunset Cove beyond it to distract me.

A hand landed on mine, making me jump before my gaze met Fox's as he wound his fingers through mine and squeezed, just like he had that night when we were fifteen and out to cause some trouble. But instead of excitement and rebellion filling me like it had then, now all I felt was fear for my boys and frustration over us ever heading out to that damn boat in the first place. But back then fear hadn't come into any of the decisions we'd made, we'd been running on dares and adrenaline rushes, thrill seeking and laughter and we never worried about the implications of any of the choices we made or cared about getting into the kind of trouble that we couldn't just run from.

"Are you sure there's no one on it?" I whispered as the steady roar of the speedboat's engine tried to steal my words from my lips.

"The thing is just sitting out there, all abandoned and alone, crying out for someone to come party on it," Rick replied, grinning at me from his place driving the boat which we'd liberated from Luther for this little night time voyage. Sometimes I feared what might happen if the king of The Harlequin Crew realised we took joyrides in his pride and joy as often as we did, but Fox had confided in me once that he was almost certain his dad knew about it and just didn't say anything. I guessed as the leader of a criminal organisation, he wasn't against his sons committing a little bit of theft and rule breaking, but I would still be running the hell away from him if he ever caught sight of me onboard it.

I glanced out towards the darkness again, squinting to see the yacht which was little more than a dark shadow on the horizon ahead of us.

"I dunno if we should be heading out here while a storm is on the way," JJ muttered from his position at the helm of the speedboat and Chase rolled his eyes dramatically while lounging back in his seat.

"Stop being a little bitch, J," he said. "What's the worst that can happen anyway? Some rich asshole catches us snooping about and yells at us. Who gives a fuck?"

Fox took my hand and squeezed my fingers between his as the two of them started bickering and I turned to look at him, his bright green eyes sparkling with the fun of the game as we closed in on the yacht.

"Are you scared, hummingbird?" he murmured, teasing me.

"Never," I replied firmly.

"That's my girl," he replied, his smile deepening as he seemed to look inside me and see all the secrets I held in my heart. I found myself staring right back, searching for his.

"Oh my god, it looks like a whale dick at night," JJ laughed and I was jerked out of the secret moment me and Fox had been sharing. I found him pointing at the huge rock that curved out of the water in front of the dark land of Isla Tigre beyond it.

"No way, that's a beluga dick if ever I saw one," I tossed back with a smirk.

"A beluga is a whale," JJ argued.

"No it isn't," I insisted, ready to die on this hill.

"Come on, assholes," Rick called loudly as the speedboat's engine cut off. "Time for the fun to begin."

JJ leapt up onto the dark yacht first despite the fact that he'd been the one complaining about us coming out here to investigate it and he quickly tied a mooring rope from the speedboat to the back of it before taking a step towards the huge, dark cabin ahead of us.

"Hello?" he called out loudly. "Anybody home?"

Silence greeted him and the rest of us grinned as we made quick work of jumping from the speedboat to the yacht and Rick strolled forward, finding a lightswitch and illuminating the luxurious upper deck of the boat. It was like a freaking mansion on the water, the thing screaming wealth so loud that I felt like little more than a grubby street urchin as I tiptoed inside.

But I was more than happy to be a street kid and this was my kind of playground.

"Looks like there's a free bar," Fox called excitedly, releasing his hold on my hand as he jogged over to the bar which sat beside a large white seating area and started pulling out bottles of liquor for us to get fucked up on.

I grinned as I accepted a bottle of Bacardi and moved towards a writing desk which sat against the far wall, opening drawers and claiming anything that looked valuable by dropping it into my pockets.

The others were doing the same, exploring the space on the upper deck and giving their sticky fingers a workout as they took anything of value that they found.

"Look at this shit," Rick called, making me turn to face him as he held up what looked like a solid gold dagger with rubies inlaid in the hilt. "Who the fuck has something like this? Would it even be any good for stabbing shit? Seems like gold would be too soft for that." He turned and stabbed one of the couch cushions with a bark of laughter as it slicked open easily and stuffing tumbled out onto the pristine floor.

"Shit," I breathed, biting my bottom lip as I looked between him and the damage he'd caused and he grinned widely as he looked right back at me.

"You like that, beautiful? Does it get your heart racing when I'm bad?" he teased and I shrugged, but my heart was galloping like a wild horse in my chest so maybe it did.

"Ripping one cushion doesn't seem all that bad to me. But maybe if you cause a bit more damage you'd earn a laugh out of me," I challenged.

The boys clearly took that challenge seriously and the sound of smashing glass made me jump as JJ threw a bottle of whiskey at a mirror which ran behind the bar, shattering it instantly.

The heathens in us were set loose with that one simple act and suddenly we were competing to see who could trash the place the fastest, destroying anything we could break, drawing on the walls, shredding the soft furnishings and drinking all of their expensive booze while we laughed our heads off over it.

Chase popped a bottle of champagne, drinking straight from the head of it as the bubbles erupted onto the carpet before holding it up to my lips so that

I could take a swig too. It tasted dry and expensive and like liquid bullshit to me, but I was happy enough to drink it all the same. He grinned at me, lighting up a cigarette and offering me a drag before jamming it into the corner of his lips and moving away to cause some more destruction.

I climbed up onto the couch and started jumping, making the stuffing fly up around me as laughter tumbled from my lips and my heart sung with happiness. We were assholes, utter fucking savage assholes, but man did it feel good to destroy something so valuable when we had so damn little. Every day of my life I had to watch yachts like this one sail past the Cove with money dripping from every polished surface while I wore shoes with holes in them and was stuck sharing a bedroom with three girls I wasn't related to and didn't even like. It was bullshit. The whole world was bullshit and now we were striking the fuck back for once. And I liked the taste of it even if it was a pointless form of anarchy.

"Oh shit," Chase gasped and we all looked around from our laughter and celebrations at the serious tone to his voice. "I just figured out whose boat this is." His face was pale and his hand shook a little where he held the champagne bottle.

"What is it, Ace?" I asked him, hopping down from the remains of the destroyed couch and moving closer with a frown. We weren't afraid of anything or anyone, so I couldn't figure out why the identity of some rich assholes was making him look like that.

Fox moved up behind me as we looked at what he'd found and a cold, sinking feeling filled my chest as fear crept through my veins like poison.

"Put it back," I breathed, feeling death's fingers clawing their way closer to me with every passing second as I looked at the medallion Chase held in his hand, a red ribbon tied to it which dangled between his fingers like an omen of bloodshed to come. My gaze remained riveted to the thing which suddenly twisted this game into something so much more terrifying. The symbol of the Castillo Cartel stared up at us like a demon promising us death with an accusation that fell firmly on top of our heads like the strike of an axe which was primed to fall at any moment. It was an ornate chalice with a venomous snake wrapped around it, its fangs poised above the cup and dripping poison into it.

"We're gonna die," JJ gasped as he saw it too and Chase quickly dropped it, but as I looked around at the fucking mess we'd made of this place, I knew that wasn't going to be good enough.

"Holy fuck," Rick said, snatching my hand and dragging me backwards like he thought he could protect me from this when he knew as well as I did that that was our deaths right there. There was no fucking way we could run from them.

"We'll just tell my dad we didn't know," Fox reasoned, panic in his normally unshakable gaze. "He'll be able to smooth it over. We didn't know. How could we have known?"

"You really think he can?" I asked desperately, looking to Fox like he might just be our salvation as the others backed away like we might be able to run from this the way we always ran from trouble.

Chase headed towards the back of the deck where a door led into the rest of the boat which we hadn't explored yet, but my attention remained on Fox as he bent down to retrieve the dropped amulet, turning it over in his fingers as his face twisted with fear.

"Shit, we need to put everything back where we found it and get the hell out of here," JJ said in a panic, clawing his fingers through his ebony hair as he took in the destruction we'd caused as if there was any hope at all of us fixing it.

"Um, guys, it gets worse. Far fucking worse," Chase called and I whipped around to look at him where he was peering through the doorway which led deeper into the yacht with his cigarette still burning between his lips.

Fox stepped in front of me in a protective gesture as we hurried over to find out what he'd discovered and JJ's fingers curled around my wrist as he moved closer to me too, sharing a terrified look with me as we tried to figure out what could possibly be worse than this.

Chase led the way down a short flight of stairs and pushed the door at the bottom of them wide as we reached him. Bile rose in my throat as I spotted the blood staining the walls first then took in the sight of dead bodies lying all around the space. Not just any dead bodies either – the tattoos on their skin and the clothes they were wearing, in fact every fucking thing about them screamed Castillo Cartel.

"Oh fuck," I gasped and Fox caught my hand, stuffing the medallion into his pocket as he looked between the dead bodies and the mess we'd made like he was hoping for some miraculous solution to drop out of the sky to rescue us.

Maverick took a step into the death filled room, elbowing past us as he gazed around thoughtfully, not seeming the slightest bit affected by the sight of all the blood staining the walls, the bullet holes carved into the dead men or even the guy whose fucking head looked like it had been blown clean off.

"Holy shit, look at his," he said as he picked up a bottle of vodka and held it out for us to see a thumb floating inside it.

"Put it down," I hissed, my eyes widening in fear as I jerked away from Fox's hold on my hand and snatched the bottle from Rick. We needed to get rid of any evidence of us ever having been here and get the hell away as fast as we could. This was a fucking massacre and I refused to let any of my boys get tangled up in the fallout once the Castillo Cartel figured out someone had taken out a hit on their people.

I took a step back towards the main deck, not even sure what I was planning to do but as I moved, a huge wave rocked the boat and I stumbled, the bottle slipping from my fingers, and crashing to the deck. Vodka and broken glass spilled across the floor as I fought to remain upright, the severed thumb washing towards the others. JJ smacked into Chase as he tried to avoid it and Fox tried to grab them, but he slipped on the puddle of vodka and fell to his knees, bringing Chase down with him.

The cigarette fell from Chase's lips, hitting the deck in a shower of sparks and instantly igniting the vodka, making me scream in fright as I leapt away from the flash of fire.

"Christ," Rick breathed in my ear, his arm curling around my waist as he drew me closer to him to keep me away from the flames and hold me steady as JJ yanked Fox and Chase back to their feet.

"I told you there was a fucking storm coming in tonight," JJ snapped like he was angry at us for not listening to him and staying home when he had the chance. And right now I was pretty pissed at us for not listening to him too. "We shouldn't have come out here."

"Keep your panties on," Maverick barked, but the heat of the fire was *already making my skin prickle and I could tell that all of us were about three seconds away from complete panic.*

We took off, racing back out of the room filled with death and up the stairs that led to the top deck. The fire flared behind us as it found the soft furnishings and I glanced back as Rick shoved me ahead, making sure my boys were all with me as we ran from the flames.

Maverick gripped my hand tightly as we ran up the stairs and the boat rocked wildly once more beneath the force of the waves rolling in ahead of the storm.

Fox caught hold of me as I skidded sideways towards a wall, taking the blow and cushioning me against his chest as he hit it. He pushed me up the next step as Maverick yanked on my hand to keep me moving and I looked back to make sure Chase and JJ were still with us too.

Fire flared brightly at their backs, the heat of it reaching us as it began to take hold of the boat and my heart raced furiously in my chest.

"Go!" JJ cried and we ran back out onto the top deck, tearing past the destroyed living area as if the fires of hell themselves were chasing after us, and diving straight over the railing at the side of the boat into the sea beyond.

The water enveloped me as I sank like a stone beneath it, the weight of my clothes slowing me down as I began to swim, kicking towards the surface with Rick's hand still firmly locked around mine.

We surfaced fast, sucking down air before swimming straight for Luther's speedboat and our means of escape as the yacht burned brighter at our backs.

Maverick heaved himself up ahead of me, reaching down and taking my hand to help haul me up next.

When I was in the boat, I leaned over the edge and caught Chase's hand as he scrambled up the side, gritting my teeth and pulling hard to help him up and over the edge while Rick helped JJ and Fox up too.

JJ quickly untethered the speedboat from the yacht which was now burning with a ferocity that had me fearing for our own small vessel and Chase started the boat up the second we were free.

We raced away across the angry waves as the sound of thunder rumbled through the distant clouds and Fox tugged me against him with an arm around my shoulders as I just stared back at the blazing yacht. The light of the flames reflected off of the curved rock which stuck up out of the water like the jagged thumb of a giant not too far away, the lump of rock laying witness to what we'd done while we prayed that no one else had.

JJ took my hand and I exchanged a look with him which reflected my fears right back at me.

"We're fucked," he whispered.

"We're not," Fox growled fiercely. "Only we know we were there. So all we have to do is never tell another soul. Swear it."

"I swear," we all agreed instantly, the flames of the yacht reflecting in our eyes as we watched them consuming the vessel. Soon it would sink into the water and the ocean would hide what little evidence remained of what had happened there. We would just have to hope the cartel would assume that whoever had killed their men had lit that fire too.

We remained silent as we raced back to shore, the storm closing in at our backs as we shivered in our wet clothes.

We moored the speedboat on Luther's private jetty then ran up the beach, the adrenaline still pumping through my limbs with every step I took as fear of the cartel consumed me.

They wouldn't care that we were just a bunch of kids if they found out that we'd been on that boat. They'd string us up and skin us alive and let the fucking crows finish us off while they laughed in our faces.

"Come on," Fox murmured as we crept up the beach to the house and the first drops of rain began to fall on us. "I'll drive you guys home."

"Shit," JJ said suddenly, stopping dead in his tracks as we made it onto the wooden porch at the back of Harlequin House and huddled beneath the shelter out of the rain. He pushed a hand into his pocket and pulled out the golden blade with the ruby encrusted hilt. "I forgot I had this."

My eyes widened in realisation as I tugged the items I'd stolen from my pockets too and the others all did the same as we stared at each other in horror, the cartel medallion in Fox's fist seeming to stare at us all with a promise of our deaths etched into the metal itself.

"We should go back out there," Rick said. "Toss it all into the sea as close to the wreck as we can get."

"Fat chance of that," Chase pointed out as thunder crashed overhead and lightning forked through the sky illuminating the roiling, angry waves of the ocean. "We'll be as dead as the men on that boat if we try to head out in that weather now."

"Then we wait for the storm to pass and go back out there to dump it tomorrow," Rick said. "It was close to Isla Tigre. We can find it again."

"We can't go near that wreck again," I hissed frantically, the mere thought of it making my blood freeze in my veins. "The Castillo Cartel will be looking for that yacht. I'm not going anywhere near it now that its sunk. We need to keep the fuck away from it and hope to hell that no one saw us heading out there."

The boys all murmured their agreement to that fact and we looked back down at the damning evidence we all still held in our hands. We had to get rid of it. Hide it away somewhere that no one could ever find it until we could figure out a way to destroy it for good.

"The Rosewood crypt," Fox said suddenly. "We can hide it in there with the rest of our loot. No one will find it there. Then once the heat has died down, we can get rid of it."

"Yeah," I agreed, nodding firmly. "We should do that. Hide it. Make sure no one sees us with it."

"Let's go then," Rick said, grabbing my arm and tugging. "We can use the storm to hide us and sneak in around back so even Miss Mabel won't know we were there tonight."

"Okay," we all agreed and we took off running to get to Fox's truck, wanting this done as fast as possible.

I wrapped my arms around me as a chill seemed to pierce through the fabric of my sweatshirt and I remembered the fear we'd felt that night. We'd never returned to the crypt again after that. Not wanting to draw any attention to the place where we'd buried our darkest secret until we knew how to rid ourselves of it. And now it had come out and we were left with this one chance to fix it or damnation would fall on us all just like we'd always known it would.

Of course this was the thing that had reunited us in the end. It was the secret I'd come back here to unlock, the weapon I'd wanted to wield against these boys to steal their precious town from them and make them run from the wrath of the cartel when they found out about it.

But as I sat among the four of them again, drinking in the feeling of their presence surrounding me, I knew in my heart that I never would have gone through with it. Because even when I hated them at my fiercest and ached for their destruction with all I had, I still loved them more powerfully than I could ever truly put into words. My soul was so tangled up with theirs that I knew I never could have struck at them in such a vicious blow.

I leaned back in my seat, my arm pressing to Fox's as I tried to steal some warmth from him and he stiffened at the contact.

I glanced up at him guiltily, realising I was crossing the line he'd drawn in the sand between us as he gave me a tight smile and nudged me towards JJ before standing and moving to the watch the horizon with Rick. They shared a look that spoke of secrets between them and I frowned, wondering what the hell that was about.

"I dunno what Luther told them earlier but they've both been cagey ever since," JJ said.

I frowned between Fox and Rick, watching as Fox leaned in to say something and Maverick shook his head angrily, waving him off and practically vibrating with rage. What the hell was that about?

I let JJ pull me closer as the cool air continued to make me shiver and we were soon slowing down close to Isla Tigre and the large rock that curved out of the water.

Chase pulled out a couple of big flashlights from beneath the seats and Fox and Rick grabbed some scuba tanks and started setting them up for us to dive.

I gripped the pistol a little tighter as I stood, the boat bobbing beneath me as I looked all around us, relieved to find nothing but calm water in every direction with no sign of anyone else out on the ocean tonight.

"Do you really think we're gonna be able to find it?" I murmured, mostly to myself as doubts crept in. Because if we couldn't find it then we were going to be seriously fucked.

"We will, little one," Chase swore, tugging his shirt off and looking at me as I worried my bottom lip between my teeth. "We know it's down there somewhere. And we won't quit until we find it."

I nodded, trying not to worry too much about how much of the yacht would even be left for us to find on the ocean floor after the fire had consumed so much of it and the wreck had been left down there to rot for the last eleven years. Because he was right. We had to find it and that was that.

Chase clutched his shirt to his chest as the others glanced his way, their eyes moving over his scars, but in a way that was appraising of him, like he was a god they were taking a moment to revere.

"What?" Chase ground out as I prised the shirt from his grip, brushing my fingers over the marks on his chest as desire pooled deep in my core.

"You're our protector," I said, my voice taking on a husky tone which I seemed to have no control over in that second. "We were all just reminded of what you did for us."

His adam's apple rose and fell and he stared at me like I held the whole universe in my eyes before clearing his throat and stranding up a little straighter.

"Come on, we don't have all night," he said, trying to get the attention off of himself, but I was having a feast on his body and I couldn't stop looking.

The others all stripped down before grabbing their oxygen tanks and placing their masks over their faces, but as Fox stopped to double check the anchor was secure, I moved closer to him.

"First one to find it gets his dick sucked," Rick challenged, smirking tauntingly as Fox threw him a scowl.

"I didn't agree to that," I replied, cocking a brow at him and he laughed.

"I know. I'm nominating Johnny James - he's gotta be fucking good if he was charging for it."

"I didn't fuck guys, asshole," JJ said, tossing his shirt into Rick's face which he caught easily.

"Whatever you say, gigolo." Rick winked at him then dropped backwards over the side of the boat and sank beneath the waves.

"We'll see how much he's laughing when I find it first," JJ swore before jumping in himself.

"Why? Is he gonna make Rick suck his cock instead?" Chase joked before diving in after them and I laughed, though I really wouldn't have minded watching that show.

I caught Fox's arm as he made a move to jump in next and he paused as he looked around at me, a frown drawing his brows together.

"Don't shut me out," I begged, my voice a hoarse whisper as I let a little of my desperation show. He hadn't given me a single moment of his company since our argument in Rick's room and I wasn't sure I could take much more of it if he kept this up. "I know I can't give you what you wanted from me, but does that mean you don't want anything with me at all? We were friends first, Fox. We always had that. Please don't tell me that has to go now too."

The harsh set to his jaw loosened at my words and a sigh escaped him as he processed them.

"I'm sorry, hummingbird," he muttered. "I'm not trying to hurt you. I just don't know how to be with you now..."

"Yes you do. You were my Fox long before you turned into my Badger."

"Fuck you," he said on a laugh and I grinned up at him, seeing a little of my best friend in his expression at last.

"You can talk to me, you know," I added. "If there's something going on between you and Rick..."

"I think you might know about that already," he admitted, blowing out a breath and pushing his fingers through his blonde hair.

The moonlight broke through the clouds and illuminated his bare chest in a caress of silver light which made his muscles stand out and the dark ink of his tattoos almost seem to shift against the canvas of his sun kissed skin. Fuck he was something to look at. He always had been really. But the beautiful boy had turned into a model worthy figure of a man and the hardness in his posture only spoke of the trials of the life he'd led while I was gone.

"My dad told you about my mom and Deke, right?" he asked and my heart sank as I realised he finally knew the truth of that.

We'd always shared the fact that we'd grown up without mothers, but as I had known full well that my own DNA donor was a fuck up drug addict who gave no shits about me beyond christening me with a verb for a name, I had never held onto the pretty fantasy version of a mother that Fox had.

"Yeah," I admitted softly, moving closer to him and taking his hand in mine.

"I knew it was bad," he said, shaking his head. "I mean, where was she, you know? If she'd been a good mom then she wouldn't have been absent my whole life. I guess I never really believed she might have still been alive somewhere. But I just wanted to believe...something. I dunno. I guess it doesn't matter now anyway, right?"

"She chose you," I said, squeezing his fingers and moving a little closer, the space dividing us making my skin prickle as I forced myself not to close it. But I wanted to. I wanted to wrap my arms around his neck and press my lips to his and show him that I chose him too. I just couldn't choose him alone.

"Yeah, I guess. But she also chose to break my dad's heart and cheat on him with his psycho brother. I've heard stories about Deke. About the way he treated women. Why would she choose him when she had my dad and me?"

"I don't know," I admitted. "But love is complicated."

"I think it was more about lust," he spat, his gaze shifting away from me before he rolled his shoulders back and let some of the tension fall from his posture. "But whatever it was, it's ancient history now. Maverick is more upset about all of it than I am - not that he'll admit it of course."

"Why? What does it have to do with Rick?" I asked in confusion and Fox paused.

"I'll let him tell you that when he's ready," he said. "It's not my secret to share."

"Okay," I agreed, understanding that much even if I was burning with curiosity to figure out what else Luther had told them.

The wind tossed a loose strand of my hair across my eyes and Fox reached out on instinct, catching it and tucking it behind my ear, his rough fingers lingering against my neck as our gazes caught and held.

We didn't say anything, the two of us halting there with our eyes locked on one another while my heart thundered to an impossible beat and he swallowed thickly. His fingers trailed to my pulse point, his thumb dragging over the fading bruises which ringed my throat as he took in the furious pace of my heart.

"Hummingbird," he murmured and I tilted my chin up a fraction, inviting him closer as I drowned in the depths of his deep green eyes.

I reached for him, my fingers grazing against his forearm and curling around the thickness of the muscle there as I caressed the bird he'd inked on his skin to represent me.

The space between us charged with a static kind of energy as we remained there, acknowledging the need in us while fighting against it too. I licked my bottom lip, trying to alleviate some of the desire in me for the feeling of his mouth on my flesh and his hungry gaze fell to the motion, a low rumble of need sounding in his chest. My nipples hardened within my clothes, the aching points pressing against the fabric of my bikini.

His grip on my throat tightened the smallest amount, just enough that I was almost certain he was about to drag me closer, close this aching distance between us and end the need in me for him which was threatening to devour me whole.

Fox released me, blowing out a breath and stepping back so the contact between us was broken, and I was left feeling like my knees might buckle and my heart might plummet right down out of my stomach to splatter all over the floor.

"I guess we should get out there before the others accuse us of slacking off," I said, trying to lighten the tension as it was clear neither of us wanted to speak about that moment of temptation which we'd just endured. Fox grunted his agreement, looking down into the water where the others had headed, searching for any sign of the flashlights they were using to hunt for the wreck.

I tugged the borrowed sweatshirt over my head and dropped it, kicking off the oversized sweats too to reveal my black bikini beneath it.

"If you wanted to do me a favour, you could stop wearing shit like that in front of me," Fox teased, his salacious gaze running over my body and making me tremble as if his hands had caressed me in the same movement.

"What's the matter, Badge? Can't you handle me now we're all grown up?" I teased, tying my hair in a knot as I prepared to dive into the cold water.

"Oh I could handle you alright," he replied with a teasing grin that almost made me feel like we were okay again before he glanced away and stepped back.

Fox made sure the oxygen was flowing from my scuba tank then I hoisted it onto my back, fixing my mask over my face and putting the regulator between my teeth. Then I put on my diving fins and sat on the edge of the boat, falling backwards into the cold sea with Fox at my side.

We released the air from our BCD jackets and sank slowly, staying close to one another as we flicked our flashlights on and searched the dark water for any signs of the others.

I turned in a slow circle and spotted the beam of another light waving back and forth to our right. Tapping Fox on the shoulder to make sure he was following me as I started swimming beneath the waves.

We dove deeper, swimming on for far longer than it had seemed before making our way down to the bottom of the ocean where the others had all gathered around the wreck of the once pristine yacht.

JJ beckoned us closer and we swam over to join them as Maverick forced open the door which led down to the remains of the lower deck.

It was pitch black as we swam inside and a shiver ran through me which had nothing to do with the cold and everything to do with the familiarity of this place which had haunted my nightmares for years as I swung my flashlight from side to side in the dark interior of the boat.

Bubbles raced towards the roof as I swam along beside Chase, my heart beating harder as we made it down to the level where the bodies of the Castillo Cartel members had been the last time we were here.

The place was almost unrecognisable with fish darting to and fro and seaweed growing through broken windows. But as I swung my flashlight around and the pale white sight of a skull greeted me, a yell of fright escaped my lips and the regulator fell free of my mouth.

Chase caught hold of my hand as my heart damn near tried to break free of my chest and I snatched my floating mouthpiece, stuffing it back between my teeth and sucking down some fresh oxygen tainted with the taste of salt.

Maverick was outwardly laughing at me and I punched him in the shoulder with an irritable growl which I swear only made the asshole laugh more.

I shoved past him and swam deeper into the wreck, JJ keeping pace beside me as I headed towards the back of the boat where Carmen had told us the safe would be located.

I pushed through another door with a grunt of effort as the weight of the water resisted me and finally found myself in what had once been a lavish master bedroom. The remains of the bedding floated towards the top of the space where a pocket of air had been captured as the yacht sank and I swam beneath it, heading for the closet in the rear corner.

JJ pulled the door wide for me and I grinned as I found the metal safe exactly where she'd said it would be.

Chase crowded in close behind us, shining his flashlight on the combination lock so that I could enter the code and my pulse began to race as I carefully punched the numbers into it.

A heavy clunk sounded, echoing through the water surrounding us and JJ reached out to pull the safe open with a triumphant whoop that translated into a spill of bubbles surrounding us.

Water rushed into the space and stacks of cash floated out around me, the boys snatching them as they went like magpies chasing silver, their arms bumping against me and making me laugh.

The moment the beam of light from Chase's flashlight fell on the watertight pouch inside, I almost wept with relief. I could see the brown leather ledger bound safely within it and I grabbed it, hugging it tight to my chest like it was the only thing that mattered in this world. And as it held the safety of my boys in its possession, as far as I was concerned it was.

Fox grabbed my hand and squeezed my fingers tightly, his eyes crinkling through his mask and giving away his smile as I grinned right back.

We all turned and headed back out of the yacht once more, kicking for the surface with bubbles coiling all around us as we swam back to the speedboat and the promise of freedom from this fucking secret we'd been forced to keep for too damn long.

Fox kept a tight hold of my left hand while I kept the ledger firmly crushed to my chest with my right and kicked as hard as I could for the surface.

When we finally came up for air beside the speedboat, I spat the regulator from my lips and crowed our victory to the damn stars.

We all took off our fins and masks, tossing them into the boat and the boys all clambered up into it as I passed the ledger up to JJ before letting Fox haul me up and into his arms.

He stumbled a little as he righted me and I looked at him in the moonlight, the two of us grinning and shivering as our near naked bodies were crushed together and my skin buzzed at the contact.

"Nice work, hummingbird," he breathed, smoothing a stray lock of hair away from my eyes as I looked up into his bright green gaze and felt at home at fucking last.

"You did okay yourself, Badger," I replied with a grin, neither of us stepping away even though there wasn't any more reason for us to remain as we were. We slid off our gear, laying the tanks on one of the benches before drifting closer to each other again, seeming unable to keep our eyes from connecting. I felt like we were two poles of a magnet, drawn together by a force bigger than both of us.

A hand landed on my shoulder and I flinched at the interruption, turning to look and screaming to high heaven as I found a half rotted lump of flesh with bones protruding from all of the fingers sitting on my fucking skin.

"Rick!" I screamed, aiming a punch at his face which he ducked with a bark of laughter before I followed it up with a knee to the balls which very much hit the mark.

"Fuck," he gasped, stumbling to his knees as JJ practically fell over himself laughing.

Chase grabbed the rotting hand from where it had fallen on the deck while I continued to curse Maverick with every colourful word in my vocabulary and Fox started laughing too as he got the engine running.

"You're such an asshole, Rick," I snarled, lunging at him while he still tried to recover from the attack to the balls and Chase had to grab me to hold me back.

"Always has been," JJ pointed out.

"Yeah," Chase agreed. "This is just like old times."

He yanked me down to sit with him at the back of the boat as Fox loosed the throttle and turned us back towards Dead Man's Isle, and I let Chase keep me there because he was right. It was just like old times, having the five of us laughing and pulling insane stunts together. And for the first time since I'd been back here, I was starting to think that maybe we could rekindle what we'd all once had for good.

The Oasis Clubhouse

LUTHER

CHAPTER TWENTY EIGHT

I sat waiting in a corner of the bar of the hotel my boy had claimed for his own after coming back to live here, watching the moon pass across the sky until sunlight slowly began to stain the black to palest blue beyond the view of the Cove in the distance.

I'd been nursing the same bottle of Jack all night, though I hadn't drunk that much of it. Enough to take the edge off of the lingering pain from my gunshot wounds and that was about it. I was mostly healed now anyway. At least enough to move about properly and get back to pounding the bag in the gym again.

I needed that.

The solid thump of my fists against a target to lighten the load of the rage that lived in me. Better I find a body to take the punishment of my blows, but despite my job description, there wasn't always one of those freely available, so a punching bag made do the majority of the time.

That darkness in me was something I'd given to my boys. I could see it in them these days more than I ever had while they were growing up. Back when they really were kids, it used to show its face less often. They had a brutality to them when pushed, a cutting kind of savagery which only reared its head under the most strained of circumstances. But I'd always seen it. Always known they had what it took to live this life. And I'd always been glad of that too. But what I'd failed at in my determination to keep them strong and prepare them for the reality of his cutthroat world was to protect the light in them too.

I'd loved watching them together with their mini crew made up of Johnny James, Chase and little Rogue Easton. Always laughed at the antics they got up to and found amusement in the chaos they caused on the streets I ruled. But it had seemed like kids playing pretend to me. The four boys playing a watered-down version of the games I played to keep cash in our pockets and fear in the hearts of those who would aim to take it.

When I'd sent Rogue away, I'd thought I was doing what was needed to turn those boys into men. I'd thought she was the reason they still played at being thugs instead of fully evolving into the gangsters they'd all been born to become. Just four teenage boys all caught up with their first true taste of lust and confusing it with the foolish idea of love.

I'd been waiting a long time for one of them to claim her, for the hurt feelings and flying fists to come between them before they all realised a woman was never worth that kind of feud with your brothers. Before she proved to them how fickle the fairer sex could be. And when I'd sent her away, I'd expected her absence to be the end of that nonsense. For them to grow out of those so called feelings and realise that no matter how prettily a girl like her might draw you in, she would always leave. Always pick another road. Yet your crew would stand true at your back through it all.

But now I was having to face the reality of my mistakes in that. Face up to the cost of the choices I'd made for my boys. The pain I'd caused them. I'd thought so certainly that I'd been doing what was best for them. Pushing them when they'd been hesitant to make the leap from boys into men.

I guessed I should have looked harder back then. Should have seen what was right in front of my face. I'd thought I had a couple of defiant kids on my hands, sneaking out and getting into trouble like all teenagers do. But that devotion they'd felt to the others - even the girl - should have been as clear as the nose on my face if I'd only looked harder.

I blew out a breath, swiping an inked hand down my face as I pushed those thoughts aside. They didn't do me any good now anyway. I'd learned a long damn time ago that dwelling in regret wouldn't get me anywhere. I could only learn from my mistakes and make fucking certain not to repeat them.

Which was precisely why I'd never let any woman get close to me since Adriana had betrayed me with my brother. And it was why I hadn't followed through on my threat to kill Rogue Easton if she ever showed her face in town again.

A real man knew when to admit he was wrong and work to fucking fix it.

So as the sound of laughter drew my attention towards the large doors which fronted the hotel, a knowing smile lifted the corners of my lips.

The doors burst open and the five of them strode in, Maverick laughing at something Johnny James was saying as Fox worked to suppress a smile too. My boys each stood on the edges of their old group instead of in the middle of it like they'd always done when they were kids, but I could see that old spark in their eyes as they joked with their friends. Johnny James had an arm slung around the girl who walked at the heart of them, her smile wide as she looked up at Chase who shook his head irritably, seeming to be the butt of the joke which they all found so amusing.

I drank in the sight of them like that, almost feeling like I was sitting up on the back porch of my house like I used to ten years ago, stealing glimpses of their happiness as they played out on the sand and surfed the waves.

It made something in me settle. I knew they hadn't fully come together yet, but only a fool wouldn't have found hope in seeing them like that. My boys reunited at last. And as my gaze fell on the little wildcat I'd made the mistake of banishing all those years ago, I knew exactly who I had to thank for bringing them together again. But as I'd done her the favour of sparing her life for returning to my turf after I'd banished her, I was going to just settle on calling us even for now.

"What the fuck are you doing lurking in the shadows, old man?" Maverick barked, spotting me suddenly while the others all remained too focused on their fun to have seen me where I sat in silence.

"Waiting on you," I replied evenly. "Did you get it then?"

Fox produced a brown, leather-bound ledger which was tied closed with a tight knot, holding it up for me to see. "I assume this is it," he said. "But as the cartel didn't want us looking inside, it's pretty hard to be certain."

"And you didn't look inside, did you?" I growled.

"Well, I would have taken a peek," Rogue chirped with a grin. "But these assholes were too scared of the big bad Mexicans to risk it."

"And with good reason," I replied, tossing back the last hit of my whiskey and pushing myself to my feet before closing the distance to their group, holding my hand out for the ledger.

I wanted it out of my son's hand and I felt slightly better as he released it into my grip. The thing was more deadly than a fucking grenade until I could get it back into Carmen's hands and well away from us, and I didn't want him connected to it any more than was absolutely necessary.

"So what will you do with it now?" Fox asked and I couldn't help but notice all of their smiles had faded now that I'd joined them. Well, almost all - Rogue looked ready to go toe to toe with me if I offered up the opportunity. I didn't know when that girl had decided to stop fearing me, but I kinda liked it. Terrifying everyone around me on a daily basis got a little old after thirty odd years and it was somewhat refreshing to have someone willing to goad me.

"I'll return it to the cartel today. I don't want this thing in our possession for a moment longer than absolutely necessary." My grip tightened on the ledger and whatever secrets it held. But I sure as fuck didn't want to know a single one of them.

"I guess I could lend you a boat," Rick mused, lording his little hold over the men on this island over me and making my lips hook up in amusement. He reminded me of me when I'd been starting up the Crew. All bravado and bullshit and not a single fear in the world. It made me proud as fuck, but his balls weren't as big as mine yet.

"I actually need a word with you, kid," I said to him. "Alone."

Fox scoffed lightly then turned and walked away without a word, the others quickly following him, though Rogue looked back at us curiously while Johnny James towed her out of sight.

Rick folded his arms, looking decidedly unimpressed as he lifted his chin in a command for me to spit it out. I wondered if he even realised he was imitating me in his mannerisms half the time these days or if he did it subconsciously. Either way, I couldn't help the small smile that touched my lips at the sight of him grown into a man almost as formidable as me.

"I don't have all day," Maverick growled as I waited for the sound of the others walking away to fade into the distance. "I was planning on getting my balls waxed and my asshole pierced - you know, all things that are less painful than enduring your company."

Amusement pushed the smile further onto my lips and I rolled my eyes at him. "Careful boy, you're not too old for a clip around the ear."

"Yeah? I am old enough to give you one right back and put you on your ass though, old man. And at your age you might end up needing a new hip after a tumble like that. So I suggest you keep your fists to yourself."

"Less of the old. I was younger than you when I had you boys to take care of on my own."

"Well I'm sorry that the time I lost while locked up in prison because of you set me back on the schedule you'd set for the production of more brats like us. I'll be sure to work extra hard to knock up some unsuspecting girl as soon as possible," he deadpanned and I shook my head before turning away and heading over to grab the whiskey bottle from where I'd left it.

"Which one of us are you hoping to fool with that bullshit?" I asked him, taking a swig from the bottle before holding it out for him to take.

"What makes it bullshit?" Rick asked, claiming the Jack and drinking from it in long, slow gulps which told me he was more than accustomed to the hit of hard liquor these days.

"That girl who just walked out of here."

His posture tightened at the mention of Rogue, the bottle slamming down on the bar in front of him hard enough that I was surprised it didn't crack before his fist was in my shirt and he was yanking me so close that we were nose to nose.

I let him do it, raising my chin and offering up the challenge in my eyes. If he needed to come to blows with me so that we could move forward then so be it.

"Take a swing at me then if you have to, kid. But if you're gonna pick a fight with a king then you'd better be ready to have your ass whooped for it."

"You don't speak about her," Maverick growled, not looking the least bit put off by my warning and making my blood heat with the challenge in his eyes. There weren't many men who could face off against me like that and I was long overdue a good fight. "You hear that, Luther? Don't go making the mistake of believing I won't gut you if I get so much as a sniff of a suggestion that you mean her harm again."

"That girl is more than capable of causing harm to herself without me needing to get involved," I said. "But I already made my deal with her and she's holding up her end of it just fine."

"Oh right, the deal where you think she'll somehow manage to bring me back under your thumb?" he scoffed.

"No. The one where I asked her to help reunite our family. And here I am, talking to you face to face after ten years of you refusing to so much as hear me out. You're spending time with Fox again. And now our gangs are going to be working together too. Seems to me like the little wildcat knows exactly what she's doing."

"You're fucking deluded," Rick spat, shaking his head and making a move to walk away, but I called out before he could take more than a step.

"It's time, Rick. The Harlequins and The Damned Men have a common enemy. You know an alliance makes sense."

He pulled up short, the tension rolling through his posture making it clear that he both hated that suggestion and knew I was fucking right. I waited him out, leaning against the bar and sliding the bottle of Jack towards him again in offering.

"Let me make this clear," he said, turning to me and leaning his own forearm against the bar, his fist tightening as he tilted his chin down and looked me in the eye. "The Damned Men are my men. They follow me and only me. They're never gonna fall in line beneath you and you'd better get that through your head fast. I built this empire. I made it myself. Just like you did with The Harlequin Crew. These men are mine. Not yours. And any so-called alliance we form would be precisely that - or more accurately a cease fire in the name of destroying a common enemy. Nothing more."

"Yeah, yeah. I hear ya," I agreed easily. At the end of the day, Fox had his own men within the Harlequins too. It wasn't like I wasn't used to having a portion of my army fall under the command of one of my sons. And if Rick needed to cling to the illusion of control over his precious Damned Men, then I was more than happy to let him.

"You'd better," he grumbled, taking up the bottle of Jack and sinking a large mouthful.

"So you're agreeing that it's time for that?" I pushed. "For The Harlequin Crew and The Damned Men to come together to take down Shawn."

Maverick's jaw clenched and a sneer tugged at his upper lip before he blew out a harsh breath. "I'd pay in blood and death to see that motherfucker gutted," he replied. "So sacrificing a little of my pride seems like a low enough payment for now."

"Good." I clapped him on the shoulder and he stilled, turning his dark eyes on me and looking me over slowly, like he couldn't decide how he felt about me. Or whether or not he just wanted me dead. I was hoping he was remembering that I was the man who had raised him, loved him, nurtured that beast in him, led him to see his own potential. But maybe I really was deluded. Still, a king had every right to indulge in the idea that the world he ruled was perfect, even if our little slice of perfection held more bloodstains and pain than your average emergency room. "So I can contact my people and tell them to come here? Form a united front so that we can chase Shawn out of our fucking town?"

"How about you make sure the cartel are dealt with first. Unless you want them butchering every single one of your men on their way here," he hissed.

I placed the ledger down on the bar between us and nodded, drumming my fingers against the leather and giving one of the ties securing it a gentle tug before releasing it just as fast.

"I'll call Carmen and arrange the return of this now," I confirmed.

"Good. When it's done and she's called her dogs off, you can bring your frightened rats here. Until then, I need some fucking sleep." Maverick dropped the bottle of Jack Daniels on the bar and turned to walk away from me but I caught his arm, forcing him to look back at me once more.

"I fucked up, kid," I said to him in a low voice, looking him in the eye like the man I knew he was now. "I know it now but didn't know it then. I fucked up and I can't undo that, but I love the fucking bones of you. You're my boy, always have been. And I'm proud of the man you've become even if I have to face your hatred every time you look at me. I just wanted you to know that."

"In case your cartel whore is lying and she cuts your throat the moment you show up with that thing?" he asked, a mocking lilt to his voice as he pointed to the ledger.

"No. Because it's the truth. And I want you to hear it even if you don't want to listen." I grasped his face between my hands and pressed a kiss to his forehead, ignoring the way he gripped the gun at his hip and taking a moment to remember the little boy I used to tuck into bed, who used to look up at me like I was the biggest, baddest asshole in the whole world and all he wanted was to grow up and become just like me.

Maybe I'd fucked up on encouraging that though. Because now he *was* just like me: a king with no queen, a man on a ledge, violence given life and fucking aching for something he didn't even understand. That was what it was to be a king though. It was a lonely fucking existence when you stood above all others with no one by your side.

"I love you, kid," I growled as he fell still. "And it's okay that you don't love me back. But don't let that hatred poison what you used to have with Fox anymore. You and him were always meant to have each other. Don't let my mistakes keep that from you too."

Maverick released a long breath, his hand moving away from his gun and clasping the back of my neck tightly as he held me close there and my chest seemed to cleave apart as I drank in that moment. Tasting the love I felt for my boys and knowing that I was the reason I'd been missing it for so damn long. I'd tried to do right by them. I only hoped that in time they might come to understand that.

He pulled back suddenly and I let him go, scratching at my ribcage for a moment where his name was inked across my flesh.

"You'll be needing a boat," Maverick said, turning towards the door and calling back to me as he walked away. "Make your arrangements and I'll have one waiting for you at the dock when you're ready to leave."

I watched him walk out on me with an empty kind of feeling in my chest and just hoped that he might be on his way to spend more time with Fox. It may well have been too late for me to salvage the love my boys once had for me, but if I could repair the rift between the two of them then I could at least sleep easier at night.

I turned towards the exit then paused and changed my mind, heading back inside to the room Rick had given me to use while I stayed here, ignoring the stares of his men as I passed them. I wasn't afraid of a bunch of low-ranking douchebags like them. I could take them all out before they even realised I'd decided to end them if the notion took me. And I actually considered it for a moment before just heading into my room. I'd been taking a back seat in this game for a little too long, my injuries forcing me to hold back. But fuck that. I was born of blood and ruin and I craved the taste of carnage on my tongue once more.

I didn't need to show up for a meeting with the cartel in yesterday's clothes with the scent of alcohol hanging around me though. Or more precisely, I didn't need to show up for a meeting with Carmen, looking like I'd done little more than roll out of bed. Not that I gave a fuck what she thought of me really, but it was a matter of respect. And she was a woman who demanded a whole lot of it. For good reason too.

I took a quick shower, never once taking my eyes off of the journal the cartel coveted so dearly then changed into some of the clothes Rick had given me, his large frame a good match for my own even if his taste was a little different. But a black shirt and jeans couldn't really fail, and I took a few moments to sweep my blonde hair away from my eyes before smoothing my tattooed hand across the short beard which covered my jaw.

I stilled as I realised what I was doing. And why I was fucking doing it. Thoughts of that cold, beautiful woman filling my head for several long seconds before I blinked hard to force them away.

"Bad fucking idea," I muttered.

I wasn't a damn saint. I may have steered well clear of women so far as hearts, flowers and bullshit promises went, but I hadn't spent the years since my wife had been murdered by my brother celibate. I liked to fuck as hard and as often as any red-blooded man. I just knew well enough how to pick the right kind of woman for the fix. Namely by avoiding any complications like gang affiliations and making it clear what I was offering up front.

I grabbed the journal from the side of the sink, stuffed it into the back pocket of my jeans then strode out into the hotel.

The sun was climbing higher into the sky now and as I stepped into the already balmy heat, I knew we were in for another sweltering day in the Cove. Which was just the way I liked it.

I stalked down the jetty along the beach, casting my eyes across the boats bobbing in the sea beside it and lifting my chin as one of Rick's men stepped into my path with a key held out for me.

"Mr Stone says you're to have that one," the man said, jerking his head at a high-powered speedboat before tossing me the key to it.

"His name is Harlequin, not Stone," I grumbled, jumping down into the boat, and letting the bottom feeder untie it for me. "Don't fucking forget that."

"No, sir," the guy agreed quickly, tossing the mooring rope into the back of the vessel for me and leaning down to give the boat a little push as I started her up.

I didn't bother to reply to him, turning my attention along the coastline to the north before revving the engine and speeding away across the water.

I cut across the deep blue sea, cresting waves at speed and kicking up spray in a wide arc around the boat as I fixed my gaze on my destination long before it ever truly came into sight.

My heart hit a slow and steady pace as I closed in on the cartel's compound, that oh so familiar taste of danger lingering on the air with more and more potency the closer I drew to it. I knew that this could be insane. It could well be the end of me. I had the very thing they most desired in my possession and my boys had been responsible for its loss all those years ago. I wasn't a dumb man. I knew I could easily be headed to my own execution alongside the delivery of this ledger, but that was precisely why I was going to do this alone.

I wouldn't risk my boys here. I wouldn't even risk my men. And I didn't need to put on some pathetic show of bravado by turning up here surround by backup either.

I got how the power hierarchy worked around here and I understood my place in it. I may have been a king, but the woman I was headed to see was an empress. And above her, the man she answered to may as well have been a god. Though he certainly wasn't of the benevolent kind. More like a cruel and blackhearted demon really, one so corrupted by greed and the want for power that all traces of humanity had long since abandoned him.

Not that I was much better. We all knew how best to sin in these parts.

As the huge old plantation appeared along the coast ahead of me, I cut the speed of the engine and turned the prow towards the jetty which sat before it. The building itself was set up on the hill, the coast here having little beach while rocks took the place of sand and the properties were placed higher up to look out over the water.

Armed men appeared as I approached, enough lead aimed my way to shred me like Swiss cheese if the notion took them, while I slowly brought the boat closer to the wooden boardwalk which extended into the sea.

"I've got the item I was asked to find," I called out, hearing a few murmured words in Spanish from the men who continued to watch me hungrily. Like they would enjoy nothing more than the opportunity to pull those triggers and end me.

A man I recognised as one of Carmen's personal bodyguards stepped forward, jerking his chin at me in command without bothering to speak, though I knew full well that he could speak English if he wanted to. The asshole was just refusing me the simple respect of addressing me the way he should.

"Are you forgetting your manners there, asshole?" I called to him as the speedboat bumped against the jetty and I hopped out to land on the wooden boards, the solid thump of my feet hitting them giving me a moment to get my bearings.

There were no less than twenty men with guns currently trained on me, though I wouldn't have been surprised to find it was actually thirty if I counted the assholes who remained hidden from my sight.

The men weren't posturing in fancy suits and bullshit, which was one thing I liked about the cartel. They may have been a bunch of bloodthirsty motherfuckers, but they didn't bother to pretend they were anything else. In fact, they flaunted their scars and the coldness in their eyes just as openly as they flaunted their wealth. They were ravenous beasts always hungry for more and more, and the idea of collateral damage meant little or nothing to them. Least of all to the people who led them. One of whom I was here to see today.

The men surrounding me continued to speak to each other in Spanish, purposefully excluding me from the conversation, though I knew enough of their language to grasp the bones of what was going on. They were waiting for their orders from the woman in charge. Which meant I was safe enough for now - at least until she decided what do with me.

A couple of the men approached me, roughly patting me down and checking me for weapons. But the only thing I had on me was the ledger and they didn't lay so much as a finger on that where it still protruded from my back pocket. Like they knew it was worth far more than they could afford to pay out.

I was left to wait in the blazing sun once they were done, most of the guns still pointed my way while silence fell among the men and seagulls squalled in the air above us.

The silence that fell was of the heavy, ominous kind and I could practically feel the sharpness of a blade being primed and aimed at my heart. I didn't move from the spot where I'd been left to wait, but I sighed irritably, folding my arms and letting it be known that I didn't appreciate the wait. Not that Carmen would give a fuck about that. I swear that woman revelled in wielding her power over men like me. The kinds born with a spine that didn't know how to bend and a soul dipped in sin.

Eventually, her man Pepito beckoned for me to follow him and turned to lead the way up to the enormous house. The cartel had owned this place for a long damn time and though I'd never been particularly fond of knowing that they held a stronghold just up the coast from my town, I'd long since come to the conclusion that I preferred to know where they were when they were in the area. Which they weren't often. Just often enough to set my teeth on edge while they watched over their product and the ways it was transported into the country.

I climbed a set of steep stairs carved into the rocks which led down to the jetty, then followed him through an iron gate topped with spikes. The gardens which ringed the house were wild with flowers, an abundance of colour surrounding me and filling the air with their sweet scent as I passed between them.

We crossed a long veranda which backed the white property then stepped through a set of double doors which led into the opulent building.

Pepito silently led the way down long hallways adorned with paintings worth more than most of my cars and nothing but the sounds of our footsteps against the tiles broke the silence.

The scent of chlorine reached me a moment before Pepito pulled open a wooden door which revealed a set of stone steps. He moved aside to let me pass, the depth of his scowl letting me know quite clearly that he didn't like the idea of me heading down there.

"Remember who you're meeting with down there, hijo de puta," he hissed at me in a low tone designed not to carry. "The black widow won't hesitate to gut you if you disrespect her."

I gave him a shove, my forearm pressing to his neck for the briefest of moments as I pinned him to the door and gave him a good look at the darkness in me while offering him a deadly smile.

"Don't forget who you're talking to either, asshole," I growled, releasing him just as fast and striding through the door without a backwards glance.

Pepito cursed me before slamming the door closed behind me and locking it too, leaving me in the dark with nothing but the glow of orange light from the foot of the curving staircase to guide me on.

I started walking, pushing my fingers through my hair absentmindedly as the sound of lapping water reached my ears and the scent of chlorine grew stronger.

When I reached the ground floor, I found myself in a stunning pool room, set out to look like something the Romans would have had with brown tiles coating the floor and walls while hidden lights cast that orange glow throughout the warm space.

The pool itself looked midnight blue where it lay in the centre of the room and as I stepped closer to it, I spotted Carmen swimming beneath the water, her tanned flesh clad in a blood red bikini which gripped her round ass like a second skin, making the man in me growl with the unwanted desire to steal a taste of her.

But no matter how beautiful the creature beneath that water may have been, I knew better than to take the risk of getting any closer to her.

Carmen made it to the end of the pool closest to me where wide steps led up and out of it and I watched her as she emerged from the water, sweeping her long, brunette hair away from her face so that it dripped down her back as she strode from the pool. She cast a look my way, her scorching dark eyes scanning me from head to toe before she walked towards the small table beside me where a towel lay waiting for her.

I picked it up and held it out obligingly as she approached forcing my gaze to stay locked on her face rather than drinking in her bikini clad curves the way I wanted to. This was doubtlessly some kind of test and no matter how much the sight of her dripping wet and near naked body might have made my flesh heat, I wasn't going to be letting her win a point by distracting me with it.

"Mr Harlequin," she said in greeting, reaching for the white towel, her fingers brushing against mine as I handed it to her.

That was no fucking accident and I arched a brow at her as she proceeded to dab at the water coating her flesh while not covering up a single inch of her alluring curves.

Despite her swim, her mouth was stained red, though her dark eyes were adorned with nothing but the beads of water which clung to her long lashes. Perhaps she wasn't wearing lipstick at all. Perhaps her full lips really were that deep shade of ruby which drew my attention far too much all on their own. She looked younger without the makeup on, though she was still all woman in her mid-thirties and oozing power, nothing like the silly girls who seemed to surround me in the Cove. It wasn't even about their age - there was just something juvenile about most of them. Or maybe it was innocence that I saw. But in Carmen's eyes I could only see the life experience that being a leader in our world could offer and the cold, dark void of the monstrous nature it took to thrive in it. She was quite possibly the most beautiful woman I'd ever laid my eyes upon, and it was that look at her soul which I glimpsed from time to time which made that the truth just as much as the package she was wrapped up in.

"Carmen," I replied, watching that fire in her spark as I addressed her by her name like that. Not that she had ever once called me out on it. I think she secretly liked that I wouldn't be cowed by fear of her or the people she worked for, even though she'd never say it out loud.

"Indulge me a moment, won't you?" she asked, reaching past me and picking up a handheld scanner which she flicked on casually.

I held my arms wide as she ran it over my body, circling me like a shark scenting blood in the water, though I didn't so much as shift from foot to foot while she did it.

"Feel free to check me too - and the rest of the room if you desire. I want us to be able to speak openly today," she said, her tongue caressing each word with that sultry voice of hers, laced with Spanish inflection which I swear was specifically designed to get the attention of my cock.

I took the scanner from her as she offered it up. "You want honesty?" I asked curiously, stepping closer to her and running the device down the front of her body even though I seriously doubted there was room for any kind of listening device inside the confines of that little bikini.

Carmen only gave me a coy smile, clearly wanting the room checked before she would be more candid. She turned her back on me, tipping her head to one side and running the towel through the wet strands of her hair while offering me the opportunity to scan her back. But all she really gave me was the freedom to drop my gaze to the perfect curve of her ass in the red bikini bottoms and consider the idea of pushing her down over the small table beside us and seeing how that voice sounded when she was screaming in pleasure.

Carmen turned her head, arching a brow at me over her shoulder as she caught me looking and I raised my chin, owning it as I looked right back.

"I thought you asked me here to return your ledger?" I asked her in a low voice. "If you wanted me to fuck you then you should have just said. It would have saved my kids a lot of effort in retrieving the thing."

Carmen laughed, tipping her head back and walking away from me. "If I wanted to fuck you, Mr Harlequin, I would have done it already. But men like you are so often a disappointment in the bedroom - so much testosterone and bravado is often a compensation for a tiny cock after all. And even if that isn't true in your case, I don't fuck men who think of themselves as kings. You're all far too interested in self-gratification to know how to please a woman like me."

I considered telling her that she had no goddamn idea what she was talking about when it came to fucking me or the size of my cock, but as I caught a glint of amusement in her gaze, I got the feeling that I was falling right into her trap. This whole thing was a game to her. She was using her body to throw me off and clouding my judgement with lust. Well fuck that. I'd been played by a beautiful woman before and I'd long since learned how to avoid getting burned.

"Good," I retorted. "Because you're not my type."

She didn't take any offence at that, only laughed again. "Well perhaps you can continue to scan the room so that we can get on with this conversation then? I'm a busy woman."

I considered calling her out on the fact that she didn't exactly look busy, swimming in her private pool, but just turned my back on her and started to make a quick sweep of the room with the scanner instead.

By the time I'd given it all the once over and was sure we were speaking in private, Carmen had pulled on a sheer golden kaftan which hung open at the front and did nothing to cover her body. She sipped on a cocktail while relaxing into one of the little chairs sat either side of the metal table.

I dropped into the other chair, noticing that there was no drink there for me and biting back the irritation of that implied insult. I wasn't here to enjoy a drink with this woman. I was here to deliver a package.

I took the ledger from my back pocket and placed it onto the table between us, watching Carmen as she reached for the leather-bound book.

She picked it up and untied the cords which held it shut, flipping it open and releasing a long breath as her gaze skimmed over the handwritten words inside it. I flicked my attention away from the pages before I could read any of it, not wanting to know what was in there one fucking bit. The cartel were welcome to their secrets and I would be keeping mine too. We didn't need to know where all of each other's bodies were buried to maintain a healthy business relationship.

"Did you read this?" Carmen asked curiously, turning the pages without lifting her gaze to meet mine.

"I'm no fucking fool," I ground out. "Your secrets are your own. I'm only interested in them buying my kids out of the firing line."

"You have two boys, yes?" she asked, looking at me again as she snapped the ledger shut.

I grunted a confirmation, not liking her paying too much attention to that fact. She'd met Fox plenty of times and though I doubted she'd ever had any direct interaction with Maverick, it was no secret that he was my boy no matter what name he went by.

"I can tell you didn't have girls," she added, seeming amused by me and forcing a response from my lips despite my better judgement.

"And why is that?" I asked.

"Because if you'd been forced to appreciate the power a woman can hold first hand by raising one yourself, you wouldn't look at me with such disdain."

My jaw clenched and I shook my head. "I don't look at you with disdain," I muttered. "It's respect and caution. I know full well the power a woman can wield, and I'm not dumb enough to fall for the same trap twice."

Carmen's brow rose with interest and she pinned me with a calculating look. "Well, that is intriguing. And here I was, thinking you were just another arrogant man, believing the lump of flesh between your legs is a magic rod of power that sets you above the fairer sex."

"Oh no," I replied, flicking my gaze over her again. "I'm well aware that what you hold between your thighs is far more powerful than any cock," I assured her.

Carmen smirked at me and my blood boiled as I saw the mocking gimmer in her gaze. She was enjoying this, dangling the carrot before my eyes and seeing how far she could push me in hopes of grasping it. I couldn't say I much liked being at her mercy, but there was something about her that made me think I could trust her to be fair. She always had been in the past after all. But she hadn't gotten her reputation for nothing either.

"Give me a moment," she purred, reaching for a phone which lay on the table. I'd scanned it for a bug and the thing was switched off, but she turned it on and made a call while her gaze drifted to the ledger.

I had no choice but to just sit there while her call connected and once it did I couldn't hear the voice of the person on the other end of the line. But it didn't take a genius to figure out that she was calling the man in charge.

I'd never met the Castillo drug lord personally and I had no desire to either. If this woman was deserving of her terrifying reputation then she was still a kitten in comparison to him. No. My connection to the cartel went this far and no further and I had absolutely no desire for that to ever change.

"I have it," she said, leafing through the pages of the ledger before switching into Spanish as she continued her conversation. She said something which sounded like a confirmation then laughed, sounding genuine enough, though as her dark gaze flicked to me I swear there was a very different emotion in the depths of her eyes. She was afraid.

Carmen wet her lips, mostly listening now and still looking less than comfortable despite the casual lilt to her words. She murmured something a little reluctantly and I frowned, wondering what she'd said, but her gaze had moved away from me and back to the pool, so I wasn't certain if I was just imagining her discomfort or not. She was a damn good actress either way. She said a couple more things before agreeing to do whatever had been asked of her and ending the call.

Carmen switched the phone off again and showed me the screen so that I could see we were once again enjoying the privacy of this conversation.

"Do you have a lighter on you, Mr Harlequin?" she asked me, turning to face me once more without so much as a flicker of anything dark in her gaze. I'd probably just imagined it. Or she was just as afraid of her boss as the rest of the world - and I could hardly blame her for that if it was the case.

"Yeah," I said, taking one from my pocket and handing it over.

She smiled at me, pulling my gaze to her mouth once more even though I was fairly certain nothing about the way she was acting was real. She was temptation embodied, brutal, powerful, and deadly. And I wasn't going to forget it.

Carmen flicked the lighter to create a small flame then held the ledger open above it and set the thing alight.

My jaw ticked as I watched it catch, lines and lines of carefully handwritten notes curling up in the flames and turning to ash before my eyes as the pungent scent of burning filled the air.

Carmen dropped it before it could burn her fingers, the leather cover falling open against the tiles as the pages continued to burn within it, destroying every last piece of the thing that had supposedly meant so damn much to them.

"That's it?" I growled, unable to hold my tongue a moment longer as the pages continued to burn. "You threatened my family, my entire fucking crew over the loss of that thing and now you just burn it?"

"That's the power of knowledge, Mr Harlequin," Carmen sighed, sitting back in her chair and watching the flames as I studied the reflection of them in her dark eyes. "When it is out there in the world it is dangerous. In the wrong hands, the words written in that ledger could have caused many, many problems for the Castillo Cartel with the FBI and such. Now it is gone and it can no longer touch us."

"And what about my kids?" I pushed. "Can it still touch them?"

Carmen gave me that coy smile of hers again, making me feel like I was some dumb shmuck pleading at the feet of a goddess who already knew my fate and had no intention of changing it.

"It never did touch them," she said with a shrug, standing and moving away from me towards a small bar set up to the side of the pool. She started fixing herself a drink and I simmered as I waited for her to go on, but she didn't. She just kept fiddling with that fucking drink until I snapped and stood too.

"What is that supposed to mean?" I demanded.

"I will tell my people that I no longer bear the Harlequins any ill will," she said, ignoring me and dropping ice into her glass from a bucket set to the side of her.

"Just like that? There were a lot of people killed on that boat fifteen years ago. Are you seriously telling me that one burned up book is enough to cover the cost of that? Because I don't want this hanging over their heads. If there's more of a price to pay then I'll pay it. But I want them clear of this. I don't need to be worrying that some family member with a grudge is going to hear about them being on that boat the night all of those people were killed and-"

"You don't need to worry about anyone else in my organisation coming at them over any of that," Carmen said, waving a hand dismissively like her word on that would be enough for me to drop it. "You can go now."

I ground my jaw at being dismissed like some fucking bus boy and strode towards her with a snarl on my lips. I may have put up with a lot of shit where the cartel was concerned, but leaving here with a threat still hanging over my boys' heads wasn't gonna fucking fly with me.

Carmen must have heard me coming, but she didn't so much as stop pouring her drink as I closed in on her from behind, let alone bothering to turn and face me.

I snatched her wrist into my grasp and whirled her around, my grip tight and unyielding as I looked down into her ebony eyes and snarled at her, making her see me for exactly what I was. A man who wouldn't be disrespected any more than she would be.

"I want to know why," I hissed, keeping a tight grip on her wrist while my chest pressed to hers and she stared evenly back up at me. "I want you to tell me exactly why no one is going to come after my boys in retaliation for this. I want the answer to those fucking secrets hiding within your eyes and I want you to explain to me why you look so fucking pleased with yourself right now."

"You make a lot of big demands for a man who is one small slip of my wrist away from losing his manhood," Carmen replied, tilting her head so that her wet hair brushed my forearm as she gave a slight twitch of her free hand which was positioned between us. Something hard pressed against the side of my cock through the fabric of my jeans and I eased back an inch to look down at the sharp blade which she held at the ready to relieve me of my crown jewels.

I bit my tongue in frustration with myself for not expecting that, but I was pretty sure I'd been distracted by the sight of her ass in those bikini bottoms and hadn't noticed the knife she'd been using to slice lemon for her drink until now. Fucking devil woman.

"I just need to know that my boys are safe," I ground out, refusing to release her despite the predicament she held me in.

"You really want to know the truth of it?" Carmen asked, her voice low and seductive once more as she moved closer, her chin tipping up as if she might kiss me, though I knew she'd sooner follow through with her threat against my manhood than do that. "You want to take one of my secrets with you when you leave here?"

"I need to know," I confirmed, my palm growing hot where I still held her arm.

Carmen considered me for a few seconds then shrugged like she didn't much mind either way. "I never told anyone else about your boys and their silly little friends being on board that boat," she said slowly. "Not a single man, woman or child within the cartel has any idea that they were there. So no one would even know to come looking for them."

Shock rattled through me at that confession and I balked, trying to figure out how that could be the truth and what the fuck it meant. Why would she have kept that information to herself? What the hell was I missing here?

"Then why were the cartel hunting us down? Why did you back Shawn when he strode into my town after years of loyalty between my organisation and yours?" I demanded.

"Because he figured it out," she breathed, shifting her hand so that the knife scraped against my jeans a little and made me grunt. I did not want to be leaving here without my dick attached to my fucking body, but I did want to hear the truth of this. "And I couldn't just stand aside and do nothing while that ledger was still out there. So I told them the Harlequins had done something to anger me and made it appear to Shawn that I was hunting you over your connection to the yacht, La Princesa. My men do not question my motives, so all they knew was that I wanted you brought to me if you were found."

"Well the ledger is gone now," I said.

"It is. And so is my deal with him now that I have nothing to fear from him spreading that piece of information. If he decides to start shouting about your sons being on that boat all those years ago then I suggest you start telling everyone it was his men. No one will believe either of you then. The cartel want nothing more to do with your petty gang wars. And we no longer care about that boat now that the ledger has been retrieved. I told my boss that I discovered the wreck myself and as far as he is concerned, the matter is dealt with now. You and Shawn Mackenzie are welcome to tear each other to pieces and we will happily continue to work with the victor once the war is won."

"So tell me why you're not looking to claim retribution yourself," I demanded. "What do you know that you aren't telling me? Because it makes no damn sense for you to believe they only set that fire if you have no idea who killed those men. What makes you so fucking certain it wasn't my kids who did it?" I didn't want to dig my family into a hole over this shit, but I wasn't going to leave here without being certain that this wasn't going to come back and bite them in the ass either.

Carmen smiled this dark, delicious smile which made me still as I looked down at her. She might have been half the size of me, but I'd bet her body count was twice the height of mine. And I'd killed a lot of men in my lifetime.

She tiptoed up, her blade finally moving away from my manhood as her lips brushed against my ear and she spoke four words which I never would have expected to hear no matter how often I'd tried to figure out the mystery of

391

what had happened on that boat all those years ago.

"Because I killed them."

I pulled back sharply, wanting to see the truth of those words in her eyes and she let me see it plain as fucking day.

"Why?" I asked incredulously. She could only have been twenty-four or so back then and I was certain she hadn't even been a player on the chess board. In fact, I was pretty sure her rise to infamy and her position as the right hand of the Castillo Cartel drug lord had come in the years following the deaths of the men who had been onboard that boat, so what possible reason would she have had to kill all of them?

"My father was a vicious man," Carmen said, trailing the blade up my chest and giving my hand a pointed look where I still held her arm so that I released her suddenly. But I didn't back up. "He never paid me much attention when I was very young, but once I began to grow into a woman, he found he had a use for me. In fact, he found that his friends and brothers had a use for me too."

My brow furrowed as understanding flooded me and I was filled with a dark and potent kind of rage as I realised what she was telling me.

"I endured the wrath of weak and heartless men for many years while he owned me. But that night was different. That night he had decided that it was time for him to sell me off - give me to a husband to abuse instead of him. But I was done with being owned. I was done with men using me for their own sick pleasure and making me bow to them. So when he introduced me to the disgusting old hijo de puta he expected me to marry, I snapped. They were all drunk and off their fucking faces on their own product, so it was more than easy enough for me to steal a gun from one of them. And you and I both know how simply men die when faced with lead and wrath."

I wasn't sure I had the words to give her in response to her admission. I'd always thought of her as this cold, calculating creature who used her sexuality like a blade for no other reason than the thrill it gave her to have men falling at her beck and call. But there was so much more to her than that, and as she pressed her blade to my throat, letting me know how easily she could end me if she wanted to, I found the darkness in me liked that. I liked what she'd done and how she'd done it.

"And then you rose up and took his place?" I asked, my heart thumping hard as I pieced it all together. Fox, Rick and their dumb friends had stumbled upon something so much more beautiful than a simple FBI raid gone wrong or an assassination from a rival cartel. They'd walked in on her play for power. The beginning of her reign.

"I swam to shore when I was certain they were all dead. It was so simple to convince everyone in my father's organisation that I had just been a terrified girl who ran from the sound of gunfire. No one ever questioned me. Even when I took the reins of my father's empire and refused to let go of them. They told me a woman couldn't fill his shoes, but I have far surpassed his position within our organisation now. And every day that I sit in his place and spend his money, I laugh at the knowledge that I was the one who took it from him. I was the one who placed a bullet between his eyes and I was the one who proved that a woman could be worth so much more than he had ever even considered. No man has crossed me and lived to tell the tale since. No one ever really cared about the people who died on that boat, but the ledger was something else. Now that it is gone, the rest of those secrets no longer matter."

"I underestimated you," I admitted slowly.

"Men like you always do." She smiled slowly, dragging the tip of the blade down the side of my throat. "So now you own my secret, Luther Harlequin. And I own yours. No one will believe a man like Shawn Mackenzie if he starts shouting about your little Crew being responsible for the deaths of those men. But I can assure you that they would take my word on the matter far more seriously. So tell me, are you my friend or my enemy? Because I don't abide men who cannot choose a side."

"I have a feeling your friendship doesn't come freely," I said, though I could already tell that if I chose to be her enemy, I'd find myself bleeding out within a matter of seconds, so it was hardly much of a choice.

"Nothing worth having in this world ever does," she conceded.

I tried not to fall prey to the darkness in her eyes, but I could feel her reeling me in, setting the pieces on the board and placing me in a game I didn't even understand yet as she cemented this alliance between us. It wasn't about the Harlequins and the Castillo Cartel anymore. This was personal. Me and her. And this friendship would most definitely come with a high price. But perhaps the payoff would be worth it too.

"Friends then," I agreed, though I couldn't even think of the last time I'd called a woman that.

"Friends," she purred, pulling her blade away from me and tossing it down beside her unfinished drink. "I trust you can see yourself out?"

I watched her as she dropped the thin kaftan and dove back into the pool without another word, swimming away from me as I tried not to stare and fucking failed. I'd come here hoping to free my boys from the wrath of this creature and somehow I'd gotten myself tangled in her web.

CHAPTER TWENTY NINE

We spent hours hashing out plans to strike at Shawn and finally had a solid strategy in place for how to target him. When the cartel pulled out of Sunset Cove, it would leave him exposed and between the combined weight of The Damned Men and The Harlequin Crew, I knew we could take him. I just didn't know what life awaited us beyond his death. It was all I could think about, seeing him scream, seeing him bleed, and it wasn't even for myself that I wanted that. It was for Rogue. My little one, the girl he'd tried to destroy but was far too strong to ever truly be crushed.

But he'd left his mark on her all the same, a darkness in her soul that may never really leave, and when we were together the shared ache of those scars hung between us, binding us in a way I never would have wished to be bound.

I was starting to understand one thing though thanks to her. We weren't his victims, we were his fucking survivors, and I planned on showing him our strength before he went out of this world, our faces the last he'd ever see, the creators of his downfall.

It was getting late and Luther had headed to bed, leaving the five of us alone together and whenever that happened, Fox always slipped away. Things were awkward between us, so many unspoken words going unsaid that it was tearing me apart inside. I didn't really know what he thought of me being here, if he was angry or maybe he just didn't care anymore. Either way, it hurt me to see him so withdrawn from us, his place in our family feeling thoroughly lost.

"We should get some rest before tomorrow," Fox said as we walked down the corridor away from the lounge where we'd had our meeting. Without waiting for a response, he peeled off from our group, slipping into the stairwell and heading upstairs in the direction of the room he'd claimed here as his own.

Maverick clucked his tongue and Rogue stared after him with a look of longing in her eyes that made my chest tug. I reached out to brush my fingers across her cheek and she leaned into my touch, a sigh leaving her. Beautiful, ocean-eyed Rogue. She made my heart rate settle as my hand lingered on the smoothness of her flesh, enjoying the way it felt beneath my roughened touch.

Maverick and JJ kept moving down the hall, though JJ glanced back at us with a frown. "You coming?" he called as Mutt trotted along behind him wagging his tail.

"I'm gonna go talk to Fox," I announced, wanting to clear the air between us as best I could before tomorrow. Because who knew what the fuck might happen? I didn't wanna die knowing I hadn't tried to bridge the gap between us, and I needed him to know I didn't begrudge him for the actions he'd taken toward me. I didn't deserve this second chance I was being gifted day after day with Rogue and my brothers, but I was also far too selfish to keep myself away from them while they wanted me here.

"Should I come too?" Rogue asked, moving into my personal space. I could feel her everywhere when she was this close, her soul seeming to intertwine with mine.

"I think I need to speak with him alone, little one," I said and I resisted the demanding need in me to claim a kiss from those enticing lips. This was Rogue Easton, the girl I'd ached for my whole existence and I was going to prove to her that her body was secondary to anything else I felt about her. I'd stand at her side no matter what, let her own me in any way she saw fit and show her what she meant to me through actions alone. It was the least she deserved and it gave me something to focus on outside of the eternal nightmare living in my head.

"I love you," I told her in a low voice just for her, those words a liberation to me in so many fucking ways. I'd bottled them up inside for so long, trying to crush them, rip them apart, causing myself internal wounds and filling myself up with so much hate, anger and resentment that it had almost broken me. But now I didn't have to hold it in or pretend like it wasn't there, I could let those words free. Words weren't enough though, because we'd all used those to weave lies and betrayals against each other, so from now on every time I told her them, I'd show her too.

I slipped the piece of paper from my pocket I'd stashed there earlier, pushing it into her hand and closing her fingers tight around it.

"What's this?" She unfurled her hand, reading the name of the song I'd written on the paper. Arcade by Duncan Laurence.

I ran a hand down the back of my neck. "While I was gone, I made a playlist on my phone. Shit that reminded me of the past, but some of the present too, the good, the bad, and all the pain in between. They're about us, little one. And maybe it's dumb, but I thought I could give you a song whenever I say I love you to show you that those words represent a lifetime of us, a million memories made in Sunset Cove together, all of it so fucking imperfect, but there's something beautiful about that I think, even if it's sad too."

"Oh Ace," she breathed, her eyes drinking in my expression as her fingers curled around the song once more. I could see the ache in her to trust me again like she once had, but we had a marathon to go before that happened, and if it took me my whole life to earn that trust back, I'd do it. I was not going to let her down again, that was a fucking promise. And this small gesture was nothing to what I had planned to prove what she meant to me. "Come find me when you're done, I'll wait up."

She stepped away and I watched her go to Maverick and JJ, scooping up Mutt and tickling his ears as she walked away with them.

I moved into the stairwell, my leg giving me some trouble as I climbed through the hotel to the floor Fox and his dad were staying on. By the time I made it out into the corridor, I was spitting curses and trying to force myself not to limp as I headed to his door. I'd pushed myself too hard lately and I hadn't been doing my morning calisthenics routine with all that had been going on. I probably needed to rest it if I was being really honest, but I stubbornly wanted to keep pushing myself to fight against that feeling of weakness that was creeping over me.

I won't be made into my dad by fucking Shawn. I'll walk straight again if it kills me.

Sure you will, pretty eyes.

I shuddered at the echo of Shawn's voice in my head, frozen for a moment as I made it into the corridor and found the lights off all along it. The darkness seemed to stretch on forever and my breaths came harshly as I stood there, my heart bashing against my ribs and fear crawling across my skin.

My dad was sitting by the window with a cigarette between his lips, puffing on it as he aimed his air rifle out the open window at a seagull in the backyard.

"Dirty, rotten animal," he growled under his breath. "Let's see if I can take your eye out."

I had my pack on my shoulders and knew I could probably take the opportunity to slip out the back door and escape his wrath for today. Rogue and the boys were waiting around the corner to pick me up, but I found my feet stuck in place as I glared at the back of my father's head with hatred seeping through my veins. My gaze flicked to the bird pecking at the pieces of bread my dad had obviously tossed out there to lure it onto the ground and a snarl pulled at my lips.

I knew what that was like, my dad laying traps for me so he could take his rage out on my flesh. He'd leave the lights off in the house so it would look like nobody was home, and the moment I slipped through the door, he'd spring his attack. It left me constantly on guard, unable to ever get a good night's sleep in this house, my life lived in an eternal state of anxiety. Which was why I spent as little time here as possible. If I wasn't at school, I was out with my friends, but if I ever slept away from this house for more than a night or two, my momma called, telling me I needed to come home or my daddy would be getting angry. And what she really meant was that she was afraid for her fucking life.

I didn't know what possessed me exactly as I strode across the room towards him, but as he lined up a shot at the bird which had been lured here to die at his hands, I picked up the nearest thing to me which happened to be an overflowing metal ashtray and smashed him over the head with it.

The gun went off, but the shot went wide and gull took off into the air with a terrified squawk. I was already running, racing for the front door which was closest, knowing I'd pay dearly for this later but not giving a damn.

"Boy!" he bellowed, running after me, making my pulse elevate as my hand landed on the doorknob and I twisted it.

Locked.

Fuck.

His hands latched around my shoulders, dragging me backwards before he threw me against the wall face first, his hand slamming onto the back of my head to keep me there.

"I'll teach you some respect, you piece of shit," he snapped, his breath a fog of alcohol.

My body tensed and I shut my eyes, waiting for my punishment and it came in the form of his belt wrapping around my throat and cinching tight. I stiffened, grabbing hold of it in alarm as he pressed me harder to the wall with one hand and yanked on the belt with the other.

"You feelin' like a big man now, boy?" he crowed as I fought for air, trying to tear the leather from my throat in desperation. He somehow pulled it even tighter and the pain in my neck increased as I battled to take a breath and fear ratcheted up inside my chest. "Your momma's not here," he breathed in my ear. "Maybe I'll have ya buried before she gets home. Tell her you ran away. Ain't a soul in town who wouldn't believe that, boy. You're a worthless coward lookin' for a way outa the shitty life you're fated for anyway. It'd be a kindness to put your sorry ass in the ground."

My lungs roared for air and I tried to fight, but he was keeping me pinned in place and my head was starting to spin.

Stop. Please stop!

"Oh fuck," he cursed and the belt suddenly loosened and I sagged to the floor, pulling it from my throat as I gasped down air.

I blinked away the darkness around the edges of my vision, finding my dad hurrying towards a small fire taking root in the corner of the room, his cigarette clearly the source of it.

I managed to get to my feet, staggering as I regained my strength then *started running for the back door, moving as fast as I possibly could as I made it outside. I didn't stop there, shoving through the gate and tearing up the road, rounding the corner and spotting Fox's truck waiting for me at the end of it. I moved faster, ripping the passenger door open and climbing inside, Rogue shifting onto JJ's lap to make room for me.*

"Ace!" she squealed, but I was too shaken to respond, my hands trembling as I pulled the door shut.

"Can we go?" I asked, not looking at my friends as I tugged at the collar of my shirt, trying to pull it high enough to cover the mark that must have been darkening my neck.

"Fuck, what happened?" Rogue gasped, climbing into my lap and tugging my shirt down.

"Nothin'," I said, looking away and feeling my boys' eyes on me too. "Fox, please."

"Okay, man." Fox started the truck and took off down the road as Rogue cupped my cheek, angling my face to look at her.

Her eyes glinted with emotion but my heart rate settled as I gazed at her, finding the peace I needed right there in this girl. She laid her lips against my forehead and I shut my eyes, feeling safe at last as Maverick started telling me about a huge wave him and Fox had caught while surfing that morning and I relaxed as I listened, soaking in the presence of them and knowing that so long as I had them, everything would always be alright.

I forced myself to move and the motion sensor picked me up at last, the lights illuminating along the corridor and allowing me to draw in air again.

I limped along it and hesitated outside Fox's door, taking a moment to try and think through what I was gonna say. Except I didn't really know what I was gonna say, because shit was so messed up between us and maybe he didn't want to see me at all anyway. But I had to try.

I knocked on his door, my hand going to my eyepatch, adjusting it as self-consciousness trickled through me.

Fox opened it a beat later, his shirt off and a gun in his grip. He lowered it when he saw me, his eyebrows arching in surprise.

"Everything alright?" he asked, glancing down the corridor as if he expected to find enemies lurking there.

"Yeah," I cleared my throat. "I just thought we could...talk."

He frowned as he observed my expression then he stepped aside, ushering me into his room with a nod.

I moved into the space which had plain white walls and sheets, the place sparse yet clean. He led me out onto a balcony that overlooked the north of the Isle, the stars glittering above the dark expanse of hills that led to the sea.

He dropped down into a chair and I noticed a packet of cigarettes on the small table in front of him. He swiped them up, taking one out and pushing it between his lips before offering one to me. I took it, missing my old Zippo lighter which Shawn had stolen as I grabbed the plastic one from the table and lit up my smoke, dropping into the seat opposite him.

"Since when do you smoke again?" I asked as Fox lit up his own cigarette, taking a long toke and letting the smoke pour between his lips.

"Since I ain't got no reason not to," he said with a shrug and I frowned at that.

"Are you really out of the Harlequins?" I asked and he rolled his eyes.

"How many more times are you lot gonna ask me that?" he said.

"It's just the Crew...it's your whole life, it has been forever," I said.

"Not forever," he muttered, his eyes moving to the view beyond the railing and my gut tugged as I remembered our childhood, the best time of my goddamn life. And a time I'd never get back. No matter how much I wanted things to be like that again, there seemed to be a constant dark cloud hanging over us now. And even if we managed to kill Shawn, I wasn't sure we'd ever be free of it. Too much bad had happened, and now Fox was planning to leave our lives for good, I had the most terrifying feeling that I was never going to feel whole again with him gone.

It was always going to be a battle to keep our heads above the water, trying not to drown in the despair of all we'd lost, all we couldn't heal. I didn't even know what I had to offer Rogue in any real sense. I had no money, no job, no security at all to give her. Even if I could give her every drop of love that existed in the world, it wouldn't be enough. Because this life wasn't enough. She deserved so much more, and I had no idea how to get it for her.

"So that's it? You're just gonna leave town and be done with all of it? With all of *us*?" I asked, an edge to my tone, because it made me angry to see him giving up. He was checking out too, giving up on anything ever being good for him again, and it hurt me to see.

He leaned forward, resting his elbows on the table as he took another drag of his smoke and his green eyes flared with the reflection of the cherry. "Look, Ace, I know how it sounds. Like I'm running from all this shit, but that isn't how it is. The truth is – and please don't breathe a fucking word of this to Maverick or I'll kill you – but the truth is that I can't watch the four of you together, it fucking breaks me. But I know you're happier this way and that's all I want now. It's what Rogue needs, and I've spent too damn long trying to make her do what I want, what makes me happy. I've been a selfish prick and I'm tired of fighting for someone who was clearly never meant to be mine." Pain flashed through his eyes and he glanced away, ashing his cigarette in a tray on the table.

"Fox…" I sighed. "She wants you to be a part of this too."

His jaw flexed as he shook his head. "I can't do what you and the others can do, Ace. When she came back to town, something switched on in me, something that was maybe always in me when it came to her, but losing her made it ten times stronger. It's fucking primal, this need in me to possess her, but knowing she belongs to the rest of you, that she craves you all, it just…" He ground his teeth, a glimpse of that beast in him peering through his eyes.

"What?" I pressed, wanting to understand so I could try and find a way to fix it.

His gaze moved onto me, a predator awaiting me within them. "It's like she's splitting herself between all of you. But I want all of her, Ace. I'd never be satisfied with a piece of her soul because I need to capture every inch of it. I need to know she's mine right down to the sand in her hair and the scent of the sea on her flesh. If she's not mine in every way, then I can't have her. It's all or nothing with me, it always has been, always will be. So it's nothing, because she's made her choice and I really hope you all make her happy, I do, but I can't stay in this town and watch you become a family together, because I'll die, Ace. Inside, I will fucking die."

He snatched another cigarette out of the box and my chest crushed in a vice as I watched him, wishing he could understand that she wasn't splitting herself between us. It was so much more than that. We were offering our souls and she gave hers in return, and it wasn't easy and it wasn't going to happen overnight, but we were all fighting for what we'd had as kids and finding a way to make it work.

"I'm not gonna try and change your mind, but for what it's worth I'm not settling for a portion of Rogue, Fox. I could though. I'd settle for scraps because I don't deserve anything, but I can't sit here and tell you it's like that, because it ain't. She's ours. I can't explain it, but she isn't fractured by this, if anything it makes her more alive, like she's that girl again who we all knew and loved as kids again."

Fox winced a little, keeping his eyes averted from me. "I don't see how that can be possible."

"Because she's Rogue," I said simply. "Because she used to give herself to all of us when we were young and now she's doing it again."

"Sure," he murmured, clearly not buying it and I sighed, stubbing out my cigarette.

"Anyway, it's not just her I came to talk to you about," I said, rubbing the back of my neck. "I wanted to clear the air with you seeing as tomorrow we're gonna go fight Shawn and who knows what shit will go down."

Fox looked to me, regrets shining in his eyes. "You look like you're about to apologise," he said slowly.

"Well…" I shrugged. "I am, so-"

"Don't," he growled, reaching out and clasping my shoulder as he looked me in the eye. "Don't you apologise to me, Ace. I did what I did because I let being a leader of the Crew blur with me being your brother, and I was a damn good boss and shitty fucking friend. But I'm not part of the Crew anymore and I don't wanna be that man again. I'm sorry I treated you and JJ like I did, sorry I didn't listen to you both when Rogue showed up. Maybe shit could've been different, I dunno." He sighed, his hand sliding up to grasp the back of my neck and I let him pull me forward to rest his forehead to mine in the way he had when we'd last said goodbye. "Promise me you'll love her as hard as you fucking can, and don't let a day go by where she doesn't smile, Ace. Swear it."

"Fox…" I tried.

"Fucking swear it," he demanded and I could sense how much he needed this as I nodded.

"I swear it," I said, feeling our positions had flipped since that moment in the motel parking lot, like I was back there now only Fox was the one leaving this time. "But you know what, Fox? You never kept your promise to me, you said you'd keep our family together no matter what, and you didn't."

Fox released me, sitting back in his seat and looking to the sky. "I'm keeping it now, brother. Just not in the way you pictured because I'm not part of the family anymore."

"You are," I growled fiercely, wanting him to fight for us but seeing he'd already accepted it. "We can't be a family without you, don't you get that? It's the five of us, it always has been. It can't be any other way."

"It can and it will," he said simply as he retreated to that detached place he always seemed to be in these days.

"The Fox I know would never give up on her," I pushed.

"That Fox would have made her eternally unhappy," he muttered.

"So be a different Fox for fuck's sake," I snarled, but he didn't rise to meet my rage, simply shaking his head like the case was closed.

I stretched out my aching leg and winced as pain radiated up my calf, but I quickly schooled my expression to hide the pain as I felt Fox's eyes on me. Right, I was gonna do it. I was gonna play the best card I had, but I had to stoop really low to use it. And I was okay with that because if it got Fox to even attempt to spend some time with the rest of us then fuck it.

"Guess I'll see you in the morning then," I said with a sad smile, pushing to my feet and I placed all of my weight on my bad leg. I went down like a motherfucker and I didn't even have to act since I'd strained it running for my life the other day. I definitely didn't mean to knock the chair down either, but my plan went a little too smoothly as I made a complete ass of myself and Fox's hands locked around my arm, pulling me upright and holding onto me tight.

My mouth twisted up at the corner. "My hero," I teased and he cracked a grin. "Do you want me on my knees as thanks or shall I just bend over and spread 'em like a good girl?"

He snorted a laugh and I chuckled, breaking out of his hold and hobbling to the door, definitely putting on more of a limp than I actually had. I glanced back at him before I went, clutching onto the doorframe, about to ask for his help to get downstairs but I found him already behind me, watching me like a dad with a wobbly kid learning to take his first steps.

"I'll walk you down," he said and I nodded, hiding a smile as I turned away again and Fox took hold of my arm to support me.

I kept up the pretence as we went, making our way downstairs and along to the bar where the others had headed.

Rogue's laughter carried to us as we made it to the wooden doors and the sound was achingly good to hear. But it was far rarer these days than I liked, and I knew between the brief moments of happiness she had found since Shawn, she was never truly okay anymore. And it broke me. So I wanted to stretch out each of those moments and make them last longer and longer until one day, when Shawn was dead and he was a distant memory, maybe they'd last a whole lifetime.

"You alright from here?" Fox muttered, about to release me, but I staggered a step like a pro actor and looked to him like a puppy dog with an injured paw.

"Just a little further. Until I can sit down," I said, giving him the biggest eyes – alright eye – I had to offer. His gaze narrowed in suspicion but I kept up the innocent act, adding in a little grunt of pain as I shifted my weight. Yep, this was a low point of my life, but it wasn't the lowest I'd ever stooped, so there was that.

Fox's grip tightened again and he pressed his lips together as he pushed the door open and guided me inside. Rogue's laughter died and silence rang through the air somehow as loud as a bomb going off as she, JJ and Maverick all looked over at us and spotted Fox. They were sitting on a group of seats around a table littered with playing cards, a bottle of tequila on the go between them. Mutt was lying on his own seat, watching the game with his two front paws crossed and a look of contentment about him.

"Are you okay?" Rogue asked as she realised Fox was helping me along and I nodded, shooting her a wink which probably didn't translate because dammit how could I wink with one eye when I was wearing an eyepatch? That just made it a blink. Gah.

"Where do you wanna sit?" Fox murmured to me and I pointed to a seat beside JJ. He guided me over there while I kept up my limp, feeling Maverick's eyes on me, looking like he knew exactly what I was playing at.

Fox lowered me onto the seat and JJ reached out to pinch my cheek affectionately, looking half cut as he grinned at me.

"You shouldn't drink too much before a fight," Fox pointed out.

"Did anyone hear that?" Maverick boomed. "Sounded like a bossy asshole's voice just blew in on the wind."

"Rick," Rogue hissed. "Be nice."

"Don't worry about it. He's right, it isn't my place to comment," Fox said in a low tone, glancing between us before backing up like he didn't belong, clearly about to leave.

I'd gotten him here but I didn't know how to make him stay, and my heart didn't like that he was leaving so soon. JJ was looking at him like a hungry Labrador and I was surprised he wasn't whimpering too. It was pathetically endearing and I hated that he was pining for Fox, unable to bridge the gap between them.

"Night then," Maverick said lightly, dropping his hand onto Rogue's thigh beside him and squeezing hard.

Fox's eyes followed the movement of his hand and for a second I could see that possessive beast in him raise its head before he forced his gaze away and started striding toward the door at a fierce pace.

"Wait," Rogue called and Fox actually paused, glancing back at her with the eyes of a desperate, desperate man. "Do you want a drink?"

"He's good, aren't you Foxy?" Maverick taunted, his hand shifting another inch up Rogue's leg. "Or is somethin' bothering you, brother?"

Fox's throat worked as he watched Maverick's hand then his gaze snapped back to Rogue. "I'm fine. Goodnight, humming - Rogue."

Rogue looked crestfallen as Fox kept walking and my mind raced as I tried to think up a way to make him stay, but short of launching myself out of my seat and feigning another fall, I was coming up short.

But then Mutt leapt out of his own seat, racing over to Fox and yipping excitedly, jumping up at his legs as he looked for fuss.

"Hey boy," Fox cooed, dropping down to kneel on the floor and pet his head. Mutt licked his hands and face, seeming like the cutest, cuddliest dog in the world, even though he only switched on that side of him when it suited.

"How can we make him stay?" JJ whispered to me and Maverick's eyes flicked our way like he'd heard.

"I don't think we can," I said with a frown.

"Stay here, boy," Fox said, rising to his feet as he walked to door and Mutt trotted after him, chewing at his jeans.

"He can go with you if he wants," Rogue said and Fox nodded, not looking back again as he slipped out the door and Mutt went with him.

I turned to the others, my features tight as I felt the absence of the fifth member of our group like a hole in my chest.

Rogue continue to gaze at the door and I could almost feel her hurt over him leaving.

Maverick slid his hand off of Rogue's thigh, instead dropping it over the back of the couch behind her. "Maybe you should go talk to him, beautiful," he said, surprising all of us.

"And say what?" she sighed. "He won't listen to what I have to say."

"Try harder, pretty girl," JJ encouraged. "You're the only one of us who has a chance of getting through to him now."

She chewed her lip for a moment then nodded, getting to her feet and hope filled me as she left the room.

All I wanted in the world was our family back intact and it was clear JJ wanted that too, even Maverick for all his bravado wasn't exactly objecting to it. And I really hoped Rogue could convince him, because Fox was vital to our group and without him, it would never feel whole again.

CHAPTER THIRTY

I was glad of Mutt's company as the door shut behind me in my room because the space felt cold and unwelcoming. I trailed to the bed, dropping down onto it with a sigh and as Mutt moved to snuggle up beside me, I ran my thumb back and forth over his head.

"Are you gonna stay with me or them when I go, hm?" I asked.

Mutt glanced at me and I swear the little bastard rolled his eyes.

"Your choice, Mutt," I said and he growled at me.

I couldn't win with him.

A soft knock came at the door and I frowned, hesitating for a beat before rolling out of bed and walking to answer it. I looked through the peephole and my heart lodged in my throat as I saw Rogue there, my hand moving to rest flat against the door. I could just not answer, pretend I was asleep already, though she'd probably figure out I was ignoring her.

"I can see your shadow under the door," Rogue said, her eyes snapping up to look directly at the peephole and I swear it felt like being shot in the chest.

Fuck.

I gave in, unlocking the door and cracking it open to look out at her.

keeping the barrier of the door mostly between us.

I meant to say something, but all words abandoned me as I found her there, looking vulnerable and so fucking sweet it killed me.

"Can I come in?" she asked hopefully and apparently I was all out of refusals for today because I stepped back and simply let the door swing wide.

The moment Rogue was in my personal space, it felt so much fuller, so much goddamn warmer. Her shoulder brushed my chest and the energy that charged in my blood from that small touch was enough to raise every hair on the back of my neck.

I pushed the door closed, shutting us in together and making the change in the air permanent as she moved deeper into the room.

I followed her toward the bed, my gaze dropping down to her lower back which was on display in her crop top hoody, revealing the base of the angel wings which decorated her skin either side of her spine, then further down to the roundness of her ass in her sweatpants.

The animal in me who starved for her awoke and demanded I run my tongue and teeth over all of that exposed skin and mark her as my own. So I stopped myself from getting any closer, resting my shoulder against the wall and forcing back those carnal thoughts that had always won out in me before. Now, I fought them with all I had and hoped I could slay this beast who wanted her in ways more fitting for a caveman.

She climbed onto my bed, crossing her legs and stroking Mutt as she looked back at me. Her dark hair was a mess of waves and her eyes were so large and unblinking I couldn't escape them.

I cleared my throat as the silence stretched, struggling to breathe the air which seemed ten times thicker than it had been before she arrived.

"Can we talk?" she asked and no matter how strong a man I was, I could not deny that need in her eyes.

"What do you want to talk about?" I asked, though I knew, of course I fucking knew.

"Me and the others."

My spine prickled and jealousy warred in my chest with my need to let go, like two hungry wolves fighting to destroy each other.

"What about it?" I asked tightly, trying not to lose my temper or fall into old habits, but it was seriously fucking hard as she sat there on my bed looking like the most edible creature I'd ever met.

"We're trying to make things work again, like they used to."

"Chase told me," I said. "And I'm happy for you. Really." In all honesty, I wasn't jumping for joy over having to let go of her and them, but I did truly want them to find peace regardless of me.

"Are you?" she asked. "Because you look sad to me, Fox. You look sadder than I've ever seen you and it hurts me."

"I'm sorry about that," I said earnestly. "I don't want to cause you any more pain."

"Come here," she asked. "Lie with me, like we used to when we were kids and I'd sneak into your house while Luther was sleeping."

"Rogue…" I resisted, though the temptation was nearly impossible not to give in to.

"Please," she begged and fuck, I was only human. I moved to the bed, dropping onto it beside her and Mutt moved to the end of the mattress, curling up by our feet as I rested my head on one pillow and Rogue rested hers on the other.

"Why are you giving up on us?" she asked, the question seeming to snap some chord inside my chest, one I'd been holding onto tight to keep me sane.

"You know why," I said, my eyes lowering to the eternal temptation of her mouth before I ripped my gaze away again. She was an addiction to me, the kind that lived in every thought in my head. She was the centre of my world, my life had pivoted around this girl for years and I needed it to stop, because the truth was, I wasn't good for her. I was selfish and destructive and the more I tried to keep her, the more she suffocated. So why wasn't she grabbing the chance to run from me with both hands?

"I just don't think you're considering all the options," she said, tension lining her brow. "I think you've decided it's all or nothing, so now you're giving up everything. But it doesn't have to be like that. You don't have to leave town when this is over, you don't have to be miserable forever because you think leaving all of us to it is the answer. Me and the others are starting from scratch, trying to find our way back to the beginning again. I wanna be those kids, Fox, don't you?"

The silence stretched for a moment as that question stripped away my walls and left me entirely naked. Because of course I wanted that, I'd wanted that for years, I'd longed for it, dreamed of it. But I knew where that river ended up and it was an ocean of despair, because we weren't able to wield time.

"There's no going back," I sighed. "If there was, I'd be there now, not here."

"But we can rebuild it, Fox." She reached out, painting her fingers over my temple and fuck, she was convincing when she touched me. But the moment she did, that creature in me begged to be sated again and I knew I'd never stop wanting her like this.

"I can't watch you with them," I said, shaking my head. "I can't do what you're asking."

"What am I asking?" she pushed, gripping my cheek. "Because I think you're hearing it wrong."

"I think you're asking me to be your friend, while I endure seeing you with the men who were my brothers. Watching them kiss you, touch you. That's what you're asking."

"No, it's not," she hissed, her hand slipping down to my throat and squeezing like the ghost of a threat as she begged me to hear her. "I'm asking you to try and help us recreate our family. The five kids we were. I know it won't be exactly the same, I know we're corrupted in so many ways, I couldn't even begin to count them, but I also need to believe that there's something good left here. But I don't think it'll work without all of us trying. So really Fox, all I'm asking is for you to try. Try for me, try for you, and try for them. Because you say you want us happy, but honestly there's no happiness with one of us gone. You might not see it, but every one of us is missing you, and if you really think taking yourself out of the equation and suffering alone for the rest of your life is the answer, then you're dumber than I thought."

My head was a storm of thoughts and needs and urges, and I didn't know which ones to trust because I feared becoming the man who'd tried to own her again and it was so difficult not to make things black and white. A clear cut action to separate myself from them had seemed like the right choice, because I knew what the alternative looked like.

But maybe I was looking at this in extremes. Maybe there was some semblance of happiness left to claim here. After all, I'd spent years as a boy wanting her and never acting on those urges, I could do that again. But I couldn't ask her or the others not to act on their own desires if that was what they wanted to do.

"I'm not even sure what things are between me, JJ, Chase and Rick, but what if I promised you that you wouldn't have to see any of us together in that way? Do you think you could try then?"

I stayed quiet so long, I was surprised she didn't prompt me again for my answer, but I was battling with so many conflicting feelings that it was impossible to give one right away. On the one hand, I wanted my family back more than anything, I wanted to laugh with my friends and remember the untarnished souls we'd once had. But on the other, my love for Rogue was a red-eyed monster that would always be lurking under my bed. What if I couldn't control it? What if I lost my mind over her again and tried to steal her from them?

"I want to," I admitted. "But I don't trust myself with you. I fear one day my want for you will blacken anything good that once lived between us, and I don't want you to remember me as the villain in our story. I think if we leave it now, there's still enough good left in the past for you not to always cringe when you think of me."

Tears pooled in her eyes. "You're such an idiot, Fox Harlequin. I don't cringe when I think of you, I ache. And I'm gonna keep aching as long as you stay away from me because you're my best friend and I need you in my life. I've made shitty mistakes and hurt you too, but I want to show you how sorry I am, and I can't do that if you shut me out. Please Fox." Her hand moved to sit over my heart and the rampant, wild beat of it told her exactly what effect she was having on me, but I guessed it was nothing new.

She took my hand, bringing my fingertips to her own heart and I felt it beating like furious wings. And I could see her want for me blazing in her eyes as we lay there feeling the pounding of each other's pulses, but we'd gone down that road before and this was where it had led us, jealousy and revenge twisting us into two people who neither of us wanted to be.

She'd been enough for me as a friend once, even though I'd always believed she would one day be mine. But if I took that out of the equation, maybe I really could find my way to be there for her again. It certainly beat the alternative of losing them all forever.

"I'll try," I promised her, knowing it was going to be hard, maybe impossible, but after all we'd been through, maybe we owed each other this. One last chance at happiness.

Relief filled her expression and I pulled my hand away from her skin, rolling onto my back.

"Can I sleep here tonight?" she asked and I was about to decline when I remembered the way we'd curled up together as kids sometimes in the bed of my truck. I said I'd try, so I had to start getting used to being around her again, get used to holding back the tide of instincts that demanded I claim her as mine.

I patted my chest and she smiled as she moved closer, resting her head over my heart and laying her leg over mine.

I wrapped my arm around her, finding myself relaxing like my muscles had been tensed up for weeks on end. It felt so fucking good to just shut my eyes and hold her close, and I pictured us as two teenagers again, full of dreams for the life we one day planned on building together. And I wondered if it really was possible to feel the endless hopefulness of youth again.

We rose well before sunrise and prepared for the coming fight. I'd woken with Rogue in my arms, my hard on driving into her ass and had slipped away to the bathroom before she could notice. And yeah, maybe I'd jerked off in the shower while she slept and thought of the way she felt against me, the way she smelled, the way she lit up every dark corner inside me. And then I'd gotten dressed, woken her up and gone back to pretending I wasn't obsessed with her as we left the compound.

The Harlequin Crew and the Damned Men were combining forces as they took boats out across the water. Maverick drove the speedboat they'd borrowed from Tatum's family across the water, and I stood beside him with a gun in my grip, gazing at the few lights on in windows across Sunset Cove. The roar of engines rang out across the sea, the only warning Shawn and The Dead Dogs were going to get of our approach. But we outnumbered him and his men now by a mile and I wasn't afraid to go to war for the town I loved. By dawn, I planned on holding Shawn's bloody, severed head in my hand, ready to restore order to this place I loved.

I wasn't sure exactly of my plans now I'd decided to try and make things work with Rogue and the others, but I knew I wouldn't be taking up my position in The Harlequin Crew again. Dad might have thought I was just throwing a tantrum, but my decision was iron. That role had turned me into a man I despised, and I wouldn't allow myself to become that heathen again. Not when so much was at stake with the people I loved.

Luther stood on Maverick's other side, watching the shore as we approached, a dark intensity in his gaze. He was ruthless in situations like this, a cold-blooded killer who would do whatever needed to be done to regain control in this town. And I'd stand at his side in this fight no matter what.

Rogue, JJ and Chase sat at the back of the boat with Mutt, all armed and ready for the coming fight. It wasn't ideal to have the dog with us, but we couldn't leave him behind and there was no time to bring him anywhere else. I was pretty sure my dad would take a bullet for him so he was probably in the safest place he could be anyway.

We reached the shore, using the fishermen's jetty to tie the boat off and climb up onto the boards. I took Rogue's hand as she made it to the edge of the boat, helping her up and her fingers remained in mine for a moment as she stood at my side. I squeezed her hand before letting her go and though I was struggling to accept her coming on this dangerous mission to reach Shawn and destroy him, I also knew she deserved to be there and that it wasn't my call to make regardless.

JJ helped Chase up out of the boat and we all moved along the boards, heading onto the street and hurrying up an alley along the route we'd planned to take towards the Rosewood Manor. While the Harlequins and Damned Men dealt with any rogue Dead Dogs stationed in the streets, we were going to sneak in through Shawn's back door and cut him down before he even knew what was happening.

My pulse climbed as we drew closer and closer to the manor, bloodlust and determination tangling inside me as I scented Shawn's death on the air. We were going to make it bloody and last as long as possible, and I couldn't wait to hear his screams as Rogue stuck him with any sharp object she fancied and the rest of us held him down. I was practically salivating for it.

As we took a side street that skirted the property, I glanced back at Chase just behind me, seeing an apocalypse in his gaze as he drew closer to Shawn's death. I offered him a stiff nod, telling him with a single look that I'd help hand him the revenge he needed, the revenge we all fucking needed. Because his scars lit a fury in me that rivalled a titan, and I wanted blood for them so bad, I knew my inner demons would come out to play tonight when we got our hands on fucking Shawn. For him, for Rogue. I'd use my knife to gouge and maim and disembowel that piece of shit who had dared try to destroy them.

We followed the outer fence down a dirt track that led into the trees to the south of the property, and Mutt trotted at Rogue's heels the whole time, keeping quiet like he knew the importance of that tonight.

"Here's good enough," Luther said.

"No it ain't, old man," Maverick tossed back. "There's a tree further up here we can use to hop the fence easier."

"If you're sure," Luther said with a frown I could only just make out in the dark.

"We know these woods," I said darkly and Dad's eyes found me.

"Yeah, I did too once," he said in a low tone, and I half wondered what my dad's childhood had been like around here. He never really spoke about it, though now definitely wasn't the time to ask.

We followed Maverick along to the old oak which had a branch high enough to give us a leaping jump over the fence. The ground on the other side looked pretty soft, but I guessed we'd find out for sure when we landed.

Rogue moved to the tree, dropping down to a crouch and petting Mutt's head. "You'd better stay here, boy. It's not safe for you in there." She kissed him and Mutt whined, but did as she asked as if he spoke perfect English, moving to sit and watch her instead.

Rogue was about to get a foothold on the tree when both me and Maverick swooped on her, pulling her back.

"Hey," she hissed, trying to jerk out of our grip, but there was no chance of that.

I glanced at my brother over her head, the same thought shining in his eyes.

"Someone needs to go first to make sure it's safe over there," I murmured, fully intending to be that person, but the look in Maverick's eyes said he was also planning on being the one to go.

"And why can't that someone be me?" she growled, looking up at us.

I went to answer but a soft thud made me turn and I spotted JJ on the other side of the fence. "Are you guys gonna stand around out there all night?" he asked with a smirk, moving to the bushes behind him and peering through to check for any signs of guards.

"Asshole," Maverick muttered and I nodded my agreement.

I moved forward to grab hold of the tree, but his shoulder smashed into mine as he tried to do the same and we shoved and pushed as we fought to clamber up in front of one another. We wasted so much time fighting our way up that by the time we got to the branch, Rogue was already there, clearly having taken a different path up, her eyebrow arched at us.

"You know, if you spent half the time you do fighting as you did helping each other out, you'd have beaten me up here and wouldn't have to suck on this." She offered us her middle finger then leapt over the fence.

JJ moved like a whippet, catching her out of the air and swinging her around in a move that simply had to be from one of his shows. A smile lit her face and I was surprised when it lit one on mine in return, even though she was offering it to him. JJ made her happy, and fuck him for betraying me, but I was glad he was capable of that, because I definitely wasn't.

Maverick leapt over next and I looked back down behind me, finding my dad climbing up with Chase further down the trunk.

"You okay, Ace?" I called to him in a whisper and he lifted his head, his expression determined.

"I'm fine. If anyone tries to help me I'll punch them in the face," he hissed back, heaving himself up and I could see the strength in his body was not in question at all.

Hang the fuck on, wasn't he limping about last night like he couldn't even walk that far without my help?

I pulled myself onto the branch, lining up the jump and taking the leap, the air rushing over me before I hit the ground. I stumbled a step and Maverick caught my arm before releasing me just as fast with a grunt like he'd burned himself.

"Thanks," I muttered.

"My arm happened to be there, Foxy boy, don't go getting any ideas. It's cute that you think I'd stop you from falling though," he said, turning his back on me as he moved to join Rogue and JJ by the bushes. I hung back, waiting for my dad to jump down and he did so with all the smoothness of James Bond then we all looked up as Chase readied to follow.

"Stop looking at me like I'm gonna fuck this up," he growled.

"Come on, everyone take off their shirts and make them into a parachute to catch Ace," Maverick mocked, folding his arms as he watched him.

"Fuck you, Rick," Chase snarled.

"You got this, Ace," Rogue said.

"I know," he huffed. "Just back it up. I'd rather fall flat on my face than you all catch me like a damn injured cat falling out a tree."

"Yeah, yeah, just hurry up about it," Maverick said.

I forced myself to fold my arms, my instincts to help him making my hands twitch, but I had to give him what he wanted.

Chase took the jump, hitting the ground and cursing as he jarred his bad leg, but he stayed upright, even if he did stumble a few steps.

Maverick silently mimed clapping him and Rogue elbowed him in the gut, making him cough out a breath.

JJ slung his arm around Chase's shoulders, kissing his temple hard before letting him go and a weird moment passed between us all where we sort of just smiled at each other. Even my dad was involved, which was weird as shit. So I quickly broke it, striding through the group and leading the way into the bushes and deeper onto the property. I had a head to cut off tonight and I was hungry to get started.

We snuck deeper onto the grounds, closing in on the house and finding all of the lights off. My senses prickled as we gathered together in the dark shadow of a horse statue, searching for any of The Dead Dogs manning the doors. But there was no one there.

"Where the fuck is everyone?" JJ muttered, his shoulder pressing to mine as we crouched side by side. I adjusted my grip on my gun, running my tongue across my teeth.

"I don't like this," I said.

"Do you think it's an ambush, kid?" Dad asked.

"He couldn't know we were coming," I said in confusion.

I took out my phone, the light on the screen low as I cupped my hand around it and found several messages from the Harlequins.

"Our boys are saying there aren't any Dead Dogs out on the streets. Not one," I whispered, my nerves on edge over this. This wasn't right. Where the fuck were they?

"We should retreat," Luther said decisively.

"No, what about Miss Mabel?" Rogue growled. "I'm not leaving her. Look, the cars are gone, maybe they're not even here."

"Or that's what they want us to think," Maverick said in a deep tone, his eyes finding mine again over her head.

I could see what he was thinking, we'd always had a way of silently communicating with each other, but it had been a long damn time since we'd done it. He wanted to get Rogue out of here, which was exactly my feelings on the matter too. Though knowing my brother, he likely planned to remove her from the situation before ploughing on in there himself, painting a bloody nightmare for anyone he came across. If he found Shawn, I knew he'd end up at Rogue's feet, ready to do whatever she wanted with him. And with the way I was feeling tonight, that was a plan I could get on board with.

"Let's back up," I said.

"No," Chase growled. "He could be in that fucking house. And I'm not leaving Mabel again."

"Agreed," Rogue said and I glanced at JJ as he scored a hand over his head indecisively.

"Your call, Fox," Luther said to me and I almost opened my mouth to make it when I snapped my teeth together, stopping myself.

"It's not my call," I said, though the urge to take control of this situation was burning in me, the need to gather everyone up and force them to leave almost impossible to hold back. But I did. Because I wasn't anyone's leader here anymore, and this wasn't just my mission.

JJ looked to me like he wanted me to make the decision, but I wasn't gonna do it.

"Why don't we make a distraction?" Rogue suggested. "If it's an ambush, we can draw The Dead Dogs that way, figure out their plan and how many of them are here. And if we can't handle it, we can get out."

"Sounds good to me," Luther said.

"Okay, so how do we-" I started but Maverick stood up, launching a rock at a top floor window and smashing it to bits.

I instinctively threw an arm over JJ's head beside me in case gunfire came in return, but all was quiet.

"Jesus fucking Christ, Rick," Chase hissed as Maverick released a low laugh.

No men came running, no shouts of alarm sounded. All was quiet.

I released JJ, feeling his eyes on me as I pointedly didn't acknowledge what I'd done and focused my attention on the house.

"Looks like no one's home," Luther said.

"Or not many people are," I said.

"Come on then," Rogue said firmly, getting to her feet and we all did too, grouping around her as we crept toward a ground floor window.

"Johnny James, you and me will run a circuit of the property," Luther commanded and JJ nodded before they took off towards the back of the house.

We kept low as Chase jimmied the lock and slid the window up to give us access inside. Maverick climbed through first and I kept tight behind Rogue as Chase went next and she glanced back at me with her lips parting.

"You okay back there, Badger?" she asked and a smirk twisted my lips at that old nickname I'd hated so goddamn much. But as I'd spent a lot of time thinking I'd never hear it again, I found I didn't hate so much anymore.

"Just watching your back, hummingbird," I said and she smiled.

"You sure you're not just hoping for a view of my ass when I climb inside?"

"No," I said tightly and she frowned when I didn't flirt back, but lines had to be drawn now and I wasn't going to cross them ever again. Though as she climbed inside, my gaze fell traitorously to her ass to undermine my point. *Dammit.*

I glanced up and down the front of the property one last time before climbing inside and listening for any sound of movement in the house. But there wasn't anything, not a creak of a floorboard or a shuffling footstep. The whole place was eerily silent. And if I wasn't entirely losing my touch, I had to admit, I was starting to think no one was home.

We moved through the dark lounge we'd climbed into and the air immediately changed between us all. Rogue and Chase drew closer together like the memories of this place suddenly bound them with ropes and my teeth crushed together at the thought of what they'd been through in this house. My mind went to a cold, ruthless place where I could kill with a brutality that would make most people shudder, but I had to be the worst monster I could be tonight if we caught Shawn. Because he deserved the worst kind death, the most suffering my hands could offer him.

We crept deeper into the house, checking room after room for any signs of life, but we came up short every time.

When JJ and Luther appeared at the end of the hall, all of us raised our guns, but instantly dropped them again.

"This end of the house is clear," JJ whispered as we started climbing the stairs to the next level. But after another few minutes of searching, it was clear the house was empty. The beds weren't warm and it looked like Shawn had hightailed it out of here in a hurry. I didn't know if he'd been tipped off or just gotten cold feet the moment the cartel had left him exposed, but either way, it looked like the rat had gone to ground. It was fucking frustrating.

Maverick let out a growl of anger as we made it back downstairs, flicking lights on as Rogue started leading us all to the basement, an urgency in her movements.

My throat thickened and I shared a look with JJ that spoke of our concern for Miss Mabel's life. If Shawn had run, why would he bother to leave her alive? Then again, I wasn't entirely sure why he'd bothered keeping her alive in the first place.

The basement door was locked, but Chase dealt with that by ramming the butt of his gun down on the padlock, breaking it clean off before unlocking the bolts. I noticed him hesitate as the door swung open and a slight tremble to his hands made me sure he was affected by this place.

Rogue took his hand, giving him a reassuring look that said she understood and my heart twisted for them as they led the way down into the dark and I forced myself to let them go first.

"I'm gonna keep watch up here," Luther said and JJ agreed to stay too which was probably a good call. All of us heading down into our enemy's basement together was undoubtedly a stupid way to get us all cornered.

I walked down the dark stairs beside Maverick, the cool air making the hairs raise on my arms and I squinted into the gloom a moment before someone switched a light on.

"Bless my pearls!" Mabel cried as she sat bolt upright in her rocking chair, aiming a knitting needle at us. "Don't shoot!"

I realised my gun was raised, finger on the trigger, my instincts having taken over. Rogue turned back, pushing it down and I nodded to her before she hurried over to Mabel and hugged her tight.

"We're getting you out of here," she said.

Mabel gazed at us in surprise as she released her and the old woman who'd once been so good to us as kids stared around at us in shock as she seemed to recognise us.

"I'm going to see the sea again?" she asked, the desperation in her gaze making my stomach knot at how much she'd been deprived all the years she'd been trapped down here.

"Yes, Mabel," Rogue said through teary eyes. "And everything and anything else you've missed."

"Oh goodness, gracious. I can't thank you enough." Mabel pushed out of her seat, a bright, watery-eyed smile filling up her whole face. "What are we waiting for? Take me to see it all."

ROGUE

CHAPTER THIRTY ONE

"**O**h, this is nice," Mabel said appreciatively as she looked around Harlequin House, brazenly opening doors and checking inside cupboards. "Airy. Even if it is a little bit chockablock with modern thingamebobs."

Luther raised an eyebrow at Fox from behind her back as if to ask if he was sure about this and Fox just nodded. I trailed along behind her while JJ, Chase and Rick did a sweep of the house outside to make sure there really was no sign of Shawn still hanging around or him having done anything to the place while we were gone.

"There's a guest suite at the far end of the house downstairs," Fox said. "I figured that would be easier for you-"

"Because I'm old and my legs can't manage a few steps, is it?" she asked, whirling on him.

"Well...yeah," he said, shrugging innocently. "But if you want a room upstairs instead-"

"Up the stairs? With my old legs? Don't be daft, boy. Now tell me which is my armchair?" Mabel asked, pointing between the chairs in the living room while Luther shook his head and moved to get himself some coffee.

"I'll get on to my contacts in the Sunset Cove PD," he said. "They can sort out the little issue of your death being registered."

"Yes, yes. And someone will need to fix the mess that nephew of mine made of the estate too. Orange walls...whatever was he thinking?" Miss Mabel muttered as she wriggled her ass in the armchair Fox usually favoured and sighed. "This one it is. Come on big fella, it won't carry itself to my room."

"Oh, you want me to move it to-" Fox began but Miss Mabel cut him off.

"Has all of that tattoo ink addled your brain?" she asked with a tut. "I always said it can't be good for the mind to soak in ink like that."

"The ink doesn't soak into your bloodstream-" Fox tried but she was already on her feet and snapping her fingers at him to follow her as she headed towards the corridor which led to her new room.

"Ah, there's a good boy," Mabel said, patting Luther on the arm in thanks as she took his cup of coffee from his hands and strode away with it like it had been intended for her all along. "Next time let's have a dash less creamer and a spoon more sugar though," she called back to him as she headed away and the biggest, meanest motherfucker in the whole Cove just stared at her back as she went.

Fox hurried after her, carrying his favourite armchair and I grinned broadly as I dropped onto one of the stools by the breakfast bar. "Isn't she great?" I asked as Luther moved to make himself another coffee.

"Of course you would think she is," he muttered, though he looked amused and I could tell he liked her too.

"Not right in the window! I'm in my nineties, are you looking to cook me up like a shrimp on a barbecue in all that sunlight?" Miss Mabel cried from the room where Fox was getting her set up and I laughed as I heard him apologising.

Luther placed his fresh coffee down on the breakfast bar and stood facing me across it, scrubbing a hand over his stubbled jaw as he considered me. I wondered if his generosity might stretch as far as his most favourite Crew member, so I leaned forward and grabbed his coffee cup to test the waters.

Luther's hand snapped out and he caught my wrist before I could pull it even an inch towards me.

"Watch it, wildcat. Don't go forgetting who I am," he snarled, all big bad boss man. But I'd gotten a look at his gooey insides so I wasn't buying it anymore. I mean, a jolt of pure terror had just shot through my body and I may have peed a little beneath the force of his scary gangster glare but it was an incontinence of love.

"Just checking, Papa H. I needed to make sure you weren't going all soft in your old age or anything." I gave him an innocent smile but he didn't release me.

"Old age?" he questioned and I was like seventy percent sure he was playing with me by this point. Or I was about to die. Hard to be sure. Luckily, I was saved by the bell. Or more accurately, saved by the not so mini mobster who strode into the room with Chase and JJ and released a snarl like a feral animal as he spotted my wrist in his dad's hold.

"What the fuck are you doing?" Rick growled, closing in on us fast and Luther rolled his eyes as he released me.

"Your little hellion tried to steal my coffee is all. Don't go getting your panties in a twist over it, Rick. I taught you better than that. You should know not to lose your head over a woman."

"It's a bit late for that," Maverick responded. "Because I lost my head, my heart, my entire fucking being to that particular woman a long damn time ago. And you'd do well not to forget it."

Luther looked between me and his adopted son and I slowly reached out to snag his coffee again.

He snatched it away from me with a bark of laughter then drank the whole lot in one hit. Holy hell. How hot had that shit been? That was scolding fucking coffee and he'd just sunk it like a lemonade. Why was I so impressed by it? Hard to say, but Papa Harlequin was a badass for that one act alone.

Luther strode around the breakfast bar and reached out to scruff up my brunette locks as he passed me by. "Catch you kids later," he said as he went. "Oh and wildcat?"

"Yeah?" I looked around at him, watching as he tucked a pistol into the back of his jeans. Prime place for shooting off an ass cheek, but I held my tongue on that one.

"Fix your hair - normal just don't suit you."

I stilled at his casual compliment, feeling the brush of Shawn's lips against my ear for a moment, hearing the words he whispered to me. The way he'd pushed me into dying it brown again. I hadn't been letting myself think about it all that much but now it was just out there, hanging in the air between us like the toxicity of Shawn's touch was written all over me with that one simple fact.

Luther left, not noticing the atomic bomb he'd just dropped on my head and Chase slipped into the seat beside me, his hand finding mine and squeezing tight.

Maverick looked at me across the breakfast bar, his jaw working as his fists balled against the work surface.

"I'm okay," I promised as JJ placed a mug of coffee down in front of me and I gave him a rueful smile as I picked it up and took a sip. It was in the Green Power Ranger mug that I'd bought him so that definitely helped.

"You don't have to be," Chase said, his thumb rolling across the back of my hand and making my flesh heat.

"I am," I said firmly, shaking off the sound of Shawn's voice in my ears and raising my chin. Because here I was, surrounded by my boys and back home. He couldn't take that from me, and I refused to let him taint it either. Though it was hard to ignore the damage he'd done to this place while he was here. "So was everything clear outside?"

"Yep. All good," Rick agreed. "So I was gonna get going..."

"Going?" I asked in a small voice, looking up into his dark eyes.

"Back to the Isle. I don't have a place here, beautiful. You know that."

"Yeah you do," Fox interrupted as he strode back into the room. "And you fucking know it too. So don't bullshit her or yourself over that anymore."

Rick looked like he was willing to step straight into a fight as always, but I leaned forward, taking his hand in mine and making him look at me.

"Please stay," I begged, looking up into his dark eyes and letting him see how much I really wanted that.

Maverick glanced to the others then blew out a harsh breath and rolled his eyes. "Fine. Whatever. I can stay here while we're working on finding fucking Shawn, I guess."

The tension in the room seemed to pop like a balloon as he agreed to that and I swear we all sagged with the relief of being united beneath one roof for at least a little longer.

"Rogue has your old room," Fox said as he moved to make himself a coffee. "So I dunno if you wanna-"

"Rogue's room, my room, makes no fucking difference to me. I'll be sleeping where she is either way," Maverick interrupted and Fox's jaw ticked, but he just nodded like he'd been expecting that anyway. It didn't look like he was taking it all that well internally, a dark veil cloaking his eyes, but still he said nothing. And I kinda missed the badger in him. Not the kind that kept me from my boys, but couldn't he just be a teensy weensy bit possessive? Touch me like he couldn't bear to let go, look at me in that way that lit me up inside?

"We should all probably try to get some rest," JJ said. "As much as I wanna believe that Shawn really has run for the hills, I just don't think it's gonna be that simple. Tomorrow could be one hell of a day."

"Agreed," Chase said and as I looked at him, I swear I caught a flicker of pain in his gaze.

I pursed my lips then pushed to my feet. "Come on then, bed," I commanded like a mother hen trying to round up unruly chicks and to my surprise, the four of them all moved towards the stairs with me.

I slipped under Chase's arm, letting him lean on me a little as we climbed and he sighed, squeezing me to let me know he appreciated it.

Upstairs the place was more of a mess than it has been downstairs, Shawn and his men having tagged the walls with graffiti and rifled through everything.

JJ, Rick and Fox wordlessly started clearing up, gathering heaps of laundry and taking them downstairs, stripping the beds and clearing away all signs of the destruction that had been caused here.

We all started in Chase's room and when he made a move to help us, I just gave him a shove that knocked his ass down into the chair by the window which overlooked the pool.

"Stay," I barked at him, pointing aggressively and forcing his obedience before I headed into his en-suite to find his pain pills. He'd stopped taking them before Fox sent him out of town but there were plenty left over and I was glad when I found the medicine cabinet untouched above his sink.

It didn't seem like The Dead Dogs had spent long here. I wondered if they'd even come back again after the exchange Shawn had made between me and his mother. It looked like they'd just trashed the place and left. And I was glad of that. A splash of paint and a bit of tidying up was nothing compared to what they could have done here.

Downstairs I could hear the sound of some of the Crew members changing the locks on the doors and when I glanced out the windows, I saw them tossing broken items and anything too damaged to save into the back of a large van. The place would be looking like new again in no time.

I filled a glass with water and headed back into the bedroom, finding Chase leaning his head back on the chair I'd forced him into with his good eye closed and the eye patch still covering his bad one, a frown pulling at his brow.

The others had already gathered up the clothes that had been thrown around the space and any broken items, carting them downstairs. Only JJ remained, stripping down the bed with quick, practiced movements.

I climbed onto Chase's lap and he opened his eye as his hands slipped around my waist to hold me there.

"Open up," I commanded, showing him the pills I held between my fingers and he frowned.

"I don't need those anymore."

"You do tonight," I argued.

"No, I-"

"Open your mouth, Chase Cohen, or I'm going to punch you in the dick, and shove them down your throat while you're screaming," I warned.

His gaze flashed with irritation then amusement and he finally parted his lips, letting me place the pills on his tongue. I held the water up to his lips so that he could wash them down and I watched his throat bob as he swallowed, my gaze riveted to the motion as my skin burned where he still held me.

I knew that he was giving me space. That all of them were giving me space to work through the shit that Shawn had put into my head, but as I shifted in his lap and felt the hardness of his dick driving into me, I couldn't help but want him. I wanted to feel the power of his body against the softness of mine again, I wanted to feel the heat of his passion and the beat of his heart while I fell apart for him.

I placed the empty glass down on the windowsill beside us and Chase leaned in, his stubble grazing along the side of my jaw as his lips made it to my ear.

"Can I Be Him by James Arthur," he murmured, his fingers shifting where he held me so that they brushed my skin beneath the hem of my shirt.

I turned my head to place a kiss on his cheek the way I had every time I'd given him his pills while he'd been recovering and my lips found the corner of his mouth, my chest tightening as that simple brush of his skin against mine set an explosion firing off within my veins.

Chase groaned and leaned back, making it seem like pulling away from me was harder than any pain he'd had to endure at Shawn's hands.

"The bed is good to go," JJ said behind us and I turned to look at him, finding him smiling at us and offering me a hand to help me up.

I accepted a little reluctantly and let him pull me out of Chase's lap. Chase stood too and the air between the three of us seemed to come alive with an aching kind of promise as he pulled his shirt over his head and moved towards the bed.

I stepped forward and slid my fingers into Chase's belt, unbuckling it for him as he watched me, my heart thundering with want and need while I tried to block out the echoes of Shawn's words in my head, telling me that this was why they wanted me here. This was all they really wanted.

I hesitated for the briefest moment and Chase's fingers curled around mine, halting my movements where his pants hung open and catching my chin in a light grasp as he tipped it up and made me look at him again.

"Get some sleep, little one," he urged. "I'm good now."

"If by good you mean unable to place your weight on that leg then, yeah, you're great," JJ joked. "But sit your ass down and I'll help you with it."

"Help me how?" Chase asked, looking to him as I stepped back and JJ pulled a red bottle from his back pocket.

"It's massage oil...and it's also lube if I'm being totally honest, but mostly it's massage oil because your tits aren't really big enough for my tastes and I'm only planning on feeling up your leg."

"Dude, I don't need you to-" Chase's protests were cut off as JJ gave him a shove that sent him bouncing back onto the bed behind him and I laughed as he cursed loudly.

JJ ignored him and caught the hem of Chase's pants before yanking them off of him, leaving him on the bed in his boxers which were doing very little to cover up his hard dick.

"Jesus, Johnny stop manhandling me. I don't need a massage from you - especially not while I've got a fucking hard on."

"Oh please. I've seen it all before. Just point your dick away from me if you're gonna deal with it because I don't really wanna have to wash cum out of my hair before I get some sleep tonight."

I laughed even louder as Chase looked like he wasn't sure whether he should be trying to punch JJ or grab a pillow to hide his solid cock and he turned a glare on me next.

"I dunno why you're laughing, little one. It's your fault I've got this fucking problem," Chase snapped which only made me laugh more.

"Keep laughing like that, pretty girl, and I'm going to be hard too," JJ warned. "Your voice is too fucking sexy for your own good."

"Which is why I came to steal her away for myself," Maverick said as he strode into the room, casting a half interested look at the two of them as Chase tried to back away up the bed and JJ dumped a dollop of massage oil on his bad leg, ignoring him. "You ready for bed, beautiful?"

"Err, yeah. If you're sure you're okay now, Ace?" I added but JJ chose that moment to wrap his hands around Chase's shin and start massaging it and the only thing that escaped Chase's lips was a groan.

"Fuck, that actually feels really good," he muttered.

"Yeah man, I've done a bunch of massage courses. You don't get to be the best paid male escort on the west coast without knowing all the ways to pleasure people," JJ said, rolling his eyes as Chase gave in and let him keep working on his leg.

"Right, well you two have fun pleasuring each other. I'm just gonna steal our girl for the night," Rick said, his arm wrapping around my shoulders as he guided me from the room and the others bid me goodnight.

The sound of Fox's door snapping closed reached me as we stepped back into the corridor and I chewed my lip anxiously, wondering if me sleeping in a room with Rick was crossing the lines of the promise I'd made him. Then again, I'd slept in a bed with all of them over the years when we were kids so it wasn't like this was an entirely new prospect for him to have to deal with. I'd even slept in with him last night. And as Maverick practically shoved me over the threshold to our room, I didn't get any more time to over think it than that anyway.

A lamp was on beside the bed, but the shade was missing now and I had to assume it had been broken. The rest of the room seemed tidy enough though and fresh linen covered the bed.

"Your clothes were all shredded," Maverick said as he casually stripped out of his clothes and made my freaking mouth dry out at the sight of all of those inked, bulging muscles. "Do you wanna sleep in my shirt or naked?"

A pang of loss twisted through me at the realisation that all of my stuff had been destroyed, but I wasn't even surprised. Shawn was a controlling asshole. He'd been dressing me up in Mia's revealing shit and trying to change my appearance to suit his preference the whole time I was with him in the Rosewood estate.

I wondered briefly if Mia had followed my instructions and found her way to Di and Lyla. I really needed to reach out to them tomorrow and explain why I'd disappeared this time. Honestly, they were probably sick of my disappearing act by now.

I took Rick's offered shirt then moved toward the bathroom to change, but he caught my wrist and stopped me before I could leave.

"You think avoiding sex means you're proving a point against that asshole?" he asked me, cutting the truth of me in that one simple question and making my breath catch as I looked up at him.

"It's not..." I trailed off, not even sure where I was going with that before I shrugged. "I don't even know anymore. I hear him whispering his poison inside my head and I hear my own doubts and questions about myself and-"

"Then fucking stop it," he snapped at me, making me blink in surprise as he stalked closer.

"Stop it?" I asked, tipping my head back to look at him as he towered over me in nothing but his black boxers.

"Yeah. He doesn't own your body any more than anyone else does. The only person it belongs to is you. So fucking own it. You don't wanna fuck me?

Then don't. But don't go hide in the fucking bathroom to get changed like I'm some kind of fucking animal who can't control myself."

"You're trying to tell me you're not a fucking animal?" I teased and he gave me a dark grin that made everything inside me clench with need.

"Oh you know I am," he replied, moving closer and making me back up until my back bumped against the door where he placed his hands either side of my head and dipped his head low to put it on a level with mine. "And when this anger between us snaps and you fucking beg me to take possession of your flesh again, you'd better believe I'll be stamping my name all over every delicious inch of your golden flesh for the whole fucking world to see. But you're the one in control of that. Not me. Because you've always been the one to hold all of the cards, you're the one with all of the power. And when you remember how to wield it again, I'll be more than ready to fall at your fucking feet where I belong."

My skin burned with his nearness and the taste of his breath on the air which divided us was laced with the most tempting kind of sin. The way he was looking at me filled me with this delicious sense of power which only I could claim.

I kept my gaze on his and tugged my shirt off slowly, letting it fall to the floor before dropping my pants too. My underwear followed and my toes curled as he stared at me, his muscles tensing as he held himself entirely still.

I let him look, the fucking need in his eyes making my heart pound and my thighs clench together as my pussy throbbed with want. I was heady with this power I held and the longer he looked, the more I understood his words. This wasn't about being their whore. It was about being their fucking end. Their desire. Their love. Their girl.

I licked my lips, my chest heaving as Maverick's gaze roamed over my body with a hunger so fierce it had me starving too.

"Tell me what Luther said to make you so angry," I breathed, needing to know the source of the pain in his dark eyes.

Rick flinched like I'd slapped him, his gaze raising to mine in a warning glare before he jerked back and turned away from me, stalking over to the bed and leaving me exposed and alone against the door.

I swallowed the bite of rejection that pierced through my chest and quickly snatched his shirt, covering my body with it once more.

"Oh, so you can try to force me to face my issues but you're just gonna hide from yours?" I demanded, stalking after him as he dropped onto the bed and got himself comfortable, linking his fingers together and clasping the back of his head as he leaned against the pillows.

"I never said I wasn't a hypocrite," he replied, giving me a challenging look, but if he thought I was just gonna back down over this then he was dead wrong.

"Just tell me," I said, moving to kneel beside him. "You've shared every other secret of yours with me. So why not this one?"

"Because..." Maverick sighed and looked away from me. "Because this one isn't about the things I've been through, beautiful. It's about the thing I am. Where I came from and the blood that runs in my veins."

"Luther told you about your birth parents?" I asked in a hushed whisper, understanding filling me as I realised why he had been so angry again since speaking with his adopted father. "I thought he told you a lot about your dad already-"

"No. He told me stories about a man who had been in the Crew before I was born. Some stranger who had died and who he'd pretended was my father to cover up the truth."

"He lied?" I breathed, shifting closer to him so that my knee nudged against his side.

"Yeah, he lied. Turns out my mom was just some poor terrified bitch who came begging him to take me in because someone was after her. He never even found out her name, only that she was afraid for both of our lives and needed Luther to keep me safe from whoever was after her."

"And Luther just took you in? Even though he had no connection to her?" I asked in confusion. It seemed more than a little odd to go to a notorious gang leader and ask them to adopt your fucking baby out of nowhere. Surely there was something else to the story beyond that.

"Oh he had a connection to her alright," Rick muttered bitterly.

"He's your real father?" I breathed, my eyes widening in understanding.

"No," he snapped. "Though if you can believe it, I wish he was rather than have to own the truth of who my father really was."

My frown deepened because I really wasn't getting this. "Rick, I don't understand. If Luther isn't your father, then why would he have taken you in? What reason did he have to-"

"I was his brother's bastard. You know, the same brother who fucked his wife before killing her and robbing Fox of his mother," he snarled, turning away from me and suddenly looking so like the lost boy I'd once known that my heart broke for him and I couldn't help but lean forward and pull him into my arms.

"Oh Rick," I murmured. "I'm so sorry."

He grunted, trying to pull away from me but I held on tight and after a moment of vaguely trying to push me off, he wound his arms around me instead and tugged me tight against his chest, giving in to the bond between us.

"I guess it explains a lot," he muttered. "Like why Luther trained me up for all the dirty work. How he knew I could handle the bloodstains on my hands and the damage to my soul. It also explains why he never wanted me to be in charge. He knew where I came from, the traitorous, brutal blood that tainted my veins and he-"

I leaned up and silenced the vile words pouring from his lips with a kiss so hard it bruised, the ache in him and me colliding in a brutal, angry clash of mouths that allowed no room for anything else aside from the two of us and all the loss and hurt we'd both suffered through when we were apart.

"There's nothing tainted or dirty about you, Maverick," I snarled, biting his bottom lip as he tried to shake his head and forcing him down beneath me as I moved to straddle him, my hand curling around his throat in a warning. "I don't care if your father was the Devil himself and he dressed you in sin at the moment of your birth because you're still you. Still my Rick. And there isn't a single thing in this world or the next that could ever make me want you any less."

"Fox lost his mom because of my father," he said, trying to pull back but I wouldn't let him, my mouth pressing to his again as my grip on his throat tightened.

"That man wasn't a father to you. He's nothing but ash and bone. Fucking nothing."

"So what does that make me if I came from nothing?" he asked, his

438

voice hollow and hopeless as his grip on my waist tightened to the point of pain like he thought he'd fall forever if he made the mistake of letting me go.

"Mine," I replied simply. "You're mine, Rick. And I'm not letting you go no matter how much you might want to run."

A groan spilled from his lips that was so animal it made my back arch like a cat as I leaned away to get a better look at him pinned beneath me.

He was so fucking beautiful, this painted god held at my mercy and prostrated beneath my body like I was the one thing in this world which he desired above all else. The one thing he would bow for, break for, die for.

"Big words for a frightened little girl," he growled, his hands fisting in the oversized shirt I still wore and making my heart thunder with the challenge he was offering up.

"Yeah?" I asked, my gaze meeting his as desire lit his dark eyes on fire and made me burn all the way through to my core.

My pussy was slick and throbbing, and my nipples were so hard that it was a shock that they hadn't punched a hole right through this shirt already, and instead of hearing Shawn's poisonous words in my ears all I could hear was the thundering of my pulse and the heady fucking need I felt for this man.

"Come on then, wild girl, show me you own me if you think you really do."

"I do," I assured him, my grip on his throat tightening.

"I dunno about that. I'm still pissed at you for running out on me," he said in a low tone, anger flashing through his gaze to back up his point.

"And I'm still pissed at you for showing Fox that sex tape," I growled back, squeezing his throat and getting a little thrill from the act. There was something about it, a power which stoked that carnal desire in me for this man as I reared over him and pinned him at my mercy. And yeah, he might have been letting me do it, but there was still power in that because Maverick never let anybody dominate him and yet here I was, pressing him down beneath me and digging my fingernails into his skin as I asserted my position.

"I'd do it again," he goaded and I bared my teeth at him.

"Fuck you."

"That's what I'm hoping for," he replied and my whole body buzzed at the challenge in his words but my grip loosened all the same, the reality of that challenge forcing me to remember the reasons I'd had for holding back on this.

Rick saw it and a snarl tore from his lips as he shoved himself up on his elbows, forcing me to lean back as he sat up and faced me eye to eye,

"He's in your head, isn't he?" he said, not a question, a fact.

"Yes," I breathed, my hand slipping from his neck and trailing down his chest as I began to withdraw.

"Tell me," he commanded, raising his chin in challenge.

"It's nothing," I muttered. "I just need a bit of time to-"

"No," Maverick snapped, grasping my hips as I made a move to get off of him and driving me down into his lap more firmly. "Fuck that. Rogue Easton never needed a bit of time to figure her shit out. Besides, even if you did, you've had it. You've been back with us for a week now so cut the shit and tell me what it is he's said or done to you to make you think you can't fuck me or Chase or Johnny James whenever the hell you want to."

I bit my lip, fighting against the desire to hide and listening to his words. Because he was right. I didn't hide from anything. Never had.

"Come on, beautiful. What would the Green Power Ranger do?" Rick taunted and I broke a laugh.

"He'd face his fucking demons," I said.

"Well come on then. Don't go all Pink on me. Give me what you've got."

I sucked in a sharp breath at that implied insult then blew it out again and just fucking said it.

"He made me feel like my value to you only went as far as what it took for you to get full access to my body," I admitted, plucking at the loose fitting shirt and letting the material fall against my skin once more as he looked at me. "All of you have lied to me, hidden things from me, tried to keep me out of the way whenever there's something dangerous to deal with-"

"He'd made you believe that you're just some girl to us? Some body to fuck and use and forget again the moment our dicks are satisfied?" he asked me with clear disgust written into his features.

I shrugged, feeling the sting of a lie in those words even as I spoke them aloud, because that wasn't what it felt like when I was with my boys and I knew it.

"I don't even know anymore, Rick. He told me you all lied to me and made me believe what I wanted to so that I'd keep on being your pretty little whore and I know that that's fucked up, but I can't help but think that we never had the problems we all have before I started sleeping with all of you and-"

"When have I ever lied to you, beautiful?" he demanded, his gaze going cold with anger at that accusation and I shook my head, hating how that had sounded.

"Rick, I-"

"No," he barked. "No more of that horse shit. I won't fucking hear it. You're not our fucking whore and you know it. You're our girl. And when we're with you, we aren't just fucking some piece of premium pussy for easy kicks. We're worshipping our motherfucking goddess. You think I'd share some random girl with my brothers the way I'm sharing you? It's not because I like watching you get fucked so damn much, beautiful, it's because I know that you deserve to be worshipped by all of us. That it takes all of us to even come close to being the man who would deserve you."

A blush rose in my cheeks at the intensity of his words, the raw and brutal truth of them sinking beneath my skin and lighting me up inside as the last traces of Shawn's venomous influence on my feelings towards me boys was pushed right out of me and banished to the fucking gutter where it belonged.

"Say it again," I growled, holding his dark gaze and as my chest rose and fell heavily.

"You're our girl," he said, his eyes blazing with those words as his fingers gripped my thighs. "And you own me in every way that a man can be owned. So show me you own me, Rogue. Remind me why I worship you."

I bit my lip as I looked at him, this demon clad in the skin of a man who was pledging all he was to me with the certainty of all the stars in the sky and all of the water in the ocean. He was mine and I was his and I was a damn fool for ever doubting that.

I'd been trying to reclaim something with these men without sex getting in the way of it, but now that I was looking down at him while he baited me with the pure temptation of his body, I was starting to realise I'd been a fucking idiot for thinking I could do that.

I couldn't take sex out of the equation with them. My whole being burned for them, my body shook and trembled with need at the mere sight of them and owning that need and my own sexuality was nothing to be ashamed of. I wasn't their whore. I was their girl. And they were my fucking boys. Which meant I could claim them all as often and in as many ways as I liked, and the only thing I should ever have felt about it was pride.

I tipped my chin up and curled my fingers into the hem of the shirt that covered me before slowly peeling it off of my body and revealing myself to him once again. I tossed it aside and instead of focussing on the carnal hunger that grew in his gaze as he drank in the sight of me exposed before him, I bathed in the worship which poured from his eyes, the fucking need in him to belong to me just as I needed to belong to him.

"There's my girl," Maverick rumbled, his hands flexing where he still held onto my hips and my skin erupting in goosebumps at his touch. "I see her looking right back at me out of your eyes, beautiful. And that's what I desire most about you, because I've been obsessed with that fucking girl for my whole life and no matter how far we've been from each other or how long I go between each time I lay my eyes on you, I still carry you with me right here in my chest. You're the good in me, Rogue. You're the only good I got left."

I leaned down and kissed him again, and this time there was nothing left dividing us, no hesitation, or whispers of doubt. Just the pure, blazing fire which always flared so goddamn hot between the two of us, its burn so fucking good that I would never get enough of its beautiful agony. Our kiss deepened and he didn't hold back, the dark in him coming to consume the light in me until the two of us were left hanging in this perfect twilight where we merged as one and the press of his lips, the bite of his stubble and clash of our tongues became a hungry, desperate animal which would never be satisfied.

He fell back against the pillows as I ground against him, trying to relieve some of the tension in my flesh with the friction I could gain along his hard cock through the barrier of his boxers.

My body was humming and buzzing, my pussy so wet that I was practically whimpering with the desire to take what it was fucking begging for and as Maverick's fingers dug into my sides more forcefully, I pushed a hand between us and released his cock from his boxers.

I didn't waste any time, needing to take what I wanted as fast as I could and I wrapped my fingers around his thick length, positioning him exactly where I needed him to be before driving my body down over his.

A throaty moan escaped me as his huge dick filled me so completely that it stole my breath from my lungs and made my pussy clench greedily around him.

"Fuck yes," he groaned, sounding like a ravenous beast who had finally made the kill it needed to survive.

He gripped my ass and tried to lift my hips, claiming control of the motion in that dominating way of his, but I grabbed his wrists and pulled his hands off of me as I sat back, panting around the fullness of his cock lodged deep inside me.

"This is me owning you, Rick," I warned him as he looked up at me. "So I'm in charge. All I need you to do is make sure no one else hears me screaming when I start coming all over your dick."

Maverick laughed as I placed his left hand on my breast before pressing his right down over my clit, but he obediently kept them there as I wrapped my hand around his neck once more and looked into his dark eyes.

"Mine," I claimed him and his snarky little comeback got caught in his mouth as I raised my hips and sank down over his cock again hard.

I moaned as I began to fuck him, his thumb pressing hard against my clit just like I'd wanted while I rode the entire length of his huge cock as roughly as I wanted to, tilting my hips just right until he was slamming into that perfect fucking spot inside me to make me see stars.

He watched me with the intensity of the sun, his breaths coming heavier and a groan rolling from his throat that was so hot, it made me nearly cry out in response.

I bit down on my bottom lip, trying to stifle the noise I was making so that the whole house didn't have to listen to us, but Rick seemed to realise that I was struggling to control myself and his big hand wrapped around my mouth to help me.

It felt like it had been fucking years since the last time I'd claimed his body and his massive dick was already bringing me to a climax which I wasn't going to be able to hold off.

I squeezed his throat tighter as I fucked him harder and harder, taking with every thrust of my hips but giving back to him too. His gaze darkened as I cut off his oxygen and the sight of him pinned beneath me like that at my utter fucking mercy was enough to send me crashing over the edge with an explosive orgasm which had me screaming into his hand so loud that I was sure the sound had still carried.

My pussy pulsed and throbbed around him and he groaned as he came too, his body shuddering beneath me as his cum shot deep inside me and made me moan once more.

I released my grip on his throat, panting heavily as he took his hand from my mouth and let me fall forward so that my forehead was pressing to his as we took a moment to recover in each other's arms.

"You like that, baby girl?" Rick asked me and I could feel his smile against my skin as he turned towards me before running his tongue up my neck and making me shiver in his arms.

"Yes," I admitted, biting down on my bottom lip as he continued to kiss my neck, his dick still buried inside me. "I think I might get a taste for being the dominant one."

Maverick chuckled then slapped my ass hard enough to make me yelp before lifting me off of him and dropping me onto my back at his side.

"Nah, beautiful. That isn't really the dynamic I'm built for. But if you wanna make Chase and Johnny James into your obedient little subs then I'll happily watch that show." He rolled onto his side and reached out to tuck a lock of hair behind my ear, propping his head up on his arm so that he could look at me.

"You really like the idea of that, don't you?" I asked curiously.

"Watching you get fucked so good you can hardly walk after? Yeah, baby, I like the idea of that. But only with them. Any other man tries to lay a fucking finger on you and I'll break him in half without a moment's hesitation."

"Break him in half?" I laughed and he leaned down to kiss me.

"Fuck, I wanna drink that sound," he growled against my lips, his hand moving to my side and trailing along my flesh so that a shiver broke through my skin and my nipples ached with need.

"I love you, Maverick," I said, knowing he wouldn't say it back, that he couldn't. But that didn't mean he didn't need to hear it all the same.

He made a satisfied kind of sound, dropping down and sucking my nipple between his lips before tugging on it with his teeth and making me gasp.

"Do you ever think about your parents?" he asked as he released me, his hand brushing along my skin in that insatiable way of his and I dropped my gaze, noticing his cock was already half erect and wondering how much longer we'd keep talking before he was making me moan his name again.

"No," I replied with a shrug. "I've read the file on my mom. She was a drug addict and a hooker, Rick. Chances are she overdosed somewhere long ago, and I doubt she even had a clue who my father was. It doesn't matter to me. Never did."

"Why not?" he asked.

"Because I always had the four of you. I don't need some deadbeat mom who loved shooting up more than she loved me. I don't need some dad who has no idea about my existence having to pretend he gives a shit that a woman he paid to fuck ended up pregnant without him ever wanting me. Honestly - I realised when I was real young that I wasn't missing anything from the people who donated my DNA."

"Yeah, but you used to wish you had a real mom and dad when we were kids," he pointed out, knowing me all too well.

"Sure. When Stacey Roberts had that huge princess party and a cake bigger than my entire body, I wanted to punch her and steal her mom from her. I think all of us did," I agreed. "But her mom isn't my mom. I might have wished I had someone to love and care for me when I was a kid. I might have wanted birthday parties and bedtime stories, but if my mom had been on the scene, that wasn't what I would have got. I'd have had a fucking weight around my neck. Someone more interested in getting a fix than putting food on the table. Honestly Rick, I saw how Chase grew up living with his dad and I know in my heart that I was better off in the care home. And that's saying something because I fucking hated that place."

"Remember when Rosie Morgan stole that chocolate bar I gave you and stuffed her big mouth with it?" Rick asked, smiling down at me as he leaned in closer, his hard on pressing against my thigh.

"Yeah," I grumbled. "Bitch. I still hate her. I can't believe Chase fucked her."

"Mmm. Well do you remember what I did to her in revenge?"

I thought on it then smiled as I remembered him drenching her with the garden hose when she left the house for school the following day before throwing a bucket of sand over her head so that it stuck to her.

"She squealed like a stuck pig," I laughed at the memory and he nodded.

"Yeah she did. And all she did was steal a snack from you." Rick's hand moved between my legs and I moaned softly as he stroked his fingers through his cum which had trickled out of me and started using it as lubrication to toy with my clit.

"She deserved it," I murmured, my head tipping back as he slowly circled my clit and set my nerve endings tingling.

"Yeah. So what do you think I'll do to a man who got into your head and made you question our feelings for you?" he asked, moving his fingers back and forth and making my breath hitch at the pleasure he was giving me.

"Rick," I begged, forgetting the question as he continued to toy with me.

"What do you think I would do to a man who laid his fucking hands on you? Who put bruises on your skin and made you fear my touch?"

"You'll kill him," I gasped and he pushed two fingers into me instantly like he was rewarding me for those words.

"Yeah, baby girl, I'll kill him. I'll kill him real good," Rick growled, his fingers driving in and out of me and making me whimper as he built my body up so fucking easily that I knew I'd be crashing into another orgasm at any moment. "I'll cut him up bit by bit and I'll only pause to fuck this tight cunt of yours while we listen to him screaming together. Would you like that? Do you wanna look into that motherfucker's eyes while he's bleeding to death and I'm fucking you raw right in front of him?"

"Fuck," I moaned, my pussy pulsing hungrily at the thought of that, his fingers driving in harder, his thumb owning my clit and making me weak beneath him.

"I'll paint your pretty flesh red with his blood and fuck you dirty in a puddle of it so deep that you'll think you're fucking drowning."

"Jesus," I gasped and he drove his fingers into me even harder, forcing me to come for him hard and fast all over his hand just like he'd wanted me to. Just like he'd known he would when he spoke those sinfully wicked words into my ear. He stamped his mouth to mine to swallow the noise I made as my pussy clamped around his fingers and I shuddered beneath him, knowing he wasn't done yet.

"Fuck, I love the sight of you covered in my cum," he said in a low voice, drawing his fingers back out of me and wrapping them around his solid cock, pumping it the way he liked and putting on a show which had me panting for a taste of him.

I pushed up onto my elbows, my body still trembling from the aftershocks of pleasure he'd delivered to me as I leaned forward and ran my tongue over the tip of his dick.

Maverick fisted my hair and fed me his cock like I wanted, driving it in to the back of my throat and making me gag around his huge, inked shaft.

My eyes began to water as he fucked my mouth hard and I gripped his ass, my nails biting into his flesh in encouragement, loving when he was rough with me and wanting him to own me just as I'd owned him.

"You're so fucking perfect," he said as he watched me. "My perfect, beautiful, lost girl."

I moaned around his shaft but he jerked back suddenly, leaning over me to the side of the bed and returning with his belt in his hands as he reared over me.

"I told you I was angry with you, Rogue," Maverick said, holding the belt out between us and creating a loop with it. "So now I need you to tell me if you're ready for your punishment? Because I'm gonna need my pound of flesh before I can forgive you."

I licked my swollen lips, tasting his arousal mixed with my own on them as I considered what he was asking of me. I'd been afraid of so many things recently and Shawn's poison had worked itself so far beneath my skin that I couldn't have even imagined being in this position with him this morning. But as I looked into his dark eyes, I found the answer to my question there.

Because there might have been a lot of things for me to fear in this dark world we lived in but there were some things which I could trust in implicitly and this man was one of them. I loved him. And I'd hurt him. So I was willing to let him work through whatever punishment he needed me to so that he could move on from that betrayal and find his way back to me again.

I nodded slowly, offering up my wrists and Maverick's grin turned wicked as he gripped my hip and flipped me over beneath him.

He caught my wrists and secured them at the base of my spine, cinching the belt tight enough to make me suck in a sharp breath before grabbing my ass and tugging it up into the air.

My face was pressed to the comforter and I was instantly glad of that as it muffled my cry when he drove the full length of his dick inside me without any further warning.

I cursed as he drew back and slammed into me again, his cock striking deep and hard and selfishly as he used my body for his own pleasure and gave me the punishment he needed to with an animal ferocity.

It was all I could do to push my hips back to meet his and take every thrust of his dick deep inside me as he slapped my ass and pulled my hair and fucked me so hard I could barely breathe.

My pussy took each punishing thrust he could deliver and still it begged for more, and I flexed my fingers at the base of my spine, wishing they were free for me to stroke my clit.

As if he could tell that I needed so much more, Rick grabbed me suddenly, flipping me onto my back and pinning my arms beneath me as he lifted my legs up onto his shoulders and sank back inside me again.

His hand came down over my mouth to stifle my cry of pleasure as he ground himself against me and gave my clit the friction it had been desperate for.

He slammed into me again and I bit his palm, the taste of his flesh and blood coating my tongue as my teeth pierced the skin but he didn't let go. He only held me tighter, his eyes alight with pleasure and the taste of his blood still lingering in my mouth.

Maverick kept fucking me hard but his movements grew slower, his eyes on mine as he seemed to drink me in and the rest of the world just faded away.

We were this single being, utterly united in our lust and love and blissful pleasure of our flesh.

He rolled his hips against mine over and over, grinding against my clit until he could see the orgasm building in my eyes and I was moaning into his hand once more.

"I love you too, baby girl," he said in a low voice just for me and with those obliterating words, I came hard, crying out into his palm as my pussy gripped him tight and begged him to follow me out of the dark.

Rick drove his cock into me a few more times, not pausing in his pace as my body spasmed around his then he pulled out suddenly, coming all over my tits with a roar of pleasure which made all of my attempts at staying quiet seem utterly pointless.

"Fuck, yes," he groaned, looking down at the mess he'd made of me while I panted beneath him and he reared back, placing my legs down on the bed again as he reached over to the nightstand before grabbing his phone and taking a picture of me.

"Asshole," I grumbled, unable to do a damn thing to stop him with my arms still tied beneath me and he grinned widely, turning the phone around so that I could see the shot.

"Just fucked looks damn good on you, beautiful," he purred, leaning down to kiss my neck and as I looked at the image of me laying there covered in sweat and trails of his seed, I could admit that he had a point. My eyes were a bright and vibrant blue, my full lips puffy and kissable and the utterly satisfied look on my face made me look like I really was happy. And as I looked at Rick, I realised that was the truth.

"You're still an asshole," I muttered.

"If I was an asshole, I'd make you sleep like that - all tied up and marked as mine. Would you like that, beautiful?" he teased though I would be willing to bet he'd really leave me like this if I pushed him.

"I think I'd like a shower," I said, giving him a pout. "But if you wanna help me get cleaned up then I might let you eat me out for breakfast in the morning."

Maverick barked a laugh and my heart lightened as I found such a genuine smile on his face. I could see the boy I'd known and loved in that smile, the light-hearted daredevil who wasn't afraid of a thing looking back at me at long last.

"Alright, beautiful. But that will only be the starter," he said before sweeping me into his arms and walking us to the en-suite. And I was seriously okay with that.

I woke with a start, wondering what the fuck was going on before remembering where I was and taking note of the heavy arm draped over me and the other hand which was currently shaking me.

"Back the fuck off or I'll blow your head off," Rick snarled beside me and as I cracked an eye open, I found him aiming a gun at Fox over my sleeping form.

"Terrifying," Fox deadpanned, barely sparing the gun a glance. "But I'm not here to see you, asshole. I'm here for Rogue."

"Me?" I mumbled sleepily.

"Yeah. I was wondering if you wanted to catch the morning surf with me?" he asked, seeming kind of unsure now that I was blinking up at him sleepily. He glanced at Rick, a struggle in his eyes which said he was trying to hold himself back from snatching me away like a thief come for a diamond. And for a second, I wanted him to, to see that fire in him again for me. But he schooled his expression, his want for me vanishing and leaving me aching for it.

"She's busy," Rick grumbled, tossing the gun back down on the nightstand before pulling me further into his arms.

I wriggled free though, kicking him when he wouldn't release me willingly and he cursed me before letting go and rolling over to go back to sleep.

I pushed out of bed, glad that I'd tugged Rick's shirt on again last night after we'd got done losing ourselves in one another.

"I picked up a few things for you at the store," Fox said, holding out a brown paper bag which looked pretty heavy. "You'll probably wanna go shopping yourself too but seeing as Shawn destroyed all of your things I figured you'd need a bathing costume and stuff."

"Thanks," I said, shooting him a smile as I accepted the bag of clothes. "Give me two minutes," I added, heading away to the bathroom.

Fox sank down onto the chair in the corner of the room which still sat facing the bed from all the times he'd snuck in and watched me sleeping. I narrowed my eyes at him as he picked up his phone from the table beside it and Mutt leapt up into his lap.

"How long have you been in here?" I asked suspiciously.

"An hour or so," he said, giving me a look which I couldn't determine. "Rick needs to work on his reflexes if he expects to defend you with that gun in the night. He's not much protection if he sleeps through someone entering the room." He shot Maverick's back a glare, and I drank in the possessive little badger in his gaze before he smuggled it away again.

"I knew you'd just come in to jerk off in the corner, so I decided to leave you to it," Maverick said from somewhere within the pillows. "Makes a change from the amount of times you've done it over that home video I sent you of me, J and our girl, doesn't it?"

Fox's jaw ticked and he shoved himself upright suddenly. "I'll go make us coffee," he announced, not bothering to respond to Rick's claim and heading out of the room with Mutt on his heels.

"Told you he kept it," Maverick muttered and I rolled my eyes at him before quickly stripping out of his shirt and finding the bathing suit to change into.

I arched a brow at Fox's choice of swimwear, the navy blue one piece covering up so much of my body that it was practically criminal and made my ass look all kinds of flat. My ass – the ass which would never be contained! How the hell had he even managed that?

"Boo. Where did he get this from, Grandmas-R-Us?" I asked, turning back and forth to get a look at it in the mirror.

Rick appeared from beneath the covers and fell about laughing as he got a good look at me, and I scowled at him as I folded my arms.

"Foxy boy is trying to stop himself from eye fucking you every time he looks at you, beautiful," he decided, still laughing at me as I turned around to show him the front which was practically up to my goddamn neck.

"Fuck off," I shot back, plucking at the material. "It was probably all he could get."

"Yeah, sure it was."

I left Rick laughing in the bed as I headed downstairs to find Fox.

He was waiting for me by the back door, a thermos of coffee in his hand for me while our surfboards leaned against the wall outside.

"How's the surf looking?" I asked, moving to stand beside him and deciding not to comment on my less than hot bathing suit. Though as I ran my gaze over him, I couldn't help but notice how fucking good he looked in the low hanging, bright orange board shorts he'd put on. His blonde hair was pushed back out of his face and his green eyes reflected the waves as he turned to look at the sea.

"Good. You think you can keep up with me?"

"Oh, I can keep up," I promised him, taking a swig of my coffee which had been made exactly the way I liked it.

"Big words."

"Always."

We shared a smile and I set my thermos down carefully, the challenge hanging between us and setting butterflies warring inside my stomach.

"Don't do it," he warned.

"Do what?' I asked innocently, readying myself for the race we always used to have as kids - last to the water had to drink it.

"I'm a lot faster than I used to be when we were kids," he warned.

"Yeah, but you have that big old head to carry around now too," I pointed out and he barked a laugh.

"You're asking for it."

"No doubt," I agreed before turning and looking over his shoulder, my eyes widening as I pretended to spot something behind him. "Oh shit..."

"What?" Fox asked, turning to look like a Badger on high alert and I pounced. I grabbed the back of his shorts and yanked them down to his ankles before kicking him in the ass as he bent to try and grab them.

Fox fell to the floor with a yell of surprise and I laughed wildly as I threw the back door open, knocked his board over then grabbed mine and started running.

Mutt yipped excitedly as he raced down the sand beside me, the rising sun cresting the hills at my back as I sprinted towards the water.

"You'll pay for that, asshole!" Fox yelled.

"Bite me, dickbag!" I yelled back, laughter tearing from my throat as I splashed out into the sea and dropped my board onto the water with a sigh of pure joy.

This bitch was finally back where she belonged, and I was fucking loving it.

CHAPTER THIRTY TWO

Everything felt...better. Like the world was righting itself at long fucking last. But sometimes I woke up fearing it was all going to crumble beneath me and we'd fall into everlasting chaos for good. Things weren't perfect. Fox and I still hadn't worked out our shit and we were getting by on surface level conversations, but I was really hoping that might change eventually.

The problem was, every time Rogue touched me, or we shared a look for too long in his presence, he shut down again, retreating from our space, from me. And it broke my damn heart. I'd never considered being able to call Rogue mine would equal me losing one of my closest friends in the whole fucking world. But of course I should have considered that. I'd just never seen myself as a real option when we were kids, and I'd naively thought nothing could really be strong enough to break us, even when I'd feared her choosing. But now, this arrangement we'd formed felt as fragile as glass and I knew it couldn't go on forever because I already saw the cracks forming in Fox's eyes. Eventually, he was going to shatter. So I decided that I was going to do everything I could to prevent that and though Fox had rejected every advance I'd made to bridge the gap between us, this time I wasn't going to take no for an answer.

While Rogue was playing in the pool with the others, and Mabel was taking a nap in the lounge, I slipped inside where Fox was cooking lunch in the kitchen, his tanned back to me as he focused on the task at hand. Practically every meal he made was a feast these days and sometimes I wondered if that was because he wanted to spend as much time as possible in this room avoiding interacting with us as a group.

There was fresh bread, cheeses, olives, fruit, pasta and three different kinds of salad. I mean, who the fuck needed three different kinds of salad? Not that I was complaining exactly, I hadn't eaten this well for this long in fucking ages, and I swear the five of us had glowing skin and richer hair because of it. But the intense trance Fox seemed to be in as he worked made me think all this cooking was an anxiety outlet for all the things he had no one to talk to about. But he'd had me once, and I really, really, *really* wanted him to have me again.

I got some fresh lemonade from the fridge, pouring it into a glass and making myself known in the room, though he didn't look around. So I guzzled down my lemonade then cleared my throat, hip bumping a stool to make it screech across the floor a little. He still didn't look around.

I cleared my throat again, placing my glass down hard to make a noise, but it slipped out of my fingers, fell over and rolled off the counter, hitting the floor and smashing hard.

"Shit," I hissed, dropping down and trying to gather it up between my hands, immediately cutting myself and cursing.

"What the fuck are you doing, JJ?" Fox growled and I sensed him coming up behind me.

I looked over my shoulder and he swooped down with a dustpan and brush, batting me away from the glass on the floor.

I stood up, sucking my index finger which now had a slit along the tip of it and tasting blood on my tongue.

Fox cleaned up the mess then turned to me with a sharp frown on his brow. "Show me," he commanded and the little bitch in me who used to be under his thumb plucked my finger from my mouth and offered it up to him.

It was stupid, but I'd liked our little dynamic before now. I was good at playing his second, it made us a dream team. I'd only ever hated that he extended his bossy shit to my personal life.

"Who picks up glass with their bare hands?" he muttered, grabbing some white rum from the fridge and pulling me to the sink where he proceeded to pour the alcohol over the cut.

"Me?" I offered, hitching on my cutest smile and he glanced at me with a hint of a smile in return before flattening it.

"There," he said, placing the bottle down and returning to his cooking.

"So um…" I started.

"You don't need to make small talk with me, JJ, go enjoy the sun," he said and my heart felt like a kicked alley cat, curling up in a ball in a lonely dumpster.

"I want to talk to you though," I said, pulling out a stool and dropping onto it.

He glanced over his shoulder at me and I arched my brows hopefully, making him shake his head and turn away again.

"What about?" he muttered.

"Stuff…and things," I said, picking an olive out of a bowl, throwing it in the air and catching it in my mouth.

"You know this cute kid act doesn't work on me," he said dismissively.

Dammit, how does he know what I'm up to?

I sighed. "Come on, Fox, talk to me." I rested my elbows on the table, cupping my head in my hands as I gazed at him imploringly and as he turned around, I could see him considering it.

"About what?" he asked. "About how you lied to me? Went behind my back? Fucked the girl I love in the house I grew up in right under my nose? Is it those things you wanna talk about?"

My throat turned to stone, unable to allow in a single breath of air, so I just nodded instead.

"Fine, I'm all ears," he said, folding his arms across his bare chest, cocking his head as he waited.

Shit, I didn't think this through.

"Well…I know what I did was a little underhanded, but I thought… Honestly? I thought you'd shoot me in the head if I ever told you I wanted her. And I'm not saying that metaphorically, I literally thought you'd kill me.

I'm actually ninety nine percent shocked I'm still breathing." I laid it out how it was, figuring there wasn't much more harm I could do to our relationship at this point. It was already knocked to the ground covered in stab wounds, twitching its way into death.

Fox inclined his head, not biting back as I'd expected him to but looking like he really was trying to hear what I had to say. It looked like it was a real fucking struggle for him too, but he was trying and that gave me hope. "Yeah, I guess I can see why you'd have thought that," he said eventually and my eyebrows shot up. "But, that doesn't excuse you not having the balls to come talk to me before you started fucking her."

"And how do you think that conversation would have gone, Fox?" I asked in a growl. "Because I'm pretty sure it would have ended with you telling me to never touch her no matter what my feelings were towards her, wouldn't it?"

Again, he took a moment to think on that, clearly biting his tongue on his instinctual reaction to snap at me.

"Yeah," he said at last. "It would have."

"So, you get it?" I asked, hope rising in my chest.

"No, JJ," he said, hurt crossing his features. "Because I know I'm an unreasonable asshole, but I was your friend too. And I'm not saying I would have taken it well, but you didn't even have the guts to find out."

"And risk being executed by you for being a traitor?" I scoffed. "You can't have it both ways, Fox. You can't treat my personal actions towards you as actions against the Crew, like you did with Chase."

Fox winced at my words, and I could see they'd hit home like a dagger to his heart. "I know," he snarled. "I fucking know, Johnny James."

"Don't call me that," I said in frustration, shoving to my feet. "Look, I may be in the wrong here, but you are too. And I'm sorry I fucked up, sorry I lied, but I'm not sorry I love her and I'm not sorry I laid a claim on her any chance I got because she's all I've ever wanted and if the tables had been turned, you'd have claimed her right in front of me without ever considering what I might feel about it."

"You never told me!" Fox snapped. "I was clear from the start how I felt about her."

"It wouldn't have changed anything," I said firmly. "You know it wouldn't have. And regardless of that, maybe if you'd thought about it for one second you might have realised it was damn obvious I loved her, like we all fucking love her."

Fox opened his mouth to retort then his eyes slid over my head and I turned, finding Rogue walking indoors in the tiny pink bikini she'd bought when she went shopping for new clothes, her smile falling as she realised we were arguing.

"What's going on?" she asked.

"Nothing, pretty girl." I glanced away, but I felt her gaze narrow on me as she moved closer and I took her hand.

"Don't give me that," she pushed and I sighed, knowing we'd vowed to be honest with one another, but I didn't wanna bring her mood down.

"We're just trying to sort our shit out," Fox said and I looked over at him in surprise.

"Are we?" I asked. "Is that what we're doing?"

He glanced from me to Rogue, to the place where our hands were locked together. His eyes burned with the most intensely possessive beast behind them and he forced his head away to look beyond us like he simply couldn't bear seeing us together. Sometimes it seemed like he was getting used to it, but it was clear from that one look alone that he wasn't. He was suffering, burning in a hell of his own making day in and day out. But he was still here, still trying and that just made me seriously fucking sad for him.

"It doesn't need to be this way," I said and Rogue tried to pull her hand from mine, but I wouldn't let go.

"Do you wanna go for a walk, Badger?" Rogue asked but he shook his head.

"I'm good, hummingbird. Lunch is nearly ready." He drew a smile on his face that didn't touch his eyes. "Go enjoy yourself, I'll call you when it's done."

He turned back to preparing our meal, his shoulders rigid with tension as he tried to mask his pain, but it was right here, living in this room like a demon. And I couldn't stand it.

Maverick ran inside, soaking wet and dripping water everywhere, clearly not picking up on the awkward vibes in the room as he grabbed Rogue, flipping her over his shoulder and slapping her ass, making her yelp in surprise.

"Having fun, kitchen wench?" he called to Fox who didn't answer.

Maverick looked to me, pulling a moody face in mockery of Fox than strode back out to the pool and threw Rogue into it before diving after her.

"Go have fun, JJ," Fox said, not looking at me.

"Why don't you come too?" I asked, not wanting to give up on trying to cross this void between us.

"I'm making the food," he said.

"You've made enough for a hungry army," I said, moving over to him and grabbing his arm. It was a bold move, but fuck it, I needed to get past this awkwardness with us because it was driving me crazy.

I tugged him toward the door, glancing at the chopping knife in his hand then looking up at his frowny expression. "You're gonna cut me up with that salad knife, aren't you?"

"Well I did forget to pick up cucumber," he said, pointedly looking at my crotch and I gasped, clutching Johnny D.

"You wouldn't."

"Seems like it would solve both of my issues." He gave me a devil's smile, twisting the blade in his hand and a grin spread across my face.

"Was that a joke?"

"Maybe." He shrugged like it was nothing, but it wasn't. It was a step towards old times, me and him messing around. And I was so here for it.

"Let's just put the knife down, hm?" I reached for it but he swung it out of my way, a dare in his eyes and I smirked at the challenge. That was definitely the face of someone who wanted a play fight and I was as down as a clown in a gown.

I lunged forward, grabbing his wrist, my fingers tightening on his pressure points, but he knocked me back with his other hand, sending me stumbling out onto the patio. I dove at him again with a bark of laughter and he held the knife behind his back while trying to fend me off with one arm. But that was his mistake. I locked him in a choke hold, forcing his head down and reaching for the knife, but he wrapped his leg around mine, throwing his weight sideways and knocking us both to the ground.

I threw the heel of my palm against his jaw and he cursed as I tried to get my leg over him to pin him down. A clang said he'd dropped the knife and he used both hands to shove my shoulders down beneath him and my ears pricked up as Chase started counting.

"Five, four, three, two, one. Fox wins," he announced and Fox smiled the brightest smile I'd seen on him in ages.

"I went easy on you because you needed the win," I said with a smirk and my heart lit up like a bonfire when he smirked back.

"Sure, J," he taunted, getting to his feet and pulling me up after him.

I glanced at Rogue, finding her and Maverick out of the pool and standing with Chase as they watched us.

"Winner faces the next opponent," Maverick ran at us, thumping his chest like a gorilla and slammed into Fox with the force of a freight train.

They crashed to the ground and started wrestling like kids with the strength of men, the two of them seeming so evenly matched that they could never quite pin the other one down.

Rogue dropped onto a sun lounger where Mutt was resting in the shade, grabbing her glass of lemonade from beside it and taking a long gulp as she watched the show. I shared a look with Chase which told me he knew exactly what Rogue was thinking as her gaze remained rivetted to Fox and Rick.

"Do you need a napkin for all that drool, pretty girl?" I teased and her eyes snapped to me, full of heat and dirty thoughts.

Damn, she looked like sex embodied, Aphrodite in human form. I could have watched her all day long. Though as much as I didn't give a damn about her hungry eyes feasting on the others, I wanted her attention on me in that moment, so I stepped into her view, her mouth perfectly aligned with my cock from her low position on the lounger. I pushed my fingers into her hair, a carnal energy coursing through my veins as I observed her parted lips and dilating pupils.

"You keeping this dark hair?" I ran my fingers through it, liking the way it reminded me of the girl I'd once known, but also despising the fact that fucking Shawn had chosen it for her.

"I haven't decided," she said, worrying at her bottom lip and Chase appeared, dropping down onto the lounger beyond hers and lighting up a cigarette.

He was shirtless, his scars on show but his eyepatch was in place and every now and then he'd pick up his shirt like he was thinking about putting it on before placing it down again. I knew he was trying to brave out this new version of himself, but I could see his fragile walls and I was sure a few hard strikes would bring them crumbling down.

"What do you reckon, Ace? Brunette or rainbow or something else?" Rogue asked, dropping back to lay on the lounger and my gaze fell down the perfect gleam of her sun kissed skin, the swell of her tits in that tiny bikini and-

Mutt savaged my leg and I cursed, stepping back and dropping onto my own lounger. *Little hellion.*

"It doesn't matter to me," Chase answered, smoke pluming from between his lips. "All I see when I look at you is colour anyway. You're like the sunset that never ends."

He said it so offhandedly like it was a straight up fact, and it sure as shit was, but it left even me kinda fuzzy, so Rogue must have been pure fuzz inside. Her cheeks flushed as she gazed at him, but he didn't seem to notice the affect he'd just had on her as he continued smoking and watching the wrestling match Maverick and Fox were still locked in.

They'd moved close to the pool and as Maverick tried to hold Fox's head down, Fox bucked and rolled and the two of them crashed into the water, making me breathe a laugh as they continued fighting even then.

Rogue leaned over, pressing her lips to Chase's cheek and he looked at her in surprise, always seeming so taken aback by her love for him. And dammit, I was tired of him thinking he was worth nothing to no one. Between his damn father and fucking Shawn, his confidence had been obliterated and I for one wasn't gonna stand for it any longer.

And as an idea came to me, I smiled like the Grinch with a plan to ruin Christmas, because tonight, Chase was going to get his confidence back whether he liked it or not, and baubles be damned.

Evening arrived and I was way too fucking excited to get back to Afterlife after

so long away from it. Estelle had been keeping me informed of how business was running, working overtime to keep everything in order and I was going to be giving her a fat bonus for looking after the place. And my pet starfish.

I entered through the back door in low-riding sweatpants and a pink wifebeater with a shark on it, finding all the dancers there with Estelle and a little welcome back banner hanging across the wall that had been made out of G-strings.

"Surprise!" they all cried and Di walked forward with a small tank of water in her hands and a pink starfish inside.

"We got you a new starfish!" she exclaimed, holding the tank up for me to take and my jaw dropped.

"You *guys*, you didn't have to do that," I said, taking the tank and gazing in at my new little dude. Or dudette, because she looked like an absolute beaut of a starfish.

"Well, your other one looked kind of sad on its own. We decorated his tank, look." She pointed across the room and I took in the row of sparkly nipple tassels stuck all along the top of it with a bright smile.

"That's fucking amazing. You guys are the best." I walked over to Sparkle's tank with his new friend, waving at my carnivorous little psycho and I swear he twitched a star finger at me.

"What are you gonna call the new one, boss?" Adam asked, appearing at my side and I grinned at him.

"Errrr, Jigglypuff," I decided.

"Isn't Starmie the starfish Pokemon?" he asked.

"Yeah, and?" I tossed back. God, couldn't he see that she obviously looked like a Jigglypuff? She wasn't some bog-standard Starmie.

I poured her into the bigger tank with Sparkle and she floated down to the bottom of it, landing near to him and latching onto a rock.

"That's my girl," I cooed. "Now don't eat each other, you hear me?" I pointed at Sparkle then Jigglypuff. "Daddy won't be pleased if I come back later and one of you has bite marks."

"Oooh *Daddy*," Bella giggled from somewhere across the room. "Don't spank me, Daddy."

I glanced over at her, finding her swaying on her high heels and clinging

463

onto Lyla's arm.

"Is she drunk?" I growled and Lyla gave me an apologetic look, though it wasn't her fucking responsibility.

"She had some bad news today," Adam murmured to me. "Her friend's step-brother's cat died."

"That's a very far removed cat," I balked. "I mean, it's sad and all, but was she really that close to her friend's step-uncle's-"

"Step-brother!" Bella shrieked. "And you didn't know Mr Whiskerton like I did, JJ. So don't you go around telling me whose cat I can and can't care about." She came apart, wailing and burying her face in Lyla's shoulder.

"Alright, alright," I gave in. "Take a night off for the cat." I pointed to the door. "I'm not having you dancing drunk out there sobbing about Mr Purrington to clients."

"Mr Whiskerton!" she snarled and Lyla had to hold her back as she came at me like she wanted to fight me.

Jesus.

Lyla guided her out the back door and silence fell, the noise suddenly broken by a slap, slap, slap sound. All eyes fell on Texas where he stood with a towel around his waist, jerking his hips left and right so his dick slapped between his thighs.

"Thought I'd break the tension," he said, booming a laugh and dammit that shit was funny.

"You're such a weirdo, man," I said, moving over to clap his shoulder in greeting before heading to the door that led into the bar and gesturing for Estelle to follow me.

She smiled brightly, trotting along at my heels and filling me in on everything that had been going on here since I'd left. By the time I was caught up, I was ready for tonight's show and couldn't wait to get out dancing again. Estelle had even put out a notification across our social medias saying I was re-joining the troupe tonight after my extended vacation and we'd sold out tickets in under a day after the announcement. If that wasn't good for my ego, then I didn't know what was.

"Oh sorry sir, we're not open yet," Estelle said and I followed her gaze to Tom Collins who'd apparently shown up an hour early to see his favourite dancer return. Maybe tonight he'd finally pluck up the courage to shove a few dollar bills down my asscrack. Aww, that'd be great.

"Nah, he can stick around Stelle," I said, waving a hand, but then I noticed the wide eyed, panicked look on Tom's face and frowned.

"You okay there, big boy?" I laid it on thick, hoping to get a smile out of him instead of that strange look he was giving me.

"No, I'm not okay," he said, shaking his head then he strode towards me at a furious pace and I got up from my seat by the bar, my right hand curling into a fist in case this got ugly. I'd had pouncers before – mostly women – but their hands could get down a man's pants faster than you could say sexual assault.

"Woah, woah, back it up," I tried, but he kept coming and I was about to flatten him when he wrapped me in a tight hug, clapping his hand against my back.

"I was so worried. Where the hell have you been?" he asked, squeezing me tighter.

Crazy with a capital C. But maybe I shouldn't have been so harsh, I knew some of the regulars we had in here could get pretty attached to the idea of us dancers. We were a fantasy painted into their minds and brought to life on stage. It all got a little too real for those who were lonely or suffering through heartache.

Estelle took a taser from behind the bar and I shook my head at her to hold her off, the woman a pure savage when she needed to be. I'd seen her use a G-string as a garrot against a guy who'd groped Di in the parking lot once. It had been damn poetry to watch.

"Where have you been, Johnny James?" Tom demanded once more, an edge to his tone I'd never heard from him before. He was always so soft, so nice, but this was a new look on him and if he kept that up, I bet he could get himself a nice boyfriend who'd regularly suck his cock. Aww, I'd like that for him. Maybe I could ask around the club, find someone who looked a bit like me…

"Vacation," I said.

"Bullshit." He released me, giving me a hard look then glancing at Estelle. "Is there somewhere we can talk in private?"

I patted his shoulder. "I'm sorry, I don't do private gigs anymore. But if you'd like a nice little BJ, I can ask Texas if he-"

"No, JJ," he said, seeming flustered.

"Honestly, it's fine. Texas has the softest lips," I said encouragingly. "And he might be big, but he can be real gentle too if that's what you like? Or he can go rough. Whatever floats your boat. You look like a guy who loves a good deepthroat."

His cheeks pinked and he shook his head ferociously. "I'm not gay."

I winked. "It doesn't have to be gay, Tom." I knew some guys struggled with being open about things like this, they needed to pretend it was all just some bro time between men. "You and Texas can just go for a drive…no harm in that, is there?" I winked again and he gripped my arm tightly.

"Johnny James, I really need to talk to you. I'm not looking for any kind of funny feely business." He looked even more flustered as he said that and I took pity on the guy, leading him through to my office. He might just wanna talk for a bit, get comfortable then I could call Texas in and they could go off somewhere together. Or hell, maybe I'd let him go to town right there with my friend because from what Estelle had told me earlier, Tom had been keeping this place afloat on the nights the clients hadn't been flowing and I was seriously fucking grateful to him for that.

I grabbed a bottle of spiced rum stashed in my desk drawer with a couple of glasses, offering him a shot. He took it, throwing it back and wincing so hard his entire face screwed up before he gasped down a breath.

"Christ." He grimaced.

"All good things hurt a little. If you embrace the pain, you'll find the magic sweet spot." I grinned, leaning back against my desk and letting him get a good eyeful of me for his little daydreams later when his cock was in Texas's mouth. He wanted me so fucking bad it was almost a shame I hadn't given him a pity hand job pre-Rogue coming back to town. But here we were.

"JJ, I…I've wanted to tell you this for quite some time," he rambled and I waited patiently, the inevitable love declaration coming. I didn't wanna let the old guy down, but I'd had to do this quite a few times in my line of work before, so I was a pro at it by now. I'd tell him I wasn't interested, that it wasn't him, it was me, while giving him a hug and steering his cock between the lips of a friend. It was beautiful really.

"I don't know quite how to…to tell you this but I…I-"

"Love me?" I offered with a knowing nod, but he finished his sentence at the same time.

"I'm your father."

Cold, dead silence hung there like a wet fish brought to shore.

"I'm sorry what?" I asked, sure I'd misheard him or else I was about to find out Tom had some seriously messed up kinks that I was not interested in playing out with him. I'd had enough of that shit at the Dollhouse. And I would not be donning a dress and pretending to be his pretty little daughter or some shit, no matter how much money he offered me to do it.

"I'm…your father," he said again, clearing his throat and shuffling from foot to foot.

I glanced around the room, half expecting my troupe to jump out and announce I was being pranked, but no one showed up. No camera team led by that dude from Stranger Things, no Ashton Kutcher laughing at me for being 'Punked.' The room was roaringly quiet and Tom Collins let those words simply hang in the air like a potent fart.

"I know I should have said something a long time ago. I meant to, really. The first time I came here, I was going to wait until the show was over and tell you right away, but then I saw you dancing and I -I -oh JJ it was wonderful, you really are an incredible dancer. And I suddenly feared you turning me away, saying you didn't want me in your life. And why would you? I haven't been around, but you see…I didn't know. Your mother never told me, not until many years later. And then it seemed too late, and I really wanted to be a part of your life, so I just…kept coming here. To see you. I just wanted to see you."

I gawped at him, probably looking like a slack-jawed seal as I tried to process the words he'd just launched at me.

I shook my head. "But you're Tom Collins. You want my dick." Oh how I wished those words had been said inside my head as he cringed, looking like he always did when I suggested shit like that. And I suddenly recognised it for what it actually was. He didn't want my dick. He was my dad. He was my fucking father and I'd made multiple – MUL-TI-PLE – suggestive comments about him fucking me on countless occasions. To his face.

TO.

HIS.

FACE.

"Prove it," I demanded, going on the defensive because no. Just no.

He reached into his pocket, taking out a photo and shakily handing it to me. It was him with a moustache – a fucking moustache! – with my mom on his lap and his hand on her knee. She was in full hooker gear, tits half out, stilettos in place and Tom looked like he was fucking in love as he stared up at her.

"It's the only picture I have of her," he said. "It was just one summer, but I'll always remember the magic of it. One, long, hot summer full of thrills and romance and all the things you see in movies. I was undercover, see? It was meant to be a job, but oh my, it was so much more than that. Your mother was a whirlwind I have never forgotten."

God, what was happening? Was he talking about fucking my mother now? Was he telling me for one whole summer he'd banged her repeatedly and somehow I was supposed to find that endearing?

I handed the photo back to him, refusing it. "I don't have a dad. He didn't know about me. You couldn't know about me."

"Like I said...your mother reached out to me. You were twenty, you'd just opened the club. She was drunk, I'm not sure she'd even remember it honestly. When I tried to call her back the next day, she blocked my number. But she'd told me about Afterlife, how you were a dancer and how she'd been afraid to tell me the truth about you because, well..." He rubbed a hand over his thick, dark hair. Hair that was so like mine.

No. Tom Collins is not my father. He wants my dick. Oh god. Oh god.

"Well what?" I pushed, but my voice came out like an echo of its usual ferocity.

He gave me a guilty look then took something else from his blazer pocket, showing me a badge. A cop's fucking badge.

"I'm a detective. And obviously me having liaisons with a woman of her...profession-"

"You're a cop," I interjected.

"Yes, but-"

"You're a cop," I repeated.

"Yes."

"A dirty cop?" I pleaded but he shook his head in horror, confirming my very worst fears. He was straight laced. A good guy. I bet he filed all of his paperwork. Oh Jesus, how could I be related to a fucking goody two shoes cop?? Why would I be cursed this way?

"I'm not here to cause trouble, JJ. I've been looking out for you. I'm not going to tell anyone about the illegal prostitution that-"

"Oh my god, you're my father and you're a cop," I spoke over him again, staring at him with wide eyes. This news was an explosive even worse than the father bomb he'd just dropped.

"I just want to get to know you some more," he started.

"Know me? You don't know me," I said, my chest compressing like it was in a compactor. "You're just a customer. You're Tom Collins."

"My name is Gwan Park. You can ask your mother about me."

"Your name's not Gwan," I refused.

"Um…it is Gwan."

"No it isn't." I pointed to the door. "I need you to leave now, Tom."

"Yes…I, okay." He dropped his head in defeat, drifting out the door like Wilson the ball in Castaway. He glanced back just before he left, his eyes full of some gleaming emotion. "I'm very proud of you, Johnny James. And if I don't see you again then I – I need you to remember that." He walked back over and placed a business card down on my desk – a fucking cop's card with a cop name and cop phone number and all that shit – then walked out the door, leaving me in the torturous company of my own thoughts as my heart bucked and jerked.

I breathed heavily and deeply for a very, very long time then compartmentalised that sack of shit which had been dropped at my door and slapped on a smile.

Right, time for the show of a lifetime.

469

CHAPTER THIRTY THREE

I drove along the cliffside road in my red Jeep with Chase in the passenger seat, Mutt in the back, the roof down and the wind blowing through my hair while I sang Bad Habits by Ed Sheeran, which was the latest song Chase had given me for my playlist.

Every time I glanced over at him, I found a smile playing around his lips which sent my mood soaring higher. I was taking the long drive around to meet JJ at Afterlife for his show so that we could enjoy the sunset and I could steal some more of this time in his carefree company. Because as much as it sucked ass, I knew he'd be uncomfortable once we arrived at the club and were surrounded by people who could gawp and stare at him again. This right here was his happy place, alone with me or the boys where no one else could pop our bubble.

I glanced to my right where the sun was already halfway beneath the horizon, the last of its rays gilding the ocean in gold and pink tones and making my heart ache with a sense of home.

I turned the wheel sharply and the Jeep bumped up off of the road and onto the grassy verge which ran closer to the cliff's edge, ignoring Chase when he asked me what the fuck I was doing.

I kept bumping along over the grass until I passed behind a thicket of thorny weeds which hid the car from the road and gave us some privacy then turned us to face the water and parked up.

"What are you up to, little one?" Chase asked curiously as I unclipped my seatbelt then leaned over to unclip his.

"Watching the sunset, duh," I said, flashing him a grin before getting out of the car and rounding it so that I could jump up onto the hood and take up the prime position to watch the show.

Chase appeared a moment later, pulling a red baseball cap on and using it to shadow his features seeing as I'd stolen his eyepatch yet again. I was pretty sure he had another eyepatch stashed in his pocket for when we got to the club, but I would deal with that in due course.

Mutt leapt out of the open car door to go pee on everything in the vicinity and I patted the hood beside me to encourage Chase to climb up.

"You know, we'll probably bend the hood by sitting on it like that," he pointed out. "And the buttons on your shorts might scratch the paintwork too."

"Boo, stop being a Debbie downer and come watch the sunset with me, Ace. And if you're that worried about my shorts scratching the precious paintwork then I guess I could take them off if you ask me real nicely?" I arched a brow at him and he pushed his tongue into his cheek as the tension between us settled in the air, the secret which wasn't a secret just screaming for our attention. Because I may have bitten Maverick hard enough to draw blood in an attempt to keep my screams of pleasure stifled when we hooked up a couple of nights ago, but it was clear that everyone in the house had heard me anyway. None of us had mentioned it or what it might mean though, and I still wasn't even entirely sure if it had been the right thing to do at all given my current mental state over fucking Shawn and his poisonous words but…I didn't regret it. In fact, just thinking about it made my skin heat and desire pool between my thighs. And being here alone with Chase only heightened the need in my flesh to claim so much more from my boys than I had since I'd returned to them.

Chase wet his lips, his gaze trailing over my bare legs and exposed stomach beneath the white crop top I wore to complete my outfit. I'd been tempted to wear a dress, but the booty shorts had called my name and the day had been so freaking hot that I mostly just wanted as little material covering my flesh as possible. So I'd dressed it up with a pair of Barbie pink killer heels which currently sat on the backseat of the Jeep and I'd gone all in with curling my hair and doing my makeup. Besides, I knew the guy who owned the club, so I was pretty sure I was exempt from the dress code anyway.

I'd left the music playing in the car and the song switched to This Town by Niall Horan - another of the ones Chase had picked out for me. My playlist was five songs long and counting now, and if the way his gaze darkened as he listened to the music gave anything away then I was willing to bet he really did feel that these songs reflected us and the tangled mess we'd made of our relationship.

"You're missing it," I said casually, turning my attention back to the setting sun which only had about a quarter of its mass left to sink beneath the waves. It really was stunning tonight, seeming to stretch out across the entire span of the ocean and paint the sky and sea in a plethora of colour which made my chest ache with happiness.

Chase gave in and came to sit beside me, placing his ass carefully as if he was trying to avoid dents though at least he could calm his socks over any scratches from his black shorts as he was zipper free. He was wearing a short sleeved white button down with the top couple of buttons undone and as I cut a glance at him, I couldn't help but stare a little. He was so gorgeous it hurt, his dark curls tangling at the nape of his neck beneath the ball cap made me wanna run my fingers through his hair and the dark shadow lining his jaw made me ache for the feeling of it scoring against my skin. Even his scars only added to his beauty, he didn't look soft or sweet anymore, it was like the brutality which lay within him had been painted onto his flesh for all the world to see. And I liked looking at the savage in him. I liked knowing what he was capable of with one glance, and I really liked the way his shoulders filled out that shirt.

He shot me a look as he noticed me staring and I stifled a smile, gazing back out to the sunset as if I hadn't been looking at all.

I could feel his eyes running all over me again and I wondered what he was thinking, what thoughts were spinning through that brain of his as he looked at the girl who had always been the creator of chaos in their lives.

"What?" I asked, glancing back at him again as he reached out to run his fingers down the sleeve of tattoos which covered my left arm.

"Sometimes I still can't believe you're really back here," he said in a low voice that made my toes curl against the heat of the hood.

"Me either," I admitted, reaching over and twisting the red baseball cap on his head so that it faced backwards and gave me a better look at his features.

A flicker of vulnerability flashed through his expression but as I ran my fingertips down the edge of his scar, he softened, relaxing once more and turning back to watch the sunset with me.

We remained silent while we watched it dip beneath the horizon, its reflection on the water brightening as the last rays of light clung to the rise and fall of the waves before it was finally gone.

I glanced at Chase and found him leaning in close to me, his mouth the barest distance from my own and my heart leaping with his proximity.

We hesitated there, looking into each other's eyes and waiting for something to push us over the edge while all the want and need and pain we'd lived with for so long filled us up and made us ache.

"We should go," Chase said, still hanging there in that suspended moment with me for another few seconds and I nodded, leaning in closer so that our lips almost touched.

"Don't wanna be late," I agreed, dipping my fingers into his pocket while his attention fell to my mouth.

But before he could distract me with those sinful lips of his, I drew back, flashing him a smile as I hopped off the hood and skipped to my car door.

Chase frowned as he took in my sudden disappearance and as he got up too, I snagged the silver sharpie I had stashed in my car door pocket before jogging away to the far side of the bushes and calling out to tell him I needed to pee.

I found Mutt as I stopped out of sight, the little monster cocking his leg against a tree stump despite the fact that he was clearly out of urine to mark anything with.

"Hey boy," I greeted him before biting the cap of the sharpie and pulling it off with my teeth.

I balanced the eyepatch in my left hand and quickly wrote on it with the pen while Chase still thought I was peeing. I wrote 'Ask me about my buried treasure' on one side of the black material then flipped it over and wrote 'Call me Long John Silver Cock' on the other.

I grinned at my handiwork, hid the pen in my pocket then skipped back to the Jeep with Mutt on my heels.

Chase looked at me curiously as I jumped back in behind the wheel and I leaned over to him, placing a hand on his thigh and sliding the eyepatch into his pocket once more as I spoke into his ear.

"I'm done letting fucking Shawn into my head, Ace. So if you decide to kiss me tonight, then make sure you fucking mean it when you do."

I sat back before he could answer that, flashing him another wide smile then starting the engine and jerking the car around so hard that I almost knocked us both out of our seats.

Mutt yipped excitedly as he stuck his nose in the air to sniff at the wind and I hit the gas hard as we raced back through town towards Afterlife.

As we drew close to the club, we found people everywhere, cars double parked down the street outside and the parking lot overflowing.

"Looks like everyone wants to get a piece of Johnny James now he's back in town," Chase commented and I scowled at a girl who jogged across the road in a dress so skimpy I could practically see up her asshole.

"Well they can't have a piece," I replied scathingly. "Only a look. And even then, I might have to cut a bitch if she looks too hard."

Chase barked a laugh. "Are you jealous, little one?"

"No," I snapped. "I'm possessive. And that goes for you too. So don't go letting your eyes wander tonight either."

"Eye," he pointed out. "And I wouldn't worry about that, little one. Nobody is thinking those kinds of thoughts when they look at me anymore."

I jerked the wheel hard and bumped the car up onto the sidewalk, making several girls scream as I yanked the parking brake on and left the car sitting right in front of the entrance to the club.

I leaned over and pinched Chase's thigh hard enough to bruise. "Don't talk like that," I growled as he cursed me and batted my hand away.

"Ow, you asshole," he growled.

"Oh, did that hurt? Well try spewing that bullshit in front of me again and see which body part I tackle next." I gave his junk a pointed look and he shielded it with his hand.

"Jesus, haven't I been through enough without you going all psycho on me too?" he muttered, glancing beyond me at the crowd of people who had been queuing for the club and who now all seemed to be trying to get a look at who the hell had parked here.

"If you wanna see me go psycho, Ace, then just push me on this," I said sweetly before quickly checking my lipstick in the rear view mirror and grabbing my heels from the back seat.

One of the bouncers was walking over to us, no doubt planning on telling me to move my car but I just ignored him and got out.

"Gah when the fuck did you get hold of my eyepatch?" Chase cursed from behind me as he took the thing out to put it on and I laughed to myself.

"Oh no, looks like you'll have to either go without or wear it with my new decorations intact," I called back, holding the door open for Mutt to hop out before tossing it shut in Chase's pissed off looking face.

I smiled at the bouncer who was looking all red in the face and ready to tell me off like the bad girl I was, but he stumbled to a halt as he seemed to recognise me.

"Oh, err, Miss...Rogue," he said hesitantly, tossing a look beyond me as Chase got out of the car too and slammed his door aggressively. I looked around to find that he'd spun the cap on his head again and had pulled the peak low to shadow his face, but the death glare he gave me told me in no uncertain terms that he was pissed at me over this.

"Barry, is it?" I asked, having no idea what this dude's name was.

"Jerry," he corrected with an uncertain smile and I was pretty fucking impressed with myself for how close that guess had been.

"Right. Jerry, I can't get parked anywhere and I might already be running late for the show. JJ will be all kinds of pissed if I'm not front and centre when he gets on stage so..." I placed a hand on his tattooed arm and batted my lashes all sweet and innocent like.

"Oh, erm, yeah. Okay. Well, you can't park there but maybe I could find a spot for it and leave the keys back in the dressing room with Mr Brooks' things?" he suggested, glancing at Chase again as he closed in on us.

"That would be amazing," I said, handing over the keys and flashing

Jerry a smile half a second before Chase's arm fell around my shoulders and he jerked me away from the dude.

"Okay, I'm on it!" Jerry called after us as Chase swept me into the club, bypassing the line outside.

Chase dropped his mouth to my ear as we walked. "If I catch you flirting with some random asshole like that again, I'm gonna break every one of his fingers off and make a necklace for you out of them. Got it, little one?" he asked in a dark tone which got me all tingly.

"Got it, boss," I agreed easily. Damn I liked it when these boys got all dominant with me. I might have been a badass in my own right, but I had to admit that I was a sucker for being made into their sub from time to time.

Chase kept the peak of his cap pulled low and his arm tight around my shoulders as we moved through the club between the press of bodies. Girls were dancing up on some of the podiums and the atmosphere was lit, the music pumping and people chasing shots at the bar.

Chase led me straight through the crowd to the centre of the stage, a couple of Harlequin lackeys hurrying forward to usher some eager girls out of the best seats in the house so that we could take them.

I moved to take my seat but a squeal of excitement reached me before I could plant my ass down and I suddenly found myself in the arms of Di and Lyla as they launched themselves at me.

"Hey bitch, where the hell have you been?" Di asked as I squeezed them tightly.

"Yeah, you dump that crazy chick on us then drop off the face of the planet - what the hell is that all about?" Lyla teased and I was relieved to finally find out that Mia had made it to them after all.

"Sorry. I need a new phone," I explained, not mentioning the fact that JJ had told me Rick threw my last one in the sea not too long after I left them to go to Shawn. "And things have been...crazy."

"Err, yeah, we know," Di admitted. "Gang business is not our business, obvs, but The Dead Dogs and The Harlequins being at war is a pretty fucking big deal even for those of us who are on the outside of all of that."

"It's been pretty fucking intense," I agreed, glancing around and finding Chase had headed off to the bar, giving us a few minutes to talk alone.

"So Mia made it to you guys then? How is she?" I asked, feeling guilty that I hadn't been able to check up on her yet while wondering if she'd really want a visit from me anyway.

"Oh yeah, she found us. Honestly, we almost kicked her out when she showed up here looking like a crazy person, her feet bleeding from walking fuck knows how far to get here. All she kept saying was that you'd sent her and that she had nowhere else to go," Lyla said, lowering her voice.

"We figured she had to be telling the truth because the poor bitch seemed so damn desperate," Di added. "So as McCreepy is too afraid to rent your old trailer out to anyone since Fox almost killed him for trying to sell off your shit, we put her up in there."

"How is she doing?" I asked, glad that she was safe even if I had no real idea what else she needed.

"Erm…" Lyla glanced at Di who shrugged. "She's calmer. But she still won't talk much. We've been making sure she gets food but mostly she's just hanging out in the trailer. I think she'd afraid of someone finding her, but she won't talk about that with us."

"Estelle has been giving her some counselling," Di added. "She did an online course once, so she thinks she's practically got a PHD. It does seem to be helping though."

"Good," I said, really meaning that. I may have hated that clam vag for hooking up with Maverick before me, but in all honesty I found it pretty hard to hold on to any bad feelings for her now considering that she'd fallen prey to Shawn. "I'll come pay her a visit as soon as I can. Maybe she's got some family somewhere she can go be with or-"

"She has been asking for one person-" Lyla began but Di jammed her elbow into her side and gave her a warning glare.

"I thought we weren't gonna mention that," she hissed and my gut twisted as I realised who it had to be.

"Maverick?" I asked, biting my tongue on any less kind thoughts that might have sprung to mind.

"Yeah," Di admitted as Lyla shrugged.

"I figured it was better if you knew. She says she needs to talk to him and I get the feeling she won't move on until she does."

I blew out a breath, trying to stamp down the jealous bitch who was rearing her head at that suggestion and nodded. "I'll talk to him," I said. "Maybe he can fit in a visit…"

I wasn't particularly thrilled over that prospect, but after all Mia had suffered through it seemed like a bit of a dick move to point blank refuse her based on me not liking it. Besides, I trusted Rick, so I could suck it up if I had to.

The lights suddenly dimmed and the crowd started cheering excitedly as a guy cried out over the mic for everyone to take their seats.

Di and Lyla took off, calling out to say they'd see me later and I dropped into my seat just as Chase returned with a pair of shots for us and took his chair at my side.

I downed mine, cringing at the potent taste and turned my eyes to the stage as fog poured from smoke machines and obscured the back of it from view.

Red lasers came on, piercing the smoke and illuminating the silhouettes of five stacked male dancers as they prowled out onto the stage.

JJ was front and centre, his swagger and the wide set of his shoulders enough to let me recognise him instantly and have my thighs clamping together in anticipation of this show. Johnny James had been fired up for this performance ever since we made it back to town and from the few snippets I'd managed to sneak a peek at him practicing, I knew the whole thing was going to be obscene in the best fucking way.

A deep, booming beat started up, making the walls vibrate as women all around us screamed in anticipation and when Promiscuous by Nelly Furtado and Timberland broke out over the speakers, the lights came up and the dancers all began to move.

JJ looked fucking edible in an army uniform, the front of his shirt already undone to reveal the sculpted edges of his abs and I screamed just as loud as all the fan girls as he dropped into a move that had him in a half press up, grinding his hips over the floor and letting every fucker in the room know exactly what kind of skill he was working with.

His eyes found mine as I watched him and the dirty smirk he shot me told me exactly who he was thinking about.

He was fucking unreal to watch and as the show went on, I swear it felt like everyone else in the room just faded away, their presence melting into the background until it seemed like there was no one in the entire place aside from him.

JJ danced like he was made for it, his body this fluid vessel for movement which had me aching for the feeling of his hands on my flesh and my body bending to the rhythm of his.

As if he'd read my damn mind, when the set drew close to the end, Sleazy by Kesha came on and JJ strolled straight towards me, holding out a hand and staring me down until I complied and let him drag me up onto the stage with him.

My cheeks flared at the feeling of hundreds of eyes pinning to me, but as Johnny James pulled me into his arms, that all just fell away until it was me and him again, alone with the music.

He stepped into me and I automatically stepped back, his hands falling to the base of my spine as he encouraged me to bend backwards, dipping me towards the ground before yanking me back upright again, my chest pressing flush with his.

Our lips almost touched and his honey brown eyes flared with heat as he looked deep into my gaze and rolled his body against mine, making me move with him. My flesh burned at his touch, every movement feeling like liquid sex against my skin and I swear that if he'd peeled my clothes from my body and claimed me then and there, I wouldn't have had a damn word to say against it.

JJ caught the back of my neck and spun me away from him suddenly before catching me from behind, his front pressing to my back as he ground his cock against my ass and stole a breathy moan from my lips.

"Fuck, pretty girl, I've never wanted anybody half as much as I want you," he growled in my ear, his words heating my blood and making my pussy throb as his hands traced down my sides and he dropped down low behind me.

When he pushed to his feet again, he drew me back into his arms, taking control of my body as I let him move me against him, the two of us finding a rhythm together as easily as breathing while his body undulated against mine and I panted in his arms like a weak bitch who was utterly cock blinded by him. And shit, I really didn't mind that at all because if he kept grinding against me the way he was, I was pretty certain I'd be coming right here and now through friction and sexual tension alone.

"JJ," I gasped as he ran his tongue up the side of my neck and released a growl in my ear which had me going weak at the fucking knees.

"Everything about you screams sex, pretty girl, but that's not something you should feel ashamed of or fear," he said in a raw, carnal voice, his hands moving down my body like he was worshipping me as the two of us put on what I was pretty sure was a damn near pornographic show. "It's power. *Your* power. And you can use it any way you want to. If that means you have all of us whipped and at your mercy, then so be it. You can claim us with that power, but it doesn't change the love we have for you. We loved you long before the idea of sex occurred to any of us."

He pulled back and spun me beneath his arm as the music hit its final notes, his hand grasping my hip at the final second and his leg stepping between mine as he dropped me into a dip for the finale and froze us there as the song came to an end.

The crowd was screaming and throwing money up onto the stage as we remained in place, my whole body thrumming with need as I panted in his arms and the feeling of his thigh pressed up against my clit had me damn near to coming apart for him.

JJ drew me back up slowly and I pushed my fingers into his hair as I leaned in close to him and spoke words for his ears alone.

"I'm done being afraid, Johnny James," I said. "I want you. Every piece of you. And I'm not hiding from that anymore."

He gave me a smile which was designed to shatter hymens and break hearts for miles around, but it belonged solely to me.

"You'd better mean that, pretty girl. Because once I get done stripping for all of these nice people, I fully intend on making good on this promise that's hanging between us," he said, making every muscle in my body clench with desire.

"I mean it," I swore and his gaze ignited as he forced himself to release me and I dropped back off of the stage and into my chair where I proceeded to drool over him and melt into a puddle with every thrust of his hips and shake of that perfectly toned ass.

CHAPTER THIRTY FOUR

I put on the performance to top all other performances, the crowd going wild for every thrust, grind and hip roll but the only ones I cared about watching were Rogue and Chase who were currently grabbing drinks by the bar, cheering me on.

I loved the way Rogue's eyes felt on my flesh. It was almost as good as her tongue felt, and fuck did I miss that. Not that I was complaining about the lack of sex in our relationship despite how hard I woke up every morning and how much Johnny D begged for more of her. But we were building a new foundation for our entire family, and I wasn't going to fuck it up by crossing any lines she didn't want crossed. Even if she had said she was ready, I wanted to be sure, to test the waters before I pushed her further than she could truly handle.

Rogue was the epitome of every dark fantasy I'd ever had, but she'd also been hurt so deep that I wanted to make sure whatever actions I took now healed those wounds, not cut them open again.

Fuck, my dad is Tom Collins and his name is Gwan.

Nope.

Nope.

Nope on a rope.

Not gonna think about that.

I finished the show to raucous screams and after a sexy as fuck encore, my troupe headed off stage while I remained there. I walked to the end of the platform and gestured to Phil in the light booth to give me a spotlight. He did so and excited chatter broke out among the girls gathered at the edge of the stage, looking up at me hopefully like they wanted me to pick them out of the crowd. But there was only one person coming up here tonight.

"Please welcome a very good friend of mine to the stage. He's only here for one night as his ship will be setting sail for Aruba tomorrow. He'll plunder your heart and bury his treasure between your thighs, it's the one, the only, Cap'n Chase Cohen!"

The crowd cheered as I pointed him out and the spotlight swung onto him, making him stiffen at all the attention that was suddenly on him. Rogue clapped excitedly, bouncing up and down and I bit my lip as her tits bounced with her.

"No," Chase called, turning his head and taking his eyepatch from his pocket. He removed his hat, pulling on the eyepatch before tugging his hat on again, all while facing the bar instead of the crowd.

"Captain Chase, Captain Chase, Captain Chase," I started up the chant and the rest of the crowd took it up, clapping and catcalling him.

Rogue prodded him then whispered something in his ear and he looked at her with a frown before looking resigned and walking toward the stage. *Well done, pretty girl.*

The crowd parted to allow him up to the stage and his throat worked as he made it there, glaring up at me like I was the source of all his misfortune.

I smirked at him, leaning down and yanking him up onto the stage by the back of his shirt, slinging my arm around his shoulders as I spoke into my mic. "Can I get a fuck yeah for the pirate in the house?" I called and the patrons complied with a fuuck yeaaaah!

"I'm gonna kill you," Chase said to me through a false smile.

"Don't be so hasty," I said with a lopsided grin then tugged his hat off and threw it into the crowd like a frisbee. A girl caught it with a squeal, waving it victoriously and Chase stiffened in my hold. I looked at his eyepatch, realising the words Long John Silver Cock were written on it in Rogue's handwriting. *Pretty girl, I fucking love you.*

"Perfect." I barked a laugh then turned back to the crowd and put on a pirate accent. "So who here wants a night with a pirate? He'll board your vessel and ride your high seas until the *kraken* of dawn."

"What?" he hissed, trying to pull out of my grip, but I held on tighter. "I'm not riding anyone's high fucking seas."

I ignored him, talking to the crowd again in my amazing pirate voice as they all got excited, gazing at Chase with lust in their eyes, but fuck if he'd noticed yet. "He'll loot your booty and spill his pearls all over your doubloons. He'll make you spend time on his plank while fingering your Davey Jones' Locker."

"Alright, I think they get the point," he growled at me. "And I'm not doing any of that shit."

A bunch of girls were reaching for him like they wanted an early taste of the goods and I grinned wickedly as I spotted our girl drawing closer to the stage, trying to get through the surging bodies with a look of rage in her eyes. *Jealous, pretty girl? You'd better get bidding then.*

I leaned in close to Chase's neck, running my tongue up to his ear and making him gasp in surprise, meeting my gaze as I smirked like the Devil.

"Sorry about this, Ace." I winked, then grabbed his shirt, tearing it down the back and tossing the shredded pieces to the crowd.

Chase looked like he was about to make a run for it, but I grabbed him again, locking my arm firmly around his shoulders once more as the girls in the bar screamed and their eyes lit with a wild, unbridled hunger.

"Look at them," I growled in his ear in a command and he fell still. "Look at how much they want you."

His shoulders stopped heaving with the oncoming storm of a panic attack and he turned his head to look at me, our mouths just an inch apart as our gazes met and realisation filled his expression.

"You're a fucking wet dream, Chase Cohen," I said powerfully, wanting him to know that with every fibre of my being. "Every girl in this bar would fall to their knees for you and suck your cock like it was the gift to eternal youth, they'd spread their legs and scream for more while you fucked them raw. But you know what's even better than that?" I raised my hand to the back of his head, fisting his hair in my grip and forcing him to look down at Rogue as she fought her way toward the stage, taking on two busty women who were waving wads of dollars at Chase. I spoke directly in his ear, a note of amusement in my tone. "Rogue would fight them all to the death to keep you from them."

"Alright, game's over," he said breathlessly, looking like he wanted to climb down there and go straight to our girl. But I wasn't done having my fun yet.

"We'll start the bidding off at fifty dollars?" I spoke into the mic.

"Fifty!" one girl screamed, waving the money at us as I kept a firm hold of Chase and fought a laugh at Rogue as she battled her way towards the stage, the women in front of her thirsty as hell. *You'll have to try harder than that, sweetheart.*

"Sixty!" another girl screamed and my eyes narrowed on Rosie Morgan. "Chasey!" she screamed. "I'm sorry about what I said. We can fix your scars – I know a great plastic surgeon."

Chase stiffened in my hold and a growl pulled at my lips. *That fucking bitch.*

"One hundred to be swashbuckled!" an older woman cried, elbowing another in the face as she tried to get some cash out her purse.

"JJ, it ain't funny anymore," Chase snarled. "I'm not going home with some woman."

I just laughed as the bids kept climbing and Rogue snatched a fistful of cash out of Rosie's hand, waving it up at me.

"One-fifty!" she shouted and I grinned from ear to ear.

"We have one-fifty on the table," I said into the mic.

"You whore, give me back my money!" Rosie dove at Rogue but she slapped her with the cash before tit punching her and slipping away into the crowd.

"Two hundred to have that pirate jolly roger me!" a woman with a hairy upper lip yelled.

"JJ!" Chase snapped.

Rogue snatched more money from purses, hands and pockets and practically started a brawl as angry women dove after her to get it back. She was a wild thing though, slipping away through the ranks of horny females and making it to a barstool where she climbed up and waved the cash triumphantly.

"Rogue Easton, you ruined my boyfriend – you give him back so I can fix him!" Rosie shrieked and Rogue's foot snapped out, kicking her dead in the face and making her drop flat to the floor like a rotten turd.

"All of this cash and a thousand more after you pillage my poop deck!" Rogue yelled and I burst out laughing.

"Do we have any counter offers?" I managed to say, but no one could top that and I tossed Chase a wink. "And the pirate goes to the wild-eyed girl on the barstool!"

She was still batting off the women she'd stolen from and she threw us a salute before leaping onto the bar, jumping down behind it and running for the exit. She made it outside and I tugged Chase after me backstage, laughing as we ran for the back door past the half-naked dancers as they got changed and making it outside into the warm night air.

Rogue pulled her Jeep around, throwing the passenger door open like it was a getaway car and one look sideways at the women swarming after us told me it was. Mutt barked at us from the backseat, and I swear the little bastard was telling us to hurry the fuck up.

I shoved Chase ahead of me and he climbed into the back of the car as I dove into the front and pulled the door shut. Rogue took off with a whoop and laughter fell from all of our lungs as she raced down the road, leaving the robbed women in her dust.

Rogue leaned over, punching me in the thigh with a growl and I chuckled, settling back in my seat.

"Don't hate the player, hate the game," I teased.

"You created the game, asshole," she said. "That wasn't funny."

"I can't believe you ripped my shirt off, man," Chase grumbled.

"Who cares? Did you see those women drooling over you? Every one of them would have you fucking the doubloons outa them if-"

"Can we stop with the pirate jokes?" Chase growled.

"And can we stop talking about him fucking some random bitches?" Rogue hissed, her eyes tinted with jealousy.

"It's alright, pretty girl, you can admit it's *your* doubloons you want tickled," I taunted, and she fell silent in a way that was so telling it made heat rush into my veins. Wait, was this on? Did she want him? Us?

Your dad's name is Gwan.

Fuck.

I carved my hand over my face, dropping the window beside me and hanging my arm out of it as I became distracted by the bombshell dropped on my head tonight.

"So…something happened earlier on," I started, unsure how to say this or if I even wanted to. If I said it out loud, it made it true. Then I'd have to deal with it. Go talk to my mom, get the full story. Then what? Fuck knew.

"Oh yeah?" Chase asked.

"I met my dad," I said, just like that, like it was nothing when it was everything.

"What?" Rogue gasped, taking her eyes off the road and I cursed as I grabbed the wheel.

"Yeah, he's a regular in the club. Been coming in for years. But I didn't know…oh god I didn't know." I thought of all the innuendos I'd made to him through all this time, calling him big boy, wishing him well on his jacking off endeavours after the shows. *Oh no. No, no, no, no.* "Anyway, he said he's a cop. And he spent a summer hooking up with my mom. And my mom didn't tell him about me 'til I was older. And now…now…"

"Fuck, J." Chase rested a hand on my shoulder. "Are you alright?"

"I think so. I mean, no. Mostly because he's a cop. And that he's called Gwan. I mean, what am I even supposed to call him? Gwan?" I snapped then lowered my tone to a mutter. "I can't call him Gwan."

"Well that's a shitfest of a name for sure, but what's he like?" Rogue asked hopefully as she took over driving again.

I shrugged and Chase flicked my ear.

"Come on, man, you can't drop that on us and not give us more details," Chase urged and I sighed, fixing my gaze out the window as the breeze rushed over me.

"He's fine, I guess. I mean he's our best patron. He tips everyone, but me the most. And I thought that meant…" *Ergh.* I shuddered.

"Oh my god," Rogue breathed. "You flirted with your dad!" she accused and I had to grab the wheel again as she turned fully to face me with a finger pointed at my face.

"I did not!" I balked, but fuck, I couldn't hide it. My lie was as thin as a piece of lettuce and they could see right through it. "He just…he was nice. I thought he was hot for me. Why else would he come to the club so much and give me so many tips?!"

Chase roared a laugh. "You so flirted with your dad, man. What did you say to him? Did you ever offer to escort for him? Did you tell him you'd let him bend you over his workbench and call him Daddy?"

"Did you tell him he could dress you up for school and pack you a big sausage for lunch?" Rogue asked, laughing openly. Even Mutt was giving me a judgmental look, one of his little eyebrows arched at me like he was questioning everything he thought he'd known about me.

"No!" I shouted. "You guys are sick. I assumed he was going home and jerking off over me, so sometimes I wished him well with that, that's all. I gave him a little wink, a little touch on the arm, something to think about when he - *oh god.*"

Rogue lost her shit, laughing so loud she squeezed her eyes shut and I fully took over steering.

"That's so messed up," she choked out.

"I know, I fucking know," I snarled as Rogue took back over driving. "But why am *I* to blame? He's the one who should have said something!"

"Did he ever actually say he wanted your cock?" Chase asked, fighting back another laugh.

"Of course not," I snapped. "He was always friendly though, and in my line of work, I assumed that meant – ergh."

I gagged and Chase couldn't hold his laughter back any longer, slapping me on the shoulder.

"It's not funny you guys," I growled. "He's a cop."

Their laughter died just like that and they exchanged a glance which said they were finally taking this seriously. Mutt whimpered then looked away from me out of the window like he couldn't even bear the sight of my face anymore.

"He hasn't got anything on you, has he?" Rogue asked in concern.

"I don't think so," I said, running a hand down the back of my neck. "He said he wasn't gonna do anything about the prostitution connected to my club but, fuck…how do I know that's true? And even if it is, what then?"

"Maybe you could talk to him?" Rogue suggested.

"But he's a cop. And I know the names of every cop under Harlequin rule so he ain't one of ours. That means he's clean. I can't be the son of a fucking clean law enforcement officer."

"Yeah…that sucks, dude." Chase patted my arm.

"Maybe it's not him," I said hopefully. "He said my mom was drunk when she called him so maybe she called the wrong guy."

"Well… there's one way to find out, JJ," Rogue said seriously then pulled over and put the Jeep in park.

I looked out the window, realising she'd driven me to my mom's damn apartment and my spine straightened.

"No," I barked. "I'm not talking to her."

"Don't be stubborn," she huffed, unbuckling her belt and climbing over to straddle me and cup my cheeks. "Just talk to her. We can go with you."

Dammit, she was hard to refuse when she was sat on my dick giving me the big eyes.

"I don't want to," I said stubbornly and Mutt barked at me like he was telling me off.

"Come on, brother, it's best you find out the truth," Chase encouraged and I glanced between the two of them, finding my willpower shattering.

"Fine," I huffed. "But if she says she doesn't remember, I'm leaving it at that, putting it to bed and never mentioning it again. It's not like he could be any kind of dad to me anyway, so what does it matter? I never had a dad before and I don't need one now."

It wasn't exactly true. I had missed out on having a dad when I was a kid, sometimes conjuring up visions of what he was like, who he could be. The closest thing I'd come to it was Luther after he'd enrolled us in the Harlequins and taken me and Chase into his home. But I'd been so twisted up with hate over what he'd done to Rogue, I'd never really bonded with him in a way I could call paternal.

When I was really young, I'd tell kids at school my dad was in the army, out saving lives in some foreign, faraway place. But I'd dropped that story around the time I hit puberty and started singing fuck yous at him for being absent instead, deciding I didn't need even the idea of him in my life. I was just a sperm donation from a client who'd bought and paid for a night with my momma's body. He'd wanted her, not me. And I was fine with that. Except now this revelation was dragging up some long-lost feelings on the matter that didn't feel all that resolved after all.

If he hadn't known I existed, could I really blame him for never being in my life? No. But he had had a chance to be in it for several years now and hadn't had the balls to say anything until tonight. He'd let me make filthy comments to him, knowingly let me talk to him like I would any paying client. What the actual fuck?

But he'd also done so much for my damn club. He'd kept it afloat, given me tips when I was desperate for them, helped out a bunch of my dancers who were struggling financially. But for what reason? Was he gonna hold it over me now? Ask me to pay him back? Blackmail me with all the shady shit he'd no doubt taken note of over the years? Or would he expect some kind of father-son relationship in return for his silence?

I couldn't give him that, but what if he threatened my club? My troupe? The girls?

I realised I was chewing on my thumb, anxiously staring at nothing as Rogue watched me patiently and brushed her fingers through my hair.

"You've got a lot of questions in your eyes, Johnny James, and sitting here isn't gonna get you any answers," she said soothingly.

"What if I hate the answers?" I grumbled.

"What if you don't?" she tossed back.

"Let's revisit what if I do," I said with a pout and she brushed her fingers over my forehead, trying to smooth out the lines that had formed there, but I was keeping those motherfuckers taut.

"You know, when I was locked down in Shawn's basement, I had a lot of time to think about my regrets," Chase said and I turned to him with my heart clenching. "And I've realised that doing the stuff I'm afraid of is way better than looking back and dwelling on how I should have done it. So I guess the most important thing you need to ask yourself is…are you going to regret it if you don't ask about your dad?"

I stared at him, then to Rogue, then out the window, then up at the sky, then down to Mutt who was giving me a look that said I was taking up too much of his damn time right now, then I sighed heavily. "I can't believe you pulled the locked-up-and-tortured-in-a-basement card on me, but fuck it, let's go."

Rogue grinned, kissing me on the lips fast before leaping out the open window like a damn alley cat and leaving my mouth burning for more of her.

I licked the taste of her from my lips, but it wasn't nearly enough to sate me as I shoved the door open and hounded her onto the sidewalk. I had a lot of pent-up energy when it came to her and as she tossed a glance back over her shoulder at me that was all fucking lust, I wondered if tonight she'd want me to burn some of it off. *Damn, she was so fucking fine.*

Chase followed me out with a smirk, knowing exactly what he'd just pulled on me and I scruffed his hair hard.

"You feeling better about those scars yet?" I asked and the immediate tension in his posture said he wasn't over it yet. "Come on, brother." I pulled him close, nodding to Rogue who was far enough down the pavement not to hear us now, Mutt trotting along beside her like he could protect her from any foe. "The hottest girl in Sunset Cove just robbed half my bar to keep her claim on you. And didn't you see the way they all looked at you in there? Fuck it, I'm half considering training you up to dance because some of my troupe haven't even had that reaction from those women before."

"How are you gonna teach me to dance when one of my legs is busted? Are you gonna strap a peg-leg on me?" he joked, trying to deflect away from the real issue which was that his confidence was in a body bag, in the morgue, waiting to be put six feet underground.

Visions of my new pirate dance act filled my head, making a slow smile spread across my lips. He seemed about as keen as a mouldy coconut to be on stage, but I was Johnny James Brooks, I could totally convince him.

"That ain't a half bad idea, Ace." I grinned at him and he scowled.

"Pretty sure my dancing days are done, J." He pulled out of my hold, walking after Rogue down the street and I cocked my head to one side, watching his limp as he walked. It was way better than it had been, barely noticeable really. So it had to be only a matter of time before he walked straight again, and if he could walk straight, he could dance straight.

Hell yes. I have a new dream. One day, I'm gonna get Chase Cohen on stage stripping like a pro.

I followed them to my mom's house, my mood descending again as I focused on why we were here. It wasn't like I didn't want to know the truth, more that I'd prefer to go on believing Tom Collins was not blood related to me in any way, because even worse than him being some rule abiding cop was all the things I'd said to him while thinking he was my number one fan.

I shuddered, my feet dragging as we climbed the steps up to Mom's front door and my lips pressed firmly together. If he'd been undercover when he'd met my mom, what was to say he hadn't been undercover all this time, gathering intel on my bar, evidence to use against me? I was, on paper, a fucking pimp. A decent one who gave really good job benefits, but I didn't think that was gonna fly in court, no matter how winning my smile was.

Rogue knocked on the door when I made no move to and she threaded her fingers between mine, giving me an encouraging look. That made things a little better, knowing she was here, that she cared. *Oh god, I'm gonna have to see her once a week during a conjugal visit in some grubby little room, aren't I?*

"Johnny James," Mom said brightly as she opened the door, dressed in a tiny black skirt and a blue top that was little more than a push-up bra. "And if it ain't Rogue Easton again, well how are-" Her words cut off midsentence as her gaze fell on Chase, or more specifically, his eyepatch.

"Hello, Mrs B," Chase said with a polite nod, trying to angle his face away slightly so she couldn't look directly at the scars peeking out from under his eyepatch.

"Don't overreact," I warned my mom but she shrieked, launching herself at Chase and wrapping him in a hug. Even on five inch heels, her head didn't even come up to his chin as she hugged him and sobbed dramatically into his chest. Mutt barked excitedly, sniffing my mom's ankles and I nudged him away from her with my toe as he looked about two seconds from taking a piss on her legs.

"Johnny's been keeping you from me," she sniffed. "I had to hear about what happened to you through all kinds of other sources before my son came and explained."

Chase seemed alarmed by how much my mom gave a shit about what had happened to him, but she always had been fond of my friends. For all her faults, she did love me and I was pretty sure she loved them too.

"It's alright, Mom, let go." I prised her off of Chase, glancing at his awkward expression and doubting he'd had an adult react like that about him his whole life. Which then made me feel really shitty and made me wanna let go of my hysterical mother so she could hug him again.

She gathered herself together as we made it to the living room and I led her to the couch, sitting her down.

Chase sat in the armchair while Rogue perched on the arm of it with Mutt on her knees, her hand on Chase's shoulder and her fingers brushing back and forth like she didn't even realise she was doing it.

Mom dabbed at her eyes, sitting up straighter and rearranging her boobs which were almost spilling out of her tiny top. "It's so nice to have guests over, Johnny doesn't let me see anyone anymore."

"Don't be ridiculous," I said. "You can't see dodgy ass men in your house, that's all. You can have all the girl friends you like."

"I have needs, Johnny!" she begged.

"Your needs lead you to doing coke out of the butt cracks of moustached thieves who take you for all you've got," I growled.

She pushed out her lower lip but she couldn't argue with that shit. Yeah, maybe I was overbearing with her. But I paid for her life, kept her off the drugs and the streets, her body was hers now and I wasn't ever going to let some lowlife scumbag change that. And when someone I deemed worthy showed up to court her like a nineteen twenties gentlemen for twelve to eighteen months before he proposed to her, then maybe I'd be more lenient with my rules.

"JJ has something to ask you, Mrs B," Rogue said, helpful little cricket that she was.

"You do?" Mom looked to me and I chewed on the inside of my cheek, trying to work out the best way to start this discussion. But I came up short so just dropped it on her like Tom had done to me.

"A regular at my club came and told me he was my father today."

Mom froze, her body becoming as still as an ice sculpture. "What man?" she demanded, seeming flustered, breathless.

"He said his name was…" I swallowed back the bile in my throat with a grimace. "*Gwan.*"

For all the reactions my mom could have given, I didn't expect her to scream, but she did, like a goddamn virgin in a horror movie, she fucking screamed and nearly leapt out of her seat too as she clutched her throat.

"I assume that means something to you then?" I asked through clenched teeth.

"Oh my god, Johnny. Oh my god," she said, flustered and panicked.

"He's a cop," I growled and she winced, screwing up her eyes.

"I know – I know!" she cried.

"You said my father was a client," I snapped. "You said I was the result of a split condom. How could you take that dream away from me?"

"Johnny you have to understand," she begged, gripping my hand and holding it tight. "I didn't know he was a cop."

I winced at the word. "It's worse than that, Mom, because he's not even a corrupt cop. He's a fucking detective - with fucking accolades for all I know."

"I know," she choked out. "It's part of the reason I didn't tell you."

"What was the other part?" I demanded, the truth really sinking in now. I was the son of a cop. I had law abiding blood in me and that was never going to sit right with me.

"He and I…it was complicated," she said, her eyes watery and desperate. "You really were the result of a split condom, Johnny, I promise."

"That doesn't make up for it, Mom. Because it sounds like my dad wasn't some guy who blew into town for one night with you. He said you spent a whole summer together."

She nodded several times and I felt Rogue and Chase's eyes glued to us over this conversation. Mutt seemed almost as interested as them, his head cocked to one side and his ears twitching as he listened.

"We did…oh Johnny, it was the best summer of my life. He was such a good lover, I'd never been touched by a man like that."

"Stop it, I don't wanna hear about you and Gwan fucking. And couldn't you have picked someone with a better name than that?"

"He went by Kai back then, his cover name," she breathed and a flash of anger entered her eyes. "He was so handsome, he whipped me off my feet. But after months and months of fucking like rabbits, he eventually told me the truth. He was undercover, looking to bust some big drug ring connected to the man I worked for back then. I was so angry, Johnny, I sent him away." She squeezed my hand harder. "I knew it was the right thing to do. He'd lied to me all that time, he'd made a fool of me. I could never tell anyone I knew who he was, they would have outcast me. I'd never have gotten any work again." She teared up, looking genuinely heartbroken for a moment and I frowned, squeezing her hand back. "I thought about calling him a few times, I imagined up this life for us where we got married, moved into a nice house and made an upstanding little family together, but it was just a pretty dream, Johnny. Whores don't get happily ever afters."

I frowned, hating that she felt that way. But men of the law were the exact opposite of people like us. We weren't built for normal lives living in pretty houses while paying taxes and showing up to nine to five jobs. But it did make me sad to think my mom had dreamed of a different life for herself. And for a second I pictured what it might have been like to grow up in some stable household with a dad who loved me, and a mom who didn't have to spread her legs to put dinner on the table.

She glanced away from me, chewing her lower lip. "After he left town, I never saw him again. I found out I was pregnant a couple of months later and I was so close to calling him, I really was. I needed the support, the money, but I didn't wanna be some dirty secret to the man. For all I knew, he had a wife of his own somewhere, a family he could be proud of."

I winced a little at those words, but the truth of them was what cut deepest. I would never have been the apple of my father's eye; I was just a street kid, born of nothing worth valuing to people like that.

"I'm sorry, Johnny," Mom said earnestly. "I don't mean it like that."

"I know, Mom," I muttered.

"So what did he want?" Mom asked nervously.

"Nothin'." I shrugged. "He just told me he was my dad, that he'd been coming to the club ever since you called him years ago to tell him about me. Then I kicked him out."

"I see," she whispered, looking anxious. "Did he look…okay?"

"What's that supposed to mean?" I rounded on her.

"You know, is he bald or does he have missing teeth or has he grown a big old wart on his nose?" She looked hopeful about those words but I shook my head.

"His hair's like mine. He looks…normal, I guess."

"Oh," she whispered.

"So what are you gonna do, J?" Rogue asked and I looked over at her, shrugging my shoulders.

"I just need to make sure he's not looking to get me arrested," I said darkly.

"He wouldn't, baby," Mom said reassuringly.

"How do you know?" I pushed, but she didn't have an answer.

"I mean, he's not a great undercover cop if he just blew his cover to you," Chase offered and I considered that, guessing he was right.

"So what am I supposed to do? Have a stroll along The Mile while we eat ice cream and go splashing in the ocean together?" I scoffed.

"It kinda sounds like that's what you wanna do," Rogue pointed out and I glared at her.

"No it isn't," I hissed.

"Okay, dude," she said lightly like she didn't believe me.

I didn't wanna talk to him at all. I mean, yeah I was curious about some shit. And yeah, I liked ice cream and splashing in the ocean, but not with my cop daddy. No way.

I sighed, getting to my feet and looking down at my mom. "If he shows up here, you'll turn him away, right?"

She hesitated for several seconds then nodded.

"Why'd you hesitate?" I asked suspiciously.

"I didn't," she said quickly.

"You did, you hesitated. Listen, Mom, he's no good for us. In fact, he's no bad for us, because he's a good guy and we're the bad guys. So it doesn't work, that's why you sent him away the first time."

She nodded and I hoped I'd driven the point home.

I slid some cash from my pocket from the show, holding it out to her and her eyes brightened as she took it.

"Thank you, baby."

I leaned down to kiss her cheek then nodded to the others before leading them to the door. We said our goodbyes and headed back to Rogue's Jeep, my mind a whirlpool of thoughts that left me feeling drained.

As we drove back to Harlequin House, I fell into the darkness of my own mind, thinking over everything and trying to process all this news.

When Rogue parked up in the garage, we spilled out of the car and I noticed Fox's truck was missing. I shot him a text to check all was okay and he replied as we made it up into the house and Mutt scampered off down the hall with a yip.

Fox:

I'm pulling a job with Maverick. We need the cash.
Mabel's in bed so don't wake her up.

JJ:

Be careful.

Fox:

Always am.

JJ:

Love you.

Fox:

You're an idiot.

JJ:

An idiot who loves you.

Fox:

Love you too, douchebag.

I gasped, catching Rogue's arm and waving the screen in her face, my mood brightening by fifty thousand watts. "Look! He said he loves me too."

"He also called you a douchebag," she pointed out.

"Yeah, *affectionately*," I insisted. "This is definitely progress."

"How do you know he was being affectionate? You can't tell someone's tone in a text," Chase said.

"Pfft, I can," I said confidently. "A client once sent me a thumbs up emoji and I went to her house with a lubed up cock because her tone said she was bent over and ready for me to fuck her in the ass."

"La la la la," Rogue covered her ears, squeezing her eyes shut too as Chase laughed.

"That's bullshit," Chase accused.

"Then why was I right?" I smirked then caught hold of Rogue's wrists, prising her hands from her ears and pushing her back against the wall. "I don't want to lube my cock up for anyone but you ever again, pretty girl. And only if you want it lubed. I can totally go in dry if you'd prefer."

Her scowl broke into a laugh and she bit her lip, her gaze falling to my mouth, so much lust in her eyes that it made me grow rock hard for her just like that. I pressed forward, her wrists still within my grip as I drew them above her head, pinning them to the wall and moving my mouth close to hers.

"I'm fucking dying to kiss you."

"Then why don't you?" she asked huskily.

"Because I'm not what Shawn painted me as in your mind, and I want you to know it, pretty girl."

"I know it," she breathed, her chin lifting as she tried to make our lips touch, but she couldn't quite breach the gap. I soaked in the expression on her face as she hungered for me, yearning for my touch. "Kiss me, Johnny James."

The words were a divine ruling by a goddess of my heart and I could no easier disobey them than I could stop the world from turning. My lips fell against hers and I pushed my tongue between her lips, kissing her with the passion of an endless fire.

I loved this girl so fiercely, it was written into the essence of my flesh. And the thirst with which she kissed me back finally healed me from the vicious words she'd spoken to me in that video. She loved me, I couldn't deny it because I could feel the strength of it in this kiss, and I could taste it too. It was the flavour of a thousand sunsets, of two kids laughing on the beach, our fingers threaded. It was sheltering in the woods from the rain and holding her close beneath my leather jacket, it was the scent of her skin and the glint in her eyes when she decided to do something wild. Our love had been forged in the dirt we'd grown up on, and it had lived in us both this whole time, waiting for us to collide.

My forehead fell to hers as our lips broke apart, our frantic breaths tangling as we stood in the immensity of our feelings for one another.

I released her wrists and watched her throat bob, the heat building in her eyes, a demand there that I was a slave to answer the call of.

"Shall we go upstairs?" I asked and she nodded, her eyes shifting over my shoulder and I suddenly realised I'd forgotten about Chase.

I turned, but found the corridor empty and guilt pulled at my chest. "Damn, I got lost in you."

"That's cute, but let's go." Rogue captured my hand, towing me to the stairs and we headed up in search of him while she threw me another burning look.

Johnny D was rocking out in my pants, ready for the party, but I wasn't going to take this any further than she wanted.

We made it to Chase's door which was cracked ajar and I nudged it open, finding him pulling his shirt off to reveal the ripped muscles of his abs. Whatever that intense yoga thing was he did at the buttcrack of dawn every day, it was doing his body miles of miracles. I mean, he'd been cut before, but now he was as shredded as a Weetabix.

His attention fell on us as he gripped the shirt in his hand and I glanced at Rogue, finding a savage heat in her eyes that had my dick throbbing. She took a step toward him, but I caught the back of her crop top, tugging her against my chest and locking an arm across her shoulders.

"It's okay if you guys wanna be together tonight," Chase said, tossing his shirt away and folding his arms in a less than subtle move that proved how self-conscious he was feeling. And that just wouldn't do.

I dropped my mouth to Rogue's ear, feeling her shiver for me as my breath fanned against her skin. "What do you want, pretty girl?"

"I want Chase to know how desirable he is," she said in a deliciously sexy voice, her ass grinding back against my cock and drawing a deep noise of excitement from me.

"Ditto," I agreed.

"I get it. I was at the show. I saw the girls screaming, but honestly, I think they'd get excited for anything you pointed at JJ," Chase said, his shoulders tensing. "I know you guys mean well, but-"

"Fuck that," I growled, my murderous side awakening. "You think I'm the reason they acted like that? You're pissing me off now, Ace."

Chase's folded arms only tightened, making his biceps bulge. He looked like a fucking gelato dick with a cherry on top, and I wasn't gonna be leaving this room until he believed it. But I wasn't going to play nice anymore.

"How far do you want this to go, pretty girl?" I whispered in her ear, so low that Chase wouldn't be able to catch it. I needed the green light from her before I crossed any lines. I may have been about to play god, but she was the real power in this room and the moment she said no, I was done.

"I told you, J. I'm all in. I want you...I want him." She bit her lip, gazing over at Chase and he definitely heard that alright.

"Then follow my lead." I released Rogue and we prowled closer to Chase as he glanced between us in surprise.

"I'm not touching you, little one," he said. "I promised I'd prove I'm here for you, not your body."

"I didn't ask you to touch me," she said in a playful tone and I took hold of his folded arms, wrenching them apart, making his eyes spit hellfire at me.

But any retort he had for that died on his lips as Rogue leaned forward to kiss a scar on his collar bone and I leaned down to kiss one beside it, making him inhale sharply.

His hand landed on my shoulder, his fingers digging in like he was about to push me back, but he didn't. He let me continue working from scar to scar as Rogue moved down the opposite side of his body. Most were just pale lines, barely noticeable at all anymore, but he acted like they were gaping wounds all over him. It was time he saw them for what they really were, which was shit hot décor for a shit hot body.

Rogue reached up, pulling the eyepatch from his face and tossing it across the room with such accuracy it landed in the trash can.

"Argh," he growled, trying to step forward to go after it, but I shoved him back so he hit the wall, pinning him there as Rogue kissed her way down his body and I touched my mouth to more and more of his scars. It didn't feel weird doing this with him somehow, it felt necessary and sort of…right.

Chase's breaths came heavier as Rogue sank to her knees, her hand riding over the huge bulge straining against his jeans.

"Rogue, stop. I don't need you to," Chase growled, but I slid my hand up to his throat, gripping tight and forcing him to look me in the eye.

"But she wants to, don't you pretty girl?" I asked her without breaking my stare with Chase.

"Yes," she said, sounding hungry and I couldn't resist looking down at her.

Her eyes were full of sex as she rolled down Chase's zipper and I leaned forward to run my tongue along his jaw, making him curse, but he didn't move away, and Rogue's eyes sparked with encouragement.

"You like that, pretty girl?" I asked and Chase's attention fell to her once more, the same question in his eyes.

She nodded keenly and Chase relaxed a little more, looking to me with trepidation in his expression but curiosity too.

"You good?" I asked and after a beat, he nodded, like the tiniest fucking nod but I guessed he didn't wanna seem too eager for my mouth again. I didn't know why this felt okay, but as I leaned in to lay more kisses on Chase's flesh, the way his chest heaved with every touch we gave him made me want to do it more.

His fingers trailed down my arm, squeezing hard into my bicep and I glanced up at him again before sliding my hand down his abs, my fingers lingering against his waistband.

"You gonna tell me to stop?" I asked through a smirk and Chase's throat bobbed.

"Fuck you," he said in dry voice.

"That wasn't a no," I pointed out and Rogue laughed, her hand still riding over the swell of his cock beautifully.

I arched a brow at Chase, seeing the want in his eyes, a fierce need which was so familiar to me I knew I already had my answer. But I was gonna hear it from him all the same because I was an asshole like that.

I decided to play with him, drawing my hand away instead, about to step back when he caught my wrist, drawing my palm back onto his abs.

"That's what I thought," I growled then pushed my hand beneath his waistband, fisting his hard cock as Rogue tugged down his boxers, watching us eagerly.

Chase let out a curse, his nails driving into my arm and I laughed like a cocky motherfucker as I held his dick ready for our girl's lips, my own breaths starting to match the uneven beat of Chase's.

This wasn't exactly something I hadn't done before. I'd been in plenty of orgies in my line of work and even just for fun. But it was the first time I'd crossed that line with a friend and something about doing this with him and Rogue was so fucking hot, I was getting high on it.

Her lips closed over his cock and he let out a groan that was rough and dirty, his hand moving to fist in her hair. He turned his head towards me and our lips grazed in the lightest of touches that sent a buzz of adrenaline through my veins.

We both watched Rogue suck and lick every inch of him, looking like the most perfect fucking creature I'd ever seen. My own cock was aching, longing for the attention Chase was getting, but I wanted him to have this pleasure. To have as much as we could possibly give him to try and overwrite the dark and painful memories I knew haunted him.

I leaned in to kiss his throat and he tilted his head to grant me more access. I could feel his pulse thrashing beneath my lips and his hand slid around the back of my neck, drawing me closer as a curse slipped from his tongue.

"Fuck, I'm gonna come already." Chase tried to pull back, but I didn't let him go and Rogue only increased her pace as her head bobbed and she took him right to the back of her throat like some sort of blowjob athlete.

I dropped my hand down to join his in Rogue's hair and he came with a growl, his hips rocking as he gave in to the inevitable and fucked her mouth through the pleasure of his orgasm while she swallowed him down like a good girl. Though I knew she wasn't that and as she sat back on her heels, looking up at us in a haze of lust, her lips puffy and her eyes hooded, I had just the thing in mind for her.

Chase tucked his cock away, though left his pants open as he reached down, pulling Rogue to her feet and I stepped back, watching them as dark ideas flitted through my head. He pulled her into a sinful kiss, his fingers knotting in the back of her crop top as she tiptoed, practically held up by him as he clutched her against his body.

"Chase, on the bed," I commanded, taking charge and they both looked over at me, seeming in a daze of their desire for each other. If Chase didn't realise he was the fucking shit yet, then maybe this would drive it home.

Chase obeyed me and I made him lie sideways across the mattress on his back before grabbing hold of my beautiful girl and guiding her up to straddle him.

"We can't fuck," Chase insisted, propping himself up on his elbows as he gazed at Rogue. "I'm not just after sex, little one."

"I know, Ace," she said earnestly, trailing her fingers up his chest.

"Let me prove it," he implored.

"You're just gonna return the favour to our girl," I said lightly as I knelt on the bed beside them, gathering her hair away from her shoulders and pressing a kiss to her neck. "You want that, don't you, Rogue?"

"Yes," she panted and I chewed on her ear as I ran my hand down her back, bending her forward until she got the message and knelt with her knees on either side of Chase on all fours.

I unbuttoned her shorts, drawing them off of her with her panties and leaving her pussy bare for us. I pushed her back down to straddle Chase's cock which was growing hard again already and rocked her hips for her, making both of them groan.

"Don't take your eyes off of Ace," I commanded her. "Show him how hot he makes you."

She nodded excitedly and I pulled her top off nice and fucking slow for Chase before unclipping her bra and freeing her perfect tits.

"So fucking beautiful." I nipped her shoulder as I positioned myself out of view a little behind her, running my hand down the length of her spine and over the curve of her ass. She continued to grind on Chase's cock, but I forced her hips up as I slid my hand beneath her, finding her pussy soaked for us.

I slid two fingers into her and she gasped, resting her hands on Chase's chest as she raised her hips higher to give me more access. But I drove her back down, encouraging her to ride my fingers as the back of my hand chafed over the swell of Chase's thick cock.

Both of them groaned, staring at each other as Chase gripped her hips, taking over the movements of her body so we were working as this perfect fucking unit. Her pussy started to tighten on my fingers almost immediately and as she drew closer to release, I tugged my hand free.

"Fuck, Johnny James," she snarled, but I just laughed, grabbing her hips and lifting her as I moved over Chase, dropping her knees down either side of his head instead.

Chase's hands came up to cup her ass and she gasped as I pressed her down and Chase pulled her in the same motion, his tongue running over her clit and drawing a cry from her lips.

"Fuck yes," I growled, guiding her hips and making her ride his mouth.

She gasped and moaned as me and Chase held her in the perfect position, and though I couldn't see exactly what magic he was working on her pussy, the screams starting to leave her throat was enough to know he was killing it.

Before he could have all the fun, I sat back on Chase's lap, his hips jerking as his hard cock rutted between my thighs instead and I breathed a laugh before leaning right over toward our girl.

"Spread her cheeks for me, Ace," I ordered and he did so, his fingers biting into her ass as he offered her up to me and I slid my tongue between them, making her moan like a woman possessed.

I rocked my hips as I tasted my girl, circling my tongue around her tight hole while grinding the swell of my cock over Chase's hard on. He cursed and grunted almost as much as she did and one of his hands slid from her ass to fist in my hair, forcing my head forward and holding me there to pleasure our girl. It was hot as fuck and got me so hard, it was like a volcano was about to go off in my pants. The feel of his cock rutting against mine was getting me off too and though I'd never have considered myself to be into men, maybe I was a little bi for him tonight.

Rogue came with a cry, her back arching, her hair tumbling down her spine as she rode her way through her orgasm and I sat back to watch the end of the show, catching her as she fell back against me.

I chewed on her ear, drawing her ass back onto Chase's chest as he smirked smugly up at her, his mouth wet with her arousal and a greedy look in his gaze as he sucked her taste from his lips.

I toyed with Rogue's nipple as she shivered in my arms, prolonging the pleasure in her body as she continued to moan softly.

"You're fucking everything, pretty girl."

She flopped out of my arms onto the bed, lying back against the pillows with her hair spread all around her, exhaustion in her eyes and her body looking so fucking good.

"Mark me," she growled in a primal sort of voice that made my spine straighten. She squeezed her tits, her eyes beckoning us closer. "I want you both to come on me, make me yours. I know it's fucked up, but I don't wanna feel him on my skin anymore. I wanna feel my boys."

My throat thickened as I nodded my agreement, moving to her side as Chase scrambled up onto his knees on her other side. She bit her lip, her eyes moving from me to Chase as we both freed our cocks and started jacking off over the tight curves of her body.

We leaned so close over her that our heads kept knocking and I braced my hand on his shoulder as he braced his on mine, our gazes meeting for a moment as we gave into this maddening act between us all before looking to our girl as she writhed and moaned beneath us, playing with herself and putting on the best show I'd ever fucking seen. I was so close already and the way Chase was cursing made me sure he was too as he pumped his fist up and down the length of his huge cock.

"Ace…Johnny," Rogue moaned and that was it for both of us, the two of us coming on her stomach, her pussy, her thighs, marking her as ours as she arched into the thick stream of our cum.

Spent and fucking tired, I dropped down onto the bed beside her as Chase did the same on her other side. I snared her hand, kissing the back of it as we surrounded her, two wolves protecting their mate. And as I glanced over at Chase, I swear I saw a gleam of his old confidence in his gaze as he slid one hand under his head, his body on show without any attempt to hide it as he lay beside the girl of his fucking dreams. And my heart filled with a contentment I hadn't felt in a long damn time.

"So..." Rogue laughed, the sound filling up the whole room. "That just happened."

"It did," I agreed with a snort and Chase started laughing too.

"Shower?" he suggested.

"Last one there is a rotten seagull turd!" Rogue leapt to her feet, diving off the bed and sprinting into Chase's en-suite.

"Seagulls don't even do proper turds," Chase complained, shoving to his feet and I let him get a head start seeing as he had a limp and all. But I still jumped up and dove past him at the last minute, punching him to give him a dead arm as I went.

"I once saw a seagull do a poo the size of dog shit," Rogue called from the shower, the sound of running water reaching me as I stepped into the room and pulled off my clothes.

"Bullshit," Chase accused.

"No, dog shit," she corrected with a smirk.

I got into the shower and Chase joined us a beat later, the space not really big enough but we did it anyway.

Chase and Rogue started bickering about the apparent dog-shit-sized-bird-shit Rogue had witnessed and I soaked in the company of my best friends, loving that a dirty as fuck three-way made absolutely no difference to how we were with one another. And though it had taken us a long ass time to get here, I was glad we'd finally arrived.

CHAPTER THIRTY FIVE

I woke up with a smile on my face and a lightness in my soul which was so alien to me that for a moment I just lay there, waiting for something bad to happen or for panic to set in, maybe even for me to realise that I wasn't awake at all and that this was just some pretty dream I'd been lost in and I was actually still trapped in Shawn's company back at the Rosewood Manor. Or worse than that - that I'd never left him at all and I was still in Sterling living a half life that left me wanting so damn much.

But as a strong arm tightened around my waist and another hand flexed against my hip, I knew that wasn't right.

I was free. Back with my boys. And happy.

I arched my back as I stretched and Chase grunted something as I accidentally ground my bare ass back against his dick which seemed more than okay with the contact, driving into me through the fabric of his boxers.

A sigh breached my lips and JJ's hand slid up beneath the hem of my shirt, his fingers brushing against my ribs and inching towards my breast as my nipple hardened in anticipation.

I shifted a little, but found my foot trapped beneath a heavy weight and as I blinked my eyes open, I found Rick there, sprawled across the end of the bed still wearing a pair of jeans with specks of blood marking his bare chest.

"What happened to you last night?" I hissed, pushed myself upright as I raked my eyes over him, hunting for a sign of a wound. He wasn't dumb enough to fall asleep with evidence like that painted on his flesh so I had to assume the blood was his.

"Nothin'," Rick grunted, cracking an eye and yawning. "But Foxy took a bit of a hit-"

"Is he okay?" I gasped, shoving myself upright and causing Mutt to fart himself awake from his position curled on the pillow behind JJ's head, my little buddy glaring around in suspicion like he wasn't sure where the noise had come from.

"Yeah, yeah," Rick said dismissively, reaching a hand out towards me as his eyes fell shut again. "You know Fox, he doesn't let anything stop him."

I bit my lip as worry continued to coil in my gut and I scrambled out from beneath the covers as I made my decision to go check on him myself.

Chase and JJ groaned their protests as I escaped them and Rick took the opportunity to move into my vacated position between the two of them so that he had more room as I hopped out of bed.

I was wearing one of Chase's tanks, the white material falling down to cover my ass while my tits were mostly concealed behind the surfing slogan which ran across the front of it - there was a fair amount of side boob going on thanks to the wide arm holes, but I was like eighty percent sure I wasn't gonna flash an accidental nipple.

I pulled on some panties and hurried out of the room, leaving the others to their man pile and pushing the door closed behind me before crossing the corridor to Fox's bedroom.

I hesitated for a moment, unsure if I should knock or not before deciding I didn't want him to have the chance to refuse my entry and just pushing it open anyway.

But as I looked into Fox's room, I found it empty, the light pouring in through the window bright enough to let me know it was morning already and the perfectly made up bed suggesting he hadn't come up to bed at all.

I wasn't entirely sure how long Maverick had been in the room with us, but he'd clearly been asleep when I first woke so it had to have been a little while.

I pulled Fox's bedroom door closed again and headed downstairs, the scent of coffee drawing me on like a dog to a bone and when I made it to the kitchen, I found the pot full and ready to go. But still no Fox.

I frowned around at the empty space then noticed the door to the basement cracked open with the lights on inside as I peered down the corridor.

I wasn't sure why he'd be down there at this time of day especially after having been out on a job all night, but I grabbed a couple of mugs and filled them with coffee - Green Power Ranger for me and a pink unicorn mug for Badger - before heading towards the basement to find him.

I hesitated as I reached the top of the stairs, remembering a time when Fox had snuck me into his room only to realise the Harlequins had been holding a meeting here after I'd arrived. He and Rick had about shit themselves in the panic to sneak me back out of here and we'd crept right past this very door, holding our breath and tiptoeing the whole way until we made it back down to the garage.

I'd glanced back as we drove the fuck away from here and I could have sworn Luther had been looking out of one of the windows at us, his eyes dark and terrifying as always. But as neither Rick nor Fox ever heard a word on the matter from their dad, we'd decided I must have imagined it. Though now I was beginning to wonder if I had been or not.

Either way, this door which had once seemed as terrifying as the gates to hell itself was now all that stood between me and my badger, so I nudged it open with my hip and crept down the stairs on bare feet.

Fox was sitting at the desk there, his head bowed low over some papers lying on it and his posture tight despite the fact he hadn't noticed me arriving.

"Hey," I said and he jerked upright, lifting a gun from the desk for a brief moment before setting it back down without even getting so far as aiming it at me.

"You shouldn't sneak up on gangsters, hummingbird," he muttered, leaning back in his chair and swiping a hand down his face as I drew closer.

"I thought you weren't a gangster anymore?"

"Gotta kill fucking Shawn before I'm out," he reminded me and I nodded, padding close and placing his coffee down on the desk beside the map he had laid out in front of him.

I perched my ass beside it, placing my own coffee down too and inspecting the bloody cut on his shoulder which he'd stuck a couple of strips over to keep it closed.

"What happened?" I asked, tipping my chin towards the wound and he dropped his hand into his lap, looking up at me where I perched in front of him.

"Rick got cocky as always."

"Rick did?" I teased, knowing all too well how damn competitive the two of them got when we were kids and I was pretty certain that they were even worse now.

The corner of Fox's mouth lifted and I knew I'd caught him out. "We had a disagreement over the best way to get inside the property and I scaled the wall - the razor wire was an unexpected complication."

"You didn't expect the razor wire?" I asked in clear disbelief.

"I didn't expect it to cut me," he clarified.

"Ah, that sounds more like it. And so the great Fox Harlequin had to suffer through the bitter taste of his own mortality."

"Something like that," he agreed with a smirk and I smiled back at him as I picked up my coffee and took a long sip from the Green Power Ranger's head.

It was cold down here and a shiver tracked down my spine as I clung to the mug for some warmth.

"So did you give up when you got a little boo-boo, or…"

Fox grinned and the sight of that devilish smile on his lips had my heart jumping right up into my throat as I looked down at him, seeing so much of the boy I loved in that expression alongside the man I lusted after all too often.

He reached out and tugged open one of the desk drawers, revealing a thick pile of cash and a bunch of jewellery which was probably worth more than my car.

"Nice," I admitted, trying to suppress another shiver as I wrapped my arms around my chest.

"You're cold," he pointed out, catching my leg beneath the knee and lifting it so that my foot was in his lap.

He fell still as the motion gave him a pretty unrestricted view right up the shirt I'd stolen to wear and for a moment I just let him look at my black panties, my heart racing as desire spilled though his green eyes and I wondered if the air might just combust around us from all the tension that hung in it.

Fox cleared his throat and caught my other knee, closing my thighs with a growl of determination and landing my cold toes in his lap.

I bit my lip before taking another sip of my coffee, watching him over the rim as he stared at me hungrily and I knew he could see the colour rising in my cheeks, the way my nipples pressed through the thin material of the shirt I was wearing and even the way I was clenching my thighs together to try and stifle the thoughts that had come rushing through me like a freight train at that one, carnal look he'd given me.

He started rubbing my calves for me in an attempt to bring some warmth to my flesh, and his gaze cut back to the map my ass was now half covering like he was hunting for a distraction.

"I've been going over all of the reports I've had back from the Harlequins as they search the town for Shawn and his men," he said, changing the subject and dumping ice cold water all over my libido.

"And?" I asked, already knowing from his tone that they'd turned up nothing.

"I guess we can rule a bunch of places out. But he hasn't shown back up in Sterling either so as of right now, I have no fucking idea where he is or what he's up to."

"He won't have given up that easily," I said.

"I know," he agreed. "But for now, all we have are dead ends and silent streets. I'm pretty sure he's planning something big, but I'm starting to think we won't know anything about it until he makes his move."

I nodded, shifting a little in my seat and my toes flexed in his lap, grazing against the rock hard length of his cock as it strained against his jeans.

Our eyes met again and my pulse rocketed, making me brave or stupid or I wasn't even sure what because the words that poured from my lips might as well have been designed to fracture this moment with utter perfection.

"Do you really have that sex tape Rick made of me, him and Johnny James?" I asked and Fox fell utterly still, his hands circling my ankles as his jaw ground and I was almost certain he was about to storm off on me when he spoke instead.

"I guess I like to torture myself with it," he said in a dark tone. "Every time I start to lose myself in fantasies of having you, I can just take my phone out and watch the two of them fucking you instead, remind myself of why you can't be mine and what you really want."

I licked my lips and set my coffee mug down beside his untouched one, unsure if what I was planning to ask him next was brave or fucking stupid.

"And is that all you feel when you watch it?" I asked, my voice taking on a low, seductive tone unintentionally.

"What else would I feel?" he asked, the anger in his eyes scorching while his cock seemed to get even harder beneath my feet.

"Sometimes I think about being with you and I can't help but touch myself," I breathed, my hands curling around the edge of the desk as I held his eye and let him see the truth of that. "I pant your name in the dark and fuck my own hand imagining you in its place, and I come so hard and fast at the mere thought of it that I can't help but want more every damn time."

"Rogue," he growled in warning, but I had promised no more lies and I wanted him to know how much I wanted him.

"Do you do that too?" I pushed. "Do you watch that video and listen to my moans while you pump your cock in your fist and think of me?"

Fox shoved to his feet abruptly and I thought he was going to storm out on me, stride away and leave me there with my truth hanging in the air and his buried deep and hidden away yet again.

But he didn't leave.

Fox stepped into me, shoving my thighs apart and stepping between them as he placed his hands on the desk either side of me and looked into my eyes, rearing over me like a king demanding subservience.

"Is that what you wanna hear, hummingbird?" he growled. "You wanna know that I watch that fucking video and I get so fucking angry that I can hardly even think straight while my cock gets so fucking hard that I can't help but take it in my hand. You wanna know that I watch you with two of my best friends while I grind my teeth and pump my cock and come to the sound of you calling their names? That I fucking hate myself for it, but that I can't help but do it again and again. Jerking off over one of the worst moments of my life like some fucking masochist getting off on my own heartbreak?"

"Yes," I breathed, knowing that was wrong but unable to deny it too as the wetness between my parted thighs made it all too fucking clear.

"Prove it," he demanded, looking down at me as I panted beneath him, my fingernails biting into the desk as I fought to keep my hands to myself. "If my pain gets you as turned on as you say then show me, hummingbird. Or are you all bark and no bite?"

I lifted my chin at his challenge and shook my head. "I'm not the one who's afraid of this, Fox," I reminded him. "You're the one who would rather run than taste it."

"Well for someone who isn't afraid, you aren't doing a whole lot besides baiting me, hummingbird. And you should know better than to do that."

I held his eye for a long moment before dropping my gaze to his chest, the Ferris wheel that dominated it and the Harlequin jester on his bicep. The lines of his ink cast dark and dominating shadows over his cut body and as my body pulsed with need for him again, I gave in to that desire and leaned in.

My gaze fixed to his mouth as I arched my spine and closed most of the distance between us. But he didn't lean down to meet me and he was too tall for me to breach the gap on my own.

"You want me to prove it for you, Fox?" I breathed. "You want me to fuck my hand while you watch me and see for yourself how worked up I get over you? You want to film it so you have something else to jerk off over the next time you ache for me but can't bring yourself to come to me directly and just take what you want from me?"

His gaze filled with wicked urges and his lips parted as I wondered if I really would do that, just lie back on this desk and pleasure myself in front of him to prove how fucking much I wanted him too. I knew he desired me. So it should have been simple for me to do that, but it wasn't because his want for me wasn't enough if he still couldn't see a way to be happy with me as I was. With my love for the others intact and my lust for them as fierce as it was for him.

Fox's throat bobbed but he still held himself there. "You know why I haven't taken it, hummingbird. And yet you still work to tempt me at every fucking turn while claiming to be my friend."

"I am your friend," I protested, the space between us crackling with expectant energy. "But you're the one who drew the line there."

"You always told me no before," he growled.

"Only because you didn't understand then. Now you do. I'm not going to pretend that I don't want you to be all in with us now." My gut tightened with vulnerability as I laid myself out for him like that, but it needed to be said, needed to be fucking heard.

The sound of a door closing upstairs snapped the tension between us like a balloon bursting and Fox cursed as he drew back.

"That's my dad," he muttered just as Luther called out asking where the fuck everyone was. "He's come with an update about The Dead Dogs and we're gonna strategize on how to proceed now."

I sighed, shifting forward and making Fox back up as Luther's footsteps sounded on the basement stairs.

"I'll catch you later then, Badger," I said, shifting around him and heading towards the stairs.

He snatched my wrist as I went, jerking me back to look at him with something burning in his eyes that he seemed on the brink of spilling, but Luther made it to the foot of the stairs and he just held my eye instead.

"Christ, wildcat, put some damn clothes on would ya?" Luther barked as he strode towards us, not seeming the least bit put off by the tension hanging around us as he strode to take the seat Fox had been sitting in at the desk.

Fox released me, the words dying on his lips and leaving me aching for them as I forced my attention to Luther instead.

"Yes, boss," I mocked, dipping into a curtsy which made my bare ass hang out the back of Chase's shirt as I pulled it wide and Luther laughed loudly.

Fox still said nothing so I just blew him a kiss, sidestepped him to get past - subtly dropping my hand into the open drawer on the desk and fisting a wedge of that pretty cash - and took off up the stairs, trying to ignore the need between my thighs as I went and the way my nipples were aching.

I made it upstairs and tossed the basement door closed to leave them to their Harlequin business, pausing as I spotted myself in the mirror that hung from the wall in the hallway.

I tilted me head as I looked at the shitty brown hair dye which was fading even more now, revealing a patchwork of tones where the rainbow job was kinda showing through. It looked fucking awful. I needed to make a decision on it. And as I focused on the sound of the waves that I could just make out outside and the fullness in my heart at being home where I belonged, I made my mind up.

Fox had left his cell phone on the kitchen side so I snagged it, unlocked it with his passcode - which was still the same one he'd used when we were kids - and dialled Saint Memphis. It only rang once before I got my answer.

"I take it you are calling to discuss the behaviour of your little friends in my abode?" he asked in a clipped tone which made me snigger despite how pissed he sounded. That guy had the scary motherfucker thing down.

"Actually, this is Rogue. I still don't have a cell phone so I stole Fox's and thought you wouldn't mind passing me over to Tatum."

"That is very presumptuous. Though I suppose I am not surprised that you would take such liberties," he replied.

"So can you pass her the phone?" I pressed.

"Perhaps she is otherwise occupied," Saint replied, seeming to enjoy running me around.

"Perhaps she is," I agreed. "Shall we just shoot the breeze while we wait for her to come to the phone then? I saw a squid when I was out on the boat the other day and I heard you have a thing for-"

"Tatum. Your undereducated friend with the verb for a name wishes to speak with you," Saint cut me off and I grinned to myself as Tatum took the phone from him.

"Hey," I said. "Do you fancy a girl's day? I need a trip to the salon to sort my fucking hair out."

"Err, hell yes. Shall I come pick you up? I can be there in half an hour."

"Perfect. I'll need to get dressed and sneak out. Wanna wait for me down on Palm Avenue?" I asked.

"Sounds good to me."

"I suggest she purchases a new cell phone while you are out to avoid the inconvenience of this rigmarole in the future," Saint called, clearly listening in on us.

"Sure thing," I agreed. "I recently came into a whole chunk of money and it's just burning a hole in my pocket, waiting to be spent." I fanned myself with the cash I'd just stolen from Fox, though I guessed the effect was lost as no one could see me. Still, it made me feel like a trashy bitch and I couldn't say I hated the feeling.

"See you soon," Tatum said and I agreed before hanging up on her and tossing the cell phone back on the counter.

I turned and jogged up the stairs, heading to my room and jumping into the shower to get ready before anyone caught on to what I was up to. I spun the dial to cold to try and alleviate the need Fox had awoken in my flesh then gave up on that and parted my thighs, sinking my fingers into the wet heat between them and moaning in relief.

My clit was throbbing with need already and as I closed my eyes I thought of Fox going full dominant badger on me, pinning me down and fucking me with all the rage he felt over watching me with the others.

I was gasping his name and coming hard within moments, my body rippling with pleasure so intense that my breath caught as I shuddered around my fingers and bit down on my bottom lip.

It only really took the edge off of my desire for him, but there wasn't much more I could do about that so I just shut the water off, dressed in a cute pink sun dress and grabbed my white sneakers before creeping out onto the landing again.

I snuck across the hall, cracking open the door to Chase's room and checking on the others who were all still fast asleep in his bed. They were gonna be pissed at me for heading out without any of them playing bodyguard, but I was confident that I could handle myself with a gun now thanks to JJ's continued lessons and I needed to do this alone.

Mutt hopped up as he spotted me and he hurried to follow me out of the room before I silently closed the door again.

I tiptoed down the stairs and I swear Mutt copied me, keeping his little paws silent as we made it back to the kitchen and I quickly took the desert eagle Fox kept stashed behind the cereal boxes and dropped it into my purse.

I grabbed a notepad and scribbled out a note for the boys, knowing they'd be pissed when they found it and feeling a little thrill at the prospect as I left it on the counter for them.

Gone out - it's important - nothing dangerous - be back later.
P.S. You can punish me for it if you must X

Was I hoping they would choose to punish me? Maybe. Was I extra hoping all four of them got together and learned one of JJ's strip routines to teach me a sexy dance lesson? Definitely maybe. But all in all, I was guessing they'd mostly just be pissed. Still, this needed to happen and I wasn't gonna chicken out now.

I took my skateboard from its place beneath the stairs and slipped out to the pool, moving one of the patio chairs over to the wall and lifting Mutt and my board up ahead of me, balancing them on top of it.

Mutt sat his little ass down on the white bricks and I put my sneakers on before scrambling up after him.

I tossed my board into the bushes then lowered myself down too, lifting my arms for Mutt who leapt into them instantly, wagging his tail and licking my face in excitement though he still stayed quiet like he knew he had to.

I grinned at him, tickling his ears and setting him down before grabbing my board and leading the way away from Harlequin House to the streets beyond, managing to avoid the Crew members on lookout as I went.

When I was clear of the house, I dropped my skateboard and jumped on, racing away down the hill with Mutt running ahead of me, his ears flapping in the wind as he barked excitedly.

The sun was beating down on us and I sighed as I soaked it in, loving the taste of salt on the air and the warmth on my skin.

We reached Palm Avenue and Tatum waved to us from an ice white convertible BMW, throwing the door open so that Mutt could leap in ahead of me and I dropped down into the seat a moment later.

We took a leisurely route through the town, making our way to the upper quarter and the fancy boutique hairdresser that JJ always took me to as we chatted shit about nothing and everything and I just enjoyed some girl time.

We parked up and I led the way into the salon, smiling widely as I stepped through the door with Tatum at my side.

"Hey Lucy - it's time," I announced, striding into the salon like I owned the damn place.

"Time?" she asked curiously, looking at me over the top of a head half filled with highlights as she worked.

"Yeah, time for the return of the mother fucking rainbow," I said with a grin.

"Oh. Okay, cool. We are pretty busy today though so we don't actually have time to slot you in this morning..."

I stalled in my badass 'the bitch is back' moment and nodded sheepishly, realising I really should have called ahead and made a damn appointment. For fuck's sake. This shit never happened to the Green Power Ranger when he went on a mission.

"We had a cancelation at one though," another girl piped up helpfully.

"Okay, cool," I agreed and Tatum laughed. "Then at one on the dot, the motherfucking rainbow is gonna be coming back-"

"It'll take hours. I'm gonna have to strip that cheap bottle job out before we can even begin," Lucy interrupted me again.

"Guys, you're seriously dampening my dramatic vibe here," I admitted and Lucy laughed.

"First world problems, amirite?" she said.

"Goddammit you are," I agreed with a sigh. "Okay, new plan. I'm gonna go shopping and get something to eat then I'll be back at one o'clock, ready to spend hours preparing for my badass bitch moment which will happen at around five-"

"More like six or seven actually," Lucy interrupted.

"Dammit. Okay, fine. But by some point later on this evening, I will be ready for my damn moment."

"Okay, see you after lunch," she agreed, waving as me and Tatum headed back out into the sunshine.

Mutt had already wandered off, sniffing all around for scraps as I tried to figure out what we should do with our morning.

"How about we get brunch, have a few cocktails then hit the shops?" Tatum suggested and I nodded, though as I did, my gaze snagged on a tattoo parlour a little further down the street.

"And maybe we make time to get some ink too?" I said as I thought came to me because I'd already marked my body for two of my boys and it had been bothering me for a while that Johnny James and Chase weren't getting fair representation.

"Oooh, I wonder if they do henna tattoos too? I could get a squid and pretend it's real. Saint would lose his fucking mind," Tatum said on a laugh and I grinned at her.

"Girls days are the freaking best," I said with a sigh as we headed down the street to get ourselves some fancy ass brunch and I grinned like all of my worries had just floated up into the sky and disappeared.

After getting my tattoos, having my rainbow hair reinstated, buying hundreds of dollars worth of clothes and drinking rather a lot of rum with my new bestie, we called it a night. It was dark and a trio of Harlequin thugs had shown up while I was getting my hair stripped out to lurk around me, all of them staying close by this entire time, clearly under JJ's command. I wanted to be pissed at Lucy for ratting me out, but at least she'd convinced him not to show up in person, leaving the hair colour I'd decided on as a surprise until I headed home.

Saint showed up to collect us, one of Tatum's other guys collecting her BMW as we were both way too wasted to drive anywhere. He passed me a cell phone as I dropped into the back seat, the flashy rose gold model clearly worth a bomb, but he just rolled his eyes when I questioned him on it.

"I would sooner you don't contact Tatum via me again," he said, eyeing the two of us in the rear view mirror as we laughed in the back seat together. Mutt was riding shotgun, looking out of the window and I was surprised to find that Saint didn't seem to have any objections to that. "Besides, I don't despise the way you make my siren laugh. Even if you are an uncouth vagabond."

I fell into hysterics at that assessment, cupping a hand around my ear and leaning in close to Tatum as I whispered my question to her.

"I bet he's a spanker, isn't he?" I asked and she giggled loudly.

"Oh you have no idea," she hissed back. "I'm going to be in so much trouble when we get home."

Saint eyed her in the mirror with a smirk tugging at the corner of his lips which confirmed that, clearly having heard everything we'd said. "I'm not the only one who will be punishing you tonight, siren," he warned and fuck me, if I hadn't had my own bunch of bananas to deal with then his dominant daddy tone would have gotten me all kinds of hot.

"Shit," I said, laughing again. "You'll have to give me tips on that. So far I've managed a couple of three ways but the thought of having more than two of them is bit full on."

"No, babe, you just have to fucking go with it," Tatum said, waving a hand dismissively. "I mean, you have enough holes for three plus enough hands for two more if you need them."

"Jesus," I said, imagining the reality of that with a little too much excitement as we rounded the corner onto the road where Harlequin House stood at the top of the hill. "Maybe you could send me some how-to videos-"

"Absolutely not," Saint said. "Those tapes are not for public viewing."

I gaped at him and his casual reference to 'those tapes' and Tatum laughed even more.

"Maybe if you wanna come over and drink rum with me again one night, I'll let you watch a couple of them in the cinema room so you can see the best angles to make it all work."

She winked at me and we both cracked up at the thought of that. "Oh yeah, who doesn't love a movie night with their bestie, watching home videos of her getting fucked by four dudes at once?"

Saint sighed like we were the most bothersome bothers that ever did bother him, and I cracked up at that thought as it ran through my head and he parked the car.

I was too busy laughing to even notice the big bad gangster who came stalking out to open the back door for me and I squealed as Rick hauled me out of the car and tossed me over his shoulder in his favourite caveman way.

"Thanks for bringing her back," Fox said to Saint as Mutt leapt out of the car and I called out to tell them to grab my bags from the trunk.

Chase and JJ took that job on and I grinned at them as I lifted my head to peer out between my rainbow coloured curls as they carried the bags of designer shit towards the house.

Tatum waved to me and I waved back, watching as she climbed into the front of the car with Saint who leaned close to say something to her which made her blush. Damn, that girl was getting laid tonight. Total, daddy Dom, full on punishment laid. Probably with those four dicks too. Lucky bitch.

Rick swept me inside the house and the others followed close at my heels as he strode into the front room and tossed me down on the couch before them.

They all stood there, arms folded, shoulder to shoulder as they glared down at me and waited for an explanation, and I just grinned as Mutt headed over to pee in one of the potted plants.

"Goddammit," Fox growled as he spotted him. "The little bastard has been outside all day. He fucking saved that piss for when he got back here."

"He likes it here," I said, slapping a hand over my mouth as a hiccup escaped then laughing as the room spun. Shit, those last few shots were hitting me hard.

"You're wasted," Chase accused and I shrugged innocently.

"Don't you have anything you wanna say?" Fox barked and I frowned before nodding and grabbing my purse.

"Here's your change," I said, pulling out the one dollar and thirty-eight cents I had left over from the money I'd stolen from him.

JJ broke a laugh then smothered it again, his eyes dragging over me and my rainbow locks appreciatively even though he was trying to keep the whole, big bad gangster thing alive with his scary posture.

"You stole almost four grand," Fox pointed out, not taking the money as I waved it at him. "What the fuck did you even spend it on?"

"Oh, you'll like it," I promised, reaching for the bags Chase and JJ had brought in and rummaging in them while trying to focus on seeing straight.

I started pulling things out to show them. There were several bags of clothes which held various dresses, shorts, shirts and shoes which they didn't seem all that interested in, but when I made it to the lingerie bag, they perked right up.

I flashed the scraps of lace at them one after another, biting my lip as they remained there, glaring down at me and making me feel like a really bad girl.

When I pulled out the leather handcuffs Tatum had suggested I buy, Chase cursed and Rick chuckled darkly. And when I continued to pull out items from the sex shop, including a spanking paddle, some ankle restraints and a vibrating butt plug, Fox swiped a hand down his face and snatched the bag away from me.

"Enough. Stop trying to distract us and get to the bit where you tell us how sorry you are for freaking us all out over you pulling yet another disappearing act," Fox growled.

"I didn't disappear and you totally had your goons watching me for most of the day so don't go pretending you've been here pacing the walls, Badger," I said, rolling my eyes and maybe slurring my words a little. "Besides, I needed to fix my hair."

"Rainbow looks fucking good on you, pretty girl," JJ said, breaking character and smirking down at me while I beamed back.

"You're still in trouble," Rick said in a low voice and I nodded seriously.

"You haven't seen the best bit though," I said firmly.

"What's that, little one?" Chase asked and I grinned up at him as I took in the fact that not only was he shirtless, but he didn't even have his eyepatch on. I hoped he did that more often from now on because he was a sight for sore fucking eyes and I wanted to look at him like this as often as I could.

"This." I got to my feet, only stumbling a little bit, before turning my back on them and bending forward to grasp the back of the couch as I flipped my skirt up to show them my new ink.

"Fuck me," Chase muttered and JJ groaned as Rick stepped forward to grip my ass cheek, pushing me further forward so that they could all get a better look at my two new tattoos. I'd gotten them done above the two I had for Rick and Fox so now the back of both of my thighs were covered for my boys.

"I'm gonna enjoy bending you over even more now," Maverick said in dark tone and I couldn't help but look forward to that.

Chase's rough fingertips skimmed the edges of the ace of spades tattoo I'd gotten inked above the Harlequin jester. The artist had embellished the white of the playing card with a swirling pattern while filling the spade itself with a demon skull with flames burning in its eyes.

JJ brushed his fingers over the tender skin of the tattoo I'd gotten for him above the grim reaper I had for Rick, a groan of desire escaping him as he traced the dark lines of the hourglass tattoo which had an entire beach trapped inside it, making my flesh prickle.

"You once told me that loving me was like trying to keep hold of sand while the tide tried to claim it back from you," I said, looking up at JJ as he continued to caress the ink I'd gotten for him. "And I wanted you to know that you don't have to work to keep it anymore because nothing can steal it away. It's as permanent as the ink on my skin and as endless as the tide which tried to steal it from you."

"Fuck, pretty girl," he murmured, his cheeks colouring a little as he took in the truth of my words.

"Are you still going to punish me?" I asked, unable to entirely hide the eager lilt to my voice as I looked over my shoulder at the four of them and found them openly staring at me as I remained bent over before them.

"Tomorrow," Maverick said firmly, reaching out and flipping my skirt back down to cover my ass. "Because you're wasted right now, beautiful, and I want to make sure you remember every moment of our wrath when we deliver it."

Fox frowned at his brother then stepped forward and hoisted me into his arms. "You need to wash those tattoos then sleep off that rum," he commanded, all bossy badger and I grinned as he manhandled me out of the room.

"Yes, sir," I agreed and he grunted, keeping his eyes off of me as he climbed the stairs and left the others behind. They didn't look entirely pleased about him kidnapping me, but they didn't complain either, and a moment later I found myself in his room as he herded me into the shower.

"What are we going to do tomorrow? Are you going to help them punish me?" I asked casually as I dropped my clothes and moved into the shower.

Fox looked away then back to me again then away once more.

"I have other plans for the morning," he replied, shaking his head like he was trying to keep it clear while I soaped up my tits and put on a bit of a show for him which he was working hard not to watch.

"What plans?" I asked and he fully turned away from me as I continued to rub the suds over my body.

"We're all going to the beach. We're gonna catch the surf and just...

hang out. Like old times."

"Really?" I asked hopefully, letting the water wash the soap away again before stepping out of the shower.

"Yeah, really," he said, his tone softening as he glanced at me and I smiled at the idea of us all having a day together like we always used to. "Shawn has dropped off the grid and I'm tired of our life just passing us by. So I think we deserve a day off."

"I'd love that," I said, taking the towel he offered me and drying myself before dressing in one of his shirts and climbing straight into his bed.

Fox stripped off and followed me without another word and I rolled over to lean on his chest as I let my eyes fall shut, soaking in the warmth of his arms around me and drowning in his rich cedar scent.

Between the rum and the long day I'd had, I pretty much passed out right away and I dreamed of the sun and the surf without fucking Shawn ever once making an appearance. Because that motherfucker was my past and now all I cared about was the future I planned on having right here with my boys.

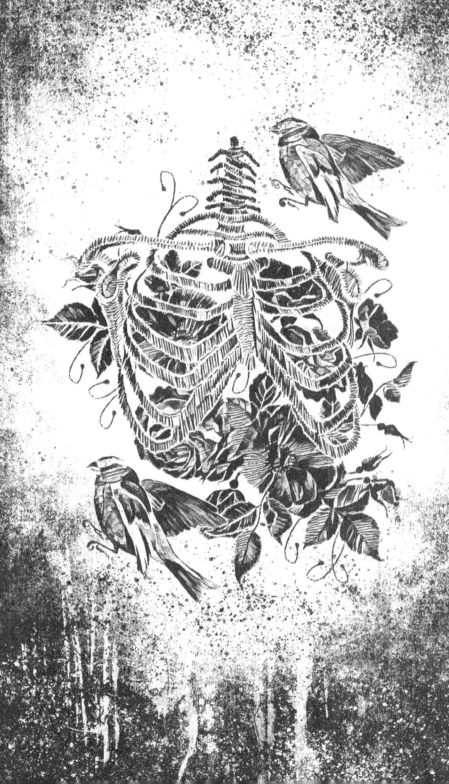

CHAPTER THIRTY SIX

There was one thing every man, woman and child on earth should have known about me. I don't go down easy. I don't bow out of fights. I win them with cunning and bloody brutality. So no, I had not run from Sunset Cove like a mouse afraid of its own shadow. Instead, I'd calculated Fox and his daddy's next moves the moment the Castillo Cartel had pulled their men outa my domain.

I prided myself on not being a fool. And so, I'd made a decision which would pay off in the long run. Delayed gratification was my favourite kind of gratification, and oh baby I was getting close to the moment I reaped the rewards for all my efforts here in this town.

This game I was playing with Rogue and the Harlequins was like a slow fuck with the tightest of pussies. I was building towards an inevitable high, but the longer I held off my final thrusts, the better it would feel when I reached my climax. It was gonna be a beautiful damn thing, and today I'd get a glimpse at the high that was coming.

I drew my baseball cap lower as I parked the inconspicuous silver Honda I'd had one of my men steal for me, gazing out at Sunset Beach, the blazing sun having brought a crowd here today, giving me the cover I needed to move about stealthy like.

One of my boys had tipped me off that my sugarpie was down here with her Harlequin boys and as my gaze settled on them out in the water, a smile curled up my lips.

"Well, well, if it isn't my sweet cheeks playing slut again."

My men had been sending me videos of her whenever she was about town, always in the company of at least one of these assholes. But I had to say I was kinda surprised Maverick had re-joined their ranks so easily, but it looked like he was putting his hatred for them aside for the sake of gaining access to more pussy.

They were playing right into my hands. Maverick had returned to Fox's side and Luther no doubt thought his family could actually be happy again. But there was fat fucking chance of that in the long term. Luther would end up slit from neck to stomach, his insides becoming his outsides and his eyes on his sweet baby boys as I gutted them too. Mm, it was gonna be a damn massacre.

I watched them for a while longer, loving the power I felt buzzing in my veins over how little they even knew about my plans. How easy they all were to manipulate. Rogue was the dumbest of them all. She couldn't even see the truth of this situation right before her eyes. What kinda man shared his woman with his friends?

Though I had to admit I was curious about this arrangement they seemed to have going on. Was she passed cock to cock, or did they share those tight holes of hers whenever they felt like it?

They were probably off fucking whatever other good pussy they could find whenever they wanted something different. It was the way of men. We weren't satisfied by one thing, always looking for the new, the exciting. And right now, Rogue might have supplied that to them in some way, but no girl who whored herself out so willingly ever became a wife. The only kind of woman worth keeping around for a lifetime was the kind who did as a man asked, who never questioned his actions and let him appease his appetite for various wet pussy whenever he needed it.

Of course, I liked them wild first before I broke them down to pieces then built them back up into an obedient little slave who wanted only to please me. Rogue was becoming something of an obsession of mine, and I couldn't say any woman had had this kind of grip on me before. She was a project I needed to see through. And it was becoming clear to me now that I could never truly own her until I stripped away the source of her strength: those boys. So one by one, I'd cut them down, make a real display of their deaths and when they were buried in the dirt, I'd claim her. I'd dry her tears and offer her a place in my bed again. She'd fight it at first, but she'd come to realise there was no other place for her in this world. She'd have no one to turn to but me, and I'd welcome her home with open arms. Then I'd make her see that she was always meant to belong to me.

I ran my finger over the scar on my cheek from the pen she'd stabbed into my fucking face. "It could have been easier than this, sugarpie. Those boys didn't have to die. But you've gone and pissed me off, so here we are."

My gaze shifted onto the little Jack Russell that was always trotting after Rogue like her farts smelled like fresh chicken. He was sitting beside Miss Mabel who was set up on a sun lounger beneath an umbrella on the sand, the dog looking like it was guarding their bags while they swam and surfed in the waves.

It had not passed by my observation that this animal was the sixth member of their circle, and I may not have been able to watch a Harlequin die today, but I could sure as shit watch a Harlequin's dog die.

I slipped out of the car, grabbing my bag from the passenger seat and taking out the bacon treats I had stashed in there before heading down onto the beach. I blended in well enough with my white t-shirt and black board shorts, and one glance into the sea told me Rogue was busy distracting all of her fan club as she climbed onto her surfboard and they stared at her body with a hunger that would no doubt end in them fucking her raw later on today. Her hair was dyed rainbow again which made my upper lip curl with distaste. But you didn't get rainbows without rain, and I was most certainly willingly to play the part of the storm.

I hoped she was enjoying her free time being a whore, because her days of offering her pussy up on a platter to multiple men were numbered. Soon, she'd offer it to me and no one else, and I'd be sure to get many, many apologies from her body before I even considered offering her an ounce of kindness.

When I'd triple checked Miss Mabel was fast asleep, I hummed Hound

Dog by Elvis Presley as I approached the dog, figuring what was to come would be kinda poetic considering the name of my gang. We never did have a mascot, and it was a mighty shame there'd be nothing left of him to string up on the front of the Rosewood Manor once I secured my victory over this town again.

"Here boy," I called, tossing a few bacon treats onto the towel beside him.

He sniffed the air, looking around and diving on the treats, making a smirk pull at my lips. I kept throwing them, making a trail directly towards me and the little beast moved from one to the next, drawing closer and closer. I tossed a few down to distract him while I bent down, rummaging through the Harlequins' things and whistling softly to myself. When I was done, I turned to the dog and grinned wolfishly.

"That's it, come to papa," I encouraged and as he stepped into my shadow to grab the last one, I fisted my hand in his scruff and lifting him into the air by it as I got to my feet.

He started wriggling and growling, trying to bite me, but I had a damn good hold on him and as I clutched him to my chest, keeping my fist tight around the back of his neck, and my other closed over his tiny jaws, he was forced to fall still against me.

I walked back to my car, not drawing any attention at all from the families playing around me on the beach. I was an invisible predator, always here, always thirsting for blood. And it looked like I was finally gonna get some blood and watch my sugarpie lose the first of her friends.

Because this furry little beast was about to go boom.

FOX Sunset Beach

CHAPTER THIRTY SEVEN

My eyes were glued to Rogue as she sat on her board out in the water, tipping her head back to soak in the sun, the light making her skin turn to liquid bronze.

Maverick's fat head moved right into my line of sight and he smirked at me, making my jaw tighten. "Sorry am I in the way of your spank bank material, brother?" he taunted and a growl scraped along the inside of my throat, but I didn't let it out.

I schooled my features and shook my head. "I dunno what you're talking about."

I turned away from him, but the motherfucker never could allow me to have the last word.

"I suppose you've got plenty of material since I sent you that video of me and JJ making her scream. Tell me, Foxy, do you picture yourself in our place when you watch it, or do you secretly like seeing our cocks in her?"

"You fucking prick," I snarled, lunging at him, but he dove under water like a fucking dolphin and swam away, his board bumping hard into my arm as it was dragged after him by the tether on his ankle.

I turned away, placing my attention on Chase and JJ as they started paddling to catch a wave behind me. Chase had been struggling to keep his balance on his bad leg, but he was as stubborn as a mule and when he popped up this time, he remained on his feet. JJ whooped and cheered for him and a smile ripped across my face as I heard Rogue crying out encouragements too.

"Go on, Ace!" Maverick cried and I couldn't help but throw a look back, finding him with his elbows resting on Rogue's surfboard as she straddled it.

I should have swum away then, got on my own board and tried to catch the next wave, but instead I couldn't stop staring as Maverick's hand slid onto her thigh and they started talking in low voices I couldn't hear, just for each other.

Jealousy roared a battle cry in my chest, ready to go to war for her attention. But I forced myself to remain there. I could have turned around, I could have put some distance between us so I didn't have to suffer like this, but Maverick was fucking right – not that I'd ever tell him that. But yeah, sometimes I watched that video. It was like having an addiction, only I was never allowed to get high, all I did was crave and crave and crave while I watched someone else feed their habit. It was insufferable, and yet I couldn't stop myself. She came alive for them in the way I'd wished she'd come alive for me, and I guessed seeing that was reassurance I'd made the right decision. But that didn't give me an excuse for watching it time after fucking time, did it?

Maverick's hand took a path north, his fingers sliding over her ass and scrunching in the material of her pale blue bikini.

My throat thickened as I continued to stare, all rational thought slipping away from me bit by bit. I was used to seeing his hands on her by now and the only thing that stopped me from losing my fucking shit was looking at her face when he did it. I wasn't even sure she realised how bright her eyes got when one of the boys were touching her. In the depths of her gaze, there was a truth there I couldn't deny. She was happy. Happy with them. And so long as that remained the case, I could find something close to peace. Though I didn't think I'd ever truly be free of the torment I felt over her.

Maverick dropped his hand, turning and swimming for his board before climbing on it and paddling hard to catch a wave. I bobbed in the water as the swell of it rolled past me and watched as Maverick caught it just as it broke, riding it all the way to shore.

My gaze travelled back to Rogue and my eyes immediately sharpened on two guys paddling over to her on their boards.

"Hey, babe," one of them called. "What's a hot chick like you doing out on the water alone?"

"I'm not alone. I've got this." She raised her middle finger at them and they chuckled, taking her sass as a sign to come even closer. It fucking wasn't.

She ignored them, shutting her eyes again and dropping her head back as she enjoyed the sun. The two guys started pointing out her tits and one of them cupped his hands against his own chest, pretending to squeeze them as they paddled even closer. I was already moving, swimming under the waves and circling around the back of them like a shark in the water, the only sign of my movements the board tailing after me on the surface.

I came up behind them, finding one of them had moved their board right up next to her and as his hand landed on her leg, I lunged at him, grabbing a fistful of his surfer dude hair and ripping him backwards off his board into the water and holding him under.

"What the-" the other one wheeled around, finding himself eye to eye with Fox Harlequin and the scream that left him was entirely female.

"If you want your little friend to live I suggest you lie down on your board," I commanded and he nodded several times before doing as I'd asked.

"Rogue, will you pull his leg strap off?" I asked and she grinned at me wickedly before paddling closer and tugging it off the guy's leg. His friend continued to thrash beneath the water and I finally let him come up.

"Up you get, you piece of shit." I half threw him out of the water and he scrambled on top of his friend with a wail of terror as he looked back at me. I ripped off his leg strap, letting his board float away on the tide.

"Hand me that, hummingbird," I asked and she smirked as she offered the long length of cord in her hand attached to the other guy's leg strap and I wrapped it round and round the two of them, pulling it so tight they couldn't move before knotting it in place.

"Wait, please," one of them begged but I was already pushing them, swimming toward the surf and Rogue suddenly appeared beside me, laughing wildly as she pushed them too. The second the surf took them, we swam backwards so the tide didn't take us too, watching as they rode the wave for a few seconds before spiralling out of controlling and disappearing under the water. They were eventually spat out on the sand and the sound of my friends' laughter drew my attention to Chase, JJ and Maverick who were standing on the beach together and beckoning us to join them.

"Your inner badger can be pretty fun." Rogue prodded me and I turned to look at her, taking in the water droplets on her cheeks and the ones she licked off her lips.

"I thought you hated my inner badger," I pointed out and she moved closer, resting her hands on my shoulders to help her stay afloat in the water. I should have pushed her off, but I was a slave to my want for her in that instant and instead my hands hooked around her waist. It was like a half embrace, neither of us touching any more than that, but it was all it took to make my heart beat like a drum.

"It turns out there's a badgeriness scale, and I like it set somewhere in the middle," she said with a grin and my fingers curled against her back, drawing her an inch closer. She came with ease, her hands sliding down onto my shoulder blades, making my breath catch and my need for her sharpen. The world became a muffled grey blur until it was just me, Rogue and the sea. My favourite place in the whole fucking universe.

"I'll always protect you," I said, the smile falling from my face.

"You protect all of us. It's what you do. It's how you're made." She slipped closer again and I ceased to breathe as she wound her legs around me and my hands pressed hard against her back, betraying every vow I'd made as I clutched her to my chest and our breathing space became shared.

"And how are you made, hummingbird?" I asked, my world narrowing in on this girl and the heat of her skin, the depth of her eyes. I couldn't think clearly when she was this close, never had been able to. I was just a kid with a desperate crush, but now that crush had become a furious love and it felt far too big for me to control. It was the one thing I'd never been able to bend to my will, and I'd never wanted to until now. Because now I'd relinquished her, I needed that love to free me from it. But I knew with all my heart that I never would be free, because freedom to me had always been Rogue.

"I think they're waiting for you," I said.

"They're waiting for *us*," she corrected. "And they can wait, Fox, because right now I only want to be right here."

"Rogue," I said in vague protest, but I only drew her closer, contradicting myself immediately. This girl was my bittersweet curse. The embodiment of all I had ever wanted and yet I wasn't enough for her.

"We should go to shore," I breathed eventually, knowing I was selfishly stealing as many seconds as I could with her this close, but it would only make parting more painful in the end. But as she leaned in closer, her cheek pressing to mine, I had the feeling she was doing the same as me, the rampant pounding of her heart against my skin like an admission of its own. She'd said she loved me. She'd spoken those words, and I hadn't truly believed them because how could anyone be in love with more than one person?

Her breaths fanned against my ear and she whispered words that made me ache. "My skin misses the contact of yours every fucking day."

I pulled her flush to me, giving in to this magnetic pull between us for a moment and shutting my eyes as if that could make it last longer.

A sharp whistle came from the shore and I finally let Rogue go, looking over at JJ as he waved at us determinedly.

She twitched a sad smile at me as I released her, and I felt the divide like a wall going up in my chest.

We swam to shore, wading out of the water as JJ came running over.

"Mutt's missing," he said, running a hand through his inky black hair. "Miss Mabel fell asleep. She said she hasn't seen him."

"He's probably just found some vendor to beg for scraps from," Rogue said and I nodded, but we still followed JJ up the beach and started looking for him.

Maverick and Chase were up by the ice cream parlour searching for our little dog and Rogue started whistling and calling him as we walked towards the beach huts further along the sand.

"Here boy!" JJ shouted.

I looked around as I heard my phone ringing and left them searching as I jogged over to where Miss Mabel was set up under a large umbrella on her sun lounger.

"I'm sure the little scallywag will show up any moment now," Mabel said assuredly, and I nodded as I grabbed my phone, finding an unknown number calling.

"Hello?" I answered.

"Hello sunshine," Shawn purred in my ear and my blood turned ice cold. "Oh, you didn't think I'd left town without a fight, did ya? Surely you didn't think Shawn Mackenzie hightailed it out of your pretty cove without even a goodbye?"

"What do you want, asshole?" I spat, the phone locked tight in my grip as blood thundered in my ears.

"What do I want?" he laughed. "The whole word, Fox Harlequin, the whole damn world. And a nice boat. But right now, I want a little blood, a few screams, some tears. Yeah, I'd say that'll tide me over until the real end of days arrives."

I glanced up, finding the others returning to me, looking worried as they eyed my expression and I was relieved to see them all there. I wanted to get them all in my truck, get back behind the Harlequin gates and keep them there until we could pin down fucking Shawn's location.

"You think you can touch us?" I hissed. "I dare you to try. Because then you'll find yourself mutilated and bleeding out at my feet." I hit speaker on the phone and they all stiffened in shock as Shawn roared a laugh.

"Those are mighty big words for a little Harlequin prince. Now listen closely, boy…"

The boys all closed ranks around Rogue and I stepped closer to my bag which was concealing my gun. Miss Mabel watched with rapt attention, her eyes wide and her hands balled into fists like she was equally ready to fight Shawn if he showed his face here.

"One of your little gang is missing," Shawn said and I looked at the others.

"Liar," I spat.

"I'm no liar. This member just so happens to be of the furry variety," Shawn said, and my heart plummeted.

"Mutt," Rogue gasped, stepping closer to me with terror in her eyes.

"What have you done with him you piece of shit?" I snarled, my muscles tightening with a violent energy.

"We're gonna play a little game," he said, ignoring my question. "When the music stops playing, the dog will go boom."

"What music, what the fuck are you talking about?" I growled then my head snapped around as music blared out of a car parked up beyond the beach. Bohemian Rhapsody by Queen echoed out and Shawn cut the call, a text coming in a second later. I opened it with my heart thrashing as Rogue took to my side and the others clustered closer to see the photo Shawn had sent. Mutt was somewhere dark with no distinguishable features around him, his small body wrapped in what looked like a fucking bomb.

"Mutt!" Rogue screamed, breaking free from our group and racing up toward that car in a panic.

I grabbed my gun and sprinted after her with the others.

"Rogue – stop!" I roared. "It could be a trap!"

She made it to the car a second before the rest of us, tearing the door open and looking inside. I made it there a beat later and Chase dragged Rogue back against his chest as Maverick and JJ searched the inside of the car.

I checked the trunk, finding it empty as well and panic tore at my heart as I hunted around us, looking for our dog.

"Mutt!" I yelled as the song played on then looked to the others. "Stay with her and someone cover Mabel," I commanded before taking off down the beach.

I made it to the beach huts, forcing the doors open one by one and checking inside as I hunted for Mutt. I couldn't let that dog die. He was a part of this family just as assuredly as the rest of us. He was Rogue's friend, and yeah he was a little shit sometimes, but dammit I still loved him.

"Mutt!" Rogue cried and I glanced back at the parking lot where she, Maverick and JJ were checking all the cars. Chase was back on the beach watching Mabel, a phone held to his ear as he no doubt called in the Harlequins for backup.

"Bark dammit," I called as I continued my hunt, but nothing came in reply.

I checked the photo on my phone again, searching for a clue, anything at all to give a hint of where he might be. But maybe this was all just a ploy. Maybe Shawn had him somewhere far away and we weren't meant to find him.

I couldn't give up though. I wouldn't.

In the corner of the screen was just a hint of rope. It wasn't much to go on, but it was green and maybe it could have been a fishing net. I set my gaze on the boats further along the shore and started running, pinning all of my hopes on this tiny possibility as I sprinted as fast as I could towards the fishing boats bobbing in the water along the dock.

It was far, almost too far to hear the music and the sand was burningly hot on my feet. But I didn't slow, not for one second because if he was there, I had to be down to the final minute of the song and I couldn't fail him. I'd failed my family far too many fucking times when I had sworn to protect them. When I'd promised to keep them safe.

"Mutt!" I bellowed, frightening some kids as they went running back to their parents.

I leapt onto the jetty, tearing along the boards and the faintest bark carried to me from somewhere up ahead.

"Keep barking!" I begged, praying he understood and maybe he did because he barked louder.

I barrelled into a guy as he stepped off of his boat, sending him flying sideways off the boards into the water with a cry. But I didn't fucking slow, racing toward that sound and leaping onto the fishing boat at the far end.

I yanked on the door to the cabin, but found it locked and my foot slammed into the centre of it a second later, the wood splintering from the impact as I broke it. I could just hear the final notes of Bohemian Rhapsody by Queen in the distance, telling me I had only seconds to save Rogue's little friend.

I stumbled into the cabin and Mutt dove at me with a bark that was all terror and I bent down, ripping through the material holding the bomb onto his body and sprinting straight back out onto the deck.

I threw it into the water as hard as I possibly could and the explosion went off at the exact same moment, a plume of water spitting up from the sea as I dropped to the floor on my ass, exhausted and breathless as the little dog jumped on me and I clutched him to my chest like the most precious of gems.

It had only been a small blast, but it would have been plenty to kill Mutt and I cursed fucking Shawn for all the good it did.

Mutt licked my face, my ears, my goddamn mouth and I collapsed down onto my back as my breaths heaved in and out of my lungs, dropping a hand onto the dog and petting him as I about died beneath him.

"Do you like me now, you little beast?" I panted and he sprang off of me, trotting to my feet and peeing on them. "Argh!"

"Mutt!" Rogue cried from somewhere close by and I scooped him up, not letting him go even when he bit every finger on my right hand. I stepped off of the boat, finding Rogue running up the jetty toward me with tears streaming down her cheeks.

"I heard the explosion and I thought – I thought-" she fell apart, colliding with me and wrapping her arms around us both as Mutt licked her face and yipped excitedly, his little tail wagging like crazy.

"It's alright," I promised her, holding her tight and watching as JJ helped the guy who'd I'd knocked into the sea climb out of the water.

When JJ started towards us, Maverick caught his shoulder, forcing him to stay at his side and I shut my eyes, resting my head on top of Rogue's as I held her and let the panic run out of my limbs.

"You saved him," she choked out and I kissed the top of her head.

"He's family," I murmured and she squeezed me tighter, crushing Mutt between us so much that he let out a fart.

"Goddammit," I laughed, stepping back and she took him into her arms, smiling up at me through her tears.

"We'll go look for him. Fox, take her and Mabel home," Maverick called to me and for once I didn't give a fuck about obeying an order from him.

I nodded and he ran off with JJ as I dropped my arm around Rogue, knowing I shouldn't but I was still on an adrenaline rush and feeling concerned as hell about how close Shawn was to us right now. And I wanted every one of them behind locked gates ASAP.

I shot a message to the Harlequins, making sure they were heading here and starting to look for any sign of that motherfucker in town. He'd lulled us into a false sense of security, but he'd just proved he was still very much a threat to us. And we needed to deal with him soon, because the next time he wanted to play with us like that, we might not win.

Harlequin House was on lockdown, several men at the front and back of the house and even more out patrolling the streets. There was zero chance of Shawn getting in here and yet I couldn't relax in the way the others had managed to. They hadn't managed to find him despite searching every corner of town and eventually Chase, JJ and Maverick had returned home, tired and defeated.

Now, they were all lazing out in the dark on the sun loungers, smoking and drinking – though I noticed Chase never touched the rum bottle being passed around and Rogue wasn't drinking much either. Mabel had retired to bed, but asked us to wake her if we caught that 'pompous hooligan' so she could 'beat him with a hat stand'.

Rogue kept looking over at me with an expression that left an imprint on my soul, and I didn't know what the hell she was thinking only that she kept biting her lip and turning away again every time I looked back.

Mutt was the centre of attention over there, being fussed and petted by all of them as he sat between Rogue's legs on the lounger. I'd given him the best meal I could cook up for him earlier and he seemed seriously pleased with himself at all the attention he was getting.

When I'd told Dad what had happened, he'd shown up at the house with a bag full of treats and spent an hour washing him in the shower before grooming him with some fancy ass products he'd bought for him. I swear the guy had never been such a sap over anything but that dog, and Mutt seemed to love him right back. He'd warmed to me a lot more since I'd saved his life too, but I still got the feeling he wasn't quite done holding his grudge against me for shouting at him that one time. One fucking time.

I stood up, slipping away into the house before the others could notice, leaving them to their night as I jogged upstairs. I knew I'd hardly get any sleep, not now I knew for sure that fucking Shawn was out there plotting against us, but I didn't wanna linger down by the pool because the others no doubt wanted time with Rogue. And as I was the reason they couldn't touch her, I figured I'd better fuck off, no matter how much it hurt to do it.

I checked my messages for the hundredth time to see if the Harlequins had had any sightings of Shawn, but there was no news. It would be a waiting game now, trying to figure out exactly where he was so we could strike against him. I despised the idea that he was still slinking around the streets of our town, infecting it like a fucking virus, but I'd cut him out eventually.

I headed into my room, pulling my shirt off and tossing it onto my bed before I walked out onto the balcony. The night air caressed my skin and I sighed as I dropped into the chair there, leaning back in it and rubbing my fingers over my eyes. While Shawn remained a threat, I was never going to relax.

I felt the absence of the others as I sat there alone, wondering if it was always going to feel this shit or if one day I'd get used to the pain. I'd weathered it before, I supposed. Ten years without Rogue had been an agony of a different kind, but this was its own brand of hell and I had to find a way to get accustomed to it if it was ever going to work long term. The problem was, some part of me was still fighting it. Every time we got too close, I lost all rational though, started giving in to the urge to touch her, just fucking feel her. And I had to stop letting that happen because it was only going to make it harder in the long run. Boundaries had to be set and not crossed, lines had to be drawn.

"Fox? Can I join you?" Rogue stepped out onto the balcony looking like every wish I'd ever made, and I nodded before I even knew what I was doing.

Great, well done asshole. Nice boundaries. Real effective.

It was nearly impossible to deny her anything she wanted, especially when I knew what she'd been through all these years. She deserved every good thing on this earth to be hand delivered to her, but I wasn't the guy who should have been the courier. Still…here I was letting her in, letting her get close enough to pull on every chord in my heart.

There wasn't another seat out here and I was about to get up to go and fetch one when she dropped onto my lap and gripped my face in her hands.

"Rogue," I said in a lame protest as she leaned closer, a hundred really convincing reasons to give in shining in her eyes.

"Fox," she breathed then her mouth was on mine and I was a weak,

weak fucking man because I couldn't resist the heat of her tongue and the sweetness of her lips.

I yanked her against me, traitor to every declaration I'd made as I surrendered to this honied sin, wanting more, needing fucking more. I kissed her in the dark and pretended it didn't matter for a stolen moment as I drowned in the girl I craved with every fibre of my flesh.

"You've been drinking," I said, breaking the kiss in the same moment as my heart tried to burrow its way out of my chest.

"Not much," she insisted, her eyes blazing as she closed the distance between us again and my hands slid under her top at the back, dragging up her burningly hot flesh and making her shiver with need.

Oh god, how am I supposed to resist her?

Stop, you idiot.

I couldn't stop. I was in a dreamland where all I'd ever wanted was coming true and I couldn't resist taking a taste of it.

Her tongue chased mine and she moved to straddle me, her pussy grinding over my cock so I was hard within seconds.

"We can't," I groaned, my fingers sliding up her back, finding her without a bra. What was it with her and never wearing underwear? I swear it was a fucking trap designed to capture me with the knowledge that so little divided me from the sweetest of oblivions at all times.

Knowing how exposed she was beneath this material made the tip of my cock throb and all I wanted to do was give into my instincts and claim her, take a bite of this apple and let myself gorge for one fucking night even if I wasn't able to offer her more than that. Because she wanted this, wanted me and I wasn't sure how I was supposed to resist that when it was all I'd ever hoped for.

"We can," she breathed.

Fuck, maybe we can.

I slid my hand around to her breast, skimming my thumb over her hard nipple and she gasped, biting down on my lower lip.

"You drive me crazy, Fox Harlequin," she growled, her fingernails biting into my shoulders. "Every day I can't have you I get closer to being committed. And today you saved my dog and God that gets me so wet for you, you have no fucking idea."

"Technically I saved him twice," I revealed and she pulled back.

"What? When?" she demanded.

"Some Damned Man tried to shoot him on Dead Man's Isle. I drowned him in Maverick's swimming pool."

She moaned like a pornstar, kissing me again and tearing at my body like she wanted to climb inside it. "Why are you fighting this?"

"You know why," I hissed, my anger spiking and when I dragged my thumb over her peaked nipple again, I did it with force, making her nails dig deeper into my shoulders.

"Hasn't anything changed? Can't you see we're meant to be together?" she pushed, the ache in her for that to be the truth so fucking clear to me that it rang like the chime of a bell.

"That's a collective we." I leaned forward, biting her neck and making it hurt, but she arched her back like she enjoyed it, her hips rolling as she ground herself over the length of my solid cock again. I may have had a lot of willpower, but it was being whittled away right now, leaving nothing but goddamn sawdust in its wake.

"Yeah, it is," she said firmly. "Get with the fucking programme."

"Fuck you." I tugged her earlobe between my teeth, raking my fingers down her sides and stopping her hips from rocking in that torturous way. "Maybe you're just fucking greedy, did you ever think of that?"

"Why are you so angry, Badger?" she asked, sliding her hands up to fist in my hair. "Is it because you're not man enough to share?"

"You little brat," I growled, but the words came out full of sex and I didn't stop her when her mouth fell on mine again. She was too delicious and I was losing this fight as surely as the sun lost its fight with the horizon every night.

Her hands dropped from my hair to my shoulders, my chest, one hand pressing me back into my seat while the other reached lower. As she scooted backwards on my lap and gripped my cock through my pants, the last of my willpower fell away and I picked her up by her ass, sinking my tongue between her lips and carrying her into my room. I was a selfish fucking asshole. I knew I couldn't be what she needed, I knew tomorrow I'd regret pretending I could, but I'd never regret this. I was consumed by her, this girl born of the ocean, the perfect embodiment of every desire I'd ever had.

I laid her on my bed, crushing her to it as I gripped her thighs and tugged her flush to my body, showing her how hard she made me. She said my name like it held everything she had ever wanted within it, and some foolish part of me pretended that was truly the case because I wanted to believe it so bad. But then a creak sounded beyond my door and I jerked around, snapped out of the daydream I'd been buying into, my thoughts scattering.

"Chase you idiot," JJ hissed and the shadows under the door told me exactly what was going on.

I shoved myself up, pulling Rogue after me as rage simmered in my veins and heat bled up the back of my neck, feeling like a complete fucking idiot. This was all just a game to them, some fucking dare they wanted fulfilled for fuck knew what reason. But I wasn't fucking playing.

I ripped the door open, finding JJ, Chase and Maverick there looking guilty as hell and I pushed Rogue into their arms, the loss of contact with her body stinging like a burn as I was left adrift without it. Without her. Because she was theirs and that meant she couldn't be mine.

She turned, staring back at me in alarm.

"Fox," she tried, but I cut her off.

"Enjoy the rest of your night," I said, my tone flat as I kept any emotion out of it, not letting them see the pain I was in over this. "I didn't mean to steal her from you. And if you dared her to come up here or some shit, I'd rather you didn't in future, yeah?"

"There was no dare," Rogue insisted, her eyes blazing, but I didn't really know what to believe. Why were they all clustered around my door like giggling teenagers if this wasn't some game to them?

"Fox, that's not why we were-" JJ started, but Maverick slung an arm over Rogue's shoulders and spoke over him.

"Night, Foxy boy. Thanks for returning her to where she belongs."

"Don't be an asshole, Rick," she hissed, shrugging him off and trying to catch my eye again.

"Goodnight." I shut the door and locked it, standing there for what felt like an eternity as they stood on the other side of it.

"Come on, beautiful, he doesn't wanna play with us," Maverick said.

Those words fucking hurt more than he could have known, because I knew that was all she really hungered for and I'd promised her I'd provide it. Someone to play with, to bring her light and joy and fun. Yet here I was, closing the door in her face and breaking some of the pieces which had begun to heal between the two of us once more. I wasn't mad at them, or even her. She'd told me straight how she felt about me so it wasn't like I could deny that, but none of that changed anything.

I swear I heard Chase sigh and JJ muttered something dejectedly, then they left. And I kept standing there, resting my forehead to the door as I missed being a kid, missed the days it had been simple, but most of all I just fucking missed *them*.

ROGUE

CHAPTER THIRTY EIGHT

The next day Fox was back to acting like nothing had happened between us and I was left with whiplash intense enough to have left me reeling. He was up early, waiting to surf with me like he had been every day since that first time and even his smiles seemed genuine enough while we rode the waves together out the back of Harlequin House, but when I'd tried to speak to him about last night he'd just dived beneath the water as if he hadn't heard me and swum back out to catch another wave.

He'd then proceeded to make us all a feast for lunch and had spent the rest of the day talking Crew business and plans for Shawn with his dad and a bunch of the other gang members. I'd sat in on some of it, using my newly acquired gang status to get myself the invite, but in all honesty, I'd found it dull as hell. There was a lot of blustering and big talk about all the things those violent men would do to Shawn if they caught him and not a whole lot of great ideas that seemed likely to actually work.

My suggestion had been slammed down by both Fox and Rick, but I still stood by it. Shawn wanted me for his sick games and I would have been willing to play bait for him. But one look at the fury and fear in their eyes over my suggestion had made me back down on that one. Not that that had stopped

Chase and JJ from sticking to me like glue ever since I'd ditched the meeting.

I was pretty sure they'd been tipped off about my idea and even though I'd assured them that I wouldn't do anything without their agreement, they seemed disinclined to trust me. I kinda wanted to be pissed over that, but I guessed we all had a bit more work to do on the trust between us yet.

Not that I minded having the two of them sticking close to me all afternoon while we swam in the pool and I sunbathed butt naked, giving the two of them anxiety over the possibility of some random gang douchebag spotting me while he left the basement for a pee break.

Miss Mabel seemed to be living her best life amongst us too, happily barking out orders to the boys for more drinks and adjustments to her parasol while Mutt kept her company in the shade. She was also totally V blocking me by hanging out with us, but I was okay with that. I was just so freaking happy to have her here, away from that damn basement and in the company of people who loved her.

By the time the Harlequins emerged again, I was dressed once more and the sun had sunk beyond the sea.

JJ had taken it upon himself to lay out a feast made up of various dishes Fox had created over the last few days alongside a salad which he'd even made himself.

I took a seat between Chase and JJ on the patio while Miss Mabel sat at the head of the table, pointing out the things she wanted on her plate.

"Pass me some of that bean thing," she commanded Chase who leaned forward to heap it onto a spoon. "No, not that one! The other bean thing," she cried and he quickly grabbed a spoon of the next dish along which was made with pomegranate seeds and didn't have a bean in sight. She kept going in that vein, scalding him constantly and catching my eye across the table to wink at me as he worked to keep his patience over the task.

JJ dropped his hand onto my thigh beneath the table as she continued to boss Chase around and he tugged my legs apart so that his fingers could slip between my thighs, his thumb scoring a line along the bottom of my shorts and making me shiver.

"Don't forget that you've been a bad girl, Rogue," he murmured in my ear, making the hairs prickle along the back of my neck.

"What?" I asked, my heart thumping a little harder at the dark tone to his words.

"You know what. You snuck off again, you went to the salon and shopping and got yourself some nice new ink, but you did it all alone and wouldn't tell us where you were. Don't go thinking we've forgotten about that."

I swallowed thickly because I had kinda assumed they'd forgotten about that. I'd passed out drunk that night and after the whole Mutt drama with Shawn I'd just moved on from it. But apparently I was the only one.

"So what does that mean?" I asked in a low voice, glancing up at him from beneath my lashes and he smirked down at me with a devilish secret in his honey brown eyes.

"You'll see," he promised, withdrawing his hand and making himself a plate of food while I was left with heat burning in my core from his touch and anticipation of the unknown making me.

Fox, Rick and Luther appeared as Chase finally finished piling Miss Mabel's plate to her satisfaction and she leaned back in her seat muttering about her never being able to finish all of the food he'd given her because she was just a little old woman.

Chase grinned at me, rolling his eyes at her as she dug in and I grinned back.

"Did you decide anything?" I asked as Rick, Fox and Luther sat down to join us, each of them looking tired from the gang politics shit they'd spent the day engaged in.

"You'd already know the answer to that, wildcat, if you had ever come back from that pee break you took after the first fifteen minutes," Luther said, spearing a potato on his fork before demolishing it.

"It was longer than fifteen minutes," I protested.

"It was more like ten," Fox disagreed and I laughed.

"Well, maybe you should spice up your meetings if you don't want members to ditch on them. We could have some dancing, snacks, maybe a little midway stop for some karaoke-"

"This is why I never let a woman in the Crew before," Luther teased and I scoffed.

"Because you suck at karaoke? Boo. I'll have to teach you some vocal tricks. You just need to pick the right song, something dark and gravelly for you. Like some Johnny Cash or-"

"The day you get the old man singing karaoke will be the best day of my fucking life," Rick laughed and I grinned at the challenge.

"Yeah, that's seriously unlikely, wildcat. Maybe go bark up another tree for someone to fulfil that little daydream," Luther agreed and I sighed in disappointment.

"So are you gonna tell us the plan then or is it 'Crew business?'" I pushed and both Chase and JJ shifted a little uncomfortably either side of me. I guessed it was a bit awkward for them to be sitting here as outcasts from the Harlequins cool kid gang, but I personally believed we'd had a much better afternoon than they had anyway so I gave no shits.

Fox glanced between his two best friends who he had banished from the gang then shrugged as he seemed to decide that they could be trusted with the diabolical plans that had taken an entire day to create.

"The Crew are gonna sweep the streets again and we've come up with a couple more places to check out tonight. Me and Dad will go after this. We aren't too hopeful, but we figure it's better to keep our presence up on the streets to make it as difficult as possible for that rat to scurry around them. Shawn clearly isn't done yet, so we all need to be ready for anything at all times."

We all agreed to that easily enough, but I had to say that it sounded like they'd spent an entire fucking day locked up in a basement only to come up with a plan that involved doing the exact same thing that they'd been doing since Shawn disappeared.

Chase and JJ took more interest in the plans than me and I zoned out a bit as I ate my meal, not really paying attention as they all talked strategies around me. It seemed to me like everything they were planning to do was pretty pointless anyway. Shawn was smart and as slippery as a damn snake in the grass. He wouldn't be showing his face again until he was good and ready. So that meant I was now keeping a gun close by at all times and just playing this damn waiting game while drinking in the time I got to spend with my boys.

The shiny new phone that Saint had bought me buzzed on the table and

I reached out to pick it up, expecting a message from one of my friends but finding one from Rick instead.

Rick:

You look tired, baby girl. I hope your stamina isn't lacking tonight.

I hid a smirk as I read the words then looked up at him across the table and shrugged before replying.

Rogue:

I'm pretty beat actually. I'll probably head to bed first.

Rick:

Nah. I don't think so, beautiful. You've got amends to make.

My bare toes curled against the cold tiles and my pulse got all kinds of jumpy at the dark look Maverick was giving me across the table.

Rick:

Oatmeal.

Rogue:

What?

Rick:

That's your safe word. If you can't take it or don't like it then that's your out.
Got it?

I looked up at him, wondering what the fuck he meant by that but the way his jaw was gritted and his fist remained clenched on top of the table made it clear he wasn't going to give me any further information than that so I just nodded like a good girl and shot him back one last reply.

Rogue:

Yes, Daddy

Maverick gave me a filthy fucking look over the table and Chase shifted beside me so that his thigh rubbed against mine and I glanced at him as the corner of his mouth lifted, letting me know he was in on this too. Shit. Would I really be able to handle all three of them if they seriously wanted to punish me the way they were implying? Because any one of them at their worst was a damn lot to handle, but all three?

My attention moved to Fox as I felt his eyes on me, my skin heating at the memory of his body pressing me down into his bed last night and confusion filling me as I tried to figure out why he was so intent on fighting our happiness.

When we all finished our meals, Fox and Luther said their goodbyes and headed for the door while Chase and JJ started clearing up.

Rick played at being a gent and escorted Miss Mabel back to her room and I hurried after Fox as he headed towards the door to the garage.

Luther spotted me coming and nudged Fox to make him wait for me at the top of the stairs before nodding in goodbye and heading down them himself.

"Hey…" I began awkwardly as Fox held himself still, his gaze roaming over me. "Just, be careful out there, okay? I can't lose you again, Fox."

Some of the rigidity in Fox's posture fell away and he stepped closer, pulling me into a hug with a sigh.

"Don't worry about me, hummingbird," he murmured. "I'm fucking bombproof."

I breathed a laugh and he released me, offering me a genuine smile before he headed down the stairs and out into the night.

I closed the door and locked it behind him to keep the house more secure and by the time I made it back to the kitchen, the others had finished tidying up. Silence fell at my arrival, a heavy kind of weight settling in the air as I looked between Chase and Johnny James.

Chase's gaze burned into me and I focused on him, shifting from foot to foot as I looked up at him.

"What?" I asked curiously and JJ gave him a nod before muttering something about checking up on Rick and Mabel and heading out of the room.

Chase moved closer and I stepped into him, my hands sliding around his waist as I looked up at him, smiling as he wore his scars proudly. He'd been doing that more often than not in the house now and I fucking loved it.

"Look," he said slowly. "Tonight Rick and J have come up with this plan to punish you for running out on us the other day…"

"I know," I said, unable to keep the lust from my voice as I tried to figure out what the hell they were planning.

"But I told you I wanted to prove to you how I feel before we-"

I tiptoed up and kissed him hard, showing him how much I wanted him with that kiss and moaning as he instantly met my passion with his own.

I grazed his tongue with mine, reaching between us and unbuttoning the front of my shorts before taking his hand and guiding it beneath my waistband.

"Do I feel like I'm not ready for you, Ace?" I asked breathlessly and he groaned as he pushed his hand lower, his fingers finding me soaked for him as he pushed my panties aside and sank two of them into me without hesitation.

"No starting the party without all of us," Rick barked and I flinched as I found him and JJ standing in the kitchen doorway, watching the two of us together.

Chase reluctantly withdrew his hand from my shorts and I whimpered with need as Maverick strode towards us. He reached for me and I turned to him, expecting a kiss or a fist in my hair or something other than him buttoning my fly and scowling at me.

"When you say all of us," Chase began slowly, his gaze moving from me to Rick then JJ as he took a step closer to us. "What does that look like to you, little one?"

I licked my lips, my gaze travelling to Maverick in front of me and JJ to my left as they all just stared right back, silent, waiting.

"I've been in love with all of you since before I understood the meaning of the word," I said as I looked between three of the men my boys had grown into. "And I could no sooner pick between you than pick between the stars in the sky. You already have my heart and I've given each of you my body too. So if you're asking me what I want then it's more of that. All of that. All of you. Together." I bit my lip as Maverick chuckled darkly and Chase and JJ exchanged a heated look.

JJ was the first to say something, his eyes slipping from his brothers' faces to mine as he released a deep breath and took a step towards me. "None of us have been happy since the moment we first lost you, pretty girl. We haven't been whole and we haven't really been together either. Not fully. Because we weren't fully here. We were empty without you and I for one want to see all of the people I love happy. So if that means we all share you then that makes perfect fucking sense to me. I love the way you look when you're with them, pretty girl, I love the light in your eyes and the fire in your soul. I want to fill you up with so much happiness that you can't take it and that means I wanna fulfil all of your fantasies too. So I can handle it - I guess the only question is whether or not you fuckers can." He aimed that last part at Rick and Chase and my heart raced as I realised this wasn't a game anymore. It wasn't a what if or a fantasy. This was about to get a whole lot more real and I was going to have to figure out first hand what it was like to own all of these men at once.

Chase was already nodding, his lust filled gaze moving between me and JJ like he was waiting for something else to happen but the distance between us remained there, unbridged like the final divide between us and the decision it felt like we were all waiting on.

"Good," Maverick said, the cruel smile turning his lips up. "So now we all know where we stand and pretty little Rogue Easton knows her safe word, don't you?"

"Oatmeal," I breathed, my body throbbing with expectation as I looked between the three of them, wondering how we were going to start this.

"Okay then. I think it's time you went to bed." Rick caught my arm and whirled me around towards the stairs.

Mutt barked in a half-hearted kind of way then just scampered along beside us as we went.

I gasped in surprise, but didn't fight him as he tugged me up them and led me to the room I shared with him.

When we made it into the bedroom, Maverick leaned in close like he was going to kiss me but he paused just sort of tasting my lips, speaking in a deadly tone instead.

"Bad girls don't get to call the shots, beautiful. So go to sleep and think about what you did to deserve this punishment – and don't even think about touching yourself either. Because if you come without my express permission tonight, you'll pay for it."

My lips popped open and I glanced over his shoulder to where Chase and JJ stood in the doorway, but they both held equally fiendish expressions on their faces and when Rick stepped back and closed the door between us I was left gaping at it in shock.

The lock sounded a moment later and I cursed. "What the fuck?"

"Get some rest, pretty girl," JJ called back, sounding altogether too amused. "You'll need your energy later."

I didn't know what the fuck that was supposed to mean but I didn't exactly have much choice in it either.

"Fucking men," I grumbled, heading away from the door and stripping off as I took myself for a shower. Mutt just ignored my strop and curled himself up on the chair Fox liked to sit in when he watched me sleep.

By the time my shower was over and I was dressed in a pair of soft shorts and one of Rick's tanks, I was left with no other choice but to climb into my bed and switch out the fucking lights.

The house was quiet and as I closed my eyes, I was left with an ache between my thighs and a seriously pissed off vibe that followed me into sleep.

And as I drifted away, I was thrown into our past, to another night where the sound of a storm howling had pressed in all around us when we'd been hanging out inside the summer house at Rosewood Manor.

"You have to pick a team, Rogue," Fox urged, his grin saying he already thought he knew what I'd choose and that it would be him. *Cocky asshole.*

"Yeah, come on, tell us who your favourite is - and make sure you don't forget which one of us bought you that cotton candy earlier," Rick added, *elbowing Fox and earning himself a shove right back.*

"You stole that cotton candy," JJ protested. *"And you made that kid cry."*

"That was a dick move," I agreed, *though I'd still eaten it happily enough.*

"Pick me and I'll take you for a ride on my bike at sunrise again,"

Chase offered, his cheeks colouring a little as the others all started cussing him out and accusing him of trying to take me on a date while he protested his innocence.

"Enough!" I snapped, making them shut up at last as they all looked back to me. "I've got a new idea - let's just be on one team and go find some other kids to beat. I'm not picking anyway."

All four of them protested, pushing and shoving each other while I rolled my eyes and turned towards the door. We were going to end up drenched if we went out in that storm, but it had been a hot day and I didn't mind a little rain on my skin.

"I'm going, with or without you," I called and their arguments fell away in favour of them all rushing to follow me out into the rain.

We ran down the lawn together, whooping and screaming while the storm drenched us and by the time we remembered that we'd been heading out to find some other kids to join in our games, we'd already changed our minds. We didn't want anybody else anyway. Never had. Never would. It was the five of us or nothing and that would be the case until the day I fucking died.

A hand pressed down on my mouth, silencing my scream as I jerked awake, finding a huge guy leaning over me with a black ski mask covering his face and the shadows of the dark room shrouding his eyes.

Panic gripped me and I thrashed against his hold as I tried to lurch towards the nightstand where I kept my gun, but another set of hands grasped my wrist and stopped me, my gaze swivelling to take in a second huge shadow, his face covered like the first.

I screamed louder, trying to bite the hand that still pressed to my mouth and kicking at him as I fought to get free.

I was wrenched off of the bed, the second man securing a leather cuff to my wrist before I was tugged into the arms of the man who had woken me.

I kicked and fought and as the hand released my mouth, I started to scream just before a black hood was yanked down over my head and I was tossed over someone's shoulder.

I kept kicking and fighting as I was carried out of my room, fear finding me as I wondered why the hell Mutt hadn't been barking or coming to my rescue.

Someone grabbed the cuff which was hanging from my right wrist and managed to catch my left hand before securing them together.

I screamed louder but there was no sign of any of my boys coming for me as we headed down the stairs and out into the cool night air and fear filled me as I tried to figure out where the hell they could be.

I was dropped on my ass on something cold and hard and the next thing I knew the sound of a van door closing filled my ears.

The engine rumbled to life and I shoved myself to my feet, struggling to try and rip the hood from my head with my bound hands as I scrambled towards where I assumed the door was.

But before I could reach it, the van pulled away and I fell backwards at the motion, unable to steady myself with my cuffed hands and falling back onto my ass hard.

The van swerved violently from side to side as we drove on, making it impossible for me to get to my feet again as I was forced to concentrate on holding myself as still as I could while ending up rolling back and forth time and again.

I lost count of how long the vehicle had been moving by the time it screeched to a halt, but it hadn't been too long. Which meant I had to still be near enough to my boys for them to find me. If they were okay. Because why the hell hadn't they come when I was screaming if they were still alive?

A choked sob escaped me at the thought of something happening to any of them and as the van door was yanked open again, a scream of fright escaped me.

There were lights on wherever they'd taken me, just enough of it showing through the black hood for me to tell I was inside somewhere and to see the silhouette of the hulking figure that was closing in on me.

I waited for him to get close enough to strike at then kicked him as hard as I could, aiming for his fucking balls.

A grunted curse escaped him as he managed to shift just enough that my foot collided with his thigh instead, the rough scratch of denim against my bare foot telling me he was wearing a pair of jeans.

Then his hands were on me again, his grip tight around my ankles as he dragged me out of the van and I screamed like a banshee.

The second asshole grabbed my bound wrists as I made it to the edge of the van and they carried me between them, swinging me from side to side like their entire goal was to disorient me.

I called them all the best curses I could think up, promising them their death at my hands when I got free as they carried me wherever the fuck they were taking me.

The combination of them swinging me about and me fighting like an alley cat caught in a net meant that it was almost impossible for me to figure out where they were taking me before they finally came to a halt.

A third guy grabbed my waist and shoved me face first down onto a cold, wooden surface, my toes barely brushing the floor as he bent me down over it.

I fought harder as he held me there, fear and adrenaline crashing through me as another one of them caught my bound wrists and secured them to something in front of me, stopping me from straightening and making me scream even louder.

The kiss of a blade touched to my spine and I froze as it moved down the length of my back, cutting through the clothes I wore before yet another set of hands ripped the remains of the fabric from my body, leaving me naked beneath them.

"Stop," I begged as hands gripped my ass and the unmistakeable feeling of a hard dick ground against me through a barrier of denim.

I was blind within the hood, completely at the mercy of these men as they held me down and kept me chained and I knew my pleas would fall on deaf ears, but as tears began to burn the back of my eyes, a mouth pressed to my ear.

"Do you remember the safe word, beautiful?" Maverick growled and my adrenaline ratcheted up as I realised who the fuck had kidnapped me.

"You assholes!" I screamed, my fear overtaking me as I bucked against the table I was bent over and the man behind me continued to hold me in place. It had to be Chase or Johnny James but they weren't giving me any damn clues.

"Do you remember?" Rick snapped in a demand and I gasped as the guy behind me rolled his zipper down and pressed his bare cock against my core instead.

A whimper built on my lips as the fear and adrenaline shifted into a dark and deadly thing. A thing I wanted more than I should have. A punishment I craved more than I'd even realised until this moment and as I gave in to the idea that I hadn't truly been kidnapped and that these were my monsters toying with me, my pussy pulsed with need and I panted as I felt myself growing wet for them.

"I remember," I confirmed and when I didn't say anything else, the guy behind me drove his cock straight into me.

I cried out, my hips crashing against the edge of the table as he slammed into me again, the thrill of not knowing who was fucking me and not being able to see a damn thing making my pussy so wet that I could already feel my body tensing in anticipation of the pleasure they were going to deliver to me.

Another set of hands moved down my spine, trailing something cold and smooth down my skin while I was fucked so hard I saw freaking stars, my tits chafing against the table beneath me in the most delicious way as I was forced to bend to the will of these demons of mine.

The guy fucking me gripped my ass cheeks in his hands as he leaned back and suddenly the cold thing was pressing against my ass, lube running between my cheeks while his thick cock kept slamming into me with a merciless pace.

As the butt plug was pushed inside me I moaned, my pussy clamping around the cock that was fucking me so brutally and the moment it was fully seated within me, I came.

JJ swore behind me, confirming that he was the one fucking me as he dove his cock in one last time and came too, his cum filling me as I pulsed around his length and screamed from the pleasure he'd delivered to me.

"Get on with it, Johnny James, some of us are fucking waiting here," Maverick snapped as JJ remained inside me for a few more seconds and a hand cracked down on my ass cheek which I knew just had to be his.

"Fuck you," JJ muttered before pulling his dick out of me and leaving me prostrated there before them with my ass pointed at them and the toy still very much inside me.

"We're gonna run a train on you, beautiful," Maverick growled, fisting my ass cheek and making me whimper. "And when we've all fucked you raw and marked you as ours, I hope you'll remember who you belong to. Who you fucking belong *with*. And you won't ever go running off on us again."

"Yes, boss," I panted, my body trembling as I remained in the dark, unable to see any of them as they moved behind me.

And as rough hands stroked down my spine, I expected Rick to take me next, but it was Chase's lust filled voice I heard as he sank his cock into my soaking heat.

"Our girl," he growled possessively, his hands moving down the angel wings which lined my spine while he kept his dick buried in me and I lay whimpering at his mercy.

"Yes," I agreed, my fingers flexing while the cuffs still held my hands in front of me.

"No going back now."

Chase didn't let me reply to that as he started moving, fucking me with deep, hard thrusts which slammed my hips against the edge of the table so hard that it hurt. But it was the best kind of pain.

"Fuck, I don't think I could ever get enough of this," Chase breathed against my neck as he leaned over me and his hands roamed down my body, pushing beneath me so that he could tug on my nipples and deliver even more pleasure to me.

"I love you, Ace," I moaned, turning my head to try and look back at him through the darkness of the hood, this scarred and fractured man who I burned for so fucking much. I'd been in love with all of them for as long as I could remember and doing this with them, being with them all like this felt as natural as fucking breathing. This was what we'd all be born for. Me and them. All in.

He drove his hips forward harder and I cried out as his cock filled me, the thickness of him stretching my pussy and feeling like fucking heaven inside me.

Chase claimed me roughly, his grip possessive and his whole posture dominating as he reared over me. This wasn't like the first time where we'd both been admitting what we felt for each other and working through all of the shit we'd done to one another. No, this was different. This was him showing me he fucking owned me and as I fought to keep pace with the punishing thrusts of his hips, I knew he was right. I was his. And I wouldn't have wanted it any other way.

Chase gripped me hard and fucked me harder, his dick slamming into me over and over again until he was growling his release and his hot cum was filling me alongside JJ's. It was so fucking dirty and so fucking right all at once, and as his weight pressed down on me and I turned my attention to Maverick next, I knew I wouldn't feel complete until I'd felt him taking ownership of me like this too.

Rick's footsteps stalked towards us, and the heavy thump of them telling me he was ready to rip Chase clean off of me unless he got out of the way fast which luckily he did.

The hood was suddenly yanked from my head and I blinked as a fountain of rainbow curls tumbled down to fall around my face. We were in the fucking basement of Harlequin House, and I cursed as I realised that they must have just driven around the block in that damn van to freak me out.

Maverick moved to stand behind me as I remained lying on the top of the desk at their mercy, his heated gaze drinking in the sight of my naked body as his fingertips slid onto the backs of my knees and he pushed my thighs wider.

I licked my lips as I looked around at him, watching the way his gaze fixed on the mess of cum which was currently running down the insides of my thighs while my heart raced furiously and the urge to snap my legs shut filled me like some dumb sense of modesty rearing its ugly head.

But I wasn't modest. I knew what I wanted now and I wasn't going to be making any dumb attempts at covering that up or trying to apologise for it. So I let him look and I turned as far as I could manage with my hands tied so that I could watch him more closely.

"Are you satisfied now, Rick?" I asked him, wetting my lips as I looked at his dark eyes through the ski mask that he still wore. All three of them were shirtless, wearing nothing but their jeans and the masks like a pack of fucking psychos and I had to admit I was seriously here for it. "Do you like what you see?"

"Oh beautiful," he murmured in a low tone which sent a shiver down my spine as he shifted one tattooed hand from the back of my knee and ran it up the inside of my thigh until his fingers were sliding through the cum the others had left there. "I don't know if you're insane or deluded to be agreeing to this. But either way, you're the property of heathens now." He pushed two fingers into me so suddenly that I gasped and his smile darkened as fucked me with his hand, smearing Chase and JJ's cum over my clit and using it as lube while he teased me. "And I hope you understand that we won't ever let you go. This right here, is just the warmup."

"I understand," I gasped as his skilful fingers fucked me harder and my pussy throbbed around them. I was so close to coming again that it was hard for me to say even that much, but the moment the word left my lips, the asshole tugged his hand away and left me fucking reeling.

"Good." Rick grabbed my hips and released his dick so suddenly that I barely even knew what was happening before his hand cracked down on my ass cheek and his cock slammed into me.

I cried out, trying to brace myself against the top of the desk as my tiptoes barely even reached the ground with my thighs widened with the way he'd positioned them while he started fucking me so hard that I could do little more than just take it.

His dick was so fucking big that it was making me see stars and despite how many orgasms I'd already been gifted tonight, my greedy pussy was clamping tight around his length and begging for more.

Chase and JJ moved to stand in front of me, watching us from the other side of the desk with heated expressions that burned me through the eyes of the masks they still wore.

"You're so fucking stunning, pretty girl," JJ praised, reaching out to push some rainbow hair from my face and pushing his thumb into my mouth so that I could bite down on it. "You were made for taking our cocks, weren't you? Look how fucking much you love it."

I moaned loudly as Maverick continued to pound into me mercilessly and I managed to gasp a "Yes," which earned me another, harder spanking and had my pussy fucking spasming around Rick's length.

"We're going to make you come so many times you lose your damn mind," Chase added, licking his lips as he watched us. "Do you want that?"

"Yes," I panted again and I could see how much they loved it every time I agreed with them.

"Have you been dreaming about us doing this to you, pretty girl?" JJ added.

"Yes," I agreed. "So many times. I've wanted this for so fucking long," I gasped, and Maverick chuckled darkly as I swear he actually found a way to fuck me even harder.

"Do you want Maverick to fill your tight cunt with his cum like we did?" Chase asked me, his hand fisting his cock through his jeans and letting me know that he wanted even more of this.

"Yes," I agreed, begging now because I wasn't sure how much more I could take. "Please, Rick."

"Look at me then, beautiful." Maverick fisted a hand in my hair and twisted my neck so that I was looking back at him over my shoulder, the sight of his powerful, tattooed body slamming into mine enough to make me whimper as my pussy throbbed and tightened. "You like that?" Rick taunted.

"Yes. Fuck me harder, Rick, make me come," I demanded and with a bestial snarl, he slammed his dick into me so hard that I instantly fell apart for him.

My pussy gripped him like a vice as I screamed my release to the whole room and with a few more savage pumps of his cock inside me, Maverick came too, his cum filling me like I'd wanted and every bit of tension falling from my body as I collapsed beneath him on the desk.

Rick took hold of the butt plug and tugged it out of me just as the waves of pleasure began to fade, chuckling as I trembled beneath him and he tossed it aside, slowly taking his cock back out of me.

JJ knelt down to release my hands from the leather cuffs that were keeping me locked in that position and as I met his gaze, he leaned in closer to speak to me.

"The things you said in the message you left us, pretty girl," he began slowly, his honey brown eyes roaming over my face with an ache in them which made my whole body quake in anticipation. "You said I was a pathetic, lovesick boy-"

"JJ, I'm sorry, I know what I said in that video was awful and I hated myself for every moment I spoke those words. It's haunted me knowing how much I hurt all of you, but I was just trying to-"

"I don't need more apologies from you, Rogue. I'm just trying to say that it hurt because it was true," he interrupted, shifting forward and cupping my face in his hand gently, his thumb tracking over my lips and silencing me. "I have always been pathetically, hopelessly in love with you. I've been

567

dreaming of this mouth every night since I was about twelve years old. Always aching for a kiss I never truly believed I could earn. So instead of daring to try and kiss these lips, I concentrated on making them smile for me. I wanted your eyes to see only the sunniest of days, for your body to feel the rush of riding a wave just as often as you could, for your heart to pound with the exhilaration of the adventures we all had together so that it could match the way mine pounded with the exhilaration of simply being near you."

He leaned in to kiss me as he removed the cuffs from my hands, my lips claiming his as the fabric of the mask he still wore brushed against my skin. I was high on the rush of adrenaline that acting out this dark fantasy gave me and it filled my body with an impossible need for more.

I pulled back reluctantly, pushing myself up to stand with my heart so full of the joy of being surrounded by my boys again that I felt dizzy with it. Though as I looked between Rick and Chase, I couldn't help but feel a pang of longing for the member of our group who wasn't here.

But as my mind turned to Fox and I wondered where he was tonight, JJ dropped his mouth to my neck and coaxed a moan from my lips.

His hands moved to my waist and he backed me up until the backs of my knees hit the couch which stood to the side of the basement. He pushed me down to sit on it and parted my thighs as his mouth claimed mine once more, his hand dragging against my wetness and making me moan for him as the others closed in behind him. I half wanted to tell them to take their fucking masks off, but there was something about them wearing them that had my heart racing and the thrill of what we were all doing together seem all the more forbidden. But I was done being ashamed of wanting this, of loving it. Shawn might have enjoyed making me feel like a whore, but he was wrong. That wasn't what this was. This was dirty and carnal and so fucking raw that it made me ache, but it was love and worship and the purest of pleasure too. Far beyond anything he could ever understand.

"No more sneaking off, pretty girl," JJ growled against my lips as he dropped his jeans, his cock hard already and letting me know that we were in no way done yet. "No more self-sacrificing either. This is it now. Promise us."

"I promise," I gasped as he pushed me down onto my back and his cock drove into me as he kissed me again, his hips rolling as he took his sweet time filling and stretching me to accommodate every last inch of him.

I wound my legs around his waist and kept kissing him as he gripped my ass and took control of our movements, his hips flexing in a slow and delicious rhythm that had my body buzzing and my fingernails digging into the back of his neck as I clung on.

JJ continued to roll his hips as he fucked me, this incredible friction building between us as he ground against my clit with every move and my spine arched, my shoulders pressing into the couch cushions so that I could feel even more of it.

His tongue dominated my mouth, making my lips ache with the intensity of his kisses as he fucked me harder, his fingers biting into my ass and groans of pleasure escaping him.

JJ flipped us over so suddenly that I had to brace myself on his chest as I found my balance riding him, my tits bouncing as he fucked me from below, his movements slow and building as he drank in the sight of me on top of him.

I could feel Maverick and Chase watching us and as I turned my head and found the pure fucking lust in their eyes as they soaked in the sight of my body being owned by another man, I couldn't help but moan louder. My cries of pleasure practically echoed in the space as I pawed at my tits, tugging on my nipples to take even more pleasure from my flesh.

I should have been exhausted from the first round these boys had taken with me, but I wasn't. I was like this pure wanton creature, built for sex and utterly insatiable and as I looked to Chase and Rick, I knew I wanted more.

"Fuck me together," I begged and JJ cursed beneath me as I rode his cock harder, my hand dropping to my clit as I began to massage it and claim even more pleasure for myself.

Rick grinned, his salacious gaze drinking me in as he picked up the bottle of lube that had been left on the desk and tossed it to Chase.

"I wanna watch you fuck her tight ass while she chokes on my cock, Ace," he said, his gaze staying fixed on me as Chase grinned wickedly within his own mask.

"I think I can manage that," he agreed and I moaned as he unbuttoned his jeans dropping them to the floor and making a show out of slicking his cock with lube for me.

I panted as I watched him, my orgasm building as JJ fucked me harder and my own work on my clit sent my head spinning.

But just as I was about to come, Rick caught my arm and tugged my hand away from my pussy, growling possessively.

"You're gonna come for the three of us together, beautiful," he warned. "Or not at all."

I nodded like a good girl as Chase moved onto the couch behind me and I bent forward, pointing my ass at him as I gripped the armrest behind JJ's head and braced myself.

JJ slowed his pace as Chase pushed his slick cock against my ass and I moaned loudly as he drove himself into me, my lips parting in pleasure at the impossibly full feeling of having the two of them inside me at once.

Maverick unzipped his fly and released his cock as the others began to move, his eyes on the sight of them plunging their dicks into me and his precum coating my tongue as he fed his huge length to me.

JJ reared up beneath me, sucking my nipple into his mouth as Rick fisted my hair and drove his cock to the back of my throat. The taste of him was like a cocktail of all four of us as I licked and sucked at the juices that had been left on his shaft when he'd fucked me. It was so fucking dirty and it felt so good. I gave in to that joy as the three of them fucked me hard and delivered so much sensation to my body that I could barely take it.

My pussy clamped tight around JJ's cock and as he dragged his thumb over my clit, I exploded, my orgasm coming at me hard and fast, a cry escaping me as my muscles contracted around both him and Chase and they slammed into me faster and faster, making that feeling go on and on until I was forcing them to come with me as I screamed around Maverick's cock.

My spine arched as pleasure radiated through every single inch of my flesh and Rick thrust into my mouth harder and harder until he was coming too, an animal groan of pleasure leaving him as I swallowed his cum like a good girl before collapsing onto JJ's chest.

The others fell around us too, forming a heap of sweaty, sated bodies as we all fought to catch our breath and take a moment to appreciate what we'd just done.

"I've never come that hard in my entire life," I murmured as hands brushed against my skin in loving caresses and their masks were finally cast aside to reveal my boys beneath them.

"Shit," JJ said as Rick shifted to get more comfortable on his other side and I just stayed where I was, utterly fucking spent and buzzing with pleasure. "I think we just formed a reverse harem. I'm officially living a fantasy lifestyle."

A breath of laughter escaped me but that was about all I could manage as my eyes fell shut and I bathed in the presence of their company.

Strong arms plucked me up off of the couch after five minutes or five hours – I wasn't even sure - and I was tucked against a broad chest. I just kept my eyes closed and let whichever one of them it was carry me away to find a bed. And as three huge bodies joined me beneath the sheets, I fell asleep with a smile on my face which I knew was going to stay there for a long damn time.

MAVERICK

CHAPTER THIRTY NINE

I woke early among a tangle of limbs and slipped away for a shower and a piss. I'd slept better in this house than I had during any time on Dead Man's Isle, knowing in my bones it was because I was home at last. But of course admitting that out loud would have proved Luther had been right all along, so there was fat chance of that happening. I didn't wake early because of nightmares here, I woke early because apparently I was an early riser. Go fucking figure.

I pulled on a pair of black shorts before walking downstairs, the sound of Foxy cooking in the kitchen like a thoroughbred housewife bringing a smirk to my lips.

For some reason he hadn't woken Rogue for their morning surf bonding sessions or whatever the hell they called it, instead making us all a feast. And oh look, I was just in time for the feast part.

I stepped into the kitchen, the scent of freshly brewed coffee making my mouth water, but it was nothing compared to the scent of pancakes carrying from the pan.

He was dressed in a white tank and some dark green shorts, and he looked over at me as I took a seat at the kitchen island.

"Hey Foxy," I said, not meaning for that to sound so genuine. It was just a fucking hello, and yet he quirked a smile at me and nodded.

"Hey Rick." He turned back to what he was doing, then a shout came from Miss Mabel's bedroom down the hall.

"Are my eggs ready yet? I don't want any of that watery nonsense like last time. A good egg is cooked to its core."

"I don't make watery eggs," Fox growled beneath his breath before calling back. "Just coming Mabel!"

I snorted in amusement. "Do you make the old bird breakfast in bed every day?"

"Don't you take that tone with him, Maverick," Mabel called, apparently able to hear me all the way from her damn room. I swear she was selectively deaf whenever it suited her though. "You could be a little more helpful around here. In fact, I need someone to apply the cream for the eczema on my back. You'll be just the man for the job."

"Great," I huffed, though I wasn't gonna deny her shit. She'd been locked in a basement for fucking years, the least we could do was make her more comfortable. *Bet I can bribe Chase to do it though.*

Fox laughed at me, dishing out a plate of well cooked eggs alongside some buttered toast and avocado. He grabbed a glass of orange juice and some cutlery then headed away to give it to Mabel. I eyed the pancake stack he'd been working on and slipped off of my stool, snatching one off the top of it and grabbing the maple syrup from the side. I squeezed it all over it, rolled it up, but before I could take a bite out of it, Fox reappeared, snatching it from my grip and tossing it in the dog bowl on the floor.

"Sit down. If you're gonna eat my food, you eat it properly not like a fucking savage," he commanded, shoulder checking me back in the direction of my seat.

"But I am a savage," I countered, but I gave in, dropping back onto my stool and playing house. I didn't know why I bothered, but as I watched my brother drizzle maple syrup onto the perfect stack he'd plated up, then decorated it with chopped fruit and some freshly whipped cream, I had to admit I wasn't complaining.

He placed it down in front of me with a knife and fork and I glanced up at him, finding him lingering there like he was waiting for something.

"What? You want a thank you?" I asked and he shook his head and walked back to the pan to make some more. "What is it?" I pressed.

"Nothin'," he muttered and I shrugged mentally, grabbing my fork and using it to cut a wedge out of my stack, spearing it on my fork with some banana and pineapple before shoving it into my mouth. Fuck me, he really knew how to make good food.

I noticed him stealing a look at me and realised what his deal was, smirking as I swallowed.

"Oh, you want my approval, don't you little chef?" I taunted.

"Fuck off." He turned away again and I continued eating my way through the food.

When I'd finished every last bite, I tossed my fork on the plate with a clatter and Fox looked around again, grabbing the plate and putting it in the dishwasher, his eyes still flicking my way like he wanted me to say something.

"Fine," I gave in. "It was half decent."

"That's it?" he asked, looking like I'd kicked him in the dick.

"Yup," I said, moving to the fridge to grab the milk, twisting off the cap, about to guzzle the whole lot when Foxy snatched it and poured me out a glass.

"You need house training," he said, twisting the cap tightly back on the milk and returning it to the fridge.

I sighed wearily. "I'm used to doing whatever the fuck I like, brother."

"Yeah, back when you lived like a mongrel in a barn. Now you're home. Everything's communal. Miss Mabel doesn't want your backwash milk in her coffee, does she?"

"Fair point," I had to agree. "So you kept up with the cooking bullshit?"

"What do you mean?" he asked, dishing out some more pancakes onto a hotplate for the others.

"When we were teenagers you were always making me dinner and shit when Luther wasn't around. I figured it was just out of necessity."

"It was," he said with a shrug, but I wasn't buying it. "Nah, you light up like a miniature Christmas tree in a window when you feed us. Especially her."

At the mention of Rogue, his shoulders tensed and I could see his shutters going up, but he couldn't just avoid talking about shit whenever it suited him. I wanted answers, so I was gonna get 'em.

"So?" I pushed, jabbing him in the kidney and he released a heavy breath before looking back at me.

"Isn't it obvious? I like looking after you. Always have. And now you're all back here and we're trying to be something again, it's the only way I can still be valuable to the group."

I saw the truth of that statement in his eyes and frowned as I realised how much he believed that. And I didn't much like it.

"Your pancakes are good but they ain't that good, brother," I scoffed, but he just looked dejected at that like I'd pissed on his pancakes and told him they had the texture of a hairy ballsack. "I mean your value ain't in your pancakes, idiot."

He frowned at me like he was trying to find the insult in those words and I couldn't really blame him for that.

Dammit I was gonna have to get real with him, wasn't I? Be a fucking marshmallow and spew out my mushy insides. Fuck me, it was too early for this.

"For the love of fuck, do not repeat what I'm about to say to anyone, you understand, douchebag?" I demanded and he nodded, seeming confused. I lowered my voice, stepping closer to him and sliding a hand around the back of his neck as I made him look me in the eye. "You're my brother. And yes, I have fucking hated your guts for a very long time, but I've also missed you every day on that godforsaken island. Your value to me is more than I can put into words, because it's our whole fucking childhood, it's every night in this house we spent together, it's playing video games 'til four am and laughing like idiots at our stupid little inside jokes. And okay, maybe there's a thousand miles of mistakes between us, and yeah, maybe I shot at you. But I shot wide on purpose, Foxy, I'd never really put a bullet in you. At least not one that'd put you in the ground." I moved my hand around to carve my finger over the scar lining his neck that my bullet had put there and he suddenly shifted forward, wrapping his arms around me and clapping me on the back. I surrendered to the sappy moment, hugging him too and feeling so much goddamn relief to heal some of the old wounds between us.

"Oh, I'm so glad you're getting along again!" Mabel called from her room and we both laughed as we pulled away from each other.

Someone cleared their throat and my walls slid back up as I twisted around, finding our fucking father standing there, apparently having snuck into the house like a damn spider.

He was smiling at us, looking like he had on our first day of school, all sunbeams in his eyes and rainbows in his face.

"No." I pointed a warning finger at him as he walked towards us, opening his arms wide. "Stay back, old man. This doesn't mean shit."

He kept coming and I stiffened as his arms closed around us, pulling us against him like we were just little kids again even though we were just as big and mean as him these days. I struggled for a moment but as Fox melted, I gave in too, hugging my asshole of a father as my brother was crushed against me and feeling a rush of relief that I would never fucking admit to. But shit. I'd missed this. Missed them, my home, my fucking life. And suddenly it was right here surrounding me like it had always just been waiting for me to step back into it despite how impossible that had seemed such a short time ago.

"I'm so damn proud of you boys," Luther said and for all the walls I'd built against him, I couldn't help the river of warmth that flowed through my body over that.

"Fuck you, Luther," I gritted out.

"I love you too, son," he whispered in my ear and yeah, alright, it felt okay to hear that I supposed.

When we'd stood like that for a while and I was pretty damn sure a hot rainbow haired chick had peeped on us with a just as curious Jack Russell in her arms, I pulled away from my family and found Luther taking something from his pocket.

"This was in the mailbox," he said, showing us the envelope with the words THE TRUTH written in bold lettering on it below our address.

"What is it?" Fox growled, immediately on edge and Luther shrugged, opening it up and taking out a couple of folded pieces of paper inside, reading it aloud.

"Dear Maverick Harlequin," Luther started and I frowned, wondering who the fuck this was from. "I can't reveal my identity for my own safety, but after all these years, I know it's time for the truth to come to light. Your mother was Rhonda Rosewood, daughter of Mabel Rosewood of the Rosewood estate."

Those words fell on me like an axe and I backed up from Luther in surprise. "What?" I balked as Fox stared from me then back to the letter.

"What else does it say?" Fox demanded as my father's eyes widened.

"What's that about my Rhonda?" Mabel entered the kitchen in her floral nightgown, rollers in her grey hair and her hands trembling as she looked to Luther.

"Your real name is Augustus Rosewood," Luther said, his voice tight and I wrinkled my nose at that name while looking to Mabel, confusion making my head rattle. *Bullshit, someone was having us on, they had to be.* "And your mother drowned in a tragic boating accident."

"Codswallop," Mabel growled. "My Rhonda was murdered by Kaiser's father, Joffrey. That man was a violent monster who wanted my diamonds. My husband, Neville, saw him for what he was. He told me to hide them from Joffrey, hide them so well that not even my Neville knew where they were." Her eyes watered. "But my poor Rhonda fell prey to that awful Joffrey, I just know it in my heart. He was a gangster with endless sins to his name, and he was always sniffing around my home, snooping around my house, accusing me and my girl of hiding the diamonds away from him, claiming he had a right to them. He wanted to get his hands on them so desperately that he killed her so that he'd be the only relative I had left to pass them on to when I died. I was glad when he kicked the bucket – he was always a fucking pig of a man and he choked to death in a restaurant while stuffing his face with a surf n turf. Got a chunk of lobster claw stuck in his throat – I laughed when they told me he messed his pantaloons in front of every other diner in the place. But it seemed his son took up his torch in the end. I thought he was better than his father, but that little cretin was a good for nothin' scoundrel."

Luther glanced up and I caught hold of Mabel's arm as she looked a little weak.

"Are you truly my Rhonda's boy?" Mabel begged of me like I could possibly have the answer and I just shook my head weakly.

"I don't know," I said, looking to Luther in shock as Fox stared from me to Mabel like he was hunting for the resemblance. Was this woman my grandmother?

"I never knew the name of the woman who asked me to take him in, but she was afraid for her life," Luther explained to Mabel. "Did she ever tell you she'd been seeing my brother Deke?"

"She never mentioned him to me," Miss Mabel said sadly. "She didn't tend to confide in me about the men she did the rumpy pumpy with."

"Err, right, yeah," Luther muttered, glancing at me like he was trying to find an answer in my face but I sure as shit didn't have one. "I know a guy who can do a DNA test for us fast," Luther said decisively, taking out his phone and making the call.

I heard muttering in the hallway and breathed a laugh as I called out to the others. "You can come in."

Rogue led Chase and JJ into the kitchen, rushing over to me and Mabel and hugging us both.

"I hope it's true," she said, looking from me to our old friend with tears in her eyes, and funnily enough…I did too.

It took my dad's guy twenty-four hours to process the DNA test results and I sat outside on the patio with my friends, chain smoking as I waited to hear the news. Mabel was set up on her own lounger while we all continually brought her drinks and Chase even fanned her for a while as she told stories about Rhonda. My mother. Or my maybe mother. Everything about her sounded good. She'd owned an orange grove a couple hours north of town and it had been her passion in life.

"Rhonda was a sweet girl, though she worked a lot of the time. I didn't see her nearly as much as I'd have liked to," Mabel said with tears in her eyes. "And those last couple of years before she died, I barely saw her at all. She was a bit of a wild child at the weekends, hitting the clubs and bars in Sunset Cove. I warned her about some of those gang men, but she always did have a thing for ragamuffins." She glanced over at me. "Not that you're a ragamuffin, Maverick. The five of you always showed me so much kindness. I wasn't sure at first, but I saw the cloth you were all cut from when you began sneaking onto my property. You'd always leave somethin' good behind ya. You'd do some weeding or fix one of my daddy's old garden tools."

Luther stepped onto the patio and we all fell silent, looking to him as he walked over to us. Rogue took my hand and I squeezed her fingers tight, a knot growing in my chest. And I realised I wanted this. I wanted to know where I came from, I wanted answers and everything Mabel had told me about Rhonda had made me hopeful that I really had been born of something good, not just the bad.

My father swallowed, pushing his hands into his pockets as he looked from me to Mabel. "It's true, the test confirmed it. You're a Rosewood, Maverick."

Stunned silence filled my ears and my heart thumped to a maddening tune as I looked to Mabel. Rogue leaned in, laying a kiss on my cheek and JJ and Chase stared between us in shock. Fox clapped me on the shoulder and suddenly I broke away from them, moving to Mabel and leaning down to hug her.

"Oh my sweet boy," she started sobbing and I held her tight, the lilac scent of her so familiar, so homely that it felt entirely right that this was true. My heart filled with so much light that for a second I forgot all about the darkness that infested me, and there was only pure fucking magic in the world. "You're the last heir," she choked out and I didn't know what she meant until she stumbled on. "The heir to my diamonds."

"Diamonds?" JJ piped up and I threw an elbow back that winded him.

"Wait…the Rosewood diamonds?" Luther asked, clearly having heard of them.

"Yes," Mabel said as I released her, moving to sit at her side as she linked her arm through mine and patted my hand.

"We don't need to talk about this now," I said firmly, not caring if I was the heir to the whole fucking world, nothing meant more to me than knowing Mabel was my grandmother.

"But my boy, I have waited so long in the dark for so many years, and I have no more days to spare," Mabel said, reining in her tears as Rogue moved to sit on her other side and wrapped her arm around her. I looked at her over Mabel's head, finding tears sliding down her cheeks too and my heart squeezed with all the fucking love filling the air around us.

Mutt jumped up at my legs, licking my hands and wagging his little tail like he knew what was happening and I stroked his head as we all gave Mabel our full attention.

She worked to get a ring off of her middle finger, the large golden thing engraved with the Rosewood crest. She twisted the top of it and the crest sunk into the ring to create a shallow groove. "This can be used to open the box I hid them in. My dear Neville had them made for me," she breathed mysteriously, placing the ring in my palm and folding my fingers around it.

"Where are the diamonds, Mabel?" Luther asked and all of us leaned closer as she spoke her next words.

"Paradise Lagoon."

CHAPTER FORTY

We rode over to Paradise Lagoon in Fox's pickup like we used to in the old days with the four of them piled across the bench and me sitting on one of their laps. Sure, it was dangerous, but it was the most beautiful kind of nostalgic too and I couldn't bring myself to worry about car crashes while I sat on Johnny James's lap, and Rick and Chase bickered over missing out. I swear if I closed my eyes I could pretend that we were sixteen again - aside from the fact that the four of them were all so freaking big now that their shoulders were all rammed together and I had to keep listening to complaints about foot room.

Luther had stayed home to look after Mabel, and on our way out I'd heard her asking him to watch Pride and Prejudice with him. The old girl sure had sway with the Harlequin king because after only a few grumbled words, he'd given in and agreed to watch it. Either that or he had a secret crush on Mr Darcy. Couldn't rule it out. I still had zero clue on what his sex life looked like – not that I wanted to know because ew – but maybe he liked to put on an eighteenth century dress and twirl an umbrella while a ruggedly unobtainable English gentleman pretended to court him like a true lady.

The moon was a slim crescent which hung low in the sky tonight among a sea of endless stars, its silvery glow just bright enough to banish the deepest shadows and cast Sunset Cove in an iridescent light that made my heart happy. We had to do this at night in case anyone saw us, though it would be far more dangerous this way, but I'd promised Miss Mabel we weren't going to let anything happen to the treasure she'd guarded for so many years. After all she'd been through, we owed her this.

The radio was playing I Gotta Feeling by Black Eyed Peas, the song bringing back happy memories for all of us and JJ leaned in to brush a kiss against my neck where no one else could see.

"Who knew home could be found so simply?" he murmured, bringing a smile to my lips.

Rick squeezed my knee where my legs were slung over his, letting me know he'd heard that too and my smile widened.

Mutt had taken up position on Fox's lap while he drove and he held his nose in the air like he was the king of the world as he watched the streets whip by outside.

"Would you rather be an onion with feelings or an emotionless apple?" I asked casually and Rick groaned while Chase laughed and Fox cast me a sidelong look which I had trouble interpreting.

"Emotionless apple," Maverick decided first despite his complaints. "At least I could hang from a tree and watch the world go by."

"Yeah but you wouldn't care about it because you'd have no emotions," Fox pointed out. "So it would mean nothing to you."

"Well why am I not surprised that Foxy wants to be the onion with emotional layers?" Rick shot back. "Crying all alone down in the dirt."

"He wouldn't be alone because I'd be down there with him," I decided and Fox shot me a grin as I smiled back at him.

"Yeah I'm with the onion gang," JJ agreed. "Besides, we could be dug up and then we'd see the world and be able to feel all kinds of things about it."

"You'd probably just feel pain while someone chopped you up and put you in a fajita," Chase pointed out and we all laughed.

We kept playing the game as we drew closer and closer to the lagoon, and when Fox finally pulled the car up to park in the empty lot at the top of the hill which overlooked it, we all fell quiet.

"Do you really think we're about to find some hole full of diamonds up here?" Chase asked disbelievingly as he looked out the windshield towards the lagoon which was sitting to our right.

We were up on the rocks here, but narrow trails led down to the water which looked almost black tonight but usually shone cerulean blue beneath the midday sun. The sandy beach which surrounded the lagoon seemed to be empty, though it was often a favourite spot for bonfires due to its sheltered location. I squinted to make out the little island in the middle of the water and smiled at the familiarity of the place, silently vowing to come back out here for a bonfire soon.

"I dunno," Rick said. "But if Mabel wants us to get them for her then I'm game to look."

"Can we make a crown out of them so that I can wear it casually around the house?" I asked. "I feel like it would fancy up my booty shorts to the point where they don't even look trashy anymore."

"There's nothing trashy about you, pretty girl," JJ objected.

"Yes there is," I disagreed. "I'm the perfect combination of trash and sass which means I don't give a fuck if anyone doesn't like it."

Rick chuckled like he agreed with that assessment and Fox shook his head in amusement as he opened his door and climbed out.

The rest of us followed him and Mutt yipped excitedly as he raced off into the long grass which coated the hill up here, the stalks shivering around him as he went.

I turned to look down into the lagoon itself where we had all partied not so long ago and I bit my lip as my gaze ran over the still water which filled it.

"We should go skinny dipping to celebrate our victory when we find them," I decided and when the boys didn't reply I turned to look at them, finding nothing but hunger in their gazes.

"There's only one way that would end up, beautiful, so if you're not up for indecent public displays you might wanna keep your clothes on," Rick said, licking his bottom lip as he ran his gaze down my shorts and crop top combo, letting me know that my clothes weren't likely to hold him off for long regardless.

I opened my mouth to tell him that I had no objections to indecency in public and that I was more than up for being violated multiple times in celebration of our win if we found those diamonds. But then my gaze fell on Fox and I held my tongue, smiling coyly instead and moving towards the truck to grab our stuff from the back.

The boys all crowded around me, grabbing ropes, flashlights and climbing anchors, loading themselves up before I could take a single thing to carry myself.

I probably should have objected to that on some sort of feminist principle, but if I was being honest, I was glad that chivalry wasn't dead with my boys. I mean sure, they were all some form of sociopath, psychopath or masochist, and they robbed people and ran with gangs for a living, but they still looked after me, opened doors for me, carried shit for me and generally treated me like I was special, and I couldn't say I had any objections to that. What was wrong with a guy treating a girl like she was different anyway? We deserved a little bit of worship on account of our vaginas - they were a whole lot more complicated than a penis and they were capable of way more too.

When we had everything ready to go, Fox got his phone out and pulled up the satellite image of the area. He'd gotten Miss Mabel to pinpoint the location on it when she'd told us where to find the diamonds.

She'd wanted to come and show us herself, but the hills here were too steep and the terrain too rocky so she'd settled for us promising to video the moment we recovered them so that she could watch it after we got back.

The Smugglers Caves where she told us she'd hidden them was around the far side of the lagoon, up on the cliff that ringed it and protruding out into the sea beyond.

We passed warning signs as we went, telling us not to climb on the rocks and to be careful of uneven ground and blowholes, but we knew this place just like we knew the rest of the Cove and we weren't afraid.

Chase slipped his hand into mine as we walked at the back of the group, bringing a smile to my lips as I looked up at him, not an eyepatch in sight.

"You remember how I used to give you a kiss on the cheek every time you took your medicine like a good boy?" I asked him in a low voice.

"Hard to forget when that was the highlight of my day for weeks on end," he replied, squeezing my fingers.

"Well what if I start paying you in blowjobs for going out in public without covering up your scars?"

Chase arched an eyebrow at me and I grinned back, releasing his hand and skipping away from him as Fox called out to say he thought he'd found it.

I clambered up onto the rocks where Fox and Rick were already standing, shivering a little as a cool breeze blew in off the sea to raise goosebumps along my bare skin.

A huge hole opened up before us, a red rope circling it held up by rusted poles that had warning signs on them, telling us to keep back.

I could hear the sound of the sea echoing up from the darkness and as Rick shone his flashlight down into the pit, the glistening rock walls of the cavern caught the light.

"We're sure there's no water down there at low tide?" I asked because it sure as hell sounded like there was water in that hole.

"I dunno about that," Fox muttered. "I think there's always water in there, it just won't be dangerous at the moment. Miss Mabel said there's about an hour where this is possible before the swells make it impossible again."

I nodded, swallowing down the lump of fear that rose in my throat. This was the most impressive blowhole in the area and when we were kids, everyone from our school used to come and hang out up here regularly. When the tide was high, water would be forced into the hole through some underwater tunnel with such force that it exploded from the top and drenched anyone nearby.

We all used to play a game of jumping between the rocks and trying not to get drenched. Or at least we did until Sammy Jessops slipped and fell in. I swear I could hear the echoes of her screams before the tide ripped her away down there. That had been the closest I'd ever come to seeing death back then and I'd had nightmares about it for weeks. We were only ten at the time and we hadn't come up here all that much after that. I glanced over my shoulder and saw the little memorial cross that had been erected for Sammy after she'd died. There were fresh flowers by it which I guessed meant someone was still missing her even after all these years.

"We don't all have to go down there," Rick pointed out as he took the rope anchors from his bag and moved to hammer them into the ground at the edge of the gaping hole.

"Bullshit," I replied before any of them got any ideas about trying to make me stay up here. "We're all in this together. An adventure like the ones JJ always used to try and make us go on. Besides, I'm not letting you find buried treasure without me."

"I'm not sure diamonds hidden in some metal box in a rocky hole fifty years ago count as buried treasure," JJ said. "More like hidden treasure."

"Yeah, yeah." I waved him off. "I'm still not missing out."

"Let's get on with this before the tide turns then," Fox said urgently, moving to help Rick with the ropes and I stepped into my harness before tightening it around my body.

Mutt barked happily as he continued to scamper about, exploring the rocky terrain and peeing on anything and everything. He couldn't come down in the hole with us, but he'd be fine up here waiting and there was clearly no one else anywhere nearby to bother him.

I tossed my cellphone down beside the bags we'd brought with us and the others did the same as we prepared to head into the dark.

I moved closer to the edge, claiming a flashlight as the boys all worked to secure the ropes and shining it down into the hole.

My heart began to pound as I looked at the sheer rock faces that led to an inky black pool of water at the base of the cave far below us.

"Shit," I breathed, wondering what the fuck Miss Mabel had been thinking when she chose this terrifying as fuck location for hiding her diamonds. She really was a badass in her own right.

The others finished securing the ropes and moved to look down into the dark with me.

Fear made my palms clammy and adrenaline sped through my veins as we listened to the water echoing in the hole below and prepared ourselves to head down there.

"If the sun rises tomorrow, we'll watch it together," Maverick murmured to me, his fingers brushing mine and I looked up at him, smiling at our old saying.

"Ready?" Fox asked and I nodded.

"What could go wrong?" I teased.

CHAPTER FORTY ONE

I stepped backwards over the edge of the blowhole with Rogue at my side, the two of us abseiling down into the dark towards the echoing sounds of Fox and JJ's voices below. Maverick stood watching at us at the top, the moon behind him casting the edges of his body in silver before a cloud rolled over and the darkness deepened.

The cold air gusting up around us sent a chill deep into my bones and I glanced at Rogue with a grin, the buzz of adrenaline in my veins making me feel like a kid again.

"You okay there, little one?"

She looked to me with the biggest smile pulling at her lips and excitement bubbled in my chest.

"Yeah I'm good, Ace. Fuck, this is wild."

My foot slipped on the wet rock and I cursed as I jarred my bad leg, trying to swallow the sound, but Rogue reached out to steady me all the same. I fucking hated that and I straightened fast, taking her hand from my arm, squeezing her fingers tight before releasing her.

"Watch it, Ace," Maverick called down to me, his deep voice echoing around the cavernous chamber. "If you fall, I ain't swan diving in to save your ass."

"You couldn't even swan dive in your dreams, Rick," I tossed back and he stepped right to the edge of the sheer drop, making my heart jack-hammer.

"Wanna bet?" he growled, switching a flashlight on to look down into the hole.

"Rick, don't be an idiot," Rogue growled as he opened his arms wide, teetering on the edge like a mad man.

"How deep is it down there, JJ?" Maverick called.

"As deep as your mom's vag!" JJ shouted back.

"You're an asshole," Maverick laughed then leapt off the edge, stealing the air from my lungs as he plummeted past us into the dark. A huge splash sounded and I craned my neck as Rogue let out a scream of fear for his life. Maverick came up with his flashlight wheeling above his head and Fox grabbed him by the shoulders.

"Are you alright?" he demanded and Maverick boomed a laugh.

"I'm good, brother."

"You're fucking crazy." Fox breathed a laugh of relief and I let one out too as Rogue groaned.

"I think my heart just fell out of my chest," she said then released her own laugh.

We made it down to the surface of the pool that filled the bottom of the blowhole and detached ourselves from the ropes, sinking into the ice-cold water with swear words leaving our lips as we swam towards the others.

JJ was the only one of us with a helmet on that had a little flashlight on the top of it alongside the Go Pro camera which was recording all this for Mabel. I snorted at him as he caught my arm and helped me onto a concealed shelf of rock at the edge of the cave. The water was still up to our waists, but we all managed to get onto it and huddle close.

"Hey, Tintin, where are we going next?" I mocked JJ and he shoved me.

"I'm not fucking Tintin." He folded his arms and the others started laughing.

"Mabel said they were in a hole somewhere around the edge of the cave not too far above the level of this shelf," Fox said. "Let's split up and find it as quick as we can."

None of us complained about that as we slipped back into the water and I swam across the wide hole to the other side, taking my flashlight from my belt and treading water as I hunted along the wall for any sign of a gap. And there were gaps. Tons of them. "Shit, which one is it?" I called.

"Check them all," Maverick barked and we started shoving our arms into any of the holes we could reach.

"Ah!" Rogue screamed and we all whipped around, panic sliding through my veins as I lunged toward her across the water. "It's okay, just a feisty little crab." She pulled it off of her finger and tossed it into the water.

"Aw, you could have let JJ take it home for his collection, beautiful," Maverick taunted.

"I keep starfishes, not crabs," JJ muttered as we all returned to searching the holes around the edge of the cave.

"Not in your pubes you don't," Maverick said and JJ swam over to punch him in the head which Maverick responded to by dunking him beneath the water.

I rolled my eyes at them as they continued to play fight, exchanging a smirk with Fox as we went back to hunting for the diamonds.

After a while, I was so cold I could barely feel my hands as I pushed them into hole after hole and my fingers were bloody from scraping against the sharp rocks.

My arm brushed Rogue's as I reached her, her body shivering and as the cold water started to rock and splash with more vigour around us, I wondered if we should call it quits and come back another day.

"How long before the tide comes in far enough for it to get lethal in here?" I called to Fox and he checked his waterproof watch.

"We're probably pushing it already," he said, sounding concerned.

"Maybe we should get out, come back tomorrow?" I suggested.

"Don't be a pussy, Ace," Maverick teased.

"I'm not," I snarled, and we continued working along the edges of the cave, trying to find the hole Mabel had stashed the diamonds in.

The water had definitely risen a fair bit and some of the holes we'd searched already had now become submerged. Who could say if the diamonds were underwater or further up than we could even reach? Miss Mabel hadn't given us any more information than 'it was in a hole' but she'd failed to mention the multitude of holes down here.

A sudden swell sent me flying sideways and I slammed into Rogue, her head knocking against the wall and drawing a curse from her lips.

"Fuck, are you alright?" I grabbed hold of her, pulling her against me and checking her hair for blood with frantic fingers.

"I'm okay," she breathed, shivering against me and I held her close for a second as the rest of the guys swam over in alarm, all checking her over and huddling around her protectively.

"Alright, maybe Ace has a point," Maverick conceded as the water rocked around us more threateningly. "If I'm gonna die in a wet hole I can think of a much better option than this one." He smirked and Fox glared at him for a second before focusing on the dark water around us.

"Come on. Let's get to the ropes." He led the way across to them as we swam after him, disappointment swirling around us as we were forced to give up the hunt.

When we reached him, I pulled Rogue against me with one arm while holding onto a gap in the wall with the other, bobbing as Fox took hold of one rope and brought it over to Rogue to hitch her onto it.

As another swell of water rose beneath us, my fingers slid into the hole I was gripping and my hand slammed against something metal.

"Holy shit," I muttered, grabbing onto it and trying to pull it out but it was wedged in there tight. "I think I found something. Gimme a light."

Rogue let go of me, raising a flashlight to shine into the hole and we all crowded close together to peer into it, finding a metal box with a lock on the side of it which matched Mabel's ring.

"Fuck yes!" Maverick cried, swimming forward to reach into the hole and unlock it with the ring which he was wearing on his little finger. As he drew his hand out a second later, he raised a silver pouch triumphantly into the air.

"No way," JJ breathed.

"We found them," Rogue gasped, all of us grouping together in a messy hug as we laughed and whooped like kids.

"Well thank you kindly," Shawn's voice fell on us like the wings of death from above and my heart clashed against my ribs as I looked up, finding his dark silhouette glaring down at us. Shadows shifted closer all around the top of the blowhole and guns were aimed at us from every angle, making fear drive deep into my bones. "Now which one of you fine, upstanding people will be bringing me my diamonds?"

CHAPTER FORTY TWO

"**W**ell don't all come running at once." Shawn boomed a laugh which reverberated around the inside of the cave and terror inched into my chest.

I didn't know what to do. Didn't know how to save the people I loved as I stared up at the monster who had us cornered. We were entirely at his mercy down here, we had no weapons, no phones and no fucking way out of this freezing cold hole filled with water aside from by climbing up towards the men standing there ready to kill us all.

"How did you find us?!" Rogue shouted at him in fury.

"Oh sugarpie, you really do underestimate me at every turn, it's quite disconcerting." He casually swung his gun between our heads and my fingers burned for a weapon I didn't have. "Now are you gonna be a good little whore and climb your way up here, or will you be sending one of your boyfriends? How about pretty eyes? He's already missing chunks 'o himself, you can spare that one surely?"

"Shut your fucking mouth," Rogue snarled. "I'd rather stay here and drown than give you those diamonds."

"Rogue," Maverick hissed as we all grouped closer around her. But we weren't fucking bulletproof despite how much we wanted to believe it sometimes. And right now we were fish in a barrel, ready to die just as soon as Shawn decided it. And the fear of that had me frozen, because I couldn't protect them, couldn't do what I had sworn to do.

"You can have the fucking diamonds, just call your men off and then we'll talk," Maverick barked.

"Oh lord, Maverick Harlequin, it almost sounds as if you think you're the one in control here," Shawn mocked, then raised his pistol and fired.

We all lurched to cover Rogue as best we could as she screamed, trying to protect us in turn and as Maverick grunted in pain, jerking backwards from the shot, my fear rooted deeper.

"Rick?!" I cried in alarm, grabbing hold of him and turning him to me, thoughts of the brother I'd grown up with flitting through my head, us playing as kids, laughing as teens. I couldn't live without him, it didn't matter about anything that had happened between us. He was my blood and I wouldn't see him die.

He was clutching his bicep and I ripped his hand away, finding a chunk torn out of his flesh and blood running down his arm, but nothing life threatening, a breath of relief leaving me. I looked into his eyes and saw his desperation to protect Rogue shining back at me as fiercely as I felt that need. And not just her...JJ, Chase. He was asking me what to do with that burning expression and I didn't have a fucking answer.

"The next bullet won't be going wide. In fact, it'll be going right in someone's skull. I might just play eenie, meenie, miney, mo to make it fair. You remember that game, don't you, pretty eyes?" Shawn called.

"Fuck you," Chase spat.

"Well that ain't no way to talk to an old friend, now is it?" Shawn asked. "You and me had a bond down in that basement, there's no denying that. I see my mark on you. I'm still with you in the dark, aren't I? I crawl beneath your skin and I live there just like I promised, don't I?"

"Shut your mouth," JJ snarled.

"Oh, hello little dancer," Shawn's gun flipped onto him. "I don't think we've spent nearly enough time together. When I have my moment with you, I think I'll shoot at your feet and see how fast they really move, it'll be the show of a lifetime. How's that sound, huh?"

"We're not coming up unless you call off your men," Rogue snapped.

"I am truly astonished by how little you all know about the meaning of the word negotiation. You see, sweet cheeks, to be in a position to negotiate, one must have something to bargain with. And as you currently have absolutely nothing-"

"I'll drop them," Maverick snarled, raising the pouch of diamonds in his fist. "I'll scatter these motherfuckers to the bottom of this pool and let the damn ocean have them. You'll never fucking find them."

"An interesting bargaining chip to play," Shawn mocked. "Because you see, if you do that, Maverick Harlequin, I will have no choice but to rain down the full force of my men's arsenal on all of you. There will be nothin' keeping me from laying ya all to rest in this here dark hole and pretending I am none the wiser to your disappearance."

I looked to the others, the flashlights from above skimming over my family's faces, showing the fear in their eyes, the blood draining from their cheeks. It made me feel so helpless that I wanted to tear down this whole cliffside to save them from Shawn's wrath, but I was just a mortal with no more power in his veins than an ant floating in a coffee cup.

The water suddenly swelled again and we clashed together from the force of it, my head knocking against Maverick's.

I fisted my hand in the back of his shirt to steady us both while Chase and JJ kept Rogue pinned between them to stop her from hitting the wall.

"There's no choice here," I hissed to my brother. "Someone has to go up."

He looked to me with his throat bobbing and I reached for the diamonds in his hand, his fingers locking tight around them as I tried to prise them free.

"That someone ain't gonna be you, Foxy," he growled under his breath.

"He's going to start shooting any second now," I snarled as Shawn started monologuing again and the others stared up at him as they listened.

"You know, you all played into my plans quite beautifully," he said in a wistful voice. "If I wasn't so damn pleased with how easy it was to pull your strings like a puppet master with a fetish for seeing his playthings burn, then I mighta been disappointed in you."

"What the fuck are you talking about?" Rogue growled, her teeth chattering a little from the freezing water.

"Oh I am so glad you asked," Shawn replied, clapping his hands excitedly and I ground my teeth, my hate for this self-obsessed motherfucker only growing with every fucking word that spilled from his poisonous lips.

"Whoever goes up is likely dead," Maverick hissed to me as Shawn encouraged his men to huddle round and listen closely like this was some campfire story being told between friends.

"Which is why it has to be me," I whispered back and his eyes widened in horror at that declaration as my heart jerked out of rhythm. "You're all what she needs," I breathed so low that he had to lean closer to hear it. This was the right choice, the only choice that made sense. Rogue was whole with them, she had a chance at happiness so long as they lived. I had to give her that chance, no matter what it cost me.

"She needs you too," Rick insisted through his teeth. "And I ain't gonna let my brother die."

"It all started with some tasty, tasty bacon bites," Shawn cooed. "That lil dog of yours really ain't the sharpest tool in the shed, is he?"

Rogue sucked in a breath which held Mutt's name on it and worry clawed into me as I wondered where the little guy had gotten to up there. I hadn't heard any barking, so we could only hope that he was hiding, hopefully recognising Shawn from the last encounter he'd had with him and getting the fuck away from him to safety.

"So there I was, just tossing the mongrel treats while you all splashed about in the sea like a pack of dolphins psyching themselves up for an orgy. You wouldn't believe how easy it was for me to snatch him and strap that bomb to him. And while you left defenceless old Miss Mabel resting on the beach with her neck exposed and just asking to be slit by my blade, I decided to spare her life and instead plant a tracking device or two onto your cell phones." Shawn laughed loudly and I glared up at him as he went on. "You all got yourselves in such a panic over trying to rescue the little bastard, you didn't even spot me watching you all from the ice cream parlour across the street – damn, do they do good raspberry ripple by the way. Anyways, I will admit that I was disappointed the little mongrel didn't go boom in the end, but I figured

I'd get him the next time."

"What kind of monster tries to kill a dog?" I yelled and Shawn laughed again, his men joining in like the mindless goons they were.

"The kind who will take great pleasure in killing each and every one of you in turn too before taking back my little whore and returning her to her place on her knees before me," he replied darkly.

The waves swelled again, water crashing over us as we cursed him and fought against colliding with the rocks. We needed to get the hell out of here and the longer that motherfucker kept blathering on, the more dangerous it was getting.

"My sugarpie really is a good lay, isn't she boys?" he taunted as we all gasped for air. "Just built for taking cock, or is it *cocks* in the multiple now? Because she was most reluctant to give me those details, but I will admit that it has run through my mind a time or ten and I really wanna know how many of you she can fuck all at once. Does Daddy Harlequin set a schedule, or do you all just pick a hole and have at it?"

"Jealousy is an ugly look on you, asshole," Rick snarled and Rogue just scowled up into the flashlight which Shawn had aimed right at her.

"Fine, fine, keep your secrets. I'll just let my men take a few turns with her to figure out how many she can take at a time once she's back where she belongs anyway. Otherwise the curiosity is just gonna keep on eatin' at me something chronic."

"I'm gonna fucking-" Chase began, but Shawn fired his gun again, blasting a chunk of rock from the wall beside JJ and only missing his head because the water swelled at that exact moment and saved his fucking life.

Rogue cried out, throwing her arms around JJ and checking him over to make sure he was alright while he murmured reassurances to her.

"I am not done recounting my story, boy," Shawn snarled, the flashlight moving to point at Chase. "You'd do well to remain silent until I do."

We all glared up at him, but none of us said another word, knowing full well that he meant it.

"Where was I?" Shawn pondered. "Oh yes. So once I was certain you hadn't noticed my little tracking devices and I had made sure that you had that sweet old lady from Rosewood Manor all tucked up and cosy in your home, I sent an anonymous letter detailing a secret I had found out about poor young Maverick's heritage. Or should I be calling you Augustus now?"

"You sent that letter?" Rick demanded, his brow furrowing as he tried to figure out why, but I had the feeling I knew exactly why.

"You knew she'd tell him where to find the diamonds," I gritted out, furious at myself for not figuring that out sooner. Why the fuck hadn't we questioned who had sent us that damn letter? We'd all been so caught up in the information that had been in it that we hadn't even given any thought to the conniving bastard who had sent the fucking thing.

"Oowee, we have ourselves a winner!" Shawn cooed excitedly, applauding me and a sick feeling swarmed in my gut as I realised how easily he'd played us. "That I did! But, as much as I am truly enjoying this conversation, I really am impatient to meet my new, glittery friends. So which one o' you will be hand delivering them to me? I vote my sugarpie, but I'll accept other options."

"I'll go," Rogue said firmly.

"No chance, pretty girl," JJ growled as we all nodded our agreement over that.

"Hold onto her," I commanded and her eyes widened in fury as Chase and JJ listened to my order, keeping a tight grip on her arms.

"Let go of me," she demanded, trying to fight free of them, but they weren't gonna release her. I could trust them on that.

My heart wrenched as I looked to Maverick, gripping his shoulder tight. "Give them to me," I begged, but he shook his head, shoving past me and swimming for the nearest rope.

I swam after him as the others started shouting at us to stop and Rogue screamed and thrashed in their hold.

I didn't look back. I couldn't. If I saw the panic in her eyes, I'd go to her, and I'd never let go. This was what had to be done, and if I failed her now I'd never forgive myself.

The water swelled just as I reached Maverick and I was thrown against him as he hit the wall with a snarl of frustration. I got my hand over his, wrenching his fingers apart and tugging the diamonds from his grip.

"No!" he bellowed, swinging a punch at me, but I got hold of the rope beside him and started hauling myself up it, not bothering to clip myself into the gear just fucking climbing for my life. For *their* lives. And for that, I could be a god, because there was no force in this world which could keep me from saving them.

Maverick started climbing the other rope, but I was well ahead of him already and as I looked up, I found Shawn watching us with intrigue, his gun swinging casually onto Maverick.

"You want me to slow down your competitor a little there, Fox?" Shawn called.

"No!" I shouted so loud, my throat was cut raw. "If you kill him, I'll drop them."

"Alright, alright, keep your head screwed on. I don't want it fallin' off before I get a chance to cut it loose myself," Shawn said with a bark of laughter.

"Fox! Rick!" Rogue screamed and pain scored a hole through my chest.

I made it to the top, my muscles burning as one of Shawn's men dragged me firmly over the edge and pulled me to my feet in front of his boss.

Maverick was cursing me as he climbed, sounding only feet away but then Shawn clicked his fingers and I turned my head, finding his men standing ready with knives in hand. They sheared through the ropes and panic slashed through my chest.

"Rick – jump!" I bellowed, lunging back towards the edge, strong hands latching over my shoulders as I made it there, just seeing him hit the water with a splash. He came up with a roar of anger, staring up at me with utter desperation in his gaze.

"Fox!" he cried.

"Don't hurt him!" Rogue screamed at Shawn. "I'll come back to you – I'll do anything you want!"

My eyes locked with Rogue's for an endless second and a thousand apologies and regrets fell in the space between us. I should have kissed her more often, I should have loved her with all I could give, I should have tried harder to be what she needed me to be.

"I'm so sorry, hummingbird," I rasped, the words lost to the wind as I was dragged backwards and I lost sight of the most beautiful girl I'd ever known alongside my brothers. The boys I'd learned to be a man with, the family who knew me inside out like no one else in this world.

I was patted down and shoved to my knees in front of Shawn and he reached out, casually pressing his pistol to my forehead with one hand while prising the pouch of diamonds from my fingers with the other.

He gestured for his men to aim their guns at me before he holstered his own, glee filling his eyes as he opened the pouch and poured five fat diamonds into his palm. They were each the size of a damn grape, catching the light of the moon and twinkling beautifully as every one of us stared at them.

"Goodness gracious, you are simply the prettiest things I have ever seen in my life." Shawn's eyes glittered with the reflection of them, his men's flashlights making them sparkle as they shifted closer to see. His hand clenched around them greedily and he dropped them back in the pouch before putting them in the inside pocket of his leather jacket.

"Oh don't pout at me like that, sunshine," he spoke to me, beckoning one of his men closer to take his shotgun from their hands.

The frantic screams of my friends filled my ears, the noise becoming a din as it echoed around the cavernous hole behind me and the sound of the incoming tide surged loudly.

I didn't feel afraid for myself, a dark kind of acceptance washing through me, but I was afraid for them. Afraid that the second Shawn's gun raised and his finger tightened on the trigger, my world would go dark and I'd leave my family at his mercy.

Out of nowhere, a bundle of fluff dove at Shawn's legs and sank its teeth into him. Mutt growled and snarled, putting all of his effort into the attack despite how small he was and I lurched forward with a gasp, trying to grab him before Shawn's boot collided with his little body.

But I was too slow, and I shouted out in terror as Shawn kicked him and he was launched over the edge of the blowhole with a yelp of fright.

"Mutt's falling!" I yelled to the others and a splash sounded alongside Rogue screaming his name. "You fucking monster."

I lunged at Shawn, seeing red but I found myself with his shotgun to my head and his teeth bared in my face.

"Back down," he growled as I felt the kiss of more guns pressing to my shoulder blades.

"He's alright," Chase called and relief rushed into my chest, my body sagging forward as hatred coursed through my blood.

"How disappointing. That dog's got more lives than a cat," Shawn mused, some of his men chuckling at his words. "I wonder if he can survive a gunshot to his belly though..."

"You shoot one bullet down there and I'll kill you," I hissed.

He regarded me, pressing his tongue into his cheek as he tipped his head to one side.

"Lighten up, little Fox," Shawn breathed, leaning down as he lowered his gun from my head. "I'll cut ya a deal, huh? How about that?"

"What deal?" I gritted out.

"One death tonight, that's fair now, ain't it? I saw how you sacrificed yourself for them and all, and I respect that. I do. But I need some blood, see? We've been playing cat and mouse for too long and maybe killing that little dog of yours would have fed some of my more vicious instincts, but he just keeps on kicking. So here we are. A hunter and a fox, and it's only fair I get my kill after all the effort I put in tonight."

"Just me?" I confirmed, my voice tight as I prayed he could keep his word on this.

"Just you." He scruffed my hair and a tremor ran through me as the weight of my fate fell on me, dragging me down into a pitch black pit of despair. "Come on now, up you get. I promised to make a spectacle for your daddy after all."

His men dragged me to my feet, binding my wrists with rope behind my back and I turned my head, shouting to my family, the only words worth anything now. "I love you!"

"Fox!" Rogue screamed and I felt her heart break in that single word. But I knew this was the better choice. She had the others; they'd find a way out of that fucking hole and then they'd protect her. I had to believe that, even if the word of this monster meant nothing. I knew he liked his theatrics, maybe he really would be sated by one death tonight. And if my blood bought my family time to escape, time to plot Shawn's downfall and seek revenge for this night, then so be it.

I was guided across the wild terrain towards a line of cars behind my truck and I was dragged to the one at the front and shoved in the trunk of it.

Shawn lit up a cigar as he stood above me, one hand on the open trunk hatch as he stared in at me victoriously while a couple of his men continued to aim their weapons at me.

"You good, boss?" one of them muttered when Shawn lingered there.

"Yes, boy, I'm just enjoying the night air and the taste of glory. A man needs a little time to dwell in his victories, you should remember that." Shawn's blue eyes fell to me again as he smirked then leaned in. He stubbed his cigar out in the centre of my chest right in the middle of the Ferris wheel tattoo I had inked there, making me hiss through my teeth.

"You're mine, boy. All mine," he growled, his gaze alight with hunger. "And you're going to die beautifully, Fox Harlequin, I promise you that."

CHAPTER FORTY THREE

The water swelled in the cavern once more and we fought to brace ourselves against the rock wall as it thrust us into it, the freezing bite of the salt water washing over my head as the wave slammed into us.

I smacked into JJ who fought to stay between me and the rocks while I clung to Mutt who cowered against my chest fearfully like he knew I was his only chance of survival.

But as I breached the surface again, the water pulling back out of whatever cavern or tunnel must have allowed it in here, all I could do was suck down air and try not to panic.

"Fuck!" Maverick roared, the blood from the wound to his bicep running down his arm and into the water around us, gleaming a deep red in the light from JJ's helmet.

"Get us out of here!" I yelled, but there was still no reply and I was almost certain Shawn and his men really had gone and left us down here to drown.

"Shit," Chase cursed as the water swelled again and he lost hold of his flashlight, the beam of light spinning in circles as it sank to the bottom of the cave somewhere far below us.

"We have to try and climb out," Rick snarled, tipping his head back to look up at the sheer walls of the blowhole.

There were more gaps and holes lining the dark rock like the ones where the diamonds had been hidden so there was a chance, albeit a slight one that we could manage it.

"We need to hurry if we wanna get out of here before the water really starts crashing through that cavern," JJ warned, his eyes on me and full of worry as the light from his helmet blinded me.

"Give me the dog," Rick commanded, reaching for him and I complied despite the way Mutt fought to stay with me. But Maverick was bigger than me and far stronger - much more likely to be able to climb out of here with the little dog in his arms.

"It's okay," I promised him. "It's okay, boy. We're gonna get out of here."

The fearful look my little pup gave me was stolen from my sight as water slammed into me again, crashing over my head and sending me spinning beneath the surface until I smacked into the rough rocks, pain exploding down my spine.

I dropped my flashlight too, the direction it disappeared in helping me figure out what way was up as I kicked towards the surface once more.

A hand found mine in the dark and I was wrenched into Chase's arms, coughing up sea water as I surfaced.

"Climb, little one," he snarled, shoving me towards the rock wall and pushing me up ahead of him as I scrambled for something to cling on to.

A curse escaped me as the sharp rock bit into my fingers as I worked to find purchase on the slippery rocks, lumps of seaweed making them slick and even harder to climb.

"That's it," Rick encouraged as he heaved himself up too, Mutt wedged under his left arm as he gripped the wall with his right.

Another wave slammed into the cave before I could reply and I clung to the rock with all of my strength, crying out to Chase and JJ who hadn't managed to start climbing yet.

They were both forced beneath the waves and I lost sight of them as the water roiled dangerously beneath me, spray coating my back and making me close my eyes for a few brief seconds.

Chase emerged a moment later but my pulse skyrocketed as JJ failed to follow him, my eyes straining in the dark to try and catch sight of him while panic took hold of me and I screamed his name.

"JJ!" Rick bellowed too, looking like he was going to dive right back in after him as Chase dunked his head beneath the water to try and spot him too.

Another wave slammed through the cave, this one even more powerful than the last and my foot slipped as it slammed into me, my hand cutting open on the sharp rocks as I fought to hold on with all I had.

A huge splash sounded as Rick was knocked free of the wall and Mutt yelped in fright a moment before they went under the water.

"Maverick!" I cried, my heart thrashing wildly in my chest as I scrambled for another foothold.

Chase and Rick emerged again, Mutt still clasped tight in Maverick's arms as the two of them sucked down another breath.

"Johnny James!" I roared as he still failed to reappear with them and terror unlike I'd ever felt consumed each and every piece of me.

This was so much worse than fearing for my own life because without them I was nothing. Without them I really was a dead girl walking and my entire point of being would cease to exist. They were my sunshine, my moonlight, my joy and my fucking soul. If there was no them, there was no me.

"JJ!" both Rick and Chase yelled, the two of them hunting for him in the dark as the water began to surge again and I saw all of our deaths lurking in the depths of that wave.

It crashed through the cavern with such force that I was ripped straight off of the wall, my shoulder slamming into the rocks and pain blinding me as I screamed, bubbles tearing from my lips as I was tossed beneath the waves like a rag doll, unable to do anything aside from clasp my head in my hands and wait for the tremendous power of the water to release me.

And as I was torn deeper and deeper beneath the icy surface of the sea, I began to lose hope that any of us would survive this. We couldn't escape a force this powerful no matter how desperately we ached to live the life that had been stolen from us ten long years ago.

We were going to die down here.

Rogue and the Harlequin Boys. A legend that never came to be. A story with no happily ever after. Just an unfulfilled wish and a dream too beautiful to ever become reality.

CHAPTER FORTY FOUR

The car drove for what felt like an age as I shut my eyes and filled my head with every good memory I'd ever had. And they were all full of my family. Days spent basking in the freedom of our youth, never truly knowing how bad things could get for us.

All I could hope was that if I went anywhere in death it was somewhere I could one day find them again, but as my heart fractured down the middle, I feared only darkness awaited me in my grave. People always said your life flashed before your eyes before your death, but it wasn't some furious flashes of the past I experienced, it was whole memories surging up in my mind, begging for another moment in the sunshine of my thoughts. And that was somehow worse, because seeing my favourite memories replay made me ache in a way I hadn't known possible.

I watched Rogue across the playground in her second hand pink jogging bottoms which were an inch too short for her as Mrs Land told her off for something. I sat up on the picnic table we'd claimed for our group. Rick had helped me carry it under an apple tree at the edge of the concrete while JJ and Chase had gone off to steal snacks out of Kevin Nesbit's pockets. Because Kevin Nesbit was a dick.

When she was finally released from Mrs Land, Rogue came jogging over to us and jumped up to sit on the table beside me.

"What was that about?" I asked as Rick dropped down on her other side, his sleeves rolled up to his elbows.

"Mrs Land thinks I should make more of an effort to make some girl friends." Her lip curled back and mine did too.

"She never liked us," Rick growled, casting a glare over at the woman.

"What did you tell her?" I asked as Rogue casually slid her hand into mine and my heart thumped out of rhythm.

"I told her I'm more than happy with the friends I have, and she suggested I think 'long and hard' about my life choices." Rogue scowled and my spine prickled.

Chase and JJ appeared with snacks in hand, diving onto the bench our feet were resting on and tossing bags of chips and candy at us.

"You okay, pretty girl?" JJ asked Rogue at the sight of her expression.

"Yeah, Mrs Land is just being a bitch again," she sighed.

"What's new?" Chase said.

"She thinks Rogue should find some different friends," I bit out and Chase and JJ exchanged a furious look before turning their attention to Rogue.

"Why?" JJ demanded.

"She thinks I should have girl friends," Rogue said with a cluck of her tongue.

"Well what if you do want that one day?" Chase asked, looking concerned for a second and that made me even more worried.

Rogue glanced between us and I realised Rick and JJ were giving her that same worried look too.

"What if you need girls to talk about periods and vagina things with?" JJ asked in a horrified whisper.

"She can talk to us about them," I insisted, looking to her. "Right, Rogue?"

She bowed her head, biting her lip and my heart thrashed like a wild animal. "No…he's right."

"What?" I snarled, squeezing her fingers hard. "You can't be serious?"

A ripple of panic ran through my boys as we all exchanged glances and Rogue nodded solemnly.

"I can steal some of mom's books," JJ suggested desperately. "I'll read all the stuff about vaginas."

"Yeah and we can Google stuff too," Chase agreed while Rick and I nodded seriously. "Like how to take care of your…vulva."

Rogue burst out laughing, lifting her head as she looked around at us and relief fell through me in a wave. "You fucking idiots." She dropped my hand, throwing her arms around me and Rick, tugging us close while nudging Chase and JJ with her knees. "I don't need girl friends, you guys are all I need. And all I'll ever need."

"Swear it," I ordered, my heart still feeling fragile from her shitty joke.

"I swear it." She offered her pinky finger out into the middle of us and we all worked to wrap our own around it until we were all locked together. "Always and forever. It's just you guys. No one less and no one else."

I came back to my reality with those final words circling in my head. *No one less and no one else.* She'd said she wanted us all from the start and I'd ignored it, blinded by my own selfish need to possess her. And now look what I'd done. Wasted the time I could have had with her, squandered every perfect second that could have existed between us. I'd loved her the wrong way for so long and now there was no time left to love her right.

The car rolled to a halt and panic cut me open because it was just dawning on me now that though I'd made this sacrifice willingly, I wanted to goddamn live. I was realising how much fucking time I'd wasted, let drift away and never put to the right use. Everything could have been so different if only I'd learned to listen to Rogue sooner.

After she'd left town ten years ago, I'd formed a new version of her in my head, this fantasy one where she chose me and all was good in the world. But that wasn't the version of her I really loved, it was the girl who had never chosen, who had stood by us all and loved us with the entirety of her heart throughout our childhoods. And I had stupidly believed that kind of love didn't exist as adults, but I'd been so fucking wrong because I'd witnessed it time and again for weeks now. And if I had only gotten out of my own way, perhaps I could have claimed the girl I'd loved when I was a boy, back when all that had lived between us were the good things in life.

The trunk popped open and two massive goons dragged me out of it. I started fighting for my life, wanting to remain in this world so badly that I was sure if a blade was placed in my hand, I'd find a way to kill every one of these motherfuckers and make my way back to her. But with my hands still bound at my back and more men surrounding me than I could easily count, I knew the chances of that were fucking low.

As another set of hands landed on me and someone pistol whipped my fucking head, I knew that was never going to happen. I was shoved in front of Shawn in a daze, pain splintering through my skull and my last hope dying before my eyes. There were no more chances to fight, my death was set in stone. And leaving them behind was the most terrifying part of it all.

I blinked away the darkness veiling my vision, taking in the concrete beneath my feet, the rushing sound of a river close by.

I knew this place.

I was on Gallows Bridge which crossed The Divide near the hills in the east of town, the place illuminated by streetlamps along the road. The bridge was an imposing grey structure which stretched across a ravine between two hills that rose up high either side of us, like two hulking beasts looming in the dark.

A crowd of Dead Dogs surrounded me, so many that my chances of escape were absolutely zero. They were watching me with hungry eyes, excitement brightening their features as Shawn moved to climb up onto the low concrete wall at the side of the bridge with a knife in his hand.

"A day of reckoning has come, boys," he called and his men cheered, pumping their fists and pounding their chests, looking at Shawn like he was some kind of god.

I jerked against the hands still holding me in place, but their grip only tightened and as I looked around for an escape, the only answer that came to me was throwing myself from this bridge into the river below. But that was a death sentence in itself, the river wild and dangerous, filled with sharp rocks. I'd never make it, especially with my hands bound. But it was worth a shot.

I lunged without thought or reason, trying to break free of the men restraining me but a mammoth of a guy stepped into my way and between them all, they shoved me back.

"Good lord, did you just try to launch yourself into a raging river of death, sunshine?" Shawn asked with a wild laugh. "I really do have a fondness for your spirit, boy. It'll make it all the more satisfying when I watch that spark snuff out in your eyes."

"Fuck you," I spat and he smirked, turning away to face his men.

"Tonight, the Harlequin Prince dies!" Shawn roared to another round of excited cheers and my blood turned icily cold.

A gunshot sounded suddenly, making my heart jolt and the way Shawn flinched made me hope upon hope that somehow, someone had shot at him. But he just looked around, patting his chest with a laugh of relief before pointing out the perpetrator.

"Well good evening, Luther. I wondered when you'd arrive. You got my message, I see," Shawn called and my breath stalled at those words.

I turned, finding my father stood on top of his truck parked beyond the bridge, the headlights on as he held a gun pointed at the sky where he'd shot the bullet to get our attention. Even from here I could see the terror in his eyes as they fell on me then wheeled back to Shawn.

"Dad – get out of here!" I barked, fear filling me at how many enemies surrounded us.

"I'm here to trade!" Luther roared, ignoring me as he spoke with Shawn. "My life for my son's."

"Dad, *no*," I snapped.

"Oh my word," Shawn laughed, looking between us with a wide smile. "How touching, your sweet daddy has come to sacrifice himself for you. You're one lucky boy, Fox Harlequin, you know that? My daddy would have traded me for a bottle o' half decent whiskey. But that's your weakness, see?" Shawn toyed with the knife in his hand, clearly enjoying all the attention being on him. "This love business is the root of all your problems, because in the end, it's people like me who win the game of life. I'll be sitting pretty in your empire while you're rotting in a hole in the ground all in the name of love."

"Shawn!" Luther bellowed again. "Enough of this. Unhand my son and let me take his place."

"And what in the world makes you think you have any kind of advantage over me, Luther? Did you really come alone like I asked because I threatened to make a nice mask outa your son's face? Are you just that fucking dumb?" Shawn taunted, making every muscle in my body tense.

I looked to dad again, desperate to see some hidden plan in his eyes, but he just looked panicked, like he really had acted out of fear and come here alone to save me.

"Well, Fox, what do you say to your daddy's trade?" Shawn asked me, jumping off the low wall at the side of the bridge and strolling toward me with his chin raised. "Are you gonna let him take your place, watch him die like a good daddy would for his kid?"

I swallowed back the lump in my throat, my breaths falling furiously from my lungs. "Let him go. Send him away from here."

"Gosh you're dumb, but you sure are pretty." He raised his knife to my face, brushing the tip along my jaw and I remained perfectly still, not wavering even a little in the face of this motherfucker. I wanted his death so keenly it licked along the inside of skin and called my name like it was spoken by fate itself. I would never cower before him, I'd die like a man, I'd die for the people I loved. And it would mean something, unlike this asshole's death when it came for him. He'd die alone without being able to claim he was loved by anyone but his delusional momma.

"Maybe you'd like to match your little boyfriend, Chase, hm?" He circled his knife around my right eye then ran his tongue across his teeth. "Or maybe these soft looking lips that have been all over my girl should go first." He slit my lower lip with the blade and I didn't flinch at all, making his eyebrows arch as the tang of my blood slid over my tongue. "You Harlequins sure have gumption, I'll give ya that. It gets me real riled up." He slid his hand around the back of my neck, smiling like the Devil at me. "I fucking love it." On the word love, he jerked the blade back and slammed it into my side with a blow that drew a roar of pain from my lips.

He yanked the blade back out of me and shoved me to the floor, kicking me hard in that same spot, the crowd exploding with noise as the Dead Dogs cheered.

"I'll kill you – I'll fucking kill you!" My dad's shouts drew closer and gunfire went off.

"Lord have mercy on my soul, that felt so fucking good," Shawn crowed, flicking the knife so my blood splattered across the concrete before me.

With my hands bound behind me I could do nothing but curl in on myself as the blood ran freely over my skin, hot and wet and reeking of death.

"Get away from him!" Luther bellowed, the sound of him firing his gun again and the cry of dying men reaching me as I tried to get up but failed.

Go back, don't come here. Please don't die for me.

But I couldn't get those words to pass my lips as the wound in my side flared like a demon was reaching into my flesh and clawing at my insides and it was all I could do to stop myself from screaming from the pain of it.

"Hold fire! Luther's death is mine - get hold of him!" Shawn barked and a moment later Luther was thrown to his knees before me with blood wetting his face, a gun pressed firmly to the back of his head. His eyes were wide with horror as he reached for me, but Shawn stepped forward, forming a wall between us.

"Now, now, everybody calm down. You just killed five of my men, Luther," Shawn said, though his words sounded kind of appraising and he didn't exactly seem upset by the fact.

"You're next," Luther spat at him, a monster burning out of his eyes. This was the Harlequin King, a man so ruthless his name was whispered through the streets of Sunset Cove, never spoken too loud for fear of summoning him to your door.

The men around us were shifting, seeming anxious for blood, especially now my father had laid some of them out on the ground.

The cold concrete against my cheek seemed to be draining all of the heat from my body, and as I started to shiver, Luther tried to get to me again.

"It's okay," I rasped, as a father's fear for his son's life stared back at me, full of all the years he'd fought to protect me, and the failure of him being unable to do so now.

"Alright, one little kiss goodbye." Shawn stepped aside. "But hurry up about it, Luther, I'm anxious to break your heart in penance for my brother's death."

Dad hurried towards me, ripping his shirt off and cinching it tight around my waist as a tourniquet, making me groan in pain. Then he wrapped his arms around me as Shawn laughed at his efforts to save me. He felt so warm and he smelled like home. Fuck, did I wanna go home.

"It's okay, kid," he promised, though we both knew that was bullshit as he rested his forehead to mine. "I'll get you outa here. Just hang on." But the hopelessness in his eyes made me uncertain whether he really had a plan or if that was just wishful thinking. I couldn't help but fear that he really had made a grave fucking mistake in coming here to trade himself for me with no backup. But surely he wouldn't have been so stupid as to trust Shawn's word? Then again, maybe he had, maybe he'd thought this was the best chance of saving me and I knew he'd make whatever sacrifices he had to to give me that shot.

"I love you," I told him, meaning that so deeply it burned. "I shouldn't have spent so long hating you."

"Shh. There's no need for all that," he tried, his eyes welling with terrified tears as he tried to refuse that this was happening, but it was. We both knew it. I just wished he hadn't come because now I didn't know how he was ever going to get out of here alive.

"Maverick and the others are stuck in a blowhole at Paradise Lagoon. The one where Sammy Jessops died when we were kids," I told him, praying he might have a chance to get to them. Luther's eyes widened in horror at that and he reached for my binds, trying to get them loose but Shawn's men grabbed him, ripping him off of me.

"That's plenty o' time, Daddy Harlequin," Shawn said, stepping between us again and I noticed he had a noose in hands, a dark and vicious smile on his lips as he stroked his fingers over the rope.

Luther fought like a maniac to get free as Shawn slid it over my neck and cinched it tight. My heartbeats seemed to slow, my breaths coming harsher as I tried to process what was about to happen.

"There now, gotta live up to this bridge's name, haven't we?" he purred in my ear before hauling me to my feet beside him.

I was weak from blood loss and my head was starting to spin, but as he drew me towards the edge of the bridge where the end of the rope was tethered, I knew I had to fight.

If my life is over, then at least let me take fucking Shawn down with me.

His men shoved me up onto the concrete wall at the edge of the bridge and Shawn stepped up beside me, his fingers locked around my arm. My dad started shouting my name and I looked to him with all the love in the world in my eyes, mouthing an apology to him.

I wished he didn't have to be here to see this, but there was nothing I could do now but pray it ended fast.

Shawn was rambling on in some grand speech about my death and as he turned to push me, I stamped down so hard on his foot that bone crunched beneath my heel and he wailed like a wounded animal as I shattered something. But he shoved me in the same moment and with my hands bound, there was nothing I could do but kick and hope my foot connected with the asshole's legs as I fell. Miraculously, my boot slammed into the back of his knee and he slipped, falling with a wail but I lost sight of him as I fell too.

I had three seconds. The air whipping up around me, my stomach lurching as I tumbled and I filled up every thought in my head with Rogue, my eyes squeezed shut as my pulse roared in my ears.

The rope yanked tight as I reached the end of it and I jerked from the ferocity with which I'd fallen, my breath cut off immediately and pain ripped through my neck as I swung from the rope.

"Holy moly, did you see that? He almost took me with him?" Shawn called from up on the bridge and my heart sunk with that final hope of taking him out as I jerked and thrashed at the end of the rope like I might somehow manage to break it. But I knew I wouldn't. It was over. The last few seconds of my life rushing past in a blur which refused to pause at all.

The pain intensified and all I could hear was my father calling my name while the seconds ticked by and blackness swept over my mind. It was stealing me away and I had no choice but to go into it, trying to cling onto every drop of sunshine left in my mind as I went, every liquid golden piece made of her.

As all went dark, I was forced to say goodbye, to let go of all the good and set it free. I'd lived a cursed life, but I had been blessed in so many ways too. And I counted each of those blessings now as I slid away into death, thankful for every one of them, no matter how heart breaking it was to leave them behind.

Maverick.

JJ.

Chase.

And my beautiful hummingbird Rogue.

AUTHORS NOTE

Watermelons!

I kinda feel like I start a lot of these things the same way, so I decided to change it up with fruit this time.

Maybe that put a smile on your face after the er, let's call it 'action packed' ending of this book.

I don't know about you guys, but I can't say I ever thought we'd be ending a book with a bunch of characters soaking wet and rammed inside a blowhole, but here we are. Did you like that? Did you, like us, discover that you now have a fear of falling down a fucking blowhole?? Because if you did then I do not suggest Googling that shit. It's a scary fucking world out there, you guys. Much safer to stay inside and relax with a book.

Ahem.

We were also imagining a shark ending up in that blowhole. Like how awful would that be?? And then we were looking up how many shark attacks happen in a year and it's a lot. Like not a lot to really be concerning yourself with but enough to make me stay out of the sea for a nice long while. I mean, we are heading into winter here in the UK so I doubt I would have been going into the sea any time soon anyway. And we don't have much of a shark issue. But fuck getting stuck in blowhole with a shark. Or ending up in the hands of fucking Shawn for that matter.

Isn't he the worst? Fucking Shawn, man. I can't with him. And just when it seemed like he couldn't get any worse, he starts going after Mutt!! Damn he needs to die so hard. And I guess he might in book 5 Gallows Bridge which is the final book in the series! But also, he might not. You'll have to read it to see.

Anywayyy, I know this book got pretty heavy in places and it might make you feel a little better to know that it hurt our souls too. But sometimes the stories just do that to us, they demand a certain level of pain and sacrifice for the characters to grow and develop in the way they need to, and I really hope you agree that it helped to bring them all to where they needed to be by the end. They've still got some shit to sort through – assuming any of them survive this cliff – but I think it'll taste all the sweeter in the end if they manage to do it.

So thank you for reading, for diving off of the cliff and for living this story with us and the characters. As always we love and appreciate each and every one of you and we gladly accept all donations of readers tears into our jar of inspiration in our reader group so please come there to talk all things books with us and thousands of other amazing readers such as yourselves. Oh and if you're on TikTok we're also super cool and down with the kids these days, so we're on there too. Come watch Caroline make a fool of herself daily and check out my super cool Flynn Ryder smoulder.

The next Harlequin Crew book will be the last and we can promise you that it will be one hell of a ride. So hold on to your eye patch, call up the Green Power Ranger, stash a starfish in your pantihose and get ready to go to war with fucking Shawn for the final time because all stories have to end and this one will be going out with a bang.

Love, Susanne & Caroline x

ALSO BY CAROLINE PECKHAM & SUSANNE VALENTI

Brutal Boys of Everlake Prep
(Complete Reverse Harem Bully Romance Contemporary Series)
Kings of Quarantine
Kings of Lockdown
Kings of Anarchy
Queen of Quarantine
**

Dead Men Walking
(Reverse Harem Dark Romance Contemporary Series)
The Death Club
Society of Psychos
**

The Harlequin Crew
(Reverse Harem Mafia Romance Contemporary Series)
Sinners Playground
Dead Man's Isle
Carnival Hill
Paradise Lagoon

Harlequinn Crew Novellas
Devil's Pass
**

Dark Empire
(Dark Mafia Contemporary Standalones)

Beautiful Carnage

Beautiful Savage

**

The Ruthless Boys of the Zodiac

(Reverse Harem Paranormal Romance Series - Set in the world of Solaria)

Dark Fae

Savage Fae

Vicious Fae

Broken Fae

Warrior Fae

Zodiac Academy

(M/F Bully Romance Series- Set in the world of Solaria, five years after Dark Fae)

The Awakening

Ruthless Fae

The Reckoning

Shadow Princess

Cursed Fates

Fated Thrones

Heartless Sky

The Awakening - As told by the Boys

Zodiac Academy Novellas

Origins of an Academy Bully

The Big A.S.S. Party

Darkmore Penitentiary

(Reverse Harem Paranormal Romance Series - Set in the world of Solaria, ten years after Dark Fae)

Caged Wolf

Alpha Wolf

Feral Wolf

**

The Vampire Games: Season Three

Hunter Trials

*

The Vampire Games Novellas

A Game of Vampires

**

The Rise of Issac

(Complete YA Fantasy Series)

Creeping Shadow

Bleeding Snow

Turning Tide

Weeping Sky

Failing Light

Printed in Great Britain
by Amazon

41769856R00354

... AND FOREVER

EVERNIGHT PUBLISHING ®

www.evernightpublishing.com

... AND FOREVER

DEDICATION

To all of my amazing readers, my family, and to Evernight Publishing for their love and support.

... AND FOREVER

...AND FUREVER

Next Generation: Chaos Bleeds

Sam Crescent

Copyright © 2020

Prologue

The night that changed it all

Tabitha stood in the freezing cold. It had been a week since Simon killed Ryan. A week since he took the gun, pointed it in his face, and didn't just shoot once, but multiple times.

There was no doubt Devil had arranged for his best friend Dean to come and take him. Lash had sat her down with her father and they'd discussed why Simon killing Ryan was a problem. Their association with the Billionaire Bikers MC, as well as with the law, meant they couldn't just hide the body. Arrangements needed to be made, deals done. War stopped.

She wrapped her arms around herself and glanced down the street. The text message had been cryptic and had come from an unknown number. She'd known it was Simon. Knew deep in her heart he was coming for her.

They were meant for each other. She stared down at the ring on her finger that claimed her as his.

Tears spilled down her cheeks as she thought about everything that had gone down in less than a month. Anthony helping her. Daisy's arms surrounding her as she tried to sleep. She'd given her best friend a black eye as she'd woken up terrified, and when she'd lashed out, Daisy had no choice but to restrain her.

She hated it.

Hated her life.

The only sure thing for her right now was the message that asked her to be here. The one piece of salvation she'd experienced.

The sound of a motorcycle had her tensing up. She expected it to be Anthony or her nephew Simon, but it wasn't. It was her man.

He was alone. Gone was the Chaos Bleeds leather cut marking him as one of theirs. In that instant, she knew he was different. Staring at him now, Tabitha knew she'd lost Simon. Lost that part of him that made him part of her.

He turned the bike off and threw his leg over the side, coming toward her. She didn't move, watching him. Knowing he was different.

She'd heard her family, all of The Skulls talk about killing people. How it changed them, how you were never the same again. She figured they were all trying to sound normal. In their world, killing happened. It was part of who they were. They didn't run from it. Looking at him now, she knew they hadn't been lying. They just hadn't delved into great detail about it.

Tears streamed down her cheeks.

"It wasn't supposed to be this way," she said.

"No, it wasn't." He didn't reach out to touch her.

She was tainted. Ryan had ruined her.

Staring at Simon, she wondered what to do.

There was a distance between them. This had never happened before. She kept on looking at Simon, waiting, but he stared at her.

Then he closed that distance, cupped her face. He stroked her cheeks. She promised herself she wouldn't cry, but as he stared at her, she couldn't help it. The pain was too much because she saw past the comfort, the touch. She knew Simon. They'd been kids, nothing more than children, then grew up into teenagers, and now, married, they were not just boy and girl. They were man and woman. Tears continued to fall down her cheeks.

"Don't cry."

"You're giving up."

"I'm not giving up. I'll never give up. Not on you."

"Then don't go."

Simon sighed. "I've got to go. There's no way I can stay here, Tabby."

"Then you're giving up."

"I want to kill every last one of them." He paused. "You see, if I stay here, I want to slaughter them. I want to wipe them out like the Savage Brothers were. If I stay here, I can't be put in control of what I do." He took a breath.

She saw it.

The murder.

The rage.

If she begged him, he would stay, she knew that. She'd lose him though. Everything that made Simon who he was would be gone. He'd be on a quest to take on an entire MC club, removing himself from ever becoming the Chaos Bleeds President, taking his father's place.

"We promised each other forever. That's the way it has always been right from the beginning." She couldn't take it from him. Wanting him with her was selfish. She couldn't do it. Leaning forward, she kissed his cheek and took a step back.

Inside, she broke apart, shattered. The pain was unlike anything she had ever felt. She'd been to hell and back more than once, but she couldn't handle this.

Simon stepped back.

She kept on looking at him through tears. He was blurred.

He got on his bike and she stood, waiting.

The rain kept on coming. Wrapping her arms around her waist, she stood alone.

Tabitha watched as the car pulled up. The driver's side door opened and Anthony climbed out. He didn't grab a jacket. He walked around the car and stood in front of her, waiting.

She watched him.

He didn't speak.

Anthony never spoke unless he wanted to. She wondered if he was ever tortured, if they would get him to crack, or if he would be a stubborn bastard who refused to budge. He'd probably die silently.

"He's gone," she said.

"I know."

She sniffled. "What do you care? You probably saw this coming."

"He did what he had to do."

"He didn't have to kill him." She covered her face. "Why? Why did this have to happen?"

She was shocked when Anthony wrapped his arms around her. Out of all the people she knew, he was the last person she expected to get comfort from. "Leave me alone."

"Not going to happen. You think this is easy for him? He didn't protect you. He fucked up, and so did I. I should have been here. I should have made sure this didn't happen."

"It's not your fault. It's mine. I … I don't know what I was thinking."

"No!" Anthony pulled away, grabbing her shoulders. "Don't fucking do that. You know what, it's not my fault, your fault, or Simon's. It's fucking Ryan's. That piece of shit had what was coming to him. Simon dealt him a mercy I never would. If it had been Daisy, I would have stripped him piece by piece, and kept him alive, begging for death."

"This doesn't make me feel any better. I don't want to talk to you. I just want to go home."

"Then we'll go home."

"Take me to Daisy's." She pushed past Anthony, climbing into the car. Anthony was a psychopath, no doubt about it. He hid it well, but she knew who he really was, what he was capable of. She didn't want to be alone with him right now.

He was silent as they rode to Daisy's. She needed the quiet now more than ever. Rubbing at her chest, she didn't know how she was going to go on. They were married, a family.

She wiped at her wet cheeks, hating her weakness. She wanted it all to stop.

Anthony arrived at Daisy's. She climbed out to find her friend already waiting for her. She was unaware of when Anthony had texted her, but she went straight into her friend's arms. "I've got you," Daisy said.

"I feel like I'm dying inside. I can't stand it."

"Come on. My parents are at the clubhouse. They're still trying to deal with, you know."

Tabitha covered her face, sobbing.

"Shit, I'm sorry. I … just ignore me. Whatever I say, I just make it worse."

"It's fine," she said, sniffling. "It's all good. I don't care." She waved her hand in front of her face and took several deep breaths.

"Don't do that. Don't pretend you're okay with this."

"I've got to be though, right? This is the way it is. The way it's always going to be. He's gone and he's not coming back."

Before she fell apart, Daisy held her close, but no matter what, she was never going to be the same again.

****

"You'll take care of her?" Simon asked as Anthony climbed out of the car.

He watched him, waiting for an explosion. Anthony leaned against the hood of his car, arms folded.

"You think I don't already? You think I haven't been taking care of her all this time?"

"Look, I know you're pissed."

"You don't know anything."

"I … I had to," Simon said.

"Yeah, you had to. Ryan needed to be dealt with. He needed to be punished, but what you did was fucking stupid." Anthony shook his head.

"I get it, you've killed a man."

"No, I've killed more than one," Anthony said.

Simon paused as he looked at him.

"That has your attention, doesn't it?" Anthony chuckled. "Tabs has probably told you about Daisy's dad. He wasn't much of a challenge. The guy would do just about anything for a drink. He wasn't my first kill, nor was he my second."

"You're no different."

Anthony stared at him. "In case you didn't notice, I'm not like everyone else. If people need to die, it's not my problem. I get shit done, but I know when the best time to do it is."

"I don't know how you can be so glib."

He smiled. "I'm not the one running away from the woman I love."

"I'm not running away. I need to leave."

"Then go. Do whatever shit you need to do. She'll be waiting."

"You'll protect her?" Simon asked, gripping the back of his neck, hating the decision he was making.

"Of course. It's what I do."

He nodded. "Right, yes, right." Simon ran a hand down his face. There was nothing more to be said.

The truth was, he wanted Tabby. He wanted to take her with him, but right now, he couldn't. He had no choice but to leave. Climbing on his bike, he took off, not looking back. He left Fort Wills behind. He'd already left Piston County.

He no longer had a home.

Dean waited for him at the checkpoint they'd agreed to. It was a rundown garage that had gone out of business years ago.

After pulling his bike to a stop, he turned off the ignition.

"You okay?" Dean asked.

Simon shook his head. "Why did you come for me?"

"I had a hunch."

"No, there wasn't a hunch. You came for me and now you're willing to ride with me. Why?"

"We came from different backgrounds, Simon, but that doesn't mean you're not my friend. I don't want anything to happen to you. It's why I'm here. It's why I'm going to stay."

"You don't have to."

"No, but I will. There's nothing back home. You

need me now more than ever."

"What about Eddie?"

"What about him? He still wants the cushy life. Let him have it. I never wanted it and now, I get to live the life I wanted. Where are we headed?"

Simon looked up the long, dark street. The rain had lessened. The pain in his chest hadn't. As he thought about Tabby, he saw the smug look Ryan had given him. He'd pointed his gun, but Ryan hadn't believed he would shoot. Even then. Knowing what he'd done, Ryan had doubted him.

It pissed him off to even think the son of a bitch thought he was going to live. Like Simon was less of a man because he couldn't shoot someone. Ryan had raped Tabby. He'd taken from her what wasn't freely given and because of that, Simon had seen nothing but death. In his head, he heard screams, Tabby's. The ones begging for help, telling Ryan to stop. He had no doubt she'd fought but because of Ryan, she'd been hurt, and he just couldn't live with that.

The Skulls and Chaos Bleeds had an agreement with the Billionaire Bikers MC, along with an understanding about their past being put to rest. There wasn't going to be another life lost, but letting Ryan walk just wasn't the answer.

He knew deep down in his gut if it had been Lexie, his dad would have killed anyone. He would have painted the streets red.

"I don't know where we're going, but we're not coming back, not for some time." With that, he turned over the ignition of his bike and took off.

****

Daisy glanced over to the window to see Anthony waiting.

She walked to it, sliding it up, and Anthony

climbed through the window.

He looked toward the bed and nodded. "How is she?"

"Fine. I think. No, she's not fine. I had to give her a sedative. The ones you gave me that you got from Sandy. I don't like having stuff like that in my room."

"She needed it and if she was going to lose control on anyone, it was going to be you."

"It's stolen."

"It's not your fault."

"Damn it, Anthony. It's not about this being my fault or taking the blame or anything. I mean, seriously. I don't get it. Ugh!" She threw her hands up in the air and left the room. "How can you be so calm?" She didn't have to look back to know he followed her. He always followed her.

For the longest time, she hadn't realized he actually had feelings for her, then of course, he had to go and tell her, but she wasn't going to think about that right now. There would be a time and place for her own feelings and it wasn't today.

Heading into the kitchen, she paused.

Whizz, her dad, had redecorated again not long ago after Lacey decided she could do what every other woman could do, only she couldn't. Not even by a long shot. Running fingers through her hair, she glanced left and right, trying to figure out what to do.

This was insane.

Crazy.

"I'm not freaking out about this," Anthony said. "Simon made his choice."

She whirled around and laughed. "Are you fucking serious right now? I mean deadly serious? Can you even hear yourself?" She shook her head. "I don't even know what's going on anymore. We watched him kill someone. He shot Ryan in the face and he didn't just do it once, he did it a couple of times. Doesn't that scare you?"

"No."

"Why the hell not?"

"Because it's who we are. You know this." He shouted the words, making her pause. "For fuck's sake, Daisy. You can't for a second believe that all of this is— I don't know what the fuck you want me to say right now. Look at how you beat down Danielle."

"Don't you dare bring her into this."

"No. You liked it. It's why all these years Tabs has kept you away from fighting. You have a thirst for pain and blood that scares the shit out of you. The only thing you're scared about right now is the fact that you don't understand how Simon could have stopped. How he made it so fucking easy for Ryan. That piece of shit raped our best friend. He raped one of our own. I saw it. I saw the fucking damage and all he did was fucking shoot him in the face."

Tears flooded her eyes as the anger filled her to the core. She clenched her hands into fists. "Get out."

"No. You can hide who you really are, if that makes you feel better. I get it, but I will not run from you." Instead, he stepped close into her space.

She flinched away from his touch and he tutted. "You don't need to do that."

"I don't want to talk to you right now."

"No? Then don't talk to me." He didn't walk away. His arms wrapped around her and held her close to him. "I'm not going to let you go. Not even for a second." He kissed the top of her head. "I'm going to stay here for as long as you need me."

She closed her eyes, breathing in the scent of leather and grease that always seemed to linger on him.

He always played with his bike, even when it didn't need fixing, and she knew it helped to calm the beast within him.

Holding on to him for dear life, she sniffled.

"I wanted to hear him scream," she said, whispering the words for only him.

"I know."

"I ... I don't know what to do. I feel so much anger."

"I've got you. I will always have you." He kissed the top of her head.

She pulled back, clearing her throat. This wasn't about her. Tucking her hair behind her ear, she focused on him. "What do we do? What happens? Will Simon ever come back?"

"I doubt he will come back now. He spoke to her today. I don't know what he has planned." He rubbed at the back of his head.

"Did you call Dean?"

"No."

"Who do you think did?" Daisy asked, wrapping her arms around her waist.

"Devil."

"Really? Even with the whole agreement they've got going on?"

"Yes. Simon is still his son and I'm guessing they're going to do everything they can to protect him."

"What happened to the body?" Daisy asked.

Anthony opened his mouth and closed it.

"No! You don't get to hide stuff like that from me. I won't have it. Just tell me the truth. I can handle it."

"Can you?"

"Yes."

He stared at her, driving her crazy. In some way

or another, he always tried to protect her. She understood it but hated it at the same time. Nibbling on her lip, she waited.

"I believe Lash and Devil scrubbed the place clean. There will be no evidence of Ryan ever existing."

"What about the club?"

His gaze moved past her shoulder.

"Don't. I'm not fucking stupid. You said so yourself. I've been here before, right? I know you don't just kill someone and everything is okay. Tell me. Now."

Anthony turned his back, his hand running through his hair. She knew he was pissed.

"They made a deal with the Dogs to stop an all-out war."

She gasped. "You're wrong."

"I'm not wrong."

She shook her head.

"They did that. He was part of their fucking club."

"I know." Glancing toward the stairs, Daisy didn't know what to say. "This is going to kill her."

"It won't. I'll fix it."

"How? How can you fix it?"

"One day, I will." He went to Daisy, cupped her face, and slammed his lips down on hers. She knew he had no choice but to kiss her. If he didn't, he was likely to go and find the sons of bitches who hurt their best friend and take them on one by one. Or knowing Anthony, he'd take on the whole club without even thinking.

Chapter One

Five years later

Tabitha glanced down at her cell phone and cursed.

"I've got to go," she said, getting to her feet. She felt Angel's, Daisy's, and Darcy's eyes on her. Way too much attention for her liking.

They were all at The Skulls' main clubhouse. Angel had offered to organize some kind of potluck, helping to raise money for the school to go on a trip.

"You need to go?"

"Yes, I'm needed." She pulled her satchel over her head, resting it across her chest, and lifted her head. All three women looked nervous. "What?"

"Nothing," Angel said. "It's just, we wanted you to have fun today."

"I did have fun. Lots of super fun." She forced a smile to her lips. "Duty calls though." Without waiting for one of them to offer her company, she moved through the clubhouse that had changed so much in the last five years.

Since graduation, Anthony had become glued to Lash's side, working with his father in improving The Skulls' position. They owned more businesses within Fort Wills that had also expanded out to the city. Their time of dirty deals, deaths, and bullshit was long and truly over.

Tabitha rubbed at her chest, hating the way her thoughts were going. It was impossible for her to even think of the time when The Skulls had nothing but enemies, she'd have been happier. Simon wouldn't have had to leave because her family, even Chaos Bleeds, would have supported him. She wouldn't be all alone. These moments were what she hated. The thoughts she couldn't turn off.

Gritting her teeth, she counted to ten inside her head.

One, two, three, four, five...

"Tabs, wait," Daisy said, catching her attention.

She stopped and turned to look at her friend. There was no denying it, Daisy had been a rock to her.

"What's up?" she asked.

"You don't ... let me come with you."

"It's nothing bad. I can handle this."

"I know you're doing this all alone and you don't want or need my help. I get it. I do. But you're not alone."

"I'm very much aware of how not alone I am." She forced a smile to her lips. "I've got you. I've got all the guys. Miles. The club. Believe me, I'm completely surrounded by how not alone I am." There were times she felt guilty because she believed they were trying to smoother her. They were constantly trying to show her how important she was, how she belonged to them.

"Do you want to be alone? Is that what you're saying?"

"Daisy, just go back inside. We both know that's where you want to be." She went to turn away.

"That's unfair. You don't think I understand? Life handed you a shit deal and you've been coping the best way you can, but that doesn't mean you get to blame it on me."

"I'm not blaming it on you." She growled out each word. "Damn it. Does it ever occur to you that I don't want to be part of some stupid potluck organization? That I don't want to have to deal with all of this crap? You're worried about me. Fine. Do me a favor and stop. I mean it. Just stop. I'm not you. I didn't get my happily-ever-after. You did. Right now, you're living the life that was always supposed to be yours, right? You've got the mother-in-law, the title."

"Stop it."

"Stop trying to turn me into you," Tabitha said. "I'm not like you. I will never be like you."

"I hate this. I'm trying so hard. You think I don't see you dying inside? That I haven't seen it all this time? I've watched you for five years and it kills me."

"Then stop looking. Stop trying."

"Tabs, please."

She tried to walk away. Clenching her hands into fists, she turned back to her best friend. Daisy was one of her favorite people in the whole world. Darcy had been as well, but there was a bigger age gap between them. Also, Darcy had married Ink, who was much older and she'd become an old lady. In her mind, she and Daisy were part of the new generation of Skulls. Darcy was the old.

Even still, watching them all with their happy lives. Their men. Their perfect families. She loved them all dearly but that didn't stop the envy.

"You got what you always wanted, Daisy. I'm happy for you. It wasn't supposed to be this way for me and I know you all get tired of hearing about it. I don't want to be that person anymore. Just leave me the fuck alone. Go back to your perfect life, and let me go."

This time, Daisy didn't call her back. She wasn't stopped as she left the gate of the clubhouse.

Being a Skull was in her blood, but the moment Simon walked away, with each passing day she got further away from who she was, who she used to be. Nothing made much sense to her.

Keeping her hands clenched, she walked into town, not stopping, not waving at anyone. So many people knew her and she'd grown up being part of Fort

Wills that it was impossible to be left alone.

Was that why she never left?

Why she didn't go to Piston County?

Lexie, Simon's mother, had offered her a place to stay many times. Had even given the suggestion of her actually living in her own place.

She was torn.

Deep in her soul, she wasn't a Skull anymore. Hadn't been for a long time. She still attended all the necessary picnics and parties, the family get-togethers, but something was missing. Something had been missing the past couple of years and she wasn't an idiot. She knew what it was.

Simon.

He'd ridden off into the night, leaving her behind, and rather than being able to find herself again, she'd lost everything.

He was just gone.

You're also angry.

All the fucking time.

She didn't think about her anger. There was no point. It never helped her. It didn't get her anywhere. All her anger did was feed the beast within and that was never good.

The last thing she wanted to feel was the anger, especially with where she was going.

She clenched and loosened her fists, trying to gain composure again.

Picking up the pace, she held the handle of her bag and pounded out her anger. The tears were so close to the surface, but she sucked them right back inside. There was no time for tears, not for her.

They were pointless. Useless.

Taking deep breaths, she saw the building up ahead and picked up her pace. She also made sure not to look miserable. Turning her frown into a smile, she pushed all of her thoughts to the back of her mind. By the time she arrived at the reception desk, she was a little out of breath but she gained control quite easily. That was what all the power walking did for her. No matter what she did, she was able to gain control.

Always had to be.

No one wanted to hear about her sad little story or how she struggled.

"I'm here to pick up Nathan," she said.

"I'm here."

She glanced toward the chairs and immediately went to him. "I'm here, sweetie."

"It hurts, Mommy."

"I know, baby." She caught him as he threw himself at her. Holding him tight, she cupped the back of his head and picked him up.

The receptionist at the desk got her to sign a form for taking him out of school early.

Carrying Nathan out of the school, she didn't look back.

"You never told me this morning you were feeling poorly." She kissed his cheek, rubbed his back, and tried to offer him comfort. Nothing she did seemed to help him though.

"I know. I didn't. I felt great but it started to hurt in class and Miss Andrea said I was just being a baby. That big boys don't complain. How you might be busy."

Tabitha was even more pissed now than ever before. "You don't listen to her. If you ever feel sick, you come straight to me. You call me. I will always be waiting. Always." She kissed his cheek again, blowing a raspberry on his cheek.

"I love you, Mommy."

"I love you too, sweetheart. So, so much."

Nathan had been a surprise. There was always a risk. On one of the last times with Simon, the condom they'd used had broken. Not long after, she'd been attacked by Ryan. Gritting her teeth, she forced her thoughts elsewhere. Whenever she was with Nathan, she refused to allow bad memories to come forward. It wasn't Nathan's fault.

Finding out she'd been pregnant had come as a shock. There had even been talks of ending the pregnancy. There was an equal chance between Simon and Ryan being the father. She'd gotten her son tested years ago. The piece of paper was still in the envelope. Unread. She hadn't opened it. Hadn't wanted to know the answer.

Her son was her baby.

Her boy.

She didn't care about his father.

Ryan was rotting in hell and Simon, well, he was doing his little repentance or whatever the fuck it was. She couldn't even give him the energy of thinking what it could be that he did that was useful.

He'd ridden away.

Asshole.

Carrying him toward Millie's place, she opened the door. The young woman looked up and her smile turned into a frown.

"Oh, no, is everything okay?"

"It's fine," Tabitha said. "He's feeling a little sick and so I figured I'd pick up what I ordered before I headed home."

"Yes, of course." Millie turned and quickly headed into the back of the shop. Millie was one of the club women and was married to Baker. A lovely woman, kind and sweet.

Nathan wriggled in her arms and she let him

down to go ahead and play.

She loved to watch her son enjoying all the toys and gifts the shop had to offer. He was the one and only joy within her world.

A couple of minutes later, Millie came out of the back, carrying a large bag. Tabitha's phone rang, interrupting them.

"Can I take this?"

"Sure. The signal in here is bad. You might want to take it outside. Don't worry about him, I'll take care. Nathan and I are good buddies."

"Of course. Thank you." Pressing the phone to her ear, she stepped out the door. "What's up, Mom?"

Glancing at her watch, she saw it had been exactly a half an hour since she left the clubhouse and only now her mother called. Eva was certainly getting sloppy.

"I wanted to check up on you. See how you're doing."

"I'm fine. Nathan's fine." Tabitha rubbed her head, feeling the beginning of a headache. Her family, she loved them, she did, but they were always hovering. Expecting her to have some meltdown crisis.

She'd been fine for the past five years. She would continue to be fine. There was no reason for them to stress about it. Freaking out, breaking down, was not part of who she was.

"Oh, well, if you want, I can take Nathan."

"It's fine. He just wants me. Thank you though."

"I thought you were looking forward to helping with the fair. You know it's important."

She took a deep breath. "Actually, Mom, you wanted me to help. I didn't sign up for it. I will go, spend some money, you know, do the right thing and all, but that's about it."

Silence met her answer.

"I assumed again, didn't I?" Eva asked, groaning.

Everyone did.

The one good thing about having your heart broken, stomped on, and rubbed in the dirt was that everyone around you assumed they knew the perfect solution to all of your problems. No one listened.

No one paid attention.

Assumptions.

Pushing you in whatever direction they want to go.

Never fucking listening.

"It's fine." And like so many times before, rather than be pissed about it, she accepted it. This was her family.

She'd been hurt in one of the worst possible ways, and then there was Nathan. When he was first born, Tiny, her father, wouldn't even look at him. In fact, the first time she took him to The Skulls' clubhouse, no one would even offer to hold him.

Now, that wouldn't usually bother her.

Possible stinky diaper to change and all that, but she'd seen the guys and the old ladies, even some of the club sluts, they loved to help out. To hold babies, to love them.

Not hers.

No one had touched hers until Angel had come out of the kitchen, holding a large lemon cake, which she shoved into Lash's arms, and immediately went to her, holding Nathan, kissing his head.

In fact, Angel had sat beside her the entire day, held Nathan, changed his diaper. The next little event after that, everyone had taken a turn in holding her son. She didn't know what Angel had done, but it had helped her a great deal. The only problem was the damage had already been done. They had already shown their true colors.

Since then, little by little, month after month, her feelings for The Skulls had broken down.

They were no longer perfect.

Family was who they accepted. Nathan, no matter the fucking father, was her blood. No one was going to change that, but they hadn't accepted him. After everything she'd been through, they could have at least given her this. Since then, it was like the happiness had been slowly withering and dying.

Pulling out of her thoughts, she tuned back in to Eva.

"Well, there's this spa event that all of us ladies are going to."

"Look, Mom, no. Okay? No spa day. No helping out with the charity events. I do have a full-time job." Of all the places for her to work, she'd decided to apply at the library. With a sudden influx of investment, the library had expanded, adding in a computer room, more books, even rooms for conferences. They'd needed more people to help run the place, and she'd signed up. Put her name on the dotted line, got a call, and had been working there for the past three years. Before that, she'd bounced from job to job at The Skulls' many businesses.

Her parents had told her she didn't need to work. How she could go to college while they'd take care of Nathan for her. The same people who hadn't even held her son. It had all been Angel. There was a time she truly believed Angel was weak, but now she saw the truth. Angel's kindness wasn't a weakness, it was a gift.

On the school front, she was in the process of taking a few courses at the local college, slowly getting her degree in English. Until then, she was happy to be around books. She loved books so much. They didn't talk back to her, unless she got audio, but she didn't listen to them. Once she was done with them, she could close them up, take them back. Her job was amazing. Nathan also happened to love going there, especially to the children's section when she had to work late.

The new building ran until ten at night. He'd often be curled up with the soft toys, and she'd carry him home.

"I know. I know. It's just, you're taking a short vacation."

"I'm not, Mom. This is my day off." That reminded her, she'd have to call them and ask about a couple of sick days so she could care for Nathan. "Look, is there anything you need? I want to get Nathan home."

"Where are you?"

"I stopped off at Millie's, why?"

"Oh, you didn't go straight home."

"You know I'd ordered the board game he wanted. This will make him feel better." Her patience hit an all-time low. "I've got to go. Talk to you soon." She hung up the phone, pressing both hands to her head to try to alleviate the headache already getting to the point of making her head explode. If she got out of this alive, it would be a miracle.

I can do this.

Her cell phone started to ring again and she immediately put it to vibrate.

"Funny seeing you here."

Hearing Luke's voice made her tense. Lash had organized some kind of deal with the Monster Dogs and every now and then, one of their crew would arrive in town. Most of the time, it was Luke, which wasn't a welcome sight. All it ever made her feel was anger at what she'd lost.

"What the fuck are you doing here?" she asked.

Luke had always been nice to her. Ever since the truth of her pregnancy, he'd been the perfect gentleman.

She hated him.

"I've come to pick up a few things. A couple of the guys at the club, their kids' birthdays—"

"And you're being perfect, right?"

"I know you don't like me, but I'm trying here."

"No, you're not. You're not trying. You need to leave this town and stop coming here."

"I know this is hard for you."

She laughed. "No, you don't have a fucking clue what this means to me."

Luke looked toward the shop and she followed his gaze to see Nathan hugging a cuddly toy. Whenever he did that, it meant he was in pain and trying to be a big brave boy. "If you excuse me, I've got to go."

"You know, if he's Ryan's, then he has a right to—" He didn't get a chance to finish what he was saying. She was done hearing him. Hearing all of this bullshit, and so she wrapped her fingers around his thick neck.

In the past five years, Luke had gotten taller, bigger, more muscular. He was fitting right in with his club.

"You don't get to say his name to me. Understand? Nathan is mine. No one else's. He is mine. He is my blood. My son." Tears filled her eyes.

"I would help you if you let me, Tabs. You know that. You know I'm here for you, always."

She gritted her teeth and pulled her hand away. "And I've told you every single time that you offer, no. I don't want you, Luke. I'm not going to allow you to think there's a chance for you. I'm not yours. I will never be yours."

"You're still saving yourself for him?" he asked.

"After all this time, you still think he's coming back?"

As she stepped back, her heart shattered into a million pieces. "He's coming back."

"And after all this time, you're going to forgive him? The Skulls and Chaos Bleeds handled this shit. The Monster Dogs covered this as well. We're all in this together and you're telling me, what? All is forgiven? He could have come back by now, but he's still gone."

She tilted her head to the side and stared at him. "Do you really want his castoffs? Is that it? You see me and you, and you think we can, what? Be friends, be together? So what if Simon never comes back. You'd be happy being second best? Knowing that the moment he did come to town, he was where my heart truly lied."

Some people believed she was cold by telling him exactly how this was going to go down. She wasn't. The truth hurt, and rather than let Luke continue to believe there was even the merest hint of a chance with the two of them, she cut him down.

He deserved to find someone who could love him for him.

She would never love him.

One day, there might be a chance to fall in love with him, but again, it wouldn't be the same. Her heart belonged to Simon, and being with anyone else just wouldn't cut it.

"I will always go to him, always." She turned her back on him and went into the store. It was time to take her son home to allow him to get well.

****

"You're baking," Anthony said.

Daisy looked up and shrugged. "You're pointing out the obvious."

"I heard what happened."

"Of course you did. It if wasn't down to a couple

of prospects, I'm sure Rachel had a fun time sharing, or was it Darcy this time?"

"I heard my parents talking."

"Right, of course, yes. You have those." Daisy pounded the cookie dough, anger rushing through her body.

"Why are you so mad?"

"I'm trying to bake here and you're distracting me. Don't you have somewhere else to be?" she asked.

His brow went up.

"Of course not. That would be easier for me to be pissed at something."

"You're cursing out loud. I know something's up."

She slammed the bowl to the surface and gripped the edge of the table. The Skulls' clubhouse had a large kitchen. For as long as she could remember, this place had been her home, her family. Every single year, the old ladies would gather together, cook up a whole lot of food to feed everyone. If some of the nomad crew stopped by, they'd be right there, enjoying it with them. Her mother though, Lacey, she didn't cook. The one time she was allowed to cook something, she set it on fire and Whizz came to the rescue to put it out. No one was injured but Lacey had merely been allowed to taste test. She was too much of a hazard to be left alone in the kitchen.

Brushing the back of her hand across her brow, she shook her head. "I'm fine."

"You're lying."

"So deal with it. People lie all the time and we have to put up with it. It's the way of the world, remember?"

"It's not like you to lie."

"Well, it's not like me to have to deal with everything I have to. I'm adapting."

"You're pissed off."

She growled, glaring at him. "What do you want?"

"I want you to get it off your chest. I know it builds up inside you until you explode and when that happens. it's not good."

She took a deep breath. "It's Tabs."

"I know."

"Then why ask?"

"You need someone to get it off your chest. I'm here. I'm not going anywhere."

She picked up the wooden spoon. Baking usually helped to relax her. It wasn't doing that. Far from it.

Pushing her hair out of her eyes, she sighed. "It has been five years, Anthony. Five years. I know something happened to make all the sticky details of Ryan's death go away. I get it. He shouldn't be hiding. He should be right back here with her, but still, he's being selfish, doing what he wants to do, while we have to continue to pick up the pieces."

"Are you pissed that he's not dealing with her, or that we have to?" he asked.

"I don't know and that's what is so frustrating to me." She dropped the spoon and stepped away from the dough. "I don't even know if I want him to come back. He doesn't deserve her. She's twenty-three years old and hasn't been on a single date. It has always been Simon and where is he now? Where was he when she went through all that crap? You and me. We've been the ones to keep her together. Miles as well. Us."

"She's ours, Daisy. You know this."

"But what if he comes here, and she doesn't get angry? What if she forgives him easily?"

"And you don't want her to?"

"No." She shook her head. "He did what he did,

and how he created all this mess and then he just left, like it was no big fucking deal. Tabs has been through enough. If he truly loved her, he wouldn't have left, and it makes me so mad because deep down, I know she'll forgive him. They're soul mates." She shook her head and turned, needing some air. Opening the door, she stepped out into the night, bending over, putting her hands to her knees, and taking big gulps of air. Once, twice, three times.

Anthony followed her. He placed a hand on her back, and she kept on taking big gulps of air.

"It's going to be okay."

"You keep saying that, but I don't see it. I really don't. He has no right to her, or to Nathan. He just left."

Anthony pulled her into his arms. "We're going to be here for her. We always are."

"But will she listen to us?"

"Tabitha will always make her own choices. You know this. We're her friends. It's our job to keep her up when she falls. It's all we can do."

Chapter Two

Tabitha wiped at her brow. Sweat still slid into her eyes but she wasn't going to stop until every single weed was out of her garden path. She hated weeds; they always made her lawn untidy.

Sitting back onto her feet, she brushed the dirt off her gloves and rested her hands on her thighs, watching her son.

Nathan sat near a flower bed, digging into the soil and planting the flower bulbs she'd picked up at the florist the other day.

I can't believe I'm actually gardening.

This was a far cry from the days of fighting and running around causing trouble. Tomorrow, she'd be taking him to the fair. He was excited about it. She hadn't been back to see Daisy since their cross words and she wasn't in a rush to go see how happy her best friend was.

Her back ached a little from being bent over for so long. Gardening helped her to pass the time. It gave Nathan time outside and she got a pretty decent-looking front yard out of it. She'd been blessed with an adorable kid.

"Do you want me to get you some lemonade, Mommy?" Nathan asked.

"Of course. I'd love it. Can you reach?"

"Yep, and I will only use the unbreakable glasses."

She chuckled as he quickly brushed his hands and rushed inside. She'd be lucky if he remembered to wash his hands.

Getting stuck back in, she gave the dandelion weed she was currently fighting a nice big tug, grunting as she did.

She looked up as a large, somewhat wrinkled hand wrapped around the weed and pulled as if it was nothing more than a tiny little weed that hadn't gotten a chance to grow.

Tiny, her father, smiled down at her as he threw it into the pile of other dandelions. "I've got to say, I didn't exactly see you as the gardening type."

"We're all so very different."

"That's true." He glanced toward the house.

"Nathan is getting me a drink," she said. She pressed down the mud on the patch and hoped the grass would grow over the nice little indent she'd created. Once done, she stood and glanced up at her father. He was always so much taller than her. "What are you doing here?"

"That's not a nice way of saying hi to your father."

She chuckled. "Dad, in the past four years of me living here, you've rarely come around for a visit. What gives?"

He sighed. "I was just looking forward to visiting with my daughter. Is that such a shock?"

"Not a shock. You normally have better things to do."

"Now you're being hurtful."

"I'm telling you the truth. It sucks, doesn't it?" She reached down, picked up the now-dead leaves, and carried them toward the compost bin. She was doing everything she could for the environment. Composting, avoiding plastics, eating healthy. Nathan liked to do his part for the planet as well. It was their little adventure. For every plastic not bought, or at least recycled, was another that didn't end up in landfills or the ocean. One day her son wanted to be a pirate, but a good one. The kind that went around helping sea life out of man-made products. It was where he was going to find himself a nice mermaid and marry her.

It was one of her son's many dreams and as usual, she didn't have the heart to tell him mermaids didn't actually exist. She hoped he'd go to high school, see a sweetheart who she'd hate, and they'd take it from there.

"Grandpa!" Nathan let out a squeal as he ran out of the house. Of course, he didn't pay any attention to the lemonade he spilled over the side of the glass.

Tabitha took both glasses out of her son's hands, laughing at how little was in them as he threw himself at Tiny.

Her father wrapped his arms around him and held him close. This moment was always a double-edged sword for her. She loved that Tiny had gotten over his issues with Nathan, but at the same time, it reminded her of how he wasn't accepted in the early years of his life. She doubted he would be if it was left to other club members. This was why Angel deserved the right to be the President's wife. She was an amazing woman.

There was a time she truly thought Angel was a little too weak to play the role by Lash's side. Now, though, she saw the inner strength in the other woman and was glad for it. Even her own mother hadn't been quite so accommodating with Nathan. Still, that was for her to know, not Nathan.

"You're dirty."

"I've been gardening."

"Your mom's got you out here gardening?"

"Yep. We've got to make it all look pretty so the bees come. We're helping the bees."

Tabitha chuckled. "And you're doing a wonderful job. I'm going to go and fill up our glasses. Head around the back for me. You know I don't like you out here all alone."

"Okay, Mommy." Nathan wriggled out of Tiny's arms, made a dash for his little gardening bag, and headed toward the fence. He reached the string, gave it a tug, and the gate opened.

She walked over, locking it before heading into the house. Her father followed close behind.

"This must be a very important visit if I'm going to have your company for a lot longer than a few minutes. I'm going to fire up the grill. You want something?"

"Is it real meat or that fake stuff?"

She laughed again. Ever since she and Daisy agreed to not eat meat, she'd never gone back. Of course, there were plenty of options at the supermarket. Nathan happened to love them as well, so she never bought actual meat.

"It's the fake stuff that you love." A couple of years ago, Angel got fed up with all the guys complaining about how difficult she and Daisy were being. At a clubhouse cookout, she served them all plant-meat, and well, they were all shocked into loving it. Of course, Adam, the British member, said he could tell the difference. They all knew he was lying.

Tiny snorted. "I'd love to stay."

"Great, I've got potato salad and macaroni salad as well. Both are going to be delicious." She headed to the kitchen, putting the glasses into the bowl of water and washing them. She always kept a bowl full, ready to wash anything.

Having an accident-prone son, she was always cleaning up his messes. Again, it wasn't something she minded doing. She'd also learned to have a medical kit of Band-Aids and antibacterial wipes just in case. He liked to scrape his knees, knock up his elbows, and the worst was bruising his cheek from falling down on a toy. That one had scared the hell out of her.

Tiny pulled out a chair at the table. She filled up three glasses, handing one to her father before taking the other out to the small table for Nathan, who drank it in a few gulps and disappeared again back into one of the flower beds.

From the kitchen, she could keep an eye on him.

She'd drained the potatoes for the salad and had allowed them to cool down while she'd been out in the garden. Taking out some celery, herbs, and dressing ingredients, she got to chopping them up as Tiny sat at the chair.

"Dad, you may as well come out with it, whatever it is."

"Simon."

She paused in her cutting. "What about him?"

"He's been seen."

"Of course he has." In the past five years, there had been a few rare sightings of the man who'd crushed her heart. She tried not to think of just how painful that moment had been when he'd walked away from her. She didn't want to think about it or remember it. That night would forever be one of the worst of her existence.

She finished chopping, putting her ingredients into a bowl. Angel was all about the measuring, whereas she liked to just go with the flow. No measuring. Going by eye and taste. She added the mayonnaise, a few dashes of vinegar, and her personal favorite, some pickles, which she'd diced up.

She poured all the potatoes into a bowl and gave it a nice big stir, making sure everything was evenly covered.

It looked lovely and she took a bite. Closing her eyes, she was happy.

Next, the macaroni salad.

"Honey, are you even going to listen to me?"

She went to the fridge, finding the rest of the ingredients for the next salad, and paused to look at him. "Why do I need to listen to you? So he's been seen again. There's nothing you guys are going to do about it. The first year he was gone, I begged you to go and find him, and you refused."

"It wasn't like that. We were still dealing with the fallout of him killing—"

"Don't say his name." She held up her hand for him to stop.

"Honey, have you ever considered going to therapy?"

She burst out laughing. "When I go and talk to a bunch of people I don't know to tell them about my pain? No, thank you."

"You've never spoken to anyone about what happened."

"Because I don't need to. I don't need to do any of this." She put the tomatoes and cucumbers on the counter.

After pulling out a fresh bowl, along with the jar of olives, she got to work chopping, trying to ignore the pain in her body.

Simon was once again seen.

She'd spent way too much time hoping it meant he was coming back to her. There had been so many nights she'd lain awake hoping and wishing. A few sounds of a bike's engine had filled her with excitement but nothing had come. She'd stopped expecting a long time ago.

"You went through a lot."

"I know. I went through a lot. I dealt with it. No one needs to talk their feelings to death, Dad. I've got a handle on all of this."

She dropped the diced tomatoes and cucumbers into a bowl, more herbs and mayo. She couldn't think of what else to put in it, and so she added the pasta, stirred, tasted, and then remembered some cheese.

Grabbing a pack of pre-grated, she tipped the contents into the bowl, gave another stir, and then she was done.

"Don't walk away from me," Tiny said.

"Dad, I'm not walking away. I've got a son to take care of. I don't need to go thinking about stories of my husband. Believe me, it's ... I just need to focus on Nathan. That's all I need right now and you and Mom should be happy about that. Why aren't you?"

"We know you're hurting."

She licked her lips. "Look, I spent way too much time hoping for him to come back. Simon's got his own life now and so have I. I've got a son I love more than anything. My life isn't so complicated. I work. I take care of him. I'm fine."

"You're not living at all. All you're doing is getting from one day to the next."

"And it's working. I don't need anything else. Not right now. Please, don't make me think about more of this."

"We could reach out."

She shook her head. "No. If you were going to reach out, you'd have done it years ago. Now it's just, it's sad. That's what it is. I don't need Simon. I never did. I'm not waiting around for him anymore."

"So does that mean you're dating someone?"

"Is that what all of this is about?" she asked. "Me dating?"

"What if your mom and I set you up with someone?" Tiny asked.

"No."

"Come on. It will then give us peace of mind that you are fine here."

"My word means nothing?"

"Your word does mean a great deal."

She laughed. "I can't believe this. You do realize in my entire life I've only been on one date. That's all. One."

"So it will be good for you."

"Dad, really?"

"Come on. You've got nothing to lose, and dating could be fun."

"I don't know."

"Please?" he asked.

"Fine. I'll go on a date. If that will make you happy. I'll prove to you I'm doing fine." What her father didn't know was she had no intention of enjoying the date. She didn't need any of that to make her happy.

No men.

No dating.

She was fine and happy. Why couldn't they see that?

"How about tonight?" he asked.

"Not happening. It will have to be after the fair."

"Fine. Deal."

"Deal."

****

Nathan giggled as he grabbed hold of a big, fluffy teddy bear that she'd won for him.

She'd been able to shoot a gun for a long time and the guy manning the stand had been so cocky that taking the biggest prize from him had thrilled her. She got to wipe that smile off his face and her son got a teddy.

This was why she loved the fair.

She could give Nathan a whole host of toys and a

good time. He just loved it.

"Where to next, darling?" she asked.

"I'm hungry."

"Of course, you are. Let's see."

"Baked potato," he said.

"That's what you're wanting?" she asked. "A baked potato?"

"Yep. Lots of cheese."

She chuckled. "Let's go and get you one."

Tabitha spotted Daisy right up ahead. Rather than avoid her friend, they both walked to each other, Nathan keeping up with her strides, and they hugged.

"I'm so sorry for being a bitch to you," Tabitha said.

"You've always been a big bitch. I accept. Damn, I don't want to ever fight like that again. Promise me we won't?"

"We won't." She hugged Daisy close.

"We're all eating over there. I saw you and I had to come and get you."

"I want a baked potato," Nathan said.

Daisy laughed and picked him up. "Wow, you're getting to be so big. I don't like this at all. You need to stop growing."

"Mommy says that all the time."

"I know. She's always very bossy," Daisy said.

"Hey."

"There's a baked potato stand over there. You coming?" Daisy asked.

She glanced at Nathan and smiled. "Of course we are."

Heading over to where a large cluster of The Skulls stood and sat eating, she went to the potato stand, ordering what her son loved and one for herself. After walking over to the table, she sat next to Nathan and put the tray next to him. He took the fork and started to break up the potato, mashing it as he went. She couldn't help but laugh at his antics. He was so darn cute.

She ate a few bites of her potato, very much aware of Daisy watching her.

"Are you going to keep freaking me out?"

"You don't eat a whole lot. I worry."

"I eat a great deal." She rolled her eyes. "You've got to stop being a worrywart." Past Daisy's shoulder, Tabitha spotted the woman she'd been wanting to have a private word with for a little while.

Taking another mouthful of food, she watched her move. When the woman went to the bathroom, she returned her gaze to Daisy.

"Will you keep an eye on Nathan?" she asked.

"Sure."

"Great. I've got to go to the bathroom." Getting to her feet, she left her potato on the table. One of the guys would eat it. She wouldn't have to worry about the waste.

Entering the bathroom, she closed the door and saw there was a lock on the inside. She flicked the lock into place, slowly, so as not to alert the woman who'd entered. She removed her heels and walked down the stalls, checking underneath. Only one was in use.

Putting her shoes back on, she leaned up against the sinks, waiting, watching, anticipating the woman coming out.

She gripped the edge of the counter.

The bathroom door opened and Miss Andrea came to a stop. She let out a little gasp. "You startled me."

"Good."

Andrea paused, her hands lifting slightly as if to ward her off. "Do I know you?"

"You know me and you're very much aware of why I'm here."

Ever since Simon had left her, she hadn't hurt anyone. Not threatened. She'd been the good mother, the standup citizen Fort Wills loved. She hadn't done anything to hurt anyone. The days of beating girls up or taking on guys, it had all stopped.

All she'd been granted for herself was the pain in her body, the memory of being a hard ass, and nothing else.

"Look, Tabitha, I know you think I was being hard on your son." She let out a cry as Tabitha wrapped her fingers around the woman's neck.

"My son was ill. He was sick. He wasn't faking it to get attention. He told me what you did. How you talked to him. So I did a little digging. I hear you've been trying to worm your way around The Skulls. Well, that ends today. None of the guys will ever be near your rank, bitchy pussy. They've got a lot better in their club. You know why? I'm Tiny's daughter."

She saw the realization in the woman's eyes. Slamming her back against the door, she didn't let her go but loosened the hold to help her to breathe. "The next time my son is ill, you will send him to the receptionist. He will call me the very fucking second he even whimpers. Do you understand? I'm one of them, Miss Andrea, and believe me, I've got no problem hitting women, especially sluts like you!" She threw her into the bathroom stall. The woman crashed to the floor, collapsing around the toilet. "Have a wonderful time."

Flicking the lock, she stepped out, walking back to where her son was still eating his baked potato.

Her heart raced but she made herself look toward the restroom. Miss Andrea came out and Tabitha kept her gaze on her until she was out of sight, stumbling away as she did.

Returning her attention to the table, she saw Daisy watching her.

"I'm guessing she deserved whatever happened in there," Daisy said.

"Whatever do you mean?"

Daisy snorted. "It's been a long time since I've seen that look on your face."

"What look?" She tried for innocence but probably failed miserably.

"You're not a very good liar."

"I don't have a clue what you mean."

"Of course, you don't. Who would?"

"Mommy, can I go on the bouncy castle? Uncle Anthony is going to take me."

She looked toward Anthony. His brow rose as he waited. He was giving her time with Daisy to properly make up.

"Sure, of course. If you want to."

"I do."

Daisy had stepped away from the table but returned holding a couple of drinks. "He's not very subtle, is he?"

"Who, your boyfriend?"

Daisy sighed. "Now tell me. What is this I hear about you agreeing to go on a date?"

She rolled her eyes. "It's not a big deal."

"I'd say it is. You're assaulting teachers, offering to go on a date. Tell me what has happened to the sweet, quiet Tabitha, or was that all a lie?"

"None of it was a lie." Tabitha took a sip of the hot coffee. It was bad, but it was a drink, and she needed it. It wasn't alcohol.

"And what's going on now?" she asked. "Do you want to go on this date?"

"No, I don't. You should know me by now. I don't want to date."

"You're still hung up on Simon?"

"No. Of course not."

"Did they tell you the news?"

"About his latest sighting? Yeah, they told me. Dad stopped by. It was around the time I kept saying I was fine and he wanted me to go on a date to prove it. You know, all of these 'sightings.'" She air quoted the last word. "It makes him sound like some kind of alien."

"I think, in a way, he kind of is."

"How?"

"He disappeared into the night, and if you think about it, there have been rare occurrences where he just pops up."

"You and I both know they didn't exactly put in a great deal of effort to find him." She took another sip of her coffee.

"Why do you think that?"

"We both know this club. When they want to find someone, really find them, they do."

"Their hands were tired with this one."

"It doesn't matter." She shrugged. "I've accepted that I'm alone."

"You're not." Daisy reached across the table. "You're far from alone. I've always hated it when you thought you were. I'm here. I'm always going to be here and that's not going to change."

That was true. Her best friend had opted for a local college rather than get out of Fort Wills.

"Can I ask you something?" Tabitha sat up, trying not to show she cared or that the answer mattered more than it did. This was very hard for her, but she needed to know the answer.

"Sure, go ahead."

"I know there have been a lot of sightings with Simon. What makes this one so different?" This one had warranted her father coming to see her. He'd stayed for dinner, helped to tuck Nathan into bed, and they'd talked. It had been nice.

Looking back, she'd realized there had to be something important that she was missing when it came to Simon's latest appearance.

Usually, she got a nice little text or a phone call. Most of the time from Lash or from Angel, depending on where he was.

This was different.

Daisy sighed. "I don't think I should tell you."

"Now you're going to start keeping secrets for the club?"

"It's not about keeping secrets. It's where he suddenly appeared."

Tabitha's heart raced. "Where?"

"I don't think I should tell you. It's not going to give you any kind of real closure."

Tabitha gripped her friend's hand and held it tightly. "Please, tell me. I know, I get it. You want to protect me. To spare me the pain. You're the only person I know who won't sugarcoat this. Just give it to me real. Please. It's all I'm asking."

Daisy licked her lips and she saw how uncomfortable her friend was.

"Simon … he's in Vegas."

Tabitha froze.

"More importantly, he's been spotted by one of Butch's crew. He was fighting at Ned Walker's place. One of the underground fights." Daisy frowned. "Look, I only know this because I overheard, okay? I also happened to hack into the computer. I know Ned likes to keep security footage of the fights. He has a lot of important people who bet on the life and death of his fighters. It's his insurance."

"I get it. I know what my grandpa is capable of." Ned Walker was a very old man but nothing seemed to be slowing him down. He wasn't much older than Tiny, and her dad was starting to show his years.

Clearly, Ned Walker had lived a lot better and more peaceful life than her father. Either way, how was she supposed to deal with this?

"Wait, he was fighting?"

"Yes. Simon was fighting and, Tabs, it got real ugly. Simon is … he's a machine. I mean, I barely recognized him."

She frowned. "What do you mean? How did you know it was him? It might not be him."

"He had your name inked on his heart. Tabby. I saw it. I could read it. He's the only one to call you that. It's him. No doubt."

He was in Vegas fighting, killing people, while she was in Fort Wills, living a nice peaceful life, trying to stay out of trouble. This was his way of dealing with killing Ryan. She didn't know if she should laugh or cry. When they were younger, all he wanted to fucking do was settle down in Piston County so he could prospect at Chaos Bleeds. There was a time she wanted to travel to explore the world. That had all changed, but it was so ironic to her now. He'd gone off to travel and do whatever the hell he wanted to do, while she had to stay at home and take care of everything.

She let out a laugh. "I guess this is the way he deals with what he caused, huh? Excuse me."

She got to her feet but didn't get far before Daisy hugged her. Her best friend hugged her tightly, trying to help her, but she didn't need help. There was nothing out there that was going to help her.

All the tears had been cried. The pain, it was still there but now, she felt anger. A bitter rage rushing through her body, ready to explode at any minute.

He could do whatever the hell he wanted. He was in Vegas fighting. She knew what was in that city; her grandpa who was known for his fights. Not only did he invest in the legal kind, but he also ran the illegal fighting ring in the city. He was a deadly fucker and the men who fought for him, well, she would never want to meet them on a good day.

Simon was there.

He wasn't getting over killing but doing more of it. He'd rather kill than be with her.

She was done with him. Through.

Simon wouldn't ever come near her again. While he was taking the time he needed, she'd fucking show him.

Chapter Three

Tabitha wanted to kill her parents.

She'd murder them both in their sleep.

She wasn't an idiot. They both knew what they'd done.

Niles Walsh. A very nice, very straight-laced man who worked at the bank. No, he didn't just work there. He was the person who ran it and didn't he like to let everyone know it. The moment she opened her door to his smug face, she'd wanted to punch it. This wasn't a good way to start a date.

A deal was a deal. She'd grabbed her coat and now they drove, side by side.

"You know, you didn't have to go to so much trouble," she said, glancing over at him. A part of her wished Tiny had asked Luke. At least then she wouldn't feel so uncomfortable and she'd be able to drop the fake niceness.

Niles had shown an interest in her years ago. She'd been standing in a long line and he'd singled her out to help. There had been older people and gorgeous women waiting in the long line, but he'd helped her. He'd opened up a till, been nice to her, only to close it once they had finished.

The next time, she'd gone to the bank with Nathan. He'd given her the same treatment, but he'd been more polite, constantly looking down at her finger.

She was still married.

Simon hadn't divorced her ass yet.

Maybe now she should file the papers. The thought shot a pain through her body, but why not?

Simon was out fighting, getting over killing a man by killing other men. She'd gotten Daisy to show her the footage. It had taken a couple of bribes and the bonds of sisterhood and friendship, but it had been worth it. She'd stood with her best friend and watched Simon.

He was bigger, harder, more muscular, but there was no mistaking who that was or what he was doing. He was a fighter. He'd found some kind of peace in fucking killing people. All this time she'd been waiting for him to return, taking each day at a time, waiting, wondering when he'd come back, and this was her payment. So much for waiting for the love of her life.

They were supposed to be together forever and always. That was their thing.

"You are going to love this Italian place. Their Bolognese is just the best."

She glanced over at him. This date was going to be a disaster. He'd picked an Italian place, just like Simon had for their date. She didn't want to make comparisons, but she couldn't seem to help it.

"So Tiny tells me you like gardening."

Her father had seen her in the garden once, and that was to try to organize her on this date. She didn't like gardening at all. It was a necessary evil. "Yep. Don't like weeds growing in my yard."

"Is that what you want to do as a professional?"

"No. I like to keep my yard tidy and it keeps my son happy." She didn't want to talk about her son. Unless it got him off her case. If he told Tiny the date was awful, her father would back off. It would be a win-win for her.

Folding her arms, she released a sigh. "Are we there yet? I'm starving. I forgot to eat earlier. I made Nathan some pasta. I'm not big on the whole Italian. Nathan farted in—"

Niles started to laugh, which she didn't like. As she stared at him, he didn't stop. "Want to tell me what is so funny?"

"Your father. He told me that you're not the

easiest woman to get along with. He also advised me that you might try to be a bit of a pain."

"And you still wanted to go on a date with me?" she asked.

"I doubt it escaped your notice that I'm always on the main floor when you enter."

She had seen him. "You're a stalker."

"No. I'm not a stalker. I like you, Tabitha. I just didn't know how to approach you."

"Look, I want to be straight with you. I didn't want this date."

"I know. You don't have to make it bad for either of us."

"I don't want to give you the wrong impression. Believe me. There's no chance here."

"Is this because of Nathan's father?"

She didn't know who Nathan's father was. Simon or Ryan. Both were the same problem. "You could say that."

"I'm not a bad guy. Yes, I am a pompous ass. I make a good living and I'm a workaholic. My life has been in that bank, but when I look at you, Tabitha, I see a great deal and I just, let me at least take you on this date as friends. Can you give me that?" he asked.

She wanted to tell him no. "You're not … you're not going to assume that if I say yes that it will mean we're going to be dating all the time?"

Niles laughed. "You certainly know how to make a guy feel special."

She thought of Luke. "I don't want you to get the wrong idea. I don't see this going anywhere. I have a son. A whole lot of issues with his father. To be frank, if I get my hands on him, there's a chance I'm going to beat the crap out of him." Tabitha nibbled on her lip. "You and I, we don't mesh well."

"Then let's have a nice meal between friends. I won't expect a second date and you can be assured I will enjoy the food and the company, but not expect anything else."

"Okay, Niles. You surprise me."

"I have that wonderful way about me." He reached over and patted her leg. "Now, do you like Italian?"

"I don't eat meat but I do love pasta."

"Don't worry, Tiny told me you don't eat meat. I checked with the restaurant and they've got plenty of pasta dishes for you to pick from."

"If you're so nice and accommodating, why are you still single? I'm sure a lot of women would love to have you."

"Ah, but it is also my choice. I'm … picky."

She burst out laughing. "You're picky and you think I'm the perfect candidate to date? You do know my dad was once President of The Skulls. I'm his daughter. The club life is all I know. I used to beat people up. I've got an attitude."

"Yes, I know all of this, but you see, I also saw that you're a fighter. You don't allow anyone to walk all over you. You fight for what you want. You're kind even if you don't want me to see just how much you are. You're considerate and above all else, you love family. You're a family woman. I don't see a single thing I don't like. You're incredible."

"I suggest you hold your judgment there, Niles. You don't know me."

"But I'd like to. As a friend, of course. Even if it does scare me a little. You're very passionate," he said.

She chuckled. "I don't think this date is going to be so bad."

They arrived at the restaurant. She tried not to

feel overwhelmed as it was fancy. There were a valet and a maître d'. They were seated at a nice, cute spot, private. The lights were low. The music soft.

"This is as friends?"

"This is one of the best restaurants around. Trust me. You're going to love this." They were handed the menus and she noticed hers didn't have any prices on.

"If we're doing this as friends, I need to know the cost."

"No, you really don't."

"Niles, I can't have you paying for me."

"I'm a gentleman. I asked you on a date, I picked the place, and I will pay."

"My dad set this up."

"He did, but that didn't mean I couldn't turn him down."

"You're being sweet. Is he paying you to be sweet?" Tabitha asked.

"No, this is who I am. But believe me, I can be a real bastard when I want to be. Would you like some wine?"

She shook her head. "Just water for me." The last occasion she'd relaxed, drank some beer, and partied, Angel had called her to tell her about Nathan's fever and how he'd gotten really sick. She'd been too drunk to drive and at the hospital, the guilt had overwhelmed her. Even though Sandy had told her not to worry about what other people thought, she hated looking like the idiot young girl who'd gotten pregnant by accident but wanted to continue living her life. She didn't want that.

So, she never drank. Sure, she went to parties and danced. They were always few and far between.

"Would you trust me to order for you?"

"Why not? Have at it." She didn't see a reason to argue with the man. He'd taken care of everything else.

This was supposed to be a relaxing evening. The waiter took their menus and she glanced around the restaurant.

"It's a nice place."

"I'm glad you think so."

"Do you take all of the women here?"

"No," Niles said, laughing. "I don't date a whole lot."

"You don't?" She looked at him. He had to be in his thirties. He was older than her. Why was her father setting her up with older men? "Do you mind me asking your age?"

"Oh, of course not, I'm thirty-five."

"Right," she said. "I'm twenty-three."

"Yes, your father did say."

"What else did he say exactly?" she asked.

Niles's face went a nice shade of red.

"That flattering?"

"He said that you've … I don't feel comfortable with this."

"Oh, please, do continue."

He sighed. "You're making this very difficult."

"I imagine it's hard for everyone on a date," she said. The only person she'd been with, the only guy who'd ever made her heart soar, was Simon. The very man she was angry with right now. Who she wanted to forget more than anything. He could go around fighting, doing whatever the hell he wanted while she had to remain at home being the good little girl. No, she was done waiting around for him.

"Your father told me you were in love with a man, a man who he didn't think deserved you. You've been waiting for him to come back to town. How from a young age, you'd both promised yourself you'd be together for a lifetime?"

"It seems my father likes to talk a whole lot."

"He cares."

She pressed her lips together, trying not to be hurt. "His name's Simon. The guy. The one I'm in love with." She no longer wore the ring he'd given her. Not on her finger at least. The ring was around her neck. She kept it on her person, always.

Damn it.

Was she really waiting for someone that was never going to be hers? The security footage Daisy had shown her hadn't exactly given her an insight into Simon's life.

She'd waited for him. Had he done the same? There were a lot of women at that fight. All of them had been over him like he was a fucking drug.

Niles reached over, taking her hand, making her jump.

"Are you okay?"

"Yeah, yeah, I'm okay. I'm so sorry. I zoned out a little."

"Simon hurt you a great deal, didn't he?"

"No, of course not."

"You don't have to lie to spare my feelings. You've been pretty clear where I stand."

She took a deep breath, licking her lips. "I'm sorry."

"You don't need to apologize."

"I kind of do." She took a deep breath. "I … I don't know where to begin."

"How about you don't begin? Why don't you just speak and see where that leads you?"

"Do you think five years is a long time to be waiting for someone? He promised me he'd be back. I know he keeps his promises, usually. I sound like a sucker right now. I can even hear it myself. I suck at this." She hated how desperate she sounded. This wasn't like her. This wasn't her, period.

"Ugh, I've turned into that woman who waits around for a lifetime for a guy who's never going to turn up. I can't believe it." She shook her head, dropping her head into her hands.

"I love the weird glares I'm getting, but could you please keep it together?" Niles asked.

She lifted her head up and groaned. "I'm sorry. I'm not normally like this."

"I have no doubt. I bet you're usually really funny."

"Not in a long time. The most excitement I get is when a pair of Nathan's socks goes missing. Especially if they're his favorite. He likes everything to do with the sea. He's going to be a pirate one day. He has to have these socks for bed." She shook her head and laughed. "This is so awful."

"It's fine."

"Why are you being so nice to me?"

"I'm a nice guy."

She sighed. "You are and thank you." She held his hand, giving it a squeeze.

"I think this can go down as the weirdest date in history though. I will have you to thank for that." He smiled as he said it, and she joined in, laughing.

It was nice to not think. To just be.

The waiter brought their food and she had a beautiful rich tomato sauce that was so delicious. She closed her eyes, basking in every single bite, enjoying the taste as it exploded on her tongue. It was really good.

For the remainder of the meal, she listened to Niles, hearing about his life. He had two sisters, both younger. One was a lawyer, another a doctor. Both were very competitive. His parents lived over in Italy. They'd retired there a couple of years ago. He often traveled to see them.

They wanted all of their kids around them, but understood they were living their dreams. Niles always wanted to work in banking or accounting. He was good with numbers. She listened to him talk and it was a lot of fun just to relax, not having to take charge of the conversation. He was fun to listen to.

By the end of their meal, she enjoyed a chocolate dessert while he ordered the cheesecake. Afterward, she wasn't ready to head on home, and so they decided to take a short walk.

She put her hand through his arm, linking them up as they enjoyed the night air.

It was dark and there was a slight chill to the air. They were due another heat wave. Nathan had already asked if he could get the pool out and she'd agreed. If it was going to be as hot as they said, she was going to enjoy it by the small pool, after work.

"You know, I think we've walked far enough," Niles said, coming to a sudden stop.

Tabitha lifted her head and glanced around. The buildings with the intricate designs and pretty titles were gone.

She saw the rundown buildings, broken windows, and graffiti all over the wall. She'd been enjoying their walk and hadn't paid attention to where they were heading. Up ahead, she saw light filling the night. She and Niles stood near the last lit lamppost.

Noise.

Heavy grunts.

Yells.

Cheers.

Groans.

All of it filled the air, making her heart race. She didn't know what the cause was, but she knew she wanted to find out. Would it be so hard to go and see what all the fuss was about?

"I think we should head back."

"Do we have to go?" she asked. She had to go and see what was up ahead.

"Really, Tabitha, I don't think that's a good idea," he said. "I promised your father I'd take care of you."

"We're only going to go and check it out. It'll be fun. You said yourself you wanted adventure."

He pulled against her hand, not moving an inch.

"Niles?"

"Look, I'm not ... I'm not a fighter. I've never been in a single brawl. I run a bank. I'm not ... I don't know how to protect you."

"You don't need to protect me, Niles. Come on. You said you'd give me a good time. I want to go and see what all the fuss is about. It'll be fun. You'll be surprised." She didn't know if it would be fun for him but it would be for her.

She honestly didn't know if she was making the biggest mistake of her life. Ever since she'd had her altercation with Miss Andrea, something had been woken up inside her. She'd found herself going to the Quad. She didn't know if it was still used by the latest bunch of Skulls and kids. There had always been rumors spread about what happened there. She heard them but didn't partake.

The fight was back inside her.

She pulled Niles along behind her. His name was so close to her twin brother's, who she hadn't seen in a short time. He was prospecting for the club and Lash wasn't taking it easy on him, or on Anthony.

Pushing those thoughts to the back of her mind, she walked up to the main building. A large guy had his arms folded, ink displayed.

"You got to pay to get in."

"See, we can't go in. Come on, let's go," Niles said.

Tabitha pulled out some cash and handed it to him. "Now we can." She took Niles's hand and marched him into the fight.

They stuck out. This wasn't like Ned Walker's fights. People here were dressed in jeans, coveralls, and not a whole lot of anything else.

The scent of blood, smoke, and sweat was heavy in the air. Her heart raced. She hadn't been this excited in a long time. It was exhilarating.

Glancing around, she saw men raising their fists in the air.

"Kill him!"

"Hit him!"

"Get it over with!"

"Stop toying with him."

"Kill! Kill! Kill!"

She looked toward where they were shouting and she smiled.

The podium was raised. It was a fighting ring. Two men she didn't recognize were pretty much killing each other.

She put a hand to her chest, feeling the pounding. Moving her way through the crowd, she saw the ref move toward the two men. One of them was in a chokehold. The other flailing around.

The ref slammed his hand to the mat.

The crowd shouted out the countdown and finally the man patted the mat, wanting out. This wasn't an underground fighting ring. If it had been, this man would have been dead already.

They got to their feet and the crowd roared with

approval. It was so vibrant, intense, and everything she'd been wanting. Watching the men walk off, she saw one had an arm across the shoulder of the other, like a team. There was no animosity.

"Now, ladies and gentlemen, I know you all go crazy for a bit of girl-on-girl action." There were some whistles and screams of *fuck yeah*. She shook her head and glanced over at Niles, who kept looking toward the door.

Poor him.

She wasn't ready to call it a night just yet. She felt like she'd found the payload of fun.

"Let's give it up for the undefeated champion right now, Melanie, The Dog, Tigers." A muscular woman came into the ring, holding her hands up, begging for the cheers. Tabitha saw the strength in the woman, the confidence. This woman wasn't waiting for life to come to her. She'd run headlong into life. She had some ink on her body as well. She wore a pair of tight shorts and a vest top. At first, with the reference to The Dogs, she worried this was about the Monster Dogs MC, but looking at her know, and knowing fighting the way she did, this woman was no relation to the MC.

She was clearly on top of the world and at that moment, Tabitha envied her.

The announcer was called to one end of the mat. Tabitha watched him nod and then turn to the crowd with a smile.

"I'm afraid we're going to have to miss our most prized part of the evening."

Boos descended on the mat. No one was happy about being kept waiting.

Tabitha's heart hadn't stopped racing and she watched as people shook their head.

"Her opponent is not going to be able to make it

tonight, but if you stop by tomorrow—"

"I'll fight her!" The words were out of her mouth within seconds, before she could take them back.

Attention turned toward her.

"Tabitha, what the hell?" Niles asked.

She looked toward him.

"You're going to get yourself killed."

"No, I won't. Besides, if anything bad happens, you can call my father." She moved toward the mat, but he grabbed her arm, stopping her.

"This, all of this, is insane."

"I know, right? It's completely crazy, but here's the thing. I'm doing this. I want to do this and I'm going to." She looked at the mat and smiled. "Please, try to understand."

"If anything happens to you, your father is going to kill me."

She shrugged. "He won't. He knows what a pain in the ass I can be."

Heading toward the mat, she climbed into the ring and approached the middle of the ring. Melanie scoffed.

"You think you've got a shot against me, princess? You don't have a chance."

Tabitha wasn't threatened. "I want to fight."

"What are you, twelve?" Melanie asked.

"I can do this. I can fight," she said, ignoring her opponent.

The crowd had gone silent, all waiting to see where this was going to go. The energy in the room was insane. She loved it.

"How old are you?" the announcer asked.

"Twenty-three and believe me, this isn't my first fight."

The man looked down at what she was wearing. The dress came to her knees, but it wasn't tight at all.

She had a lot of movement within the outfit, even if it wasn't exactly the best.

"The heels will have to go," he said.

As the announcer got the crowd ready for the action, she removed her shoes and tossed them toward Niles, who only shook his head.

"Please, it's going to be okay. I promise."

Without waiting for his response, she came back to the center.

"What's your name, sugar?" he asked.

"Tabitha … Skull." It seemed only right to use her club's name.

Stepping back from Melanie, she watched as the other woman raised her fists.

What are you doing? This is fucking crazy. You're not a kid in high school anymore. You shouldn't be on this mat. There's no way you're going to win this. Slapping around Miss Andrea isn't winning a fight.

Melanie came at her.

She dodged the first fist, and the second. She spun and made Melanie chase her.

You're a mother. You should be setting a better example.

Tabitha grunted as Melanie struck out, hitting her in the gut and then slamming her fist against her cheek. That was so going to bruise tomorrow. Rather than go down, Tabitha stepped back.

"There's no fight in you. Come on, end this, it's going to be a bloodbath," Melanie said.

Tabitha stayed where she was. Another couple of punches, one to her chest, the other to her stomach. She got slapped around the back of the head and her hair was tugged.

She got away, facing off against Melanie, who she had yet to hit.

You're better than this. You're not him. He left. Simon left and he's enjoying beating the crap out of people for fun. He killed someone and left to get his shit together. It has been five years. Five years and he's still not here. He's gone. He's gone and he's not coming back.

In her mind, she saw her husband. The man she was supposed to be with. He'd promised her forever, but it had been lies. Every single part of their life had been lies. He hadn't stuck around. All he'd done was what he wanted to do.

Melanie swiped at her. This time, she blocked her arms and swung. She connected with Melanie's jaw. It was a hard hit, making the woman stumble.

The pain. The anger, it washed over her like rain, pouring out of every single pore and nerve ending.

Simon could go and live his life while she had to wait around, always waiting around, but no more. She wasn't going to take his shit again, or ever.

Over and over, she lashed back, hitting Melanie, taking the woman by surprise by the sheer force. She slammed her fist, once, twice, a third time, and she went down. Stepping back, she waited.

Melanie got back up.

The crowd was going wild, but Tabitha didn't care.

She hit back. Melanie hit her.

Pushing out the rage and pain, she just unleashed hell, and her opponent took it.

Finally, after what felt like an hour, the ref called it a draw. There was no winner, but she and Melanie were both bleeding, panting for breath.

Her dress was torn in a couple of places but she didn't care because she'd never felt so alive.

The last five years, without Simon, she'd been

dying inside. The only saving grace for her was her son.

"You know, you are one hell of a fighter," Melanie said. "It was an honor to fight against you." She held her hand out and Tabitha took it. "Until next time."

She didn't agree. Climbing out of the ring, she went to Niles, who looked ready to vomit. "I called your parents."

And just then, Tiny walked in and from the look on his face, she was well and truly fucked.

Chapter Four

"Are you fucking insane?" Tiny asked, pacing the length of The Skulls' clubhouse. In the corner, she spotted Devil. She hadn't realized he'd turned up in Fort Wills. Did that mean another family get-together was happening or was this about Simon?

They all had a tendency to meddle where they didn't belong and she was sick of it, and sick of them.

"Tiny," Eva said, going to his side.

He shook her off. "Niles is a nice guy."

"Yep, he is a nice guy. You shouldn't be blaming him for what happened."

"I'm not blaming him. I'm blaming you."

Sandy stood in front of her, patching up her face. "You took a couple of good hits."

"The woman I faced was a damn good fighter." She smiled at the other woman and winced.

"Yes, a damn good fighter and this is going to sting for a couple of days. I don't know what you're going to tell Nathan."

"I fell down or something. He doesn't need to worry. There's nothing he needs to deal with. He's just a kid." In the past few hours, the aches had started up. Her knuckles were split and bruised. She also had nice discoloration on her stomach and chest. Melanie had even kicked her a couple of times for good measure.

It had been fun.

There, she said it.

"I don't know what the trouble is. Niles and I, it's never going to happen. We're not going to be anything other than friends. Especially now, I feel like he's a little tattler. There was nothing to worry about."

"You were fighting!" Tiny yelled. The sound echoed around the room. A couple of the guys didn't look happy. Daisy held her hand. Anthony was in the corner with Miles. She didn't know where everyone else was.

She'd slowly been distancing herself from the club. She didn't know why, just that it felt right to do.

"And? It's not like I was in Vegas, was it? At Grandpa's place, killing people. No. it was civilized." She spat the words right back at him, watching as Tiny and Devil shared a look. "Is that why you're here? To go and see Simon?"

"I'm aware of his sudden appearance in Vegas," Devil said.

"Yeah, so am I. He's making quite a name for himself."

"We believe he may try to reach out to you," Devil said.

"He can kiss my ass." She wasn't going to forgive him or have anything to do with him. "What do you want from me?"

"I was wondering if you would consider a move to Piston County," Devil said.

She huffed. "No. I won't consider a move. This is where I live."

"I want to deal with Simon and to do that, I'm going to need you to lure him there."

"Piston County isn't my home. You think I'm just going to move Nathan to somewhere he doesn't know?"

"Nathan and you are family."

She shook her head. "No, we're not."

"You're still married to my son."

"And guess what conclusion I came to today. I'm going to be divorcing him as well."

Silence rang out across the clubhouse. She winced as Sandy dabbed at her cheek.

"What? Have I surprised everyone?" She looked

at her dad, Devil, and Daisy before returning her attention to Devil. "I went on a date tonight and deep down, I felt like I was betraying some kind of pact I have with Simon. He's not here. He's off playing around and I'm done. I'm done waiting for a man who doesn't have the balls to come back to me."

"I don't believe you've thought about this."

She forced a laugh. "Are you kidding me right now? I have thought about this. Since we were kids, you were both trying to keep us separated. Always meddling. Always doing whatever it was you do to keep us apart. Guess what, it worked. We're apart. I want a divorce!" She pushed Sandy away.

"I don't want this. I had fun tonight. Do you even realize that? The first time in my life I actually had fun and it was fighting. I'm not going to give that up."

"Tabitha, if Simon comes to Fort Wills, it could start a war," Lash said.

This made her pause as she turned to the club president. One look at Lash had her gaze going to Anthony.

Her friend stared back at her.

"What do you mean?"

"As part of the turf agreement, Simon is never to set foot on Fort Wills land. If he does, we breach the peace agreement, and our club goes to war with the Dogs." Lash held himself up tall.

"So we're a bunch of pussies now? Is that it? We're scared of the other club?"

"If Simon sets foot in this town, not only will it put The Skulls in an all-out war, it will put my son at risk," Devil said.

"This is the agreement you made?"

"The Monster Dogs are not a club to mess around with."

"We're The Skulls," she said.

"Yes, and you think I haven't lived through enough death? I had to make a judgment call at the time. None of us could afford a war, and I'm not about to start one now."

She stepped away from them. "That's why you want me to come to Piston County. He's safe there."

"Simon can approach you and he'll be safe."

"Still, we're protecting him while he does whatever the hell he wants. I need some air." She walked away, shaking them off as she headed outside toward the benches. So many memories swarmed her but rather than fight them off, she embraced them, basking in the feelings of a time when life was simpler.

Their love.

Tears filled her eyes. One of which was starting to swell.

She heard footsteps and then felt Miles's arms around her.

"Why didn't you ever tell me?" she asked, burying her head close to him. She knew a deal had been made but not the ramifications of that deal.

"I wanted to, but you were always hurting. I didn't want to make it worse. Lash and Devil made the right call at the time. We all knew it. Also, in the beginning, there was no risk of Simon coming back."

"And you think he will now?"

"Yes. Showing up with Grandpa, it shows he's close to us now more than ever. He's coming for you, Tabs."

She didn't believe it. "Tell me, have you talked to him? Called him? Anything?"

"No. I haven't spoken to him. Simon and I, we were never close, not really."

She sniffled. "I hate this."

"I know."

"I want to be over him. I do want a divorce."

"Simon won't give you a divorce and he's coming for you, no one else."

"Come on, you can't believe that." She pulled away, wiping at her eyes and wincing. There were certainly consequences for being in a fight and for not being in a fight for a very long time. "I don't want to make this choice. I forgot how much it sucked getting hit." She was in so much pain, physically and emotionally.

"That's what you get for fighting. Was the chick hot?"

"Even now, you're all about the sex."

"Hey, I've got to keep my reputation up some way."

"What about Constance?" she asked, groaning. "I've been such a crappy friend." With Nathan, work, and her life doing a complete three-sixty, she'd turned her back on close friends.

"You're not a bad friend. Constance is away at college. She's studying art or design or something."

"Yeah, I did hear some fancy college was willing to pay for her scholarship." Tabitha looked at her brother. "You know, the same scholarship she didn't apply for or have any knowledge of."

"What are you getting at?" Miles asked.

"I know the truth. What I'm wondering is why you'd do it."

"She's talented and I want her to have the best life she can."

"Being halfway around the world."

"She wanted to travel," he said, shrugging.

Tabitha shook her head. "So the girl you've been crushing on for a lifetime is halfway around the world, traveling, for what? For you to miss her?"

"No, for when she gets back, for it to be all out of her system."

"Do you think she's going to come back?"

"One day."

"And you're waiting for her?" Tabitha asked.

"Yeah, I'm waiting. I'm not living like a monk and she's, you know, living her life."

"You never told her how you felt?"

"Didn't want to." He shrugged again.

"You're as stubborn as Dad."

"Yeah, and the stubborn gene completely missed you." The sarcasm dripped from his lips.

"Wiseass," she said. "I've missed this."

"You need to come around the clubhouse more often."

"Why don't you come and see me at home?" she asked. "I can cook, you know."

"Yeah, but you see, being a prospect doesn't exactly come with a whole lot of perks."

"Meaning?"

"Meaning, I've got to do a lot of shit I hate doing. It's all part of the job and most of them fucking suck, but once I get my patch, I'll be there."

She looked toward the clubhouse and sighed. "I've got to go to Piston County, don't I?"

"You don't have to go, but if we're all right, then Simon's coming back for you. If you want to see him dead, stick around. I'm sure we can take on the Monster Dogs and Chaos Bleeds. We're badass. If you don't, then you're going to have to consider it."

"Even if I stay long enough to serve him with a divorce?" she asked.

"Yeah."

"Will you come and visit me?"

"I'll try to."

She stared at her lap. Her hands were a mess. The fight tonight. The fun she had, it was starting to ebb away, leaving nothing but the memory of the pain and loss.

"I'm tired of waiting, Miles. I ... the date tonight. Niles, that's my date's name."

Miles burst out laughing. "Talk about keeping it close to family."

"You're disgusting."

"I can just see it now. What a way to dampen the mood. Like mid-sex, you accidentally call my name."

She hit him in the stomach. "You're gross."

"I can't believe you went on a date with a guy named Niles."

"He wasn't that bad. Dad set it up."

"That's just worse. Dad set you up with a bore. Wait, is this the guy from the bank?"

"Don't start."

"I'm not saying a word."

She felt his body shake with the chuckling. "It's not funny."

"I'm not saying anything."

"No? But I can feel you laughing."

"I'm sorry. It's just, you on a date with a banker. Is he still alive? And how are you still awake?"

"It wasn't too bad."

"Really?"

She shoved him with her shoulder. "It wasn't."

"You decided on this *not so bad* date to go and enter a fight. You're telling me that was just for the good of what? The universe?"

She sighed.

"Look, Tabs, I know this has been hard for you. I get it."

She glanced at him. "I don't think you do. There's nothing for you to understand." She blew out a breath. "What happened can't be taken back." She ran her fingers through her hair only to find more pain points, so she stopped. "I think fighting was a bad idea."

"I bet you were a badass, though. You always were."

"How did we get here, Miles? Seriously. I feel like I'm all alone in the world and I know that's not true."

"Maybe it feels that way to you," he said. "After Nathan was born, you stopped coming around so much. I guess it can be pretty tough."

Staring down at her hands, she felt this huge, empty hole deep inside her core. An emptiness that never seemed to be filled.

The Skulls hadn't pulled away from her. She'd come away from them. It had been easier for her to do that than to take every single day waiting for them to hate her or Nathan.

"I'm going to go to Piston County."

"Tabs?"

"It's the right thing to do." She pulled away from him. "I'll miss you. I will. Always, but I've got to do this. Either to get closure on it, or to just get some answers."

"He's already taken so much from you."

"Not really." She reached for her necklace and held up the ring Simon had given her. "You see this, this is important. This is everything. I love him. I can't stop loving him, but I know I can't live like this anymore. I don't want to. It's not good for Nathan."

"What about school?" Miles asked.

"They have schools over there. It's all very civilized."

"Ass, I don't mean it like that." This time, he nudged her shoulder. Finally, he wrapped his arms around her and held her close. "I'm going to miss you."

"I'm going to miss you too."

"You'll be safe though, right? No funny business."

"Nothing. I promise. I'll be good."

Chapter Five

Two days later

After dropping Nathan off at school, Tabitha headed back to her brand-new apartment. It wasn't too far from where Devil and Lexie lived. It was a new build and expensive. She couldn't have afforded it on her own, but it turned out Chaos Bleeds liked to invest in housing and apartments. She was living here rent-free.

After letting herself in, she made herself a cup of coffee and got to work putting her and Nathan's stuff away. She'd done a lot the past couple of days. She hated living in mess. As she set up Nathan's room with the toys he loved and the clothes already hanging up in his closet, there was a knock on the door.

Rubbing her hands down her jeans, she went to answer to find Lexie on the doorstep.

"Morning. I thought I'd come around," Lexie said.

After recovering from breast cancer five years ago, Lexie looked like her old self. Her hair had grown back, richer in color than ever before.

"Sure, come on in." Tabitha left Lexie to close the door. "You want coffee?"

"Love some."

Heading to the machine, she had no doubt Chaos Bleeds had intended for her to live here from the start. The apartment was fully furnished. There was no need for her to buy even the simplest of things like pillows or lampshades. Everything had been catered to her every need, even in colors she liked as well.

Did Simon have something to do with that?

Lexie joined her in the kitchen as she added some milk to the coffee before handing it to her.

"You're kid-free for a change," Tabitha said.

Her mother-in-law laughed.

Mother-in-law. It seemed rather odd to think of her that way, even after all these years. She poured herself a cup, the second one of the day, and sat down at the small table. The first sip had her closing her eyes, enjoying the taste.

"School days just lately, I'm always on my own," Lexie said. "Not that it's a problem. I'm always keeping busy."

Tabitha smiled.

The awkwardness built with every passing second.

She took another sip, hoping for something to crop up so they could talk.

"How are you settling in?"

"It's okay. Nathan's trying to make the most of it."

"He doesn't like it?"

"This is his first time living in an apartment. He's used to a yard so he can play. There's a small park across the street. I'm going to take him to it regularly, so that should keep him occupied."

"Crap, we took you both from what you knew and now you're having to adapt already."

"It's fine."

"No, it's not." Lexie closed her eyes, pursed her lips. "I honestly thought Devil was kidding. Why would he even agree to allow Lash to make that kind of deal that put Simon at risk? It's fucking stupid."

"It's what needed to be done."

Lexie frowned at her. "You're not pissed?"

"I'm a lot of things, Lexie."

"You haven't answered my question."

"Some shouldn't be answered." She reached out, putting a hand on Lexie's arm when she got the sense the other woman wanted to argue. "Please, don't let me open whatever that will. It's not going to be good for either of us."

There was a hole inside her and it was fast growing into something she didn't like. The fight had helped her to let it out. Nathan had been shocked by the bruises on her face and the truth was she liked them. The pain helped her to feel alive. To know she was still human. She was still … herself.

Fighting had become second nature to her during high school. Since having Nathan and living her life, she hadn't allowed herself even the luxury of watching people fight.

This was the first time she'd done something so selfish, just for her. She wanted to do it again.

Instead, she did the right thing. Drinking coffee, taking Nathan to school, unpacking.

"You're so grown up, Tabitha. You make me so proud."

And yet, little by little, she was dying inside. It didn't stop. The pain, the fear, the anger. It kept on multiplying. She couldn't get it to stop.

Finishing off her coffee even as it burned her throat, she stood. "Is there anything else I can get you?"

The frown was back on the other woman's face, but she didn't care. She had to do something. Dwelling only served to make her realize Simon was off killing people rather than getting his shit together, and she was here, alone.

Nathan might not even be his kid.

She shook her head, trying to clear the toxic thoughts from her mind.

"Tabitha, what's wrong?"

"Nothing's wrong. Believe me. I'm fine. Perfectly happy. So, er, I've got a lot of stuff to clean away. I wanted it done rather pronto. I'm sorry if I'm seeming in a rush. I want to find a job and provide a little stability for my son."

"Oh, a job, well, I was going to ask if you would like to help us out at the shop."

Lexie and a great deal of the Chaos Bleeds old ladies had opened up their own fashion line.

From what she recalled Simon saying, it had been a huge success. Forcing a smile to her lips, she said, "Thank you, I'd like that."

Are you fucking crazy? You don't want that. You want to live your own life and still, you're being offered.

It's the polite thing to do.

Fucking polite, yeah right. They're just putting you in a little box. They're trying to keep you contained.

"When do you want me to start?"

"Tabitha, is everything okay?"

"Yeah, everything is fine." She finished washing up her coffee cup and slid the milk right back into the fridge. "Look at that, I've got to go shopping as well."

"I'm getting the message," Lexie said, finishing her coffee.

"No message."

"How about I come with you to the store?" Lexie asked.

No!

"Great, I'd like that."

Why are you lying? Tell her to fuck off and to go look for the son who just left to deal with his shit.

It's not Simon's fault.

He shouldn't have shot that piece of shit.

You wanted him to.

Shut the fuck up.

She had to stop speaking to herself in her own mind. It was starting to make her sound like a crazy person and that was never, ever, any good.

Grabbing her bag from the corner of the kitchen, she slid it across her body and she followed Lexie out of the apartment. After locking the door, they walked toward the elevator. She normally took the stairs, but with Lexie, she took the elevator.

Standing in the metal box, she stared at the numbers taking her down to the ground floor.

"You can talk to me about anything. You know that, right?"

"I certainly do."

"We're all here for you."

"I get that. Thank you. I do appreciate it." She took another deep breath. *Come on. Open up.*

"I know this is hard for you. All of the Chaos men are hard."

"Simon, right now, is not a Chaos man. He's not anything. He's living his own life without a care in the world. I saw the footage, Lexie. He's living it up." She pressed her lips together. "I'm sorry."

"You're angry."

"I'm fine."

The elevator doors opened and she quickly stepped out.

Making it toward the main door, she took a deep breath the moment she hit the air.

I can do this.

Why was she struggling now? Why wasn't she able to keep her shit together? She'd been doing just fine back home. Why was it so hard now?

Pushing all of those thoughts to one side, she focused on just putting one foot in front of the other. Lexie caught up with her just as her cell phone rang. "I've got to take this."

She stopped walking and waited.

"Crap, I've got to get to the school. It would seem a bug is going around and well, I'm needed," Lexie said.

She forced another smile to her lips.

"Will you come around for dinner?" Lexie asked.

"One day soon. I want to get Nathan settled into a routine. This is all new for him and I don't want to make it harder for him than it has to be."

"Of course. I completely understand."

Awkwardness again.

"I better go. Those groceries won't buy themselves." Tabitha wanted to kick herself. What the hell was she doing?

Still, she kept on playing along. Lexie suddenly pulled her in for a hug, holding her tightly.

"It's all going to work out one day. You'll see and there won't be any more confusion or pain. I promise."

Pulling away, she smiled again and headed in the opposite direction. She didn't have a car and she much preferred to think.

Yeah, you want to think. Every single thought you have is filled with anger.

Closing her eyes, she took a couple of steps, came to a stop, and then focused on her breathing.

In and out. She made sure the air went deep into her body before exhaling it out. After a couple of minutes, she felt better, more grounded.

She started to move forward. One foot in front of the other.

From the last time she lived here, she remembered where the grocery store was. She gripped the handles of a cart and made her way inside. Nathan was a weird kid and liked to have a lot of vegetables. She didn't mind that about him at all, seeing she was supposed to feed him at least five of them. It made cooking food for him easy.

She picked enough food to feed them for two weeks. Shopping was fun, but she hadn't suddenly become addicted to food shopping. With everything bagged, she was able to carry it home without too much trouble. Her arms ached but this was the price she paid for a kid and some food.

One step in front of the other.

Her thoughts returned to Simon, like they always did.

Had he slept with other women?

Other than the date with Niles, she hadn't been with another man. She hadn't kissed anyone else.

Not even been near anyone else.

Luke had been around and he'd wanted to be a support for her, but like the last time she saw him, she shot him down. She wasn't about giving men the disbelief they had a chance with her.

Did it make her a bitch? Probably.

Did she care? No.

She wasn't going to give anyone the false impression of her wanting them.

Back at her apartment, she put the groceries away and finished with the last of their boxes. With a neat pile near the door, she took a seat and simply stared away.

All it had taken were two days to move her life from one MC to another. She wasn't part of Chaos Bleeds, but now, she was in their territory.

In the last five years, all it had taken were two days. All of her possessions were put away. There was nothing waiting for a home. It was all just neatly organized.

It's fine.

Tears filled her eyes. Putting a hand to her chest, she leaned back on the sofa.

"I won't cry. I won't cry."

The one good thing about having a job and a son, she'd been able to keep on moving. To not allow herself these random moments, but now she didn't have that. Checking the time, she saw she had another three hours before she had to pick up Nathan.

"I'm fine. Everything is fine."

The tears didn't stop.

Closing her eyes, the first two tears fell.

The loneliness swarmed around her like a virus infecting every single particle of who she was. This had been her life for so long.

In her mind, she saw Simon as a kid, the way he came and pushed her. She kicked him back, and she believed that was what started their love. She hadn't taken his shit and Simon had adored her for it.

The letters. The phone calls. The memory of hanging out and coloring together. Even when her father and Devil had their fight and nearly tore both clubs apart, she'd seen Simon.

Lexie and her mother had seen to it.

They'd been through so much together, but Simon hadn't stayed when she needed him the most. He'd gone to do his own thing and what was that exactly? Oh, yes, to go and fight. He was getting over killing someone by actually killing more people.

As she wiped at her eyes, the tears didn't stop.

Alone. He'd left her all alone and she'd been fighting that feeling for so long, she didn't know how to deal with it. Taking a deep breath, she tried not to let it consume her, but with nothing to distract her, she felt it.

Her cell phone went off. This was a lifeline.

Checking the caller ID, she saw it was Daisy.

Accepting the call, she closed her eyes. "Hey."

"Tabs, you okay?"

"The polite way to answer the phone is with a hello," Tabitha said. "I know, it's a new thing all the cool kids are using."

Daisy chuckled. "Really, is that what people do? I would never have thought it. I guess that makes me a rebel then."

"Yeah, a total rebel. What's up?" Tabitha asked. "Not that I don't mind your call."

"If you must know, I'm missing you. It's not the same here without you."

"I miss you too."

"Tabs, are you crying?"

She touched her cheek. The wetness was still there. "No. Of course not."

"You're a shitty liar, you know? You were bad when we were kids but you're even more so now."

"You wouldn't have the first clue what you're talking about," Tabitha said, smiling. "It's good to hear your voice."

"How are the bruises? We didn't get a chance to hang out or you tell me what the hell was going on. It must have been a bad date."

"You know Miles said the same thing."

"He did?"

"Yep. It wasn't a bad date."

"I don't know. I have this feeling that if you date someone who owns a bank, he'll be talking stocks and shares, and boring you all through the meal."

"He was a gentleman. He did talk about work, but it wasn't too boring." She leaned back. Her face was still bruised. Dropping Nathan off today at school, she'd gotten a couple of weird looks from the mothers.

She'd been good at ignoring glares and unwanted looks. It was what she did.

"So, come on, tell me what the fight was all

about."

Tabitha explained what happened. How they were having a nice walk, talking, and she'd been enjoying herself. The fight had merely called to her, and before she realized she'd volunteered, she was in the mat, and well, the fight had begun.

Silence met her explanation.

"Daisy, you still there?"

"I'm here. I'm wondering, though, if you purposefully went to the fight to have one? You looked more like yourself that night, Tabs. I watched you. I haven't seen that smile or that fight since high school."

"As you know, a lot has happened since then. I've had to grow up a lot."

"I get that. I guess I just didn't realize how much you'd changed until I saw what that fight did to you."

"It didn't do anything to me, Daisy. I just, I don't know what it was I needed, but it gave me something." Not that it had stuck around for long. She'd been crying in her apartment when she called, but Tabitha kept that little piece of information to herself. No one needed to know what she was thinking or doing.

"You know I'm here if you need me."

"I know." Everyone was always available if she needed them. It was always the same old story. Forcing another smile to her lips, she realized no one was around for her to pretend to.

"Look, Daisy, I've got to go. I'm settling into the apartment. I want to make Nathan his favorite dinner. Can we take a raincheck and talk about this another time?"

"Sure, sure. Call me anytime. I'll pick up."

"I will. I promise."

She hung up the phone, dropping it against her chest and releasing a breath.

It's fine.

Everything's going to be fine.

Tabitha only hoped she took her own advice.

****

"She's falling apart," Lexie said.

Devil sat on the edge of the bed, removing his boots. "I know."

"How could they not see it back at home?"

"It's not our place to judge." He put his boots on the mat his wife had put out for him. She hated it when he brought dirt into the bedroom, unless it was the right kind of stuff. He slid his jacket off and placed it on the chair in the corner. His wife's clothes were already neatly folded.

"It has only been a few weeks, but I can see she is hurting. I know Eva told me that Tabitha is strong, and I know she's strong. I can see it. Did you see her face?"

Devil went toward his wife, cupped her cheeks, and kissed her deeply. "I saw everything."

Lexie held on to his shoulders. "We've got to do something."

"I've spoken to Lash and Tiny. They all say she's a fighter and that allowing her to have her own space will help."

"They clearly don't see what's happening."

"Honey, we don't know what's going on."

"We have a very good rough idea." Lexie groaned. "I'm being judgey, aren't I?"

"You're worried. Do you think we need to be concerned about Nathan?"

"No, she loves her son. I can see it. I've, you know, gone and checked on them a few times. She takes him to the park regularly. Of course, they've been around town as well."

"You're spying on them?"

"I don't have a choice. It's not like she accepts any invitations I give out," Lexie said. "Has she even been by the club?"

Devil shook his head. "No. I heard she got a job at the coffee shop. The new one that just opened at the edge of town."

"It's like she's trying to get as far away from us as she can."

"Can you blame her? She's here because of Simon," Devil said. "She's not here because she wants to be and if the girl has any sense, she'll be pissed at my son. I know I am."

"You can't be angry at him."

"Yeah, I can. I taught him better. Killing that little prick the way he did, it was selfish."

"Even after what he did?" Lexie asked. "I don't want to have this conversation."

"You as well as I know that kid had to die. Simon, he wanted it dealt with. He's smarter than that, and since then, that girl has been alone. She hasn't had anyone. Sure, her family is there, but we all know the real person she needed couldn't be found. Now, once again, her life has been changed to accommodate him. It seems to me all she does is help Simon when she can. It has to stop."

He looked at his wife as Lexie pulled away. "You mean to tell me that if Tabitha requests it, you're going to help her get the divorce?"

"Yes. She's dying, Lexie. I've caused a lot of pain and suffering in my time, but we've known her since she was a little girl. I'm not going to allow even my own flesh and blood to continue to taint her world. The moment Simon arrives, if Tabitha asks for it, I will make sure he grants her the freedom she deserves, and I will even take her and Nathan wherever she wants to go, set her up in a new life."

"You're serious about this. Like actually serious."

Devil nodded. "I think it's only right for us. I won't be responsible nor will I help her die. For five years her life has been put on hold."

"Because she's waiting for our son."

"Exactly. I don't think it's right."

She laughed. "What if it was you? Would you expect me to move on?"

Devil went to her, capturing her lips, showing her just who she belonged to. "It's pretty fucking simple, baby, you belong to me, and there's no way I would've walked away from you. No way at all."

"Simon loves her."

"And he better hope that Tabitha is willing to stay. I mean it, Lexie. Simon will learn his lesson one way or another."

Chapter Six

Life wasn't too hard.

Tabitha cooked, cleaned, took Nathan to school, worked at the coffee shop, and picked him up. They ate breakfast and dinner together. While he showered, she packed his school lunch. If they had time, she'd take him to the park, watching him play. After taking him to school, she'd go to work, then pick him up.

She'd found a pattern.

Every now and then, she'd go to the supermarket for groceries.

Come back home.

The pattern was the same just with a few variations.

This made life easy.

She didn't have to think.

Lexie would show up, or Devil. Each time they did, it reminded her of all that she'd lost. Of everything she tried to forget.

The bruises on her face disappeared. No show for Simon.

Nothing.

With Halloween around the corner, Nathan had begged her to go trick or treating and she just couldn't say no to him. The Chaos Bleeds were having a Halloween party, and Lexie had told her Elizabeth had opted to take all the kids walking the streets in costumes with Josh's help.

It was why she was dressed in a black dress, some heavy makeup on, and kissing her son on the cheek and wiping off the residue with her thumb.

"Mom, please, I'm supposed to be Dracula."

"And you look like a very scary Dracula. You don't suck too much blood tonight, okay?"

Nathan giggled. "You're so silly."

"Yep, this is what I am."

Halloween was proving to be a little bit of a problem for her. She and Simon always found a few moments to talk or be together that night. If he couldn't make it to Fort Wills, they'd chat over the phone.

Damn!

Why was this so hard? It wasn't like Halloween had been on hold for the past five years. Nope, just this sixth year was clearly cursed and she had to pay the price.

"Don't worry, I'll take good care of him," Elizabeth said.

"Thanks," she said. "Don't let him eat too much candy." Now she was starting to sound like her own mother.

"I won't, Tabby. You can count on me."

Before Tabitha could snap at Elizabeth for using that name, she had already taken Nathan and they were heading out of the parking lot.

Putting a hand to her stomach, she felt suddenly sick.

"Don't you worry about a thing," Lexie said, taking her hand. "Come on, the party has started."

Following Lexie inside, she entered the Chaos Bleeds clubhouse. It had been set up with Halloween banners, fake webs, spiders. Some ghouls hung from the walls. The decorations and atmosphere reminded her of home.

Going straight to the table of drinks, she was tempted to take the entire bottle of vodka. Instead, being the good mom she was, she grabbed a soda.

"You okay?" Dick asked, coming toward the table.

She glanced at his costume, some kind of doctor

with lots of blood all over the uniform and a fake hand coming out of the pocket.

"Yeah, I'm fine."

Stepping away from the table with her soda, she made her way to the corner and watched as some of the guys danced with their old ladies. There were a couple of club women around for the men who weren't taken. She didn't know if the women slept with the married men or not. There were always rumors of cheating, but she doubted it. It was the same back at The Skulls.

People liked to spread gossip. No matter how nasty it was, or whose relationship they could destroy.

Lexie and Devil were on the dance floor. She was dressed as a princess while Devil dressed as himself. There were a few fake scratches down his cheek but nothing else.

She watched them.

Tabitha saw their closeness. She could imagine they didn't see or even care about anyone else as they were with each other. The entire world faded away and all that remained was the two of them. Like she'd been with Simon.

In that moment, she went from being able to deal, to feeling squashed.

She sipped on her soda, trying to count to ten. Trying to do anything that would ground her rioting emotions.

Her control slipped.

Stepping out of the clubhouse, she took deep breaths, but the music, it was like a drug to her mind, pulling her back. Taking hold of the memories she had and drawing them one by one to the forefront of her mind, and she couldn't do that. She didn't want to.

Gritting her teeth, she forced herself to keep on moving.

Lexie had told her to stay at the clubhouse for fun and games, but it was hard. Everywhere she turned, be it in Fort Wills or Piston County, they had nothing but memories. Constant, never-ending memories. All of them centered around her and Simon.

It wasn't like he'd died, making the memories special or in any way different. That hadn't happened at all. No, Simon was still out there, living his life to the fullest, and she, she was dying. There was no mistaking what had happened. He'd gone on to live his life and she was still stuck in the past.

Did Simon have moments of utter despair?

Did he wonder about her?

Or was he too busy fucking fighting to even think about her?

She kept on walking. Adults and children walked the streets, singing their little hearts out. A couple of kids were already vomiting from too much candy. She ignored it all and kept on walking.

The night consumed her, swallowing her whole, and she welcomed it.

If she could keep walking and not think, she'd be back in control.

"Well, well, well, what do we have here?"

Tabitha frowned as she looked up. She'd kept on walking and now, she was in a part of town she didn't recognize. It was dark. The street lamp up ahead was dead, and she glanced up to see some rundown shops. Windows had been smashed, and some of the letters were missing from what the signs used to say.

Spinning around, she saw a man carrying a brown-wrapped bottle. His gaze ran up and down her body.

The look reminded her of that day. Of the way Ryan looked at her.

Rather than run or scream, she dropped her hands and clenched them into fists.

"Now how did I get so lucky as to have a nice, ripe peach like you wander into my humble abode?" he said.

"I suggest you back off," she said. She was more than ready to take him on.

Another chuckle, this time behind her. She turned and now saw two men.

Great. Just great.

Looking between each of them, she kept them within her sights, waiting, anticipating. Wondering who would strike first.

"You know, you're making a mistake," Tabitha said. It was on the tip of her tongue to say Devil's name, but he wasn't here. No one was here. Like usual, she was on her own. No surprise there. Being alone was fast becoming second nature to her, just like everything else in her life.

Always, forever alone.

Looking between each man, she knew they were going to hurt her. There was no way she was going down without a fight.

"I guess you guys want to party. Who's going to take the first shot?" she asked.

You can do this. They're drunk and disgusting. They don't know you can take care of yourself.

She waited.

The man who spoke to her first came forward. She waited, the anticipation riding inside her.

Come on, fuckface. Let me see your best shot.

It wouldn't hurt her to attempt to kill him. In fact, she hoped he came at her. She wanted to feel the pain as she took him down.

A woman she may be, but she wasn't weak.

He reached out and she made her attack Slamming him in the nose, she felt the bone give and heard the crack as it echoed through the night.

There was the pause. The unearthly silence that seemed to last a lifetime but was in fact only a few seconds. Neither knew what to do, and then at once, the man howled in pain as he charged at her. At the same time, his friend came. Grabbing the man who'd tried to touch her first, she shoved him against his friend while also nailing him in the crotch. He went down, crying out.

As she was shoved against the ground, she didn't have time to stop her fall before the second man gripped her hair and tugged her head back.

She screamed, sank her nails into his hand, and tore.

He dropped her down.

Getting to her feet, she wasn't fast enough as a fist went for her face. Someone grabbed her around the waist and threw her against the brick wall.

She whimpered but didn't stop.

"Play nice," the man said, but she simply reached between his legs and took hold of his cock, squeezing him hard.

Her death grip was broken as she was tackled to the floor.

Someone was on top of her, and in the distance, she heard a whimper, a cry, a beg, and a sudden crack.

The guy on top of her was suddenly gone, and she stared up at the dark sky. Nathan had told her he didn't like her with the bruises, and now she was going to have a couple more.

No one had come back to attack her.

Lifting up onto her elbows, she stared straight ahead. Both men were dead on the ground. She could tell by their necks being at odd angles. No one lay like that, not on purpose.

Someone else was there, though. He stood near the bodies.

His jeans tight to his body.

She lifted her gaze up, knowing, feeling it in every single part of her.

Tabitha paused at his chest and then forced herself to look into his eyes.

Simon stared back at her.

The boy who had left her now stood a few feet away, a man. His gaze cold. He panted. It was Simon, but he looked different. Gone were his boyish charms.

"You fucking bastard," she said.

It was the last thing she said before the world went black.

****

"Did she faint?" Dean asked.

Simon stared at his woman. She lay on the ground. It was freezing cold and she wore a dress that didn't exactly protect her from the elements.

After removing his leather jacket, he wrapped it around her and picked her up.

"She's probably tired or something."

"Or something?" Dean looked around. "Did you have to snap their necks?"

Simon had debated passing the woman fighting in the street. He'd watched her, the long blonde hair, and it made him ache for his woman. Tabby.

He didn't know the pull, or at least he hadn't understood it, but now he did. The blonde hair had reminded him of his woman because it had been her.

He'd been so fucking stupid.

Never would he make that mistake again.

Five years.

She was in his arms where she rightfully

belonged.

"They don't deserve to breathe the same air as her," Simon said.

"Do you think she recognized you?" Dean asked, coming toward his side.

"Yeah, she did." He held her in his arms and he didn't like how light she felt. Tabby had always been a curvy woman. She liked her food. Ate a lot, and he loved that about her. He loved the smile on her lips after she smeared a fry in ketchup and popped it into her mouth. The big bites of burgers.

What had happened?

You know what had happened. You left.

Holding her close, he refused to let her go. "You're good to clean up this mess?" he asked, looking toward Dean.

"Dude, you need to call your dad."

"I don't. Not yet." He walked down the street, holding his woman. The scent of vanilla filled his senses.

"Where are you taking her?"

"Back to the cabin."

"Seriously? What am I supposed to do?" Dean asked.

"Lay low for now. I won't announce our arrival or the guys until I'm ready." He moved toward the van and slowly slid her into the passenger side. To stay out of sight, he'd left the bike out of town at the cabin he'd found. It was rundown. No one owned it until one of his guys had purchased it.

Now it belonged to him.

Just like this woman belonged to him, and he wasn't ever going to let her go again. Not ever. He'd promised her right from the start he'd come back for her, and this was him keeping his promise.

Once she was safe within the van, he walked to

the driver's side and slid in. Turning the ignition over, he pulled the car out of the space and headed out of town.

Piston County.

Not much had changed.

Some of the signs had moved and of course a few were now different, but the basic structure, it was all the same. His father still ran this place and Simon doubted Devil would let anything ruin it. His old home.

Pushing those thoughts out of his mind, he glanced down.

Tabitha was so fucking beautiful. All the photos he had no longer did her justice. They were all from a time that was so distant, he had to wonder if he'd really lived it. Neither of them was the same. Over the years, they had both changed.

Five years wasn't a long time, but it was enough to change a person. He wasn't the same.

Reaching out, he touched Tabitha's hair. Still as soft as he remembered, but she wasn't the same. The fighter in her, she was still fierce, but those men tonight, they'd been too much for her. She could have killed herself facing them. Why didn't she run?

She was never a runner.

Always a fighter.

That's not going to change.

Of course, his woman would stay and fight. It was who Tabitha was. Deep down, she hadn't changed, and he never wanted her to.

This was his woman.

He drove all the way to the cabin. Tabitha didn't stir once and he was thankful for that. With how she greeted him, he had no doubt she'd be fucking pissed at him, and rightfully so.

You fucking bastard wasn't exactly the warm welcome he'd hoped for. He'd known she was in Piston

County. He'd known the moment she left Fort Wills.

Calling Anthony had given him the few little details he hadn't been aware of. The deal his father and Lash had come to. The ultimatum. He hadn't been told when he first left what had happened. It was a good thing he hadn't come back for Tabby all the times he'd wanted to. He'd be no good to her six feet under. So the Monster Dogs wanted to kill him. He couldn't blame them, but for now, that was a fight for another day.

Arriving at the cabin, he went to the door, opening it up before returning to Tabitha. He held her in his arms as he carried her through the house, toward his bed.

He laid her down gently, going back to lock the van and close the door, and then return to the bedroom where she lay looking oh so peaceful.

Removing her shoes, he was tempted to take off the dress but thought better of it.

Again, her three words to him rang in his head. She wouldn't appreciate him touching her any more than he had to at this point. Even though all he wanted to do was touch, to memorize her body once again.

Stepping away from the bed, he lowered himself into a chair and watched her.

Just how tired was she? She didn't bang her head.

Getting to his feet, he moved toward her, touching her head and feeling for any lumps that would mean she had to go to the hospital.

Nothing.

He moved away, removed his clothes, and wondered if he should go to the sofa.

If she woke up, she'd be confused.

After changing into a pair of sweatpants, he slid beside her, not touching, just watching.

She let out a little gasp, and her body seemed

drawn to him.

Did she know it was him?

They'd slept together so many times. He loved to watch her, like he did now. She'd come to Piston County to protect him.

He saw that.

Loved her even more for it.

She was the only light in his world.

Stroking her cheek, he gently kissed the tip of her nose and settled beside her.

He didn't fall asleep.

Sleep wouldn't come to him, not yet.

Nights were the longest times for him.

He had to sit around waiting for his mind to be at peace.

"Simon!" Tabby's scream filled his head. He saw the Quad again as if it was like yesterday. Not five years ago. It was longer than that now.

Simon saw the tears in her eyes. The pain. He knew what Ryan had done to her. Anthony had told him what he'd seen. What he walked into. His woman had needed him and he hadn't been there. This was all his fault and nothing he did would ever ease her pain.

"I promised you I'd take care of you," he said.

"And you will. Please, come with me. Let's go. You and me? We've got our whole summer ahead of us, remember? We made plans. It wasn't this. Please, don't let it be this. I'm begging you. Don't walk away. Please."

He'd been tempted to follow her. His Tabby made a lot of sense. She always did. Only he'd made the fatal mistake of turning back to look at that prick. The way he looked. The arrogance, the confidence. It sickened him. Ryan believed he was going to get away with it.

Tabby called his name again.

"I can't. I'm sorry."

He'd heard the bike in the distance, but he didn't care what it meant. They could have been police sirens. Anything. All he saw was Ryan. The visual in his mind of what Tabitha went through was a constant echo. He couldn't stand it. The gun in his hand had been a lifeline he hadn't realized he needed. Ryan thought he was going to get away with it, but that wasn't justice. He'd fired the gun and with it, satisfaction came. He didn't expect to be happy or relieved, but he had been. He'd been so fucking thrilled, he kept shooting. He'd wiped the smirk off Ryan's face. He'd kept on shooting until nothing else remained.

It was wrong of him to do it, but he didn't regret it. Even now, looking back. He didn't see any part of what he did as a mistake.

Far from it.

He'd done the right thing.

The best thing for all of them.

Ryan was dead, but as he'd put each load into his body, piece by piece, a part of him had died, and it wasn't ever going to come back.

That was his punishment, but he had a horrible feeling it wasn't going to be the end of it.

Chapter Seven

Tabitha opened her eyes.

She wasn't in her apartment, nor was she back at home in Fort Wills. This wasn't the Chaos Bleeds clubhouse.

Brand-new aches and pains filled her as all of the memories from last night came tumbling back toward her.

Simon!

She'd seen him. Had actually looked him in the face and spoken to him. She glanced around the room and she just knew this was his place. Wherever this place was. She placed a hand to her chest, trying to control the rioting beat of her heart.

It didn't help.

The sound of him walking around was like a bomb going off inside her head.

Throwing off the covers, she put her feet onto the carpeted floor. It was nice, soft. She had to get in touch with Lexie to ask about Nathan. If she was here, who had taken her son? There was no phone and she didn't have her cell either. She'd left her bag at the clubhouse.

Fuck.

Padding to the door, she stopped.

Five years.

This had been one of her dreams for so damn long and now, she was petrified. Anger rippled down her spine, threatening to crush her at a moment's notice.

Ignoring it, she stepped through the doorway and followed the noise he was making.

Hands once again clenched at her sides, she turned her full attention to the man who had saved her last night.

He stood shirtless, showcasing all the brand-new

tattoos decorating his body. Her attention was caught by the ink, some tribal, others with more detail. The unmistakable graveyard across the base of his back was somewhat disturbing, but it was so tastefully done at the same time.

This was Simon.

This was the guy who owned her heart.

He turned, catching sight of her, and they both froze.

She looked at him, waiting.

They weren't the same people. He'd snapped those two guys' necks like it was something easy to do. It wasn't easy. The last person she knew who could do that was Lash. Probably Killer. To snap a guy's neck, it took strength.

Staring at him now, words failed her.

Neither of them spoke.

The kettle on the stove whizzed, breaking into the silence.

Simon turned away.

"Do you want a coffee?"

"Where am I?"

"You're safe. That's where you are. Coffee?"

"I need to call Lexie."

"I suggest you don't." He pulled the kettle off the burner, turning toward her.

"Because what you say counts now?" she asked. "It's what I've got to do because you as my lord and master, I now have to follow your rules, is that it?"

"I don't want to fight."

"Neither do I." She dropped her gaze from him. "I need to talk to Lexie."

"Not going to happen."

"Is this your attempt at kidnapping?"

"Yes. You're not going anywhere, Tabby."

"Don't you fucking dare call me that."

"I'll call you whatever I want to. You're still mine, Tabby."

She burst out laughing. "Oh, I'm yours now? The big, bad man has come back to town and he thinks we're just going to pick up where we finished. Is that it? You think you can come here and have me again?"

"You're mine, Tabby."

Staring at him, she shook her head. "I used to think I was yours. I believed in us, but you, you only take care of yourself."

"What the fuck is that supposed to mean?"

"I saw the tape," she screamed at him.

He frowned.

"Yeah, I saw the tape of you in Vegas. At one of Ned Walker's fights. I'm not stupid, Simon. I know what those fights mean. I know how dangerous they are. To the death. You were in an illegal fight. The same guy who told me five years ago to wait for him because he had to get his shit together because he killed someone!"

"I did get my shit together."

"By killing more people? That's not getting your shit together. That's living on a never-ending excuse."

"No, what I realized, Tabby, is that some men and women have to fucking die! They don't deserve to breathe the same air as you."

Her mouth opened and she closed it. "You've got to be kidding me. You're going to blame all of this on me now? It's my fault you had to do what you had to do, is that it?" She pressed her lips together. "I guess it is my fault. If I hadn't been in the wrong place at the wrong time—"

"Don't."

"Then I guess Ryan wouldn't have had the perfect oppo—"

"I said fucking don't." Simon picked up a knife and threw it across the room. The hard blade embedded in the wood of one of the posts.

Tabitha was nowhere near it, but she saw the violence simmering beneath the throw, waiting to erupt.

Silence rang between them.

She watched him, waiting.

"What happened was not your fault. None of this was your fault, Tabby. Never ever for a single fucking second believe it."

Tears filled her eyes as she looked at him. "I have to call Lexie."

"No, you don't."

"Yes, I do because I have to speak to my son," she said. There was no point hiding Nathan. She couldn't do it.

Simon stared at her. "Your son?"

"That's right. My son. He's five years old, nearly six."

He stumbled back as if he'd been hit. "He's mine," Simon said.

It didn't sound like a question.

This time, Tabitha looked away, the tears she always tried to control spilling down her cheeks.

"I don't know," she said. "That one time the condom broke, it was so close to … what happened."

"He could be Ryan's?"

She sniffled. "I don't want to talk about this."

"You didn't want to risk it?" Simon asked.

She looked at the man she loved more than anything. Even now as she hated him with a passion, she loved him. That was what sucked the most. She loved and hated this man. Right now, hate was stronger but she couldn't be the reason he died. It was why she'd come to Piston County.

"I … the test to determine his paternity was too risky for me. I … I felt him move. I felt him, and I couldn't go through with losing him. There was always a chance he was yours and I couldn't kill a part of you."

"You could find out the truth," Simon said.

Tabitha wiped at the tears in her eyes. "And do what? Put him up for adoption? Give him to someone else?" She clenched her hands. "Nathan is my son. I took the test but … I never opened the results. You weren't around. I couldn't even get in touch with you. I talked to Anthony, Lash, my dad, Devil. None of them would help. We'd get random sightings."

She pressed her lips together. "Regardless of who his father is, I loved him, and for me, that was all that mattered. I love him. He's my son, and I've been taking care of him. I have to call Lexie."

She stared at Simon.

His jaw clenched.

He shook his head. "No."

"Are you fucking kidding me right now?" she asked.

"I've told you. No. My parents will take care of him."

She picked up the nearest object, which looked like a vase. She threw it at him. The first throw didn't make her feel any better. Picking up item after item, she kept on throwing them at him, screaming out as she did.

Simon dodged them and he came toward her. Turning on her heel, she rushed toward the door, but she didn't get anywhere. He was a lot stronger than her. He wrapped his arms around her waist, spun her around, and pressed her up against the hard wood of the door.

She slapped him hard across the face.

He captured her hands, each one, pressing them above her head. She stared into his eyes, waiting.

Simon didn't let her go.

"I hate you," she said.

"And I'm still in love with you."

"You left."

"And now I'm back, to stay."

She shook her head. "I don't trust you."

"One day, I will earn that trust right back."

Before she could stop him, he slammed his lips down on hers. The touch was so unexpected. She hated her body's reaction to him. He let go of her hands, his going to her back. One traveled to her ass, cupping the flesh, as the other sank into her hair, holding her in place.

She released a little moan, wrapping her arms around him.

Damn.

It had been too long and yet, not enough time.

He smelled the same, just muskier, sexier. Again, in his arms, even bigger and more muscular, he was still Simon.

His tongue stroked across her lips and she opened up to him. He sank inside, and this made her moan again, even more desperate for more of him.

He gave it to her.

Both of his hands moved down, gripping her thighs, and lifted her up. Circling his waist, she melted again, but sanity soon began to flood her.

This was Simon. Five years stood between them. Too much history.

She pulled away, breaking the kiss. "No," she said.

Simon didn't argue with her. "You're mine, Tabby. You can go on pretending you're not, but your body and your mind know who you belong to."

Her lips were swollen. "My son needs me."

"And our son will be taken care of."

Her chest tightened. He'd said *our son.*

She hadn't been wrong.

He saw Nathan as theirs.

As she watched him, he returned to the kitchen. "You need to eat and drink something. You're not leaving until I'm ready."

"You can't keep me here. Simon, this ... it was wrong of us to even think for a second that you and I could make this work."

"Nothing has changed," he said.

"Everything has changed."

"Not this. Not us. We're never going to change, Tabby. We promised each other forever."

"Things change," she said.

"You're being stubborn." He glared at her.

"And you're being a pain in the ass," she said. She didn't like how easy this was. How normal it felt to be talking to him, even after all this time.

He chuckled, turning to place a cup in front of her. "Drink up."

"Simon, come on, be serious."

"I am. We've got a lot of unresolved issues. I know you're angry. You want to fuck my brains out and gouge out my eyes. I know which one I'd prefer more."

Her treacherous body certainly responded to the thought of fucking him. They had been enjoying each other, and their short-married life had been perfect. Their time in the bedroom even more so. They'd both been virgins, but fast learners as well, and they had loved exploring one another. Staring down at the coffee, she wanted to fight this. He'd been gone so long. It wasn't fair.

None of this was fair anymore, and she was tired of it.

"I want a divorce." She said the words she truly

believed she was never going to say, but they had to come out.

This with Simon, it hurt too much. She was done, and it was time to move on.

****

"You do know the way to get a woman to forgive you is not to tie her up in a basement to a chair," Dean said.

"Noted."

Simon looked down the street. So far, no one was aware of his presence. He had five guys living in Piston County and they had been able to make themselves blend into the neighborhood. It wasn't that he didn't trust his father, it was that he simply didn't trust him. Yeah, made no sense, but he understood his thoughts.

"You're going to fuck this up," Dean said.

They had gotten closer with their time on the road. Riding from town to town, sometimes not having any money to find a nice motel or even a run-down, rat-infested building. They had become well-acquainted with the night sky, and of course thunderstorms as well.

They'd been through a lot together. Finding hell and working their way out of it. Dean was no longer the nice little rich boy he'd been. Gone were the soft edges and easy smiles. What stood in its place was a hardened man life hadn't been nice to. He'd seen what the hard life was all about.

During their travels, they'd gotten hurt a time or two. Their shit stolen.

Simon had become hard, as had Dean. It was what they did. Like his father before him, he'd managed to somehow draw people to him. Pa, Felix, Knight, Twig, and Teddy were amazing guys. They were the kind of people he could trust. In their own way, they'd become a family. He wasn't sure exactly if this was how his father had found the club he now had, or how each member gravitated to Chaos Bleeds. Either way, it had worked. He'd always been clear to the guys that he intended to go home. Piston County was where he belonged. There were always odd moments when he truly believed he would never return home, but each time he thought of his woman, there was no doubt in his mind. She was where he was meant to be. Wherever Tabby was, he'd be. He'd already spent so much time away from her, there was just no way he'd be able to let her go.

He wouldn't be without them now. When he'd told them what he had to do, where he was going to go, they had followed him. No questions asked. They knew how important Tabby was to him.

Now he had her tied up.

"I'm not going to fuck anything up," he said, finally answering Dean's statement.

"No? The girl of your dreams is locked up back at the cabin. She wants to talk to her son, which could be yours, or the rapist you killed."

"Enough, Dean."

Dean held his hands out. "It's not good for you to hide out."

"I'm not hiding out. I'm simply not going to think about him. Not right now."

"Why don't you just go to your dad?" Dean asked. "All this sneaking makes me feel like you're going to strike out. Take the club from him."

"I'm not taking the club from him."

"Then what is all of this about?" Dean asked.

Staring out of the window, he watched his father step out of the shop. His mother, Lexie, was in the doorway. A young boy with dark hair stood in front of her. Devil crouched down and gave his cheek a squeeze.

The kid was too young to be his brother or sister.

He didn't know if any of his siblings had kids. Elizabeth would be of age, but she'd always been about studying. He stared at the boy and he just knew. This was Tabby's baby. This was Nathan.

Simon didn't know what he expected, but a sudden wave of love washed over him as he looked at that boy.

He knew from his own coloring and Ryan's, Nathan could be either of theirs, but knowing he was Tabby's, it did something to him.

Devil stepped away, kissed Lexie's cheek, and moved toward his bike.

Did his father know he was in town?

Devil was always two steps ahead of the game. Simon had watched him closely and he expected him to strike any minute, but he didn't.

"Do you want to meet him?" Dean asked.

"My dad?"

"No, your son. Or not your son."

"He's my son," Simon said.

"You don't know that."

"What is Tabby's is mine. She loves him and that's all I need to know, and I love him as well." Simon fired up the van and pulled out from the curb.

"Well, do you?"

"Do I what?"

"Want to meet him? He's your son."

"Yeah, I want to meet him."

"Simon, I can't help you here if you don't talk to me."

"There's not a whole lot to do right now. Make sure the boys lay low for the time being."

"You're going to make this last longer?" Dean asked. "Don't you think that's a little stupid?"

"My parents know Tabby's missing. I imagine

they'll check where she lives if she's not staying with them. It won't be long for my dad to figure out I'm in town."

"You sure they're going to naturally assume it's you?"

"You don't know them like I do."

"Si, hate to break it to you, but five years changes a lot of people. You could be overthinking this shit. For all they know, Tabby might have run off. Had a life of her own. She's young and she doesn't want to be with a kid." Dean clucked his tongue.

Simon pulled the van to a stop near where Dean was camping out now that the cabin had Tabby inside.

"You're right. Five years is a long time. It can change a lot of people. You don't know Tabby. If she was going to do that, she'd have done it already. When he was born, she'd have made sure there was no memory of her for him. I know her. She hasn't changed."

"This is the same woman who wants to divorce your ass."

While he'd been tying her to a chair in the basement, Dean had arrived, hearing her swear at him, threatening the divorce.

"I didn't marry a weak woman. She's fierce and right now, she's hurting. I've just got to prove to her I'm not going anywhere. I'm here to stay. I'm going to love her forever."

Dean sighed. "You're still as pussy-whipped as you always were. You know the guys think you're some kind of saint?"

"I'm not a saint."

"No, shit. We all know that." Dean laughed. "I think the guys are shocked that you were never once tempted by the pussy that threw themselves at us. It was always available, and not one chick could make you stray."

"It doesn't make me a saint."

"To men who don't give a shit, I guess it does. Try not to get yourself killed," Dean said, climbing out of the car.

"I won't die."

Dean closed the door and Simon waited for him to get inside his place before taking off, going to the cabin. The drive didn't help to clear his mind. Normally, being on the road, either on a bike or in a car, had the power to settle his thoughts.

Nothing was helping.

Nathan.

Tabby.

Both were playing in his mind on replay. Tabby telling him she wanted a divorce and the little boy smiling up at Devil as his dad said something funny. Anthony hadn't told him about a kid.

That was where he'd gotten updates. Anthony had given him enough to get by but clearly not the truth.

What had Tabby been going through?

Arriving back at the cabin, he looked toward the door. Tabby was going to be so pissed at him. Not a day went by when he didn't think about her. She had to understand that he tried to be a better man for her.

Running a hand across his face, he took several deep breaths, trying to calm his nerves, but nothing was happening.

He tapped his fingers on the steering wheel to a beat inside his head. The right thing to do would be to let her go. It was what any sane person would do.

Simon hadn't claimed to be sane.

He climbed out of the car and headed toward the cabin. Closing the door behind him, he went straight toward the basement.

No sound.

Had she gotten out?

He'd tied her up really good. It would be next to impossible for her to get out. After flicking the switch, he walked down the stairs, taking his time.

She still sat in the chair and glared at him across the room.

Lowering down onto the step, he rested his elbows on his knees and looked at her. "How are you feeling?" he asked.

"Fuck you."

He smiled. "I see you've still got your sense of humor."

"I don't see anything amusing about this. I can't even believe I opted to come here rather than let you get killed. Next time, your ass is on the cutting block."

"I seriously doubt that. You came here for a reason. You're still in love with me."

"I hate you."

"Well, there is always that fine line. At least that's what people say."

"Fuck you." She repeated the words from before.

Simon looked at her, really stared at her, watching her as tears ran down her face.

"I saw him," he said. "Our son."

"He's not yours."

"You can say that all you want, but he is mine. He will always be mine because he's part of you."

"I meant what I said, Simon. I want a divorce."

"I'm not going to grant you one."

"You're being a dick."

Again, he smiled and approached her. Crouching down, he put his hands on her knees and looked up at her. "I love you."

Her jaw clenched. She looked away.

"I don't mind that you hate me."

"I want to go and see my son. Nathan hasn't been without me since he was born. He needs me."

"And when we resolve whatever is going on between us, you can go."

She shook her head. "You can't keep me here."

"I can."

"Do you think Devil doesn't have a clue that you're here? It's Devil. He knew the moment you arrived."

"Did he tell you I had? Did he let you know there was a risk I was coming?" Simon asked.

"I knew the moment I saw the footage of you at Vegas that there was a chance you were coming. Why else would you be so sloppy?"

"I wasn't being sloppy, Tabby. I was letting the world know I was back. I hadn't gone far, not really."

"You'd gone far enough. You were never close by. You didn't see me pregnant, nor did you know how bad the labor was. That I almost died? You didn't know anything. The club didn't want anything to do with him. It took Angel to allow him to even be accepted. My own mother didn't hold my son until after…" She sobbed and shook her head.

Gripping the back of her neck, he pressed his head to hers and tried to control his rage. "I would be there for you."

"He might not be yours, Simon."

"I don't give a fuck. He's mine. He will always be mine." One look at Nathan, and he hadn't seen Ryan. All he had to know was that he was Tabby's, and that made the little boy's life worth everything to him.

He pressed a kiss to her lips even as she fought him.

"I don't know what other women you've been

with. Let go of me."

Simon stroked her cheek. "You're going to fight me, aren't you?"

"It's not like you're going to give me any other choice. Let me out and we can talk like civilized adults."

He snorted.

Getting to his feet, he started at her back, then her hands, and finally, her feet.

The moment she made a dash for it, he was on her, drawing her to the ground but also protecting her so she didn't hit her head.

When he was sure she was safe, he grabbed both of her hands and locked them by her side, his cock pressing between her thighs.

Tabby's curves had gotten softer, her tits larger, and fuck, he wanted her. He'd never stopped wanting her.

"Get off me."

"One day soon, Tabby, you're going to beg for me. You're going to want me and I'm not going to do a damn thing until I hear those sweet words coming from your lips."

"I'm never going to ask you for anything." She gasped as he rolled his hips, touching a part of her he had a feeling she'd been denying existed for a long time.

"Your body remembers me. We had only just gotten started. I'm not turning my back on you, and we're going to see where this goes."

He kissed her hard, sliding his tongue across her lips as he let go of her hands.

She didn't fight him.

Tabby pulled him in close, just as he knew she would.

His woman could fight him all she wanted to. The real fact was she craved his touch, and he was going to make sure she didn't forget it. Not for a second.

He broke the kiss first, getting to his knees and offering his hand.

She didn't take it.

Still, he followed her upstairs, knowing he was going to be in a fight for his life to win her back.

Chapter Eight

Simon cooked.

It had been so long since anyone had cooked for her.

Tabitha glanced around the cabin and couldn't help but admire the beauty of it. This would have been a perfect spot to take their honeymoon.

They'd never had one.

Wrapping her arms around herself, she tried not to think of all the things they should have had.

"What are your plans then? Stalk to the shadows? Never letting your dad know you're here?"

"Like you said earlier, I believe my dad is very much aware of where I am, and I'm happy about that. I don't know what he's waiting for."

"Are you going to prospect for the club?" she asked. "Is this a little pit stop before you move on again?"

He stirred the sauce in the pot. She noticed he put meat in a separate one and had split down the sauce. She wasn't going to think of his actions as sweet. They weren't, anyone could cook a plain tomato sauce.

Pushing her hair off her face, she needed a bath. This was all a little too much. She missed Nathan, but she couldn't help but enjoy being around Simon.

Her heart raced and there were moments her body tingled. Her lips were swollen from his kisses. The pressure between her thighs was pleasant. She hadn't experienced anything bad or scary.

Her parents had wanted her to go to therapy to talk about what happened. Instead, she'd talked to Lacey and to Sandy. Lacey had experienced serious horrors as a child in an MC that was now annihilated, and Sandy was a doctor. Both women had told her she would know what to do to help her. Lacey didn't go to any therapist Tabitha didn't want to talk about any part of what happened. Anthony saw enough to know it had been bad.

The nightmares had stopped after a year, and she was stronger. She didn't get scared in a room full of men.

She had control.

What she hadn't experienced was sexual desire with a man. In the privacy of her bedroom, reading some dirty books, she'd enjoyed exploring her fantasies, but again, no man. With Simon, her body betrayed her.

She wanted him.

Craved him.

And that scared her.

What she wished was to stay mad at him. To make him pay for leaving her for so long.

It was stupid, but again, nothing about this had made real sense.

"I'm not leaving Piston County again. Unless you decide you want out of the club life forever. You were always going to be my queen. My old lady. I don't need the club. I've lived without it."

"But it's in your blood. You must have missed it. Isn't that why you're back?"

"I'm back because it's time. I'm ready."

"Great, because you're ready, everyone else has to be."

"What you need to understand, Tabby, is when or if I take over from Chaos Bleeds, if Anthony or Lash haven't made the necessary adjustments, I will be cutting all ties with The Skulls."

Tabitha opened and closed her mouth. "It wasn't all of them."

"I know, but I want nothing to do with them. I don't want a single association with that club. I will find a way to end them."

"What you're after is wiping out the club's existence, and this has nothing to do with me, not even a little bit."

"It has everything to do with you."

She laughed. "You could have fooled me. The entire club wasn't there, Simon. One man. You took care of him."

"And I made a mistake that night."

"Really, you made a mistake?"

"Yeah, I should have taken Ryan. I could have kept him alive for many months, making him pay for what he did to you. Instead, I showed him a kind death. Don't worry, I won't make that mistake again."

"So, what you want to do is go back to the old days when there was a risk of death at every turn. You know, being shot at, invaded, sent into hiding. We lived through all of that shit that our parents created."

"I know. Once the Monster Dogs are gone. I'm done."

"No," she said. "If you want your queen by your side, then no. You will back away right now."

He smirked. "You're my queen already."

"If that's so, you will listen to me."

"Of course. I will listen to whatever you have to say."

"Damn it, Simon. Stop patronizing me."

He stopped stirring and moved toward the counter where she sat. His hands flat on the surface, he leaned in so he was so close it wouldn't take much of a stretch to kiss him. His lips looked so tempting.

Seriously, what the ever-loving fuck? Stop thinking about him and sex. It's ... not good.

She wasn't going to become this person. No way. No fucking way.

Staring at him, she waited for him to say what he

needed to so they could both move on.

"When I take over as president of Chaos Bleeds, I'm going to need to talk to Lash."

"They will make the necessary arrangements." She stood up, putting her hands between his and touching the tip of her nose to his. "I will not live in a prison nor will I put my son in danger." The irony wasn't lost on her how less than a few months ago, she wanted the old days back where death and destruction were the norm. She couldn't go back. As a child, she'd gotten hurt, beaten in fact. The fear as gunshots rang out. She and Simon even had matching gunshot wounds for a through and through. It hadn't killed them, but that was their reality as kids. Seeing the worry, the fear on all the adults' faces, or even the rage. The blood. She didn't want that. Between them, Lash and Devil had found a solution that had brought peace between the clubs. Yes, something needed to be arranged between Chaos Bleeds and the Monster Dogs but until then, she didn't want a war.

"If you loved me, really loved me. Where you couldn't think about anything but me, then you will stop this path you're on, Simon."

"You deserve for them not to be walking around."

"It wasn't them. It was one man and you never punish the entire family for one person's wrongdoing. It's not all their fault." She also had just gotten Simon back. To wipe out a club, it would change him, and she doubted it would be for the better. The men in the clubs were always holding on by a thread. The thought of anything happening to Simon, of losing what she had now, she couldn't stand it.

"Let me put this to one side for later. I won't go after the Monster Dogs, and you will give me a chance."

"Simon, it's not like I have a choice."

He smiled. "You have a choice and you know it.

Stop trying to play the victim. It doesn't suit you." He kissed her lips.

It was a quick kiss.

No tongue.

She wanted to reach out, grab him, and deepen the kiss, but instead, she sat back in her chair as he went to the stove.

"Did you ever find a place to stay?" she asked.

"No. There was no reason to set down any roots. Dean and I, we moved from place to place, picking up work where we needed to, or entering fights to earn money. We kept a low profile for the most part. No one knew who I was, and Dean, well, he wanted to completely remove his prissy boy look."

"Is that why all the ink?" she asked, pointing at him. He wore a shirt but she remembered the tattoos.

"Pretty much. Found a couple of guys along the way who are good with needles." He drained the pasta and then split it between each pan.

Her mouth watered.

Simon served them both up two generous portions. He added some garlic bread to the mix.

"Let's take a comfy seat."

Getting to her feet, she moved toward the sofa and sat down. Her body still ached from the attack, and she had a whole host of new bruises. She was pleased Nathan hadn't seen her. He'd have been upset and she hated to see her little boy upset.

This fight hadn't been any fun and had in fact put in another reality to her need to fight. Not all fights would have a great outcome or allow her to walk away feeling invigorated or alive.

Simon put his food down on the wooden coffee table and handed her a pillow to rest her bowl.

She placed it on her lap and held the bowl of food

in her hands as he lowered himself beside her.

"How are you feeling?"

"Fine."

"I meant after being hit. You took a hell of a beating."

"It's not the worst one I've been in."

"You mean the club allowed you to get hurt?"

His voice deepened and she glanced at him.

Reaching out, she put a hand on his arm. "No. I … I was on a date and afterward, we both kind of stumbled into a fighting ring. Nothing too serious. There was this woman and her opponent didn't show. I volunteered. It was stupid of me, I know. I hadn't really fought in such a long time."

"Did you win?"

"No, it was a draw. The woman was one hell of a fighter." She smiled, remembering the feeling.

"You were on a date?"

"Ah, so you heard it."

"I hear everything you say."

"Apart from the fact I hate you?" She twirled her fork in the spaghetti, enjoying every single part of this.

"I hear you. I just don't believe you."

"You're fighting a losing battle."

"It's going to be a battle I keep on fighting for." He put some pasta into his mouth. "Always."

She licked her lips and picked up the garlic bread, taking a huge bite. The buttery taste exploded in her mouth, giving her a distraction.

They ate in silence.

With every passing second, Tabitha grew more aware of his body pressing against her. The feel of his thigh right beside hers.

Simon finished his food first and once she had, she handed him the bowl. He took them and she stayed seated, listening to him wash the dishes.

"Do you want me to help?"

"Stay. Relax."

She looked toward the door. Had he remembered to lock it? Getting to her feet, she saw she wasn't wearing any shoes. Simon's back was still to her.

She tiptoed across toward the door.

"It's locked," Simon said. "You can give it a try, though. I don't mind. See if it will budge."

He hadn't even turned away from the sink.

"You're a smart ass."

"I like your resilience. One day, you're going to realize you don't want to leave."

"Why? Because you say so?"

"No, because this is where you're supposed to be."

"I have a son."

"I know, and you'll get to see him soon."

She wrapped her arms around her body and went back to the sofa. Sitting down, she stared straight ahead.

Waiting.

Licking her lips, she lowered her hands and placed them on her stomach. This was the first time in a long time she'd eaten a meal and actually been full. He'd fed her and she'd accepted the food without a single thought.

She wasn't hungry anymore.

Sated.

Simon returned, carrying two large mugs.

She stared down into the dark liquid and smelled the hot chocolate. It was a comforting smell to her. Closing her eyes, she breathed it in.

"It's not like Angel would make, but it'll do the job."

Tears filled her eyes and she took a sip, scalding

her top lip but not caring at all. It tasted so nice,

"Don't cry, please, don't cry."

She stopped the tears. This wasn't sadness. She didn't know what it was, but it felt good. It felt pure, and she didn't want the moment to end.

Finishing her hot chocolate, she settled against the sofa.

"Do you want to have a bath?" he asked.

"Yes, I'd like that." And for now, she wasn't going to keep on fighting him. It was way too exhausting to keep it up.

****

Simon sat in the bedroom.

He'd drawn her a bath and now he sat waiting.

She was naked.

In the bathtub and all alone.

He'd put in some vanilla scents that she loved. Rubbing his hands together, he rested his elbows on his knees and waited.

There was nothing wrong with being the perfect gentleman.

You need to keep her on her toes.

Tabby was hurting. He got it. Five years without a single word, not that he didn't want to talk to her. There were so many times he lifted his cell phone, ready to talk to her, only to stop himself at the last number.

She didn't need him to constantly be calling.

He wanted to.

Instead, he'd kept on fighting. Turning all of his anger into the force he needed to win. It had been a long time since he'd lost any kind of fight.

Getting to his feet, he paced the length of the bedroom, which wasn't long enough.

Fuck.

He'd known for some time he'd fucked up. How

he should have come to her sooner. Everything had moved by so fast and he'd simply rode until he was done with waiting.

Stepping toward the bathroom door, he'd seen the desire in her eyes. The tightness of her nipples. She wanted him, but was also afraid. She wanted to fight and he was okay with that.

Simon made up his mind.

He opened the bathroom door. Tabby lay within the bubbles. Her clothes a pile on the floor. She'd bound her hair up on top of her head.

"What are you doing?" she asked.

He pulled his shirt over his head, dropping it to the floor.

The gun he carried was in his drawers, locked in a compartment. Traveling the streets, seeing the kind of dirty shit he had, he'd learned to carry a weapon and conceal it.

After dropping his jeans, he lowered his boxer briefs.

He stood, letting her have her fill, allowing her to watch. His dick was rock-hard and he wasn't ashamed of it.

Her gaze traveled all the way down to his cock and then back up.

He moved toward the tub and she didn't argue with him.

She slid forward and he climbed in behind her, opening his thighs for her to settle against him.

"I don't trust this submissive you," he said.

"Good, I wouldn't if I was you."

He chuckled. Resting his hands on the edges of the tub, he felt her. Skin to skin.

Five years, nearly six he'd been without this.

Unable to waste a single moment, he put a hand

to her stomach, stroking the delicate flesh. Nathan had been here. His son.

She didn't move.

He waited and slowly, she softened against him.

"There has never been another woman. You can ask Dean and the guys when I introduce you to them. I haven't been with anyone else nor will I ever be with anyone, ever."

Her hands went to his thighs. "It was only a date. Nothing happened. I haven't been with anyone either."

She covered his hands with her own on her stomach.

"So, we've both just had each other. Like always," he said.

"It seems that way." She tilted her head back. "It doesn't mean anything."

"Of course not. Who else would save themselves for a loved one if it didn't mean anything? It's nothing. I get it," he said. She'd lied about it not meaning anything and he saw it.

If this was what she needed to help her, he got it.

Slowly, he moved one hand up and cupped one of her large tits. He teased the nipple, stroking over the bud, going back and forth, pinching the tip. She gasped, arching up. Her legs opened a little wider, and with his other hand, he moved down, cupping her pussy. He held her within his grasp, letting her get used to his touch, before he finally moved a finger down her slit.

He teased from her hole, up to her clit, stroking over the bud.

She whimpered and he stopped but continued again when she thrust up against his hands.

Leaning down, he teased over her neck, sliding his tongue back and forth, biting down on her flesh until she moaned his name.

She was such a fucking temptation. One he couldn't control.

"Simon, please!"

She lifted up and he growled against her throat as her hand found his dick. Her fingers circling the hard length and moving up and down.

Fuck.

He didn't know how he was supposed to keep sane during this.

Her touch set him on fire. Closing his eyes, he tried to think of hundreds of different things, but with how she rocked her cunt on his fingers and pressed against the palm on her tit, it was next to impossible.

She was so close, and he wasn't going to come before her.

Using two fingers, he slid them over her clit, teasing her, getting her used to the feel of him. Her body tightened and the sounds coming from her mouth were so sexy and sweet.

"Yes, yes, yes," she said.

Her cry filled the air and he followed her soon after with a grunt, his cum filling the bathtub as he did.

Her hand let him go, and they both came down to earth panting.

He kissed her neck.

Neither of them spoke. No words were required. They knew what had just happened. What it meant.

Simon reached behind him, pulling the plug and standing up. Drawing the curtain, he turned the shower on, buffering Tabby's body with his own, so she wouldn't get the first spray of cold water.

He gritted his teeth at it, but it didn't take long to warm up. Once it had, he drew her in front of him. Picked up the bar of soap and a sponge, lathered it up, and pressed the cloth to her body.

She was sexy as fuck with a nice flush to her body. One he was going to remember always. They weren't teenagers anymore, fooling around. They were adults and with it, they could play in ways they never had.

He took one arm, then the other, washing her back, carefully moving to the front, down her body, her legs, between her thighs.

Rinsing out the sponge, he washed the suds from her body, paying attention to each part of her.

Once he was done, he removed the clip that bound her hair.

Running his fingers through the length, he got it nice and wet. He started with shampoo, massaging the gel into her hair, staring into her eyes as he did. She closed hers as he moved her back beneath the spray of the water. Once her hair was rinsed, he grabbed the conditioner and repeated the process.

When he was done, he expected her to leave, but she didn't. She took his place, lathering up his body. This time, her hands explored. The sponge and her fingers, stroking along his body.

He hardened just from her touch, but he wasn't going to push her. He'd already put her through so much.

Simon had to crouch down for her to do his hair and once it was rinsed, she wrapped her arms around his neck, kissing him.

He lifted her up, and her legs circled his waist. He didn't like how light she was. Did she take care of herself? Have a good meal every single day? He'd take care of her from this day forward. Never would he rely on anyone else to give her what only he could.

After carrying her through to his bedroom, he pulled the blankets back. Their bodies were still slick from the shower, but he'd put the heat on. It wouldn't be long before they dried.

Pressing her to the bed, he kissed her neck, moving toward her lips, taking possession of her mouth before gliding down her body.

She gasped as he got to her tits. Sliding his tongue across each peak, he pressed the mounds together and teased each one. Glancing up, he watched her as she looked at him. He waited for her to tell him no more. There was no way he'd do more than she could handle.

Finally, he took one nice plump nipple and sucked it hard within his mouth, using his teeth to create a bite of pain but soothing it out with exquisite pleasure.

She cried out. Her hands clenching into fists.

Slowly, he moved down her body, kissing every part of her. Licking a path from her belly button toward her pussy.

Once he was settled between her thighs, he stared down at her pretty pussy. Fine hairs covered her lips and he slid them open to see her swollen clit. She was soaking wet.

He had to taste her.

Pressing the tip of his tongue to her clit, he circled her bud, going down to her entrance, back up, and taking her into his mouth, sucking her.

She screamed.

The pleasure echoed off the walls. He didn't stop his ministrations, teasing down to her hole, then up again, sucking her hard.

Using his fingers, he pushed them inside her tight cunt, pumping them as he worked her pussy. He felt her walls tighten around him, her orgasm getting closer, and he didn't stop. His name spilled from her lips as she came, and he relished it. Licking at her clit, drawing her orgasm out, he rode her body right along with her.

Drawing her back down to earth, he pressed a

kiss to her clit and moved up behind her. Wrapping his arms around her, he kissed her neck.

"What are you doing?" she asked.

"We're going to go to sleep?"

"What about you?"

"I can wait."

"You don't want me to?"

"No, not tonight. This was all about you." He kissed her again, content and happy.

At first, Tabby was stiff in his arms. He didn't let her go.

Slowly, she relaxed, falling against him and trusting him as she fell asleep. This was how it was supposed to be with them from the very beginning.

Chapter Nine

Simon lay beside her.

Tabby had woken up a couple of minutes ago. Her body ... was different. In a good way. Simon had given her two orgasms last night and other than her using her hand, she hadn't given him a second one.

Why wouldn't he let her touch him? Glancing over at him, she saw that the sheets had ridden down to rest at his waist.

Licking her lips, she glanced down then back up. Her name was still inked on his chest. More ink covered his abdomen and sides, but she wasn't interested in any of them.

What are you doing? Get the hell out of bed and go home.

I don't want to.

Oh, yeah, and why not?

Because.

Because? Are you freaking kidding me? He gives you two orgasms and already you want to bang his brains out.

Tabby cut off the thought. This wasn't something she was going to control. Last night had been ... amazing. When he'd walked into the bathroom, seconds before she'd been hoping he would. This was crazy. She was so pissed at him for leaving her. Five years without a single phone call or nothing, and yet, she wanted him.

There was no denying that.

She didn't see a reason why they couldn't play. They were grown adults, and well, if Simon was going to keep her locked up here, she may as well enjoy it.

Also, you really, really, really, really want him.

She should be ashamed of how badly she did.

But she wasn't.

This wasn't the worst thing to want. Admittedly, she didn't forgive him and this didn't mean they were okay. Far from it. She was still pissed at him, and she wasn't going to cave to his every single request or demand.

Moving the blanket out of the way, she exposed his dick for her gaze. Watching him, she waited for him to stop her.

What are you doing?

You have no experience with this.

This was Simon. Not some random guy. Everything with him always felt natural. Even as they'd changed, his arms still made her feel safe. They were normal to her. The scent of him, his feel, it surrounded her and gave her comfort.

There was no changing that.

She moved down the bed to straddle his waist with her hands.

He'd gotten to taste her last night, but she'd wanted to reciprocate last night, only for him to turn her down. This morning, it wasn't going to happen. She and Simon were doing this.

"If you're going to suck me off, don't you think you should wait until I'm ready to enjoy it?" Simon asked.

His eyes were open and he looked down at her.

"Do you want me to stop?"

"No." He grabbed her pillow and plumped it up beneath his head, lifting him up. "But I want to be able to watch you."

Damn. She should hate him. *I do hate him.* This shouldn't turn her on either.

Wrapping her fingers around his length, she stared into his eyes, waiting for him to tell her to stop.

He didn't.

His hands moved behind his head and he looked relaxed, calm, ready.

She moved her fingers up and down his length and stroked the tip of him with her tongue. There was already a bead of pre-cum leaking out of the head, and she tasted him. Pulling her hand back, she licked the whole head of him, drawing him into her mouth. She released a little moan and this time he groaned.

"Fuck, that feels so good."

"You like it?" she asked, letting go.

"Yeah, you have no idea how pretty you look with a mouth full of cock. My cock."

She covered the tip with her lips and took him to the back of her throat, loving his growl. The noise filling her senses, teasing her with the lack of control he showed.

Bobbing her head up and down his length, she took him as deep as he could go without gagging, and pulled up, looking at him.

"This isn't what you wanted last night?" she asked, smiling.

"You think I didn't want this? I did, but last night was all about you."

"Are you feeling bad about leaving me?" She worked his length with her hand, going up and down. She watched him, seeing his eyes close.

"Yeah, I do. I didn't want to leave."

"But you did."

"Not now, Tabby."

She didn't want to fight now. No, she wanted him to beg her. She covered his length with her mouth and using her hand, she worked the entire length of him, drawing him close to an orgasm but keeping him there.

"Please, Tabby, fuck, yeah, fuck." He rocked his hips, trying to take control, but she wouldn't let him.

She was the one with the control here, not him.

"Please, Tabby, please." Only when he changed out his begs did she thrust him over the edge. She didn't know what to expect, but as he filled her mouth, she swallowed him down. It was so natural to her. Tasting him.

Afterward, when he was finished, she climbed off the bed and went into the bathroom. Once she'd closed the door, she used the toilet, flushed, washed her hands, brushed her teeth, and ignored him as he followed her around.

She grabbed a pair of his sweats and a shirt, leaving him in the bedroom to go and make herself a cup of coffee.

He entered the kitchen, completely naked.

"What the fuck is this? Did I hurt you? Upset you?"

She wanted to throw the cup in her hand at him. Instead, she blew across the top and glared at him.

"I still hate you. You cannot use sex to control me."

"We haven't had sex. My dick hasn't been inside you, Tabby. I'm not trying to control you."

"And you never will."

Simon advanced toward her. He took the coffee and threw it down the sink, putting the cup into the bowl.

She shoved him hard.

"If you need an excuse to want to be with me, that's fine, but I will never hurt you, Tabby. I will never use anything to control you. I've never wanted to control you. I love how fucking fiery you are. I don't need anything to get what I want. You give it to me, free of fucking charge."

He lifted her and dropped her ass on the edge of the table. Tabby couldn't explain it. She was so wet, so hot, so hungry for him.

None of it made any sense.

Just give in.

Take.

Use him.

She lifted up and pushed her sweatpants down her thighs. Gripping the back of his neck, she pulled him in close. His cock pressed against her pussy, but it wasn't enough. Even as she hated him, she wanted him, and right now, she wanted his dick balls deep within her.

As she kissed his lips, he wrapped his fingers in her hair, tugging her back. He shoved the large shirt she'd picked up over her head. There wasn't enough time to get it completely off her body.

He grabbed his cock with his other hand and teased the tip against her core.

She moaned, spreading her thighs, wanting him to fuck her.

Sinking her teeth into her bottom lip, she watched and waited for him to make the next move.

She'd given him all the permission. There were no words of refusal coming from her. The meddling bitch inside her head was surprisingly quiet. Clearly, they were all in agreement, she needed this.

Simon aligned the tip of his cock at her entrance and in one hard thrust, he filled her to the hilt.

They both cried out.

He was hard. A lot harder than she remembered. Part of her had been a little afraid she couldn't have this. That the two memories of two entirely different experiences would mold into one and it would make for one of the worst moments of her life.

It didn't invade.

All she felt was a deep sense of calm. A pulsing need of pleasure rushing through her body, consuming her.

Simon stayed perfectly still within her. They were both panting. He was so close. Cupping his face, she kissed him.

Deep down, they were still the same people. Their exteriors had hardened up a little, maybe more like a lot.

He kissed her back. His hands going to her hips, holding her in place, he started to rock gently within her. He took his time, letting her get used to the feel of his cock, and it felt fucking glorious.

It was everything she remembered him being and so much more.

In and out.

He fucked her.

The pace sped up, but she didn't care. The pleasure was out of the world. It was more than she could stand.

One of his hands moved between them and he stroked over her clit, teasing the bud.

She cried out. His name once again fell from her lips as he brought her to the peak. He didn't keep her waiting. She cried as he threw her over the edge, and he swallowed the sounds with his kisses.

There was no doubt she belonged to him. Her mind, heart, body, and soul, they all belonged to Simon.

His thrusts deepened. He held her in place and she stared into his eyes as he came. For a split second, his closed, but she didn't care. Seeing the release cross over his face meant everything to her.

Afterward, they were once again panting for breath. She didn't know where they both stood. The anger would come once again like it always did, but until then, she was just going to enjoy the moment.

****

Simon had wanted the sex.

He stood out at the edge of the cabin, giving himself some air. Tabby was inside waiting for him. Since they'd had sex on the edge of the table, they hadn't spoken. Breakfast had gone by in silence, so had the cleanup.

The silence had driven him crazy. He needed to know he hadn't gone too far but of course, he was too fucking afraid of bringing it up in case she had bad memories, or it was the last thing on her mind.

Running fingers through his hair, he took a step toward the cabin and then backed up.

"Please tell me she's alive in there."

Simon turned to see his father, sitting perched on one of the fallen trees. Most of the bark had been scraped off.

Devil looked calm and relaxed. One leg crossed at the ankle, his hands clasped together like he didn't have a single problem with the world.

"I would never hurt her."

"No, but you would decide to disappear on her without a trace. You haven't physically hurt her. Mentally? Emotionally? I'd say it's right up there."

"You're supposed to be my parent and take my side."

"No, as a parent, I don't pansy to any whims. I give it to you straight. You don't like the shit you're feeling, you change it, simple as that."

He stared at his father. Devil had aged well. Living the good life, the peaceful life suited him. There was no denying that.

"You never were one to sugarcoat anything."

"I give it to you real, son. It's how it is, and I'm telling you, you fucked up, big time."

"I had to kill him."

"I know what you had to do, but I'd hoped you'd have done the right thing. Instead, you made me have to make a fucked-up agreement with Lash to keep the peace. It kept you safe, and well, that's a problem I need to fix."

"I want to wipe that club off the face of the earth," Simon said.

"That's great, but what does your woman want?" he asked. "You asked her about it?" Devil watched him and laughed. "Ah, she wants something different. That's what you're going to have to come to peace with."

"Why are you here? You came to take her back?"

"No, I came to talk to my son who seems to know how to fuck everything up. You think I didn't know about the men you have with you? After five years, I didn't know where you were every single day?" Devil asked.

Simon tensed up.

"That's right. You're my son, and no matter what you do, I'll be there with you, every step of the fucking way. This shit you needed to do and I get it, I do. I get it more than most would. It's part of who you are. This is what you were made to do. No one can take that away from you."

"You knew?"

"Who do you think contacted Dean? Who do you think got him to show up?"

"Has Dean been your contact?"

"No. I told him after our last phone call he was to get rid of the cell phone. He did that. I don't need a little mole to keep an eye on my son. I have my resources. You seem to forget, Simon, before I settled in Piston County, the road was my home. I made enemies but I also made a whole lot of friends and believe me, they're loyal that if I give them a word, they will look out for who I want." Devil stood up. "I'm not saying you didn't slip off the radar a time or two, but I just knew, whatever it was you were hunting for, you'd find it and then I'd need to be ready."

"Ready for what?" Simon asked.

"Ready for you to return to claim your woman. Tabitha has always been yours. It took some time for me to accept it, but I have. She's yours. You've made that abundantly clear. I'm not going to get in the way of that. But there are some things you should know."

"I know about Nathan. I saw him."

Devil smirked. "I know. Who do you think told Lexie to bring Nathan to the door?"

"You're a meddling bastard."

"I'm a father and one day, you're going to know what it feels like."

"Is he? Do you know if he's mine?" he asked.

"Does it matter?"

Simon opened his mouth, closed it.

"Think about it, Simon. Does it matter?"

He thought about Nathan. The little boy. He'd looked so sweet.

"No, it doesn't matter."

"I don't know the answer, and you've got to ask yourself, do you care? Tabitha loves him, your mother does. I do. He's a great kid, Simon."

"I want to meet him," Simon said, nodding. "I want to be his father."

"That's a fast decision without knowing all the facts."

"What does that mean?"

"Look how you reacted when you found out the truth about Lexie. You ran out of town."

Simon ran a hand down his face. "I was a teenager."

"And?"

"I'm not a kid anymore. I know what I want. That boy belongs to her and that makes him mine. I'll love him no matter what."

"Then what are you going to do about this?" Devil pointed toward the cabin.

Licking his lips, he smiled. "I need some time with her. She's … I fucked up. Five years is a long time and she waited for me. I've got to make it up to her."

"Keeping her locked up in a cabin isn't going to get her on your good side. Being nice to her kid, it could get you some points."

"And you know the answer to everything?" he asked.

"I know the answer to a great deal of many things, Simon. I'm your old man and I haven't gotten to where I am by being dumb."

"If I tried to win her back out there, she would hide from me. I wouldn't be able to have this with her. At least locked up here, I can win her back. You know how damn stubborn she is. I need this," Simon said.

"Good, moving on because we can argue about this all day long. What's going on with the other guys you brought along, and Dean? You going to be prospecting at the club again when you get all of this straightened out?"

"Yes." The club was part of the life he missed. He wanted his leather cut, to earn his patch.

Once again, Devil smiled. "Then you're going to have to bring your boys around. I've got to vet them for myself. I don't just allow anyone into my club. Also, when you see Dean, tell him we'll have his patched party."

"Patched party?"

"Yep. He earned his patch. I've got the jacket

ready for him."

"You've got to be kidding me. I've got to continue to prospect and he'll be patched in?"

Devil shrugged. "You're alive. He did everything I asked of him. I couldn't ask him for more."

"You're an asshole, Dad, a real big one."

"Don't I know it. Your mother is going to want to see you as well. Don't take too long at this."

"Does she know I'm here?" Simon asked.

"Of course. She misses you and she hopes you work everything out with Tabitha." Devil walked toward him and patted him on the shoulder. "It's good to have you back."

Simon watched his father disappear amongst the trees and bushes. Anyone else, he'd be worried they'd get lost or die. Not his dad. Devil could find his way out of anywhere.

Turning back to the cabin, he headed on inside.

Tabby was in the kitchen, pouring boiling water into a cup. "Do you want a drink?"

"Yeah, I'm parched." They weren't the words he wanted to hear. "Talk to me, Tabby."

She paused in filling his cup and sighed. "I honestly don't know what to say to you."

"There was a time you could talk to me about anything."

She lifted her gaze to his. "There was." She handed him the cup of hot coffee. She hadn't bothered with cream or sugar. He took a sip of the bitter liquid and winced. Getting to his feet, he made the coffee how he liked it.

"Are you saying you can't talk to me about anything?"

"Simon, I'm confused, okay? I don't know what to say or do right now. What do you want from me exactly? Tell me and I will try to work on it."

He took her hand and held it tightly as she took a seat opposite him at the table. "I want you to be my woman."

"And I've asked for a divorce."

"With how you released on my cock, I'd say you weren't ready for a divorce."

She tried to pull away.

"Sorry. That was, fuck, I'm sorry. I'm not good at this."

"You're right you're not good."

"I love you," he said.

She lifted her gaze to his.

"It has never changed how I feel about you." He continued on even as she didn't say a word. "I'm going to be staying in Piston County. I'll be prospecting at the club."

"You're going to stay?"

"Yes. I've got nowhere else I want to be than with you. These past five years, I've wanted you."

Once again, tears filled her eyes and he hated himself. Why did he keep on fucking up with his words?

"I know you've been through hell. I put you through that, but I'm here to fight for you, for us. I'm going to make this work."

She swiped at the tear that fell. "What if there is no us to fix?"

"There is. Didn't you feel it last night?" he asked.

"That was just attraction. Lust."

"No, I'm not talking about the se … foreplay. I'm talking about holding you in my arms. Feeling you against me. You, in my arms, it's where you're supposed to be. You know that. Just give me time. It's all I'm asking for. Time."

****

Lexie looked up from washing the dishes as Devil came in.

"The kids are doing homework. Nathan's asleep. He misses his mommy but hopes she's feeling better," she said.

Devil nodded and moved toward her side. He put a hand on her waist, kissing her neck.

"How is he?" she asked. She'd promised herself she wouldn't beg to know any more than he was willing to give.

Simon may not have been her flesh and blood son, but she'd raised him. He was hers in every single way that counted and no one could take that away from her. She'd been with him through sickness and even now, when he'd ran.

"He's fucking tall. Big. He's twice the size that he was."

"So he's a little more like you?"

"Probably." Devil wrapped his arms around her. She heard him inhale and she chuckled. "You always smell so good."

"And you have an insatiable appetite." She put her hands on his, loving these moments. They were most precious to her. "How is Tabitha?"

"I didn't see her but I know he's taking care of her in his own way."

"Do we need to worry?"

"Not yet. I think we will soon." He sighed.

"What is it?"

"She's keeping him on his toes. He looks so fucking tired. I hope he realizes what he's taking on."

"Did he ask about Nathan?"

"Yep. Of course, he did."

"Do you know what's going to happen there?" she asked.

"He'll be a damn good father."

Lexie agreed. "Did he ask about ... you know?"

"He did, I told him I didn't know."

"You lied to him."

"It's not for me to tell him." Devil pressed his face against her neck. "He's going to be trouble, though. His thirst for blood is still there. At this time, I think he'd go to war with The Skulls to get the heads of all the Monster Dogs."

"Do you blame him?" She didn't want her son going on a killing spree. The last one had cost him five years. More would only take the time he had.

"I don't blame him, but he needs to understand he can't go after the whole club. That kind of war will destroy clubs, this one included, and I'm not going to let him implode on himself. A time will come when he needs to sit down with them. They are all going to need to come to some arrangement. I'm not going to hand Simon over and I won't start a war."

She cupped his face. "Do you think you can make this work?"

"Yeah, I do. If I didn't think it couldn't work, I wouldn't have agreed to such an arrangement. I'm not a pussy, Lexie."

She laughed. "I didn't say you were. Your mind is going a thousand miles a minute at times. I don't know how I can keep up with you."

"You want to know how I know there's a chance here to avoid war?"

"Yes."

He smiled. "Tune in tomorrow."

She swatted at him. "Don't do that. Tell me."

"The president will not be on the throne forever. The kid, Luke, Ryan's friend. He's going to take that place. Lash has told me he's a good kid. Hard, got the skills to be a good leader."

"How does that help?"

"Luke was there the night Simon shot Ryan in the face. He's also the kid who happens to have a big crush on Tabitha. I have a feeling we can make this work."

Lexie frowned. "You're going to use Tabitha?"

"In time, when she doesn't want to kill Simon, she'll convince Luke to abandon the agreement and start afresh. She's got what it takes. You've seen the way she's been. She's a fighter and I've got a feeling she will be one hell of a lioness for her family and for her club."

Chapter Ten

Time!

Always the same.

The tick-tocking of a goddamn clock.

She hated it.

Tabitha stared out the window to where Simon was training with Dean. The other guy hadn't been invited into the house, but she was getting bored of being locked up. She couldn't remember how many days she'd been here, but not being out in the fresh air was starting to piss her off.

Slamming her hand against the window, she caught their attention.

Simon looked at her and returned to Dean.

"I swear, Simon, if you don't let me out, I will smash this window and then you won't have another choice but to let me out." She glanced behind her, seeing the lampshade. She didn't know if it would be strong enough to smash the window, but she was willing to give it a try.

Seconds passed, and she lifted it up with every intention of throwing it.

Simon came to the door. "You're not running away."

"As you've pointed out, I wouldn't know where I was going. I don't have a death wish." She breezed past him, stepping into the sunshine. It was a rare warm day. Global warming was a huge concern, seeing as it was supposed to be fall.

Tipping her head back, she enjoyed the rays of sunshine, basking in the warm glow of vitamin D.

The sounds of grunting had her opening her eyes and looking toward the two men.

"You're just pissed," Dean said.

"Yeah, and I thought you were my friend."

"I am your friend. I kept you alive because I like you. Not for the damn patch."

"Is he still moaning over you earning your place at Chaos Bleeds?" Tabitha asked, taking a seat on the porch steps.

Dean lowered his fists and laughed. "He told you?"

"Yep, in his moaning voice."

"I'm standing right here. I didn't moan."

"You totally did. You're a grade-A moaner." Tabitha watched them, seeing them spar. Simon had some skills. Dean at times was a little sloppy, but he had power as well.

For a few blissful seconds, she could forget about what happened. It was at these moments she felt the saddest and most alone. The last five years did happen. She couldn't sit around forever, waiting for the world to fade or for her to wake up as if it was some kind of dream. This was her reality.

Getting to her feet, she stepped toward the men. Both stopped fighting. "I want to train."

"Not happening," Simon said.

"I want to fight. You saw what happened. I'm good taking down women, but I need to know how to attack men."

Dean chuckled. "You want to learn how to beat the crap out of Simon?"

"Fuck off," Simon said.

"What? You're the dick in this situation. It must be tough."

"I can still take you," Simon said. "Don't forget that."

"The guys are going to love you," Dean said, patting her shoulder. "Simon never stopped talking about you. You're somewhat of a legend to them."

She turned her attention to Simon.

He stared right back at her.

"You talked about me?"

"Yeah, I had no reason not to. You're my woman. Of course, I was going to talk about you."

"Yep, and we got everything from how he was going to get you pregnant. The dozens of babies he wanted. All of them boys. He didn't want to have any girls as he would have to shoot all the boys who came near them."

Tabitha raised her fists. "It's good to know I made an impression."

"You really do." Dean stepped away, taking a seat where she'd been sitting only moments before.

"Come on, Simon."

"Tabby?"

"What? You think I can't handle this? I've fought against Anthony, remember? When I get out of here, I might give him a call. Ask him to come here so I can fight someone who'll treat me like a person."

Simon's jaw clenched. They used to spar before. He never went too hard on her. He was always worried about hurting her. There was no reason for him to fear. She was strong.

He tensed up, but he didn't raise his fists. He moved a little closer and she stepped back.

"I wouldn't raise my hands to my opponent. It gets them prepared," Simon said. "They'll know you're ready to attack. You're waiting for it."

She lowered her hands, keeping him in her sight as they circled one another.

"Wow, this is like mega foreplay. I'm surprised you two aren't just naked and fucking. Only stopping for food and water."

"Shut the fuck up," Simon said.

Tabitha didn't avert her gaze.

"This is good. Keep your focus on me. Always on me. Don't let anyone else in your sight. I'm your enemy right now."

She saw his headlights in her mind. The feel of the cold wrapping around her. The chill. The pain. It was all too much.

She attacked, slamming her fist toward his stomach, but he blocked her. She went again, and he stopped her. His touch hard yet not painful.

Falling back, he moved toward her. As he went to land a blow, she stopped it. She put her hand up and felt how he held back.

Simon was strong, but he wasn't going to hurt her.

Rather than continue on, she turned her back on him and entered the cabin. Silence met her exit.

She went straight to the bathroom. Removing her clothes, she turned the shower on, and the cold spray of water hit her body, shocking her. She wanted it. Anything right now would be better than the feelings consuming and tightening inside her chest.

"Why did you walk away?" Simon asked.

Tilting her head left and right, she ignored him.

The shower curtain opened up and she turned. He was still fully dressed and she was naked.

"Leave," she said.

"You want to spar, we'll do it. I don't have a problem."

"I don't want to spar with you, Simon. I want to fucking hurt you." She glared at him.

"Then hurt me."

"No, because then I feel guilty. I don't want to hurt you at the same time. You did what you did and you left me. You got on that fucking bike and without a damn care in the world, you rode away like I was nothing."

He pulled his clothes off and stepped into the shower. "I didn't want to leave you."

She laughed. "You didn't want to, but you could. Don't you see that? You were able to get on that bike and you've lived. Look at you, you made the most of what happened."

"Do you think I've lived? Is that what you think this is?" He cupped her face, tilting her head back, forcing her to look at him. "I didn't live, Tabby. Nothing about this was fun. I survived. From day to day. It's all I did. Whenever I entered a fight, I thought of you. I saw your tears. I saw your pain."

"Then why didn't you come back to me?" She slammed her hand against his chest. "I needed you here and you left. Why didn't you come back to me? Why didn't you love me enough to stay?"

He pulled her close so her face was pressed against his chest. She tried to fight against him, to pull away. To have distance between them.

Simon wouldn't let her.

His grip remained firm and all she did was exhaust herself until she finally relented and sobbed against him.

He stroked her hair.

"I wasn't a good enough man for you. I don't regret killing Ryan. For a short time, I thought I did. I didn't. Killing that smug bastard wasn't a mistake, not to me. No, what was the mistake was doing it in front of witnesses. I wasn't patient. I fucked up. I had no choice but to leave and to do so, I had to control this ... rage. I needed to become a man for you, Tabby. It showed me that I was still a fucking boy. I thought I was a man, but I had yet to grow up."

He kissed her lips, pulling her away from him. She stared up into his eyes. "That's why I walked away. That's why I did what I did. This wasn't easy. I saw how weak I was and I couldn't allow that to touch you." He stroked her cheek. "I'm not letting go. I'm not walking away. Where you go, I go. I will follow you everywhere, Tabby. You own my heart and soul."

****

When it came to Tabby, Simon knew deep in his soul he was always a little selfish with her. He never wanted to share her. Always wanted to be around her. Ever since they were kids, he'd been obsessed. He didn't consider it that dangerous. For him, it had always been and would forever be love.

Tabby sat in the center of the sitting room. She'd moved the coffee table to one side, her legs crossed, hands on her knees.

She was meditating. He knew the moves as he'd watched Dick do that and yoga for many years. He watched her take a deep inhale and slowly exhale.

Sipping at his coffee, he couldn't take his eyes off her.

She was beautiful. No doubt about it in his mind.

"Why do you keep on staring?" Tabby asked.

He smiled. Her eyes weren't open. "Because you're the most beautiful thing in the room."

"I'll believe that when we're in a room full of women."

"You know you'll always win."

This time, she opened her eyes and smiled. "You can't sweet talk me."

She had yet to say she loved him back.

He got it, more than she realized. He'd hurt her deeply by leaving. Maybe if she hadn't seen him actually kill another man, she wouldn't be so pissed at him, but for now, she was still in the hatred part of their relationship.

Simon knew it wouldn't last too long, he hoped not.

You've got to take her back to her son.

It had now been a week and if he knew anything about kids, Nathan would be missing his mother dearly.

What he didn't want to do was let her go. Not until they resolved these issues.

Getting to his feet, he walked closer to her and sat down. He placed his coffee cup beside him.

"What are you doing?" she asked.

"Did Dick show you how to do this?"

Her eyes opened again and she nodded. "During pregnancy. It was a tough time. My blood pressure was up. I couldn't relax. I felt sick all the damn time. I was of course miserable, and yeah, it was a hard time." She shrugged. "I coped the best way I knew how but one day, Dick saw me struggling."

She giggled. "Who knew he could be so persistent when he believes he's right about something, huh?" She waved her hand in front of her face. "Anyway, moving on. Daisy joined me and even Miles and Anthony. Dick had me and my big giant belly on the ground, and at first, I did nothing but called bullshit on the entire thing. He wouldn't give up and so, I finally relaxed. Before long, I realized I'd been sitting for nearly an hour and I felt more focused. Calm. I'd never experienced anything like it. He spent a good couple of days showing me all the necessary moves, and when he left, I started to do it regularly."

"Then show me."

"It's more about taking deep breaths and finding a place of calm."

"I don't mind."

She offered him a sweet smile.

He watched her get comfortable and it suddenly dawned on him that the couple of times they had sex, he hadn't used a rubber.

Shit.

Protection had been the last thing on his mind.

All he'd wanted was to be inside his woman. To remind her who she belonged to. Running a hand down his face, he realized he was constantly fucking this up. It didn't seem to matter that his heart was always in the right place. Tabby suffered.

"Can I ask why you're meditating?" he asked.

"Shh, be silent. Be still."

He reached over and took both of her hands.

"That's not being any of those things."

"I know. I don't want to." He brought her hands up to his face and kissed them both.

"Simon, this isn't helping."

"I love you."

She opened her mouth and he waited for the words, but her lips closed. No sound came out. He sighed. Kissing up the inside of her left arm, he trailed his lips up and up, going toward her neck.

Tabby released a shaky sigh. "You're not helping."

"I hear there is another good reliever of stress." He flicked his tongue across her neck, right over her pulse. They had a lot of time to make up for.

She could be pregnant.

Talk to her about that little piece of info.

He didn't ask. There was no way he intended to break this moment by putting them down another argument path. Sure, it usually led to sex or at least him holding her, but for now, it wasn't going to work. All he wanted was to feel Tabby without any of the fighting or the worry or the fear.

He didn't believe that was too much to ask. At least he hoped not.

Sliding his tongue down from her neck, he teased across her collarbone. He didn't linger. This was about her, not about him, at least not yet.

The shirt she wore was way too big and all he had to do was slide it down her arms to expose her chest. He probably should buy her some additional clothing but for now, he loved seeing her in his stuff.

"Simon, this isn't helping."

"I think it is. You're breathing deep so you're doing the right thing. Your nipples are nice and hard. I bet your pussy is wet for me too."

She moaned.

As he nudged her back, she didn't fight him.

He cupped her between her thighs, feeling the heat, and shoved his hand down her large sweatpants to finally cup her pussy. He found her soaking wet. He smiled. "See, you want this."

"This isn't going to solve anything."

"You're right, it won't solve anything, but it's going to make us feel good for a little while."

"For how long?"

"For however long we allow it." He tore the shirt from her body, not caring about the item of clothing. Once it was in shreds, he dropped it away from her body. Next, he took the baggy sweatpants in his hands, sliding them down her legs, and he groaned at the sight of her.

She was beautiful.

So perfect.

And she belonged all to him.

She didn't have any spare underwear, which meant he didn't have to fight to remove them.

Lifting her foot, he brought it to her lips and

pressed a kiss to her inner foot. She let out a moan.

Trailing his lips up the inside her of her leg, he got to her apex, stopped, and lifted her other foot, doing the same. This time, she gasped, arching up, but again, he kept her waiting, kissing her, and then to her stomach where he saw some stretch marks from where she'd been pregnant.

She put her hand over them and he pushed it out of the way.

"Simon?"

"Every single part of you is beautiful and I won't have you thinking or believing anything else." He kissed her stomach, tracing his tongue down. The scent of her arousal drifted toward him.

Lifting her legs, he sat back and reached toward her pussy. He spread her lips and stared down at the wet slit. Her clit was swollen and he got a nice peek at her cunt. She was tight.

He eased a single finger inside her, feeling just how tight she was. Adding a second, he began to stretch her open. Pressing his thumb to her clit, he stroked her, feeling the answering pulse of her pussy as she tightened around him. In and out he thrust.

He couldn't stand it any longer and he removed his fingers, replacing them with his mouth. First at her clit, he stroked over the bud, sucking it into his mouth, using his teeth, creating a little pain before softly stroking her.

Twirling his tongue around, he moved down and fucked her pussy. Plunging inside her. He held on to her hips, keeping her in place as he ravished her pussy, tasting her.

He wanted her to come on his tongue.

His cock was so hard it was a tight fit inside his pants. He didn't care. Tabby thrust up against him, moaning his name. He loved the sound more than anything.

Moving back up to her clit, he focused on the tight nub, drawing circles, sliding back and forth. Her body changed as the orgasm started to take effect. A nice flush crept up her body, and the instant she spilled over the edge, he saw it, felt it, and he rode that wave with her, using his tongue.

His name a perfect mantra spilling out into the room.

Afterward, he pressed a kiss to her pussy.

Tabby suddenly shot up into a sitting position. She nudged him back and before he knew what was happening, she had his waist straddled. Her arms were around his neck, and he ran his hands up her back, cupping the back of hers as she ground herself against him.

Together, they reached down to deal with his jeans, both of them wanting them out of the way. All he wanted was to be inside her.

With his dick out, he worked the length. Tabby positioned herself over him, lining the tip to her entrance, and he watched as she took him.

Inch by inch, she slid down, and he fucked his way up inside her. They both moaned together.

The pleasure instant.

Intense.

Tabby's arms came around him, holding him close.

He thrust up against her as she bounced on his dick. Their movements in perfect synch, as it was always supposed to be.

She arched up. Those gorgeous tits pressed against his face, and he took one, licking the tip of each one.

He couldn't let her go, not that he wanted to.

She was perfection.

"Fuck, Tabby, do you have any idea what you do to me?" He growled the words against her lips, but she didn't say anything. All she did was ride his cock. Her eyes closed and his orgasm began to build. Feeling her slick, pulsing pussy. It was more than he could stand and no way he could make this last any longer.

He came, grabbing her hips, holding her firmly in place as he spilled every single last part of him inside her, flooding her pussy with his cum as he did so. Over and over, he gave her it all.

She collapsed against him as the last of his release ebbed away.

"I love you too, Simon. I just don't like you."

Chapter Eleven

Tabby rolled over, wondering why she was in bed at five o'clock in the afternoon. She never took naps during the day. Only when Nathan had been little had she allowed herself that kind of luxury, and it had been right after her parents had advised her she do it, otherwise, she was perfectly content to not ever do it.

Sitting up on the bed, she heard voices. Loud male voices. It kind of reminded her of home.

Swinging her legs off the side of the bed, she lifted herself up and slowly made her way toward the window in the sitting room. The front door was closed but she wasn't willing to just go and see what all the fuss was about without at least having a peak first.

Nibbling on her lip, she looked out the window to see Simon in the center, slapping hands with—she frowned. Five guys? No, six. There was Dean loading something off the back of a small pickup truck.

She didn't recognize it.

Folding her arms, she watched the men. They were close, she saw that. Were these the men he'd met during his time away? Why hadn't he come and gotten her? Was he embarrassed by her?

One of the men headed toward the door. She didn't move away from the window. She kept her stance, waiting for him to enter.

He was a large man, but then they were all large. One of them was huge though, well over six feet, and seemed to tower over the group. He stood next to Simon, head thrown back, laughing at something said.

Simon wasn't that funny.

This guy glanced over at her.

"Oh, hi," he said. "Si said you were sleeping. We didn't wake you up, did we?"

"I wasn't sleeping." She kept her gaze on the window.

"You're Tabby, I take it."

She turned toward him. "You know my name."

"Of course. All of the guys know your name. Simon wasn't exactly secretive about the woman he had back home. He talked about you a whole lot."

"He did?"

"Yep. You're pretty special to him. We all know that."

She nodded. "I'm sorry, I don't know your name."

"Pa."

Tabitha frowned. "Pa?"

"Yeah, that's me. I'm Pa. The real name is Patrick but because I'm the oldest one of the guys, they decided to name me Pa, as if I'm some kind of dad to all of them." He started to chuckle. "I guess I am. I was the one who always made sure we had something to eat. A place to stay. That kind of shit."

"You kept an eye on him?"

"On all of them, Tabby, but yeah, I made sure Simon stayed safe."

"Tabitha," she said. "That's my name. Only Simon ever calls me Tabby." She rubbed at her temple.

"Ah, right. Yes, of course. It's his name for you. Sorry. Anyway, I brought a barbeque for us to have a bit of a cookout if you're hungry. Don't worry, Si gave me the heads up on you not eating meat, and so I got you some like mushrooms and peppers and stuff. That okay?"

"It's fine." She went to push her hands into her pants pocket, only to discover she didn't have any pants. With nothing to do with her arms, she quickly folded them again, feeling like a complete ass. This was awkward. While this man knew a lot about her, apparently, she didn't know squat about the guys.

"What's taking you so long?" Simon asked, coming to the doorway.

He glanced between them.

"Ah, you've met Pa?"

"Yep, I have. Hi, Pa." She gave a little wave and then wanted to kill herself for how silly that seemed. She was a grown woman. This was the last thing she needed right now.

"I'm going to set the grill up. The guys can't wait to meet you. You're a legend," Pa said. "It's been a pleasure."

Pa left the cabin and Tabitha dropped her hands by her sides. "He seems nice."

"He is. He's a great guy."

"How did you meet him?"

"At a fight. His family had been killed in a shootout a couple of years ago. The cops didn't do anything about it. He believes they were on the guys' payroll, so he packed up his shit, and decided to try and find the men, handle the problem himself."

"Did he?"

"No, he's still finding them. He's a good guy, though. He has a big heart."

"A big heart on a road to revenge is going to get himself killed."

"I won't let it."

"Simon, you're not God."

"Can we not fight today? I know you and I have got a lot to get through and I know it's going to be tough, but can we just hold it together for a couple of hours?"

She stared at him. "I hate fighting. I don't ever want to do this. I hate that we're at this place. It sucks."

"Yeah, it does suck." He rubbed the back of his head. "I love you and I know this is going to be tough.

Other than Dean, everyone else I met on the road. Away from you. I don't want to hurt you."

"Simon, I get it. Believe me, I do. I mean, they're your family."

"And so are you."

She wanted to argue, but for once, for now, she just didn't want to have to think. "I'd like to meet them. I'd like to meet the men you call your friends and family." She smiled, not holding back.

Simon moved toward her. His hands going to her cheeks, he cupped her face, pulling her close. "Do you have any fucking idea how much I love you?"

As she covered his hands with hers, it would be so easy to tell him exactly how much she loved him, but she held back. They still had all their worries and she wasn't going to use today to put all of that crap on hold when they had a lot to go through.

"Take me to meet your friends."

It would be so easy to hide everything.

Simon stroked her cheek, pressed a kiss to her lips, and then took her hand. She didn't fight him as he walked across the room, heading toward the door.

Once they stepped outside, the cold hit her, and she gave a little shiver. Simon let go of her hand and was already removing his jacket, draping it over her shoulders.

"Guys," he said, whistling for their attention.

Conversation stopped.

She looked over the group. The men all wore smiles as they looked toward her.

"You've heard me talk about her, but this is Tabby."

"Tabitha," she said.

"Only Simon calls you Tabby," the group said together, making her chuckle.

"Pa just gave us all the update. Damn, it is finally good to meet you," a brown-haired man with short hair came barreling toward her.

"That's Felix," Simon said. "He's a talker."

"Yeah, right. I'm the talker. I was lucky to get a word in edgeways with this one constantly singing your praises."

She smiled, liking him. He seemed nice and sweet. Easy to talk to, which made him dangerous, but oddly a benefit to any club, especially when they were in trouble. Women would open up to him, spill their secrets.

Tilting her head to the side, she watched as one by one the men lined up.

"This here is Knight, with a K."

She chuckled. "Hi, Knight."

"It's nice to put an actual face and voice to all the stories."

"I've heard he's talked a lot about me."

"More than a lot. Some of us wanted to sew his mouth shut just to get some peace."

"They're all lying of course," he said.

She laughed, loving the banter, not wanting it to end.

They were all friends, all close. She saw that even before she was introduced to all of the men.

"This is Twig. He's one hell of a fighter."

Twig didn't say anything, just nodded at her. She also noticed a scar across his lips and down his neck. Growing up in an MC club, she was used to scars and didn't react.

Next, and the final guy in line, was Teddy. He was the biggest one, towering over all of them. He kind of reminded her a little of Killer back at The Skulls, but this guy had to be taller, bigger in every way.

"Teddy, really? You think Dick's going to like

that?" she asked.

"It's something he's going to have to deal with. Kid can't be responsible for his name."

"Kid? I'm older than you," Teddy said, laughing.

"If you're planning to prospect for Chaos Bleeds, be careful around Dick. He might be a touch sensitive."

Teddy nodded. "Simon has already told me about all the guys and their names. Don't worry."

"You've met Pa and of course you know Dean."

Pa and Dean were already seated at chairs while smoke came from the grill. This wasn't a gas or an electric one. There was a bag of charcoal bricks beside it.

Simon led her toward some seats and she sat down.

"I'm going to go and grab a couple of beers," he said.

"They're in the cooler in the truck," Dean said.

"So, you're all one big happy family," she said.

"I wouldn't say we're one big happy family, but we've gotten by," Pa said looking at all of them.

"And you all took care of Simon?"

"We did," they all said in unison.

"Damn, Pa, I'm starving. If you'd gotten one of those gas grills, we could have hooked up the pipes and be grilling steaks right about now." Teddy looked toward her. "No offense."

"None taken."

"I told you the best kind of barbeque is over hot coals. It makes everything taste better. Not some fancy shit and besides, did you see the cost of those things?"

"I'm starving. I could snap a leg off you and start eating."

She looked toward Knight, who chuckled. "Are they always like this?"

"Pa and Teddy are. In all honesty, the big guy is

always hungry."

"I heard that."

"You were supposed to, crazy ass," Knight said, laughing.

"Be careful with that one. We should have named him jailbait," Dean said.

"Jailbait?"

"I'm the youngest."

"Nineteen."

"When did you meet Simon?" she asked. These men made her curious about the time Simon had been away. What had he been doing to find these men? What was it like? He'd been on an adventure, that was for sure. All of the men doted on him, cared about him. She hadn't been in their company long, but she saw it.

"When I was fifteen," Knight said. "I ran from a bad situation. Packed up what shit I could and get the hell out of there."

"You did, you didn't look back?"

He shook his head. "There's no real reason to look back when you've got nothing to look back at. Believe me, I didn't have anything to look at, or to enjoy, or to love."

The group went silent.

"I met Simon three years ago," Felix said. "I was fucking starving. Living on the streets. My parents kicked me out when I was sixteen. I lived from bed to bed until I graduated, then hit the streets. Doing petty crime and shit. Nothing big. I was begging on a street corner. One moment begging for food, the next offering up my dick and asshole to anyone who'd pay me for a hot meal. Simon had come out of a fast-food joint. He had this big whole cardboard box filled with food. I offered him everything. Even to suck him off in front of everyone. He could humiliate me. He told me to get my shit together and follow him. The rest is history."

Teddy cleared his throat. "Mine was at a fight. I … I accidentally got on the wrong side of people."

"Accidentally? You screwed the owner's daughter. Don't make yourself out to be an angel," Knight said.

Teddy's cheeks were on fire. "She's a lady."

"Dude, I grew up with big guys talking shit about who they screwed and whatnot. I have a son. Believe me, I know all about cock and pussy." She snuggled into Simon's blanket, enjoying the scent of him surrounding her.

She shouldn't enjoy it or allow herself these few peaceful moments, but she didn't want it to stop.

"Fine. I didn't like this guy. He was always taking a large cut off his fighters. They were always indebted to him. Anyway, I got it into my head to take something from him. So I did, I took his daughter's cherry. In my defense, he had put her up for auction to the guy who would pay the highest price for it. She asked me, and I didn't say no. My debt to him was large, and it was Simon who took a bet with the guy, won me back, and well, he gave my life purpose again. I won't ever forget it."

She looked toward Twig. He was the one guy who hadn't spoken.

"Twig isn't much of a talker," Pa said.

"I talk," Twig said, speaking up. "Only when it's important."

Simon returned with a whole load of beers.

He handed one to her. She shook her head.

"Why not?"

It was on the tip of her tongue to mention Nathan, only, she wasn't taking care of him. He was back in town.

"I don't drink."

"I'll go and grab you a soda."

****

Simon grabbed a soda from the fridge, closed the door, and rested his head against it. The guys being here, Tabby, he knew this was going to hurt her. They weren't supposed to drop by, not for a long time.

"Twig isn't talking about how we found him," Dean said, coming into the cabin.

"It's not exactly a great story. We found him on a bridge, gun at his temple, ready to end his life." He opened the soda and went to move past Dean.

"What's going on, man?"

"Nothing."

"Do you want us to leave?"

"Not now."

"You told us to keep our distance. You didn't say for how long. The guys, they worry."

"Of course they worry, but you had to give me more time with her. You've seen the way she is. Fuck!"

"It's going great out there."

"Yeah, because for today only, we're not going to fight but come tomorrow… These guys, I met them while I was away from her. She's already hurting about everything else. This is a fuck-up."

"Or maybe this is a chance for her to see what good you've done away from her."

"Don't," he said. "Don't say shit like that. I'm not a good man away from her. I could do this with her."

"I don't mean it like that. Fuck, look, I mean, you've found these guys. You gave them all a reason, a purpose and that's not something you should be upset about or embarrassed by. You've helped them. At least she can see during the time apart you found something good."

He took a deep breath. "I hope you're right."

"I'm not wrong."

Heading back outside, Pa stood at the grill and the scent of meat was heavy in the air.

He offered Tabby a drink, and she took it with a smile, which twisted his gut. All he ever wanted to do was make her happy, but he knew that was a big complication.

"You okay?" he asked, pulling a chair toward her.

"Yeah, I'm fine."

"So, Tabby, how have you been?" Felix asked. "We thought we were going to have to head to Fort Wills but the moment Simon heard about you being here, this was exactly where he was headed."

"Great," she said. "It's good you all found each other."

"We're one big happy family."

"Yeah, you are," Tabby said.

"I've got some mushrooms ready. I've got a burger bun. You ready, Tabs?" Pa asked.

She nodded her head.

With it wrapped in some napkins, Pa handed Tabby her mushroom burger. She took a bite and he watched her eat.

"Why do you keep looking at me?" she asked, dabbing her lips with the napkin.

"I like watching you eat. It's good for you."

"Damn, you said you were fucking besotted, but none of us realized exactly how much," Felix said. "You should have heard him, Tabby. Sorry, Tabs. I wonder what she's doing? Does she miss me? She had the prettiest smile. She's a fighter. She's not afraid to get hurt for the people she loves. You're like a goddess or something."

"You're going to make me blush."

"It would," Pa said. "If it wasn't so true. We spent many nights camped out under the stars hearing tales of you both when you were kids. It got kind of tiring just how perfect you are."

"I was going to kill myself," Twig said, speaking up.

The group went completely silent.

Tabby's burger was poised at her lips.

"When I first met Simon and Dean. They were the two I'd met. I met Knight a little later. I was going to kill myself. I was ready to end it."

Another round of silence met Twig's confession. He took a swig of his drink, licking his lips as he did.

Simon took Tabby's hand within his own. He needed to be touching her, to be doing anything at that moment. He couldn't stand the thought of not being around her.

"I don't know what it was. I was married, you see. My wife, we'd been sweethearts, at least I thought we had. It turns out she was just using me for an easy ride. The moment a richer guy came along, she jumped from me to him. I had no house. No money. No wife. My entire life I'd been living a lie. I'd been fired that day as well because my wife had decided to shack up with my boss. I had nothing. No one. So I took the only thing I had, my gun. I'd only ever gone to firing ranges to use it. I don't even know why I had it in the house. It wasn't like it was any use to me."

He snorted. "It's probably a good thing I didn't think about it sooner. I might have shot them both and then I'd be in jail." He took another sip of his beer. The smile on his lips looking slightly crazy. "I wanted to end it. I didn't see how I was going to ever be whole again or make it out alive. Everything seemed to have gotten all fucked up so fast. I walked to a bridge. The first one I came to, and I stood for a good half an hour looking at the water. The way it rushed on past. People came and went. A few cars stopped by asking me if I needed any help. I told them no. I was fine. When I was sure I was alone, I pulled out the gun, feeling the weight of it in my hand. I figured there was no purpose for me to be here. No reason for me to live. I had no one. I put the gun to my temple and your boy, he was walking right toward me. I don't know what would have happened that day but as you can see, I didn't shoot myself."

Twig nodded toward Simon, raised his beer, and took a sip.

"Holy fuck, you know how to bring down the mood of a party," Felix said.

"That's what I do. It's why I don't talk. At least I try not to. It's nice to finally meet you, Tabs."

"Likewise."

For the next couple of hours, the guys relaxed, talking, reminiscing about old memories. Tabby sat beside him, listening, laughing, enjoying each moment. At least he hoped she had. Not a moment had gone by when he hadn't missed her and the guys were making that perfectly clear.

When it was close to midnight, the guys decided to head home, and Tabby had already made her way inside.

He helped clear up the yard, saying goodbyes to the guys and promising to have everything resolved soon.

They all gave him a hug, slapping him on the back before getting into the truck. Each of them had told him they liked Tabby. She was good for him.

As their headlights diminished, he held up his hand in a final wave before going to see his woman.

She'd already taken a quick shower and changed into a nightshirt.

"Are you going to say anything?" he asked.

"They seem like good guys."

"They are. Do you like them?"

She ran a brush through her hair. "Does it matter if I do?"

"To me it does."

"I … I've only just met them. Do I think they'd be a good fit to the club? Sure, I don't see why not. You can't judge someone in a short amount of time, Simon. If you're looking for me to give you a slap on the back and a job well done, I can't do that. You and I both know this is going to take time."

"I never meant to hurt you."

"I know that."

"Then why do I feel like you think I did this on purpose?"

She sighed. "I don't want to fight. We promised ourselves tonight. Can't we stick to that promise?"

"We could, but I know this is hanging over our heads."

"Simon, it will always be hanging over us. You made your choice that night. You picked revenge over me."

"I picked justice."

She rolled her eyes. "See, I just can't talk to you when you're like this." She moved toward the bed. "Please, give me tonight. I gave it to you. I'm not running away. I met your friends and they seem like good people, but that's all. I'm not going to pass judgment. We're not in charge of Chaos Bleeds, and whatever you may think, I'm not your old lady."

He walked toward her, sinking his fingers into her hair and drawing her close. "You are my old lady. We're going through a rough patch right now, but that doesn't mean you don't belong at my side."

Slamming his lips down on hers, he kissed her hard, almost bruising. He figured she was going to hit him but Tabby always surprised him. She ran her hands up his chest and circled his neck, kissing him back.

Simon broke the kiss first. "I'm going to shower. You'll be here?"

"I keep my promises, remember? One night. I'm not going to try to run."

He nodded.

"But come tomorrow, we're back to where we started."

Gritting his teeth, he made his way into the shower to take one of the quickest washes he'd ever taken.

Chapter Twelve

"Are you being serious right now?" Tabitha asked.

"Yeah, totally serious." Simon stood at the door with it open. She heard the car in the front yard running.

"You're taking me back?"

He nodded.

She stepped toward him and paused. "Is there a catch?"

"Yeah. I want to meet our son. I want to know more about him and be a part of his life. You've also got to give me a chance."

"So what you're saying is this is an ultimatum."

"No, Tabby. This is me trying to do the right thing and also keep you. I'm selfish like that. You should have realized it long ago." He smiled.

He looked so sad. They'd had a good couple of days. She got to meet his friends and see a part of him she hadn't known in a long time. Simon was amazing. There was no doubt about it. He'd just proven to be a lousy husband.

"Can I just go and see my son? Talk to someone?" She glanced down at her body. "Maybe wear my own clothes?"

"You don't like my stuff?"

"I do, but it's not me." She liked having Simon's scent wrapped around her. Little by little, she found herself no longer angry at him. Again, she didn't know if that was a good thing or not.

The pain had lessened a little bit, which she was thankful for, but there was still so much damage between them. She honestly didn't know if they were ever going to repair it.

Tucking her hair behind her ear, she smiled at

him.

Closing the distance, she cupped his face and went on her toes, kissing him. "Thank you."

"Don't thank me yet. I want to steal you away forever."

A part of her wanted that. The part of her that wished they could be locked away forever, close off the world, and throw away the key. It wasn't going to happen. They weren't designed like that.

"Take me back to him, please."

She missed Nathan so much. Just the other night, she'd been sitting there, and all she wanted to do was read him a book. To be near him. He was her son, and she loved him more than anything in the world.

Passing Simon, she moved toward the truck and climbed into the passenger seat. There was no sign of his friends or Dean.

Dean liked to stop by.

She ran her hands over the sweatpants. The shirt she wore was creased. Simon didn't own an iron and so she didn't have any way of making his clothes look neat. Even though large shirts and sweats didn't exactly require an iron.

"Don't worry about how you look. He won't care."

"How do you know?" she asked.

"I had a mom, remember? I know how this goes."

She chuckled. "Lexie wears creased sweatpants and a shirt?"

"Yep, and she also had the vomit stains as well from the milk. I'm used to it and if Nathan loves you, he won't care."

"What a way to strain a relationship. What if he doesn't love me?" she asked, glancing toward him.

"It's not possible. He will love you."

"But what if he doesn't?" She ran fingers through her hair. "I never thought about that. I mean, do kids always love their parents?"

"Yes, they do," he said, laughing. "You loved Eva and Tiny, didn't you?"

"Well, yeah, but I hated them as well."

"And one day, Nathan is going to hate you. I wonder if you'll be the mom that stops him from going on dates." Simon chuckled.

"Did Lexie hate you going on dates?" Tabitha asked.

"No. I didn't go on any dates. My heart was owned by you. That never changed." He smiled. "I rarely brought a girl home and when I did, most of the time she arrived with a whole MC. It was a family thing."

"This girl of yours sounds awesome."

"She totally was. You should meet her. She was fearless."

Tabitha sighed. "We were different back then. Kids. We didn't know how the world worked."

"We did, Tabby. We knew what we were getting into. Our parents always thought we were kids, but that is so not true. We were more than that. We were fearless." Simon took hold of her hand, and she let him, not wanting to fight. "It's the way we will always be. We're the ones in control. No one else." He brought her hand to his lips, kissing her knuckles. She remembered what happened the last time he kissed her like this. How sweet, and then of course the sex.

The sex was better than any other time.

Pulling her hand away, she clasped it with her other, trying to keep herself in check. It wasn't good for her to allow her mind to wander. She needed to be in control.

"It's going to be okay, you know? Nathan loves

you and he's going to adore me. I swear it."

She nodded but didn't say a word.

This was the longest she'd been away from her son, ever.

Simon turned on the radio to some tune she didn't know. The music filled the silence, and she was able to not worry. Listening to the words, she tried not to think about her son, about Simon. What if Nathan adored Simon but in time, he couldn't stand to look at him?

So many problems she didn't want to face.

The time for her to decide if she'd allow Simon to see him faded as they pulled up at Lexie and Devil's house. The front door opened and there stood Devil.

It was cold, but he only wore a pair of pants, his arms folded.

After opening the door, she climbed out and walked toward the house.

"Is he here?" Tabitha asked.

"He is." Devil embraced her in a hug. "Are you okay?"

"I'm fine. Really."

"If you want me to keep him out of the house, I will," Devil said. "He already took you without your permission. You get to decide when he meets Nathan."

She glanced back, seeing a scowl on Simon's face.

He would fight his father if he had to.

Not today.

She wasn't going to get between family, nor was she going to allow this to happen.

"No, it's fine. I want Simon to meet him. It'll be good for the both of them." She hoped.

Brushing past Devil, she stepped into the house and smiled as her name was called.

"Mommy!"

So it wasn't her actual name, but she bent down as Nathan came barreling toward her, throwing himself into her arms.

"I missed you so much, but Grandpa Devil and Grandma Lexie showed me how to ride a bike."

"They did?" She looked up to see Lexie smiling.

"Not a bike with an engine. A normal bicycle."

"I'm good, Mommy. At first, I kept falling down and then I didn't stop. No, I didn't. I kept on going. I knew my mommy would want to see. Do you want to see? Do you?"

She laughed. "Of course I do. It's so awesome you can ride a bike. I guess that's what you're asking Santa for this year?"

His eyes went wide. "I could. Couldn't I?"

Pulling him in close, she pressed her nose against his neck. Damn, she'd missed him so much.

Simon cleared his throat and she glanced behind him.

Fuck!

How could she introduce him?

Did he want to see the answer to the test that was still back in Fort Wills?

She hadn't exactly thought this one through.

Not even a little bit.

Fuck. Shit. Fuck.

"Er, actually, before you show me just how amazing you are on your bike, there is someone I would like you to meet."

"Is it Santa?"

"No, bud, it's not Santa," Simon said, moving close.

Lexie gasped and Tabitha turned toward her to see tears in her eyes.

Simon crouched down so he was on a level with

Nathan. "I'm a friend of your mom's," Simon said. "And Nathan, buddy, I'm your daddy."

Nathan cried out. "You're my daddy! Mommy, it's Daddy."

Tabitha smiled but the tears and the pain were still there. Was she doing the right thing? Would Simon resent her for this? Neither of them knew the truth.

She kept on smiling, keeping up her façade.

Nathan held Simon close and she watched the two of them. They were always going to have kids, but Simon had wanted to complete his prospect status first to become a fully patched-in member.

This hadn't gone to plan. None of their life had gone the way they wanted.

She held her shit together.

Nathan grabbed Simon's hand and tugged him outside. She laughed, following behind them as he was determined to show his skills.

They stood at the edge of the driveway. Nathan walked up to the top of the street. She kept him in sight as Lexie threw herself at Simon, hugging him close.

"I want to kill you and kiss you," Lexie said.

Tabitha understood completely. She was in the same mind most of the time.

Arms folded, she kept an eye on her son.

"It's fine, Mom, really."

"No, it's not fine. You didn't call. You didn't allow us to know you were okay."

"Dad kept an eye on me. You should know that."

"Yeah, but it's not the same thing and you damn well know it," Lexie said. "You're not going anywhere?"

"No, I'm here to stay."

Tabitha jumped as Simon put his hand on her waist. His body pressing against her back.

"What are you doing?"

"I'm standing with my wife, and we're watching our son."

"You don't have to do this. I know this must be difficult for you."

He chuckled. "None of this is difficult for me. I knew this day was going to come eventually. I'd hoped that it wouldn't be so soon. I'm a selfish prick, Tabby. You know this. I want to keep you to myself, always. That is never, ever going to change."

She kept her hands folded but sank a little closer to him, desperate for him. She did love him.

When he'd left, a part of her had died and only now, with him close, did she feel herself being awakened again. They were soul mates. She'd always known the truth. They were indeed meant to be together. There wasn't a time in her life when it wasn't Simon and Tabitha, and she had a twin.

Sure, there were times it was Miles and Tabitha, but everyone always thought of Simon. Not her brother.

"Can you see me, Mommy?" Nathan asked.

"I can. Come on, sweetheart!" She cupped her hands over her mouth, watched, and waited.

He started off a little slow at first. Wobbly.

"You're sure he can do this?" Tabitha asked.

"He's been doing it for days," Devil said.

Lexie chuckled. "One day he refused to come in for dinner until he'd learned. He's such a smart kid."

Tabitha watched. The first few feet, he wobbled and she tensed, ready to sprint toward him. He didn't give up. She cheered for him, clapping her hands as he rode all the way to their backyard, pressing on the brake to stop.

"That was so amazing." She rushed to his side, pulling him off the bike and spinning him in the air.

Simon was there. Lifting him up and catching

him. Nathan loved it. She did as well. She wanted to freeze the moment. This was perfect and every time she'd known perfection, something happened to shatter it apart.

****

Later that night, after putting Nathan to bed by reading to him, Simon looked at Tabby's yawning face. "I'm going to call it a night," she said.

"I'll be up in a minute." He stroked her cheek and she leaned into his hand.

"Thank you for today."

"Nathan's a great kid. I want to get to know him."

"He really is. He's smart and fearless, but he does cry at times. I want you to get to know him too."

Cupping her face with both of his hands, he stared into her eyes. "I want you to understand that I don't care what documents say. He's mine. He will always be mine. I'm going to be his dad, your husband."

"But—"

"No, buts. That's how it's going to be. Me and you against the world, right?"

"You won't resent me?"

"No, hell, no. There's nothing to resent. No reason for me to." He brushed his lips across hers. "What I do need to do is go and see my parents." Dinner had been an interesting affair, surrounded by his brothers and sister. There had also been some awkwardness, which he'd never experienced before at his family's table.

He watched Tabby go into their room. Squaring his shoulders, he made his way downstairs, prepared to face the music. His parents sat at the dining room table. His father drank some whiskey while his mom looked to have a hot chocolate.

"It looks like we were all thinking the same thing," he said, going to a chair, pulling it out, and sitting his ass down.

"You knew this was going to happen."

"Are you kicking me out of the house?" he asked, looking between the two.

Lexie frowned. "Where the hell did that come from?"

"I don't know. I just figured that's what you were going to say. Look at how dinner went tonight." He laughed. "The only people keeping the conversation running were Elizabeth and Josh. Believe me, their conversation wasn't thrilling as kids, nor is it now."

"You've been gone a long time, son. People don't know what to expect. They've heard the rumors about you. You scare them."

"You're going to have to clue me in on the rumors. I'm still me," he said.

"You're not, honey," Lexie said. "Even I can see that. You're hardened by life. There was a time you'd have laughed at some of their bickering or joined in. Tonight you looked like you wanted to kill them with your fork."

Simon ran his fingers through his hair. "I've changed, I get that. I'm still me, and all those years ago, I still wanted to kill them with my fork. I just covered it up." He pressed his hands flat against the table. "I'm … I have a lot of shit going on and I have no right to complain. I'm not going to complain. I left Tabby and she raised our son all on her own."

He looked toward his dad. "Why didn't you ever tell me? Why did I have to find out from her five years after the fact? You told me you knew where I was. Why didn't you come and get me?"

Devil poured himself another shot of whiskey and knocked it back. "Do you think you were in a position of being all that she needs? Raising a kid isn't just today, cheering on their success. It's coping with everything. You were hardly keeping your shit together."

"I would have done that for Tabby."

"And you'd have fucked it up big time. I made a judgment call. It wasn't a pretty one, but I made it. You weren't ready to know what happened to Tabby. The shit she had to put up with. The pregnancy was already stressful enough. The Monster Dogs came calling."

Simon tensed up. "What the fuck?"

Devil smirked. "Yeah, I happened to be there that day. It was the same time I decided not to reach out to you." Devil poured himself another shot of whiskey. "I was at the clubhouse. All the arrangements had been set in place. Lash was pissed they turned up uninvited on his turf and to top it off, it was one of the rare occasions Tabitha was even at the clubhouse. Dick had been teaching her some meditation or some shit. I don't know."

Devil twirled his glass on the table. Simon's patience was starting to wear a little thin. No, not a little, a lot. He looked toward his mother when Devil finally spoke again. "The president was there, a few of his boys, and Ryan's dad. The one who you killed."

"He had no right to be there."

"I know, so did Lash. Anyway, he was in the process of getting them off club property, and I was about a second away from shooting them all in the face, when Tabitha walked in. Damn it, do you remember?" Devil asked, looking at Lexie.

"It was the first time we saw her smile. Whatever Dick had done, he'd brought her peace."

"Yep, and within a second, it was gone because of those assholes. Believe me, a lot of people wanted to start a war that day. Tabitha had been holding her shit together but barely. One look at them, and she seemed to know. Ryan's dad, and the Monster Dogs wanted her to come and live at their clubhouse. To … I don't know, become one of them. She was carrying one of them, and it was only fair." Devil smiled. "She told them all to eat shit and die." Lexie chuckled. "I swear at times, she didn't know what her words could have caused."

Simon couldn't help but smile, imagining his woman. He also knew she would have been a mess afterward.

"She told them that what Ryan did to her, none of them had any right or claim. The baby was hers. She also explained, much to my and Lexie's embarrassment, there was also a chance it was yours, about a failed condom."

Simon nodded. "We were going to wait a month and see. Take a test if she didn't start her period."

"The Dogs weren't easily swayed until Tabitha very vividly told them exactly what Ryan did. How as far as she was concerned, they would never have any claim, and if they so much as touched her, she would make sure they never knew a quiet moment because as Ryan attacked, he'd whispered little secrets about the club." Devil sighed. "The Dogs left. Tabitha got left alone."

"She has secrets on them?"

"Not a damn thing," Devil said. He laughed. "It sure made Whizz pull his shit together and start digging. They were on a countdown. He got the dirty crap he needed. Enough to keep Tabitha and Nathan safe. That's how I knew she didn't need you. Tabitha is a strong woman, Simon. I made a judgment call and you don't like it, fine. I don't care. You've seen how amazing she's been with that boy."

"I don't want to know," he said.

"You don't want to know what?" Devil asked.

"If he's mine or not. I know you've got the answers and if you don't, you'd find them. Nathan's mine." He got to his feet. "He's my son and I want him to be seen as my flesh and blood in the eyes of the club."

"The only way to make this work is to claim her, son. You know that. Stick around. Earn your patch. Show the boys you mean business. I expect you at the clubhouse tomorrow."

Simon got to his feet and held his hand out. "Thank you for taking care of her."

Devil chuckled. "You don't need to go around shaking my hand. We both know she's family."

Simon left his parents and found Tabby in bed. She was curled up but her eyes were open.

"Hey, beautiful."

"Did you have a good family meeting?"

"Not really. I've got to earn everything back. The respect, you know, the works."

"Did you expect anything else from him?" Tabby asked.

"No, not a damn thing." He stroked her hair back from her cheek. "Can I stay with you tonight?"

"If you'd like."

"I'm going to need a place to live," he said.

"Simon, I don't want to move too fast."

"I'll take the sofa at your place. No rush."

"Fine."

He kissed her cheek. "You do know I'm not going anywhere from now on. You've got me."

"Yay, I can't wait."

He laughed. "You're a giant pain in the ass."

"And that's what you love about me."

"It's not the only thing I love about you, but it's right up there of things to love." He pressed a kiss to her cheek before getting up and heading toward the bathroom. On his way to have a quick shower, he heard some whimpering coming from his son's room.

Opening the door, he glanced in to see Nathan twitch and whimper. He suddenly jerked awake, calling for his mother. Simon wrapped his arms around his son, holding him close. "I've got you."

"I was being eaten by sharks."

"No sharks."

"I hate the water."

"Don't worry. Everyone hates sharks," he said. Nathan slowly started to calm down.

He lay back against the pillows and he stroked his son's head. "Are you feeling better now?"

"Yeah, I don't like sharks."

"I hate them," Simon said, wrinkling his nose. "They're way too big and weird."

Nathan giggled. "Mom hates them too. She likes watching movies with them in."

"You don't watch them?"

Nathan shook his head. "No. Mom says I'm too young but sometimes Uncle Miles, if he's watching me, he lets me."

"I bet your mom isn't happy about that."

Nathan agreed.

"I've got to head for the shower. I kind of stink. You good, or do you want me to stay here until you fall asleep?"

"I'm good."

Leaning down, he kissed his son on the head and stood.

"Daddy?" Nathan asked as he got to the door.

Gripping the handle, he looked back.

"Will you be here in the morning?"

He nodded. "Yep, here in the morning and the day after that, the day after. You're going to get so sick of seeing me."

Another giggle. "I won't, Daddy. Love you."

"Love you too."

Closing the door, he turned to see Tabby standing there watching. Tears were in her eyes.

"See, I've got this."

****

"You're thinking again," Lexie said.

Devil put the bottle of whiskey away and looked toward his woman. "Is that a bad thing?"

"I don't know. I think every single time you're thinking it means bad news."

"I'm not and this is good news. We should be celebrating," Devil said. "Our son has returned. He's back with his woman."

"And we know Tabitha may still want a divorce," Lexie said. "If she does, it's going to get ugly."

"Yep, really fucking ugly, but I'm hopeful. You know? I don't know what to expect and Tabitha has been known to surprise us."

"I remember that day so clearly. Never have I wanted to hold that girl so much," Lexie said.

"Tell me about it. I think we all have a love for that girl. She's tough. A fighter. She's everything Simon needs, especially now." Devil chuckled. "I've gone from wanting their silly crush to be over with to hoping she'll give him another chance."

Lexie stood up and walked into the kitchen, cleaning up her cup. "Do you think he's ever going to find out the truth?" She put the cup on the draining board and turned to look back at Devil.

"You mean the part where I found the results that showed Simon wasn't in any way the father to Nathan?" Devil asked.

He saw his wife's eyes fill with tears.

"How I wiped all the evidence of the system with Anthony's help in order to keep that shit private and so the Monster Dogs don't try to take him?" Devil asked. He took his wife in his arms. "No, my lips are sealed. So are Anthony's. We're the only two who know the true answer."

Lexie slumped against him. "I don't know how you can be so calm."

He held her close. "There's so much at stake I've got no choice but to be the calm one. Look at you, you're not helping."

She let out a giggle and he loved the sound. "We've just got him back."

"And nothing we do is going to change that. Simon is here to stay. There's no reason for you to be stressing about any of this. Trust me."

"I do, trust you, I mean. It's just, ugh, it's … I don't know. I felt like they both need a lucky break, you know?"

"They'll get it and we're here to help them. We've got Thanksgiving coming up. Christmas. The New Year. We can make this work."

"Did you see the way they were looking at him?" Lexie asked, pouting, referring to his brothers and sisters.

"Stop it. Of course, they're going to look at him like that. For now, he's the crazy big brother on a tight leash. Give them all time. They haven't seen Simon like this. He was their goofy big brother. Now he's a man and regardless of how much we protect them, they know he killed someone. Probably a lot of people. We've just got to be strong, keep it together, and move forward."

"There you go again, being the perfect model citizen."

"Clearly, all of your life lessons are rubbing off on me. In fact, I think I need a brand-new rub." He lifted Lexie up into his arms.

"You're crazy."

"I'm crazy in love with you and that, baby, is never, ever going to change."

Chapter Thirteen

"You mean after all that, you didn't kick his ass?" Daisy asked.

Tabitha laughed. It was so good to hear her friend's voice again. She'd missed her. "No, I didn't. We did a lot of other stuff instead, and no, I'm not going into the details."

"Please don't. I just can't believe it. In a weird way, it's a little romantic, don't you think?"

"You think being kidnapped by my husband is a good thing?"

"No, not a good thing, but he was willing to do whatever it took to win you. Don't you think that has merit?" Daisy asked.

"I think we're both on the wrong page about all of this. Let me be clear. He left me for five years."

"Noted."

"Yes, we're still clear. Then he tells me that he's going to get his shit together. He's just killed someone."

"And in his defense, the bastard had to go," Daisy said. "He gets points for that."

"We need to deduct him points for how he did it."

"If you feel that is absolutely necessary?"

"Yes, I do. Completely necessary. He needs deducting points."

Daisy laughed. "I'll keep a score. Does a tally chart sound appealing?"

"Stop being sarcastic."

"Okay, okay, so he left for killing someone. Move on. What else?"

"And he is supposed to be making himself a man worthy of me, but instead, all he actually does is kill more people. He becomes an underground fighter. How is that finding himself?"

"I don't know his reasoning. I haven't spoken to him in years, Tabs, but I'd say, seeing as he is back, and has claimed you once again and Nathan, that whatever he needed to go and find, he found it."

"Whose side are you on?"

"Your side and we both know you're looking for any excuse to hate him, and if that's what you want, I'm good with that. I honestly don't mind. I love you, and you know I'll help but, but we both know for you, Simon is it. He has been since we were kids. The guys in high school, you shot them all down. Even Luke and Niles said so as well. He asked about you."

"He did?"

"Yep. I said you moved out of town."

"He wasn't so bad." Tabitha sighed, leaning back against the wall. She'd dropped Nathan at the school with Simon right beside her. Afterward, he'd dropped her off at work so he could go to the clubhouse. It was all very domestic. Kind of scary at how easy it was for them to fall into a sense of a routine. It was her lunch break and she sat outside in the freezing cold, curled up in Simon's jacket that he'd given her. She wondered how his prospecting was going. Simon was due back at the clubhouse today, but the rest of the guys were there on Monday. She wondered how they would all fit into Chaos Bleeds.

The clubs were constantly expanding. They were all just one big happy family.

"Wasn't so bad?" Daisy asked. "You got into a fight."

"Miles said the same thing."

"Oh, get this, Constance is back in town and oh my, she is stunning."

"She is? She was always gorgeous."

"Yeah, but you should have seen Miles and half

the male population. The other half is The Skulls and don't care about any other than the one by their side."

Tabitha listened as Daisy caught her up to speed on Constance's sudden appearance, how beautiful and curvy she looked. They'd all been close out of high school, but Constance had been the one to get out of town, all with Miles's and The Skulls' help.

Now, she was back, after traveling.

"So, Thanksgiving is in a couple of weeks. Have you talked to your mom?" Daisy asked, changing topics.

"No. I've got to phone her after you. Between us, I'm hoping to stay on the phone with you so I don't have to deal with her. She just makes things kind of difficult." She sighed. "Is it going to be one of The Skulls' big get-togethers?"

"You got it. Angel is already organizing everything. She's in the kitchen baking all the time. The guys are constantly being sent on errands." Daisy giggled. "Anthony brought back the wrong chocolate chips four times. It was so funny."

"I bet."

"You're moody."

"I'm not moody. I … they're going to be having a big club get-together here. All the family, and well, you're my family, but if I come there, Simon will follow."

"Ah, I see."

"Yeah, and that whole the-Dogs-want-to-kill-him thing. Fuck, I hate that club." She sighed. "I'm sorry. You're having fun and I'm being a downer."

"For good reason. I didn't even think about the Dogs and Simon."

"It's been a long time without him. Why would you think of him?"

"He's still your husband."

Tabitha rubbed at her temples, feeling the start of a headache. "I think it might be best if I stay here this Thanksgiving. It'll be good for Nathan and Simon."

"How did he handle that? We've talked about everything but that."

"He's … he's amazing with him. Simon is a fantastic father. Nathan is so lucky."

"But you sound so unhappy."

"My head is a mess right now. I've just got a lot to figure out."

Daisy was silent on the other end.

"I've known you most of my life and your silences mean you disagree. Spill it."

"Okay, to be clear, you don't have a whole lot to figure out. Break it down. You love Simon or you don't. You either stay with him or leave. You come back home, or you stay there, or you move elsewhere. It's not complicated. You don't want to make the wrong decision and regret it. I get that."

"You've broken it down to make it sound simpler. It's not. You forget to add that family get-togethers from now on will have to be in Piston County. Do you think Simon is going to let me come to Fort Wills with the Dogs so close?"

"Do you think he even gets to have a say in what you do?"

She opened her mouth, closed it.

"I've surprised you?"

"Yes, no, I don't know. Maybe. I guess I've been giving him a lot more credit. Wow, I just totally had a man in control there, didn't I?" she asked.

Daisy laughed. "It's fine. You've been through a lot."

"In all honesty, I don't know if I want to make this work," she said.

"Oh."

She covered her face with her hand, knowing the tears were close. Crying wasn't something she enjoyed doing but seemed to be something that happened so often just lately. "We ... er, damn it, Daisy, we had unprotected sex."

"Ouch."

"It's not an ouch thing. Not really."

"Are you happy about it?" Daisy asked.

"That I could be pregnant again when I'm twenty-three?"

"If it makes you feel any better, you'll be giving birth when you're twenty-four and there's nothing wrong with your age. Women are having kids all the time. Teenagers, older women."

"You're not pregnant."

"Let's not talk about me."

"Yes, let's. Let's talk about your love life with Anthony."

"Not going to happen," Daisy said. "Besides, we're talking about your little confession and how you're not sure if you want to make things work with Simon. I hate to be the one to put a reality check on you, but that's a big deal."

Tabitha dropped her hand and checked the time. "I've got to go."

"This isn't fair."

"I've got to go. Talk soon." She hung up before Daisy could say another word. Guilt swamped her.

Pushing everything to the back of her mind, she made her way inside to find Dean sitting at one of the tables. Simon's best friend appeared to be perusing the menu.

Great, just what she needed.

She went to the staff room, put her cell phone in

her bag, and made her way out.

Complete with a pen and notepad, she looked at him, waiting. "What can I do for you?" she asked.

He put the menu down. "Coffee, burger, and fries."

She wrote it down. This is what she loved about working in this coffee shop, everyone had to order a coffee with their meal.

"And while you're at it, I'd like to know if you're going to put my boy through shit."

She paused in writing and glanced up at him. "None of your business."

"It is. I'm the one who's been taking care of him. Not you."

"You got a little crush on him, Dean? It piss you off that the first person he comes to is me?"

"Not at all. I've got his best interests at heart."

She dropped the notepad to the table and glared at him. "You do? You've got his best interests at heart. Let's be clear on something here, rich boy. You don't have the first fucking clue on what you're dealing with here. While you were getting fed with your silver spoon and having your ass wiped by nannies, me and Simon, we got a real hard look at the world. Take it from me, it's not pretty. We got shot at. We witnessed death. Life coming and going. People passing through intending to do harm. Believe me, you don't have the first clue what you're dealing with. What you've seen doesn't even scratch the surface. What goes on between Simon and me, it'll stay that way. You don't get a say in this. Not ever. Now, you can have your food and leave me the fuck alone, or you get the hell out."

"You going to tell Simon about our talk?" Dean asked.

"No, he doesn't need to know, but I will tell you

this. I do respect you for coming to me. No matter what goes on between us, he needs someone to have his back. Just don't ever take your eyes off it. Got me?"

"I got you." Dean leaned back. "I will have that burger. I knew there was a reason I liked you, Tabby."

"Don't call me that. Only Simon calls me that." She turned on her heel and went to get his order.

Taking a deep breath, she felt her hands shaking, her body coming alive. What was it about standing up for herself, or keeping it real, that just made her feel awake for the first time in years?

You're not weak. You fight. You don't take shit from anyone. It's time you realized it. What you're getting now is your goddamn wake-up call, and you need it.

Taking a deep breath, she turned back toward the tables, coffee in hand. She could do this.

****

Simon got a warm welcome back at the club. He expected it. The guys embraced him with open arms, applause, and it was like time hadn't moved. He was still Devil's son. The golden boy. The prince to them.

Of course, the moment he put on the prospect cut, he was someone to be tested, tried, and fuck it, he loved it. Even as he was forced to clean toilets or run errands on that first day. He was alive.

By the end of the day, he was ready to call it a night. He hadn't talked to Tabby, but he'd called Lexie and asked her to get Tabby from work. He got the call from his mom that his wife and kid were back at the apartment.

Judi, his older stepsister, sat at the bar. She had a soda and was waiting for Ripper. They weren't close, like friends. Devil and Lexie had taken her under their wing. She'd been a forced child prostitute. Devil had saved her, and together, his parents had adopted her.

"You okay?" he asked.

Judi looked up. "Yeah, I'm okay. Just tired. It's been a long couple of days. Lexie's planning this big Thanksgiving feast in your honor."

"You hate that?"

"Not at all. It hasn't been the same without you and everyone has been so worried." Judi sipped at her drink. "How are you?"

"Me, I'm good."

"Really, I mean? I know that it takes something out of you, doing what you did."

Simon pressed his lips together, blowing out a breath. "I … I'm fine. I was fine. I thought I'd feel guilt over what I'd done." He laughed. "I didn't feel anything and that scared the shit out of me."

"Nothing at all?"

"The prick hurt my woman. I can't justify keeping him alive. Do I wish I had done it differently? Fuck yeah. I made a big, messed-up mistake, but it was my mess to make. Can't change it now." He rubbed the back of his head. "Now, I've got to make it right with Tabby."

"Tabby," Judi said with a smile. "Damn, that is so cute but it did stick, didn't it?"

"She's mine and I'm hers. It's the way it will always be."

"I heard she wants to have a divorce."

He tensed up.

"What will you do if she does, Simon?"

"I'm not going to think about that. I know I'm good for Tabby. I've got to hope she sees it as well."

Judi nodded as the doors to Devil's office opened. She finished her soda. "That's my cue to leave. It's good to have you back, Simon, and between us, I'm rooting for you."

He winked at her, waved at Ripper, and got back to work, wiping down the counters.

Dean came and perched on a barstool. He puffed out his chest, showing off his patched member badge.

"I can still kick your ass."

"I don't blame you. Went by to see Tabby today."

"Don't call her that."

"Funny, she said the same thing."

Simon finished wiping a glass and turned his full attention to his friend. "Now tell me why you would go to my woman at her place of work."

"Because I'm a good friend and I like to interfere."

"Don't."

"Someone needs to watch your back."

Simon put the glass away and shook his head. "What I need is to be the one to make things right with Tabby. Not you. Not my parents. Me."

"I was on the road with you. I got to see a lot of you up close and personal and some of it is scary as fucking hell. I get it. You haven't had a good lot of luck of late. I'm going to watch your back. Your woman is certainly a fucking queen. You're not wrong about her."

"Do I even want to know why you went to her?"

"Probably not." Dean winked at him. "What I will tell you is you've got your work cut out for you."

"Simon, you can head out now," Devil said.

He stood at the bar and looked at his dad. "I can?"

"Yeah."

"Exactly where would I be heading to?" he asked.

"You don't know where Tabs lives?" Devil asked. He was typing something onto his cell phone. Seeing his dad with any kind of technology was fucking weird, at least to him it was.

"It's not something I've asked about, no. I didn't take her from her apartment." He hadn't told anyone about the two men Dean had disposed of.

"Oh, guess what I found out," Dean said. "Eddie, he's becoming like the preppy boy of kissing ass."

"That preppy boy of kissing ass has turned into a moral beacon for the whole of the town. Don't start anything with him," Devil said. "I reached out to him when you were gone but his parents have their claws in him. He does whatever they say."

"I haven't seen Eddie."

"Believe me, you don't want to."

Eddie was always the one to follow his parents' orders. He'd been too scared of being cut off not to be. The kid had grown up with money and hated the thought of going without.

"Have you seen your parents?" Simon asked.

Dean shook his head. "It makes me want to go to the country club and stir shit up. That would be fun."

"Dean, you're not a kid anymore and you're a patched-in club member. You do something to bring heat, we'll deal with it," Devil said. "That patch has to stay earned. Don't make me regret bringing you in." Devil told him Tabby's address. "That's where she's living. I'm guessing you don't have a key."

"That's right," Simon said.

"If she keeps you locked out, come back home. Don't cause any trouble." Devil turned on his heel and walked away. Something was going on. Simon didn't know what but he intended to find out.

"So the whole patched-in member thing?" Dean asked. "What exactly does he mean?"

"You've got to put the club before your own pettiness. Any kind of shit you wanted to take out on your parents, you've got to run it by the club first. They will vote on if it's good or not. Anything you do with the intention of causing shit, the club will deal with you." Simon paused on his way out. "As your patched-in member status, surely you know that."

"Kiss my ass, Si."

"Nah, I know where it has been."

He left the clubhouse and made his way out to find Dick once again meditating on a patch of cold earth, beneath the stars. His wife wasn't with him, which was odd as she normally joined him at the clubhouse. She was probably home.

"What are you staring at, boy?" Dick asked. One of his eyes was open, looking right at him.

"Nothing. I wanted to say thank you."

"You don't need to."

"Why do you do this?" Simon asked, coming to stand in front of him. "You weren't the kind of guy to meditate nor do yoga."

"I also wasn't the kind of guy to be counted on. I lived with my head in a drug-infused state. I got clean for the club and for my woman, and I will remain that way." He lifted his hands up in a circle, drawing them together and bringing them down to his chest. "I do this as it gives me peace. It allows me to think of everything I've got in the world. I remind myself multiple times a day, every single day, and I will never fall back."

"Why did you do this for Tabby?"

"She needed time. Her head was filled with darkness. I know what that's like. I've had my share of darkness. Most of it brought on by myself by being the biggest dick alive. She didn't deserve the pain. I didn't know if it would work, but she smiled. I helped to bring her peace." Dick released a final breath. "You've got a good woman there, strong. Don't screw it up."

"I've got a lot of people telling me not to screw it up."

"Good. I also wanted to warn you, a few of The Skulls are dropping by. That's the only heads up you're getting from me."

"Is trouble coming?"

"You tell me, Simon," Dick said. "You will be the judge of what's to come and what is not." Dick got to his feet. "Now I'm ready to fuck. Excuse me."

Simon stood still.

Dick, out of everyone was … an asshole.

Shaking his head, he turned to his van and climbed on inside. He'd need to get his bike down at the clubhouse soon.

Driving out of the gate, he took off to where Tabby lived. The streets all blurred as he focused on his woman.

There was a small parking lot to the side of the large apartment block.

After locking his door, he made his way over to the unit, trying the door.

"Fuck!"

It was late and he'd hoped to avoid arguing with Tabby. She might not let him up, especially with Dean meddling. People needed to learn to stay out of their business. He and Tabby would work their stuff out, one day.

Pressing her name, he waited.

"Hello," she said, sounding tired.

"Tabby, it's me."

"Devil didn't give you the code?"

"No, no code."

She let out a chuckle. "What's the magic word?"

"Really?"

"Come on, it's fun."

He glanced around at the night. "Fine, unicorn."

"Ugh, you're an ass."

The door buzzed and he smiled. Letting himself inside, he went to the stairs and walked up to the floor he needed.

Tabby was already at the door. The bolt slid into place. "That wasn't funny."

"You always think of the exact same kind of magic word. You need to become more original."

"Fine, magic words?"

"You're an ass."

He raised his brow, hand on hip, waiting.

"I will let you in but I was thinking you were a fucking ass."

He chuckled. "And here I was thinking you'd be playing it safe because of Nathan."

"He's in bed. He didn't want to go to sleep." Tabby stepped away from the door. She wore a large nightshirt with, of all things, a unicorn on the front.

"Why? What's wrong?"

"Nothing is wrong. He wanted to see you before he went to sleep. He's been talking about you all day."

His stomach growled and Tabby chuckled.

"Do you want some food?"

"Yeah, I'm starving."

"Didn't they let you eat?"

"No, I ate, but try cleaning a toilet that has over ten men pissing and shitting on it."

She wrinkled her nose. "Nah, I'll just stick with the nasty visual."

"If I was you, I would." He rubbed his hands down his thighs. "I'm going to take a shower. Do you think I can go and see him when I'm done?"

"Sure. Of course. I'll cook you something." She made to walk past him but he captured her. "Ew, please tell me you washed your hands."

"Scrubbed them." He dropped his lips down to hers and after a few seconds, she slowly melted against him. "See, we can do this."

"Go and shower. I'll feed you." She walked away and he watched her leave. Her ass was a nice distraction.

He found the bathroom, stripped out of his clothes, took the quickest shower known to man, and then wrapped a towel around his waist. He didn't have any clothes, so he had no choice but to wrap himself in her bathrobe before going to see his son.

The first bedroom was Tabby's, and he smiled looking at it.

The scent of her filled the room. Rather than stay in her room, he went to the next one and found a small light on and Nathan curled up. He had his thumb in his mouth. A book was on the floor beside the bed.

He walked into the room, being quiet as he lifted the book up from the floor.

"Daddy?" Nathan asked.

He peered over the book and saw Nathan rubbing at his eyes.

"I'm here." He knelt on the floor, holding his son's hand. "I'm here. You don't have to worry." He smiled at him.

"I … I thought you'd left again. Mommy said you'd come back."

"Of course. I'm back. I just had work."

"Club stuff?"

"Yeah, club stuff."

"Grandpa Tiny always said club stuff is important and when I hear it, I have to stop listening. I shouldn't be listening."

"That's okay. Grandpa Tiny is kind of stuffy and weird. You don't have to stop listening, what you've got to do is keep it a secret."

Nathan nodded. "Mommy said that. She said no one is to know club stuff. It's not important for them to know."

"Mommy's right."

"She says that too. She's right all the time."

He chuckled. "Yep, and we as her boys have to learn to listen. Do you think you can go to sleep?"

Nathan nodded.

"Great."

"I love you, Daddy," Nathan said as he pulled up the blanket, settling it around him, getting him comfortable.

He paused and waited. "I love you too." He leaned down, kissing his head. "Hey, Nathan, does your mom ever sing to you?" He didn't know why it had just entered his head, but Tabby hadn't sung since he'd taken her or been in her life, not like when they were kids.

"No, Mommy doesn't sing. Night."

"Night."

Nathan was back to sleep even before he left the room. Watching him for a few seconds, he smiled.

This kid was so damn smart and sweet. His woman had done a good job with him.

Stepping out of the room, he saw Tabby in the hallway. Tears were in her eyes and she tilted her head to the side, looking at him. She opened her mouth, closed it.

"Thank you," she said, mouthing the words.

He closed the distance between them, cupping her cheek. "What can I do to make this better?"

"There's nothing. I'm not sad or angry. I'm happy. I heard him. I heard you. You love him?"

"Yes."

"Even if there's a chance—"

He silenced her with a kiss. "I don't give a flying

fuck what any piece of paper says. He's my son. He's part of you and I love you. He's a good kid."

She pressed her lips together but gave a nod. "Thank you."

"I mean it, but I've got to ask something, Tabby."

"What is it?" she asked.

"Why don't you sing?"

"What do you mean?"

"When we were kids, you used to sing, Nathan hasn't even heard you sing."

"Simon, really?"

"Yeah, really."

She looked past his shoulder and released a breath. "I guess I just don't want to and don't have a single reason to." She shrugged and it broke his heart to know he'd affected her so badly.

Chapter Fourteen

Tabitha made Simon sleep all night on the sofa. It wasn't like it was a bad sofa. Devil and Lexie had fully furnished the house with all the nice things money could buy. There were no complaints from her.

Holding her jacket together, she watched Nathan as he got higher and higher on the swing. There was a time he had a fear of heights but little by little, he'd slowly learned to conquer it in order to find fun.

It was so damn cold, but she'd promised him a trip to the park if he finished all his homework. He was settling in so much better than she thought he would. She hated that a little part of her had hoped he wouldn't so she'd have some excuse to move. Not that living in Piston County was a bad thing.

Chaos Bleeds had cleaned the place up and it was actually a pretty decent place to live. A good environment to have kids, raise a family. All of it.

"Uncle Miles!! Nathan suddenly screamed.

He came down the slide and ran to the park gates. She turned to see Miles and Daisy there, watching.

She smiled. "How long have you two been here?"

"Long enough to know you need to get inside. You're freezing your ass off. Me and the little guy, we're going to go and grab a decent pizza. How about it?" Miles asked.

"You don't have to do that. I can cook. I do know how."

"I know, but my treat. I want to spoil you guys."

Daisy held her hands open, and together, they met in the middle, hugging tightly. "Come on, let's get out of here. It's so cold. What are you doing hanging out in a park?"

Tabitha laughed. Holding her friend's hand, they

walked toward the apartment building. Typing in her code, she let them in, and they went up to her apartment.

As she removed her jacket, she was pleased she left the heating on to keep the place warm while she'd been out. She would've been screwed otherwise.

"I can't believe you're here."

"In the flesh. I know it's going to be a hard time for you. With everything going on, I didn't want to give you a choice."

Tabitha went to the kitchen, filled up the kettle, and put it on top of the stove. "You want a coffee?"

"Yeah, love one. Miles will probably bring back beers. I'm the driver for tonight," she said.

"Who else has come?" Tabitha asked.

"Me, Miles, Anthony as well, but he's back at the clubhouse. Lash, Tiny, Eva. She's with Lexie. She wanted to come but I told her I'd let you know we're here first. They're trying to organize something for Thanksgiving but with Simon back, I think they're just pretending to be too busy so you can stay home."

"Oh." Thanksgiving was one of those subjects she tried not to think about. Staring at her friend right now, she knew she'd have to make a decision eventually.

"I didn't mean to make you sad."

"Believe me, you don't do anything to make me sad. Just … I can't come home."

"You still see it as home?" Daisy asked.

"It is home." She turned her back on her friend, pulling down two mugs and adding in some espresso. She needed something to do right now. Everything felt messed up.

"It's not your home, Tabs. Unless you want to come home."

She paused. "Do you want sugar?"

"No thanks."

The kettle had finished and she made their drinks. "Let's have a comfortable seat." She carried them through to the sitting room. Putting out two coasters, she placed them on top, being delicate. Inside her head, she was screaming. Ignoring the drive to let loose, she sat down and finally turned toward her friend.

"You're pissed?"

"I'm not. Honestly. You're right. Fort Wills, I need to stop seeing it as my home. It's just hard, you know. I've got a lot ... there are so many memories there."

"I miss you," Daisy said. "We all do."

"I guess it's not the same here at the moment. Simon's living here, I think. He stayed the night on the sofa. He's good with Nathan." She told Daisy what he said about her son.

"You know, I've always found Simon a pain in the ass, but I can't help but love him a little bit."

She giggled. "I know. I ... everything is so messed up. I don't know what to say or do half the time. He's a great guy. I know he is, but we have that history."

Daisy took her hand. "What you need to do is stop thinking about your history. Or if you do, put it back into a context." She held her arms open. "This here is the span of your and Simon's life together. From the first moment you met, 'til now." She pointed between her hands, circling them, showing how much life they had together. Then she circled a large chunk of invisible air. "This here, this is the section pre-Ryan. He didn't matter. You and Simon, together, forever. Remember? You were always supposed to be together and whenever anyone asked, you'd always say you were going to be together forever. Kind of creepy, but even I remember you guys constantly talking about your future together. Even when we were kids."

Tabitha smiled.

"Now this section. This is the C-Ryan section."

"C-Ryan?"

"Yeah, current Ryan section." Daisy moved her finger to a point. "This is where it all started. What he did and the decision Simon took into his own hands. It's all relevant. The only problem is when this should be the post-Ryan era, it keeps on coming back. You've either got to forgive him or make a decision to move on."

Tears filled her eyes. "Fuck, I hate this. I hate crying."

"I made you cry?"

"Yes."

"I feel like this is a big deal for me. I made you cry. You, the queen of no emotions."

"Wow, you're such a bitch. I cry. A lot actually, and it pisses me off." She moved quickly to the bathroom, grabbing some tissue.

Daisy followed her. "I'm not saying your feelings aren't relevant here or that you have to forgive him or move on. What I'm saying is, you've got a whole lot of time together to just throw it all away. I get that you're hurting and as your best friend, I'm on your side."

"But you're not going to tell me how I should pick this."

Daisy hugged her tightly to her. "I'm not the one who's going to be with him for the next fifty-plus years, or alone. I don't want to see you alone. You'll never be with anyone else. It's not in your nature. If it had been, you would've been dating a lot sooner. You're not." Daisy ran her fingers through her hair.

"We're back," Miles said, calling out to be heard.

"I'll go and take care of them. You compose yourself, okay?"

"Thank you." She hugged Daisy close. "I love

you so much."

"You're becoming soft. I remember a time you were so hard." Daisy chuckled. "You've got this. I have no doubt."

Daisy left the bathroom. Wiping at her eyes, she turned toward the mirror. Her face was a little flushed and her eyes were red. She needed to get a grip on her emotions. It wasn't good for Nathan to see her so miserable.

She wanted him to be happy.

Why were The Skulls in town? Was it to discuss family matters or something more important? She wasn't sure what was going on, nor did she know if she wanted to. For so long, she'd cut herself off from the club and being part of their world.

Splashing some water onto her face, she joined them at the table. Nathan and Miles were talking about their adventure to get pizza. She laughed, thankful no one pointed at her swollen eyes. After a short time, she just enjoyed her friends and her crazy brother.

Time ticked on by and Nathan yawned, letting her know she had to put him to bed. She waited as he had a bath and she picked out his pajamas.

Once he was dressed, she tucked him into bed, kissed his head, and went to join Daisy and Miles.

Their conversation stopped the moment she was inside.

"Okay, now that makes me nervous," she said. They were doing the few dishes they'd made while eating the pizza. The box was nowhere in sight so they must have taken it down to the trash.

"It's nothing," Daisy said.

"I'm not stupid."

"We never said you were." Miles finished washing his hands on the towel and turned toward her.

"What's going on? You guys are here and it's nearly ten. I know Simon has all of his prospecting duties, but I know there are five more guys who have taken the patch as well. Something is going on. Out with it."

Miles and Daisy looked at one another.

"Look, I can kick your asses, do you understand? Out with it."

"It's not a big deal," Miles said.

"You're supposed to keep me here? Is that it?" she asked. "Keep me distracted? This wasn't a family visit?"

Daisy shook her head. "No, it was."

"But what?"

"Nothing," Miles said. "Damn. We came here because you're our friend and my sister. The Monster Dogs, they want to talk to Simon. Lash has been approached. Tiny as well. They came by the clubhouse a couple of weeks ago making demands. Lash had a sit down with them, and then we came here. I don't know exactly what it is, but it could be arranging a meetup."

Tabitha shook her head. "No, fuck no." She stepped away from her friends and grabbed her jacket.

"Where are you going?"

"You two are staying here. Keep an eye on my son. I'll be back real fucking soon. I've got to go and talk to some assholes about what will and won't happen."

She slammed out of the apartment, anger rushing through her veins.

****

Simon stared at Anthony.

"You're looking buff," Simon said.

"I could say the same thing about you."

"Yeah, being out on the road will do that for you." He glanced across the room. His father's door was closed. He couldn't hear shouting. "You think they're killing each other?"

"No, it wouldn't be contained to one room," Anthony said.

"You talk a lot more now than you ever did before." He shrugged. "Just saying, you know. You're, er, you talk. Words come out of your mouth."

"I could always speak, asshole. I chose not to. There is a difference."

"Of course, there is." Simon chuckled. "You chose not to. You were silent on purpose."

"You know I was and you're trying to hide the fact you're nervous."

This time, Simon did burst out laughing, drawing attention from a couple of the guys.

Dean was manning the bar, and it wasn't lost on Simon that Devil had organized it so all of his boys were here. Pa, Felix, Knight, Twig, and Teddy.

Dick was also in residence.

The moment Teddy and Dick first met, it had been a little intense.

"You think it's funny?" Dick asked, getting into Teddy's face.

Teddy, for his size and just the sheer force of him, smiled. He was bigger than Dick. He towered over the other man. Dick didn't back down.

"Do I think what is funny?"

"Calling yourself Teddy?"

"It's my name."

"Yeah, and mine is fucking Teddy Bear, what you got to say about that?"

Everyone had burst out laughing, Dick included. They'd shook hands and afterward, Dick had gone to meditate.

"I'm not nervous, Anthony. I want to know what

brings you boys here, that's all."

"I guess if you'd stuck around, you'd have been a fully patched-in member."

"Yeah, but why do I get the sense that this trip is about me?" Simon asked.

Anthony shrugged.

Devil's door opened. "Simon."

The doors closed.

"I guess we're about to find out." He walked toward the door and slid inside. Lash and Tiny were there in the office.

He acknowledged both men before turning toward his prez. Right now, Devil wasn't his dad.

"The Monster Dogs want to meet with you," Devil said.

"They do?"

"Lash and Tiny here are negotiating the terms." Devil took a seat.

To anyone who didn't know Devil, they would assume he was calm, okay, and everything was fine with him. They didn't know him like he did. Underneath the surface, Devil was fucking fuming.

He controlled it.

Sitting back in his chair, he watched Lash and Tiny. The current prez and the former prez. His gaze on them more like a hawk ready to strike.

"I know you think this is a meeting to hand him off," Lash said.

"Oh, I think this is a lot more than that. I think this is a fucking trap. The last five years have been all about peace and being friends. They scratch your back, and you do the same."

"It's not like that," Lash said.

"No?" Devil laughed. "Then tell me how this little arrangement has benefitted me? My son can't go to

Fort Wills, and his woman is one of yours. You tell me how that's going to fucking go." Devil slammed his hand on the desk. "Tell me."

"I wasn't going to start a war," Lash said. "I know this is painful for you."

Devil laughed. "This shit isn't painful to me, Lash. I followed your lead because you are a damn good one. You know what you're doing, but somewhere along the way, the Monster Dogs have come out as the injured party. They fuck you left and right. They make demands, you turn them down, they scream like a child. Make threats. You're here, asking my son to go and have a sit down with them. That shit isn't happening."

"And if this had been anyone else?" Lash asked. "What he did could have started a war with the clubs. We've been there. We know how all this goes down."

Devil threw the contents of his desk onto the floor. "What they started. We didn't throw the first punch. As I seem to recall, your daughter." He looked toward Tiny. "She was the victim. They threw the first punch, and your son." His gaze turned to Lash. "Found her in that state. They fucked up. Not us. We didn't cause this. They did!" He yelled each word. "Or did you forget about that? We have been treating this wrong for too long."

"He killed Ryan," Lash said.

"And what, you're saying Tabitha's rape was less than that? What should we have done, slap him around a bit? Cut him? What Simon did is what all of us would do! Don't forget who we fucking are deep down in our core."

"I haven't forgotten who we are," Lash said. "I know the price that had to be paid, but he was the one to do it in fucking public in my town. We could have handled this differently."

"Stop acting like a pussy."

"They're on my doorstep," Lash said. "They are the ones who want to negotiate a truce."

"No," Tabby said.

Simon turned to see his woman, panting. She stood in the doorway and stepped into the room.

Tiny got to his feet but she held her hand out. "No more," she said.

"Tabitha, you need to wait outside."

"No!" She slammed her foot to the ground. "I'm not going to be told to go outside. To go and wait, to be a good little girl. I'm done with that." She looked toward Simon. "You are not going!"

"This isn't your decision," Devil said.

"This is my decision. I have stood by and watched you all try to keep the peace. For fuck's sake, you've been together for twenty-plus years. You've all had your ups and downs, but this isn't going to fall apart because of those assholes," Tabby said.

Simon couldn't take his eyes off her.

She dropped her hands by her sides, closing her eyes. "I get that you want to keep the peace, but they have taken too much." She tapped her foot. "They're not going to take any more. They don't deserve it. An eye for an eye. That's what happened."

"I do believe they want to settle this."

"No," she said. "If they want to settle this they talk to me."

"Tabby," Simon said. "This isn't your place."

"One of their sons raped me. He waited until I was alone, defenseless. I fought. I tried, and he didn't stop. I begged him to stop. He didn't listen. If they want a sit down with anyone, it will be with me. I will negotiate any future deals. They have no power and it's about time we took back what we've been giving them."

She took Simon's hand. "He's my man. I only just got him back. I'm not losing him. This stinks of a trap, bringing Simon back. Not happening. If you go, I go with you. Tonight. I want to deal with this now. I'm not waiting around anymore. I'm done."

"No," Simon said. He pulled her close. "You're not doing this."

"I am, because you're not going to pay that price."

"I'd have to arrange a time and place," Lash said.

"No," she said. "Tonight. Now. Miles and Daisy are with Nathan. I want to go tonight."

Chapter Fifteen

The drive from Piston County was a long one.

Tabitha hadn't taken no for an answer.

Rather than ride with her dad or Lash, Devil had opted to come with her. Neither of them had spoken on the journey. She didn't have a whole lot to say.

Words weren't necessary.

She'd tried to sleep, but that was a long way off. There was no way she could sleep right now. She was too wired. Too prepared.

Her hands shook a little.

Devil made a stop to fill up with gas and buy her a few snacks. Even as her stomach revolted at the prospect of food, she shoved it into her mouth. She didn't taste it.

Time ticked on by.

Her cell phone blowing up.

She'd asked Simon to stay with Nathan. He'd need someone while she was away.

"Are you okay?" Devil asked, clearing his throat.

"Yes."

"Your hands are shaking."

"I'm fine."

"You're not fine."

She put her hands flat to her knees, trying to hide the shake. "I'll be fine. I will. I promise."

"You don't have to do this. I know you were angry and it makes us do and say stupid stuff."

She chuckled. "I meant what I said. I've tried to avoid this. I've tried to be strong and to move on with my life. They can't take Simon, not now."

"Does that mean you and him are going to stay together?"

She glanced over at Devil, but his focus was on

the road. "Are you trying to get us together?"

"You and Simon have always been a pain in my ass. It was never going to be easy. I knew that. You and him, our clubs may work with each other from time to time, but other than that, our relationship can be tested."

"If you're not careful, one day it is going to break," Tabitha said. "I'm aware of how fragile any clubs' true friendship is. One wrong move, Simon is dead." She had to stop because the very thought was more than she could bear. "All friendships end. Even in high school I hated the Monster Dogs. Luke was okay but again, he was the enemy. They are the enemy and somewhere along the way, it's been fucked with. I'm not going to allow that to happen. I don't want it to happen." She breathed out a sigh.

"Thank you," Devil said.

"What for?"

"For not wanting my son dead more than you want him alive."

She chuckled. "I don't know where that leaves us. I … I love him. I don't doubt that. The kind of love we have or had, it doesn't go easily."

"It's not past tense. I see the way you two are with one another. I thought it was a crush that would die slowly. I was so wrong. What you and Simon have, it's fierce. It's love and it's loyalty. It's rare, but you and my son were lucky to have found each other when you were young. You haven't had to go through several relationships, jumping from partner to partner."

"Is Lexie your woman?"

"I'd do anything for her."

"Is that why you're not angry at Simon over what he did?"

"I'm angry at him for not doing it properly." Devil winced. "I bet not many fathers-in-law would say that."

"No, I don't imagine there are."

"He should have taken Ryan, but covered his tracks. It doesn't matter now. We can't go back in time and change anything. He did what he did, and we've all had to deal with the consequences." Devil patted her knee. "Are you sure you're ready for this?" he asked. They were on the street toward the Monster Dogs' clubhouse.

The sun was coming up. "What would you do if I said I couldn't do this?"

"I'd turn this car around and we could leave. I'm not going to force you to do something you don't want to do."

Tabitha stared at the building. Flashes of the past merged with the present, but she couldn't contain the panic, the fear. It was all a little too much.

You walk away now, you will regret this.

I'm scared.

You have no reason to be scared.

Devil will be with you. Your family. You're the one in control. You hold all the power. No one else.

This is your fight.

"What's it going to be, Tabitha?" Devil asked.

She licked her lips, watching. "Stop. We're going to do this."

Devil pulled the car up behind Lash and Tiny.

She took a deep breath.

"I'm not going to leave your side," he said.

"Good. I don't want you to leave."

She climbed out of the car, squared her shoulders, and took a step toward the closed door.

Devil caught her shoulders. "They've got cameras. We don't want them to see we don't have Simon."

She stayed perfectly still.

Lash did the talking. "You wanted to talk, now is the time."

Tiny looked toward her and she offered a smile to her father. He didn't like this, she got it. To him, she would always be his little girl.

The door opened. Lash and Tiny headed on inside. Devil blocked her from view as they made their way into the Monster Dogs' clubhouse.

She hadn't been inside their clubhouse. This was going to be the first and only time she did this.

"You want to leave?" Devil asked.

"No. I'm ready."

The doors opened up and out came Luke. He looked at them and the smile disappeared the moment he caught sight of her.

Lash wrapped his fingers around the kid's throat. "Take us to your dad." He spun him around.

It had been a long time since she'd seen Lash unleash the monster, and seeing it now, she knew they were in real danger.

What the hell am I doing?

Why am I doing this?

This isn't who I am anymore.

I can't do this.

You can.

You were born a Skull. You can do this. These men mean nothing. You have the power.

Stepping into the Monster Dogs' clubhouse, she saw the women who were still partying, gyrating up and down the pole. Men and women were fucking in a corner.

They were what The Skulls had been so many years ago. She heard the tales. The stories were all farfetched but watching this club, she had to wonder if they were all in fact true.

As they arrived at Luke's father's office, they saw the older man had a woman sucking him off. He sat on the sofa while she bobbed her head between his thighs. It wasn't exactly what she wanted to see.

Lash pulled Luke close to him and she saw he was having trouble breathing.

Tiny and Devil pulled out guns, pointing them directly at Luke's dad.

"What the fuck is this?" he asked.

"You wanted a meeting set up. This is the meeting."

Commotion at the door had her turning. She saw Ryan's dad. She only knew him because she recognized his face from the last time.

He glanced at her, taking in the scene.

"You call your boys and I will shoot your prez in the face, and then I will take out your entire club," Lash said.

"You don't have enough bullets."

"I'm the kind of person who can snap a man's neck with my bare hands," Lash said. "I also alerted my club to the fact I was coming here and I may start a war. It depends how this meeting goes."

Tabitha was a little confused. Only hours ago, Lash had seemed like a messenger with the Monster Dogs having the real power.

He was back in charge. A true leader.

"This isn't what we negotiated."

Lash chuckled. "I know, but you see, I've also been made aware of a few things that I've seemed to have forgotten. My bad, really. You no longer call the shots. Not anymore. I don't dance around to your tune. I'm Lash of the motherfucking Skulls. We don't negotiate with rapists."

Lash loosened his grip on Luke's neck. "How are you holding up there, buddy? You want to breathe? You will get the chance to fuck girls again. It's all up to your daddy and Tabitha. You remember her, right?"

Rather than hide behind Devil, she stepped away from him, holding her head up high.

I can do this.

I'm not the one in the wrong here.

"You see, I think we've all forgotten what actually brought us here and it's not Ryan. No, Ryan's death was a consequence," Lash said.

"My boy died."

She jumped as a gun went off.

Tiny had shot Ryan's dad in the foot. "The next one will go in the leg. My daughter was raped by your boy. As far as I'm concerned, your boy got off lightly. I'd have gladly severed his dick from his body and made him suffer for months to come."

Luke's dad shoved off the girl and Tabitha she stepped forward, showing him she was strong.

"This stops today," she said.

"You're in no position to negotiate."

"I am." She looked him in the eye. "I have two clubs at my back. You have one. You can start a war over Simon, go ahead, but you're not getting to him. We will pick you off one by one. You're not the injured party and remember, there's always a slim chance of who Nathan's father is." She tilted her head to the side. "You're getting old. One day soon, your spot is going to be replaced." She glanced over at Luke. Lash let him go and he gathered his breath. "Your vendetta with Simon ends today. He's safe to come and go on Fort Wills land and to go back home."

"You have no power here."

She smiled. "I can tell Lash to snap your boy's

neck," she said. "There's a lonely spot where Ryan is buried. I'm sure both friends will be happy to play around in hell. One by one, I will make sure we pick you guys off so that all that remains is a club getting constantly older. Smaller, until finally, all you are is a bitter, sad memory."

"You won't do that," he said. "The Skulls and Chaos Bleeds are kept on a tight leash." Another gunshot, and he cried out.

She glanced behind her to see Devil had shot Luke's father in the thigh.

"I'm not on a tight leash."

"We do what we want," Lash said. "You think we let a couple of billionaires dictate to us what we do and won't do? Fort Wills is my fucking turf. You want to bring on a war, go right ahead. I'm ready. It has been a long time, but you see, I'm still standing. As is my club. We've had no end of fucking shit come knocking at our door. We're still here. Our enemies, their bones are in the dirt, fertilizing the ground. Think about it."

She pushed some hair out of her eyes. "You've underestimated us for the last time."

"If your boy is a Monster, his rightful place is here!" Luke's father said.

Tabitha shook her head. "No, he's with me. You forfeited any right to him when you threatened my family. I'm not some little girl to be pushed aside or bullied. I'm a fucking queen, and I will protect my family. So what's it to be? Will you be burying a son today?"

****

"I can't stand this." Simon paced the length of the apartment. Miles and Daisy were eating popcorn while Anthony took one of the chairs. They all watched him. Nathan was still in bed. He'd only gotten up to go to the bathroom.

The time ticked on by and no one reached out to him.

No phone call.

Just a never-ending darkness he couldn't stand. He hated being kept in the dark but what he hated more was that it was his woman who was once again out there for him. Running his fingers through his hair, he looked toward the door.

"You can't go," Daisy said.

"Patience, man," Miles said.

"Screw fucking patience. I'm done waiting. I'm done with all this shit." He didn't move toward the door. "I'm not afraid of them."

"Never said you were," Anthony said. "You've got to let her do what she needs to do."

"Tabby's been on her own for far too long."

"Hey," Daisy said, frowning. "She hasn't been on her own, okay? She's always had us." She pointed at each of them. "It's tough for her to ask for help. We've always been there for her."

"Just sit your ass down. If you were worried, you wouldn't have left her," Miles said

Simon was on the verge of sitting down, but now he was up and ready to fight. "What the fuck did you say?"

"You heard me."

"Come on then if you think you've got a shot at me." He was ready to fight.

"Enough!" Daisy growled the word. "Seriously. We're in her apartment. Nathan's asleep. This isn't about the two of you or what you guys think. This is about Tabitha. What is wrong with you guys?" She threw the bag of popcorn at Miles and stood. "Stop making this about you. Can't you see what a big deal this is?"

Simon stared at her as Daisy glanced at each of them in turn. "I'm surrounded by assholes."

"This is the first time Tabitha has entered Monster Dog territory," Anthony said, speaking up. "They've always had to come onto our turf. If she's going to them now, it shows how far she has come."

"Exactly." Daisy licked her lips. "We all know what happened. None of us have talked about it. Tabs has handled it in her own way. Always. It's what she does. She's never opened up to me, Miles, or Anthony. It's just been what happened. You know?" She blew out a breath. "This is a big fucking deal and I don't want to screw it up. Not for her. Not for us. Not for anyone. This is big."

She ran fingers through her hair. "I need to use the bathroom." Daisy walked away. Simon stared at the spot where she'd stood.

Leaning back in his chair, he closed his eyes, rubbing at his temples.

"Sorry," Miles said. "I shouldn't have said the shit I did."

"You're right. I left and now look at me. I sleep on the sofa. I've got a kid that I don't know. All of this is messed up. What's more, my friend made patched member before me. How is that crap even right?"

They all chuckled.

"I never thought it would go this way, I didn't." He blew out a breath. "I'm sorry for putting you through all this shit."

"I care about Tabs," Miles said. "She hasn't been the same since you've been gone. It's like she was a shell of who she was. Her backbone bent. She was sad. Broken even. I don't think it was all because of what happened."

"We all know she was mourning his loss," Anthony said. "None of us could do anything to help her."

"I can't believe you never told me about her having a kid."

"It's not something you needed to hear and I'm not going over this ground with you again. You know what happened. I don't want to argue with you anymore," Anthony said.

They were all silent.

"Do you know?" Simon asked. Anthony had leaned back and closed his eyes. He reached out and kicked him, making him look at him.

"Do I know what?"

"Whose Nathan is?"

Miles sat up.

Anthony nodded.

"Whose is he?"

Anthony frowned at him. "Does it matter? You've claimed him as yours."

"I know but … I…"

"He's yours," Anthony said. "Don't worry about it."

Simon took a deep breath. "It wouldn't matter. I mean, of course, it wouldn't. He's innocent."

"And Tabby loves him," Miles said. "It's all that counts."

Simon agreed and leaned back. It had been a long night and there was no sign of Tabby returning soon. He wasn't going to go to bed though.

He was way too wired for that.

****

The following morning, Daisy was the first one to wake up. They'd all camped out in the sitting room. She checked her phone to see if there was any news from Tabitha. No messages or missed calls. Nathan got out of bed and she got him to get dressed and to play in his room while she set up breakfast.

Opening the cupboards, she smiled when she saw Tabitha's writing on a jug marking pancake batter.

She'd slept over a couple of times when Nathan was first born, and Tabitha had a craving for pancakes. Daisy had been doing all the cooking so she hadn't labeled anything.

Tabitha had thought the mixture in the jug at the time had been custard. She'd already taken a mouthful before she could warn her. She'd been violently sick, and since that day, Tabitha labeled everything.

Turning a couple of plain jars, she saw leftover tomatoes and even some tofu. All neatly packaged and labeled. Tabitha had changed a great deal over the years. The disorganized girl she remembered from high school was no longer there. Tabitha was a mom.

"You've been staring into that fridge for a long time." Anthony put his hands on her hips and she stood up.

He pressed his lips against her neck and she couldn't help but sink against him. His arms went around her, holding her close. She'd gladly stay in his embrace for the rest of her life.

"I'm just remembering the good old days."

"Lash called. They're on their way back."

"Do you know how it went?" she asked, grabbing some butter to help make pancakes. She went hunting in cupboards for more flour to make more batter. What was leftover wouldn't feed all of them.

"They're alive. That's all I know."

"Do you think they could start a war?"

"It's club, Daisy. Anything could happen."

"Chaos Bleeds are far away. It would draw us into it."

"There's nothing we can't handle. I hope you know that."

"I do." She put the ingredients on the board and moved toward the entrance to the kitchen, looking into the sitting room. Simon was still fast asleep. "You lied to him last night."

"So."

"We know whose Nathan is."

Anthony rubbed the back of his head.

"Don't you think he has a right to know?" Daisy asked.

"Why?" Anthony asked. "To know that his kid is a rapist's? That Tabitha carried him to term on the fifty-fifty chance he could be Simon's? Does it matter?"

"I don't know."

"Lexie took care of him, and he wasn't hers."

"That's different. Lexie is an aunt."

"And Nathan is an innocent kid who has a chance to have a good life." Anthony frowned at her. "This world is fucking shit, Daisy. We know what it's like. It's filled with guys like Ryan who turn into men. They hurt people and they continue to do so. No one stops them. Women are sold and pawned like cattle. Kids are hurt. So are animals. Nothing good would come out of telling him the truth. Not now. Not when he can walk away."

"You think he would?"

Anthony moved toward her. She didn't back away. "Would you be able to look at the evidence of what happened to your woman? How you failed? How she was hurt every single day? Simon and Tabitha are strong. They could overcome this. But what if they can't? What if he learns the truth and walks away? She's been through a lot. I'm not going to put her through anything more. She's our friend. I'm taking care of her."

"And what if the truth comes out one day? It did with Simon."

"If the truth comes out, then he would have had a

chance to influence Nathan. He'd have the opportunity to love him without that dark stain. Give them that. Besides, only a few of us know the truth. There is no physical evidence lying around. Just human word unless he demanded another test."

"I wouldn't tell. Ever."

Anthony put his hands on her neck, his fingers dancing across her pulse. "I know."

Chapter Sixteen

Tabitha climbed out of the car at the Chaos Bleeds clubhouse. She and Devil had made a stop, along with Lash and Tiny, for a quick nap. Exhaustion hit her hard. All she wanted to do was go and collapse on a bed.

"Mommy," Nathan said, running to her. She picked him up, spinning him around. Simon was there, as were Anthony, Miles, and Daisy. She held her son tightly and he wriggled out. "Grandpa Tiny!" He giggled as he threw himself at her dad.

She tucked some hair behind her ear.

"Hello, my little bug," he said. "Have you been strong?"

"Yes, I have." Nathan lifted his arm and flexed. She smiled, watching them, aware of Simon's gaze on her. She'd feel him anywhere. "Can you take me to the park?"

"Not today, scamp. I've got to head back."

Nathan groaned and pouted. One day that wouldn't be so cute.

"But you just got here."

"I know. How about Thanksgiving? You come back home and we can spend the entire day at the park?" Tiny asked.

"Actually," Tabitha said. "We're not going to Fort Wills for Thanksgiving."

"Tabs?" Tiny said.

"I know, Dad, another time."

"Nothing bad is going to happen."

"I know. I do know that, but I'm not…" She looked toward Simon, the Chaos Bleeds crew. "This is my home now. It's time I become part of it. Simon's back and we're going to be here, with his family."

"Tabby," Simon said, but she held up her hand.

She'd already come to a decision. For a long time, she'd been holding on to the illusion that Fort Wills was her home, and in a way, it would always be. It was the home she grew up in, but she wasn't a child nor was she a teenager anymore. The time for looking back had long passed.

She was a full-grown woman and it was time for her to make her own choices, and that wasn't about going back. It was time to move forward. "Maybe next year," she said.

Nathan wriggled out of his arms and she moved to stand beside Simon. He wrapped his arm around her.

Silence met her decision.

Lash clapped his hands. "Devil, we've got to talk, but right now I'm thinking we should do that tomorrow. See how the lay of the land is."

Devil and Lash shook hands. "Thank you," Devil said.

"No." Lash turned toward Tabitha. "Thank you. You … you put it back into perspective for me. I won't let anything cloud my judgment again."

She leaned against Simon, wanting more than anything to go to sleep.

Daisy came to her, hugging her close. "I'm going to miss you. Call me."

"I will."

She hugged Anthony and kissed Miles's cheek.

Finally, her dad. She walked toward him and hugged him. Her mom was there with tears in her eyes.

"I don't like leaving you here," Tiny said.

"You're not leaving me. We're saying goodbye until the next visit." She pulled away. "I'm not going to cry." She swiped at her cheeks. "I've spent way too much time crying. I'm determined to stop it. It's a bad habit I want out of."

"We're a phone call away," Eva said. "All you've got to do is pick up the phone."

"I will, Mom. I promise." She held her mom tightly.

Stepping back, she went to Simon. Sleep was what she needed right now.

She waved at them, watching them disappear out of town. Rather than be sad and alone, she knew it was the right decision. Fort Wills was the past.

"You look dead to the world and I know that feeling," Lexie said. "Come on, sport." She held out her hand to Nathan. "He and I can have some fun."

Tabitha chuckled. "It's fine. Really."

"Tabitha, you're with family. Go and relax. Simon, take her to your room."

Simon lifted her up in his arms and she let out a little squeal. "I can walk."

"I've been given orders from my mom. I'm not going to let her think I'm disobeying her."

"Really?" she asked. "You're going to do as you're told?"

"I've been naughty for too long. I've got to do something right." He carried her through the clubhouse. No one stopped them. She was glad.

She no longer had the energy to fight. Between the main club room and Simon's bedroom, she must have dozed off because the next thing she remembered was Simon taking off her shoes.

"Should you be undressing an unconscious woman?" she asked.

"Only to make her more comfortable. Do you feel better?"

"I'm sleepy. Really sleepy. I could close my eyes and not open them for a week. It's a long drive to Fort Wills." She opened her eyes as his fingers went to the button of her jeans.

"You can't sleep in them, and they'll be uncomfortable."

"I think you're trying to get me naked."

"You know me, Tabby. I don't need to try to get you naked. I could just ask."

"True."

He slid her jeans down and she turned on her side, snuggling against the bed. His pillow was so soft.

She heard him remove his leather cut, kick his boots off, and finally lower his own jeans.

He joined her on the bed and she opened her eyes. All she wanted to do was sleep, but having him so close, she put her hand to his cheek.

"Hey."

"Hey," he said. "How was it?"

"Let's not talk about it."

"You can cut everyone else out, and play the big girl with them, but not with me. I deserve more than that. I'm your man, Tabitha. Don't push me away."

She ran her thumb across his bottom lip. "You called me Tabitha."

He pushed some of her hair off her face, cupping her cheek. "Yes, I did. I'm here for you. I'm not going to go off the loose end. I'm fine. I'm here for you. I will always be here for you."

"But what if you go away again?"

"Not happening. You saw me wear the patch. I'm here. I'm going to stay. I love you more than anything else in the world. I will never be far from you."

She smiled as tears filled her eyes. "Damn it. I'm sick of crying."

He stayed still as she wiped at her tears.

Licking her suddenly dry lips, she leaned in close and kissed him. "I hated it," she said, closing her eyes and whispering the words. "I didn't want to be there and the moment I saw it, I wanted to run."

"You didn't have to stay."

"I did." She pulled back, opening her eyes. "They won. They got that stupid, messed-up agreement. I hate that they got that. They had no right. An eye for an eye. They took and took. Not anymore. They won't take another thing from me. I don't know what they wanted, but they're not getting you or Nathan. I had to put them in their place."

"And how did that feel?"

"It was scary. So scary. While I was there, it was like I stepped back in time. I didn't feel like myself. I felt weak and I don't know, something clicked inside my head, and I realized I didn't need to feel this way. I've done nothing wrong. They did. They raised a bastard rapist. That's not on me. I wasn't going to allow them to blame you." She slid her hand down, going toward his heart. "They threw the first stone. You threw it back, and it should have been finished then. Not five years later. I'm sorry, Simon."

"No, you don't have to say sorry. I'm the one who's sorry. I ... I should have done things differently. I've lost five years. I'm not going to lose any more. I know tomorrow we're going to be doing this dance until you trust me again, but one day soon, you're going to trust me. I'm going to earn back everything that was taken from us." He kissed her lips. "I'm your man. One day, you'll see it."

"I already do." She closed her eyes. "Simon, I'm sleepy."

"Then sleep."

"Please, don't leave."

"Never."

"Be here when I wake up."

"Always."

"And, Simon?" she said.

"Yeah."

"Even when I want to kill you, please love me."

He chuckled. "No doubt about it, I will belong to you. We're meant to be together." His lips pressed against her head and she sighed. Finally relaxing, she heard him breathing, and she rested next to him, sleep slowly claiming her.

****

Simon didn't want to move nor make a sound. Tabby had been out for the count all night. At first, he watched the clock, seeing the time going by slowly. There was nowhere else he needed to be other than in this bed, holding his woman. Running his hand up and down her back, soothing her if her dreams seemed to get a little dark.

Not once did she wake up.

There was so much ground to cover between them. Trust to earn back, he got that. In his relationship with Tabby, he was a prospect, having to earn her back, but he wasn't scared or worried.

He'd get her back.

She was his queen, just as she belonged to him. She let out a little sigh. The only problem he had right now was how close his dick was to her core. The only thing separating them were her panties and his boxer briefs, and he couldn't concentrate. He tried to think of gross things. Dead bodies, Dick naked, spiders, snakes, but she'd move a little and his thoughts would go to how good it felt to have her close against him.

This was a hard battle to fight. One he didn't want to.

She gave another little sigh, and all he wanted to do was spread her legs wide and lick her pussy until she woke up while orgasming on his tongue.

He had to get his thoughts back in order. This wasn't good.

One, two, three, four, Dick naked, dancing in nothing at all. Snakes slithering over my body.

She moved and let out a sigh.

He closed his eyes. The touch of her pussy was so close.

Lifting his gaze to her, he paused.

Tabby was staring right back at him.

"Why do you look in pain?" she asked.

"I'm not. I'm just trying to be the perfect gentleman."

"Why wouldn't you be?" she asked.

"Er, I'm a guy and I'm close to my woman's pussy. You were asleep and after last night..." He groaned.

"You don't want me to be angry at you?"

"No. Fuck, no." She reached down to his cock, cupping him through the boxer briefs. She pushed on him a little and he rolled to his back, getting into the position she wanted him in. Tabby straddled his waist and he put his hands on her thighs.

Her pussy rubbed against him. "You like it like this?" she asked.

"You know I do."

She wriggled on his cock and he growled. Hands moving to her hips, he held her in place.

"You're playing with fire."

"Is that such a bad thing? Playing with fire can be oh, so nice." She leaned down but her lips didn't go to his. They went to his neck, flicking over the pulse.

He closed his eyes, gritting his teeth to control his arousal as she sank her teeth against his neck and sucked.

She was going to leave a mark but it wasn't

painful. He fucking loved it and didn't want her to stop. Sinking his fingers to her neck, he held her in place as she moved her pussy right over his cock.

If they weren't wearing underwear, he'd have moved right between her wet slit. She had to be wet and if she wasn't, well, he knew how to get her there.

Moving down, he cupped her ass, sliding his fingers beneath the material of her panties, tracing over the curve of her ass to her pussy. Finding her slick heat, he stroked her pussy and she gasped.

Lifting up, he crushed his hand between their bodies.

She tutted. "No need to rush. We've got all morning."

She eased off his hand and he did no more than grip her panties, tearing them right off her body. The sound echoed in the room and he held them up. "Problem solved."

"So you're in a rush?"

"No rush. I know what I want." He grabbed her hips, spinning them both around. "And I know how to get it."

She sat up and grabbed his shirt, pulling it up over his head. Dropping down to the bed, he pushed her to it, kissing her lips as he pressed his cock against her core. His boxer briefs were still in the way.

Tabby grabbed the waistband and started to push them down. He took over, kicking them off. They were both naked, and he cupped her tits, pressing them together as he licked each mound before sucking each one into his mouth. She wrapped her legs around him, trying to get him inside her, but he wasn't in a rush.

"I want you to come on my mouth, Tabby."

"Please, Simon, I need you."

"And you're going to get me. All of me, but in

my time." He flipped her over on the bed so he covered her back. Sliding a hand between her body, he found her pussy. Circling the tight bud, he pinched her before caressing down to her entrance and teasing her even more.

"Fuck, that feels good," she said.

Pushing two fingers inside her, he pumped them in and out of her body, stretching her. He didn't want her to come on his fingers and so he pulled them away as she began to fuck him.

"Simon!"

"All in good time."

"This isn't funny."

"I'm not laughing. Well, maybe a little." He pulled her onto her knees and cupped her ass, stretching out the globes and groaned. Her puckered ass and cunt were on display. His cock was rock-hard, and he fisted it, pre-cum leaking out of the tip. Without waiting, he pressed the tip to her entrance and slammed hilt deep inside her.

They both cried out.

The sudden onslaught of pleasure took them both by surprise. He moved his hands to cover hers, locking their fingers together as he rocked inside her. Simon had no intention of coming first. No, he wanted to drive Tabby crazy, to have her begging for more. He was going to enjoy this moment before reality came rushing back. For now, they were Simon and Tabby without problems. They were the old them, not tainted by life or circumstance.

In and out, he thrust inside her. She wriggled back, taking more of him. He wasn't going to let her come like this.

Pulling out of her, he flipped her over.

"For fuck's sake, Simon." Her growl turned into a

moan as he flicked his tongue across her center, going from her clit, down to her entrance, and back up again.

"I want you to come all over my tongue, beautiful. I want you to give me everything you've got."

She wriggled and he teased her, drawing her closer to an orgasm.

Glancing up her body as he tongued her clit, he couldn't get over just how beautiful she was, and she belonged to him, in every single way possible.

"Simon, I … I'm going to come."

"Then come. Come for me. Let me have it."

He flicked her clit, focusing on the nub, building her orgasm, when there was a sudden knock at the door. They both paused and he turned toward the door.

"Who is it?" he asked, shouting to be heard.

"It's Felix. Dude, we've got to go. Come on."

"Fuck off."

"If you're not there you know it's going to be ten times worse."

Tabby released a giggle as he pressed his face to her pussy. Lifting his head, he turned toward the door. "I said fuck off or I swear you're not going to be able to use your dick again!"

"Whoa, dude, wait, are you like fucking someone?"

"Fuck off!"

"Right, noted. Okay. I'm going."

"I'm so sorry," he said, turning back to his woman. "Now, where were we?"

"You're going to have to go, Simon. We've spent a lot of time watching prospects getting fucked over because they chose their dick over the club."

"I'm not picking my dick, baby. I'm picking you. Just you."

He touched her clit, stroking back and forth,

watching her come apart beneath his onslaught.

She gasped, arching up, moaning, and flooded his tongue with her orgasm. He licked her up, relishing her taste, not wanting to waste a single moment of it. She tasted exquisite. Perfect.

Kissing a path up her body, he took a short time to lick and suck at her tits before finding her entrance and fucking into her hard. She cried out. His name spilling off her lips sounded so damn perfect. He couldn't get enough of her. All he wanted was to be surrounded by every single part of her.

She felt amazing. So tight. Wet. Hot. Everything he wanted and more.

After pulling out of her tight heat, he slammed in deep. Taking hold of her hands, he kissed her, making love to her body.

He found a pace that pushed her to the edge of release, holding her there. He wanted to feel her come all over his dick. With their hands locked together, and her surrounding him, all he wanted was her.

Simon reared back, running his hands down her body, touching her pussy. He worked her clit again. With his cock so deep inside her, there was no way he was going to stop.

"Please, Simon."

"No, I want you to come all over my dick."

"I have."

"Again."

She gasped, arching up as he worked her pussy, wanting her more than anything. He watched her and felt her pussy squeeze him. The tightness nearly made him lose control, but he held on, only concentrating on her. She was his primary focus. He used two fingers to work her pussy and it didn't take long for her orgasm to rebuild once again. This time, she came all over his cock, and before she'd even finished, he grabbed her hips and began to fuck her, slamming every inch inside her as he took possession of her mouth. Sliding his tongue across her lips.

For his orgasm, he thrust in deep and filled her naked pussy with his cum, giving her every single drop.

Wrapping his arms around her, he kissed her hard.

They were both panting, but he couldn't have thought of a better place to be than in her arms.

"This is incredible," she said. She curled up against him. "I know you're going to have to face the music. Everyone is going to be so pissed at you, but I loved this. You picked me over the club."

He chuckled. "I know in a few hours you're going to go back to hating me. I guess I wanted a little peace to remind myself of who we are after what we've been through."

She stroked over his chest. "What if we don't?" she asked.

"Don't what?"

"Hate each other."

"Tabby, babe, I don't hate you."

"I don't hate you either." She sat up. "What if we put the past to bed? We really do just start over."

"Getting to know each other?"

"No. I don't mean that." She ran fingers through her hair. "I mean, I stop holding it against you about what you did, and you stop feeling guilty for not being there. We wipe that out of our history. It happened, but it's not the only thing that happened between us. We've got so much more, don't you think?"

He sat back, looking at her. Reaching out, he stroked a stray curl. "Do you think you can do that?"

"Simon, I've never stopped loving you. In case

you didn't get the memo, I just picked you and Chaos Bleeds over everything else. I love you. I want to be with you. What I don't want is to keep on fighting over something we can't change. It happened. Can't we at least, you know, get over it? You think we can do that?"

"So." He sat up in bed, moving a little closer to her. He cupped her cheek. "Does this mean I get to sleep in your bed?"

"Our bed. Yes. Unless you stink or are completely drunk and disgusting."

"I won't drink. What else do I get to do?"

"Simon, you're my husband. I think it's time you started to act like it."

He fingered the band on the necklace around her neck. "I'd gladly do it, but you've also got to give me a little something. You need to wear this."

She reached behind her neck, unclasping the necklace. She slid the ring off and he watched as she put it right where it was supposed to be.

"See, I can do it as well." She leaned forward and kissed his lips. "This is our forever part. I want it. I don't want to keep on fighting. So it means being with each other through thick and thin. You know, the whole sickness gig."

"I'm there. I'm right there with you. There is one snag."

"What?"

"I'm still a prospect. You know what it means?"

"Long hours. You're going to come home stinking. You've got the whole loyalty thing to prove."

"You got it. It's going to be a bumpy road." He pulled her close.

"But we can do this together. You can also … get to know Nathan."

"Don't do that," he said.

"What am I doing?"

"He's mine. I don't care about the rest of it, Tabby. I'll love him. I do love him. I want to take care of him, and I will." He kissed the top of her head, loving her.

Chapter Seventeen

One month.

Two months.

Three months.

Tabitha held her hair back as she threw up in the bowl. This was becoming a regular habit. So far, she'd been able to contain it until Simon left the house. He kept such odd hours. The guys at the club had him doing a great deal of shitty work. Chaos Bleeds, since their turn to the legal side of things, had started up an array of businesses. Their most successful was indeed their clothing shop. Lexie kept asking her to come and work there, but she still kept her job at the coffee shop.

Of course, working at a coffee shop with all those smells was becoming a bit of a hazard. There was no reason for her to get a damn test, but she knew it was going to have to happen. This was no stomach bug or flu.

Nope.

This was plain old stupidity.

She and Simon.

Sex.

Fucking.

No protection.

Once again, consequences.

"Are you okay, Mommy?"

She looked toward her son with a smile. "Yes, I'm okay. I'm more than okay." She flushed the toilet. Her stomach was still doing somersaults but she was capable of moving now.

She grabbed her toothbrush and got to work on her teeth. "I'll be done soon and I'll take you to school."

"Okay."

He sounded so sad, and she hated it when he was sad. "What's the matter?" she asked. She spat out her toothpaste and crouched down to see into his eyes.

"It's nothing."

"Now, come on, you can't do that to me. We're best friends, right? What do best friends do?"

"We tell each other everything?"

"Right. I can't help you if you don't help me."

Tears shone in his eyes and it broke her heart. "What is it, baby?" she asked.

"I ... you're going to think I'm a loser."

"Hey, do not ever say that. I don't think you're a loser. You're one of the nicest people I know, and I know a lot."

He'd bowed his head. She put a finger beneath his chin and lifted his face so she could look at him. "I love you. You're my brave boy. Come on, tell me."

His chin wobbled.

All she wanted to do was protect him. To not let the world get to him, or infect him with their nastiness.

"No one..." He stopped to sniffle. "No one likes me, Mommy. I have no friends. I hear them. They call me scum." He covered his face with his hands. "They say I don't have a daddy and you don't know who he is."

The old Tabitha, the one with violent tendencies, would march down to the school and smack every single teacher in the face. Okay, the old Tabitha as a six-year-old may have also hit the kids for name-calling a few times.

Right now, Nathan didn't have a poisonous bone in his body.

"You know what, kids are just mean."

"I'm a kid."

"You're not mean. You're perfect."

"Mommy." He groaned.

"I mean it. Some people don't think this, but it takes a lot to be a good kid. A great kid, in fact." She cupped his face, wiping away the tears. "You know Angel?"

He nodded.

"Well, she is one of the nicest people in the world. Some people believe she is a bit of a pushover. She's not strong, but believe me, they are all wrong."

"They are?"

"Angel is strong. No matter what anyone has thrown at her, she has stayed strong and sweet and kind. You see, anyone can be nasty. Not everyone has it in them to be nice." She kissed his head. "I wish I was a little more like her."

"But you are nice, Mommy."

"Oh, sweetie. I'm not as nice as I could be. I know that." She kissed his cheek. "Are you ready to go to school?"

"Mommy, don't tell my teachers, okay? I don't want them to tell everyone in class."

Tabitha sighed. School politics always pissed her off, but she didn't want to hurt her son.

"Fine. I won't say anything. I'll be a good mommy."

"Thank you."

"Sweetheart, don't tell your dad about me being sick. He'll worry."

"Do I need to worry?"

"No, I can fix it. It's fine." She kissed his cheek and grabbed the car keys. Simon had gifted her with a car for Christmas, while she'd gifted him with a scrapbook of memories. He'd spoken between Thanksgiving and Christmas about wishing he'd been there for every step of Nathan's development.

Even though she'd wanted to forget she was pregnant at times, Daisy and Miles had been the main two who helped her to document everything. Every little piece of her journey. From each ultrasound photo, to the day of her giving birth.

There were baby photos.

She'd gotten pictures of it all and had taken Simon on the journey with her.

Surrounded by their family, he'd cried and held her. Simon had loved the scrapbook as he hadn't gotten one of his own. His own birth hadn't been documented. Even though Lexie had loved him, she hadn't been part of every single detail leading to his birth.

Dropping Nathan off at school, she wanted to go and wring the teacher's neck. She loved fighting a lot, but what she had come to realize, there were different ways to fight. It wasn't always with fists and rather than use them, she'd decided to fight for her life with her family. To make Chaos Bleeds, Simon, Nathan, her entire world. Rather than go in and hurt the teacher, she instead kept a nice polite smile on her face and drove to the clothing store. She frowned at seeing a line forming outside of the door. Driving around the back, she found Lexie and Natalie tossing out some boxes.

"You know they're behaving like it's Christmas out front," Tabitha said.

"I put a large poster out front saying we have a new line. We're unveiling it here, and if it goes well, we're hoping to expand," Lexie said.

"These were literally doodles I made in a sketchbook," Natalie said. "Lexie saw them and knew they'd make a perfect fit or something. I had no idea they'd look so good."

"What brings you here? Are you wanting a job?" Lexie asked, hands on her hips, giving her back a little stretch.

"Er, no, I was wondering if you knew where Simon is today?"

"It's Friday. I'm afraid Devil's taken him to one of the meetings with Lash and the guy from the Billionaires. James? Ugh, I can't remember." Lexie waved a hand in front of her face. "Can I help with anything?"

"Unless you can dress up as Simon and pick Nathan up, nope."

"Come in for a coffee."

Tabitha held her hand up. "Make mine a tea. I'm not drinking coffee at the moment."

Natalie had already made her way inside but Lexie folded her arms and smiled. "I wondered when you'd, you know, figure it out."

She wanted to deny it but she winced. "You knew, huh?"

"Your body has changed a lot, Tabitha. I see you a lot, and I can see the difference." She pointed at her chest.

Tabitha glanced down. Her buttoned shirts were a thing of the past for the time being. She was in the stretchy kind of large shirts.

"Yep. They like to grow."

"Does Simon know?" Lexie asked.

"No. I haven't taken a test to confirm it, but seeing as I spewed my guts up every morning for the past couple of weeks, I'd say I don't need a test. I have the other signs as well." She followed Lexie into the shop.

Natalie was out front. All of the blinds were pulled down.

"I'm starting to regret that sign," Natalie said.

"You might want to call in a few of the ladies to help us out."

"I can help," Tabitha said. "A bit of training on the till and I'll be good to go."

Why did I say that?

Because this is your family now. It's time you stopped fighting it.

Lexie cupped her face and kissed both of her cheeks. "You're a lifesaver." Lexie took Tabitha's hand, leading her into the office. "We've got ten minutes."

"I'm nervous."

"Don't be. How are you feeling?"

"Other than the sickness, I feel pretty good." She pressed a hand to her stomach. "It's a lot to take in. I don't know if I should tell Simon yet. You know, he's doing well with the club. His schedule is all over the place, but we're making it work."

"He wants to earn his patch. Devil has said he's always there. Each phone call, he's the first one to arrive."

Tabitha chuckled. "I think it pisses him off that Dean got the patched-in member before him."

"He's going to earn it, you know that. Devil is going to pass the patch on to him when he's ready."

"I know."

Lexie took Tabitha's hand. "No, I mean, *the* patch, the President's patch."

This made Tabitha pause. "He is? When?"

"Not right now. Simon's young, but Devil has already said he has qualities as a leader. The five men he brought, they're all showing signs of being team players. There's no doubt in Devil's mind that his son has what it takes to be the club leader."

Lexie smiled. "I'm so proud of him. It won't be today, or tomorrow, and not next year. When he's ready. When everything is stable, and he's had been patched in for a while, you know. Only when the time is right."

"Simon probably already knows."

Lexie shrugged. "So why do you need Simon to go and pick up Nathan?"

Tabitha gave her a complete rundown of her conversation with Nathan. "It broke my heart. I can't stand it."

"Kids crying are the worst," Lexie said. "You always feel like there's something you can do to make it right, but nothing ever feels good enough. I'll make a call to Devil. See what I can do."

"Thanks. I'd call Simon, but if he's in a meeting, I don't want it to look badly on him. I know he'd put me first, and—" She winced. "Am I making him sound less like a leader?"

Lexie chuckled. "Devil puts the club where he needs to. Sometimes I felt like he put the club before me, but he balances it. I know deep down, nothing will ever happen to us because his heart is always in the right place. I don't always see it where it's supposed to be, but it's there."

They both chuckled.

Lexie put a hand on Tabitha's stomach.

This was the only thing she hated about being pregnant. The unnecessary touching. Lexie was family, but when she'd been pregnant with Nathan back in Fort Wills, she'd walked around a supermarket and had no choice but to threaten people who dared to touch her. It had been a thing.

Maybe this time it would be different.

"When are you going to tell Simon?"

"Soon, I guess. Will you take Nathan this weekend?"

"I'd love to." Lexie chuckled. "I'm going to get another grandbaby. I'm so happy." She pulled her in for another hug.

"I hate to break this emotional meeting, but it's time to open the doors."

Tabitha pulled away and chuckled. She realized

she'd been crying and shook her head. Always with the damn tears.

****

"You're sure you're ready for this?" Devil asked.

Simon looked up at his father. They'd just ridden back from a three-hour meeting with all of the Billionaire Bikers MC, Lash, and a couple of guys from The Skulls.

"I'm ready."

There was a compound about a three-hour ride out of town. The Billionaires had the details, cameras, and footage. At least twenty young women were being held in cages. All of them exposed. What Simon had seen had turned his stomach. The girls were being forced to earn basic luxuries like a bath, clothes, even the use of the toilet. They were also having to beg and do things for food. The men, they were the lowest forms on earth.

He couldn't believe just how depraved some people were. Devil was giving him a crash course in what the club was doing and why they did it.

"Do you need a drink?" Devil asked.

They sat in Devil's office. He held up a bottle of whiskey and a glass. Simon shook his head. "I don't need any food. I'm sorry. I seem a bit out of it." He ran a hand across his face.

"It's always shocking at first."

"But this isn't the first time you've helped. I've witnessed some of the women and men, even kids, you've saved." The Skulls and Chaos Bleeds not only helped to protect the vulnerable, but in most cases, they were the ones who also went in, extracted, and even killed. "How does it keep happening?"

"It's what happens. Believe me, I was always aware of the kind of shit that went on, just not how close to home it could be. It's tough. These are ... those women, we don't know how long they've been there. I think the worst is the Billionaires have to wait. Gather enough intel before they bring us in. Some of these women could have been there for a year or more. Maybe longer. Those that don't crack or end up dead get put up for auction."

"What happens to those that are auctioned?" he asked.

Devil sighed. "Sometimes we find them. It's not … easy. It's tough. This entire gig is fucking hard."

"Tell me about it. I don't know how you can deal with that. I don't."

Devil took a seat next to Simon. "There have been times I've thought about backing out. This is bad, but we've encountered a lot of loss. Seeing piles of dead girls even put on display so the ones that are still alive stay compliant. I don't need to see this kind of shit. I'm very much aware of the depravity of all life forms. I've lived it every single day. But I also know that if I don't help, no one will. Sure, there will be people along the way, but I've got to help. I think about Lexie, my girls. I'd want someone to if I couldn't help them, you know?"

Simon nodded. "I couldn't think of anyone taking Tabitha. I don't think I'd be able to stand it."

"I'm not going to lie to you, Simon, when we go in, it's going to be hard. It's going to get ugly. I'm going to be taking a lot of guys. I want you, Pa, Knight, and Twig. You're light on your feet. Teddy and Felix are too loud. I've got a couple of boys. We move out Monday."

"Why not tonight?" he asked.

"On Sunday, they've got a whole wave of girls coming in. With some fresh meat, they're going to be distracted. They'll be too busy trying to show them the ropes, punish them. This is our best chance."

Simon shook his head. "Fuck, I hate this. I hate how helpless I feel."

"It's the name of the game." Devil's cell phone rang. "Hey, babe." There was a brief pause. "Yeah, we're back. I'll give you an update tonight. Oh. Okay." He held the phone out. "You're on speakerphone."

"Hey, I'm going to put Tabitha on the phone," Lexie said.

"Hello," Tabitha said.

"Hey, what's up?" Simon asked, sitting forward. Tabby had told him she'd avoid trying to call him while he was prospecting so he could focus on being what his father needed him to be. The last few months had been amazing.

They were growing closer with every passing second.

"It's a little thing. I don't suppose you'd pick Nathan up from school today and do it in your leather cut and bike, would you?"

He could see Tabby scrunching up her nose, hating that she had to ask him. Simon gritted his teeth. He hadn't even thought to offer to pick up their son.

"Of course."

"I wouldn't ask, but Nathan was upset today." He sat and listened as Tabby told him what Nathan had said. It pissed him off. "I know you're busy. I'm sorry, Devil, for interrupting."

"Don't worry about it. Family is important. I know that. I had no idea Nathan was being picked on."

"I don't think he's being picked on. I just don't think he has any friends."

"I'll pick him up," Simon said. "I'll see you at home tonight."

"Yeah, I'll cook dinner."

Devil hung up the phone.

"Shit, what time do they get out of school?" Simon asked.

"We've got twenty minutes."

"We?" Simon looked toward his dad.

"Do you think I'm going to let you be the only one to pick up your son? He's my grandson, and I'm not going to let fuckers think he doesn't have family. I'd have nipped this shit in the bud a long time ago."

"You hate being called Grandpa," he said, reminding his dad.

Devil shrugged. "I've got no problem with it. Actually, I rather like it."

He laughed. Standing up, he ran his hands down his leather cut then he ran his fingers through his hair. "How do I look?"

"Son, you're going to pick up your boy. That's all Nathan needs to see."

"You're right, but, do I look, I don't know?"

Devil folded his arms. "Like what?"

"A badass. I want to be able to give those kids a look that says back off my boy without having to say it."

Devil chuckled.

"Come on, Dad. Don't be my prez right now. Be my dad."

"I am being your dad and I can tell you you sound like an asshole."

He rolled his eyes. "Very funny."

"I'm being serious. Your son just wants you to pick him up from school. He doesn't know that is what he wants. You love him."

"Weren't you nervous about picking me up?"

"Nope, and you shouldn't be either. I'm definitely coming so you don't bring down the cool rating."

"I am cool. Do you think we could bring a couple of the guys?" Simon asked. "Nathan's one of us and with a few of the guys, it'll be good for him. He has nightmares at night about being alone. I haven't said anything in case he's worried about me leaving, or if he misses Fort Wills. I don't know what I've missed and I don't want to ask Tabby."

Devil put a hand on his shoulder, silencing him. "Tabitha withdrew a lot from The Skulls, Simon. She was rarely at the clubhouse and didn't even work for them. Of course, they were there for her, but not like it was for you guys."

Guilt flooded Simon. "Then let us take some of the guys. I want them all to see that Nathan is one of us, and that we've got his back."

Devil squeezed his son's arm. "You might make a good man, yet. Go start your bike, I'll round up the boys."

Simon headed out to his bike. Straddling the machine, he gunned the engine.

One by one, Chaos Bleeds, the men who were available, each came out. Dick, Ripper, Pussy, Felix, Teddy, and Curse. Simon watched them all straddle their bikes. The clubhouse was always full at night, but each guy had a job to do.

They all got on their bikes. Devil and him taking the lead, they rode out, heading toward the school.

Simon didn't know if he'd fucked up. It was just a school and his son, but he wanted Nathan to have the best and for Tabitha to have phoned or be with Lexie, this was important to her.

They came up a main road and he saw the school ahead. There were a lot of parked cars. Children were running to their parents, and bringing his bike to a stop, he looked out across the sea of faces, spotting Nathan. He lifted his hand and his son spotted him.

Nathan let out a squeal and grabbed his teacher's hand, pointing in their direction.

"Do not falter, son. This is his moment," Devil

said.

"I won't."

The teacher nodded and Nathan started to run toward him. Simon watched, nervous, hoping his son didn't fall down. If the kids started to laugh, he'd be mightily pissed.

Keeping his shit together, he waited, and finally, Nathan threw himself into his arms. Simon lifted him up, pressed a kiss to his cheek.

"How about we make this a party, take you out for ice cream?"

"Yes, Daddy," Nathan said.

"I didn't hear that. You shout that for me."

Nathan did, repeating the words. Simon knew he had the whole yard's attention.

"That's my boy."

He helped him onto the back of his bike and it felt so damn good.

Devil already had a small helmet for Nathan to put on. With his arms wrapped around him, he left the school grounds, letting them all know he was here, Nathan was his son, and he belonged to the Chaos Bleeds crew.

They may not start fights. Their reputation may be tame, but those who remembered the hard days, they'd be able to pass down the warnings not to mess with them. No one should ever poke a sleeping monster, just in case it might wake up.

Chapter Eighteen

Simon had dropped off Nathan at his parents' house and was due back any minute. She'd bought a test and rather than take it with Lexie and the girls, she'd opted to have this experience with Simon. Daisy was also waiting for the results as she'd talked to her best friend that afternoon to let her know.

Glancing around the apartment at the candles and the soft music, she couldn't help but groan. This all looked wrong. She wore a summer dress. The only one that didn't require a zip and was nice and stretchy over the bust.

Her tits were refusing to cooperate by actually fitting into any clothes. Natalie had sold her this after she tried it on. According to Lexie, it brought out the color of her eyes.

Fashion wasn't her thing. Clothes were what she wore. She'd never been the kind of girl to spend too long trying to find the perfect outfit.

She wasn't wearing heels and just as she was about to blow out all of the candles, the door opened.

"So I thought we'd…" Simon started to say but stopped as he took note of the lights out, the candles.

"Hey," she said.

"Hey." He closed the door, locking it. "What's going on?"

"Nothing." She pushed some of her hair off her face. Gripping the back of the sofa tightly, she forced a smile to her lips. "You stopped off at the shop." He held a small bouquet of flowers.

"Yeah, it's our first weekend without Nathan. Am I missing an anniversary here?"

"No, not an anniversary." She blew out a breath, rubbing at her temple. "I don't know what I'm doing.

This was supposed to be a little something special. This is what couples do. They light candles, have wine, but I can't drink wine. A nice romantic meal."

"Why can't you drink wine?"

She pressed her lips together. "You caught that part."

"You speak, I listen."

She chuckled. "Yeah, how about that."

"Tabby, what's going on?"

Turning toward his chair, she lifted up the box. "I had this whole thing planned in my head. We'd enjoy a meal, you'd drink a beer or wine. I'd have a nice water. Er, we'd talk, laugh, and then I'd show you this." She held out the pregnancy test.

"You're pregnant?"

"I don't know. I haven't taken the test but I believe I am. I've got a lot of signs."

"You have?"

"I vomit a lot in the mornings. Smells make me feel sick. My tits are huge."

"I had noticed your tits." He smiled. "And this made you nervous?"

"Yeah, I mean, this is like our first real … moment."

"And you think we needed all of this?" he asked.

"I don't know." She covered her face. "I'm so scared. I know we've only been together a few months and everything is going so perfect."

He put the box down and went to her. His hands covered hers, and he dropped them away from her face.

"You need to stop second-guessing all of this," he said, stroking some of her hair back from her ear.

"I don't want to spoil what we've got."

"You couldn't spoil anything." He pressed a kiss to her lips. "You're too perfect to. I don't need all of this and we haven't been together for a few months."

"You're not mad?" she asked.

He shook his head. "No. I'm not surprised about this. It's not like I was being careful."

"Did you do this on purpose?"

"What? Get you pregnant a second time so you've got less of an excuse to leave me?"

She shook her head. "You did, didn't you?"

"I didn't have an agenda with you. I never do. But this isn't a bad thing. I don't see it as a bad thing. Do you?"

She shook her head.

"Then it's not bad. Do you want to take this before or after dinner?" he asked.

"You want to know the answer?"

"Hell, yeah. This is our future right here. Me and you."

"Then before dinner," she said, smiling. "You're not going to want to see me pee, are you?"

"I'll hold your hand and turn my back."

This was going better than she thought. Her nerves were back in place but she didn't expect anything less. There was no way she couldn't be nervous about this.

This was their life. Their future.

Entering the bathroom, Simon removed the test from the box and handed it to her. She took it, thanking him as she did.

Her hands shook. He took one of hers in his own. Their fingers locking together. "We've got this. You and me."

Simon turned away but he didn't leave her.

Peeing on the stick was so embarrassing but she was glad to not be alone this time. Once she finished, she put the stick on the counter and washed her hands. Simon didn't let her go as he held on to her hips. His arms wrapping around her body, his head resting on top of hers as he looked over to see the results.

She held on to him, not wanting to let him go.

"If it's a yes, we've got to move to a bigger house," he said. "I want Nathan to be able to play in the yard. He talks about your place back in Fort Wills. He likes gardening."

She chuckled. "It was how I got him to be tired on weekends. He's got so much energy. It's almost impossible to keep up with him."

"You've done good with him, Tabby. I wish I could have been there," he said. "I'd have loved to be part of every moment, but I'm going to make up for it now."

"Simon, you don't have to make up for anything. I don't blame you. I love you so much."

"And I love you too." He kissed her neck and she leaned back so he could take her lips. That first touch and she was already on fire, her need growing by the second. They both moaned.

"Wait," she said, holding her hand up. "It's time."

They looked down at the test.

"Is that a yes?" he asked.

She turned in his arms and nodded. "It's a yes. We're pregnant."

He lifted her up on the bathroom counter, spreading her legs as he sank his fingers into her hair. He pulled her in close, ravishing her mouth. One of his hands rested on her thigh, and he stroked up, touching the edge of her panties.

"I want you," he said. "Fuck, I always want you. Can dinner wait?"

"Yes."

She wrapped her arms around his neck and he

picked her up, carrying her through to the bedroom. Her body was so soft against his. He was never going to get enough of her. She was fucking perfect.

Always.

He slid his hands underneath her ass. Taking hold of her panties, he pulled them down. Tabitha attacked his clothes, wanting him inside her, but both of them, body to body, naked.

"I never want this to end," he said.

"It won't ever change." She pulled him down once they were both naked.

She spread her legs and the tip of him teased against her core. She gasped as he slowly sank within her. He wasn't in a rush and neither was she.

They both cried out as he filled her up. At the last inch, he slammed in deep.

"I've got all night long," he said. "You don't have to be quiet. You can keep on moaning."

"Please, Simon."

"Yeah, I want to hear you beg me for it." He pulled out of her and she stared up into his eyes.

"I want you. Fuck me, Simon, make me yours."

"You've always been mine." He took possession of her mouth, swallowing down her cries as he fucked her harder.

After pulling out of her quickly, he moved down the bed, putting his mouth to her pussy. He sucked on her clit, tasting her. There was just no way this was ever going to get boring to her. He plunged his tongue into her core, and he fucked her with it, drawing back to stroke her nub, then down.

She loved it when he licked her pussy. Glancing down, she groaned, seeing him swirl circles around her. He knew what to do to get her off quickly but he was forever the tease.

"Please, please," she said, begging.

He gave it to her, sucking her clit into his mouth, using the right amount of teeth. Everything she needed. This time, he didn't stop the buildup. He let it happen, thrusting her headlong into an orgasm that had her panting for breath.

She screamed his name but he wasn't done. His tongue stroked her, bringing her to a second earth-shattering peak.

This time, he guided her so she straddled him on the bed. He held on to her hips and plunged inside. She loved the feel of him as he filled her, taking her to the edge of bliss. She rode his cock, knowing in her heart they were going to get through this. They were good. They were a team.

They were Simon and Tabitha. No club could separate them. No one could come between them. They were fire and ice, and everything in between.

He came, his fingers digging into her hips as he growled. She loved it, every second of it.

"I love you, Tabby."

"And I love you."

****

"Simon, what's going on?" Devil asked.

Simon took a breath, closed his eyes for a second. It was Monday. He'd dropped Nathan off at school and his son had been surrounded by friends, so he'd have to have a word with his son about the difference between friends and acquaintances. There was nothing he'd give more than to be there right now.

He was the lookout. He'd been able to sneak past their guards and through the cages undetected, so he had a spot within the warehouse where he heard the girls scream. Some of them were begging for their lives.

Glancing through the crates, he counted the men.

"Ten men, I passed four in total on my way here. They're not heavily armed. They have knives and other shit," he said, whispering into the comms he had.

Clenching his hands into fists, he tried to contain his anger as another whimper echoed around the room.

"I want my mommy."

The sound of a slap followed. "You're never going to see your mommy again, slut. You want to get out of here alive, you're going to have to follow the rules."

Simon looked through the crates. The girl who'd been slapped didn't look any older than fourteen. The man in front of her held a knife to her face, stroking the tip down. When he pressed, she screamed, trying to back away, but he held her in place. "You don't move until I say so."

Another slap.

"You better hurry," Simon said. He held on to his gun, ready, prepared to fight. Taking a deep breath.

"We're nearly there, son. Two guards down."

"You useless whore. You're good for nothing."

Simon watched as the man in question unzipped his pants.

"Not even good for my dick."

The man started to pee on the girl's face and Simon lost it. The crates weren't heavy and he picked one up and threw it down to land on the man beneath. Grabbing the rope, he slid down to the floor. It wasn't his best landing, but he rolled, pulled out his gun, and fired at two men. Leg shots. He brought them down.

"For fuck's sake, Simon."

He ignored Devil, no longer caring as he fired. His gun ran out of bullets, but that was why he kept a knife. He slashed the two men who came at him, and then to the man whose dick was still hanging out. He grabbed him just as the main doors were opened and the others took care of the men he hadn't harmed.

With his blade at the man's neck, he grabbed his cock and started to twist it.

"Fucker!" the man growled.

Simon drew his head back and slammed it against the man's temple. The man fell and he stomped on his dick. He didn't stop, just kept kicking him.

The man had passed out and he became aware of the guys now watching him.

"Are we done here?" James asked.

"You good for these men to be taken, or do you want to knee him in the balls a little more?" Devil asked.

"I'm good." He reached down, grabbed the gun, and shot the guy twice in the dick. "He'll still live with that, won't he?"

Simon didn't wait to hear the answer. He left the warehouse, stepping outside into the cold air. The women were all being rounded up. Ambulances and cars were waiting to take them to safe locations.

"You okay?" Pa asked, coming out to see him.

He nodded. "Yeah, of course, I am. I'm fine."

"Really, 'cause the way I see it, you went a little crazy in there." Pa folded his arms, waiting.

"I don't need to talk about it."

"I think it's time you did talk. It could be good for you."

"I'm not the kind of guy to talk about my feelings. I don't need to. I'm fine."

"You don't sound fine."

"I am," he said. "You don't need to worry about me." He paced the length of the ground between the cages. Blowing out a breath, he gripped the back of his neck, trying to focus on something other than what he'd just witnessed. "I am fine."

"Okay." Pa hadn't left. He took a seat on the ground, resting his back against the cages. "You know I thought I'd seen it all, but now I know I haven't even touched the surface of how shitty mankind can be. It's tough."

"Those women, they didn't deserve what happened to them," Simon said.

"No one rarely does."

"Apart from those fucking animals. They…" He stopped. He just couldn't finish.

"Are you worried you're going to turn into one of them?"

"No. What kind of bullshit is that?" he asked, stopping to stand in front of Pa.

Pa held his hands up. "I know you've got a lot of shit going on in your life and it took you far away from your woman."

"For fuck's sake. We don't need to be talking about that shit. Honestly, I'm good."

"I think you need to talk about it."

"I don't." He stopped, glancing over toward the warehouse where his father was helping out the women.

"He's a good guy," Pa said.

"Yeah, he's one of the best men I know."

"Do you want to be like him?"

Simon brought his attention back to his friend. "Yeah, I do. Everything he's been through. All the challenges he's faced. He's looked death in the face and laughed. Men follow him."

"Simon, we followed you because you're one hell of a guy. You don't have to worry about those men."

"I can kill so easily," he said. "I don't … I don't think about them." He looked at Pa. "Those men, you've seen the pile of dead bodies. Girls, they at one point had families, but they've been discarded like they meant nothing."

"And you're worried you're like those men."

"I would never rape a girl."

"No, but you don't care about the men you've killed. The lives you've taken."

Simon gritted his teeth. "I don't know what's wrong with me."

"You're human, Simon."

"And I don't care. I've just stomped on that guy's dick, and I don't care."

"He's never going to use that cock again."

"I want to kill him."

"And that's your problem."

"To be like my father, I've got to learn to walk away. To let this happen," he said, looking at the men being led out. The Billionaires knew their shit. There were always fuckups. Men died, as did women. They were not always so easily contained. "I don't know. I think Tabby being pregnant is messing with my head." He sat next to his friend.

"This is going to mess with anyone's head. It's a fucked-up situation. There's no getting away from that. I do think you're going to need to have that looked at," Pa said, pointing to his shoulder.

Simon glanced down and his eyes went wide. He'd been shot in the shoulder but he hadn't even felt the pain.

"Now you know it's there, it's going to start stinging like a bitch," Pa said.

"You're right. Fuck, ouch."

Pa laughed getting to his feet.

"For what it's worth, Simon. I think you're one hell of a guy." Pa shook his hand.

There was an ambulance waiting that hadn't gone. He sat on the edge as one of the paramedics saw to his arm. It was only a graze. He'd need to patch up his leather cut.

Devil finally came over to see him. There were no girls and the bad guys were all gone. The Billionaires were handling everything else.

"We've got five that we're going to need to house until the Billionaires can find the right center to send them to. Parents are already being called."

"That's good."

Devil glanced back at the warehouse.

"If you've got something to say, say it. I know I fucked up," he said.

"You did fuck up. You didn't wait for us to be in position. What you did was sloppy. Not to mention the fact you could have been fucking killed. I don't know if you've got a death wish."

"I don't."

"Fucking shut up. Death wish or not, what you did was fucking messed-up, and against all the rules, and … it's exactly what I would have done."

Simon lifted his head to look at his father. "It is?"

"Yep, it's exactly what I'd have done. I wouldn't have gotten shot, but, you saw what was going on."

"He was pissing on that girl. She was crying. I couldn't … I'm sorry. I know you expect better of me," Simon said.

"I don't. You think Lash and I didn't have fuckups all those years ago when we started this?" he asked.

Simon glanced at his father.

"We did. I can't speak for Lash, but I thought I'd seen the dregs of this earth. I'd been to hell and back, and I'd enjoyed the ride. I truly believed the Billionaires were all talk no real action. They made it sound rough but were mostly bullshitting. I was wrong. So wrong. I've been wrong about a lot of things in my time. Those men, they know so fucking much. On a couple of the first missions or operations, I nearly got myself killed. I was the lookout. I could move like you, get in and out of shit with ease. The stuff I saw, at times I thought I was looking at some kind of setup, but it wasn't. This is why I don't walk away. Why I can't. When this club is yours one day, I want you to understand that someone has to fight for those women. All of them."

"I will."

"I'm not going to lie, you're probably going to be cleaning shitters for the rest of the week for disobeying me."

"I'm sorry."

"Son, I'm not speaking to you as your prez. You're my boy. I love you, and club or not, I don't want anything to happen to you."

Devil grabbed his good shoulder and gave him a squeeze. Then he got up and walked away.

Twig came over. "You want a ride home?"

"Yeah, I could do with that." He got to his feet and Twig was there, by his side. "You ever hate that I didn't let you kill yourself?" he asked.

"No."

"You don't hate me?"

"No. You've made me realize my life can do more. Chaos Bleeds is my future. I see that now."

Simon smiled. He'd done good.

Chapter Nineteen

Four months.

Five months.

Six months.

"I can't believe how big you've gotten and you've still got three months to go," Daisy said, putting a hand to her stomach.

"You do realize you've called me fat and are warning me that I'm going to get fatter?" Tabitha pushed her friend's hand away with a smile.

"I didn't mean it like that."

"Oh, you liar," she said.

Daisy groaned. "Crap, I sounded so mean."

"Daisy has to drink. She's upset the mommy," Angel said.

"Look at you, Angel, encouraging us all to drink," Lacey said. "Clearly, we've all had a bad influence on you."

"This is supposed to be a baby shower. This is the fun part."

"When are baby showers actually supposed to happen?" Tabitha asked. "Just before my due date?"

"Who cares?" Tate, her sister, said. "So long as you get some free gifts, there's nothing else to worry about, right?" Tate clinked her wine glass with Tabitha's water glass then hugged her close. "How are you feeling, really?"

Tabitha put a hand to her stomach and smiled. "I don't know. We're good. Everything is amazing. Simon is looking at houses. He doesn't want us to raise both of our kids in the apartment. Not that there's anything wrong with that, but … we're having a girl." She and Simon had been keeping the sex of their baby private but now, she wanted to explain why they were looking to move. She didn't want Lexie or Devil to think she was ungrateful.

"We need more wine," Lacey said.

"I think this is wonderful," Constance said.

It was nice to see her old high school friend. She hadn't seen her since they were eighteen. Constance had returned to Fort Wills and was currently working with Millie at the toy shop.

"It's good to see you. You've got to tell me all about your travels," she said.

"Nope, not today," Lexie said. "Today is about you and gifts and us all talking about what your baby is going to be like."

Music played and Tabitha opened up gifts. She had a nice home spa kit, a breast pump, pacifiers, baby clothes, chocolate.

Her friends were around her.

"I need some air. I mean, seriously, you guys." She got to her feet and moved out of The Skulls' clubhouse. Simon was back in Piston County with the guys and Nathan. This was her first trip away from him since they'd been back together. Fort Wills no longer felt like home. It was odd. She'd missed this place for so long but now, she just couldn't live here. The life she once had wasn't what she wanted any longer. The only future she saw was in Piston County.

She glanced down at the leather cut she wore. Miles had given it to her as she'd left it behind. It was her Skulls cut, marking her as the property of one of the men, her father.

As she ran her fingers over the leather, it felt wrong to be wearing it.

Movement at the edge of the clubhouse caught her eye.

She stood perfectly still and there at the gate

stood Luke. He held a bouquet of flowers and a wrapped present.

"You shouldn't be here," she said.

He spun in a circle. "I'm not here as a rival or wearing colors. I heard the news and that you were going to be in town." He held up the flowers. "I wanted to offer you my congratulations."

"Oh," she said. "You didn't have to do that."

"I know, but I wanted to. I know we haven't seen eye to eye on a lot of things."

"Luke, we haven't agreed on a lot of things. I'm in love with Simon."

"I know, but, after everything, I wanted to apologize."

"What for?" She didn't reach out to take the flowers. Instead, she folded her arms underneath her breasts and with how big her stomach was, on top of it.

"Ryan. I didn't know what he was capable of and it makes me ashamed to have ever been his friend."

She held her hand up. "Stop. Really. None of this matters to me."

"I know I never had a shot with you, but ... I did love you, Tabitha. I'm not trying to win you over or anything. Just wanting to let you know how I feel. Don't worry, those feelings, they're fading. Looking at you now, seeing how happy you are, it makes me happy."

Tabitha sighed. Stepping up toward him, she took the flowers and present from him. "Thank you."

"I hope you're happy, Tabitha. You deserve it. I wish you and Simon all the best."

She nodded, stepped away.

Don't do it. Don't do it.

Tabitha turned. "This means nothing." She went onto her tiptoes and kissed his cheek. "For what it's worth, I hope you find someone, Luke. Someone who can love you. Don't ever treat her like she's second best. Ever."

With that, she turned on her heel and didn't look back. Daisy was standing at the door, watching her. She went into her friend's arms, holding her. "You okay?"

"Yeah, I'm okay. It has been a long day." She tried to stifle a yawn.

Daisy laughed. "Come on, I'll make the excuses and we'll go to bed."

Tabitha left everything to Daisy and like a pro, within ten minutes, they were in Daisy's room at the clubhouse or more, Anthony's room.

"You're proving that you can be the head old lady," Tabitha said, changing into a nightshirt.

Daisy laughed. "Yeah, right. I'm sure they only did that because you're pregnant and they don't want to stress you out."

"They never did this with Nathan," Tabitha said.

"I know. I did though."

Tabitha smiled as she thought about the party her best friend had thrown for her. Complete with ice cream, cake, and water. It hadn't been great but for Tabitha, it had been perfect.

"I do sometimes miss when we were kids," she said. "Do you?"

"Life was much simpler. We could go and have a whole lot of fun. There was no pressure. I hated high school, though," Daisy said. "That's one thing I'm glad I don't have to get out of bed to do."

"How is college?"

"I don't know. I'm taking a break at the moment. Everything seems so hectic here, you know?" Daisy tucked her hair behind her ears. "Can you imagine what my life would have been like if Whizz and Lacey hadn't adopted me?"

"Can you?" Tabitha asked.

"I wonder if I'd have been nice or if I'd been mean, you know? Would I have slept around? Would I even care for a job?"

Tabitha laughed. "You're kind of exhausting your head on pointless what-ifs."

"Yeah, you've got to learn to do the same as well. There's no point in thinking about what has been. Focus on what is to come." Daisy stroked her hair back. "I know what you're going to do."

Tabitha smiled. "You don't hate me?"

"No, I don't. Promise me that club aside, we can always talk. You'll always be my best friend."

"I promise."

Tabitha wrapped her arm around her friend and together, they fell asleep. It was going to be the last time they could have a sleepover like this.

****

Simon's head pounded. There was no way he was going to drink that much alcohol again. He'd promised Tabby he'd take care of Nathan, and once his son was in bed, well, the booze had flown freely as the guys all celebrated his upcoming child. It helped to distract him from the fact Tabby was in Fort Wills, closer to the Monster Dogs and away from him. He wanted to follow her, but she wasn't going to start a fight. She was going to have some fun with friends and family.

She was due back today.

Daisy had already texted him that she was coming back.

He stumbled downstairs. Devil, Nathan, Tiny, and Lash were already sitting at the kitchen table while Dick worked the stove, humming.

"There's no way you can be in a good mood."

"Perks of not drinking, you don't get a

hangover," Dick said. "Pancakes."

"Ugh," he said, groaning. The thought of food made him feel sick. There was no way he was going to be able to eat anything, which wasn't good. "Tabby's heading home."

Devil nodded, sipping at his coffee.

"Morning, Daddy," Nathan said.

"Morning, son." He kissed the top of Nathan's head and slid into the seat next to him. He had a bunch of crayons spread out across the table along with several sheets of paper. "What are you doing?"

"I'm drawing our family. There's me and Mommy, and you."

"What's that coming out of her stomach?"

"That's the baby."

It looked like a monster. "I don't think that's how babies come out."

"It's going to come out though, right? Mommy is not going to like explode."

"No, no, it'll come out. I promise."

"And Mommy will be okay?" Nathan asked.

"She'll be great."

Devil chuckled. "I can remember when you'd ask so many questions."

Simon groaned. "Please, don't remind me of anything."

"You once asked me why one of the guys was going to lick a pussy cat."

"I like pussy cats," Nathan said. "Daddy, can we get a cat and a dog? Please, please. Please."

He kissed his son's head. "First, let's get the right house, the baby, and you know, we'll take it from there."

"Mommy would like a doggy. I've seen her stroking them at the park. She loves doggies and she's going to love them." Nathan looked up at him with his big eyes.

"I'll talk to Mommy."

Nathan laughed. "I need to use the bathroom."

His son climbed down and ran out of the kitchen.

"Does he know how to use his mom to get what he wants?" he asked.

"Be warned, kids are sneaky little devils," Devil said. "You were the worst."

"I was a lovely child."

Devil snorted.

"Where did the time go?" Tiny asked. "One moment she was a baby, in my arms, the next, she's grown and having babies of her own. It's not right."

Simon smiled. "I will take care of her, Tiny, sir, I promise."

Tiny glared at him. "One day you're going to have a daughter of your own. You're going to watch her grow up, and there's going to be a boy who will say the exact same thing to you. When that happens, and you believe him, come back to me then."

"I'm having a daughter," he said.

All eyes turned toward him.

"Tabitha and I were going to wait to tell you but we got the news a few weeks ago. Our baby is going to be a little girl."

His hand was shaken and Devil clapped him on the back.

"Now there's two girls for you to look after. You sure you can handle this?" Tiny asked.

"Did Ned Walker ask you the same thing?"

Tiny glared at him. "Good comeback."

He chuckled.

Dick served up some pancakes. Simon didn't want to eat, but the last thing he wanted was to be smelling like booze when his wife arrived. After finishing up two pancakes, he took a shower. Nathan had already run outside to play on the swings.

Once he was dressed and ready to face the day, he headed outside. He kept checking toward the main gate, waiting for his woman to arrive.

Tiny, Lash, and the guys were gathering up their supplies, ready to go. Not only had they had a celebration last night for the baby news, but there had also been a debrief over a mission two weeks ago. This one had required Felix and Teddy. They'd wanted a distraction, not stealth.

He glanced down at his leather cut. Tabitha had stitched the jacket from the bullet he took a few months ago. Letting her go to Fort Wills alone had been one of the hardest decisions he'd ever made. He missed her. Wanted her back. These feelings for her, they never went away, never expired. They only appeared to be getting stronger with every passing day, and he craved her more than anything.

Standing behind Nathan on the swings, he kept his gaze on the gate.

"Higher, Daddy."

He smiled, loving whenever Nathan called him Dad or Daddy. It was one of the highlights of his day, and it never got old, never.

Nathan let out a giggle.

He didn't allow his son to go too high. Was this what Devil felt with him? These shared moments that seemed to mean so much?

Up and down, he pushed his son, watching him giggle and squeal with glee, and he loved every second of it.

"Mommy!"

Simon grabbed the swing chain and brought it to a stop as Nathan jumped off and started to run toward the car.

Tabitha got out with a smile and picked him up, swinging him around. "I missed you," she said, kissing his cheek.

As she pressed kisses all over his face, Nathan chuckled, and she finally let him go.

He ran back to his side, taking his hand.

Tabby walked right to him, wrapped her arms around his neck, and kissed him hard. "Hey, you," she said.

"It's good to have you back." Sinking his fingers into her hair, he brought her lips in for a kiss and they both moaned as he kissed her. "Missed you."

"I missed you too. It's so good to be home."

Simon smiled. *Home.* She actually thought it was good to be home. He was so fucking thrilled. For a long time, he'd been worried that she still considered Fort Wills her home, and in a way, it was, he got that. But he wanted her to see wherever he was, it was her home.

"There's something I've got to do."

She took his hand, giving it a squeeze and stepping away.

Simon watched her. He picked Nathan up, holding him tightly as she went to Tiny. He watched Tiny hold her tightly but then Tabby pulled away. She eased the jacket off her shoulders, folded it up, and gave it back to Tiny.

He moved closer to listen.

"I'm home," she said. "I will love you guys always. You'll always be my family, but this is my home. I love my life with Simon and I don't want to leave. I'm happy. I'm really, truly happy." She went on her tiptoes and kissed Tiny's cheek. "Love you, Dad."

Tabby had picked him. Over her family, Fort Wills, she'd picked him, and Simon knew he was never going to let her down again.

Chapter Twenty

"I love it," Tabitha said.

She walked back toward Simon who held back, watching her.

"You love it?"

"Yes, I love it. Don't you?" She tugged his hand as she moved through the house. It wasn't huge like Lexie and Devil's house. There were three bedrooms, two bathrooms, a kitchen, living room, dining room, study, laundry room, and a nice-sized yard out back. Not to mention a basement for supplies. "We can put our Christmas tree in the corner. I can have you decorate it, put a star right on top." She pressed her lips to his neck.

This was the thirteenth house they'd visited. The realtor had been getting desperate as she'd refused every single one. Her mom once had told her that when you find something and can see yourself living there, making memories, then it was only a matter of time before you found a way to have it completely. This house made her feel that way. She was already excited at the prospect of living here.

"The yard is big enough out front that we can have some Halloween decorations. We've always loved that time of year. We can dress up, taking Nathan and baby girl trick-or-treating. What do you think?"

"I think if you love it, I love it."

She stepped back. "You don't love it."

"I think the place with a pool was better."

Tabitha shook her head. "Do you know how many accidents a pool can cause, not to mention, you know, death?"

"We'd take care."

"I don't want a pool," she said. "If you do though, we can totally go for that one. I just didn't see it as a home."

Simon sighed, cupping her cheeks. "This is where you want to live?"

She nodded. "It's not too far from the clubhouse and when you make patched member, you're going to want to be close by." She took his hands, kissing each one. "But I don't want a home you're not happy with. I can compromise."

He quickly grabbed his chest, faking an attack.

"Stop it. I can compromise. Stop being so mean."

Simon looked past her shoulder. "We'll take this one. Whatever it takes to close the deal soon."

The realtor smiled and started to talk, but she didn't hear the woman. Wrapping her arms around Simon, she brought his head down for a kiss. "That wasn't so hard. We've got a place to call our own."

"We have."

"So, why don't we head back to the apartment and make the most of Nathan being in school?" Tabitha asked.

"Damn!" He grabbed her hand and she laughed as he pulled her out of the house and down the garden path toward his waiting car. With her stomach being the size it was, at seven months pregnant, she couldn't ride on the back of his bike anymore. She hadn't been able to ride on his bike in some time, and she did miss it.

Wrapping her arms around his waist, they got all the way to their apartment, inside, and completely naked when Simon's cell phone rang.

She giggled as he groaned.

"I've got to take this," he said.

"I know."

"I don't want to take it."

"Then don't."

"I hate this," he said.

"The curse of being a prospect. I get it." She started to pull on her clothes but Simon banded his arm around her waist, holding her close. "No," she said. "I know you'll be with me, and because you didn't answer whatever that call is, you'll be punished for it. I can wait. I want you and yes, I'd love to have this, but I'm not going to let you fall behind, nor am I going to help you have to be home later than necessary. Devil's not going easy on you. He never will be." She took his face into her hands. "I'm going to head over to the shop, help Lexie out."

"You want me to drive you?"

"No, I want you to answer that call."

Simon handed her the keys, and she took them with a smile. Getting dressed, she didn't linger in the apartment. Instead, she made her way over to Lexie's. Their last fashion line had sold out at the shop within a matter of hours. Not only by customers at the actual shop, but online purchases as well.

They had no choice but to close for a couple of days to restock and they'd rolled it out across their other stores as well.

"You okay?" Tabitha asked, entering the shop to see Lexie frowning over her cell phone.

"Me, yeah, just got a text from Devil. He's going to be out of town for a couple of days." Lexie sighed. "I probably sound like a petulant child, but I do hate it when he has to leave for days at a time."

"I feel the same way with Simon." As if on cue, her cell phone went. "Oh, it looks like I'm going to be alone with Nathan."

"Do you want to come to my place?" Lexie asked. "Nathan will have someone to play with and we can have some fun."

"I'd like that."

"You sure? I just realized I'm way older than you."

"Lexie, it's fine. I want to hang out. You're Simon's mom."

Lexie chuckled. "You know, I never thought you and Simon would last."

"You didn't? You mean because of what happened or…"

"Oh, I'm talking about you two being kids. You were both always so cute together. He'd ask about you and I'd get calls from Eva, you two were just so … into each other. Nothing would ever tear you both apart." Lexie smiled. "Of course, I assumed it was a crush, but it never was. You two were meant for each other, I do see that now more than ever."

"I do … love him. I don't know if that helps. I do."

"Tabitha, honey, I'm not judging his choice by dating you, far from it. I think it's good. The two of you are so good together. I love the way you both are, always around each other. You have each other's backs and for me, that is important." Lexie stood up and ran her fingers through her hair. "I'm glad you decided to stay here. To be with us. To keep Simon here."

"I decided this was my home. Simon's my family. I do miss Fort Wills, but Devil told me once I was going to have to make a choice. I couldn't wear two patches. I couldn't be on the fence or moving from one town to another." She put a hand to her chest, tears in her eyes. "So I picked Simon. I picked love. Does that make me sound weak?"

"I don't think you're weak. The choices you've had to make. They're all scary. They try to test us all the time."

Tabitha went to open her mouth to ask another

question but stopped as the door opened and women entered.

Removing her jacket, she smiled at Lexie. For the next couple of hours, they didn't get a chance to speak. They served customers until they had just enough time to close up, ring up the till, and head to the school to pick up their kids.

Elizabeth and Josh were off doing whatever it was they did, but Lexie's other kids hadn't left home yet. Nathan loved being around his aunts and uncles. After doing whatever homework was needed, they went off to play, while she stood in the kitchen with Lexie, preparing a lasagna, a lentil one.

"You didn't have to do this for me," Tabitha said.

"I don't see why not. I like trying out new things. Besides, what will you eat?"

"The salad."

"You're a pregnant woman and need to eat."

Tabitha chuckled.

"Tell me what you wanted to say back at the shop but didn't get a chance to," Lexie said.

"You noticed that?"

"I'm a mother of nearly a dozen kids. I know everything. A whole lot. Believe me, I know when someone is trying to tell me something or ask me but they're nervous or interrupted. We've got all night."

"You mentioned Devil handing over the club to Simon."

"Yep, I did."

"I never asked this before I handed my jacket over to my dad. Will my position in his son's life change the way he feels?"

"How do you mean?"

"Will he pick someone else whose partner isn't from another club?" she asked.

Lexie poured some lentils into a pot of water and turned the stove on.

"You think Devil's going to punish Simon for loving you?"

"I don't know. It's probably crazy."

"No, it's not. Devil will only hand the club over to Simon when he believes his son is ready to deal with everything it entails. You won't enter into the equation. However, if I know my husband like I think I do, then he has already made that kind of decision."

"He has?" Nerves flooded her body.

"Tabitha, you'll be the president's old lady. I'm sure you've seen how it goes with me, Angel, even your mom. We have our spot within the club. Like now, any crap that goes down, if it gets ugly, they'll come to me. If it's an argument about something, or to ask my advice, they will come to me, and I don't mind. At first, I was a little out of it because why the hell would they come to me? I'd never understood it, but they do. I get it. I'm their family. I'm their president's old lady. It's a lot to take. I don't completely know what Devil is doing but I know every single time he leaves me, there's always a risk he might not come back to me. That's something you're going to have to deal with. It's tough. It always is."

"Do you think I'm capable of being what he needs?"

"This isn't about what Simon needs," Lexie said. "You and I both know you're everything that boy needs. He can't see anyone else but you in his life, and that is a good thing. It's intense, and I don't imagine it's going to be easy for you, but I do believe you're going to make it work together. Being the main old lady, the one they come to. It's not easy. You've got to be strong, make tough decisions, and sometimes even be someone they don't like. Do I think you've got what it takes? Hell, yeah. You know why?"

Tabitha shook her head.

"Because you're strong. You've overcome so much. No one can take that away from you. It'll be odd at first, even difficult, but give it time, and you'll see exactly what I mean." Lexie touched her shoulder. "Now, how about we get dinner ready, the kids washed, and we have a movie night?"

"I'd like that."

****

Moving into the house was easy. Simon didn't allow Tabby to do a single thing on the day of. All she had to do was tell them where she wanted everything to go, to sit and look beautiful. Of course, she didn't sit. She moved around, ordering furniture exactly where it needed to go. At several points, Devil advised him that she was nesting, getting ready for their new arrival.

Nathan loved his room and had already decorated it, putting his posters on the wall. Tabby had already picked out the paint but Simon had ordered her not to decorate. Any painting she needed to do, she had to wait for him. The guys would stop by and help out, and he was able to get the whole house painted exactly how Tabby liked within a month.

From that month, they'd gone furniture shopping. Whenever he had a spare moment, he was making their house perfect and taking moments when Nathan was at school to have sex with his wife.

She wore his ring once again, and he wore hers. They were bound together once more.

She went from the seventh month, to eighth, and now she was in her ninth month. They'd already had a quick hospital trip as she thought she was having contractions, but it had turned out to be something Hicks.

He couldn't remember the name. Devil had handed him a bunch of pregnancy books but between being with Tabby, prospecting, and parenting, he hadn't gotten the time to read them.

Pulling out his cell phone, he checked to see if he had any missed messages.

"Why do you keep checking that thing?" Pa asked.

They'd both been put on a stakeout of a man who'd been reported as being a wife beater. The Billionaires had gotten a call from a young girl sounding terrified. It could have been a prank call, but the mother had turned up over a dozen times at the emergency room. The Billionaires were trying to reach out, to offer help to the young woman, to let her know she wasn't alone and had options. Until they could go for full extraction, they were on guard duty.

Felix and Twig had been on the case before. Now it was him and Pa. Teddy and Knight would take the next shift.

"It's nothing."

"Dude, we're going to be here all night."

"Hearing you say dude is plain weird, man. Isn't that a little young for you?" Simon asked, shoving his cell phone into his pocket.

"Dude, I'm not that old, dude."

Simon burst out laughing. "True, you're not too old." He lifted his arms above his head, trying to work out the kinks. "I hate it when we have to do this."

"I hate that we have to do this," Pa said. "That piece of shit has got a wife. A child. What's he doing, he's screwing prostitutes, drinking, gambling. I mean, if this kid wasn't playing around, then when he gets home, he's going to beat his wife. What do we do if she doesn't reach out?"

"What makes you think she won't reach out?"

"It can happen. I don't know what happens. Fear or they love them. I've seen this before."

"You have?"

"Yeah, a long time ago." Pa's jaw clenched. "I don't talk about my fucked-up past but my mom, she was that woman. The one who took every kind of beating, covered up the bruises. Put on fake smiles for everyone." Pa shook his head. "I hated it. She tried to protect me, but he kept on coming. One day, he hit her too hard, and she never got back up. I was ten years old. By that time, I'd learned to hide. He was easy to read when he had a temper. There were times when I couldn't hide."

"Shit, I'm sorry."

"I didn't tell you this to make you feel sorry or for us to talk about our emotions and shit. I told you because … you need to be prepared for her not making that phone call. For her going back to him even if we do pull them out. The kid too." Pa shook his head. "It's fucked. That's what it is. I get some women are nagging bitches, but they don't deserve to be hit."

"I never realized how much you talk." He checked his cell phone again.

"She'll call."

"I want to be ready," Simon said. "I missed the first one. I'm not going to miss this."

"You know, I heard a bunch of guys saying there was always a chance Nathan might not have been yours."

"Don't."

"I'm just saying."

"Don't just say. You hear shit like that again, you shoot it down. Nathan's mine and even if he wasn't, he's mine. You get me? I love Tabby and I love that little boy. Even if he wasn't mine, he deserves to have a good father and I love him."

He wasn't lying either. At first, he wasn't sure what he felt for Nathan. He was worried he'd be a little jealous of the younger boy stealing Tabby's attention. It wasn't like that. He wanted to protect him. To save him from the world. There would come a time when he wouldn't be able to do that, and he needed to prepare him, but he intended to allow Nathan to enjoy his childhood for a long time.

"Okay. I'll stop talking."

"Yes, stop talking."

They both went silent as the man in question came out of the hotel room. He looked happy and a few seconds later, the prostitute he'd entered with left as well, without seeming to be affected.

"We follow him," Simon said.

"Do you want me to go and ask about the guy?"

"Nah, we're not supposed to get involved." He turned the ignition over, started up the car, and followed behind the guy. He missed his bike but on stakeouts, only a car would do.

The man went straight home. Parking across the street, Simon looked toward the house.

"Do you think he's hurting her right now?"

"I don't know," Pa said. "I hate this."

"You think the wife could be accident-prone?"

"Yeah, and the black eyes are because she hits the doors at a perfect angle."

"No need to be pissy."

"I'm not. Sorry. This is personal for me, remember?"

"I do." Simon leaned back. Staring across the street, he suddenly felt his phone vibrate. He grabbed it out of his pocket but his hands suddenly went slippery. As he went to open it, the phone slid right on out of his grip, falling to the floor. "Fuck. Shit. Fuck. Shit." He ended up banging heads with Pa as he reached for it. "Shit, one at a time."

"Go for it," Pa said.

Grabbing the phone, Simon clicked to see it was a message from Lexie. Another one quickly appeared from Devil.

"Shit, holy shit. She's having the baby. She's at the hospital. Her water broke. Crap. What do I do?"

Pa took the phone from him. "Devil texted to get there."

Starting up the car once again, he shot out away from the curb, missing a car that had started to pass him.

"In one fucking piece, Simon," Pa said. "Fuck. She's going to want you to actually be a father in the flesh, not in the spirit."

"Shut up. I'm having a baby."

"You're having a baby."

He pressed his foot to the ground, speeding up. There was no way he was going to miss this one. Why did he have to be on a stakeout tonight of all nights when his woman was back at home with the chance of dropping any day now? It wasn't fucking fair.

He was pissed off.

"You might want to slow down."

"Not happening."

"Dude, you don't want to die before we get there."

"I'm not going to die." He knew how this car drove and even if it seemed he was acting a little crazy, and he probably was, he didn't intend to. Only, he wasn't going to allow his woman to do this without him. He had every intention of being there for her. Of seeing this birth.

He could imagine her now, refusing to give birth until his ass was in the room. If she did that with all the pain she was going to be, she was going to be so pissed.

"We want to live through this."

"We are going to live through this." He drove, by some miracle not passing a police car.

Arriving at the hospital, he brought the car to a stop. Turning off the ignition, he threw the keys at Pa. "Park it."

Devil waited for him.

"Where is she?"

"She's in the labor ward. There's still time." Devil took the lead, showing him where he needed to go. He followed, his nerves picking up.

A nurse was on hand, offering him some scrubs. He washed his hands with sanitizer and quickly pulled on a gown and a hat. Entering the room, he heard a scream.

"No. I'm not pushing. Not until Simon's here. We talked about this." Tabby had her head turned away from the door. "He wanted to be here."

Lexie was there by her side.

"And I'm right here," he said, drawing their attention.

"Where the fuck have you been?"

He rushed to her side. "Working, but I'm here now."

"I hate you right now."

"I know."

"And I love you." She sniffled.

"I love you too." He pressed a kiss to her clammy forehead.

"I smell."

"You're beautiful."

"You're lying."

"Does it matter?" he asked. "So long as I love you and I'm here." Lexie didn't leave. His father had also entered, and they stood back.

Simon didn't care. Taking Tabby's hand as another contraction rushed through her body, he held her as she screamed and cried.

"It hurts."

The doctor agreed but promised it wasn't too much more. Just another couple of pushes.

He'd gotten here in time.

Tabby tensed up, screamed, and then collapsed. Her face had gone a deep red.

He stroked her hair back.

"We're never having sex again."

"Never?"

"Never ever," she said. "I can't. I can't do this. It hurts way too much." She sniffled.

"I've got you, baby." He looked toward the doctor who held up a single finger. "One more push. Then it will all be over."

She whimpered.

"I know. I know. I want to take the pain away. I'm here. Hold on to me and give me one more good push. Come on, baby."

She held his hand, squeezed it with all of her might, and then he heard it. It was the most precious sound in the world. One he was never going to forget. The sound of his little baby girl, screaming, finally born into the world.

"Is she okay?" Tabby asked.

The nurse handed her to a doctor, and after a few minutes, she came back to them, the baby wrapped in a blanket.

"She is perfect and she has a set of lungs on her."

Their daughter was placed in Tabby's arms. He reached out, touching her cheek, but quickly pulled away to remove the gloves.

"She's so sweet. So precious," he said.

"We did this." She leaned her head against his. "I love you, Simon."

"Love you, Tabby."

This was the perfect ending to the day.

Chapter Twenty-One

Tabitha lifted her glass of soda as Pa, Simon, Knight, Teddy, Felix, and Twig were each gifted with the official patches. The prospect patch had been taken off, and now they were full members of the Chaos Bleeds MC.

Tears filled her eyes and she clapped her hands, seeing how happy her man was. Nathan did the same while Skye sat in her stroller, sleeping. She'd just been fed and burped.

The sun was out. It was a glorious day. The cold nights would start fighting back. Her husband had finally earned his patch, and she knew what it meant to him. What it meant to all of them.

They had found each other on the road, but that hadn't stopped them from becoming a family. They were a unit. United together. One person.

Devil slapped his son on the shoulder and tears filled her eyes as they embraced. This was perfect. Wiping away the tear, she got to her feet as Simon jogged over to her. He wrapped his arms around her waist, picking her up.

"I did it, babe."

"I had no doubt."

He took possession of her mouth as Nathan groaned. "Ew, gross."

Giggling, she put her hands flat to Simon's chest. "You're going to party."

"I'm going to party. Mom is taking the kids tonight so you and I can enjoy this moment together."

"This is your moment."

"No, it's our moment. I couldn't have done this without you and the truth is, I never want to do anything without you."

"You're a charmer." She wrapped her arms around his neck, kissing him again.

Lexie came over. "How would you like to hang out with Grandma?" she asked.

"Will you and Grandpa make out?" Nathan asked.

"No, he's staying here," Lexie said, chuckling.

"Then, yes, I'll come."

They all burst out laughing.

"One day, son, you're going to want to make out with a girl."

Nathan wrinkled his nose. "No. They poop and fart and throw up. Look what Skye does all the time."

Tabitha laughed. "She won't stay like that. You love your sister, don't you?"

"Yeah, I'm going to protect her. I promised her I would."

Tabitha kissed his cheek before standing up. "You're sure you don't mind taking them?"

"I've seen many patched-in nights. It's a cause for celebration. Even if you're family, you're now part of a bigger one. I'm so proud of you." Lexie kissed Simon's cheek. "So, so proud of you."

Simon went bright red. "Okay, I get it, Mom, I get it."

"I love it when he's so embarrassed."

Laughing along with her mother-in-law, she helped to get Nathan and Skye into the car. She stood watching as the car pulled out of the parking lot.

"It is going to be fine," Simon said, coming up behind her, wrapping his arms around her waist.

She spun in his arms. "I know. It's the first time. I can't help but be worried."

"Mom has had a lot of practice with everything."

Tabitha laughed. "Oh, really?"

"Hell, yeah." He kissed her hard. "Just like I intend to get you into a lot of practice."

"Is that your way of saying you're going to knock me up every single chance you get?"

He ran his hands down to her ass and she moaned. She loved it whenever he touched her. She couldn't get enough of him.

"Haven't you noticed I've already been trying to do that? I want you all the damn time, baby." He slammed his lips down on hers and she melted against him, kissing him back. "I don't think I want to stay and enjoy the party."

"Then let's make our escape now," she said. She was more than happy to cut the party short, go back to their place, fuck, and make love in every single room of their house.

"Wait."

She groaned.

"No, don't go all sad on me just yet. Hear me out." He held his hand up. "I've got something I want to give you." He kissed her on the lips and jogged into the Chaos Bleeds' clubhouse. She waited as seconds later, he came out. In his hands was a folded leather cut. "I got this for you."

She took the leather cut and smiled. "This is for me?"

It had a property of the Chaos Bleeds MC attached on the back followed by Simon's name.

Simon's woman.

Underneath his name were the words *always and forever*. Their promise to each other. They'd never been with anyone else. They were loyal to one another.

As she lifted her gaze, there were tears in her eyes.

"Don't cry."

"These are happy tears." She threw her arms around him, knowing she'd made the right choice. Simon was her soul mate. The love of her life, and she was never going to forget it.

****

Two months later

Simon didn't like this.

He heard the screams. With his cell phone against his ear, he listened to Devil.

"I've got to do something. He's killing her." The woman whose daughter had phoned finally decided to reach out to the Billionaires. They'd extracted her and her little kid a week ago. Simon had been there to help. The little girl was way too thin and looked like she was constantly afraid. It tore at his heart to see.

The little girl had sent a distress call and seeing as he was in the neighborhood where they'd placed them in a safe apartment, he'd offered to drop by. He'd noticed the husband's car parked out front. So he didn't arrive and spook the husband, he'd snuck into the bedroom window. The little girl lay in the corner, curled up in a ball. Tears streamed down her face and he saw the bruise on her cheek. Her clothing was torn, and there was blood on her hands.

Crawling toward her, he put the cell phone down on the floor.

"Hey, sweetheart, do you remember me?" he asked.

The little girl nodded. "You're a hero."

He smiled. "Do you know how long that has been going on for?"

She shook her head. "I ... I was naughty. I dropped my glass and it smashed. He made me pick it up."

This girl was younger than Nathan but she spoke

so perfectly. There was a young edge to her voice, but he also heard the nerves. Her hands shook. That son of a bitch had cut the girl's hands.

"And he hit me." Her chin wobbled.

"I'm here now. He's not going to hit you."

"He's going to kill me," she said, sniffling.

"My dad is on the phone. Can I talk to him? You okay with that?" he asked.

Another scream ran through the apartment, along with cries for him to stop.

He couldn't even get the girl to cover her ears in case there was glass in her palms. Then he remembered he'd purchased Nathan a music pod with headphones. They were earbuds, and Nathan had wanted to play in the park, and he hadn't taken it out of his jacket. Quickly pulling them out, he held them up for her to see. "You want to listen to some music?" His son liked classics as well as some rock.

Finding one of the longer pieces, about ten minutes, she tilted her head to the side and then the other, and he slid them inside.

She shook and it broke his fucking heart to see.

With the music playing and he hoped drowning out all the noise, he picked up his cell phone.

"Devil, I've got to do something."

"Backup is on the way."

"Dad, I can do this. He's killing that woman." Simon stopped at a sudden cry, a thump, and then nothing. "You hear that?"

"Fuck, Simon, get the kid. Get out of there."

"Not happening. She isn't going to be afraid of him again." He hung up his cell phone and looked at the little girl.

"Where is that little bitch!" the dad said, yelling.

He eased out one bud. "I've got to go and handle

this. Close your eyes, listen to this music. Don't come out. Okay?"

She nodded her head.

He put the bud back in and stood as the door opened. The little girl did as he asked. She closed her eyes and Simon stood.

"I bet you're that fucking whore's boytoy. Well, she's dead. You can't have her rank pussy anymore. Get out of my way. I'm taking the kid with me."

He went to move past but Simon put his fingers to the man's chest, stopping him from moving.

"Who the fuck do you think you are?"

The man shoved him and Simon didn't move. He tensed his whole body. This time, he shoved back and the man moved out of the room.

He closed the door behind him so the little girl wouldn't even see anything if she was tempted to open her eyes.

"What the fuck?" the man asked.

"You like hitting women who are too afraid to hit back? You're a fucking coward. But I'm not. I'm not afraid to hit back." He turned to see the woman they'd tried to save. Her neck was at an odd angle. Her face was covered in blood and bruises. It also looked like he'd stabbed her.

"That was an accident."

"Believe me, this won't be, but it will be far too kind for you." Simon lashed out, kicking his foot in the man's leg. He went down. Wrapping his fingers around his neck, he tightened his hold, cutting off his circulation.

With him fighting for breath, he let him flail his arms, trying to fight back. Letting go as the man tried to take in several deep breaths, he reached around, grabbed his chin, and tugged, snapping his neck.

After dropping him to the floor, he entered the

bedroom again. Staring at the girl, he saw she still had her eyes closed. He went to her, putting a finger to her foot. She jerked, opening her eyes, and when she saw him, she threw her arms around him, holding him close.

The earbuds came out and he held her. "I've got you. I've got you." He sat on the edge of the bed.

Time passed. She wouldn't let him go.

When the door opened, he turned to see Devil enter the room. Paramedics were close but when he tried or anyone tried to take the little girl away, she held on to him tighter.

"Please," she said, whispering.

"I've got you." She wouldn't let go and he got to his feet. There was only one person he knew who could help.

"I've got to take her to the clubhouse," he said.

The paramedics started to argue.

"I wasn't asking. I'm not staying here." He looked toward Devil. "It good for me to move her?"

"It is."

He looked at the paramedics. "You've got two choices, take me to the clubhouse, and I might be able to get someone to help you, or you get the hell out of my way."

The girl still shook.

Simon got it. She felt safe with him. For too long, she hadn't been safe with anyone, but he'd helped her. This wasn't the first time, but the second. She felt an anchor to him, and damn it, all he wanted to do was protect her.

As he glanced at his dad, Devil nodded. "I'll handle it."

The paramedics drove him to the clubhouse where Tabby would be waiting. He had no doubt Devil had also put a call through to the clubhouse to warn them about what was happening.

Once he arrived, he saw a lot of the guys were outside. That was his sign that Tabby was inside with Nathan and Skye. Nodding at each of them, they all stopped to watch. The girl's hands would be seen, along with her bruised face.

Entering the clubhouse, he saw the tables had been moved away but what also caught his attention was the sweet sound he hadn't heard in such a long time. Tabby was singing. It was only softly, but for the first time, she was finally singing. He looked toward her and found her. Tabby, wearing a plain white dress with her hair pinned atop her head with some curls cascading down, looked up and smiled at him. Nathan sat on the carpet. Some food was on plates. Skye lay on a mat with a toy positioned over her so she could reach up.

"Hey, sweetheart," he said. "What's your name?" He knew her name but wanted to get her to respond to him.

"Jade," she said.

"Hey, Jade, I'm Simon. This is my wife." He crouched down, turning so Jade could see. Tabby held her fingers up and smiled.

"She's pretty."

"Yes, she is. That's our son Nathan, and our little girl, Skye."

The paramedics were standing there, watching, waiting.

Slowly, Jade pulled away from him but didn't let him go.

"You won't leave?" Jade asked.

"No, I won't leave. My wife, she'd like to see if you're okay. She has the softest hands and what's more, she won't let anyone hurt you."

"She won't?"

"Nope. She will kick anyone's ass who tries to hurt you. She's like a superhero."

"Like you?" Jade asked.

He chuckled. "Better than me. She's my wife and I get my power from her."

Jade's eyes went wide. He glanced at Tabby. "We won't let anything happen to you. We promise."

Jade wriggled out of his lap and went to Tabby's arms. He watched his wife as she ran her fingers through her hair. "I've got to take a look at these hands, okay?"

Jade held her hands to her chest and then slowly eased them out.

Tabby held her hands, seeing the blood. "It looks like there might be a bit of glass. I'm going to call on my friend. She can take a look, but I promise you, if it hurts, you will tell her no."

"I don't want it to hurt."

"I know," Tabby said. "Will you trust me? We get this nasty glass out, and then I've got ice cream and chocolate sauce with your name on it."

Jade's eyes went wide. "I ... can I?"

"Yes. You like ice cream and chocolate sauce, right, Nathan?" Tabby asked.

His son walked over to the little girl, putting his hands under hers. "I'm here. It looks painful."

"It is."

"Mommy and Daddy's friends will make it all better."

Jade nodded her head. Only one of the paramedics moved closer. She put her bag down, putting on some gloves.

"You're a brave girl," the woman said. "There are some shards of glass, but I can get them out. You didn't squeeze your hands or press on anything did you?"

"No."

"That's good. Really good."

Simon stood and he turned as Devil entered the clubhouse.

"I don't know what you need to do, but I will protect her."

Tabby looked at him and he pointed at Jade, letting her know his intention. She rolled her eyes and mouthed the words *of course*. She kissed Jade's head.

"You know it can be difficult."

"I also know the Billionaires can get shit moved. Make sure by the end of this week, Jade is mine and Tabby's. We'll take care of her. She's one of us now." There was no way he was going to let Jade be taken, put into the system, or even lost. She'd been through too much and she saw him as a hero. Well, they had room in their family for her.

"I'm proud of you, son, so fucking proud."

It took the paramedic over an hour to check for glass. She shined a light to double-check. Once Jade was all bandaged up, Nathan joined her for ice cream. With them both sitting on the mat and Skye fast asleep, Tabby moved toward him.

"You don't mind, do you?" he asked.

"What? Having a new member of the family? No, I don't. The way she held you. She's been through a lot. I love her already." Tabby sighed. "But this means you're going to work on two fronts to keep me here. You're going to knock me up and bring in kids that I instantly love."

"Is it working?" he asked.

"No. You can't force me to stay when I'm already where I want to be. Bring all the kids you want, knock me up, I don't care. I'm yours, Simon, always and forever." She kissed his lips. "I never knew just how big of a family I wanted, but I love it. I love them all,

Simon."

"I'm the luckiest fucking hero in the world."

He pulled her down, kissing her lips. This was his woman. The love of his life. His soul mate. It could only get better from here.

Epilogue

Ten years later

Tabitha parked the car. "Who's ready to party?" she asked.

"Mom, really?" Nathan said. "I can't believe you made me come here. It's so lame."

She rolled her eyes. "Yes, coming to the town fair where you get to hang out with all of your friends is so lame. Next time you want to sneak out at night, I'll tell your dad to ground your ass and have him come to the school to pick you up."

"I'm sorry," Nathan said.

She smiled. "You ready, Jade? Skye?"

She looked at her girls, who nodded. There was also Candice, Jackson, Petra, and Robin. In total, they had seven kids, and she was pregnant with her fourth.

Jade and Skye nodded.

Getting out of the car, she helped Robin out of the car, putting her daughter onto her hip. In the last ten years, it had been so crazy but amazing. She wouldn't trade it for the world.

With her kids rushing onto the field, she followed them, watching as they all ran toward the row of bikes, and there, wearing his president's patch proudly, was her husband. He'd taken the lead only six months ago. The first night, he'd woken up in a sweat, panicked, scared, worried that he was going to screw up his father's legacy, but she knew the truth. She knew how amazing he was, and how dedicated to the club he was.

Devil was there in the group. Still a part of the club, but he had stepped down. It was a moment she never thought would happen, but it had.

One by one, Simon hugged his kids, shaking Nathan's hand before their oldest went off to enjoy the fair.

Robin held her arms out and Simon took their little girl.

"How are my two girls?" Simon asked, putting a hand on her stomach.

"We're good. Tired, but good."

Devil and Lexie already had a swarm of grandkids and they were constantly adding to the mix.

Simon pulled her in close as Pa took Robin from him, giving them both a little time. The guys at the club were amazing, as were all the women. Simon had been petrified about taking over as club president, but so had she. Lexie was always there though, having her back, guiding her, just as Devil was with Simon. They hadn't been pushed out.

They were one big happy family.

"This is our sixteenth wedding anniversary," he said. "Happy birthday, Tabby."

Tears filled her eyes. They'd been together over twenty years. Their love surviving so much. She loved him more than anything in the world.

"I love you, Simon."

"I love you, Tabby. Then, now, in the future."

"Always," she said.

"And forever." He took possession of her mouth and she didn't care. The world faded away. Being in her man's arms, surrounded by the club, she felt safe and whole.

The End

www.samcrescent.com

Author Note

This is the end but not the end. Chaos Bleeds and The Skulls are entering new chapters. I had thought about ending this series completely after the Next Generation, but I feel with this club, they are constantly developing, and I love this series so much. It has tested me in so many ways. All of these books are my babies. There will be more Simon and Tabitha to come for the future, with more guys coming into their lives (I'm thinking something for Dean, Pa, Felix, Knight, Twig, and Teddy). These will be the only two books that are long and completely devoted to them (possibly, you know my muse). There will be more books that are perhaps novellas for sneak peeks into their lives. I don't want to give too much away, as there will be other stories to tell in that ten-year gap, leading up to Devil handing over the club. Of course, I'm going to be working on Next Generation: The Skulls as well. So many plans.

Simon and Tabitha's story has taken me on a journey I never really planned for. I had an idea of what I wanted their story to be, and it was constantly evolving and changing. They're two of the strongest characters I've ever written. Their love was the main focal point. Whenever I thought about them, that's all I could feel. They loved one another and that was their constant draw to each other. What I also knew was their relationship would be tested. They've come from different clubs, and no matter what, Devil would never join. Chaos Bleeds and The Skulls would work together but never become one. I never knew how or in what way Simon and Tabitha would go. Part of me was afraid of where their story would lead me. For me, they were always going to be together. There was no doubt in my mind. Even with separation, their connection wasn't on the surface, but bone-deep. Thank you so much for taking the time to read their story. I really do appreciate it, and I hope you love their story.

Sam x

... AND FOREVER

EVERNIGHT PUBLISHING ®

www.evernightpublishing.com

Printed in Great Britain
by Amazon